LIE TO ME

ALSO BY
Molly McAdams

The Brewed Series

Fix

Whiskey

Glow

Fire

The Rebel Series

Lyric

Lock

Limit

The Redemption Series

Blackbird

Firefly

Nightshade

The Thatch Series

Letting Go

To The Stars

Show Me How

The Sharing You Series

Capturing Peace (novella)

Sharing You

The Forgiving Lies Series

Forgiving Lies

Deceiving Lies

Changing Everything (novella)

The From Ashes Series

From Ashes

Needing Her (novella)

The Taking Chances Series

Taking Chances

Stealing Harper (novella)

Trusting Liam

Stand-Alone Novels

I See You

LIE
TO
ME

Molly McAdams
New York Times Bestselling Author

Published by Jester Creations, LLC.
First Edition

Molly McAdams
www.mollysmcadams.com
Cover Design by RBA Designs
Photo by © Eric Battershell Photography
Editing by Unicorn Editing

Print ISBN: 9781950048014
eBook ISBN: 9781950048007

Lie to Me is written as a standalone. However, if you've read the Forgiving Lies series, you know the brother disappeared in Trusting Liam because I sort of forgot all about him—*yikes*. But a group of readers and I came up with this amazing idea that he was overseas on a super-secret mission to make up for my forgetting him, and I've stuck to that story.

Ever since, #HesOverseas has remained a fantastic constant with my readers, but I thought it was time to bring him home.

So, Monsters, for the Facebook thread that started it all . . . this book is for you.

He's no longer overseas.

PROLOGUE

EMMA

When the woman at the ticket counter asked me where I was headed, I wanted to say, 'anywhere.'

Get me a ticket anywhere. Just get me away from here.

Words I never thought I'd say.

Not when it came to Manhattan—the one place I'd chosen for myself and had fallen in love with. Not when I'd vowed years before that I would never turn into *her*.

Yet, there I was, weighed down with suitcases that made up my life, leaving everything behind. No better than she'd ever been.

I'd grown up bouncing around from place to place in an RV with my mom. It could've been fun, sure. When I was just a child, I'd pretended we were on grand adventures, always headed to the next. Really, Mom was always running away. From men, collectors, responsibilities, dealers . . . reminding me with each place we left that she and the road were all I had.

Warning me that family would try to take both from me.

But there was always some new man she met at a diner or

gas station that had us settling down for a few months, if we were lucky. There was always an addiction that had me caring for her and had us on the run after she ran out of money . . . or stole it. And there was always her mom, who we ran to every year when money and food had been absent for too long.

The last time I saw my grandma, I was sixteen—ten years ago.

"TOLD you she'd try to take you from me," my mom had hissed once we were back in the RV, repeating the same words I'd heard every time we'd left my grandma's home.

Except, that time had been different. That time, before Lala had tried to take me in—the way she always did—she'd told Momma she wouldn't give her another dime. That time . . . it had all gone so wrong.

Momma had smacked the thin wall, bitterness falling from her lips as she'd continued. "Go to her askin' for help and look what she did. Tried to take everything I have away from me."

ANYWHERE HAD BEEN on the tip of my tongue when that memory flitted through my mind. I sputtered out, "South Carolina," as I reached for my wallet and began tearing through it, taking out every card and looking in every slot.

Just as I was about to give up, I found a small, folded up paper in a zippered compartment. When I opened it and saw Lala's address in my adolescent scrawl, I sighed in relief.

"South Carolina—Colby. I want to go there," I said on a rush, suddenly wanting nothing more than to find the only person who had ever been a comfort. No longer caring just how horrifically similar I was to my mother at that moment. "Get me a ticket as close to there as you can."

Within a handful of hours of purchasing the ticket, I was on a plane and leaving everything behind. But as we lifted off the runway and the city I loved disappeared beneath the clouds, something cracked inside me . . .

A month before my eighteenth birthday, I'd woken in Ohio to a note from my mom, saying she'd gone to Vegas with her new boyfriend to get married. *Be back in a week,* the note had said.

They'd never come back.

So, when I'd finally saved up enough to move to New York City, I hadn't had any plans. I'd just known the bustling city was a place we'd never made it to in all our travels, and anywhere far away from my childhood sounded like a good way to avoid repeating my mother's life.

I'd walked for hours and took countless subways until I found a place in the worst location imaginable. But it had running water and four walls, and I was able to afford it . . . for a couple months.

I applied for jobs any and everywhere and worked at a restaurant just below my tiny apartment until I'd landed a position as an assistant in a high-rise in Lower Manhattan. I'd worked my ass off, eager to find my way and gain the respect I'd never had.

I'd reinvented myself there. I'd *found* myself in Manhattan and had wanted to call it home for the rest of my life.

In the end, none of it had mattered. Because one night had brought back dozens of memories and made me feel like a helpless, worthless girl in an RV all over again. And suddenly, all of Manhattan's loud and noisy comforts had become suffocating.

So, there I was, pulling up to the familiar, Victorian-style home in Colby, South Carolina just as the sun was setting on the day.

No longer employed. Desperate for someone to lean against.

Hoping my grandmother was still there.

Vowing to never let my guard down around a man again.

ONE

EMMA

I shouldn't have come back to Colby.

That had been painfully obvious right about the minute Lala had opened the door the night before. My relief at seeing her—at her still being in the same place—hadn't lasted more than a second before she'd staggered away and *screamed.*

Trembling hands out in front of her. Looking at me like she was seeing a ghost.

And then a little girl had come running into the entryway to see what was happening. A little girl with my eyes . . .

"How are you here?" Lala had asked, sounding terrified and dumbfounded.

"I . . ." I'd slowly dragged my gaze from the little girl who was studying me, my stomach twisting uneasily for some reason. "I still had your address."

Lala's head and hands had quickly shaken. "How? Joslin said—"

She'd glanced down at the girl and pressed her hands to the girl's shoulders. "Get ready for bed, Nora."

I'd watched her go, that unease growing and growing when she'd glanced over her shoulder to look at me one last time as she climbed the stairs.

Once she was on the second floor and out of hearing distance, a soft cry had left Lala as she studied me. "I just can't believe what I'm seeing."

"It's been a long time, I know. I'm sorry."

Her hand gripped her chest, tears streaming down her cheeks. "Emma, your momma told me you were dead."

SUICIDE.

That's what my mom had told Lala the last time she'd shown up, begging for money. What's funny about that? I would've been eighteen—meaning, I was still living in the RV at the time, saving up for New York. The RV my mom had never come back to.

The next time she'd come back to Colby had been two years later. She hadn't asked for money, just dropped off a quiet, watchful baby and said, "Ain't going through this shit again," and left. She hadn't been back since.

Which meant, for nearly six years, Lala had been raising my little sister. For even longer, she'd thought I was dead. And my mom was truly staying away because she didn't want the responsibility of a child.

For whatever reason, she'd chosen to spare Nora the life she'd dragged me through—used me to achieve.

I pushed my legs harder and harder as I crossed the street on the way back to Lala's house. As if I could outrun the sliver of resentment that had formed in my chest when I'd learned the truth about Nora.

But it remained, making me feel like the worst kind of human.

Not that I ever would've wished my life on anyone—especially not another child. But why did I have to go through that life at all? What was it about me that made her decide to keep me close and ruin me over and over again? What was it about Nora that allowed her to let that daughter go—to give her a chance at a real life?

I bit out a shamed curse as I slowed in front of Lala's house, my gaze automatically sweeping to where I could feel eyes on me.

Two old women were sitting on the front porch across the street, shamelessly whispering to each other as they stared at me. As they had been when I'd left earlier.

When one of them pointed at me and said something I didn't fully catch, I called out, "I'm sorry?"

"You're here because you got caught, aren't you?" she yelled.

I paced a little to keep my body moving, my head listing as I wondered if this was normal for them. They'd asked if I was in the CIA as I was leaving for the run. "Got caught?"

"You know what you did," the other said loudly. "Laundering money."

A bemused huff burst from me. "I'm just visiting," I said, repeating what I'd told them earlier.

They nodded in sync. "We'll figure it out," the second said. "Whatever the real reason is."

"So weird," I mumbled as I turned and hurried up the porch and inside the house, abruptly stopping when a man in a Colby Fire Department shirt came walking toward me with a grin and a plate full of food.

"Mornin'."

My lips parted on impulse, but my confusion left me unable to say anything as I followed him with my eyes alone to a table filled with three other men in similar shirts.

Next to them, a table with two police officers.

If it weren't for the busybody neighbors behind me and the staircase that haunted my dreams in front of me, I would've wondered if I'd stepped into the wrong house.

I hurried to the kitchen, where I could hear Lala banging around, and dropped my voice to a whisper when I neared her. "Lala, there are people in your house."

Police, I mentally added. *There are* police *in your house.*

Instead of seeming surprised, she asked, "Didn't you see all the cars outside?"

My mouth slowly opened to respond only to close because I *hadn't*. I'd been too focused on the gossiping women across the street. And that's when I finally noticed everything scattered around the kitchen.

The food.

The dishes.

The pots and pans.

"What . . . what is all this?"

Lala gave a little laugh as though it should've been obvious. "It's Thursday."

"What does that mean?"

"First Responder Day here in the Wade house." She sent me a warm smile. "All first responders are welcome in my home on Thursdays for any meal of the day."

"That must cost—why would you do that?"

Her features hardened into a look that made me shrink

inside. It was pure disappointment and frustration wrapped in blood-bound love.

It brought back memories of my childhood—of watching my mother beg and lie for some cash. I'd never felt more like her than I did then.

"Just tell me why the hell shouldn't I? If you don't approve of my hospitality, you are free to find another place to stay."

I stumbled over incoherent words before I finally managed to spit out, "I just don't understand why you choose to do this every week by yourself without help for the funding or cooking. That's all I meant."

She regarded me silently for a few moments before focusing on the stove. "I think New York changed you. Or your mother did. Either way, I'll pray for the girl I knew to come back."

"I haven't—"

A wooden spoon was suddenly inches from my face, effectively shutting me up. "The Emma I saw last would've asked who else we could feed. Not *why* I feed them."

She might've been right. I couldn't remember what I was like ten years before. But if Lala had ever truly known me at all, she would know I'd never willingly put myself anywhere near law enforcement.

When I didn't respond, she explained, "I've had plenty of help from the first responders in this city over the years. Even for things that aren't their jobs and they don't get paid for. They've become my and Nora's family. The least I can do is offer them a meal. Besides, this is the only way I've been able to help them in return."

"I understand," I said, then glanced around the kitchen. "Is there anything I can help you with?"

"You can go find Nora," she began in a tone that said she was done with this conversation. "Tell her to come eat. Get you a plate too."

That unwarranted resentment sliced through my chest, and my eyelids fluttered shut for a moment as I tried to force it away. When it only lingered and mocked me with its presence, I started heading out of the kitchen, murmuring, "Yes, ma'am."

My stare darted over the men and women filling the living room as I climbed the stairs, hand tight on the railing, breaths shallow as their loud voices seemed to make the nightmare that accompanied those steps even more disorienting.

I squeezed my eyes tightly shut and fortified the walls on my past as I made it onto the landing and turned down the hall. A pained breath forced from my lungs when my eyelids opened to find Nora there.

"Jesus," I hissed, staggering back a step and gripping at my chest, my heart thundering beneath my hand.

Her stare was familiar and expression curious as she studied me the way I was her.

After minutes in weighted silence, she sighed—her chest and shoulders lifting and falling in exaggeration—and curled a stuffed puppy closer to her chest.

I hadn't even realized she was holding anything until then.

"I heard my Lala talking to you," she said, voice soft.

It was the first time I'd heard her speak, and just hearing the innocence in her tone made me want to protect her from everything in the world and rage because I'd been stripped of my innocence long before I was her age.

"Me and you have the same mommy." Her stare drifted to

the wall, her little face scrunching up tightly. "She left me with my Lala. Why did you leave me?"

"I didn't even know you existed until last night," I said bluntly. "Our mom left me before you ever came along."

Her fingers played with one of the puppy's ears for a few seconds as she seemed to think over my words. "She left you with my Lala too?"

Old pains and bitterness flared in my chest. "No." Tilting my head toward the stairs, I said, "Lala wants you to go eat breakfast."

Nora just watched me with those wide eyes as I started past her, not moving or saying a word until I was almost to my room—my mom's old room. "You would have left me?"

"What?" I asked, voice maybe a little too harsh as I turned on her.

"If you knew I sixisted," she said, getting the word wrong. "You would have left me too?"

Flashes of my life burst through my mind in an instant. That box I'd tried so hard to keep closed tight breaking open and filling me with an ice-cold dread. "With our mom?" I asked, horror and wrath dripping from my lips.

Nora's eyebrows drew close as she gave a small nod.

"I would've taken you and ran," I said slowly, honestly. "I would've made sure she would've never been able to find you."

"Like hide 'n seek?"

I blinked quickly as I was slammed back into Nora's reality—into all the innocence. "Go eat, Nora."

I hurried into the room and shut the door behind me, pressing up against it as nightmares consumed my mind until I was a trembling mess. Whether because of Manhattan or being immersed in bits of my past again, I didn't know.

It didn't matter.

Because they hadn't broken me then, and they wouldn't now.

I sucked in steeling breaths until everything was trapped behind the walls I'd spent so many years building. Until I had a handle on myself again.

With one last harsh exhale, I pushed from the door and headed for my bags. Searching through everything until I'd found a change of clothes. My eyes caught on my phone, on the shattered screen, and my movements slowed. *Faltered* as that last night in Manhattan tried creeping through my defenses.

A shiver raked down my spine as I forced that night back.

"Fuck you, Chris," I mumbled as I grabbed up my phone and went to shower, dropping my phone in the bathroom trash where it and the past belonged.

I CHOKED and nearly spit the liquid back into the cup that afternoon but somehow managed to swallow it through my coughing.

"Lala," I wheezed and coughed a few more times. Holding up the Mason jar, I inspected it closely. "What the hell is in this?"

She didn't turn from where she stood at the island, just pointed behind her with a huge chef's knife. "Don't you dare use that language, young lady, you are not the owner of this house. Manners."

I swallowed back any retort I may have had. "Yes, ma'am."

"That's real tea," she explained.

"This is pure sugar."

"Mmhm. And it's good for the soul." She did a little dance as she went back to chopping, the woman never seeming to tire.

We were in a weird in-between time where lunch was ending in the kitchen and dinner was being prepped. All the while, first responders continued coming in and out to devour a homemade lunch.

Lala hadn't stopped moving, and I was exhausted. I didn't know how she did this every week by herself.

But I could see it was appreciated and she was adored. Every person who'd come into the kitchen to make a plate had stopped to give her a hug or a kiss on the cheek. Every one of them had affectionately called her *Lala* as if they all claimed her as their own. Whenever Nora was around, people doted on her as if she was their little sister or child.

I was thankful my grandma had been loved and cared for when we'd abandoned her. Despite the unwelcome resentment, I was thankful Nora had somewhere safe to grow and people who adored her . . . beyond thankful. But I'd spent most of the time at the sink doing dishes so no one would see that, with each person, I hated myself a little more for being part of the reason they'd needed a makeshift family.

"It's gonna give me a heart attack, Lala." I hesitantly sniffed the drink in my hand. "Or diabetes."

She scoffed, then turned and gave me a soft smile. "I have been drinking that since I was in my momma's belly, same as your momma and you. You will be fine."

"I don't think I'll make it through this one glass."

She rolled her eyes and went back to whatever it was she was chopping. "Come tomorrow, I'm betting you'll be pouring yourself another glass."

"I doubt tha—" I pressed harder against the counter, barely managing to keep my composure when a man walked into the kitchen.

Hardened stare that quickly scanned the room before settling on me. Corded muscles filled heavily tattooed arms. Lips twisted into a lethal smirk that somehow looked natural.

Dressed casually, when every other person today had been in some type of uniform.

Everything about him screamed trouble. *Danger*. The real kind . . . because one look at him, and I *knew* his kind.

Sinfully handsome, bad to their core, with a unique ability to get women to do anything before leaving them broken.

I'd spent most of my life surrounded by men like him.

Lala dropped the knife and made an excited sound. In the second it took me to glance at her, his smirk had transformed into a warm, charming smile.

"Hey, Lala," he said as he pressed a kiss to her cheek and enveloped her in a quick hug. "Is there any chance you need all the bread in my truck?"

Lala clucked her tongue and held a hand to her chest, her cheeks reddening. "How did you know?"

With a brief shrug, the man started backing away. "Had a feeling."

"My Reed!" a tiny voice cried out, preceding Nora as she came running into the kitchen, barreling into the side of the man and holding tight.

I watched, a mixture of surprise and wariness unfurling in my stomach as he grabbed her up and swung her onto his back with the ease of a practiced move.

"How's my favorite girl?" he asked as he headed out of the kitchen.

And Lala just let them go—let *Nora* go.

I followed a few steps, unsure if I should stop them or not.

Nora had responded softly to almost every person who had spoken to her that day. Some people, she'd just offered shy smiles or refused to speak to at all. Her reaction to this *Reed* had been unlike anything else I'd seen from her.

Clearly, she knew him, as did Lala. But for the life of me, I couldn't figure out why *he* was the one to get that kind of reaction from them.

I knew men like him. *Lala* knew men like him.

"Who is that, and why is he here?" I asked, the words bubbling up on their own accord.

"His name is Reed, and he's just as welcome as anyone else in this town." Disappointment oozed from Lala when I faced her at her sharp words. "I have never been so ashamed of you as I have been today."

"Do not look at me like that. Do not look at me as if *I* am the one going against everything I have ever said." My voice came out softer and sharper as I continued. "You are the one who told me to stay away from men like him."

Lala's eyes widened at my tone.

I felt myself cringe.

Felt that kneejerk instinct to apologize, but I couldn't at that moment. Everything she'd ever engrained in me . . . nearly every nightmare from my life . . . she'd brushed away with one short interaction.

I pointed at her. "You told me, you *told* me . . . you said, 'You see that man? A man like that is nothing but trouble. You stay away from men who look like that.' And I have. I've *run* from men like him because I was forced to watch as they ruined Momma's life."

As they ruined my life.

But the truth of my life was something I'd sworn to never burden my grandma with.

I'd seen it every time my mother and I had shown up, asking for money—the pain and worry in Lala's eyes when she looked at me.

Knowing the truth would wreck her, I was sure of it.

"Oh, Emma." Lala sighed and her expression softened. "I didn't mean the appearance. I meant the man. His aura. His soul. The men your momma hung around with and married . . . they were pure evil." She waved her hand through the air. "So Reed has some tattoos—"

"Some? Lala, he's covered."

Literally.

There were tattoos peeking above the collar of his shirt. Swirling down his arms like sleeves. Littering his hands. Decorating his calves.

I could only imagine if he took his shirt off, there would be plenty more.

"Covered in ink or not, you will be polite when he returns."

At that exact moment, the man in question walked in. Those tattooed arms weighed down with loaves of garlic bread, and Nora clinging to him like a monkey, talking excitedly.

He took one look at me and then directed his attention to Lala.

Trouble.

Dangerous.

Handsome—*no. Not.*

Lala smiled at him adoringly when he hefted the bags on the only empty space left on the counters. "Saw Peter this morning."

"Yeah?" Reed said with a bright smile. "Blush any harder over Peter Rowe, and I might start thinking I'm not your favorite, Lala."

At that, Lala did blush, and Nora giggled wildly. "Oh, you hush," she said, waving him off. "You know I love you both. Now, fix you a plate."

He held up a hand and stepped back. "I'm good."

Lala's thinning eyebrows lifted. "I said—"

"I'm not on today."

"That makes no difference to me. Make a plate, or I'll have to drive one over to you. You wouldn't want to make an old woman leave her kitchen, now would you?"

His lips formed a thin line as if he was trying to figure out how to stay firm and not disrespect her. "No."

"Sorry. What was that?"

"No, ma'am."

"I'll help you make a plate, my Reed," Nora said as he helped her to the floor.

He started to speak, then paused as his stare darted to me. Stepping forward so he could lean over the island to speak directly to my grandma, he dropped his voice low. "I'd rather this food go to whoever's working—"

"You picked up groceries for me. That's work enough."

"Lala . . ."

Lala planted her hands firmly on the island. "Get a plate and get you some food before I call your momma, boy."

Nora gasped and covered her mouth with both hands.

Reed's lips formed another tight line, this time so different than the last.

His jaw tensed and worked like he was putting too much pressure on it. The muscles in his arms rippled and twitched like he was restraining himself from reacting in any way.

My initial assessment of him was coming to life in front of me . . . only now I was enraptured. The sudden, frustrated set of his features was alarming and fascinating and edged on this side of terrifying.

I should have been horrified.

He was every man I'd hated and cursed. Every man who'd had a hand in ruining my life. But I couldn't look away.

I was captivated and intrigued and too curious for my own good.

Some small part of me was urging me to move. To put myself between him and my grandma or my sister. To protect them from a man like Reed when he was obviously struggling to remain calm.

A reflex from years of trying to protect my mom.

But I didn't do any of those things. I wasn't sure I could move at all. I just stood there, waiting for something.

For him to look at me. To speak. To give me a reason to stare at that expression for days on end. For a chance to touch him.

Anything.

All while sucking down the sweetest tea I'd ever tasted.

Reed's hardened steel-gray eyes had been fixated on a spot on the island. When they snapped up, they burned with something that awakened a place inside me.

"Lala, that was low," Reed said in a soft, rumbling tone.

"Would do you some good," she said dismissively.

Reed rubbed at his jaw and laughed, dark and husky and everything a laugh had no right sounding like. "I'm not ready. You need to drop it."

It wasn't until I was halfway through the tea that I realized what I was doing . . .

Running back to Lala . . . needing help . . . fantasizing about the quintessential bad boy.

Tall, dark, handsome, covered in tattoos and screaming how he would be the beginning of a ruined life.

Not fantasizing. Not.

Oh my God, what is wrong with me?

I set the tea on the counter harder than intended, then was out of the kitchen and up in my room in seconds. Throwing the few items I'd taken out of my bags back in and zipping them up before my thoughts had unscrambled enough for me to be able to make sense of what I was doing.

Not more than a minute later, I heard the telltale sound of Lala's steps in the hall, getting closer and closer.

Worry wove through her tone when she called out, "Emma, honey, are you okay?"

I turned in time to see her come through the door.

Disappointment and hurt etched lines on her face before she could wash them away with a look of indifference. "I see."

"I have to leave." The statement was nothing more than a whisper, but it rocked me.

The truth of it.

The lie.

The way every part of me screamed *no*.

Because I knew . . . I *knew* I needed to be there.

It wasn't that I didn't have anywhere to go. I'd been faced with that challenge before, and I'd made a life for myself. I'd figured it all out on my own. I knew I could do it again and again and again.

But there was an ache that had formed deep within me when Lala opened the door the night before, as if my soul were saying *finally*. As if the journey I'd been on all these years had been leading me here all along.

But turning into Momma . . .

That I couldn't do.

And being here, I was afraid that was exactly what would happen.

"I can't become her," I said tightly. "If I stay here, I will. I know it." I gestured to myself then her as I continued speaking. "Look at me. I'm already following in her footsteps. I wanted to have a life as far from hers as possible, and everything I'm doing leads me down the same path. I *can't* be her. I can't stay here."

Lala rubbed at her head and then hurried to smooth her pale hands over her apron. "If that's how you feel."

My entire being begged me to say *no*, that wasn't how I felt.

That I was terrified.

That I needed someone. Not just someone . . . *her*.

My head shook sadly. "Nothing scares me more in this world than becoming my mother."

After a few seconds, she nodded, a sigh pushing past her lips. "I could give you a ride to wherever you need to go. But if you don't want that, don't leave without saying goodbye."

I roughly fell to the bed and buried my head in my hands.

I wanted to apologize for putting her through this . . .

For showing up. For disappointing her. For hurting her now. But I was afraid if I spoke, I would tell her every reason why becoming like my mom was so terrifying. Reasons that Lala *couldn't* know.

There was a sigh from my doorway. "Running . . . your momma did that."

And then I was alone with my conflicting instincts and needs and packed bags.

The muted sounds from the men and women coming and going downstairs created their own sort of lullaby until I fell asleep.

WHEN I WOKE, it was dark outside my window, but the muted voices were still weaving up the stairs and to my room.

I looked at my bags and then hurried down the stairs to where Lala and Nora sat at the kitchen table with a few men in uniform.

Lala's smile slipped from her face when she saw me standing there. After excusing herself, she stood and came to me, expression guarded and questioning.

"I'm sorry I left you to make dinner and do the dishes."

All that was left in the kitchen were massive pans filled with food above warmers.

A small laugh left her. "I do this by myself every week."

I glanced at the people attempting to ignore us at the table, then back to her. "I just—I'm sorry, Lala." My mouth opened and shut half a dozen times before my shoulders fell with an exhale.

"I know," she said and then turned, grabbing Tupperware to fill with food.

When it was nearly overflowing, she pushed the lid on and held it out to me.

My brows pinched in confusion, but I didn't have time to ask before she was already explaining.

"Reed slipped out when I went after you. You're gonna take this to him."

I was so shocked, I just stood there staring at her. Not reaching for the container. Not speaking.

"Go on. Night isn't gonna get any younger."

"Lala, he is every man I watched my mother with my entire life. Why would you even ask me to interact with him?"

"Because he is not those men." She gave me a look like she didn't understand how I couldn't *see* it. "That boy has saved my life and countless others'. He cares for Nora as if she's his family. He's fixed my lightbulbs without being asked. He's planted flowers when I couldn't get in the garden. And he brings bread every week because I always forget to buy it. If you give him half a chance, you'll see exactly what kind of man he is."

A stunned laugh burst from me. "I don't want to give him half a chance."

"I didn't mean like that," she said gently yet firmly. "I'm not telling you to go looking for anything with him. I am asking you to open your mind so you can see the difference in the men you grew up around and good, honest men."

I curled my fingers around the Tupperware when she shoved it at me and sighed. "Yes, ma'am."

She slapped a sticky note on top with an address as though she'd already been expecting this.

As though she'd known I wouldn't leave.

"You be nice to him, Emma. Reed Ryan has the purest heart of them all."

TWO

REED

I woke in a cold sweat.

My arms crossed tightly over my chest.

My head aching from how strongly I was grinding my jaw.

I let out a shuddering breath and told my body to relax. Tried to force it. But thinking I could was easier than the reality. It was like listening to my brain beg my body to respond and watching my body laugh in response.

I finally forced myself from the bed, my mind racing with images I tried to push away, my limbs jittery with the adrenaline pounding through my veins.

Dragging my hands over my face, I turned for my closet and grabbed a clean shirt and shorts, then slid into my running shoes. I was out of the house and running within a few minutes of waking up.

I took deep, gulping breaths of the humid air, letting it fill my lungs before I set my breaths to my pace.

It wasn't often those haunting memories crept into my mind, even less that they made it into my dreams. I knew I was lucky in that aspect. But when they did, I felt wrecked for hours after. Unable to scrub images from my mind. Unable to get scents from my nose. Unable to stop sounds from crashing down around me.

But, again, I considered myself lucky.

I ran until it felt like my lungs would collapse, then pushed myself a little farther until I reached the waterfront coffee shop.

Once I was inside, I breathed deep, trying to smell the coffee and not the acrid smoke and copper.

"*Reed*. Reed, hi."

Jesus.

I glanced at the barista the excited, breathless voice belonged to and forced some form of a smile that quickly faded when I returned to focusing on smelling what was real. What was *here*.

"Coffee or water this afternoon?"

I looked pointedly at the woman trying to order and murmured, "I'm fine, Courtney."

The woman standing at the counter looked over her shoulder, her brows already drawn together in irritation and curiosity.

It was instant . . .

The way my body reacted to seeing her there.

My heart kicked into an uneven, wild beat, so different from the steady hammering from my exertion. My hands twitched, wanting to trace and learn her subtle curves.

The impulse to step toward her, just to be that much closer to her, had me struggling to stay in place.

Just as it had when I'd seen her standing in Lala's kitchen the night before.

One look at her, and I'd known she would be more

trouble than she was worth. Fuck if the reaction she caused didn't make me want a little trouble though.

Her expression immediately shifted into one of judgment and bewilderment. And just as it had last night, hostility poured from her as she looked me over.

With a quick shake of her head, she returned her attention to Courtney and finished ordering before walking away to wait for her drink.

I walked up to the counter, grabbing a bottled water from the display case as I did.

"Hey, Reed—hi," Courtney said eagerly. "You look like your run went well today. I mean, you just look like you ran. It's so good to see you." She jerked her thumb in the direction of the girl I was watching from the corner of my eye. "That lady totally asked if we're together. Can you believe it? *Us*?"

Courtney's laugh was slightly frantic and her stare was hopeful. And I had no fucking clue how to come off more disinterested than I always was with her.

I smiled politely and reached for my pocket, my smile and stomach dropping when I reached for the other and realized they were empty.

I didn't even have my keys.

"Shit," I murmured.

"What?" Courtney's voice was full of alarm as she leaned over the counter toward me. "What is it? Are you okay?"

"I'm fine. I just . . ." Another curse slipped from my tongue as I reached for the bottle to put it back. "I guess I left without my wallet today."

"Oh, that's okay," she said quickly, reaching for my hand to stop me. "It's on me."

"No. No, it's fine. Really." I nodded toward the faucet they used for the free cups of water. "I'll just take a cup."

"Take it," she urged, shoving the bottle toward me. "I'll pay for it."

I let out a laugh that bordered on frustration and rubbed at the back of my neck. "I appreciate that, but I'm putting this away."

"Are you sure? I really don't mind."

I was well aware of that. Every time she worked, she tried to give me something I didn't ask for.

My attention wavered when the girl from Lala's kitchen grabbed a drink and started walking away.

I wanted to get her name. Wanted to ask what could've happened in her life to make her so aggressive. Ask what it was about *me* that made her look like she at once wanted to fall into my bed and force me from her sight.

I cleared my throat and focused straight ahead. "I'm sure."

Courtney's face fell slightly, and something in my gut twisted.

It'd been like this with her since I'd moved to Colby over three years ago. I'd never once encouraged or engaged in anything with her, I was only ever polite, but she always seemed to expect something from me.

And every time she realized nothing was going to happen, her eyes dimmed, and it made me feel like the biggest asshole.

I dipped my head when she returned with a cup of water and kept my smile neutral. "Thanks, Courtney."

She sucked in a quick breath, her face lighting up like I'd just offered her the world. "Oh, you're welcome, Reed. Anything for you."

I started toward the door, tipping the cup back and draining the contents as I did.

"Do that often?"

I glanced to my right as I tossed the empty cup in the trash and paused when I saw the girl from Lala's at the condiment station, focused on the iced coffee in front of her.

Dressed in a button-down shirt and pants that fit her like a second skin and high-as-fuck heels that made her legs seem to go on forever and put her nearly eye-level with me. Looking better fit for a big city than what Colby had to offer, and exactly like the kind of girl I wanted nothing to do with.

I had a type . . .

Short girls with curves that never ended and smiles that could erase even the worst situation. Someone who preferred jeans and an old shirt over dressing up. Someone who didn't look like they'd rather I was dead . . .

If only the rest of my body could catch up with my brain.

To be honest, Courtney would've been my type if she hadn't planned out *and* told me our entire future the first time she saw me.

"Do what?" I finally asked.

She let out a soft huff and finished putting creamer in the drink. "Conveniently forget your wallet so the girls falling all over themselves will buy you things?"

My brow furrowed at her sure tone, but she never gave me a chance to respond.

"I know your type," she said as she glanced at me from under her eyelashes.

"Is that right?"

Her hazel eyes flitted over my body for only a second before she returned to her drink. That judgment from earlier was back and stronger than before.

So was the heat.

The need.

The impulse to take another step closer to her as if something was drawing me toward her.

I stepped away instead and let myself take her in the way she had me.

Her slender frame and long, blonde hair. The way she radiated anger and looked like money. But it was all offset by a soft, captivating face and wide eyes that made her look so innocent and pure.

I'd never seen anyone so contradicting.

"I had you pegged from the moment I first saw you," she whispered and turned on me.

She was so close, her expression fierce and, in the light of day, so different from how I'd remembered it.

"I was told I was wrong. Clearly, I wasn't." Her eyes flitted to the counter where Courtney was watching with rapt attention. "You have her nearly climbing out of her skin, ready to do anything for you at the drop of a hat. And last night . . ." Her eyes widened as if that incomplete sentence said it all.

"What about it?"

"I was sent to your house to deliver dinner since you ran off without a plate."

I stilled. The wild beating of my heart sounding so damn loud as I waited for her to continue.

Because I knew . . . I *knew* who'd come over. Who I'd let stay because I'd needed a release for so many reasons.

The girl in front of me being at the forefront of every one of them.

Not once during that time had anyone else shown up—that I'd known of.

A breathless, mocking laugh fell from her lips when she turned back to fit the lid on her cup. "Reed," she breathed. "Oh, Reed. God—yes—harder."

Her voice was soft. Erotic even through her mocking. And sent a shock of heat and need straight to my dick.

Those words in that voice were sure to haunt me for the rest of my life.

I dragged my hands over my face and then let them fall to my sides, my fingers curling into fists as they did. As flashes of this girl assaulted me.

On her back.

On her knees with her ass in my hands.

Against the wall.

Clinging to me.

She sent me a cold glare that successfully pushed away every thought she'd just put in my mind.

And there it was, as it had been the night before.

That look like she wanted to push me as far from her as possible. Like I was the worst kind of human.

"You may have other people fooled, but I grew up surrounded by men like you," she said through clenched teeth. "I can pick an asshole like you out of a crowd."

"Men like me?" A sharp breath worked from my chest, and I nodded slowly. Grabbing a couple of napkins, I set them beside the drink where she'd spilled, then stepped away. "Since you know me so well . . . I guess we're done here. Have a good day."

I didn't wait for her to respond. I didn't want to.

After what I'd woken to, I didn't have the patience to deal with this.

I wanted to run.

I wanted to forget.

THREE

EMMA

Exhaustion and lifelong fears wove through me as I climbed the steps of Lala's porch, but the moment I walked through the door, some of the weight on my shoulders lifted . . . eased. As if just being in that house had the power to make worries and stresses disappear. Then again, it'd been that way my entire life.

That house had given me a day or two of reprieve every year or so—a day or two where my life wasn't what it *was*.

"That you, Emma?" Lala called out from the kitchen, and I wondered what she would do if I were someone else.

"You might want to consider locking your door, Lala."

A soft snort was her only response.

I rolled my eyes as I set my purse on the entry table before heading in her direction, pausing in the archway and leaning against the frame. Watching as she baked something or other. I wasn't sure the woman had ever once stopped cooking or baking since I'd arrived.

"You were gone quite some time," she mumbled without stopping.

I lifted a shoulder. "I had a lot to do. Needed a new phone . . . things like that." I studied her for a moment as she nodded, debating on telling her about the other parts of my day and who I'd seen before the words, "I saw your *perfect* Reed Ryan," came tumbling out.

She glanced up from her creation, hands and apron and temple covered in flour and who knew what else. Her pale green eyes brightened with excitement even though her exhaustion from yesterday ran deep. "Did you? Oh, I just adore that boy."

I made some sort of condescending noise in the back of my throat.

I hadn't told her what I'd heard coming from his house the night before, just as I didn't plan on telling her what I'd seen with the barista.

Besides, Lala had been disappointed enough that I'd come home so quickly after leaving last night . . . with his dinner still in hand.

But it wasn't her business—it hadn't even been mine. I'd just been unwillingly subjected to both occurrences. Unwillingly subjected to dreams of those eyes and that smirk and what he could do with those perfectly muscled arms and body to make me say the things that woman had been screaming.

I'd woken up in the middle of the night, equal parts disgusted, horrified, and *aching*.

"I'm telling you, Emma. That boy is good to his soul."

"He's nothing but trouble," I disagreed, "in every sense of the word."

"You're taking past experiences and projecting them onto him."

I wasn't about to deny it . . . we both knew she was right. Didn't mean I was wrong about Reed Ryan.

He looked like a drunken regret and had heartbreak written over every inch of his body.

Literally.

There was nothing to guess at with him.

"There's something about him . . . I can feel it like a warning. You seem to trust him so much, and I just wonder if maybe you shouldn't."

"I know what it's like to put my trust in the wrong people," she said pointedly, irritably. "That *feeling* you have? Maybe it's because you've never been around a man as honest and good as him. The unfamiliar and unknown can do that to a heart."

"Heart? What are—" I realized then that I was pressing a hand firmly to my chest and hurried to drop it. "No. Lala, you need to stop pushing at that."

"I'm doing no such thing." When I lifted a brow, she put her flour-covered hands in the air. "What you need right now is a friend. He lives close, and he's here often, checking on Nora and me and helping around the house. You haven't had much of a good *anyone* in your life, and I can't think of anyone better than that boy."

"As a friend," I said doubtfully.

She snorted, the sound both delicate and slightly offending. "Reed Ryan deserves a girl who thinks he raises the sun each morning. You, my wounded child, would only attempt to tear the sun away from him with your doubts and pent-up wrath."

I wasn't sure if I should be insulted by that or not.

I decided against it.

"I don't want him as a friend, Lala. I don't want him as anything."

"Well, I won't apologize when he stops by," she said dismissively. "I also won't ask him to leave. He's more welcome here than you are."

I jerked back against the frame, caught off guard by her tone. It was sharp and defensive and laced with hurt . . . and it made my chest ache even though I knew I deserved it.

Because the Lala I'd known had never spoken to me that way, had never been guarded with me. She'd been all open arms and unconditional love.

Then again, I'd abandoned her. And, as she liked to keep reminding me in the short time I'd been here, *I* had changed.

I straightened from the wall. "Um, I, uh . . . I was just coming back to drop off some things and see if you needed anything before I headed back out."

"Oh?" The word screamed indifference but worry poured from her.

"I have to take back the car I rented," I explained.

"Did you need us to come with you to give you a ride back?"

"No, that's fine," I said quickly, which only seemed to increase her worry, her entire body going still and hands falling to the island. "I'll get a ride back."

After long seconds passed, she turned to the unbaked pastries with an uninterested hum.

I hesitated for a moment, but when she didn't so much as look at me, I shifted away, murmuring, "I'll be back," because it was all I could offer her.

I couldn't give her what she wanted.

I couldn't tell her why I'd suddenly left New York and shown up at her door. I couldn't tell her that what happened had shaken me in ways it shouldn't have because *nothing* had happened. And even if it had . . . it wouldn't have been the first time.

Because explaining that meant explaining the others to her. It meant describing all of Momma's disgusting boyfriends and husbands and the dirty cops that had become a revolving door in our lives.

With the way Lala had always tried to take me from a life she hadn't fully understood, I couldn't devastate her with the truth of what she hadn't been able to save me from.

I slipped away, grabbing the paperwork and box for my new phone as I headed up the stairs. Holding my breath and tightly gripping the rail as I went, unable to shield my mind fast enough from the wraiths that haunted and tormented me.

"Emma!"

I'd turned at the booming voice of Chris Dennison, my boss of the past three years, my eyebrows lifting when I saw the group of men laughing and stumbling along with him.

"Em-ma, Em-ma, Em-ma," he'd called out, pointing in the air with each syllable and dragging out my name the last time.

I'd switched the thick folders I'd worked on through my late dinner to one arm and grabbed my phone from my pocket with the other as I smiled politely at the men. "Did you lose the car, Mr. Dennison?" I'd asked as I pulled up the number for the car service that was supposed to be taking them around for his bachelor party.

"I should've known it would be you here," he'd said, his words slightly slurred.

"I'm always here," I'd reminded him. "Don't worry, I'll have you at—" I'd tried to catch my phone before it could fall to the floor when

it was smacked out of my hand, dropping the folders and spilling their contents at my feet as I did.

"Oops," my boss had said from where he was now directly in front of me.

My chest had pitched as fear and carefully buried memories burst to the surface when I straightened and looked into his glazed-over eyes.

"Weren't there supposed to be more of you?" a guy had asked from his side, pointing at me and then around me. "I thought we hired more of you." A grin that was pure charm and lust had stretched across his face as his bloodshot stare shifted down my body. "But you're gonna be worth every dime, darlin'."

FOUR

REED

My heart clenched as I read the latest message.

It wasn't much different than the others, but it never stopped pulling at me. Never stopped calling to me.

Kira: Come home.

My thumb hovered over the keypad for seconds or maybe minutes before I loosed a harsh breath and tapped out of my messages without responding.

I reached for the handle of my door, my stare darting to the street and sidewalks around me out of habit and narrowing on the car rolling to a stop behind me.

I studied the driver in my rearview mirror as my free hand automatically moved toward my off-duty weapon where it rested on my hip. This was Colby, I wasn't exactly worried something would happen here, but I'd been trained from a young age to always expect otherwise.

I noticed the sign for the car service on the windshield half a second before a blonde unfolded herself from the back.

A very hostile, tall blonde who had been plaguing my every thought.

With her alluring features and challenging expressions.

With the way she'd tormented me by moaning my name.

With the absolute mystery of her.

I opened my door and stepped out, brows already lifted in question before she ever noticed me.

"Stalking me?" I asked at the same time she sneered, "Fantastic."

Jesus, she was just so damn angry.

She gestured to me. "And I really feel that whole 'stalking' bit might be misdirected."

"That right?" When her anger poured from her and crept toward me, I took a step forward to meet it, embrace it. "I'd never seen you before last night, but there you were, in the place I'm at every Thursday night—and every other day for that matter. Then you came to my house." Her lips parted, but I continued before she could speak. "The coffee shop I saw you at?"

"I was there first," she tossed out stubbornly.

A disbelieving laugh rumbled in my chest. "But I run there every afternoon. A stalker would know that. And since we're playing that game, I was here first."

"I currently live here."

I stilled at the unexpected comment.

Lala was the first to offer others everything she had, but I couldn't imagine her taking in a stranger—especially without telling me.

She told me about her plants and what the neighbors were up to. She told me what she bought at the store and when she and Nora were going to be out of the house for a while in case I'd planned on swinging by during that time. She called to make sure Rowe and I had enough food for dinner, even if she'd just sent one of us home with enough food to last a week. The woman had a hard time keeping anything to herself, even though she swore up and down she wasn't a gossip like the women across the street.

So, to have someone move into her home without telling me?

For all of us to have been in the same room without her or Nora mentioning it?

It didn't make sense.

"How do you know Lala?" I finally asked, shock pulsing through me when I took in her soft face and wide, magnetic eyes behind all that anger and resentment. "Holy shit . . ."

Nora.

The girl's head listed and her brows lifted knowingly.

"Nora's your . . ."

Confusion and denial swirled in my chest as a wave of protectiveness slammed into me. Because I would do anything for that little girl—including keep her from the woman who'd abandoned her.

"Little sister," she finished for me. "I gave Lala the name you all use so fondly."

"Nora has a sister?" I asked, voice low with doubt even though it was there, in her eyes.

Lala and I talked about family often—too often. She'd been relentless in wanting to know why I'd shown up in Colby alone one day until I'd told her the whole story.

From the military to the job I'd been forbidden from having to the family I'd left due to dynamics no one would understand unless they'd lived it.

Everything.

In return, she'd pushed me to reconnect with my family nearly every time I saw her, saying family could be gone from your life in the blink of an eye.

Gone in the blink of an eye . . . that was all she had given me of her and Nora's story—not that I had pushed for more. The rest, Nora had told me in bits and pieces over the past three years. And yet, another granddaughter was standing in front of me.

"Yeah, well, I just found out about Nora a couple days ago . . ." The girl laughed a soft sort of breathless sound, but it was filled with pain and frustration. "Don't get too caught up on it. I would've been more surprised if Lala *had* told you about me."

"And why's that?"

Her eyes narrowed. "Why are you here again?" With that, she headed toward the house, looking like she was walking down a runway rather than a stone path.

And, fuck me, because all I could do for a moment was stand there and watch her. Take her in. Study her.

Those damn shoes.

The clothes that hugged her slight curves perfectly.

The subtle sway of her hips as if her body were taunting me with each step.

The way her hair fell down her back in waves, practically begging for me to grab hold.

The energy that both drew me toward her and pushed me away that was already becoming so goddamn addicting.

I let my head fall back and raked my hands over my face, groaning up to the sky before jogging after her. I reached for the handle of the door before she could grab it and felt the corner of my mouth tip up at the surprise that stole across her face before she could send another glare my way. But it wasn't like before.

The chill was gone. The hatred was missing.

She looked fucking adorable.

"Emma, honey, that you?" Lala called out when we stepped inside.

My smirk widened. "So, my stalker *does* have a name?"

"I'm not stalking you," she bit out before responding louder, "Lala, you should seriously rethink locking your door since I wasn't going to be the first one in here."

There was a brief pause before Lala asked, "Oh, is Reed here?" Excitement wove through her tone and the house and clearly irritated the girl in front of me.

Emma.

It fit the doe eyes and innocent, wholesome-looking face.

The lethal glares and animosity clinging to her body? They didn't seem to fit the name or the girl.

"Who else?" Emma asked, loud enough for Lala to hear her in the kitchen, but her eyes never left me. When she spoke again, her voice was nothing more than a whispered sneer. "Your precious Reed Ryan is here."

"The hell?" I murmured at the genuine disdain dripping from her lips. When she started moving past me, I reached out to stop her—the reaction involuntary. But the moment I touched her arm, her palm slammed into my chest and she jerked away as if I'd shocked her.

"Don't touch me," she snapped, backing even farther away as she did. Eyes narrowed with disgust and loathing.

I stepped back, hand raised just as Nora came running through the living room, shouting, "My Reed, my Reed! You're here!"

I wrapped my arm around her instinctively when she

smacked into my side, but I couldn't pull my stare from Emma as she hurried up the stairs and out of my sight. I didn't look away from the staircase until Lala clicked her tongue from beside me.

"Don't take offense."

I glanced at her, but my attention darted to the stairs one last time. "I don't know what I did."

"What did you do?" Nora asked softly, wrapping her hand up in mine and twirling around.

"Nothing," Lala answered her and then looked at me, her voice sad. "You did nothing. Come on, let me fix you a glass of tea."

"Why didn't you tell me you had another granddaughter?" I asked halfway to the kitchen. "Or that she was here?"

She faltered in her steps before continuing ahead. "Well, I do, and she is."

"You mean *that one*?" Nora asked, tone getting soft the way it did when she spoke to people she didn't know very well. When I looked down at her, her eyebrows were drawn together tightly. "Me and that one have the same mommy. I heard my Lala say so."

That one.

Which meant Nora either didn't like Emma or didn't trust her yet.

Then again, Nora trusted very few people. Funnily enough, they were some of the people I trusted most. Kid was smart.

"Is that right?" I asked as if I hadn't found that out just minutes before.

She nodded, the movement subtle. "That one was left too. But she wasn't left with my Lala."

"Nora," Lala gasped, sounding horrified, "who told you that?"

"That one," she explained, pointing upstairs.

Lala's head moved in fast jerks and she pointed away. "I'm about to start on dinner. Go clean up whatever you were playing with."

"But, my Reed—"

"Nope," I cut her off, tapping on her shoulder and slanting my head when she looked at me. "Lala told you to do something. What do you say?"

Nora's head lowered as she shuffled away, whispering, "Yes, ma'am."

I leaned against one of the counters and folded my arms over my chest, waiting until I was sure Nora was out of hearing distance before I asked, "You don't want Nora to know about Emma?"

Lala's head snapped up from where it had lowered to stare at the floor as she rubbed at her head. "What kind of absurd question is that?" When I gestured to where Nora had left, she heaved a big sigh and said, "Nora knowing things . . . it scares me. I've always been afraid of the day when she would start saying things she shouldn't know—worried it would mean her momma had shown up. Talked to her when she was playing outside . . . something."

I nodded in understanding and lowered my voice, trying to soothe and reassure her. "But Emma's here. You know that."

"Emma doesn't talk about her past. Ever." She lifted her hand to her head again, her stare drifting. "She wouldn't even talk about her life as it was happening."

"Your head hurt?" When she looked at me with wide

eyes, I nodded to where she had her fingers pressed to her temple.

She scoffed and rolled her eyes as her hand fell away. "Just the shock of Nora saying things she shouldn't know."

I grunted before asking again, "Why didn't you tell me about Emma?"

For a while, she just stood there, chin trembling and eyes filling with tears. "It isn't a happy story or one I like to remember."

"But you trust her with Nora?" I asked, needing to confirm even though nothing about the girl upstairs put me on alert.

"Of course. I just can't trust her not to disappear one day. But as long as she's here . . ." She shrugged. "Her being here is a miracle of a blessing."

"She disappear a lot?"

"I don't know," Lala said, sounding as if not knowing weighed heavily on her. "I don't know her anymore, but I do know that you've done nothing wrong."

A disbelieving huff burst from my chest. "The short conversations I've had with her say otherwise."

"I won't make excuses for what she's said, but I need you to know it's nothing *you* have done." She pointed toward the ceiling for only a moment before clasping her hands together. "That girl has had a life neither you nor I can imagine. I don't know most of the details, but I know she's the way she is because men made her that way. Because they terrify her."

"We're talking about the same girl? The one who looks like she eats men for breakfast?"

Lala's head shook in quick, subtle jerks as she turned to pull glasses down from the cupboard. "Don't let that mask fool you. She's terrified of them all—you especially."

Doubt flooded me, but any response I might've had disappeared when the sound of someone walking across the upper hall and descending the stairs filtered into the kitchen.

Emma walked in, having changed the button-down to a loose-fitted shirt that fell just below her hips. The heels were gone too, and her hair was piled haphazardly on her head.

Christ, if it didn't transform her completely—didn't make the cold, unapproachable woman seem a little more approachable.

Until those slaying eyes found me and told me everything without her ever saying a word.

She hated me.

She wanted to know why I was there.

She wanted me gone.

None of which surprised me, but throughout it all, there was a reluctance that I couldn't figure out.

Then her eyes dipped over me as if on impulse, and her reaction betrayed everything she was trying to keep hidden from me. She sucked in a quick, shuddering breath and her eyes darkened with a craving that only seemed to fuel her anger and bring to life the energy between us.

Just as fast, the look was replaced with indifference before she faced away.

But I had seen it. I could still *feel* it.

That unexplainable connection, filling the room and pulling at me . . . urging me closer to the girl in front of me.

Heavy, thick, and nearly impossible to resist.

As if I'd been running from shit my entire life to bring me there, to that girl, who hated the fucking sight of me.

It was probably for the best. Relationships were something I didn't want to entertain.

"Can I get you to stay for dinner, Reed?" Lala asked as she

started my way, glass of tea in hand. Before I could begin to respond, she casually tossed out the words that got me every time. "I was thinking breakfast for dinner."

I pressed a hand to my chest. "You know the way to my heart, Lala, but I really was just stopping by to check on the two of you."

She handed me the glass and shrugged as if it wasn't a big deal. "More pancakes for us then."

A low, agonizing laugh crawled up my throat. "You're cruel."

"I know a lost cause when I see one," she said on a dramatic sigh, but her smile was mischievous. "Though, I really could use some help with my porch swing since you're here. It's come loose on one side." She waved dismissively toward the entrance of the kitchen. "The rope or the hook. Something. Don't mind the smell of dinner, I'll just be cooking your favorites."

"Cruel," I repeated and pulled her in for a hug. "Tell Nora I'll say goodbye before I head out."

I spared one last glance at Emma, arms folded under her chest and attention fixed on the island, then headed outside.

After setting the tea on the porch, I jogged over to my truck to grab the small box of tools I'd gathered over the last years for this exact reason. The homes in our neighborhood were beautiful but old, and there was always something that needed fixing.

Once I was back on the porch, I headed over to the large swing, studying it as I did.

It was level. The ropes looked fine. The hooks still seemed to be perfectly tightened.

My eyes narrowed suspiciously for a moment before I finally set down the toolbox and pressed my palms to the bench, putting more and more pressure until nearly all of my weight was on it.

Nothing.

I stood and went to the side, and then the other, inspecting where it was secured, before grabbing hold of one side of the ropes and pulling myself up.

Nothing.

When the other side proved the same without so much as a groan, I dropped to the porch with a laugh that was equally amused and frustrated.

Damn you, Lala.

The laugh abruptly ended when I caught sight of Emma standing in the doorway out of the corner of my eye.

"Stalker."

Her eyes rolled, but the corners of her full mouth twitched into what might've been a smile. When she spoke, all traces of her earlier anger were gone. "I wanted to see what she was talking about. I've sat out here the last two nights, and it's been fine."

"Still is." I jerked my chin toward the doorway. "One way for her to keep me around a little longer."

"She do that often?"

"Not once."

When Lala needed help, she asked for it. When I told her I was just stopping by, she accepted it. Until a leggy blonde crashed into my world like a ball of wrath and set my head spinning.

Lala knew exactly what she was doing tonight, but this was the last thing I needed right now. Then again, I was struggling to remember that with that energy snapping and pulling and fucking *begging* me to move closer to Emma.

It wasn't until I was a foot away, watching the war rage within those wide eyes, that I realized I'd listened to it.

She swallowed slowly, the delicate movement of her throat wholly capturing my attention. "Nora was setting the table when I walked out . . . there's a place for you."

"Figures." I bent to pick up my tea and leaned against the side opposite her. "You want me to leave." It wasn't a question. It'd been written on her face from the moment she saw me standing outside my truck.

"More than anything," she said immediately, but her inner battle told me exactly how much of a lie lingered in those words.

I should've walked away then.

I should've *driven* away the moment I saw her get out of the car behind me.

But after just a few short encounters, I desperately wanted to figure out how to strip away Emma's anger and resentment. I wanted to know what she tasted like. If she'd be sweet and addicting, or if the bitterness dripping from her would bleed from her lips.

"And if I stayed?"

I fought a smile at the way her eyes flared before she could drop her stare. Her tone lacking all bite when she asked, "Don't you have somewhere to be? Someone to be *entertaining*?"

"Are you saying I'm not entertaining you?"

That gaze flashed up, all wide and innocent and holding me prisoner. Her full lips parting with a stuttered exhale as she whispered, "You know what I'm talking about."

A knowing hum left me as I stepped closer, losing the fight as a smile tugged at my mouth when she pressed closer to the frame and heat crept up her cheeks. "You didn't answer my question."

"Which one? You ask a lot—too much if you were wondering."

My smile widened and my attention caught on the way her throat shifted again, the movement faint but so telling. "If I stayed?"

"I wish you wouldn't," she whispered.

That energy pulled tighter and tighter between us with her blatant lie, but I forced myself to step away. Leaving her pressed against the frame as I slipped into the house.

She followed me in, voice hushed and demanding. "What are you doing?"

"I can't leave without saying bye to Nora." I met her wide-eyed stare, words dancing with amusement when I said, "But I think I'll stay for dinner first."

A soft laugh rumbled in my chest when I left her standing in the entryway, expression an intriguing mixture of irritation and wonder.

FIVE

REED

I closed the door to my truck, steps cautious as I took the path up to Lala's porch. Eyes darting over the house like there was something unfamiliar about it. Or maybe it was just that I knew Emma was inside, and she made everything about the house and this visit feel different.

I stopped by every day, but Sundays were special. Only today, I felt restless. Like my run had gone on forever, and I couldn't get back home and shower fast enough. Wanting to see that wild card of a girl even though she wasn't why I was here.

But she was all I could think about anymore.

I'd stayed late into the evening Friday, talking with her and Lala long after Nora had gone to bed until Lala had not-so-subtly tried leaving us alone.

It hadn't worked.

The moment Lala stood and very clearly excused herself, the energy spiraling between us had thickened and pulsed, and Emma had nearly jumped from her chair in an attempt to beat Lala up the stairs.

Not that Emma had been offering much to the conversation before, only little pieces here and there. But it wouldn't have mattered if she hadn't said a word all night because she'd smiled . . . she'd *laughed*.

And, Christ, they were both completely *her*.

Soft. Beautiful. With a slight edge as if her bitterness never truly left her.

Fucking perfect.

Yesterday had been much of the same. Lala conning me into staying longer and longer until Nora had gone to sleep, and Emma and I realizing some time later that Lala had never come back downstairs.

Emma hadn't even said goodnight. Just hurried for the stairs, her soft smile slipping away as she'd snapped, "You know the way out."

And I'd been consumed in thoughts of that hesitant girl wrapped up in a shield of ice and steel ever since.

I quickly climbed the steps and ran a hand through my still-damp hair. Dragging in deep, calming breaths as I tried to prepare myself to see Emma again before reaching for the doorknob. A smile crossing my face when I opened the door and saw Nora jumping up from where she'd been waiting at the bottom of the stairs.

"My Reed!"

"There's my favorite girl." I caught her in a crushing hug and then held her back to inspect her, my voice dropping to a whisper. "I think this is the fanciest you've ever been."

"Really?" she asked, her voice matching mine. "I worked really hard *all* morning. Everyone at church loved it."

"Of course they did." I looked around her, then gave her a shocked look. "But where's Éclair?"

She gasped and covered her mouth before turning and dashing up the stairs.

I straightened and turned for the kitchen, stopping when I was slammed with all that wild energy and need. Hazel eyes narrowed in curiosity and full lips slightly tipped up as she held a mug close to her chest. That current swirling around us nothing less than a charged minefield.

And I wanted to step right in.

"Reed," she murmured as she turned away.

"Stalker."

A hum of strained irritation left her. "So, are you just always here?"

"Does it bother you?" I asked as I followed her deeper into the kitchen to lean up against the island.

"I think it's weird," she said bluntly as she took a similar position at the counter opposite me, her eyes traveling over me before quickly darting away.

I fought a grin as she cleared her throat and continued.

"I mean, you come see a woman who is . . . what, probably twice your age and a young child?"

"Well, when you try to make it weird . . ."

She just lifted an eyebrow in response as she drank from the mug.

"Lala took me in as her own the way she does a lot of people. When she needed help, I was there, and Nora clung to that—clung to *me*." I shrugged unapologetically. "And when that little girl chooses you? That's a gift you don't refuse."

"And because of that, you're here every day?" she challenged, but there was no bite to her words, just genuine curiosity.

I wavered for a moment as I thought of what to say, what

all to tell her, then glanced over my shoulder and listened for sounds of her younger sister. When there were none, I looked back at Emma and lowered my voice. "You don't know her yet, but Nora needs stability. She . . ." I ground my jaw as my chest ached for that little girl. "She *can't* handle when things change."

Emma's eyebrows drew close, her stare darting away as if looking for the girl in question before meeting mine again. "What do you mean?"

I rubbed at my chest, hesitating again because talking to anyone about Nora felt like a betrayal to her. Felt like I wasn't protecting her when I'd sworn to do exactly that. "Your mom was using when she was pregnant with Nora."

Emma's expression fell into a mask of nothing.

"Nora's lucky, considering."

"But?" Emma asked tightly.

"She has a mild heart defect. Everything else is just . . . I don't know. I think it's part of what makes her *Nora,* you know? Lala said she started talking and walking —all of that—long after she should've, and she still learns at a slower pace. And like I said, she needs consistency. She can't handle high-stress situations or if things change. But I think she's perfect, and she's fucking smart. You'd never know she struggles with any of that unless you witnessed it."

"So, me being here . . ." Emma murmured when the sound of little feet running across the top floor could be heard.

"No," I said quickly. "You'll know when she can't handle something. But I think she's so used to people coming in and out of here for Thursdays that she sees you the way she sees all of them." I pushed from the island and walked a few steps away to be ready for when Nora came in, lips already curling into a smile when her voice preceded her.

"I found her, I found her!" she yelled before she came rushing in, holding up her favorite stuffed dog in the air. "I looked everywhere for her, but she was hiding. And then I finally found her in my bed."

"Maybe Éclair was tired," I said as I accepted the dog from her. "It's hard work keeping you safe all night."

She giggled and reached for my hand, swinging my arm wildly as she asked, "Can we read now?"

"Of course. But where's Lala?"

My arm abruptly stopped, and Nora's head lowered, her happiness disappearing in an instant as her eyes drifted to the side—where Emma still lingered.

I glanced over my shoulder at her, but she was still staring straight ahead. Expression blank and mug suspended in air.

I lowered to a crouch in front of Nora and asked, "Where's Lala?"

Nora wavered for a few seconds before moving to my side to whisper in my ear. "She left me with that one. After church, she brought me home and said it was okay if I was here with that one while she went to pick up lunch. But I don't think I like that one."

"Oh yeah?" I asked softly. "Why's that?"

"Because I don't think she likes me."

My heart twisted at the genuine sadness in her words, and I looked at her wounded stare. "That isn't true, Nora."

"Yeah-huh," she whispered. "She looks at me like she's mad at me, and she didn't say anything about how fancy I look."

"What?" I feigned shock and then glanced at Emma one more time before giving Nora a sly look. "You know what? I think it's because she's jealous that you look fancier than she does."

Nora's mouth popped open wide at the idea.

"But, hey, even if she didn't like you—which isn't the case—you'd have to be okay with that. Right? We don't need everyone to like us."

Nora nodded firmly even as her face scrunched together uncertainly. "But that one and me have the same mommy . . ."

"Nora, she likes you," I assured her. "But was it weird for you to find out you had a sister?"

She thought for a second before saying, "Yeah."

"Okay, it was probably a lot weirder for her because she's the older one. If I found out I had a six-year-old sister, I'd have a hard time with it too." I worked my jaw as messages and arguments and family bullshit flashed through my mind before I could push it away. "All right?"

"Okay," she said after a while and cradled her dog close when I handed it back to her.

"Where are your books?"

"In the living room!" she said, her excitement back in an instant.

"All right, go get them all in order. I'm gonna get some coffee, and I'll be there in a minute." Once she was dashing off to the other room, I stood and turned to find Emma pulling a mug down.

"What did she mean, I didn't say anything about how fancy she looks?" she asked softly as she set the mug in front of me.

"Thanks," I muttered, then sighed. "What she's wearing . . . she dresses up on Sundays."

Emma didn't say anything until I looked at her. And even

then, she gave me a helpless look for a moment before glancing to the kitchen entrance. "She's dressed the same as every other day."

A soft laugh pulled from me. "I know. But on Sundays, she puts on almost every piece of jewelry that she has and puts bows in her hair. She wears certain shoes . . ." I shrugged when Emma looked back at me, a crease formed between her brows. "She's obsessed with *Fancy Nancy*."

"What's that?"

"It's these books," I explained, gesturing behind me before taking a sip of coffee. "The girl in it is into France and everything being fancy. It's our thing on Sundays—I come for lunch, and Nora and I read all the books together."

"All of them?"

"All the ones she has," I confirmed.

"Seems like you're into being fancy," she whispered dryly, the corner of her mouth twitching into a ghost of a smirk.

I lifted my pinky, forcing a soft laugh from her. "She's learning to read," I said more seriously, then added, "Slowly. She works on it every day because she likes learning. But these books are helping a lot because she already knows them almost by heart and she *wants* to be able to read them. So, they're good for her."

A hint of some emotion I couldn't begin to understand swept across her face as I spoke, replacing her amusement. But I would've sworn there was a flash of resentment in her eyes.

"Why do you do this?" she asked when I started stepping back to head to the living room. "I heard what you said about stability, but she isn't your responsibility—you aren't her guardian. Lala is."

I wavered as buried truths ached to be revealed and forced

a smile. “I’d die for that little girl,” I said simply, then turned and walked away.

“SUNDAYS ARE a good day to call your momma,” Lala said when I walked into the kitchen a couple hours later, all casual indifference even though she said the same thing every week.

I held the air in my lungs for a moment before slowly releasing it, somehow managing not to grit my teeth when I said, “Drop it, Lala.”

“I’ll drop it when you make it right.”

Emma’s stare darted between us from where she was sitting at the table with Lala. Legs crossed on the chair and teasing me because she was all comfort in a threadbare shirt with her hair piled messily on top of her head. Such a contradiction from the girl I knew she could be and the way she usually dressed. And that contradiction only intrigued me more.

Forcing my gaze away from her, I leaned up against the island and told Lala, “We aren’t talking about this.”

“Oh, we never are,” she mumbled, eyes on where she was turning her cup in circles. “Because some young men I know are too stubborn to swallow their pride and fix what’s wrong.”

“Lala.”

She looked over at me, tone all dry and mocking. “Sorry . . . did I say something?”

I roughed my palm over my jaw and refrained from rolling my eyes because that would only land me in deeper shit with her. “I’m tired of doing this,” I said softly, the hint of warning weaving through my words. “I’ll fix it when I’m ready.”

"And by then, it might be too late."

"Lala," I ground out, voice sharp and irritated in response to the argument she liked to fall back on—to the same argument we had all the time.

She just raised a brow in disapproval.

Forcing out a calming breath, I pushed away the frustration and jerked my chin toward the entrance of the kitchen. "Nora's cleaning up, but she's in a mood. We didn't finish reading."

In an instant, everything about Lala changed. She straightened and her expression shifted into a mixture of worry and curiosity. "Oh?"

"She started pouting and getting upset, so I told her we were done for today. And then—" I stopped when I heard Nora's steps in the entryway and then pointed in that direction when she very obviously stomped up the stairs. "That."

"Oh Lord, no," Lala muttered as she stood.

"Yeah . . . have fun." I listened as she left the kitchen, my stare drifting back to where Emma was tracing lines on the table with her finger.

"Is that my fault?" Emma asked once Lala was gone. Her gaze lifted to meet mine as she unnecessarily clarified, "Nora."

I shrugged. "She can't do that."

"That isn't an answer."

"In Nora's mind, maybe. But . . . no. It isn't."

We'd only been a couple books in when Lala had come back with lunch earlier. I should've figured out what was going on with Nora while we were eating because she'd talked almost as little as Emma had. Her tiny face had scrunched up tighter and tighter each time Emma offered something until her chin was tucked into her chest. I hadn't been able to tell if she was about to cry or if she was just pissed in a way six-year-olds could get.

But I'd been too focused on Emma to notice the depth of it until we were cleaning up, and Nora was practically dragging me back to the living room to continue reading. Once we were settled in her favorite reading spot, it had been as if nothing had ever happened.

Until Emma came in a few books later.

Just walked in and sat down across the room without saying a word, watching curiously until Nora grabbed the book out of my hands and slammed it shut, saying, "That one can't be here."

Emma had left as abruptly and quietly as she'd appeared, even though I'd tried telling her she didn't have to go. And Nora had opened the book back up with a contented sigh as if all was right in her world again . . . until I'd taken the book away to talk to her.

"She can't do that," I repeated to Emma.

"It's because I'm changing things?" she asked. "Like you mentioned earlier?"

"No." The word was a soft laugh. "Again, you'll know when Nora is struggling with something because it's changing on her. It's . . ." I thought about the times I'd witnessed it and pushed from the counter to sit in the seat Lala had vacated. "Loud and heartbreaking."

Emma's eyebrows pulled together, but she didn't ask for more details on what happened during those times.

"She thinks you don't like her," I explained even though I was sure Emma had already heard Nora say that earlier. "And, apparently, she's getting possessive because she's jealous of you."

Surprise and confusion marred her face for a few

moments before a huff left her, all soft amusement and bitterness. "What?"

"I guess she's starting to see everything with your mom differently—the fact that she was left by her when you weren't."

Anger and resentment flashed in Emma's eyes before she could hide it, leaving a mask of ice and steel.

"She's six," I tried to explain. "In her head, she doesn't understand why you got to live with your mom and she didn't. And because of that, she doesn't want you to have Lala or me. She'll get over it when she gets to know you."

"Have Lala or *you*," she said. "Because *you* are hers the same as Lala is." She cut a cold look my way and offered me a smile that would've made lesser men shrink. "Because the two of you raise Nora together in this weird, family thing you and my grandma have going on."

"That's fucking disgusting," I muttered.

"That's how it is, isn't it?" she challenged.

"I think you're reaching because you want a reason to hate me."

A bitter laugh fell from her lips. "I hate you plenty, Reed."

A smile stretched across my face at the obvious lie. "I think it kills you that you don't."

Her expression faltered for half a second before she was able to fix it in place, but that hiccup had my smile growing. "Are you leaving yet?"

"If I go, will I see you tomorrow?"

Shock stole across her expression and filled the kitchen with silence. "What?" she finally asked after long moments, voice soft and breathless.

"Just wondering if you'll let me in Lala's house again once I leave," I murmured, the slightest tease lacing my words.

A stunned laugh fled from her as she sat back in her seat. "What'd you think I was asking?"

Her eyes rolled before settling on me with another one of those glares, but the chill behind it was gone. "Again: Are you leaving yet?"

I studied the way she was sitting, relaxed and content to be there with me. The way the corner of her mouth kept twitching as if she was fighting a smile. Lifting a shoulder, I said, "I'm good right here."

SIX

EMMA

I hurried into the kitchen and headed straight for the coffee maker. My mind racing so fast as I grabbed a mug and the coffee pot that I didn't notice Lala until she was beside me.

I jumped, nearly sloshing the hot liquid onto me, and tried to start my heart again when I realized it was *her* there. "Jesus."

"Try again."

Blowing out a steadying breath, I finished pouring the cup and set the pot back in its spot. "Morning, Lala."

Her brows lifted. "Oh, so *now* you say good morning?" When I stared at her in confusion, she huffed and pointed behind her. "I said my greetings and asked where you were off to this Monday morning looking like you forgot that you were in South Carolina instead of New York again, and you just kept on walking."

"I'm sorry." I lifted my hand, trying to indicate where my head was at, but gave up and hurried to the fridge to grab creamer instead. "So many things going on in my head, I didn't even know you were in here."

"Maybe it's because you don't slow down," she said with a huff. "Now, just where is it you're going looking like a Yankee . . . and in those stupid, four-inch heels nonetheless?"

I fought the urge to roll my eyes. They were five inches, but I didn't tell her that. "People in the south wear heels too, Lala."

"Of that, I am well aware. But from the way you dress to the way you walk and talk, you have Yankee written in big ol' letters across your forehead."

I doubted I walked or talked any differently than I ever had. I'd only been in New York for five years.

"I have a meeting," I said carelessly as I took a sip of the hot liquid.

"A meeting," she echoed dully. "What could you ever have a meeting about in Colby when you've only been here a few days?"

I choked down the next sip and hurried to say, "Interview." I met her stare, checking her reaction and praying she bought the lie. "I have an interview."

Disbelief and surprise covered Lala's face. "An interview? Goodness, I didn't even know you were applying anywhere."

I made a confirming hum as I forced down more of the coffee, thankful she'd accepted it so easily. Depending on how the meeting went, I would talk to her. But I refused to get her hopes up about something I might not be able to do for her.

"Well, that's quite something," she said. "Where's the interview?"

"Can we talk about it later?" I asked, taking another big drink and draining the rest in the sink. "I need to get going."

She pushed from the counter, talking as she went. "Oh, sure, sure. Let me get you the keys. You can take—"

"No," I said quickly. "It's fine. I have a car coming to pick me up."

"Again?" Confusion coated and slowed her words. "Isn't that getting expensive?"

"I'm used to paying for transportation. It's fine." I shrugged, letting her know it wasn't a big deal. "Besides, they're already on their way. I'll be back later."

She looked lost for words, but I didn't want to get into it with her. Especially then.

I hurried from the kitchen, grabbing my bag with everything I'd researched and gathered during my late nights on the porch, and got outside just in time to meet the car.

Research to protect that little sliver of resentment I couldn't seem to shake. Because, as Lala had told me that first night, she was always afraid that my mom would show up at any time and take Nora.

My mom hadn't left Lala with anything more than Nora—not even a diaper bag. No written word that she was giving up her rights. No assurance that she would never be back. And knowing firsthand just how erratic and desperate my mom could be, I knew Lala's fears were valid.

But I would do anything to make sure my mom couldn't put anyone else through what she'd dragged me through. So, despite how bleak my research had come back, I wanted to meet with lawyers to see what Lala's options were. Hoping they would give me better news.

Something that would ease Lala's worries.

Something that would protect Nora.

I stepped through the doors of Butler and Davis Law Offices with a minute to spare, the large building located in the middle of Colby, and offered the secretary a smile. “I have an appointment—”

“Wade?” she asked, already reaching for her phone.

“That’s correct.”

“I believe they’re already ready for you . . .” She waited for a moment before speaking into her phone and then gave me a smile. “Just a moment.”

Before I could sit down in one of the chairs, a man came walking into the reception area. Brow creased and pointing at me. “Wade? Not . . . Joslin . . .”

“Her daughter,” I said, unease weaving through me because this man knew my mom.

His head shook in disbelief, eyes blinking exaggeratedly. “Well, goddamn. Look at you, all grown.” He held out his hand for me to shake and then quickly ushered me back the way he’d come. “When I heard the name *Wade,* I was wondering why your grandma didn’t just come talk to me. Then I walked out and saw you . . .”

I swallowed through my hesitation and asked, “How do you know my mom?”

A laugh left him, but it hinted at everything *Joslin Wade*.

Frustration and sorrow and relief that she was gone. I knew the feeling.

“This is Colby—everyone knows everyone. But we go way back with your family,” he explained as he gestured me down another hall. “My wife used to babysit your momma when she was a teen. We actually live just next door to your grandma.”

“Really?” I asked, surprise weaving through the word.

“As I said: Way back. And, I’m sorry,” he continued as he pushed open the door to a conference room and ushered me in, "it's been a long damn time . . . what was your name again?"

"Em—" My name died in my throat when I saw the man already waiting for us at the table. Not much older than myself, handsome in a conventional way, with a charming grin.

I knew that grin.

"You're gonna be worth every dime, darlin'."

"This is my partner and son-in-law, Jarrod Davis," Mr. Butler said as he shut the door behind us.

My chest pitched with a jagged breath as recognition slowly lit in Jarrod's eyes.

Any hope I'd had for Lala . . . for Nora . . . abruptly vanished along with his grin.

This can't be happening. This can't be happening. How is this possible?

"I'm sorry, I think . . ." I struggled to take a breath, but the air in the room felt too heavy and suffocating. And everything in me was screaming to leave. I stumbled back and grabbed the handle of the door. "I have to leave."

"You feeling all right?" Mr. Butler asked.

"Why don't you stay?" Jarrod Davis asked as he stood from his chair, the question sounding more like a demand in his low and commanding voice. His head slanted, stare glossing over the papers in front of him before his eyes were on me and dragging over my body. "Ms. Wade, was it?"

Ice shot down my spine at the look that flared in his eyes and the sound of my name leaving his mouth. But I fumbled with the handle until the door flung open wide behind me, then turned and hurried down the hall and through the building. Avoiding the receptionist's eyes on my way out as emotion built in my throat, hot and full of shame. Anger pulsed just beneath my skin, making me shake and breathe erratically.

As soon as my feet touched the sidewalk, I felt him behind me. All hostility and fear and that overwhelming presence that screamed he was used to getting what he wanted.

"Get away from me," I seethed, head whipping around to keep him in my sight.

He bared his teeth in a feral grin. "Right now, I'm simply checking to make sure you feel all right since you ran out before our meeting could begin. So, you will not run, and you will not react. Do you understand?" Without waiting for a response, he took a step closer, his stare dipping over me and tone dropping. "What are you doing in my town, Ms. Wade? Better question: Why exactly do you need a lawyer? And know that there *is* a wrong answer to that."

A trembling breath ripped from me at the threat. "Why are *you* here—you were in New York."

"It's funny how the world works," he said in the same unforgiving tone. "Your boss was my college roommate and is still one of my closest friends. That doesn't explain why you're in South Carolina now. In my office, needing a *lawyer*," he hissed, then rocked back a step, breaths harsh and fast.

I pressed my lips closely together, refusing to answer. Refusing to ease any of his worries.

After a while, he huffed irritably. "If you're hoping for some type of retaliation, I told you that night: You can't touch me. You can't touch any of us. Now that you've seen what I do for a living, you know why."

The threat rang in my ear long after he'd stormed back into the building, leaving me on the sidewalk alone. Trembling as I struggled to make my lungs work properly.

But I refused to break down. I refused to let any man break me or make me feel like this . . .

This shameful, dirty whore.

I refused—

A sob burst from my chest, sharp and unbidden before I had the chance to slap my hand over my mouth. Sucking in quick, shallow breaths, I attempted to pull myself together and hurried away from the law office.

For a long time, I simply walked until I somehow ended up on the main streets of downtown Colby, knowing if I was there, I'd be able to find my way back to Lala's.

I could've gotten another car, but I just didn't care.

Walking gave me time to think over the morning. Gave me time to think of the absurd odds of any of the men from that night being from Colby or South Carolina in general.

If I had even thought for a second that they might be, I never would've come. Just knowing Jarrod Davis was in the same small town had me itching to pack up my things and leave.

I slowed to a stop when my eyes caught on a piece of paper taped to the inside of the window of the building I was passing.

COULD SURE USE SOME HELP.

Come on in.

I STARTED STEPPING AWAY but stepped back instead to take a long, assessing look of the building in front of me. All massive bay windows and a non-descript, faded sign that read *Books*.

And that faded sign pulled at a part of me from long ago that I'd tried to forget.

While the store was dull with chipped paint along the borders, the other storefronts on the street were bright with fresh color and care. But they had flat faces and windows that could never compare to the dusty panes before me that continued in designs all the way up to the second floor.

The store could have easily been a statement on the street, but it was muted and seemed to have settled into its place in the background decades ago. As if to say, "This is all I will ever be, and I'm content with that."

It nearly begged people to walk right past it.

But the store and that sign, handwritten in beautiful script you just didn't see anymore . . . it called to me. It begged me to *stay*.

I grabbed the handles of the thick, wooden and glass mosaic doors that had definitely seen better days, and let myself in.

And was immediately hit with the smell of dust.

"Jesus." I cleared my throat and tried not to breathe in the smell as I walked deeper into the store and called out, "Hello?"

"Have a look," a gentle voice called from the side.

I followed it, taking in the place as I did.

Dozens of memories swirling through my mind and tugging at my chest even though this store looked nothing like the others.

The place was enormous inside.

High ceilings with beams running the length, giving the store an elegant look within all the dust and dimmed lighting.

Floor to ceiling shelves almost completely lined three

walls, separated every so often by large partitions that extended farther than the shelving, so it didn't look cluttered.

But the outer shelves, along with what I could see of the inner bookshelves, were empty. All the books had been piled haphazardly on tables near the front of the store.

With every step toward the large, wooden checkout counter, I wondered why I was walking closer instead of turning right back around and walking out.

And then a sweet, old woman popped her head above the counter and let out a slow exhale as she hefted herself onto the chair.

She gave a little jolt when she saw me. "Well, hello. Was there something I could help you find?"

I cleared my throat and pointed to the side. "I saw the sign in the window."

She nodded in a resigned sort of understanding. "Oh, yes. That's been up for quite some time now." Her eyes locked on me, studying me. "This place may not look like much, but I'm not selling. So, you can turn yourself around and leave if that's why you're in here."

"What?" I always knew exactly what I was wearing and owned it. But at her words, I glanced down to inspect myself, feeling uncomfortable in my own skin even. "Oh. No. No, I had . . . no, I'm not a—I'm just here." I lifted my head and met her questioning stare. "I would like to help you."

Her chin wavered and her eyes watered. After a few seconds, she lifted a wrinkled hand to her chest. "Truly?"

"Yes."

She gave a quiet sob and looked around. "This was my grandparents' place. My parents took over after. I tried, but I . . ." She made a face as if there was only so much she could do. "My husband passed twenty years ago, and I couldn't afford help when people no longer wanted to come in. Those electronic things have taken over, you know."

I did, even though I'd never owned one.

"I can't pay you much, I'm afraid," she continued. "But this place . . . I can't give it up either."

"I can understand that." I took a step closer and said, "I don't have my résumé, but I can get it to you this afternoon."

"Well, that's something. I don't know if I've ever looked at a résumé."

"Also, you should probably know I left my last job under less-than-ideal circumstances."

She wrung her thin hands together. "Oh?"

"Yes, ma'am," I said, not giving her any more details on Chris Dennison or New York or that part of why I'd left was, apparently, in Colby.

For a long while, she was so silent, so still, that it was unnerving. Then she looked around the store and lifted her frail shoulders. "Like I said, I can't pay you much. Maybe not even minimum wage."

I nearly fell to my knees in shock and gratitude.

"And this place . . . I know how it looks." She paused. "Do you know anything about books?"

Only that they had a part in saving my life.

"No," I said honestly, throat thick with my past. "No, but I've never known anything about anything, and that's never stopped me. I'll keep going until I learn it all."

Her smile was simple and kind. Gratitude pooled from her. "You know, you might want to wear something a little more casual around here."

A laugh tumbled from my lips. "I can do that." I glanced over my shoulder, assessing the place.

"I know how it looks," she repeated. "Haven't been able to do much more than sit back here for years now."

"I can fix that," I found myself saying, then hurried to look at her. "With your permission, of course. It's your store."

A tear slipped down her cheek. "If you can make her breathe again, you can do whatever you want to her."

I turned then, taking in the quiet store that seemed to hide even within itself. "I think we can do more than that."

SEVEN

EMMA

"You back now, Emma?" Lala's voice rang through the house, meeting me as soon as I walked in.

I rolled my eyes, the corner of my mouth lifting as I did. "What if it wasn't me, Lala?"

"Well, whoever it was would be just in time for sandwiches."

I rounded the corner into the kitchen and watched as she put the last bits of food on the island for lunch.

Fruits, vegetables, dips, cheeses, and rolled meats.

Different types of bread and mini loaves . . .

She had enough food out to feed an army.

"Expecting more people, Lala?"

I hated that my heart took off at the possibility of it. Hated that a small part of me was hoping Reed would be the one she was expecting.

I didn't want him to have an effect on me at all.

She spread her hands out as if it wasn't that big of a deal. "Just a little something for us to nibble on. Nothing fancy."

"Oh yeah, nothing fancy."

Her eyes narrowed in mock irritation before a questioning look entered them. “I got a call from Ron Butler not long ago . . .”

Shit.

When Lala realized I wasn’t going to respond to her prompting, she said, “When he first mentioned you, I thought maybe that’s where your interview had been. But he said you’d set up a meeting there.” Her head slanted curiously. “And then left before it could begin.”

I kept myself tall and still and held her stare. “Is there a question here, Lala?”

Hurt and frustration dashed across her expression at the coldness of my tone. “Honey, he’s a lawyer. I’m trying to figure out *why* you need one.”

“It isn’t anything to worry about,” I said, shrugging indifferently. “Besides, I decided they wouldn’t be a good match for me anyway.”

Lala looked equally worried and upset when she said, “They’re a very nice family, Emma. We all go to church together—Ron’s wife used to babysit your momma.”

“I heard.”

“And their daughter is married to that Davis boy. She’s about your age, and their first baby is on the way.”

He’s about to be a father?

Oh God.

My stomach rolled.

“That’s great, but I don’t need a lawyer, Lala.”

She stared at me, silently begging me to give her something since she knew I was lying, but I held my ground.

After a while, she released a weighted sigh. “Well, then . . . go get you out of those clothes, then come eat.”

“I’m fine in—” I pressed my lips firmly together when she

lifted a brow. "Yes, ma'am," I muttered, then turned to go do as she'd said.

Once I was in jeans and a different top, I padded into the kitchen and grabbed a plate to load up with food.

"Nora and I popped over to the BBQ place in town," Lala said as I neared the meats. "And there isn't one thing about that place or their food that is less than divine. Isn't that right, Nora?"

Nora nodded subtly from where she was already at the table with food, barely catching my eye before studying her plate.

I looked over the different meats as I placed cheese on my bread, emotion tugging at my chest as I remembered the days we'd stop in, and Momma would beg for Lala's money. It was the only time I ever ate like *this*.

I'd grown up on peanut butter sandwiches and dry cereal —what we could afford and what traveled easily since our RV didn't have a working fridge. When my mom bailed, not much changed because I needed to save money.

The first year working for Mr. Dennison, I'd finally let myself buy real groceries when I'd received my Christmas bonus. I'd cried when I'd cooked and eaten that first meal. It'd been terrible, but it'd been mine. And Lala had been on my mind the entire time.

"Something not to your liking?"

"What?" I glanced over to see Lala's full attention on me. "No. No, of course not. Sorry . . . just a lot on my mind."

She nodded after a moment and resumed assembling her sandwich. "Always seems to be." As she was grabbing her plate and turning for the table, she whispered, "Your momma had a lot of secrets before she started disappearing too."

Frustration and fear swirled in my stomach. "What else, Lala?" I demanded as I faced her.

She turned at my question, mouth parted and brows lifted in surprise.

"Running . . . secrets . . . what else am I doing that's like her? Because, of all people, I thought you would be proud that I didn't go down her path. That I worked my ass off and tried to make a life for myself. But since I've come here, it's been nothing but snide remarks about my clothes or the way I talk or my life up until last week." I stumbled back until I was pressed to the counter, my throat tightening and words straining as I pointed at Nora. "She shouldn't be here for this."

Lala's head shook for a moment as if she wasn't sure what to do, then she hurried to usher Nora out of the kitchen. "Adult talk. We'll be done soon," she tried to assure her.

Once Nora was gone, I went on. "I thought I'd done it. A life to be proud of. A great job. I'd *done* it. And then it fell apart, and now I'm getting pushed down like I'm the one at fault. I don't need you digging at me every day, making sure I stay down."

"Oh, Emma." Lala breathed a quiet cry and fell into her chair. Placing her hand over her mouth, she just stared at a spot in the kitchen as I continued.

"You had troubles with my mom. You struggled with her before she left. You've told me all that. After, you saw her—saw us—every year or so for a couple hours or maybe a day. But you didn't really see *her*. What you saw during that time was her at her best because she was trying to get money from you. I know her life and her actions broke your heart because she's your daughter." I placed my hand on my chest. "I know.

But you don't know what it was like for me. Every day with her. Fixing her mistakes and bearing her shame and trying to keep us alive because she wouldn't. Being her permanent, reluctant crutch. That was *my* job. So, forgive me for not turning out how you hoped I would. Forgive me for having irredeemable traits like running and keeping things to myself when that's all I've ever known."

"Emma, no. I'm sorry—please . . . forgive *me*." Her hand fell to her chest as her shoulders lifted in a faint shrug. "I just . . . I always knew why y'all returned—why *she* returned. I did. And she always had an excuse for needing the money, and I knew it was a lie, but I couldn't help hoping she might be telling the truth. That she might be changing."

"I would've told you why we were really here if you'd asked."

She studied me for a moment before looking away. "When I opened the door the last time both of y'all showed up and saw you standing there, it was written all over your face that you were just . . . *broken*."

I wanted to say I hadn't been.

I wanted to say nothing would ever succeed in breaking me, but she continued speaking.

"I knew by helping you all those years, I had only hurt you. I knew by not fighting harder for you, I was to blame for that look in your eyes. That's why I said 'no' to her and fought harder than ever for you," she said, voice filled with years of grief. "I lost you that night, and the decision to stand up to your mother has haunted me ever since."

The words *I never wanted to leave you* were on the tip of my tongue, but I choked them back. Lala already knew I hadn't. She'd known that then.

It didn't change that I *had* left with my mom. It didn't

change that when opportunity after opportunity arose, I hadn't come back. I'd stayed with my mom because I'd known she wasn't capable of taking care of herself or protecting herself from the disgusting men she brought around. When she'd left me, all the fears that still consumed me had kept me from coming here . . . from letting Lala even know I was alive.

"You *should* be proud of yourself and your life, Emma. You should be very proud . . . I am," she said, voice weak. "Anyone who knew your Momma can see you're nothing like her. You weren't then, and you aren't now. But I've been guarding my heart with you because *you* are so guarded and because I've been preparing for you to walk right back out that door ever since I found you standing on my porch."

"Lala . . ." Her name was soft and twisted with regret.

"I'm sorry, Emma," she whispered sadly. "You needed *me*, not a house, and I've failed to give you that because of the past." A mixture of a laugh and a cry burst from her as she waved her hand toward the island. "If anyone should be ashamed of their actions, it's me. I did this to prove I've always been fine without the two of you here. That Nora and I are fine."

I looked behind me at the island covered in food.

"And it ain't even Thursday."

Despite the heavy tension in the kitchen, a laugh bubbled up my throat. "So much food, Lala."

"I know. I feel juvenile." She placed her head in her hand, looking at the spread.

"So, this isn't normal?" I asked, confirming.

"Not unless I'm throwing a party."

My lips tipped up but quickly fell into a frown. "The

Thursday thing . . ." The unspoken question lingered in the air.

"That is to give them a little extra lovin'."

"Every week?"

Lala dipped her head in a nod and gestured between the table and me. "Eat. Please." Once I'd gone back to putting my sandwich together, Lala came to my side. "I am sorry, Emma. I will try to push aside my fears, and I apologize now because I know it might take time before they're gone completely."

"I understand."

I had to. She was on the other side for those sixteen years. Constant coming and going for nothing other than money. I would've had the same thoughts too. I couldn't understand why she'd ever let me back in the house at all.

"I'm sorry for abandoning you," I said softly, words I should've voiced the minute she'd opened the door to me when I'd needed her most.

"Oh, hush."

"I'm sorry for not coming to you sooner. For not contacting you," I continued even when she waved my words away. "I'm sorry you had to make a family of strangers when I should've been there."

She gripped my chin in her hand to stop me and looked at me through glassy eyes. "You had a hard life. I'm sure I can't imagine the half of it, but I see it when I look at you. I *saw* it. You did what you had to in order to survive." She shrugged and stepped back. "And you *did* come back to me."

"When I needed help."

"There is nothing wrong with asking for help, Emma," she assured me. "I ask for help all the time. Hell, I receive help even when I don't ask for it. That's why First Responder Day here at the house began."

The corners of my mouth lifted before falling when I thought about a man covered in tattoos with a smirk that did traitorous things to my stomach and knees. Gray, knowing eyes that seemed to see straight to my soul . . .

And disaster written all over him.

"The difference is what you do with that help," Lala said simply. "It's how you receive it and what you do in turn. And I know asking was hard enough for you, but you need to learn how to accept the help that is offered to you."

I nodded hesitantly. "Yes, ma'am."

"Now enough heavy." She waved her hand between us as if she were washing away the conversation. "Tell me about the interview," she said before calling out, "Nora, honey, come eat."

My eyebrows drew together in confusion before I remembered passing off my meeting as an interview.

Lala must've seen the look on my face because she said, "Unless there was no interview . . ."

"No, I actually got a job."

Lala clicked her tongue as she sank back into her seat and pushed Nora's plate closer to the little girl when she sat as well. "Well, congratulations. Where at?"

"Um, I actually don't even know if it has a name," I said with a hesitant laugh. "And it isn't ideal, but I'm . . ." My lungs expanded with a deep inhale. "I don't know, I'm really excited about it."

Lala waved a chunk of fruit in the air. "Well, what is it?"

"You know that bookstore on Main street? It's almost at the corner—it has beautiful bay windows."

She blinked slowly, her eyes drifting to the side for a moment. "Is that still there?"

Another soft laugh left me. "Yes, it is, and *yes*, that one. It looks like it's hiding. The woman who owns it is older and can't do much with it. I think she kind of gave up on it after her husband died. But it's been in her family for generations, and it clearly means everything to her." My mouth curled into a smile. "When she saw me, she told me she wasn't selling and that I could turn right back around."

An amused huff left Lala. "Donna," she said suddenly as if just remembering her name.

I made a sound of affirmation as I moved to sit at the table with them. Setting my plate down, I asked, "You know her?"

"Not well, just from around church. She keeps to herself mostly." Her stare seemed distant as she ate for a few moments. When she looked at me, curiosity wove through her words. "And what is it about an old bookstore that has you so excited?"

Old memories danced at the edges of my mind, my head shaking when I said, "There was just something about that building that called to me. I had to go in."

A soft smile pulled at my lips as I thought about the dusty store with chipped paint and dirty windows.

"The place is a wreck. Looks abandoned and looted. It feels forgotten and just . . . *sad*. All I want to do is bring it out of hiding and see what it can be." I blinked away the shop and the old woman within the shadowed walls and laughed uneasily. "That sounds weird."

"Not when you did the same for you."

My head snapped to the side, but Lala was staring at the table as if it were the most interesting thing in the world.

"I like books," Nora said softly, pulling my attention to her. "My Reed got me some books for my birthday."

I tried to ignore the wings taking flight in my stomach at

just the mention of him and asked, "Oh yeah?" even though I'd already been told as much the day before.

"Two of them," she whispered, but her eyes were lit with excitement the way they seemed to whenever Reed came around.

"That's right, he did," Lala said. "And he got you some fun and pretty things to go with them, didn't he?"

Nora nodded quickly, her head lowering when she realized I was still watching her.

"I didn't know that store was still standing, let alone open," Lala said, easily shifting back to our conversation. "Is Donna gonna be able to pay you?"

"She was upfront about that . . . said what she could afford. It isn't what I was making, but it's more than I've made at other jobs. And it's enough for me to start over. Besides, I want to be there."

Lala seemed happy with that answer, sitting back in her chair with a satisfied look. "That's good, Emma. I'm happy for you. So, what is it you want to do with this bookstore?"

My chest rose and fell with an excited breath.

Ideas swirled in my mind, as they had since I was in the store.

So much to do and even more to work with.

So many possibilities.

"Everything."

EIGHT

REED

"Got it," I called out as I headed toward the entryway.

"Careful, it might be Courtney," my roommate, Peter Rowe, teased from where he was making a post-workout shake in the kitchen.

I let out a dull laugh, my mouth quirking up at his own responding laughter that was pure amusement because he knew just how much the shit with Courtney bothered me. With a steeling breath, I glanced through the peephole and felt everything in me go wild.

I don't know who I expected to be knocking on the door.

One of the guys from the department wanting to shoot the shit before work started . . . since that was a thing in Colby. Even Courtney . . . because God knew that girl had probably figured out where I lived.

But it hadn't been *Emma*.

I shifted away from the door, murmuring, "Stalker," as I pulled it open.

The corners of Emma's mouth tipped up, negating the scowl she was clearly trying to keep in place. Her gaze darted over me as if drawn, and then she went utterly still as horror blanketed her expression.

I automatically glanced down to see if something was on me but stopped my quick inspection when her whispered words slammed into me.

"You're a *cop?*"

I slowly lifted my head, unsure of what to say or think.

Because Emma's back was ramrod straight and her chin was lifted, but there was no missing the mixture of denial and disgust in the way she was staring at me.

If I'd thought she hated me when we first met, I was wrong.

For the life of me, I couldn't figure out why Lala hadn't warned me that her granddaughter hated police officers. I also wasn't sure how this was news to Emma.

She shoved a large paper bag toward me. "We had a lot of food leftover," she muttered, voice cold as ice. "Lala thought you and some guy named Peter would want some."

"I'm some guy named Peter," Rowe yelled, his steps coming closer. When I glanced over my shoulder at him, he took one look at me and quickly turned to go back the way he'd come.

I looked back to Emma and then let my stare drift to the bag but didn't move to take it. I just leaned against the doorjamb and folded my arms across my chest as the dozens of questions swirling in my mind gathered on my tongue.

Before I could settle on any one of them to ask, she asked, "Do you want it or not?"

Disappointment built in my chest as I felt that push just as strongly as I felt the pull.

"She's the way she is because men made her that way. Because they terrify her."

I hadn't believed Lala then . . . I was beginning to.

Men. Officers. Who the fuck knew what else.

I forced something like a smile, but it felt all kinds of wrong. "And here I'd thought your anger was only reserved for me."

"Sorry to disappoint you."

"So, it isn't *me* then—"

"Oh, trust me, it's you." A bitter laugh fell from her lips as her eyes slowly raked over me. "It's every single thing about you."

I nodded and worked my jaw. "The other day, you said you know my type. Said you grew up surrounded by men like me . . . but you clearly hadn't known I was a cop. So, what kind of guy do you think I am exactly?"

"Trouble," she said immediately. Her eyes narrowed and that sweet face creased with some kind of hatred I couldn't even begin to understand. "The kind of guy who knows women will ruin themselves for him, so he uses them up and leaves them broken before moving on to the next. The kind of guy who uses his position and power to get what he wants."

Anger and confusion and irritation washed over me.

I'd never had someone pin me so wrong. But I could tell she believed every word.

I stared at her until I was sure I could speak calmly. "All that because I was hooking up with someone the night you stopped by?"

Her head shook in quick jerks as she rocked back a step, her expression screaming I didn't get it . . . that she hadn't expected me to.

A sharp, berating laugh burst from me when I remembered her words from the coffee shop. "Oh, and because of

Courtney. Right? The barista," I offered when confusion lit in her eyes. "That girl who took your order? I've been politely rejecting her for three years. Never encouraging. Not my goddamn fault she doesn't stop."

"Ever consider trying harder?"

"Right, and then I'd be the asshole." I leaned forward, my mouth twisted into a sneer. "And you apparently have an issue with law enforcement, but the day *I* use my position to get what I want is the day I turn in my badge."

The bitter amusement drained from her expression, leaving an understanding that was as haunting as it was hollow. "I'm sure that's what they all said before the first time . . . and the second. Power can be as addicting as any drug."

Jesus Christ, what did she grow up around?

I swallowed thickly, afraid to go down that road. Knowing my mind would run wild, and I would only want to annihilate whoever had put that look there—whoever had made her this way.

Hesitation fueled my next words. "There are bad men and there are bad officers. Not all men or police officers are bad."

Anger flared in her eyes. "How reassuring coming from someone who is everything I've hated and feared in my life, combined into one."

For a second, I didn't respond.

For a second, I didn't move.

Then some mixture of amusement and frustration sounded in my chest as I stepped back and grabbed for the door. "Then why are you still on my porch, Emma Wade?"

Before she had the chance to react in any way, I shut and locked the door.

I stood there with my hand on the deadbolt as her last words replayed in my mind.

I'd had a girl years ago. A girl I'd thought I wanted to give the world to before she broke my heart. Ever since, there had been a string of women who were only interested in the uniform. Other than a night every now and then to release frustrations or needs when it all got to be too much, I'd wanted nothing to do with them.

For the first time in years, someone had caught *my* attention.

A girl with a sweet face and steel in her eyes . . . and she hated me for even breathing.

NINE

EMMA

"He's a cop." The three words tasted sour leaving my tongue and snapped back at me from the walls of Lala's kitchen.

They had been playing in my head again and again since I'd seen that uniform and badge, but I still couldn't wrap my mind around it.

Reed's a cop.

Disgusted.

Outraged.

Disappointed.

I couldn't get a handle on the emotions filling my veins, and I wasn't sure I wanted to.

I knew, I knew, I *knew* better than to do something as foolish as let myself *want* a man like Reed Ryan.

To want any man.

Yet, wanting him was exactly what I'd done since that first night . . . only to be slapped in the face with the reality that he was worse than I ever could've imagined.

A fucking *cop*.

. . .

I'D WOKEN to the sound of banging on the door.

Hard, incessant banging.

My heart had already been racing, my body tensed and ready for a fight that wasn't mine. I'd woken to that so many times in my life and had distantly wondered how many more nights like that we would have to endure.

People wanting what they felt was owed to them. Demanding back whatever Momma had stolen from them. Men wanting nothing more than a woman they could use for a few minutes before leaving.

Worse, when they decided to stay.

"This is the police, open up."

I'd scrambled from the makeshift bed, my already-racing heart flying so fast I'd been sure it would take off out of my chest.

Because those . . . those *was the worst of them all.*

Momma's name had been on my tongue, already prepped for a whisper, but by the time I'd scrambled to the main section of the RV, she'd been swinging the door open.

"Officer." Her voice had been husky, the word slightly slurred.

A bright beam had shone through our home, stopping on me for a few moments before going back to my mother's face.

"We've been getting calls about suspicious activity in this vehicle. Suspicious people coming and going all hours of the night."

Momma had lifted a shoulder, causing the sleeve of the shirt she was wearing to fall off of it. "Ain't no idea what you're talking about. Seeing as it's night and the only person here besides us is you."

There had been a beat of silence before the officer asked, "Mind if I search the place?"

Momma had taken a step toward him to block the entrance. "And if I do?"

"Not up for discussion."

After a second's hesitation, she'd stumbled back as he'd come barging in, turning on the lights as he did.

My heart had sunk and stomach twisted when the first thing his eyes touched were the lines of coke Momma had left on the table and the empty baggies next to them.

Not again, not again, not again.

I'd never wanted that life. I was only there because Momma had dragged me along so I would take care of her and clean up her messes and pick up the pieces of her fucked-up life. So she could use me as a pawn in her game.

The officer had glanced from my mom to me, his eyes lingering on me for a long while before he'd said, "I would love to hear the excuse for this one."

LALA TURNED from her place at the sink at the sound of me storming in, towel in hand and genuine surprise at my anger sprinkled across her face. "Who's a cop?"

"Who else?" The sound that climbed up my throat might have been a laugh, but I couldn't be sure because it was wrong. *So* wrong. Tarnished with every memory that was clawing at my brain and trying to mold itself to the image of Reed in a uniform. "Your precious Reed Ryan."

"I know," Lala said slowly, her brows lifting at the same leisurely pace. "I wasn't aware his profession was something to be angry over or that it was a surprise considering who I feed on Thursdays."

"First responders, Lala. You feed first responders."

"A police officer is a first responder," she needlessly reminded me.

"I know, but I thought he was a fireman or an EMT. Something else—*anything* other than a cop," I seethed, my voice holding a hint of the desperation I felt. "You said he saved your life. You said he has saved countless others'."

"All truth."

"But it's why I expected something else."

"Well, now that isn't my fault," she said as if I were absurd. "And what does it matter if he's—"

"Because they're evil," I cried out, my voice wavering and cracking when I continued. "Cops are evil and corrupt. Every single one of them."

"It ain't mine," Momma had said automatically.

The officer had huffed a disbelieving laugh and looked at me again. "So, that makes it yours?"

"What? No!*"*

"Either it's one of yours, or it's both of yours."

Momma had lifted her hands in the air as though she was washing her hands clean of the whole situation. "I told you, it ain't mine."

I'd pushed from the wall, fear and anger pulsing through me. "Momma, please.*"*

But she wouldn't meet my stare. She'd just stood there, twitching and eyeing the lines like a woman dying.

"It isn't mine," I'd said adamantly. "I've never touched that shit in my life. Test me, I'm clean."

"I'd have to take you down to the station for that." The officer had leered at me. "If that's what you want me to do, I'll gladly put you in the back of my car."

I'd hurried to put more distance between us. "No. No, I don't—I didn't do anything. I don't want to go anywhere with you."

He'd taken cuffs from his belt and sighed like the whole situation weighed heavily on him. "I told you how this was gonna work."

"Momma."

She'd tilted her head in my direction. "If I go, you got nowhere to go. No one to take care of you."

"I have—"

"She's dead," she'd snapped.

She isn't.

She isn't, she isn't. I have Lala.

The instant I felt a hand on my arm, I'd reacted.

Shoved my free hand against a Kevlar-covered chest and ripped away from the fingers gripping me. "Don't touch me."

It was instinctive after years of men touching me and taking things from me they had no right to.

Horror had ripped through me as I'd stumbled back and looked into the stunned and determined eyes of the officer.

"I believe that's assault on an officer."

"No. No, it's—I—" My breaths came too fast. Too shallow. "I didn't mean to."

His stare had slowly raked over me. Emotions I knew too well shifted through them. Want. Lust. Need.

All things that shouldn't be in his eyes. Not in that situation. Not when I was only fourteen years old.

"You know . . . I'm feeling a little generous tonight."

Oh God, no.

LALA JUST WATCHED me with a mixture of dread and understanding as though my outburst had given her a crucial piece of my world that she'd been searching for.

"No, they're not."

I whirled around at the soft voice to find Nora standing a handful of feet behind me, holding a stuffed dog close to her chest and looking as angry as I could imagine her being.

"They're not," she repeated. "And my Reed's not. He's the

bravest and best and he's so special. And you shouldn't say mean things about him."

"I—" I blew out a harsh breath and curled my hands into fists, trying like hell to keep my voice calm and even when I responded to her. "Nora, this is an adult conversation."

She made a little move as if she were gathering up her strength to continue defending *her Reed,* but just looked to Lala.

"Emma's right, sweetheart. Why don't you go play or color?"

"I can have talks about my Reed," she said stubbornly. "I'm a big girl!"

"Nora," Lala said firmly.

Nora stood her ground for a few more moments before leaving, looking equally upset and angry.

I turned back to Lala as she sighed and rubbed at her head. "I can't imagine what happened to make you say those words, Emma . . . I just can't. But it tears me up inside to see that hatred and fear in you because I know *where* it comes from. And that's what *I* hate—that you were subjected to that life at all."

I steeled my jaw when hers trembled, as if I could give her the strength I'd maintained over the years. The strength to will away tears and emotions that threatened to drag me under when I'd always refused to drown.

"However, it isn't fair to say what you said," she continued, her voice thick and shaky. "You're being prejudiced. The majority of the police officers in the world are *good.* And you can be damn sure one of them is Reed Ryan."

"Oh Jesus." The words were a whispered curse. "You're blind, Lala. You're blind to them. You're blinded by *him.* I told you that he was trouble—I *told* you. I could see it."

"You're seeing what you want to see." There was that Wade strength, backing each clipped word that left her mouth. Giving them bite. "You're seeing whatever hell you were put through. You're seeing a life you never should've been exposed to, and you're projecting it onto others. You can't go through life that way, Emma."

Some mix of a scoff and a sneer pushed past my lips as I turned to leave the kitchen. Two steps later, I whirled around, chest heaving, teeth clenched so tightly it made my jaw ache.

Lala stood tall and proud, waiting for whatever it was I would say next.

But when I spoke, the harsh delivery I'd planned came out frail and soft. "If you had spent a *week* in my shoes, you wouldn't be saying that to me. The thought wouldn't even enter your mind."

I'd backed up until I was against the wall, my body tensed and prepared for a fight I wasn't sure I could win.

Of the countless times Momma had been arrested, there were a few times she hadn't. A few I remembered with sickening clarity. And they'd all started like that—only their attention had been on her.

The officer's eyes had settled where my shirt ended on my bare thighs. "You offer something worthwhile, and I'll forget everything that happened here tonight. Everything I saw."

My teeth had clenched so tightly I'd been sure they would shatter. "I'm fourteen, you sick fuck."

The man's eyes had darted to my face. The hunger there didn't lessen, but a question arose. "Now, why do I have a feeling that isn't true?"

He'd rocked forward, but my mom had grabbed his arm, saying,

"You want somethin', then you got me tonight." Glaring at me as if I'd tried to take what was hers.

The officer had looked from her to me and then back again. After a hesitant nod, he'd jerked his chin in the direction of the lone room of our RV. My room.

Once Momma was headed there, his focus had returned to me. "You talk about this, I'll come back for both of you," he'd said in a low warning tone. "You scream, I'll come up with enough charges to make sure neither of you sees the outside of a prison for a damn long time. Understood?"

My head had moved in rough jerks, but I didn't speak.

I'd just tried to disappear into the thin, hollow wall as he'd pushed past me and followed Momma into my room. Once the flimsy door had shut behind him, I'd forced myself away from the spot I'd been rooted in and fumbled for the radio, hurrying to power it on and turn it up. Anxious to drown out the noises that would soon come from the room.

Once the radio DJ's voice was filling the small RV and fading into a song, I'd taken slow, calming breaths, then started the methodical process of cleaning up Momma's mess while she'd kept herself out of jail.

For that night, at least.

I STORMED out of the kitchen and up the stairs, forcing back the haunting memories and shattered screams that always accompanied me whenever I set foot on those steps, gripping the railing tightly until I was safely on the second floor.

I hadn't been in my room for more than a few minutes before I heard Lala making her way across the wood floors. I looked expectantly at my opened doorway, waiting for when she would appear there, and was surprised to see her chin raised defiantly once she did.

"I guess I'm just surprised."

When she didn't continue, I bit. "By what?"

"By you," she said, her expression and tone thoughtful. "You've had a lot of strong opinions about Reed Ryan since you first met him." She lifted her shoulders in the barest hint of a shrug as if the thought had just crossed her mind. "I noticed you aren't only exceedingly mad at his choice in profession, but you're also saddened and disappointed by it—disappointed in *him*. Odd reaction to have for someone who doesn't care."

"I don't care."

A disbelieving hum sounded in the back of Lala's throat.

"I *don't*. He's nothing to me," I said stubbornly. "I've told you that he was trouble, and that's it. I have opinions because I've been around men like him. If they're strong, it's because he keeps confirming those notions, yet you refuse to see who he really is."

"And the disappointment?" she challenged.

"I'm not," I said in exasperation, praying she couldn't hear the lie.

Because I was.

I was disappointed that he so perfectly made up everything I hated while still making me want him. I was disappointed in myself for wanting him at all.

"Ah," Lala said with a nod. "Of course. You're right, I must have been imagining things."

From her expression to her conspiratorial tone, I knew there wasn't a chance she believed me.

"I must have imagined the way he can never take his eyes off you," she said with an exaggerated sigh. "I guess I also imagined the way you steal glances at him and maybe also the way you always smile when he laughs."

My heart began racing as mortification and denial rushed through me.

I'd known she had been attempting to meddle in things she shouldn't. I just hadn't realized I'd been letting my unwelcome emotions slip to the surface.

I hadn't known Lala had seen anything she wasn't meant to.

She placed the tips of her fingers to her temple. "This old girl is just seeing things, I guess."

"Lala, he's . . ."

"Nothing to you," she offered, the words nearly sounding like a question. "Yes, I heard you. So, then you wouldn't mind if he were to, say, date someone?"

I swallowed the response that was quick to form because I honestly wasn't sure what would've left my lips once I opened them. If my tongue would betray me at the last moment.

Because I'd found myself craving Reed all too often. I'd begun fantasizing about him the first moment I saw him. And—even though I'd been trying to embarrass him—the second I'd moaned his name, my need for him mixed with my contempt. Both nearly impossible to ignore. Both growing until they nearly consumed me.

Wanting to know what he felt like. Tasted like.

Needing him to know exactly how much I detested him.

Leaving me empty and frustrated and confused when I'd finally succeeded with the latter this afternoon on his porch.

But it was for the best, wasn't it? Because I'd already foolishly allowed myself to entertain even the thought of him.

And I was still struggling to answer a question that should have been simple.

All I needed to say was *no,* and the conversation could be over.

No, I wouldn't mind.

No, I wouldn't care.

He can fuck every single woman in Colby, for all I care.

Easy. It should have been easy.

Except those lies felt harder than any of the others I'd told my grandma about Reed because the others had been tangled and encircled in truths or my pride. This? Lala already knew she'd caught me with this.

Her eyes were narrowed on me, seeming to capture every movement, every breath, every thought.

"There's quite a line here in Colby of girls vying for Reed's attention," Lala said. "One, in particular, has been trying to catch his eye. I think she'd be good for him—many people in town agree."

A surge of discontent swirled through my stomach and chest, but I cleared my throat, my head bobbing as I said, "That's good then."

"And that wouldn't bother you?" Before I could even attempt to respond, she took a step into the room and added, "Seeing him with someone? Here in this house even?"

"Why are you doing this?"

"Because you are lying to yourself to protect your heart, and it's about time you stopped."

My eyelids slipped shut. "Lala . . ."

"Give Reed a chance."

"I can't," I said immediately. "Lala, he is—God, he's everything I hate."

"*He* is not who you hate. The men you encountered in

your life are who you hate—and you encountered them because your mother made sure you were surrounded by them." She raised a hand as though she was already expecting an argument. "You've been hurt more than I'll ever understand. You do not trust men, that is more than clear to everyone—including Reed."

My chest heaved with a sad, muted laugh.

"But love comes when you aren't looking for it. Life has a way of giving us exactly what we need when we need it."

"This coming from the woman who said she only wanted Reed and me to be friends," I said skeptically. "Who said I would . . . what was it . . . take the sun from him with my pent-up wrath?"

She clicked her tongue and gave me a knowing look. "I was sure if I'd said the truth, it would've given you more of a reason to push that boy away. But you seem to be doing that all on your own, even though I see the way the two of you look at each other. I've seen it from that first moment."

"Lala, it's just not what I want," I murmured.

"You can't tell your heart that it's wrong in wanting someone. You can't silence it just because you're afraid of what could happen."

My lips slowly parted only to close again because she was right.

She pointed at me as she stepped into the doorway to leave. "Of anyone I have ever known, *you* have every right to be afraid. But you have always been brave, Emma Wade. Don't let your fear stop you from being brave now."

I UNCURLED my legs and pressed my bare foot to the wooden porch late that night, lightly rocking the swing back and forth a few times before pushing off and curling my legs under me again.

I leaned my head back against one of the ropes holding the swing up, letting my eyes unfocus and the night's symphony fade to nothing as I replayed my conversation with Reed that afternoon for the umpteenth time.

Analyzed every expression. Every piercing stare.

Remembered the tornado of fluttering wings that erupted in my belly the moment he opened the door and the disgust and denial that unfurled in my stomach when I noticed what he was wearing.

I had meant every word I said to him. If asked again, I would still mean them.

Lala could call it prejudice all she wanted.

I didn't care.

She hadn't been subjected to it dozens of times, and I'd never encountered anything different to show me otherwise.

My world had been men littered with tattoos who tried to ruin me.

My world had been cops who left me in the care of those vile men. Cops who feigned honesty and devotion between pocketing my mom's drugs and taking her bribes.

Before today, I'd found myself wanting to believe Reed wouldn't be like those men, and I knew I would continue to. I'd known it as soon as the shock of seeing his badge had faded enough for a thought to emerge.

Not him . . .

Only to be quickly taken over by the persistent, disturbing echo.

He's a cop, he's a cop, he's a cop . . . Reed's a cop.

As horrified as I'd been today, every time I replayed our conversation, I still saw *Reed*—not the badge. And I was beginning to hate myself for that.

I was falling too hard, too fast.

Despite Lala's insistence to be brave, the harder I fell for Reed, the more it terrified me and made me want to push him far away.

Even if I could take away the tattoos and the badge—and God knew my traitorous heart was battling with my mind, screaming they didn't matter—other factors made me want to keep Reed at a far, far distance.

The greatest of which was a tower of tattered baggage that had followed me around my entire life.

New York had been a place I'd found I could be free of that girl.

Funny how here, in this safe haven, my demons ran rampant. Ready to torment and torture me at every turn. Reminding me I was nothing more than a damaged girl who'd managed to escape Hell.

Maybe because running from them wasn't the answer.

I lowered my foot to the porch again, a sigh falling from my lips as I rocked the swing a few times and prepared to push off.

Blinking away the daze, I flattened my foot to stop the swing's movement when I heard the sound of a car door shutting far too close to be anywhere else other than—

I sucked in a shallow breath.

Oh God.

TEN

EMMA

My heart stuttered and then took off at a rapid pace, matching the thrum of wings in my stomach as I watched Reed walk up to the porch. But my muscles tensed instinctively at the sight of the police SUV in front of the house. A lifetime of reacting to seeing those kinds of cars and those uniforms. The deep-rooted instinct to dispose of anything illegal my mom might've left lying around—the need to protect her—still hit hard, all these years later.

By the time he climbed the steps of the porch and stopped a few feet away from me, I was a mess of conflicting emotions.

The disgust poisoning my veins? I understood it.

The anger making my blood race? Went without saying.

But I couldn't figure out why the sight of Reed dressed that way had my lungs seizing, stealing every last breath. I couldn't wrap my mind around this *betrayal* and this *ache* when I hardly knew him. When he meant nothing—he *had* to mean nothing to me.

"You should go," I whispered and looked to the door, gauging the distance and Reed's position.

"Shit, Emma, I'm sorry." It all came out rough and aggravated and on edge. "I'm fucking sorry. I'm sorry about how everything happened today and how I responded to you."

I stilled. My stare slowly shifted in his direction again as I tried to figure out what he had to be sorry for.

I'd gone through our conversation enough times to know that I was the one who'd been harsh and cruel—only I didn't know how to apologize for my life and the kind of person it had turned me into.

"I've been thinking about it ever since you left, and I just keep seeing that look in your eyes when you saw me," he said softly, dejectedly. "I shouldn't have reacted the way I did. I'm sorry."

"Please stop," I softly begged. "Stop apologizing."

"I don't know what else to do. I feel like I've fucked everything up just by breathing, and I don't know how to make it right by you."

You can't . . .

You don't understand . . .

And why did that bother me so much?

My head shook as I stood and hurried for the door. "I'm sorry, I can't do this."

"Emma."

The instant Reed's hand touched mine, I reacted.

Wrenching my hand from his grasp and shoving him away. "Don't touch me," lashed from my tongue like the cracking of a whip as I lurched from him.

Reed's hands were in the air and he was standing at the lip of the top step by the time I pressed myself to the siding of the house. "I'm sorry," he said carefully, eyes wide and worried as they searched me.

Oh God, oh God . . . "Oh God."

"I'm going to stay over here," Reed said after a few seconds, voice rough and tense. "I won't come closer."

"I'm sorry," I wheezed, struggling to see him past the flashes bursting through my mind. "It's—"

Instinctive.

Survival.

None of your business . . .

"It's okay," he said when he realized I wasn't going to finish speaking.

"Why are you even here, Reed?"

"I was going through the neighborhood for a call," he answered softly. "Saw you when I was driving back out and thought we could talk." When all I gave him was a nod, he continued, his voice pure hesitation with underlying hints of sorrow and fury. "Emma, what happened to you?"

My gaze flickered in his direction as the wraiths continued tormenting me with my past. Clearing my throat, I took a step toward the door. "You should go."

"Wait."

I hated that he had the power to make me stop. To make me go against every instinct. To have me abandoning my morals. To crumble my resolve.

"You don't have to tell me—that's okay. But will you do something for me?"

At that, I rested back against the wall. All those monstrous thoughts still there, clawing at my mind and trying to overpower me, but the wonder of what Reed Ryan could want from me quieted them.

"Will you close your eyes?"

My head was shaking before the last word could leave his lips. "No."

"Emma—"

"No."

"I will stay in this spot. I won't move unless you tell me I can," he said, honesty dripping from every word. His throat worked, the movement slow and wholly captivating. "You said something this afternoon, and I want to talk to you about it now that you've had time to process what I do. But I can't if you're already looking at me like I've somehow ruined your life."

I didn't move.

I didn't close my eyes.

I simply stood there, staring directly into his pleading eyes, silently begging him not to make me do this. Not to ask me to blindly trust a man.

"Emma, *please*."

With a defeated, broken exhale, I forced my eyelids shut and tried to contain the shaking that took over my body.

"You said I was the kind of guy who used my position and power to push people into giving me what I want," Reed said after a moment, his voice a mixture of confusion, anguish, and defeat, and just as far from me as it had been before. "Do you truly think that?"

"Why are my eyes closed for this?" I asked instead of answering, praying the softness of my voice hid the slight tremble there.

"I saw your reaction to me at my house," he responded gently. "I saw the way you looked when I walked up this porch. You're not gonna be able to give me a real answer if you're focused on my uniform—on the way it makes you feel."

"Part of me believes that," I finally answered, then relented, "*A lot* of me does. But if you would've asked me yesterday, my answer would've been *no*."

"Because you didn't know I was a cop," he assumed, his voice low.

I didn't respond. I kept my jaw firmly locked, already kicking myself for the answer I'd given him. I was positive if I hadn't spent the day worrying over our fight and my conversation with Lala, I would've already walked into the house and up to my room, leaving Reed out there alone.

After a minute of excruciating silence, he asked, "Can I take a step toward you?"

I sucked in a sharp breath and slanted my head in preparation to shake it . . . and halted.

My lungs began aching the longer I stood there, turning over a harmless question and a simple answer.

"I'll stay here," he said resolutely.

"One," I whispered.

"You're sure?" he asked after a beat.

I nodded unsteadily and wondered if he saw the way my entire body jerked when his heavy boot sounded on the porch. Wondered if he noticed the way my chest pitched and my lips parted with my shaky inhale. If he noticed my racing heart and deepening breaths were from equal parts old horrors and in response to the energy thrumming between us.

"But it's more than my job," he assumed softly. "So, if you hadn't heard someone at my house that first night, would you still think all this about me? Think I'm some asshole who uses women up and leaves them?"

My eyelids popped open to see him studying me, brow set in frustration.

Responses gathered on the tip of my tongue, jumbling and choking me. Because to give Reed a simple *yes* would mean one thing to him, and I wasn't sure I could hurt him that way—not again. To say *no* and explain my life would be a confession I wasn't willing to give.

"That's difficult to answer," I said, voice wavering in uncertainty.

"Why?"

Because my mind tries to connect my past to you at every chance, conjuring images of a man I vowed to run far away from—a man who is trouble.

Because even with the badge and tattoos and the girl that night, I still find myself wanting you.

But I hate that you evoke these thoughts and reactions and emotions in me at all—I'd rather feel nothing toward you. And yet . . .

"Unless you tell me no, I'm about to take another step toward you," he said when I didn't respond, his tone filled with an agonizing mixture of warning and longing.

I didn't say no. I didn't say anything at all.

My belly tightened nervously watching him take that step. My breaths came quicker . . . heavier. The space between us was so alive with energy, it felt suffocating. As if I wouldn't be able to take a full breath until it was erased.

Damn him for it.

When he spoke again, his voice was softer, gruff. "All I need is a *yes* or *no*—would your thoughts of me be the same?"

"I can't give you either."

His frustratingly handsome face twisted in defeat and sadness. "Why?"

"Why can't you let this go?"

The corner of his mouth twitched into some semblance of a forced smirk as those emotions came off him in waves and crashed into me. "You and I both know it would be a mistake to."

I wanted to tell him I didn't know that. I wanted to tell him he was wrong. I wanted to send him away—force him from my life.

Instead, I stood there, silently begging him to understand something I refused to tell him.

To understand that I was haunted by a horrific childhood. That I'd learned to never trust men who represented what he was. And I'd survived by running from all of them.

To fall for Reed . . . it would shatter everything I'd known and who I was.

But those demons still had their claws deep within me, and it was impossible to shake them off.

"It isn't as simple as a *yes* or *no*," I finally said. "And I can't explain why."

"Because I'm everything you hate and fear, right?"

My body sagged against the wall. "Reed . . ."

"Right?"

"It isn't that simple," I whispered because I knew Lala was right. I knew just looking into Reed's eyes that he was *good*.

He studied me for a while before faintly begging, "Close your eyes."

I didn't hesitate that time.

That earlier fear and suspicion were noticeably absent, leaving only the current that seemed to grow stronger and stronger with each minute that passed.

As if even the energy between us was mocking me for fighting the inevitable.

"Is this how we're always going to talk from here on out?" I asked. "With my eyes closed?"

The slightest hint of a laugh filled his voice when he answered, "No." A few moments of silence passed—tense and heavy with unknowns and wants before he said, "Hold your hand out in front of you."

Unease wound through me.

Because my heart was already going insane, and now my mind was going wild with possibilities of what would happen if I did as he asked.

I slowly rubbed my fingers together before reaching out in front of me.

Hesitantly.

Blindly.

Trusting a man littered with tattoos and wearing a badge.

A shock of that electricity and excitement and *Reed* bolted up my arm when his fingers circled around my wrist and slowly slid up my forearm.

His hold was both gentle and firm, enough to assure me that I was safe while silently conveying his own cravings.

Halfway up my arm, he reversed his path until his fingers were intertwined with mine.

"I'm taking a step," he said brusquely.

My lips parted.

A shuddered breath escaped.

It was all I could offer in way of consent.

He lifted our joined hands, his fingers teasing mine in a slow dance before he trailed his hand up my arm again.

"If this puts fear in you, I'll never touch you again," he said softly, unwavering in his honesty. "Open your eyes."

I did. Immediately. Already knowing his face would be directly in front of mine.

Close enough that if he leaned in . . .

His stare dipped to my mouth as if we were both standing on the edge, forcing ourselves not to fall. "Do you see me or someone you hate?"

I saw a mistake I was about to make.

My mind was screaming, reminding me of every reason this was a bad idea. But my body had taken control the moment he touched me.

I see you.

I see you.

I see you.

What are you doing to me?

Before my lips could touch his, a muffled, distorted voice had me jolting away and snapping back to my clashing reality. My stomach twisting with disgust and dipping with regret as the energy that bound us lashed between us, stronger than ever.

I wanted to break through it. Shatter it. Destroy it.

I pulled from Reed's hold and pressed closer to the siding of the house, trying to ignore the way my chest ached when the hunger and longing in his expression were replaced with understanding and disappointment.

He murmured something into his mic as he stepped back, then cleared his throat. "That one was for me."

I nodded. Jaw firm. Stare darting all around, never resting on him.

I felt restless.

I wanted to run.

To get away from Reed and what I'd been about to say—about to *do*.

"I have to go," he said, the disappointment I'd seen on his face leaking through his words.

"You should," I said quickly, already taking a step toward the front door.

"Emma," he called out before I could reach the handle.

I glanced over my shoulder to stare at the porch, at the railing, at *anything*.

"It would be a mistake to let this go," he said, repeating his earlier words, and then he was gone.

Leaving me confused . . .

Aching.

More determined than ever to push him away . . .

To let myself want him and be wanted in return.

ELEVEN

REED

I pushed Rowe into the booth opposite Nick Butler and then slid in beside him, releasing a weighted breath.

In part from the run we'd just completed, mostly from the mixture of the shift I'd recently finished and the encounter with Emma in the middle of the night.

Butler's eyebrows were raised when I finally focused on him. "You serious, y'all actually ran here?"

Rowe gestured to me.

I lifted my hands a fraction from the table before letting them fall. "Needed it."

Butler shoved menus at us. "Y'all planning on running home after eating your weight in pancakes?"

"Fuck no, you're driving us home," I said as I tossed the menu back.

"Usually make a man buy me a meal before I let him boss me around," he murmured, his expression impassive.

Rowe coughed out a laugh as he lifted a glass of water and drained it.

"Does your *wife* know that?" I asked, putting a strong emphasis on the new title.

"I stole the line from her." His mouth twisted in a wry grin as he opened the menu I'd thrown at him.

Not that he needed it, we didn't even need to place our order anymore. He and I had been getting the same thing every week since the day I'd shown up in Colby three years before, needing to get away from my family and the bullshit that only built whenever we were together.

I'd driven from Florida without a direction in mind until I realized I was coming here. Or maybe I'd subconsciously always known. Maybe I'd needed to talk to the one guy who knew it all—who would understand.

I'd met Butler on my first day of training to be a SEAL.

We weren't friends then—I didn't really care to make any when they would've just been a distraction. Besides, people kept failing out of the school or leaving.

Butler wasn't one of them.

After graduation, we were placed on the same Team. Not more than a year later, Rowe had been placed with us, and I'd ended up stuck with them for nearly six years and too many deployments and assignments to count.

That Team became my family, but Butler had been through it with me from the beginning. That's a bond some people will never have or understand.

So, it shouldn't have surprised me that my hands had steered my car in his direction when things had finally come to a head with my dad.

But after what was only supposed to be a couch to crash on and a conversation to vent, I hadn't left. There had been something about the small town and the anonymity in a place where everyone knew everyone else that had called to me—*begged* me to stay.

The next day, Butler had come to me with news that the next city over was beginning a new law enforcement academy class soon.

We hadn't taken more than a minute to decide. We'd started the process for registering that day. By the end of the week, I'd officially moved into Butler's apartment and had done everything to become a South Carolina resident. Within the month, we were sitting in a classroom, and it'd been just like old times.

A year after that, Rowe had shown up much the same way I had—freshly discharged and breaking over his divorce, needing to lean on us.

Asshole hadn't left either, and we'd started renting out the house we were still in just as Butler and his now-wife moved in together.

Just something about this town.

But after last night, I couldn't help but wonder if an angry blonde was the true reason I'd been drawn here all along. The reason I'd *stayed*.

"Bad shift last night?"

I glanced up at Butler's question and realized his menu was on the table, and he was looking at me expectantly.

"No. Just long." Made longer by everything that happened between Emma and me.

Rowe snorted and then grunted when I elbowed him.

"How was the honeymoon?" I asked before Butler could start interrogating me.

Rowe tossed his unopened menu onto the pile on the table and then turned, looking at me with a shit-eating grin.

Butler's eyes narrowed, his voice dull. "Fucking amazing,

but you already know that because we talked about it this weekend."

"Didn't know talking about your honeymoon more than once was a bad thing," I said dryly. "I'll be sure to tell Jenn."

"No, no, keep stalling," Rowe said, all amusement. "It's not at all obvious."

"I'll kill you," I threatened softly as I swung a glare in his direction.

He blew a kiss at me.

Butler sat back against his side of the booth, eyes narrowed. "All right, something's clearly up, and I can't figure out why you're trying to keep anything from me at all, especially *this*."

I looked at Rowe in confusion and accusation, but he just held his hands up, revealing his innocence.

Other than what he'd seen from when Emma had come over the day before and what I'd revealed to him about our encounter late into the night, I hadn't said a word about her to anyone since she'd come into my life like a ball of wrath. So I had no fucking clue what Butler was talking about. "*This?*"

He pushed his empty mug between his hands a few times and lifted his shoulders. "Going around the department that you and Hannah finally hooked up last week."

Shit.

The bad thing about small towns . . . they were full of loose lips and eager ears.

Rowe kicked my knee. "The hell, where have I been?"

"Wait, *finally*?" I demanded.

Butler rolled his eyes and sent the mug sliding in my direction.

I caught it before it could slide off the table but didn't back down. "What do you mean?"

"Everyone in town has been taking bets on when it would happen."

"And I lost," Rowe groaned, and Butler gave an agreeing grunt.

"The fuck," I mumbled under my breath.

"Dude, it isn't a secret that Hannah's been after you for a year," Butler went on. "There's no way you didn't know."

"I didn't," I assured him.

"*What*? There's even a pool in the department for it."

My brows slowly lifted. "For Hannah and me, or my sex life in general?" Before he could answer, I took one of the rolled-up silverware sets and chucked it at him. "You're an asshole if you went in on that. And *you*?" I said to Rowe before punching him in the shoulder.

A deep laugh burst from Rowe and was echoed by Butler. "You know I did," Butler said, "and it was just for Hannah. Man, how did you not know?"

Because I usually spent my days dodging attempts from girls like Courtney, and Hannah had never once given off any kind of vibe until recently.

Soft.

Subtle.

At the perfect and worst time.

Perfect, because I'd needed to get out all of my frustrations. I'd needed to get lost in someone for a little while because a girl had just appeared in Colby, twisting me up with her long legs and scorn-filled stares.

Worst, because that girl was rapidly consuming my thoughts and wants and needs, and she'd heard Hannah moaning . . . screaming.

We murmured *thank-yous* when the waitress set our plates down and filled the mugs up with coffee.

Before she'd even left, Butler dug into his food and said, "So, Hannah—"

"Fucking mistake."

He paused with his fork halfway to his mouth, looking genuinely surprised and a little disappointed.

Rowe choked on the first bite. "Shit," he said thickly as he reached for his mug.

"What? Why?" Butler asked. "She's—okay, yeah, she's been hung up on you about as bad as every other girl in this town, but she isn't crazy. She doesn't build shrines to you like Courtney or some of the other girls in town. And we all think she'd be good for you."

"Who is *all?*"

He shoved the fork in his mouth and spoke around the food. "Jenn, Rowe, me, the town . . . you know, not including the ones obsessed with having your babies."

"People really like her," Rowe added, but his stare was tentative. The amusement that always burst from him had vanished because he'd seen just how badly I'd been wrecked by one encounter with Emma.

"Jesus, this was really a thing?"

Butler gave me a look as if to say, once again, that he couldn't figure out how I hadn't known. "Dude. Yeah. And no *was* about it . . . it *is* a thing."

"I didn't know until recently that there was something on her side, and I didn't think it was really anything. For me? There's nothing. I—fuck." I dragged a hand through my hair and shifted lower in the booth. "I feel like a dick for saying this, but she was just . . . there. I don't even remember why she came over. Any other night, I would've turned her away."

He sucked in a breath through his teeth. "Ouch."

"I know . . . I know."

Rowe elbowed me, not bothering to be subtle in any way, and I forced out a relenting sigh.

"Lala sent a girl to my house with dinner that night. She heard Hannah. And this girl? Butler, she's . . . *goddamn*."

His eyes widened at my hushed confession, but he hurried to hold up his fork. "Lala's been on the Reed-and-Hannah train for about as long as the rest of us. Why would she send another girl to your house?"

"It's her granddaughter. Apparently, she has two of them."

Butler's head slanted as if he wasn't sure he'd heard me correctly and his eyes unfocused. When they finally snapped back to the present, his brow was pinched in concentration and denial, stare shifting between Rowe and me before he asked, *"Emma?"*

I leaned over the table toward him. "You know her?"

"Emma's here," he said in a soft tone, trying to confirm. "With Lala and Nora."

"Yes."

"Her mom back too?"

I tensed instinctively at the question . . . at the thought.

We all knew about Nora's mom. About the possibility she could show up at any time—how bad it would be if she did. We just hadn't known about anything else, including Emma. At least, I hadn't thought anyone else knew about her.

"No. How do you know Emma?"

"Yikes," Rowe mumbled when Butler took too long to answer. But Butler just gave a single jerk of his head, disregarding the implication.

Butler's piercing gaze searched mine for a few moments

longer before he lowered his shaking head and started stabbing at his plate with his fork. "Don't go getting caught up with her." The subdued warning was twisted with a hint of sadness as if he was afraid to speak about her too loudly. "She won't be here long."

"No. No, fuck that. You can't just say some bullshit like that without explaining *why*."

"Hey! Fancy seeing three of my favorite boys here."

I jolted back at the teasing voice, as if we'd been caught talking about something we weren't supposed to, and looked into the warm eyes of Butler's sister . . . and her husband.

Asshole.

"Jesus, I don't think I've ever seen a more beautiful pregnant woman," I said smoothly, earning an eye roll from Leah, and elbowed Rowe when he and Butler remained silent.

"I have to agree," Rowe added, voice hushed. Gentle almost. Completely ignoring the stone-cold glare Leah's husband sent Rowe's way before his attention returned to his phone.

Butler didn't say anything. Just stayed hunched over his plate, stabbing at the food.

Leah rubbed her swollen stomach, her cheeks tinged pink. "Y'all are sweet," she said softly. "I woke up craving the waffles from here this morning, so I begged Jarrod to bring me."

"Literally," he muttered irritably, then huffed out a sigh. "Can we go? I need to get to the office and I still have to drop you off."

"You can go," Rowe ground out. "Some of us know how to drive *and* be kind to women."

"Is she your wife?" Jarrod shot back, stare snapping to

Rowe for a few seconds before falling to the screen of his phone again.

Leah just smiled the way she always did, seemingly unfazed by Jarrod. She reached out to run her hand through Butler's hair adoringly as if she were the older one and not the other way around. "You okay?"

He finally glanced up, all his shock replaced with a genuine smile when he looked at her. "Always. Waiting for my namesake to be born."

Leah let out a soft laugh and patted his head. "Nice try."

"I'll be in the car," Jarrod said, already walking away.

"Just *such* a nice guy," I said dryly.

"Be kind." Leah swatted at me, her stare dancing across the table in Rowe's direction as she turned to go. "You boys have fun."

"Her husband's a dick," Rowe mumbled as soon as she was out of earshot.

We said something to that effect every time we saw him.

Butler grunted in agreement. "What my sister sees in him . . . then again, apparently he's a god or a saint or something. He's the son my dad always wanted anyway."

"Come on, man."

"You know it's true." He dropped his fork onto his plate and sat back against the booth. "Dad bought the house next to theirs for Leah and that piece of shit and raves to everyone about how proud he is of Jarrod and their company. When I came home? 'Ah. Looks like my son has decided to actually do something with his life.' Like serving our country for eight years had been an embarrassment to him."

"You being a cop is still kind of an embarrassment to him." It was said in a soft tease, but he and I both knew it was true.

Butler shrugged. "Exactly."

"He isn't much better than Jarrod. How you turned out normal, I'll never know."

The corner of his mouth tipped up in a smirk. "My mom," he said at the same time Rowe and I said, "Your mom."

Leah was an exact replica of her.

Warm. Loving. Always letting things roll off her shoulders as if she couldn't be bothered by stress or asshole husbands.

"To disappointing our parents," Rowe said, holding out his mug.

Butler scoffed in mock annoyance, but we held ours up and then drank to it because it was fucking true.

"I always forget you grew up next to Lala," I said once my mug was on the table again.

Butler's expression immediately fell. He knew where I was going, what I was bringing us back to.

His head started shaking, a slow, barely noticeable movement.

"No one has ever mentioned anyone other than Nora and her mom," I said when he didn't speak. "Lala hadn't ever mentioned Emma. So, you knowing Emma's name . . . your reaction to her being here . . ."

"You have your pick of women, Ryan. Literally. If you don't want Hannah, that's fine. But since you've been here, you haven't wanted anyone. Emma should not be the one who changes that."

I was sure there was a part of Emma that agreed with Butler. I was also positive every time she stopped shoving her past between us, she was right there with me . . . trapped in that energy that swirled around us and pulled us closer.

Craving a connection she'd never experienced before.

Somehow already falling.

I wanted to ask Butler *why*, but I had a feeling he wouldn't answer the question. But in the chance he did, I wasn't sure he should be the one to tell me.

"Just tell me how you know her," I softly begged instead. "Tell me why you reacted that way."

"I don't know her," he said after a while and blew out a harsh sigh. "I only ever saw glimpses of her over the years, usually when she and her mom were leaving. But I always knew when they were back in town because there'd be screaming from all three of them. Accusing, pleading . . . it never stopped until they left."

Rowe stayed uncharacteristically quiet as we listened.

As I tried to put pieces together.

"And they didn't stay long?" I guessed from his earlier statement.

Butler shook his head. "A day . . . if that. My mom knew hers, so she told us some stuff about her. Said Joslin Wade was the kind of person that, when she left here, people wanted to forget about her—Lala included. So, if Emma's anything like her, stay far away."

I stared at my food for a few moments before launching into everything that had happened since Thursday night.

From the moment I'd first seen her, horrified and disgusted, to last night on Lala's porch, a breath from crossing that unseen line between us.

When I finished, Butler let out a low whistle. "I don't know, Ryan. Maybe you should take a hint and back off."

She did more than drop hints.

She threw grenades.

But I'd tried backing off, and I'd ended up right back in front of her. That invisible tether drawing us closer the more distance we put between us.

"I don't think I can," I said honestly.

From Butler's expression, he expected my answer and was disappointed by it. "Lala might have something to say about it."

"Pretty sure she's pushing for it to happen."

"Or maybe she's expecting Emma to be here for all the old reasons, so she wants you around to stop her from stealing her shit and disappearing."

Shock and bemusement bled from me. "She looks like money and dresses like she just stepped out of a business district. I don't think she's here to steal from Lala."

"You said she freaked when she found out you were a cop." He lifted a hand as if he'd just connected every dot for me.

"She didn't look worried that I'd catch her doing something, she was fucking *disgusted*. She looked at me like she hated cops. Hated *me*." A frustrated laugh escaped me. "I don't have the information you do, I get that. But is it so hard to accept that Emma might not be anything like her mom? Were we not just talking about you and your dad?"

He'd been ready to argue his side but sagged in defeat at my last question.

"What about you?" I asked Rowe, who'd been sitting there, hunched over his half-eaten food and playing with his fork, ever since I'd started explaining the past few days.

After a while, he let out a sigh and met my stare. "I see what she does to you," he finally said, head moving subtly. "And what you're saying, I want that for you—I do. But this has disaster written all over it, and y'all haven't even begun."

My jaw shifted. Tensed.

"Just be careful," Butler added. "You didn't hear it all. You didn't *see* it. See what it did to Lala every time they showed up and left again."

A pang of sadness and protectiveness hit my chest for the woman who looked out for the town. "I understand."

Butler's head slanted in a show of denial as he picked up his fork again. "I don't think you do."

TWELVE

EMMA

Two hundred and six.

That was the number of books Donna had left in the store when she hired me, all piled on a table at the very front up until a few minutes ago.

They varied from books about cooking to travel to thrillers to self-help to romance . . . but they all had one thing in common. They looked old and worn though they had probably never been read, only touched.

I also had a feeling that no matter how much we cleaned the store, we would never get the smell from the pages.

"I think the books you already have should be discounted. Heavily."

Donna's expression said she agreed, but a sadness lingered there. "How did I let this happen?"

My heart sank.

She'd said the same thing so many times over the last few days.

"Donna . . ."

"I could've tried," she said, her voice softer than a whisper. "I could've tried harder. I could've made sure this store didn't die."

"It didn't." I held my arms out to encompass the building we were in before heading for the cart that held the boxes of books. "It's still standing. It's still open. It didn't die. It just needs a makeover, is all, and we're giving her one."

A fierce determination lit in her eyes. "It's long overdue." When I groaned opening the heavy doors, Donna sighed. "I've never liked those doors. The poor things are—well, I just don't have anything nice to say about them."

A giggle worked in my chest at her soft admission. "They can't hear you," I called out as I pushed the cart outside.

In the three days since she'd hired me, I'd quickly come to adore Donna. Everything about her was kind and gentle and graceful.

The way she moved. The way she spoke. Even the way she sat, staring out the window.

And despite letting the store fall into the state I'd first walked into, it was what kept her going. So, I was determined to make sure I held true to my promise.

I was going to make the store breathe and thrive.

First thing yesterday, Donna had gone to the bank for a loan. Neither of us had been sure what the outcome would be, but she'd come out of the meeting both hopeful and discouraged.

The bank had happily loaned exactly what we needed, unaware that there had been a bookstore in Colby and wanting nothing more than for the town to have one. But Donna hadn't understood how the woman hadn't known when the building was so large and had a prime spot on Main Street.

I hadn't had the heart to tell her that, despite the size and uniqueness compared to the other stores, the building seemed to hide the way Donna hid inside.

Instead, I'd told her that everyone would soon know it was there.

Since then, we'd gone over plans and ideas, and I'd spent hours on the phone hiring crews for all the things we would need. Last night, I'd spent hours researching bookstores until I'd ended up scrolling through never-ending pictures of books, bookstores, and readers' bookshelves. And I'd somehow managed to convince Donna to close the shop until we were done with our minor renovations.

I'd had to remind her that we would need to be coming and going to oversee the progress and to do the shopping for the store. She'd only agreed after admitting I had been the first person to walk into her store in over a month.

To prepare for everything that was about to happen inside, we were clearing out the store. Boxing up the two hundred and six remaining books . . . organizing and filing the scattered papers in the office and front desk before packing those up too . . .

All that was left were the two small boxes and shoebox in the loft.

There was a couch up there that should have been retired a decade or two ago, but the crew coming to move out the bookshelves for the cleaning company was going to get rid of it for us.

An idea came to me when I was walking back to the shop, and excitement made my tired body feel light as I hurried inside. "Donna, we need to let people know we're closed."

"I'm not sure they know we're open, Emma dear."

I gestured to the window. "You had the smallest piece of paper asking for help, and it caught my attention immediately. If we had a large sign letting people know we're closed for renovations and will be opening again soon, they would see it. They would be intrigued. They would want to come in to see what all the fuss is about when we open again," I rambled quickly. "I can have something done up this afternoon or tomorrow."

A few seconds passed before she said, "If you think it would help."

It was the first time she had been hesitant about anything so far.

"I don't have to, it was just a thought."

"It's a good thought, and I think we should." She stared at the desk for a few moments before looking at me. "Emma, I received a call from your previous employer when you went outside."

The high I'd been riding vanished.

My knees felt weak, and it suddenly felt too hot in that space.

"From HR?" My voice was nothing more than a breath, but Donna heard and shook her head.

"I'm not sure. It was a man named Dennis? Dennis something?"

My knees gave out so abruptly that I had to grab at the wall to remain standing. "Chris Dennison?"

Donna's head listed in acknowledgment. "He wanted to warn me of the person I hired."

"How does he know?" I asked anxiously. "I just—it just happened. I *just* started here."

She gave me a helpless look. "You were upfront with me. It's only fair that I return the favor. I felt you needed to know that he contacted me."

I'd left.

I'd made no threats. No *anything*. I'd just left.

Why couldn't he let me go?

"Can I know what he said?" I finally asked.

Donna's frail hands wrung for a moment before she said, "No, I don't think so."

Just as worry and fear started swirling in my stomach, she continued. "If he had been trying to help me with real information, he wouldn't have sounded so desperate—worried that I wouldn't believe him. There's no sense in upsetting you over what were clearly lies from a man I believe it's fair to say we do not like."

"I didn't—" I clutched at my stomach, feeling like I might get sick all over the stained, threadbare carpet, before forcing it all away.

Steeling my limbs, fortifying my mind, and locking away the demons as I mentally chanted:

I will not break.

I cannot be broken.

I will not break . . .

"Donna, whatever he said, I didn't do it," I finished helplessly. Numbly.

"Oh, Emma dear," was all she said as she started over to me. Genuine pain creased her face when she reached me. "I've never seen something so sad in all my years." Her hand weakly reached up to cup my cheek, light eyes never leaving mine. "We were given emotions for a reason. Given pain the same as we were given love. If we bury them away, refusing to let them surface, how will we truly live?"

"I'm fine," I tried to assure her, but she just shook her head sadly.

"Don't run from what's inside you." After another

moment, she clicked her tongue and took a step away. "What do you say we call it a day?"

I nodded, the movement stiff. "All I have left is what's upstairs. Let me get that first."

She didn't protest as I hurried past her for the hallway that held the office and storage rooms. Slipping up the nearly hidden staircase just beyond the archway and using the solitude to breathe and shake the news that Chris had called Donna from my mind.

Once I was in the loft, I stood there looking out over the store, letting the sight and possibilities wash away the remaining wraiths scraping their claws down my shield.

I could see it all . . . what I wanted to do to the place, what it could be. The boost Donna needed and the fresh start I wanted. I just hoped when it was done, the woman waiting below would be happy.

I hoped I wouldn't fail her.

With a sigh, I picked up the boxes and made my way down the stairs.

"Last chance to turn the loft into something for the store," I said when I emerged again.

Donna's head moved in faint shakes when I placed the boxes on the desk. "My grandmother always said it was our own special escape. I grew up playing in that loft . . . so did my mother." She reached for the boxes, her face drawn together in delicate curiosity. A gasp slipped from her when she lifted the lid to the shoebox. "Oh."

My attention automatically slid to the box when she pushed it so it was between us.

It was full of letters.

Very old letters.

"My husband wrote these to me when he was in the war."

Her hand shakily moved to the other boxes. "I believe those are pictures. I've wondered where these went. I must have brought them here after he passed."

I settled onto a stool when she gestured for me to open them and lifted the lid from the first box as if it were fragile.

Because I knew . . . I *knew* the contents were more valuable to her than anything I had ever owned.

My heart expanded and my lips twisted into a shy smile when I did.

The adoration and love that poured from the picture resting on top were enough to make even me believe love truly existed.

A married couple was sitting on the floor, curled up together and smiling at the camera like nothing bad could ever touch their lives as long as they had each other.

I pulled it out and turned it to show Donna. "Is that you?"

Light and love and emotion lit her features as she stared at the photo. After a while, she gave me a saucy smile. "I was quite the catch, wasn't I?"

A surprised laugh burst from me. "You still are, Donna."

We sat there for hours, going through pictures of her family and husband before finally leaving. By the time I got home, Lala was already prepping dinner for the first responders and had a glass of sweet tea waiting for me.

"Come tell me what happened with Ms. Donna today," she said as she slid the glass in my direction before going back to chopping an onion.

I hurried over to the island and snuck a sip of the death-in-a-cup before launching into the day, all the while checking on the remaining lunch, making sure the pans were full and the plates were piled for the first responders who were still coming in, before heading over to do dishes.

When I got to the pictures and letters, Lala stopped prepping and turned to listen, a hand pressed against her chest.

"Lala, I nearly cried," I admitted.

Her brows lifted, a disbelieving and amused look crossing her face. "You? Now that's just something I don't believe."

A soft laugh worked up my throat.

A group of firemen entered the kitchen then, one of them with Nora on his shoulders, their movements slow and expressions hesitant.

"Look how big I am!" Nora cried out, all excitement.

"We too late for lunch, Lala?" the one holding Nora asked.

Lala scoffed. "Now, what kind of question is that? As if I wouldn't whip something up for y'all even if I'd already run out. Get you some plates and fill them up."

Nora patted his head and echoed, "Fill 'em up!" with a wild laugh.

Whoever he was, he must be special to Nora if she was so open with him—so free.

I finished rinsing out one of the large pots I'd cleaned as the guys chatted with Lala, then grabbed a towel and dried it as I walked it over to the stove for dinner.

It wasn't until I set it down that I realized one of the other firemen was watching me curiously.

I glanced from his empty plate to the buffet-style pans Lala had lined up. "Is everything okay?"

"You were in here last week."

A couple of the guys next to him quieted in their conversations—the others continued talking with Lala and Nora.

My cheeks reddened as I tried to remember what they had seen of me last week.

It seemed so long ago, but everything had been so fresh then.

Wrecked. Agonizing over the fact that I was following in my mother's footsteps and being terrified that I was turning into her. *Reed.*

An uncomfortable laugh bubbled up my throat. "Uh, yeah . . . you'll probably see me in here quite a bit from now on."

I didn't miss the way Lala's breath caught or how it took her a few seconds too long to resume speaking. I was surprised that my statement had been shocking for her. Last week, sure, my entire life had been up in the air. But I thought she'd know by now that I wasn't going anywhere.

"Is that so?" he asked.

But I couldn't respond.

Trouble had just walked into the kitchen, dripping sex and frustration and looking every inch the regret I'd suspected he would be that first night. And his piercing stare had immediately locked onto me.

Freezing me in place.

Stealing my words.

Muddling my mind.

He started my way, looking like he was coming right for me.

I wanted to both back away and stand tall to show him I wouldn't back down, but I was unable to move. Wanting nothing more than to have him near again. Feel his touch on my arm. Have him close enough that he stole my air and I took his.

At the last second, he dipped his head close to mine and whispered, "Emma."

My body trembled when he brushed past me.

I glanced over my shoulder but didn't allow myself to turn. Didn't allow myself to look when I heard him talking to Lala and Nora.

I finally focused ahead of me and tensed when I found the three firemen watching me expectantly.

Waiting for me to respond.

I blinked, trying to remember what we had been talking about, and stumbled over my words. "Right—I'm here—yes —I'll be around." I cleared my throat and forced a smile, silently damning Reed for being able to do that to me by just walking into a room. "I actually live here now. Lala is my grandma."

"That's right, boys," Lala said loudly. "This here is my Emma. So, take care of her if you see her around, but keep your hands to yourself."

I sucked in a sharp breath when fingers trailed against my palm—light, teasing, asserting. The touch sent a spark of electricity up my arm and a shock of heat through my stomach.

I knew in an instant who it belonged to without needing to look—before he ever had the chance to continue past me and out of the kitchen.

Because although it shouldn't have been . . . it was all so familiar.

The firemen were asking questions about being Lala's granddaughter and if that meant I was Nora's sister and where I'd been up until the past week. For the most part, I think I responded. Keeping my answers as vague as possible until they realized I wasn't going to give them much. When the fireman holding Nora on his shoulders introduced himself to me as Reed's roommate and *Some-Guy-Named-Peter,* I'd awkwardly stumbled over my words as understanding dawned.

As I realized he'd probably overheard all that had taken place a few days before when I'd discovered Reed was a cop.

But throughout it all, my attention kept pulling toward the entrance of the kitchen, waiting to see if Reed would walk back in. And as the last of the firemen were filing out, he did, weighed down with bags upon bags of garlic bread.

As before, he came directly to me.

"So, firemen are okay then?" His voice was soft enough that it wouldn't carry to Lala or Nora, but it only emphasized the hurt there.

"Reed—"

"I saw you, Emma. It didn't faze you to look at them. Talk to them. So, if I were a fireman, would it all be different?"

It felt like he'd delivered a critical blow with that one question. "Don't do this."

"You know neither of us really want that," he said in a voice that had a flash of heat racing over my body.

I started to step away but somehow ended up taking a step closer. "And what if it *would*?" I bit out. "Would you quit your job and do something else?"

"Fuck no. I'm just trying to figure you out."

"Don't."

"Give me one good reason not to," he fired back.

But I just stood there, lips parted and mind racing with a dozen reasons that sounded as inane as my rhetorical question.

"Lie to me, Emma," he practically begged. "I'll know you're lying to yourself too." He inched forward, bringing us nearly as close as we had been the other night. "Or don't say anything at all. That's all I need from you to know that getting into your head is worth every fight. That you want this as badly as I do."

"You're wrong," I said through clenched teeth.

For the first time since he'd walked into Lala's kitchen this afternoon, a smile broke across his face. "How's that lie taste?"

I wanted to scream at him.

I wanted to push him away.

But all I could think of was how close his lips were to mine, what they would feel like, taste like.

Lala cleared her throat, and I quickly stepped away from Reed, having forgotten where we were . . . who was in the room with us.

"Are you going to stand there holding that bread all afternoon, or are you going to set it down?" Her question was laced with knowing humor, and her raised brows said more than words could.

I put another few steps between Reed and me until I bumped into one of the counters, then gripped it tightly as if I needed to grasp something to stay standing after the intense moment we'd just had.

Reed put the bags on one of the counters and started unloading them onto the same place he had the week before.

Though I tried to avoid looking at him again, my gaze kept pulling toward him over and over again. If it hadn't been, I might not have noticed the way his head snapped in my direction when Lala said, "Saw Nick this morning."

Brows drawn together. Eyes filled with some odd mixture of wonder and frustration and fear.

And I didn't understand it.

Reed had dropped his head almost as soon as he saw me watching him, putting his focus on creating the pyramid of garlic bread. "Yeah?"

"Didn't stay long. Just stopped by to check on me and tried to sneak out without a plate of food since he wasn't on duty." Lala swatted at Reed with a kitchen towel. "You boys, I swear."

A smile threatened at the corner of Reed's mouth but never fully formed. "You make him take one?"

"Of course, and another for his wife."

Reed made a sound of disagreement in the back of his throat. "Other people deserve the food, Lala."

"Don't you start with me today too. I've already had to fight one of you."

A sigh bled from Reed when he finished with the bread and turned to face Lala. It was obvious an argument was on the tip of his tongue, but then his head jerked back. "Where'd Nora go?"

"She probably ran off to sit with Peter, and before you even try me, young man, I'll just send Emma after you with a plate if you don't take one."

Reed's stare flashed to me and his mouth twitched. "Well, we wouldn't want that."

After what I overheard last week . . . no, I wouldn't.

Without waiting, Lala pulled out some Tupperware and began loading it with food.

Every time Reed tried to stop her, she added more until it was filled to the brim.

With a defiant grin, she handed the container to Reed and accepted a kiss on the cheek from him. "One of these days, you'll learn I get my way."

A breath of a laugh left him. "Learned that long ago, Lala."

She gasped suddenly and placed a palm on her cheek, eyes comically wide. "Oh goodness. I think . . . yes, I think I left the stove on."

"Lala, you're in the kitchen—*Lala,*" I hissed when she walked from the room as if she didn't have a care in the world.

"She isn't subtle," Reed mumbled, staring at the container in his hands.

"Not at all."

The sounds of the people currently in the house—talking, laughing, and eating—filtered into the kitchen and somehow made our silence louder.

The tension between us thicker.

The longing to be near him fiercer.

The need to run stronger.

"Emma—"

"No, don't," I said quickly. "Reed, it isn't just what you do. It's men. It's my life. It's *everything*. I can't do this—you have to let it go."

I wanted to take it back as soon as the words finished leaving my mouth, but I wanted him to leave just as badly.

After a moment, his head dipped and he pushed away from the counter. But he hadn't taken more than two steps before he stopped and looked at me again. "I don't know what you've been through or what you're going through, but I've never doubted that whatever it is, it's hard. It's taken its toll on you, I know. I see it in the way you look at me and talk to people and the way you hold yourself—I fucking see it. I heard it in nearly every word you just said."

My body went rigid against the counter.

My lungs ached and screamed for air as I waited for him to continue.

"I may not know all that much about you yet, but you're not that hard to read, and your lies are your biggest giveaway. That last line about not being able to do this and wanting me to let it go?" His lips twisted into a smile that still managed to look defeated. "Bye, Emma."

No sooner had he left than Lala came strolling back into the kitchen, whispering the same words she'd told me the week before. "Reed Ryan has the purest heart of them all."

"Lala, stop pushing this. I can't—"

"That's just it, you can."

Instead of getting into that argument, I just started clearing away the lunch pans she'd emptied out into Reed's container and took them to the sink.

Once I had all the pans cleared and the hot water running, I remembered Reed's odd expression from earlier in their conversation.

"Hey, Lala," I began indifferently, "who's Nick?"

"Oh, that's right, he hasn't seen you since you've been back," Lala said. "I wonder if he'd recognize you."

I glanced over my shoulder but didn't have a chance to ask before she rushed to continue.

"Not that I'm sure you ever met him. It's just that he's about your age . . . grew up next door."

My hands stilled with the pan halfway into the sink, quickly filling with hot water.

A night filled with screams and terror unlike anything I'd ever known quickly flashed before my eyes.

A night that haunted me in a way men *couldn't*.

Lala knew just as well as I did that I'd met Nick, though I hadn't known his name before today. From the way she'd hurried to backtrack and then trailed off, she knew when and was remembering that night, same as me.

I made some sort of noise in the back of my throat but didn't respond otherwise.

"Anyway," she said after a few moments, "Nick, Reed, and Peter are the best of friends. Nick's actually why the other two are here at all."

Reed's best friend had been witness to one of the worst nights in my life, and at the mention of him around me, Reed had gotten uncomfortable.

Shit.

He knew . . . he knew.

For the life of me, I couldn't figure out why I still had to keep Reed at a distance. I couldn't figure out why he hadn't run.

"They were on the same SEAL team," Lala continued. "When they got out, Reed came here, needing time away. He never left. Same with Peter."

I turned, all but forgetting the dishes. "Reed was a SEAL?"

Lala sent me a look from over her shoulder. "I told you he has saved many people."

"You said he saved your life."

"And he did."

My eyes narrowed into an assessing glare. "Do you mean figuratively or literally?"

She shrugged and turned back to the food she'd been prepping when I first came home. "Ask him yourself."

She and I both knew I wasn't about to do that.

As soon as I turned back to the dishes, Lala asked, "Does knowing that about him change your opinion?"

I shut the water off. "Knowing what?"

"Everything I just told you."

"Not in the least," I said honestly and risked a glance over my shoulder. But Lala wasn't looking at me. She was staring straight ahead, waiting for my answer. "You told me that first night about saving you and others. It's why I thought he was a medic or fireman. As for being a SEAL, it just confirms one of my first observations about him."

"And which one would that be?"

"He's dangerous."

Reed Ryan *was* dangerous . . .

For my heart.

For my soul.

For my already weakening resolve.

THIRTEEN

REED

The moment I stepped into the coffee shop the next day, my eyes were drawn to the side, where tables and chairs were clustered together.

There, like a beacon, was the scornful girl who refused to leave my mind.

Blonde hair piled messily on top of her head. Shirt hanging off one of her shoulders. Catching every man's eye in the café without even noticing.

It was last night all over again.

A primal need to put my claim on her swelled inside me. To let every single one of them know she was mine . . .

Except she wasn't.

I ordered a drink and paid. The entire time, my attention drifted to the far corner where Emma sat.

She never looked up from the tablet she was focused on. Never seemed to notice or react to the energy building and twisting and pulling between us.

Tormenting me.

Taunting me.

Begging me to erase the space between us even though I knew what would happen when I did.

She might give for a minute, but then she would shut down and push me away.

Not that it would stop me from going to her. From trying to get past those walls again and again until she finally let me in.

When I was a few feet from the table where she sat, she said, "I thought I'd be safe coming here in the morning."

Eyes still fixated on the tablet, finger still swiping across it while her other hand was poised over a notepad, pen at the ready.

That she'd known I was there without ever acknowledging it had a smile tugging at my mouth.

I slid into the seat across from her. "Meaning?"

She sighed and put the tablet to sleep, her hazel eyes flashing fire and irritation and desire when they shot to me. "You told me you ran here every afternoon. Ever since, I've avoided this place in the afternoons."

I clutched at my chest. "I think that hurt."

"And yet, I can't seem to get rid of you." The words were pure tease, emphasized by the twitch of her full lips.

I leaned over the table and lowered my voice. "You want to be rid of me, you know how."

That twitch transformed into a full smile, forcing one from me. "Enlighten me because I've been trying to figure out how to do exactly that for over a week now."

"Tell me you want me gone . . ."

"I want you—"

"And mean it."

Her smile slipped, and for a moment, she just studied me.

"How do you know I'm not actually telling the truth these times you think I'm lying."

Because everything about you changes when you lie.

"Not hard to read, Emma."

"You keep saying that," she mumbled.

"Because it's true." I nodded toward the tablet and notepad. "What are you doing?"

Excitement slowly stole across her face, lighting her up in a way that made her look more beautiful than I'd ever seen her.

"Research." The word came out a breath, but it said everything.

It explained her light mood and teasing banter. And it immediately dashed any hope I had that we were making progress.

I swallowed back my disappointment and asked, "What for?"

She slid the tablet over her notes when I tried to read her writing upside down. "Just something I'm working on."

"I can't know?" I glanced up and knew in the set of her stare that I'd lost her.

Guarded.

Protective.

Worried, as if I was about to take whatever it was she was working on away from her.

"Right." When I caught sight of my drink waiting on the counter, I leaned closer to say, "I'm not whatever guy you're afraid of. I'm not whoever hurt you."

"Reed," she called out when I started to stand.

From her tone, she'd been battling herself on whether or not she should stop me. From her expression, she was struggling with what to tell me.

Her shoulders finally lifted before sagging, and she placed a hand on top of the tablet. "I've had people try to take a lot of things from me. I just . . . I need this to be mine until the time is right."

I dipped my head in understanding. "Then it will be."

"Lala said something," she hurried to say when I stood. "I want to know what she meant by it."

I gave her a pointed look. "Ask her."

Hesitation warred in her eyes. "She told me to ask you."

I folded my arms over my chest and waited, mind racing as I thought of the few things Lala could've told Emma that I would need to explain.

"She said you saved her life and countless others'." She dragged out the last words, pushing her unspoken question into the space between us.

My arms dropped heavily to my sides.

That hadn't been one of the things I'd expected her to say.

"Did she?" I murmured and forced something that might've resembled a smile, but it quickly fell.

"She told me you were a SEAL," she said, voice dropping even lower. "I want to know if it's all true and what you did for her."

My head was shaking as I backed away. "She lied."

Before she had the chance to react in any way, I turned, snatched my drink from the counter, and left the shop.

What she was asking . . . I didn't want to go down that road. Not with anyone.

Especially not Emma Wade.

Because no one was ever *just* curious. They all had their reasons for wanting to talk about shit they wouldn't understand. And, eventually, those reasons all made themselves known in one way or another.

Some wanted to brag they knew someone who had done something they saw as heroic. Nearly all could be described in one word: Courtney.

Besides, what none of them realized was I'd just been doing my job. But for every person I'd *saved,* there were others I hadn't gotten to in time. That I'd failed.

"Reed!"

"*Jesus,*" I hissed and nearly lost my footing when I stumbled away from the unexpected intrusion.

To my senses.

To my mind.

To my personal space, seeing how Courtney didn't miss a beat when I shifted back, following me until she was practically pressed against me.

It was like that saying: Speak of the devil, and he will appear.

Except I only had to think of Courtney, and she would pop up like my own frenzied jack-in-the-box on speed and a strong-as-fuck love potion.

"Can you believe it?" Her smile widened so much it looked painful. "Who would've thought we'd run into each other because I'm not on right now, I'm just coming to pick up my tips. And here you are!" She placed her hand on my arm, never noticing or not caring when I shifted out of her hold.

"I, uh . . ."—I held up my cup even though it had been pressed between us—"just decided to swing by on my way home from running some errands."

"That's what I'm about to do!" Her eyes brightened with excitement and hope. "How crazy we're doing the same thing at the same time."

An uneasy laugh left me as I started stepping away.

"Right. Uh . . . have a good day."

"Oh, you too, Reed!" she called out loudly. "I'll see you tomorrow."

"Jesus Christ," I mumbled under my breath as I turned for my truck.

Once I was inside, I pulled out my phone and sent off a message to Rowe.

Me: Do me a favor and date Courtney.

I ONLY HAD to wait a few seconds before he began responding.

Rowe: Ha. Fuck you.

***Rowe:** . . . are you getting coffee because I'm about to head home and I'm pretty sure I'm dying. Coffee would help.*

***Me:** I'll give you mine. No way in hell I'm going back in there.*

BY THE TIME I made it home, I was trying to figure out who I had pissed off.

Because sitting on my porch was Hannah.

I pocketed my phone and grabbed the coffee as I stepped out of my truck and tried to prepare myself for this.

Hannah stood, already smiling as I rounded the porch to where she waited.

"Hey," she said easily, "figured you'd be back soon."

It didn't register until then that she was just waiting for

me. Because what if I hadn't come back soon, how long would she have waited?

If it had been Courtney or some of the other women in town, I had no doubt the answer would be *forever*.

"Yeah, just ran some errands." My phone vibrated in my pocket, but I didn't reach for it. "What's going on?"

Her face fell slightly when I stopped a handful of feet away from her. She eyed the distance between us again and again before she shook her head and focused on me. "Just haven't really heard from you since last week, even though I know our schedules conflict a lot. But we both have the day and night off . . . and I was thinking—"

"Hannah, I can't." I swallowed past the knot in my throat when her body visibly tensed and her eyes silently begged me not to do this. "The other night, I thought we were on the same page. I thought we both knew it was *a night*. And I'm sorry I didn't realize before that it was different for you."

Funny how it was easier to stop her. To put an end to what she wanted, no question. Funny how it made me feel like the worst kind of asshole.

But with women like Courtney, I was always dancing around the subject and struggling to find a way to let them down easy while never actually being able to.

Maybe because nothing had ever happened with them, and I knew nothing would. Maybe because they had built me up in their minds to be this guy I wasn't and turned it into an obsession, and their hearts weren't on the line.

Hannah's head shook in fierce, quick motions. "It isn't, it wasn't," she said adamantly. "It *was* just a night. I just thought we could, you know, have another one because it was fun."

If her eyes hadn't turned glassy and her voice hadn't

gotten thick, I might've been able to believe her. But she couldn't even hold my stare.

"Hannah, I'm sorry."

Her head continued shaking as she pushed from the railing and turned for the stairs. "You shouldn't be. I should have known you have a one-night limit."

"That isn't it, I just can't give you what you want."

She spun around, bringing us closer than we'd originally been. When she spoke, her voice trembled. "If nights are what you want, then I can give you that."

"I should have never let the other night happen," I said honestly and hated that everything I said was crushing her. "I'm sorry for hurting you."

She started to leave again but asked, "Is it because of *her?*"

My head slanted in question, but I didn't ask *who.*

"That girl everyone's talking about right now." Anger quickly replaced everything else on Hannah's face. "Some of the fire guys said they saw you with her at Lala's. Said it looked like you were really *familiar.*"

Everything right then was because of Emma. But even if Emma weren't in Colby, I wouldn't want anything with Hannah.

"It's because I can't do this with you," I said simply.

"With me," she whispered, the words a defeated laugh.

I blew out a slow breath and watched her walk down the steps. When she was halfway across the pathway, I called out, "I *am* sorry."

She turned, and the tears slipping down her cheeks tore at me. "Me too."

I sank to the top step just as Rowe pulled up to the house, prompting Hannah to hurry to her car.

By the time he was stepping out of his car, she was pulling away.

He watched the car go, pointing at it in question.

"She was waiting for me when I got here," I explained.

"This is what I get for going to the gym," he said as he stopped before the first step. "I miss everything." At my frustrated laugh, he grunted in understanding. "Guess it didn't go well."

I sent him a look before mumbling, "Feel like an asshole for hurting her."

"Maybe because you're making a mistake?"

"I'm not. If I would've known how she felt, I wouldn't have slept with her. I should've never slept with her at all."

A beat passed as he grabbed the coffee from me before asking, "Because of Emma?"

My head dipped slowly as I thought about that girl before admitting, "Ran into her at the coffee shop . . . there was something different about her. I kept thinking I knew why—thinking I was figuring her out. Then she says Lala told her something that she wanted explained." My attention had drifted, but I fixed it on Rowe. "Lala told Emma that I saved her and *countless others'*. Told her I used to be a SEAL."

Rowe shrugged when I didn't continue. "And?"

"And she was different today," I said, irritation and disappointment weaving through me. "If she turns into a Courtney? Or, fuck, even into a Hannah, who said shit about it the other night after we slept together? Like she knew we'd be good together *because* of it." I glanced away again.

"Look, I'm not Butler, I only know what you've told me about her. So, do you really think Emma's the kind of person to turn into one of those girls?"

"No, but all the women here have been the same. They

find out and think *hero* and start romanticizing it and me, and I don't fucking want that. Emma's complicated and argumentative and hesitant. If all that changes now . . ."

My phone vibrated in my pocket again . . . and then again and again.

My brow furrowed as I hurried to grab my phone, but as soon as I saw the lock screen lit up with messages, my face fell and a mixture of frustration and guilt pulsed through me.

Kira: *Please come home.*

Kennedy: *You're an asshole.*

Kennedy: *You're being selfish.*

Kennedy: *GO HOME.*

I TOSSED my phone onto the step and raked a hand through my hair. "Fucking awesome day."

FOURTEEN

EMMA

First thing Saturday, I'd gone shopping for the store. Looking for décor that would match the wall color and new flooring Donna and I had picked out the day before. After hours of finding more than I could've hoped for, I'd dropped it all off only to go school shopping with Lala and Nora.

Nora hadn't said a word to me.

Then again, she hadn't said anything to me for a couple days.

By the time we made it back to the house, I was exhausted from shopping and enduring Nora's silent distrust and working late into the night every night on everything that was needed for the store.

I bit back a groan as I watched Nora dash up the stairs, then followed Lala into the kitchen. "Lala, I think I'm gonna lay down for a little bit."

"If you're hungry now, you're going to wake up wishing you'd eaten. Why don't you put on somethin' comfy, and I'll whip us up a quick lunch?"

I sighed as I thought about the bed waiting for me upstairs, then glanced at what I was wearing. "I'm fine in what I'm wearing."

She gave me a look and pointed at my feet. "For the love of all that is holy, go take off those heels. They're making *me* tired."

My eyes rolled as I pushed from the counter, but a wry smile tugged at my mouth as I forced my steps to be *extra* hard and the clicking of my stilettos to be *extra* loud as I headed for the stairs.

"I hear you, child. Lord Jesus."

My chest moved with a silent giggle when Lala's scoff followed me from the kitchen but abruptly died when I set my foot on the first step of the stairs.

I gripped the railing tight with my free hand as I climbed the steps, unable to escape the nightmares that rushed to the surface.

They were always there, ready to torment me every time I set foot on this staircase.

Harsh, unforgiving words.

My screams.

Sickening thuds.

Pure horror.

I blinked quickly, forcing the flashes away when I passed the last step and hurried down the hall to my room.

I slipped off my shoes and changed into yoga pants and an old shirt since I was up there and tried not to look longingly at my bed even as I kept inching closer and closer to it. Just as I was deciding to skip lunch, the front door opened and shut, and Lala started talking away.

A flash of heat raked across my skin when the answering voice floated up to me.

Deep. Commanding. Unrecognizable.

At least, it should have been. Their words were too muffled to make out, but I knew in the tenor of that voice—in the way my body immediately reacted—who was downstairs.

I turned and stared at my cracked-open door as Nora's thunderous steps sounded just before her excited yell, confirming Reed was there. I needed to shut it and stay in the room. Tell Lala later that I'd fallen asleep instead. But my feet were already taking me in the direction of the door in hopes that he'd speak again.

My need to push him away was just as powerful and dangerous as my craving for him, and I couldn't give in to the latter.

My body was buzzing and warring with my mind because all I wanted was to see him standing in that kitchen again. See those eyes that followed my every move. See that slight twitch of his lips, like he knew exactly how crazy he made me.

Yet, at the same time, there were risks that went along with letting a man like Reed Ryan into my life.

Before I realized that I had made a decision, I was slipping out of my room.

You're an idiot.

You're an idiot.

You're such an idiot.

But by the time I made it down the stairs, the foyer and kitchen were empty.

Disappointment dipped in my chest as I turned to head back to my room.

Reed stepped into the house at that moment, looking more handsome and dangerous than any man had the right to, staring at me with that look that always nailed me to the floor.

"Emma." My name was all gravel and steel wrapped in the softest breath.

It made those butterflies inside me take flight. Made me want to move closer and run as far as I could. Instead, I stood there, wondering if it would be so bad to never move from that spot again.

His thick neck moved with a forced swallow before he ground out a low, "Lala said you weren't here."

My eyebrows lifted in question. "I was just upstairs. She sent me up there."

A moment passed before Reed's chest pitched with a muted laugh. "Of course she did." He rubbed his hand across his jaw before gesturing behind him. "She said the water heater stopped working, wanted me to check on it. When I got here, she was getting ready to leave."

Suspicion unfurled in my stomach. I knew what she was doing, and from Reed's expression and tone, he did too. "Did she say where she was going?"

"She and Nora had a lunch thing."

I let out a slow sigh. "I have a feeling you wasted a trip."

He quickly looked me over before forcing his gaze away. The muscles in his jaw strained when he said, "I should check it since I'm here. These houses are old—things break or need repairing a lot."

I blinked quickly, thrown off by the bite in his tone and the coldness pouring from him that clashed with the heated, charged tension that was always present whenever he was near.

When he'd abruptly left the coffee shop the day before, I'd thought I crossed a line in asking questions about his past. I hadn't thought twice about it since I wasn't exactly someone to volunteer information about pasts.

But in just a few sentences, I was rethinking the entire encounter.

I'd hurt Reed before, maybe even offended him, but I'd never done *this*.

"Yeah," I said softly. "Yeah, okay."

He started to say something before deciding against it and storming through the house.

The breath that ripped from my chest once he was gone could have shattered walls.

My body was trembling, and I felt weak and exhausted as if I were experiencing the worst kind of crash. I hadn't realized how tensely I'd been holding myself until he was gone.

Congratulations, Emma. You've managed to force Reed away without even trying.

The slightest bit of relief filled me and was nearly overpowered by guilt and a soul-deep sadness.

But I couldn't let myself dwell on the latter.

If I did, I would do something stupid, like ask him to forgive me. If I did, I would do something I couldn't take back, like try telling him the truth.

I went in search of food but had only scanned the contents of the fridge by the time Reed came back.

"How'd it go?" I asked as I stared blindly into the fridge.

"Porch swing all over again."

A distracted sound rumbled in my chest, but I no longer had the ability to speak when he came to stand beside me. Close enough that I could smell the subtle scent of his cologne. Close enough that our shoulders brushed when he leaned forward to shut the refrigerator door.

"For someone who has a lot of opinions about me and

demands to know about me, I don't know a lot about you," he said, voice all a rumbled breath. "Tell me something about you."

"Trust me," I said on a strained laugh, "that's a rabbit hole you don't want to fall down."

"You have to know that isn't true."

I haven't been able to stop thinking about you.

You enter my thoughts unbidden. I've thought and fantasized about you so much that I struggle to remember why you're a bad idea.

Then I see you . . . and I'm torn between wanting you and wanting to keep you at a distance. Because wanting you terrifies me.

This roller coaster of emotions is making me feel like I'm going insane.

And I was clearly wrong in thinking I'd succeeded in pushing you away.

My eyelids fluttered shut. I couldn't do this. His closeness, his words . . . they were innocent. But paired with the gentle rasp of his tone, it was all too much.

I needed space so I could breathe.

I somehow moved away from him, away from his intoxicating draw, toward the kitchen table. Once there, I finally risked a glance at him. "I'm not sure what you want me to say."

His colorful arms were folded across his muscled chest. Eyes narrowed on me like he was trying to figure me out.

I wished he wouldn't.

"I've heard talk from guys at the department," he finally said. "After this Thursday, everyone's been going on about Lala's granddaughter who won't talk to anyone. Who won't *look* at anyone."

Surprise pulsed through me.

Before I could think too much on the fact that I was a

topic of conversation between police officers, why I might be, and all the reasons why I didn't *want* to be, he continued.

"I've thought about that conversation on my porch . . . about the one *here*. I've heard what you said and seen your expression over and over again. I thought I would be the only one to notice your reactions because, well . . ." A defeated laugh broke from his chest. He looked at me helplessly for a moment before confusion and desperation stole across his face. "What is it about police officers, Emma? What happened to you?"

"You'd think cops would have something better to do than talk about me." I tried to put strength behind my words, but they came out soft and breathless.

It was the only response he would get from me.

I didn't owe him anything.

"Not when your grandma and sister mean something to all of us. Not when you came into town and started up like you were better than everyone else."

"Better than—I never said I was. I've never *thought* I was."

"But it's what everyone else thinks, and this town talks."

"Then let them talk." I forced a breath from my too-tight lungs. "I'm here for me, not the town. I don't owe them anything, and I sure as hell don't owe you a goddamn thing."

"Emma."

The last thing I saw as I stormed out of the kitchen was Reed's falling expression.

I'd made it up the third step when he grabbed my hand. "Emma, *wait*."

Ice shot through my veins.

I gripped the railing as if my entire life depended on me holding onto it. Because at that moment, it did . . .

. . .

"Momma!"

Fear and denial and body-numbing grief.

I felt faint.

My knees went weak and were seconds from giving out.

My lips were moving rapidly, but no sound was coming out.

". . . sorry, just don't—just talk to me," Reed said, his voice sounding muffled and warped.

A second.

It had been a second since he grabbed me, but it felt like minutes in that nightmare.

Let go, let go, let go, I continued mouthing, unable to put any air behind the words.

I finally twisted to look at him, my free hand still tight on the railing, my body swaying as the room spun around me.

Reed's face shifted to worry and then fear in an instant. "Sit down. You need to sit down."

"Let go of me."

It was barely audible, but Reed shook his head. "Let me help you—"

"Let go!" I shouted.

His hand was gone immediately.

The next, I was sitting on the steps, my head resting against the railing, my fingers tightening on the banister.

A banana and a glass of water were set next to me so suddenly, it surprised me.

I hadn't realized Reed had ever left.

Worry and confusion covered his face when I looked up at him. His hands were lifted slightly as though he didn't know what to do with them.

"Emma, I'm sorry. For what I said, for touching you, for . . . fuck, I don't know." His eyes flashed to mine before falling. "Drink that. Please."

"I'm fine." When his chest pitched with a disbelieving huff, I said, "I am. I just . . . I can't be—" My head moved in quick jerks.

I didn't want to give this man any part of my life, but the words were sitting on the tip of my tongue, begging to fall.

"I shouldn't have touched you," he murmured, understanding and regret weaving through his words.

I should have left it at that. Let him think that was it.

But he should have known by now that a touch from him wasn't going to send me spiraling down. It was going to set me on fire.

"Don't grab me on stairs," I whispered. "Don't touch me when I'm on them."

His brows lifted. His eyes darted from my face to the step I was sitting on to the banister I still had a death-grip on.

After a moment, his head slanted in a nod. "All right. Why don't we move away from the stairs?"

Relief flooded me, but I kept my lips pressed firmly together so I wouldn't thank him or say anything else that would reveal exactly how badly I'd wanted to get away from those steps.

Once he'd grabbed the water and fruit, I followed him to one of the couches in the living room.

He set the items on one of the end tables, catching my stare as he did. "I would feel better if you finished those."

I glanced at the fruit and water, but my head felt heavy and my stomach uneasy.

I wanted to lie down. I wanted to sleep.

The moment I sat down, curled up in the corner, my body relaxed and my eyelids felt impossible to keep open.

I reached for the water but ended up with my head resting on my arm as if it were a pillow.

"Emma," Reed murmured, slightly disapproving, mostly worried. "Please."

"I will."

After a few moments, he asked, "Is there a reason behind the fear?"

His confusion and concern were so raw and palpable that I knew without a doubt Nick hadn't told him about that night.

That thought had relief sliding through my veins.

I was sure if I hadn't been seconds away from drifting off to sleep, I would wonder what exactly Nick *had* told him to make Reed look at me the way he had the other afternoon. But I could barely focus on his question long enough to answer.

"Not one you'll ever know," I finally mumbled, voice soft and slow with my exhaustion. I tried to lift my eyebrows, but they also felt too heavy. "You're wrong, you know."

Amusement danced through Reed's tone when he asked, "About what?"

"Me."

I don't know when I'd closed my eyes, but it felt good to close them.

Felt so good to relax deeper into the couch.

Felt comforting to be watched over by the man in that room.

"Never thought I was better," I muttered lazily. "My entire life, everyone has been better than me."

FIFTEEN

REED

I hurried onto Lala's porch to escape the rain the next night, making the five steps in only two, eyes focused on the girl tucked into the large swing like she belonged there.

Like she'd been there forever.

Emma's eyes flashed to mine before darting back to the tablet in her lap, a soft smile pulling at the corner of her mouth. "Stalker."

"Is that right?" My lips twitched as I fought my own smile at her responding hum. All amusement and ease. "Hate to ruin your night, but I was asked to come here," I continued as I lowered myself to the other side of the swing, nearly touching where her feet were curled up beneath her, and considered it a small victory when she didn't try to move away from me.

Not just because I had water clinging to me, but also because it would've been such an Emma thing to do.

"I'm aware."

When I looked at her, that soft smile had turned playful, but she still had yet to look up from her tablet.

"I'm the one who texted you. Lala's asleep."

"So, is this a porch swing situation? Or . . ."

"No, I really need your help." She finally lifted her head and put the tablet to sleep. "I can't get into my room. The doorknob fell right off when I grabbed it, and now I can't get it to open."

"And you called me?" I asked dryly.

"Technically, I texted you," she said with a teasing narrowing of her eyes. "You work nights, I figured you would be awake, and I really don't want to sleep on the couch."

"You slept on it yesterday," I reminded her.

It had been the first time since meeting Emma that she'd truly looked relaxed. Vulnerable in the purest of ways.

Breathtaking.

Knowing there was no point in waking her up to get her to eat or drink something, I'd draped a blanket over her and left.

But I hadn't been able to get that look on her face out of my head since, as if the weight of the world had finally left her shoulders. It had to be exhausting . . . to constantly be on the offensive. To not trust anyone. To have so much hate built up inside you that you couldn't let yourself just *feel*.

Emma ducked her head, but not before I saw the heat creeping into her cheeks. "I'm sorry for that. For the whole thing."

"Don't be. I should know better by now than to grab you." When she just shrugged off my words like none of it mattered, I asked, "You're not going to tell me what happened on the stairs, are you?"

Instead of the immediate response I'd come to expect, she looked away and chewed on her bottom lip. After a while, she asked, "Do you really not know?"

"I scared you. Clearly."

When her attention fixed on me again, her eyes were filled with pain and uncertainty. "Your friend *Nick* didn't tell you?" I jerked back, but she continued before I had a chance to respond. "I saw the way you looked at me when Lala brought him up the other day. I saw how uncomfortable you were. I know who he is."

A stunned breath punched from my chest. "He's a lot of things, Emma. My best friend. A former teammate. A cop."

"He grew up next door."

I ground my jaw for a second and then slowly nodded. "Yeah. Yeah, he did."

She studied me, seeming to wait for me to continue. When I didn't, she asked, "Did he really not tell you about that night?"

Considering I didn't have a clue what *that night* could mean . . . no, he hadn't, and I couldn't figure out *why*.

Butler knew everything about my life the same way I knew everything about his—or, at least, the way I'd thought I'd known everything. For him to keep anything from me, especially when he knew how I felt about the girl in question, didn't make sense.

"He didn't have a whole lot to say about you," I admitted gruffly. "I've never seen him shut down about anything the way he did when he found out you were in town." One of my brows ticked up. "Seems to be a theme with you."

She nodded after a while, accepting my response, but didn't offer any kind of explanation. From the stubborn set of her chin, I knew she didn't plan to either.

I glanced at the darkened tablet on her lap. "You ever going to tell me anything about you?"

"I told you, that's a—"

"You're wrong," I said adamantly and looked into her wary eyes again. "I've never wanted to know so much about a person, and that was even before I realized you were the most guarded person I'd ever met."

"Knowledge gives people power and leaves the provider vulnerable. Why would I want that?"

"Then you've been around the wrong people." I stood and started to step away, intent on getting my tools from the truck, but stopped. "The other day, what Lala told you about me, what you wanted to know . . ." I faced her and let out a slow exhale. "That's something I don't talk about."

A curious expression covered her face, but she simply waited.

"People hear things like that and it changes them. Changes the way they react and respond to me or anyone who has done what I do." I lifted my shoulders. "They hear *SEAL* or *military* or *hero,* and it turns women obsessive. As you've already seen from Courtney."

The corners of Emma's mouth twitched in amusement. "Well, thankfully for us, those words don't do it for me. I tend to stay away from heroes."

Of course she did.

"I just wanted to know what Lala meant," she continued. "If, when she said you saved her life, she meant it literally, and what happened."

It was my turn to be surprised.

I'd been so caught off guard and in denial at the coffee shop because Emma had been diving into the one territory I didn't want her to, that I hadn't fully registered Lala hadn't told her own granddaughter what happened.

"Lala had a stroke," I said softly.

Emma's reaction was immediate. The shock and sorrow

and rejection. "No. No, because she's . . . she's fine. There's nothing wrong with—she would've said something." She looked at me helplessly. "Right?"

You would think.

Then again, who knew if Lala treated Emma the same way Emma treated the world—guarded.

"I was coming home from my run and decided to check on her and Nora. Found her on the floor of the kitchen, phone nowhere near her."

She flinched. "Where was Nora?"

"Playing upstairs. She'd had no idea."

Emma nodded, the motion subtle. "How long ago was this?"

I thought for a second. "Close to two years ago."

"I had no idea," she murmured. "I can't believe she still makes three meals a day, once a week, for so many people . . . even after that."

Amusement pulsed through me. "She was determined to keep it going, no matter what. When we tried to make her rest and recover, she made us bring her down to the couch every Thursday and had food catered in for all three meals, even when we threatened not to come."

"That sounds like her." Her eyes met and held mine. "Thank you."

"Don't."

"It doesn't change anything," she said softly. "I'm not the kind of girl to swoon over a hero. If anything, you should know that by now. But I was never there for her, so it helps to know that she had people looking out for her, loving her, and even more that one of them loved her enough to be there when she needed it most. So, let me thank you."

I slanted my head in a nod.

When I turned for the steps, she asked, "You're leaving?"

My mouth twitched into a grin because those two words were just so . . . *Emma*. Little bit of frustration and contempt, little bit of indecision and longing.

She'd been right: Not one bit about her had changed.

"Just getting my tools." I risked a glance over my shoulder. "Unless you'd rather stay out here with me all night, listening to the rain."

She rolled her eyes and dropped her attention to the tablet. "I'd rather sleep on the couch."

When I made it back to the porch with my toolbox in hand, she was still on the swing and showed no signs of moving.

I stepped out of my running shoes and asked, "You coming?"

Her fingers stilled for only a moment before she resumed tapping on her tablet. "It's the room without a doorknob."

Right.

Maybe I wouldn't have minded a little change if just to avoid that part. The coldness and the way she retreated within herself while still seeming to stand ten feet tall.

I let myself into the house and went straight for the stairs, slowing to glance at the lower step Emma had sat trembling on . . . the part of the railing she'd gripped so damn tight. Wondering what exactly happened *that night* before jogging up.

Once I was on the top floor, I kept my steps light as I passed Lala's room and headed over to the long hallway on the far side of the second floor where Nora's room and the guest room were.

And right in front of the guest room was an old, crystal doorknob resting on the floor. I bent to pick it up as I inspected the door, my brow furrowing as I did. Glancing at the doorknob, I laughed as I tried to think of what exactly she would've had to do to accomplish this.

Opening up my toolbox, I grabbed a pair of regular and needle-nose pliers, then turned back to the door.

Before I had a chance to open it, I heard the front door open and shut, quickly followed by footsteps on the stairs.

And, damn it, it sounded like *home*.

The creaks of the old wood.

Her bare feet on the floor, coming closer.

Even the way she sighed when she rested her back against the wall and slid down it to sit next to me.

It had chills creeping across my arms and my heart pounding so damn loudly and painfully because I swear I'd just been given a glimpse into our lives together.

I wanted to ask if she could hear it all the same way I did. If she could *see* it. But God knew that would have her forgetting her walls and putting a damn ocean between us instead.

I swallowed forcefully and looked her way.

She jerked her chin past me. "I figured if the ladies across the street were even awake, they were going to talk about us regardless since we'd been out on the porch at such a late hour *unsupervised*," she said dryly.

"You stayed out there because you're worried what people will say?"

Her brows lifted. "Aren't you?"

"They're already talking about us anyway." My stare fell to her mouth before I could force it away.

"Are you serious?"

My head slowly shifted back in her direction at the horror in her whispered tone. "What does it matter?"

"It—" Her head moved in small, fast jerks, and her tongue

darted out to wet her lips. "I just don't need that in my life. Not right now."

"Because it's me?"

"Because I don't need that kind of attention on me."

"You came to the wrong place for that," I said unapologetically and went back to the door. "Wrong town, wrong house."

When she didn't respond, I grabbed the remaining part of the spindle sticking out from the door and twisted, popping the door open with a soft click.

If Emma noticed her door was open, she didn't show it.

"What the hell did you do to the doorknob?" I asked softly as I picked it up and grabbed the needle-nose pliers to pull out the small piece of the spindle that had snapped off with it.

Emma blinked and slowly dragged her attention to my hands and then to her door. "I don't know. I just tried to open it, and it fell off in my hand."

"Sure you didn't break it off with a hammer?" I teased as I put the pliers away and grabbed a screwdriver to take off the plates and latch.

A breath of a laugh left her, but she seemed even more withdrawn. "No. No, but that room used to be my mom's, so who knows what she did to the doorknob or anything else in there."

I had just finished with the last of it and was palming the screws when she added, "My mom was . . . well, she wasn't a *mom*, to put it nicely."

Every inch of me locked up when I realized she was willingly sharing something about her life. Moving slowly, as if I might scare her into stopping, I placed the screws in my box and sat beside her.

Knees touching.

Eyes on her.

Her stare fixed across the hall, but distant.

"She also wasn't much of a daughter, but I don't think Lala would say that to anyone. She kept me away from here most of my life. We only came back when—" Emma swallowed slowly, her slender neck shifting with the action. When she spoke again, her voice was soft and filled with shame. "When she needed money."

My conversation with Butler quickly flashed through my mind, and I had a feeling I knew what she was going to say next before she said it.

"Lala always gave it to her, and we always left as soon as she did." She lifted a shoulder. "The one time Lala refused, I thought it might be different. I thought we might stay, but my mom had no plans to. Soon as she realized she wouldn't be getting anything, she wanted to leave . . . I didn't, but I was sixteen and I couldn't make that decision." Her eyes darted to mine before snapping back to that spot across the hall. "But I tried."

I finally looked in the same direction she'd been fixated on and felt my blood run cold when I noticed where she'd been staring . . . *the stairs*.

I'd wanted any piece of her so fiercely that I would have *begged* for her to tell me something about her. I'd wanted to know what happened yesterday so badly, what had triggered her to spiral down so quickly, that I would have waited for this story forever.

Now that she was offering it to me, I was both eager for it and not ready to hear it.

Because this girl was fierce and brave unlike anyone I'd

ever met, and whatever happened could reduce her to a trembling mess in a second.

"Everyone was yelling." Her voice was soft but somehow seemed to shatter the bubble of quiet that had built around us, eclipsing even the weather outside. "Lala was begging my mom to stop, to just wait and give it time. Or to finally let me *stay*. I was yelling that I wasn't going, that she couldn't make me. And Momma . . . God, she was *screaming* that I was selfish and a traitor and calling me every name she could think of. Said I *owed* her. Demanded I go outside on my own two legs, or she was going to drag me out there."

Emma blew out a slow, stuttered breath and shut her eyes.

If I hadn't been sitting so close, if I hadn't been so focused on her, I might not have noticed the slight tremors rolling through her body.

When she opened her eyes again, she lifted a hand to point but kept it close to her body. "Lala was there at the top of the stairs. I was down there, about a third of the way up. Momma was at the bottom. We probably looked every bit the dysfunctional family we were, standing in that line, screaming at each other." Even though there was a hint of amusement in her words, her expression only grew more severe.

"Then Momma charged me," she continued in a grave tone. "Started sprinting up and screaming that she'd warned me. She caught one of my legs just before I reached the top and yanked me toward her. My feet slipped out from under me, but I managed to grab the railing as I fell. Lala lost it, started crying. Momma was screaming and tugging on me, but when I didn't move, she started jumping."

Emma's tongue darted out to wet her lips, her chest caving with a jagged exhale.

"Literally holding on to my ankle and launching into the air and slamming back down like she was rappelling down the stairs. I begged her to stop, begged her to let go. She tore my arm straight from the socket, and I *screamed,* but she never stopped. Just kept jumping, just kept yelling and saying all kinds of horrible things."

An apology was resting on the tip of my tongue. For what happened, for grabbing her the day before even though I'd clearly had no idea what it would do to her . . . but I swallowed it back.

I knew in my gut that couldn't be the end. Because Emma was still *staring* like she was reliving a horrible nightmare. And even knowing virtually nothing about her, I had no doubt it would take a hell of a lot more to bring Emma Wade to her knees.

"The pain was so bad that my grip on the railing loosened, and I warned her—I did," she added on quickly as if trying to convince me. "I told her again and again that we were going to fall. I lost my hold, and we started falling, but Lala grabbed me and hauled me back just in time. Momma's fingers slipped and she went all the way down. Hit the stairs once near the bottom and then rolled to the landing."

"Jesus."

"Lala and I sat there, staring at her. I don't know how long. Felt like an eternity. Then I started screaming because I was sure she was dead, and it was my fault. There was blood everywhere, and we couldn't see her chest moving from where we were. I was panicking because I'd killed her. I was afraid I was going to get arrested. Lala kept struggling to pull me away from my mom every time I tried to go to her." She finally looked at me and held my stare. "That's when a boy came charging into the house."

Butler.

"Took one look at my mom laying on the floor and then looked to where Lala was trying to keep me away. Lala said, 'Get her out of here,' and he did. Took me into the kitchen and wouldn't let me leave for anything." Her eyelids slowly shut before opening again. "He didn't say a word about it, even though I was sobbing, 'I killed her. I killed her,' over and over again. He just kept asking if he could help me with my arm—not that I let him. I figured out how to do it on my own.

"But I was in the kitchen trying to get past this boy I didn't know, yelling at him to let me leave, when Lala came in trying to calm me. Saying we would figure it out, saying we needed to call the cops and just tell them the truth." Emma's head lowered and her stare fell away. "I panicked, of course, said they couldn't be involved. Suddenly, Momma starts yelling and cursing from the other room, demanding to know where Danny was." She leaned closer and explained, "He was one of her husbands, not the most recent one at that time either. Before any of us could even get out of the kitchen, she came walking into it like nothing had ever happened, looked at Nick, and said, 'Who the fuck are you?'"

A sharp, stunned laugh escaped me at her harsh drawl, and I quickly lifted a hand toward Emma. "I'm sorry. I'm sorry, it isn't funny."

"No, that part kind of was. We all just stood there staring at her. Finally, I asked if she was okay, and she started yelling all over again, demanding to know why I wasn't ready to leave. When Lala pointed out the blood all over her, my mom thought it had to have been because of Danny and was so worked up, she wouldn't let anyone tell her otherwise. It ended up being from a small cut on her head, and Momma remained adamant that we were leaving right then. I was afraid that situation would repeat itself, so I left with her. I drove, of course, but we left."

"No hospital, no nothing?"

"Oh no. There's no way you could ever get Momma in one. She definitely had a concussion, and the next day, she was covered in bruises. But otherwise, she was fine. I don't know how after a fall like that." Her voice dipped and went shallow. "But every time I set foot on *that* staircase, I hear her screaming at me. I feel that drop in my gut like when we started falling. I *see* her falling." Catching my stare, she whispered, "Yesterday, I *felt* her grabbing and pulling me."

"Emma, I'm sorry," I said just as softly. "For what happened to you, for yesterday, all of it."

"You weren't the one who did it," she said dismissively.

"I grabbed you."

"You didn't know."

"I should've just let you walk away."

Her brows lifted and eyes widened. "Hey, now there's a thought. Almost like I've been telling you to do something similar since I met you."

"Maybe one of these days I'll actually listen to you," I lied as I pushed to my feet.

A breathless laugh left her. "I wish you would."

Now if that wasn't the sweetest lie.

I held my hand out to her and helped her up, my entire body buzzing when she lingered for a few moments before pulling away. I was so wrapped up in this girl that the simplest touch from her had my head spinning.

Because her touch meant everything.

It meant trust, and if I knew anything about her, I knew she didn't give that to many people.

Clearing my throat, I said, "I'll run to the hardware store tomorrow, get everything to fix your door. But you can get in and out of your room now."

"Oh, no, you don't have to. I can get it figured out."

"You called me to take care of something. I'm going to take care of it."

"I texted you," she whispered, her mouth tipping into a teasing grin at the reminder.

The power flickered and then went out completely, submerging us in darkness. The only sounds were the rain outside and our deepening breaths. That tension that wound between us grew thicker and stronger until I had to physically fight against it to stay in place.

"Happens with these houses when we have a lot of rain," I murmured, voice pure gravel.

"Convenient."

I swallowed past everything screaming to be said and choked out, "I should let you get some sleep."

"Right. Right, because it's late, and you're here and you shouldn't be." Everything was said almost as if it were a question. Everything was said like she was trying to remember *why* I should go.

And it made me want to stay.

"Tell me you don't feel it," I nearly begged. "Tell me you don't feel *this*."

"Reed . . ."

That was it. Just my name said as a plea, wrapped in everything else I was feeling.

"Hold out your hand."

She sucked in a quick breath when the tips of her fingers

collided with my abdomen, and I hurried to collect them in mine. Bringing them up, I placed her palm flat against my chest, against my pounding heart.

"Tell me I'm the only one feeling this."

Instead of a response, her breaths quickened and grew heavier.

"Can I take a step closer?" I asked quietly, studying her silhouette in the dark.

The tips of her fingers curled against my chest as her soft *Yes* filled the space between us.

I placed one of my hands on the wall for support and leaned my head toward hers, bringing us within a breath of each other, and said, "Tell me any of those things, Emma. Lie to me."

"You're the only one feeling this," she breathed, longing and confusion wrapped around each word. "You should go."

My head listed to the side as a smile tugged at the corners of my mouth. "You lying?"

"I don't know anymore," she said honestly.

In an instant, that energy between us spun and spun and wound so tight that I could hardly breathe.

"Emma Wade, I'm gonna kiss you unless you tell me not to."

"Oh God."

I slanted my head closer until my mouth was hovering over hers. "Tell me not to, and I'll leave this house right now."

When only the sound of the rain hitting the roof and windows met me, I leaned forward and swept my lips across hers once . . . twice . . . before pressing my mouth to hers in a slow, gentle kiss.

Taking my time with what I knew was more important than any act I had ever done before.

The next breath that left her shook my goddamn soul.

I teased the seam of her lips with my tongue and groaned when she opened for me. Without hesitation, without reservation. Slanting my mouth over hers, I claimed her slowly, teasingly, letting the kiss build until we were both breathless. Releasing her hand, I traced the line of her jaw, tilting her head back and taking control of the kiss. Then my hand was in her hair, and she was grabbing at my shirt, trying to pull me closer, and I was trying to figure out how a kiss could be so *good*.

"Stop."

The hushed word registered in my mind a split second before she said it again.

"*Stop*," she wheezed, the word twisted in a horrible mixture of reluctance and self-loathing. "I can't do this. I can't do this, stop."

But I already had.

I'd already pushed away from her and pressed up against the railing before the second *stop* had finished leaving her lips.

"I'm sorry." I cleared my throat, trying to force back the need to pull her into my arms as that reluctance in her voice tugged at every part of me. "I'm sorry, I shouldn't have kissed you."

"Would you stop?" she nearly begged. "Would you stop being so nice? Would you stop just . . . God. There is so much about my life that you don't understand."

"Trust me, I got that."

"No, you don't," she said gravely. "You don't because

there are so many things you can't begin to fathom. And what would happen if you could?"

I went still at the blatant challenge.

Lungs aching as I waited, silently begging her to let me in a little more. To give me another piece of her life that I was dying to know.

"What would happen if you knew exactly why I need to hate you? Why I *do*?" Her words dipped and broke even as she struggled to put her razor-sharp strength behind them. "You would very quickly realize you don't want this. That you should've left this alone and walked away that first night."

"I fucking doubt that."

"You can't say that when you don't know," she snapped, then covered her mouth with a hand as her back hit the wall in the darkened hall. After a shuddering breath, her hand fell away with a weighted sigh. The sound sad and full of regret and confidence. "Because there is no getting past *you*. And there will be no getting past what you learn about me."

"Then tell me, Emma. Tell me everything, so I can prove you wrong."

"I can't."

I stepped toward her without thinking, but she didn't try to stop me. "You can," I assured her, voice soft and low. "You do what you did tonight. Give me a part of your world so I can know you. So I can show you not every guy is what you've encountered before. As I said earlier, you've been around the wrong people . . . *clearly*, if you're telling me to stop being nice. I'm not being fucking nice, Emma. I'm apologizing because I know better. I may not know who you are yet, but I know you. I know you need to go slow. I know you need your space, but I still pushed you because I want you in a way I've never wanted anyone."

"Reed, I can't," she said weakly. "There is—" Her hands lifted, hovering just over her head for long moments before falling heavily. "I'll never be able to let myself. You have to understand that."

The regret in her voice and the tension swirling between us, so thick and alive, made that impossible. But I'd already pushed her too far, and I knew if I pushed even the slightest bit more, this extremely rare, vulnerable moment with her would vanish.

Stepping back, I bent to grab my tools, then searched her darkened features, trying desperately to ignore the pull between us. "Whatever happened in your life doesn't scare me. I'll prove that to you someday." Before she could try to solidify any of her walls between us, I murmured, "Goodnight, Emma," and left the house.

SIXTEEN

EMMA

"That you, Emma?" Lala called out as soon as I set foot in the house the next day.

I'd come to love the way Lala always called out, asking if it was me.

Because I now knew it could literally be anyone else. Any of the other people in town, coming to check on the woman they loved. Anyone coming to pay a visit.

I still didn't love that she kept her door unlocked, but she'd told me one afternoon that her door and kitchen were always open, to friends and thieves alike . . .

I'd rolled my eyes, she'd told me to go change, and that had been the end of that.

However, today, I didn't want her greeting. I didn't want to respond. I hadn't slept at all after Reed had left the night before, replaying that kiss and every word, every emotion, every fear.

I was fairly certain I'd barely made it out of the store with my life after drowning in a sea of book-filled boxes—and we still had more coming. I was exhausted, my brain was mush . . . I just wanted to climb into bed, never leave, never speak to anyone, and never see another book again.

"Emma?"

"*Ugh*," I groaned overdramatically.

An affectionate laugh filled the kitchen and drifted to where I was pressed to the front door. "Come get you something to eat."

I managed to stumble into the kitchen. The moment I fell into one of the chairs, my head dropped to the table and my eyelids slid shut. "I'm falling asleep . . . right here."

"Don't you dare drool on my table," Lala said in warning as she slid a plate onto the table. "Tell me about the day and get this into your stomach, then you can go sleep."

I lifted my head to look at her when she sat beside me and briefly wondered if my head was always this heavy. "Half of the books came."

"Oh, how thrilling!" When I narrowed my eyes at her, she lifted her brows. "Was something wrong with them?"

"There were so many books. So many."

"Oh, I see." She lifted her hand to her mouth as if trying to solve a problem, then sighed. "I hate to be the one to tell you this—really, I do—but you work at a bookstore."

"You're funny," I said dryly, then took a bite of the sandwich she'd made. "I feel like I could sleep for a week. We didn't even make a dent, and the other half of the shipment is coming tomorrow."

"Well, Nora and I will be there for that. I just had my things to do today."

"No. No, don't do that. Donna and I have it."

"And miss an opportunity to tell you what to do?" She scoffed.

"Donna tries," I offered.

"*Tries*," Lala shot back. "She doesn't know you."

Affection pulled at my mouth. "Lala, you should've seen her today, she was . . . God, she was so happy. When they finished delivering the shipment, she went from stack to stack, touching them as if they were precious. Then she looked at me with the sweetest smile and said, 'I wish I had my old record player,' and started doing this cute, little dance."

Lala laughed. "Oh, she's darling."

"It gets better," I assured her. "I asked what she would have played, and she just looked at me like I'd grown another head. 'Well, the very best song in the world, of course.'"

I dug through my bag for my phone and opened the music app to play the song I'd had on repeat for Donna.

"Did she tell you what it was?"

I nodded and pushed play on *You Can't Hurry Love* by The Supremes.

Lala pressed a hand to her chest. "I love this song." Halfway through, she said, "Look at what you've already done for her."

I waved off her words. "She's done more for me by giving me a chance."

"There happen to be a few people in this world who can see through that diamond-tough exterior you wear."

I rolled my eyes, but the corner of my mouth was tipping up in a smile.

"We'll just be thankful that Donna Morrison is one of them." She drummed her fingers on the table. "Speaking of people who can see through that exterior of yours . . ."

Oh no.

"Reed stopped by this morning."

I tried to appear unaffected, but I knew Lala saw right through it. "Did he?"

"Sure did. Would have been nice if a certain granddaughter of mine had told me about the whole doorknob incident before she left this morning."

"I'm sorry, I wasn't thinking. I was . . ." Consumed.

Wholly, completely, thoroughly consumed in a man, and trying like hell to get out the door before he could show up again.

"It slipped my mind," I said lamely.

"Uh-huh." She clicked her tongue and continued as if she weren't interested to hear every single detail that I knew she was dying to get her hands on. "Told me about last night, how you messaged him from my phone."

"You always leave it on the counter," I choked out because it felt like my heart was in my throat as I waited to hear if Reed had told her about the kiss.

"Said he couldn't believe the way the doorknob had been hacked off, but he got it all fixed just fine." When I only nodded, she deliberately added, "He asked about you, asked if you were here."

My gaze shot to hers. "Did you tell him where I was? About the bookstore?"

"No. Sure didn't." She fluffed at her hair that was more gray than blonde as her eyes bore into mine. Waiting. Prying. "But when I said you weren't here, everything about that boy changed. I've never seen him so disappointed in the time I've known him."

A noncommittal hum sounded in my throat.

The hand that had been playing with her hair smacked down onto the table. "Don't *hmm* me, I can see the two of y'all trying to hide something from me because you went flying out of here this morning without so much as a *hello*, and he came in here looking all hopeful before I went and crushed him."

A strangled sound crawled up my throat as I admitted, "He kissed me last night."

Excitement broke across Lala's face. "*Emma Wade!*"

"You kissed my Reed?"

I turned, eyes wide at the unexpected voice. But one look at the betrayal on Nora's face, and I knew I was going to regret ever wishing for her silence to end.

"Why did you—you *can't*," she said firmly, her hands balling up into fists close to her chest.

"Nora," I began softly, but she continued.

"I knew it, I knew it! He wants to talk to that one more than he wants to talk to me when he's here," she said to Lala. "That one's taking my Reed from me just like she took my mom!"

"That is not—"

"You can't take my Reed!" she screamed over Lala.

"Nora," Lala snapped, pointing away from the kitchen. "Upstairs now."

I watched as Nora stomped away and Lala went after her, my chest and stomach tight with unease. After a couple minutes of indecision, I pushed from the chair and followed until I was up the stairs and hesitantly stepping into my old room.

"You can't take my Reed," Nora said when she saw me from where she sat on her bed, face red and wet with tears.

Lala tsked. "What did I just say?"

But Nora just looked away and rubbed at her tear-stained cheeks.

Sucking in a shaky breath, I asked Lala, "Do you think Nora and I could talk?"

Lala's brows lifted in surprise, but after a moment, she nodded and stepped out of the room as she said, "I'll be downstairs if y'all need me."

"I don't like you," Nora said soon after.

I lowered my head in acknowledgment. "That's okay. You don't have to like everyone." I shrugged and stepped deeper into the room. "I kind of resented you when I first met you too."

Nora looked around, her chest jerking with her shuddering breaths. "What does 'resented' mean?"

"Um . . ." Embarrassment flared in my chest as I admitted, "It basically means I was angry with you." I shrugged as I met her confused and hurt eyes. "But it wasn't fair because you didn't do anything to deserve that."

She stared at her comforter for a while before her curiosity got the best of her and asked, "Why are you angry at me?"

"I'm not," I said quickly, "but I was. I was angry because you didn't *have* to know our mom. Our mom was a really, really bad person. I had a terrible, scary life because of her. And it made me angry that she let you have a normal life with Lala when she refused to let me have that." I lowered myself to the floor and sighed. "But the thing is, I never should've been angry with you because all of that was her fault and her decisions—not yours. I'm also really thankful you never had to see that terrible, scary life, and I would do anything to keep you from it and from her. But that doesn't mean I took her from you. I already told you, she left me long before you were born."

"But you got to know her."

"Nora, I can't imagine what that's like for you, but I wish you knew how lucky you are to be raised by Lala. To know *her*, and to have people like Reed."

"You're trying to take my Reed," she cried out, chin wavering.

I studied her for a while before asking, "He's really special to you, isn't he?"

"The most special."

"You're incredibly special to him too—he told me." I watched as she wiped furiously at her face and said, "Nora, no one can ever take Reed from you. But he might find someone one day that he wants to date and marry, and you're going to have to be okay with that."

She sniffled loudly. "You?"

"God, no," the horrified words were fueled by years of watching my mom go through boyfriends and husbands like it was a game. But even as my mind rebelled against the idea, a pit of jealousy opened up in my stomach at the thought of Reed with anyone else.

"Then why did you kiss him?" Nora yelled. "You say mean things about him and you always tell him to leave. You're mean to my Reed—maybe you're the really bad person and not my mom." A sob left her as she crossed her arms stubbornly. "You can't kiss my Reed, and you can't take him when he's here. He used to talk to me all, all, *all* the time, and now he always wants to talk to you."

"You can't demand a person's full attention, Nora," I said as I stood. "You have to be okay if people want to talk to someone who isn't you—it doesn't matter who they are. What if I said Lala couldn't talk to you, she could only talk to me? Would that bother you?"

She murmured her assent after a beat of hesitation.

I nodded and started for the door. “I’m sorry you feel like I’m taking people from you. I promise I’m not,” I said before slipping back into the hall and downstairs.

“Oh, well, isn’t this news of you and Reed just so exciting?” Lala asked as soon as I was in the kitchen.

“Lala . . .”

“Don’t you start that with me again because I’ve seen you with him recently, and I know how you feel about him. So, don’t you go telling me none of that nonsense you’re trying to make . . . yourself . . . believe.” Lala’s expression fell when she noticed the way my chin was trembling. “What happened with Nora?”

“Nothing, no,” I said quickly, my voice thick. “Not her.”

If I hadn’t been so utterly exhausted, I would’ve been horrified that I was on the verge of crying.

If it weren’t *Reed*, I wouldn’t be at that point at all.

“Everything Reed’s done . . . God, Lala, I don’t know of anyone who would do what Reed does. I don’t think anyone would care to take the time that he has. He asks if he can take a step closer to me. He asks *me* to reach out so that I’m the one who touches him first. He told me he was going to kiss me unless I told him not to. He told me he’d leave the house if I asked him to.”

Affection softened Lala’s features, but worry still lined the creases around her eyes.

Probably because she hadn’t seen me like this in so, so long.

“In my head, I knew I needed to stop him, make him leave, anything . . . but I couldn’t. Then he kissed me.”

I sat there, replaying it as I had so many times throughout the night and early morning.

Before that moment, I’d never been kissed in that way.

Full of need in a way that was gentle and adoring and everything that was *Reed.*

I'd never been kissed by anything less than unwelcome force.

"I've never experienced anything so pure or beautiful," I whispered. "But it shook my world in a terrifying way. Because I knew I was falling too fast, and I knew in that kiss that I would give my last breath to experience it again. That's when the panic and worry and reality set in. For the first time, I knew a man had the ability to break me, and I was so afraid of giving him the power to. Of giving him any part of myself. And I freaked out and pushed him away."

Lala gave a slow dip of her head. "And are some people in this room still pushing him away?"

I tried to smile, but it fell flat. "I have to. I know you see him as this perfect man, and maybe he is, but he isn't for me. He can't be."

"Or maybe he could if you'd just let him."

"Lala—"

"You've only been around fiends and assholes your entire life. Don't count the good ones out before they have a chance to surprise you." She sighed as if what she was about to say didn't matter either way and said, "Reed doesn't have to be the one who does that, but I think it would do you a whole lotta good to consider opening up your heart to someone for the first time in your life."

I stared at the floor, but my thoughts were on gunmetal eyes and a wicked smirk.

"I think it would do you a whole lotta good to let someone heal some of those scars on your heart."

My stare shot over to her and got caught up in the worry and pain and comfort there.

I wanted to tell her she didn't understand what that meant—what that would entail. No one would understand the wraiths that lived to torment me and the demons that lingered in my bed. Baggage was something in a relationship, I knew.

But not mine.

Lala blew out a long sigh, a distant look in her eyes. "I was engaged to be married to a man." Her head bobbed subtly. "A man I loved very much. Our wedding was planned, nearly every detail in place. Oh, I was so ready to marry him." She fell silent for a while before muttering, "There was an accident at the train yard he worked at—he and a few others didn't make it."

I sucked in a quick, audible breath. "Lala, no . . ."

Her shining eyes shifted to me. "I was sure I would never love again. That I would spend the rest of my life alone—I *wanted* to spend the rest of my life alone. But then I met your grandfather." A wistful smile crossed her face. "It was a chance encounter, truly. My girlfriends and I were walking to the theater and passed by the diner just as some men came walking out. They didn't live here, were only visiting and leaving the next day. But I knew the moment I saw your grandfather that I was looking at my future. From the way he stopped at the door and just stared at me, I was sure he knew it too. I didn't go to the theater that night. He and I ended up going back into the diner and talking until closing."

"Did he leave the next day?" I asked when she didn't go on.

My grandpa had died a few years after I was born, and my mom hadn't ever talked about either of her parents unless it was about getting money from Lala. So, I didn't know a thing about him.

Lala dipped her head in a slow nod. "He did, and I was oddly heartbroken. I felt like I'd lost my entire world, yet I'd only known him for a few hours. But I was walking to the store a few days later, and there he was, asking every single person who passed by if they knew me." Her eyes brightened. "I married your grandpa not even a week later."

My mouth dropped open in shock. "*Lala.*"

"Oh, my parents were furious, but I didn't care. I knew he was it." Sadness crept across her features. "When he was taken from me, I knew *that* was it—that I would never find anyone like him again. And I was okay with that because just a few hours with him had healed so many hurts and held enough happiness and love to get me through a lifetime."

My mouth had been lifting into a smile, imagining something like Lala described. Imagining a stop-you-in-your-tracks kind of moment. A night that could change your entire world. But when she continued, my smile fell.

"It would do you a lotta good to let someone heal the scars on your heart," she repeated her earlier words softly. "When you're ready, of course."

I offered her a nod, then looked back to the floor as haunting whispers slipped past my defenses.

"Let go!" I'd screamed when I was caught around the waist and hauled back. Thrashing and connecting with another man only to be dropped unexpectedly on my back.

The air had rushed from my lungs and stars burst through my vision for a moment.

I'd blinked them away, already fighting and screaming when hands had clawed at my shirt as the weight of another man rested on my hips, and looked up to see Chris Dennison on top of me, pulling off his shirt. "Do you know how long I've wanted to fuck you? Since about the minute you stepped into my off—" His grunt and shocked yells had sounded when my fist connected with his jaw.

I'd scrambled away when he'd rolled to the side and was immediately pulled back against another body.

"Where you think you're going?"

"Fuck you," I'd cried out. "I'm not a stripper or a prostitute or whatever you think you ordered."

"Oh, it didn't take long to realize that," he'd said, lips at my ear even as I'd tried to get away from him. "But things change, and you're one hell of a nice surprise."

"I'll kill you—you fucking asshole," I'd screamed when his hand had crept lower and lower.

His dark laugh had vibrated against my skin as his other arm banded around my waist, locking my arms close to my body and keeping me tight against him. "Darlin', you can't touch me. You can't touch any of us."

I'd cried out in frustration and disgust when he'd slipped his hand into my pants despite how hard I tried to break from his hold, a sickening chill running down my spine when he'd said, "But we can touch you."

I FINALLY SUCCEEDED in forcing away the memories and tightly locking the doors on my mind. My voice was hollow when I asked Lala, "What if I'm never ready?"

MY EYELIDS POPPED open at the sound.

Heart hammering and chest pitching with shallow breaths as I was wrenched from sleep.

In seconds, I'd scrambled to sitting and shifted to my knees on the bed, trembling hands out in front of me as I waited. Listened.

Old memories flooding my mind and threatening to swallow me whole as my stare searched the darkened room.

When my phone vibrated on the bedside table, I jumped, a gasp catching in my throat.

"Jesus," I said on a wheezing breath as I reached over, grabbing up my cell and settling back on the bed when I saw there were two messages, both from within the last minute.

Both from an unknown number with an area code that wasn't from Colby or New York.

I glanced at the time, noting that it was barely half-past four in the morning, and hesitantly slid my finger across the screen. Unease swirling in my stomach as I held my breath and waited the short moment for the messages to open.

Unknown: *I'd like to see you. From what I've gathered, the only way I can do that while I'm on shift is by waking you up before the sun rises.*

Unknown: *You want to watch the sun rise with me, Emma Wade?*

My heart took off. This crazy, uncontrolled beat that was as intoxicating as it was frightening.

Glancing around the room as if Reed might've gotten through the locked door without waking me, I scooted back against the headboard and tapped out a reply, fingers trembling as a hesitant smile tugged at my mouth.

. . .

Me: Stalker.

Me: *How did you get my number?*

Unknown: *Grabbed it from Lala's phone when she heavily hinted it was in there and then left it next to me.*

Me: *Of course she did.*

I TAPPED ON THE SCREEN, saving his contact as my heart and stomach betrayed me. Just hours before, I'd been trying to fortify every wall that Reed Ryan had managed to find ways past. Sure it was for the best. That we were only headed down a path that led to destruction and pain. But as another message from him came through, I found myself anxious to see what he'd said.

Reed Ryan: So how about that sunrise?

Me: *When?*

Reed Ryan: *I'm outside.*

I SAT UP, one foot already on the floor and heart threatening to break free as my mind screamed for me to stop.

To stay. Tell him to leave and remind him that we couldn't do . . . whatever it was we were doing.

Because this was a terrible idea. Not just that I was slipping out of my room and down the hall to freshen up in the bathroom. But all of it. Letting Reed into my life—or any man.

It was all so bad and so dangerous, and it had a feeling of dread crawling through my veins as I crept down the stairs. Had those wraiths trailing icy fingers down my spine and pushing memories to the surface as I gripped the handle of the door, my head falling to the wood as I let out shaky breaths.

Go upstairs, go upstairs, go upstairs.

You have nothing to offer him. End this.

Taking a step back, I released the handle, something in my chest aching as I resigned to turn around and ignore Reed's offer completely.

Another step back, I started turning for the stairs but reached out instead. Grabbing the handle and opening the door before I could talk myself out of it again.

And then I was stepping outside, my breaths embarrassingly uneven when I found Reed standing at the bottom of the porch steps, arms folded over his chest and staring up at me as if he knew the battle I'd just endured. Looking like sin and bad memories and still somehow making butterflies erupt in my belly.

SEVENTEEN

EMMA

"How many times did you talk yourself out of coming down?" Reed asked, voice soft and rough in the predawn morning.

"Once."

His lips lifted in a slow, knowing smirk. Gesturing to the side of the porch with a subtle jerk of his chin, he said, "If it's okay with you, I'm gonna walk up there and sit on the swing."

I inclined my head in both challenge and acceptance. "What would you do if I said no?"

"There are the steps," he said as he climbed them, his stare dipping over me and voice dropping even lower when he added, "Back of my truck."

Heat flashed across my skin and stole my next breath, my stare falling to the dark wood at my bare feet before bouncing everywhere else. Anywhere other than Reed and his distracting presence and implications.

Once he was seated on the porch swing, leaning forward with his forearms resting on his knees, I let out a shuddering breath and headed that way but elected to lean up against the house instead of sitting next to him.

If it bothered him, he didn't show it. His eyes just tracked my movements with a heated interest that had me worrying over the state of my heart when any kind of interest from a man should've had my stomach twisting and souring. Should've had every hair on the back of my neck rising.

"The doorknob work out all right?" he asked as soon as I was settled against the house.

My lips parted but only a soft breath blew past them. "You got me one with a lock . . ."

His brows drew together in worry. "Uh, yeah. I couldn't find anything that looked like what had been there. But I can look online."

"No," I said quickly, trying to ease his worry. "No, it's fine. I . . ." My head shook and I looked out over the darkened lawn. "I like locks." I cleared my throat of the remnants of the confession and asked, "How much was it?"

"I got it."

My eyes shot back to him and my spine straightened. Voice hardening as I repeated, "How much was it?"

"Emma, it wasn't—"

"No, see, it broke off in my hand, which means it was my problem. So, I need you to tell me what it cost."

He straightened, arms out in a helpless action. "It's a doorknob. It was *nothing*."

"I refuse to be in debt to anyone for anything," I bit out. "It doesn't matter how big or how small those debts are."

Reed studied me for long seconds as if he was trying to understand . . . or maybe he *did*. Maybe it was that he was piecing me together in ways he shouldn't. Taking what I'd just given him and putting it with what I'd shared the other night.

When he spoke, his tone was soft and gentle, but no less firm. "That was from a door in Lala's house—do you have any idea how much your grandma feeds me?" He shrugged. "No matter what I do for her, I'll never repay her." He held my stare, voice dipping with some unknown emotion when he said, "There's no debt."

He didn't understand. Nearly my entire life had been the way it was because of my mother's debts, and I had lived every day trying to pay them while ensuring I never had any of my own.

It was one of the reasons why coming to Lala for help had been so difficult. It was why I knew exactly what day I'd arrived so I could pay for every living cost. It was one of the reasons I was so determined to make Donna's store everything she'd ever wanted, why I was determined to make it thrive, because it was the only way I could truly repay her for giving me a chance.

But those were things none of them understood, so I simply murmured, "Thank you." My gaze darted over his fitted gray shirt and dark athletic shorts before drifting to my feet again. "How long are you working?"

"What?"

"You said you can only see me before the sun rises when you're working. Just trying to figure out how often I'm going to be waking up to early-morning texts." When I risked a glance at him, he was fighting a smile.

"Just had my first on. I work four on, four off." He leaned back in the swing, resting his long legs out in front of him and folding his arms over his chest. "If you didn't hide from me all day, I wouldn't have to wake you up."

"I don't hide from you."

He lifted a brow at the blatant lie, expression all disbelief and amusement. "Where were you when I came by yesterday?"

"Out." When he looked content to wait for me to expand on that, I let out a slow exhale and vaguely answered, "Working."

"You ready to share that with me yet?" Understanding washed over him when my lips pressed firmly together. "Can I ask why you don't want to?"

Because I don't owe you anything.

The words were on the tip of my tongue, but I choked them back. Indecision warring within me for long moments before I finally said, "Because this feels very delicate for so many reasons."

I needed a job. Chris had found me and contacted Donna within days of her hiring me, and I had a horrible feeling that had a lot to do with Jarrod Davis and the size of this town. But I doubted any other employer would've responded the way Donna had—would've trusted me blindly with work-related accusations and with their business. Most importantly, Donna needed this.

This was her life, her family, and her home.

"I'm afraid of it being taken away, and I'm afraid of failing," I admitted, voice soft as a whisper. "Not that I think telling you would have an impact on that, I just . . . I feel more protective of this than I think I've ever felt of anything."

Reed grunted, his head moving in a slow nod as if what I'd said made everything make sense to him.

"What?"

His eyes darted to me. "You don't share anything, Emma.

You hold everything close so no one can touch you. Why wouldn't you keep something that means this much to you even closer?"

The truth of what he said had a self-deprecating laugh tumbling free. "The thing is, I'm not. I mean . . . it's complicated." I blew out a sigh as I tried to gather my thoughts. "The whole purpose of what I'm doing is for people to know about it. To *see* it."

"But not see you do it," he said in understanding, stunning me into silence as I stared at him.

Those wings fluttering in my belly as I wondered how he could see me so clearly.

Moments passed in our tension-filled silence before he lifted a shoulder. "Guess I'll be waking you up."

The corners of my lips lifted, a breath of a laugh dancing free even as I shook my head. "Nora might have a problem with that." At his obvious confusion, I explained, "She thinks I'm taking you from her. She's pretty upset."

Understanding lit Reed's features as a sigh eased from him. "Yeah, she mentioned something like that when I stopped by yesterday. But she'll get used to it."

I thought over his words for a moment before saying, "There shouldn't be anything for her to get used to because nothing good can come of this." The words straining with my warring thoughts and desires.

"You know you don't believe that."

"I do," I argued weakly because I *needed* to believe it.

One day, something would happen that was too much for either one of us. I was sure of it. But I was falling too fast for my heart to care.

I looked away from his amused and knowing stare and

caught on the house across the street. "Don't say it," I warned as I started for the front door.

"Emma—" Reed was already on his feet, hand outstretched and mouth still parted when I glanced at him from over my shoulder. But my expression was enough to satisfy his pleas and curiosity because he forced back whatever he'd been saying and stayed in place as I opened the door.

I strained my ear as I turned off the porch light, listening for any signs that Lala or Nora had woken, then quietly slipped back outside. Stare darting over Reed's silhouette in the dark as I started toward him again, trying desperately to catch my breath and calm my heart as I stopped directly beside him.

"The ladies across the street wake very early," I said in way of explanation. "They've told me many times."

His smile flashed in the dark. "They'll still see my truck."

A noncommittal hum sounded in my throat as I sank to the swing. "Then they can stare at a truck."

"A lot of stories can be made from that," he said as he sat beside me, movements slow and cautious as if he were waiting for me to stop him.

"Well, they've already come up with plenty about me," I muttered. "'You must've been a mistress,'" I recalled, pointing the way they had at me as if they'd finally figured it out. "'She caught y'all, didn't she? Mmhm. About time, filthy homewrecker.'"

Reed barked out a laugh and hurried to quiet it when I hushed him. "That didn't happen."

"It did," I said earnestly. "One of my first days here." I leaned my head back against the ropes, taking in his entertained expression now that my eyes had adjusted. "It wasn't their first theory, and it hasn't been the last." I shrugged, a smile crossing my face. "I think they like me."

"I think I like it when you smile."

My poor heart. It wasn't going to survive this morning or Reed Ryan.

I could feel it in the way it faltered every time he said something like that. I could feel it in the way the fierce beats warned that I was falling for him in all the other moments.

I cleared my throat, but my voice was still a strained breath when I said, "I don't want you to."

"I know I like it when you lie," he added, the words drifting over me like a caress in the dark and wrapping us in a bubble of wants and needs that intrigued me almost as much as it terrified me. "Tell me something . . ."

I tilted my head in response, my stare following his every movement as he shifted in the bench swing to face me, his hand slowly extending to me in invitation.

"When I came back yesterday morning," he began, words sure, "were you trying to avoid me?"

Hesitation unfurled inside me and bled free as I looked from his open palm to his expectant expression.

"Lie to me, Emma," he said when I'd held on to the answer too long. "Either way, I'll know the truth."

I reached forward, setting my hand in his and loosing a stuttered breath when he curled his fingers around me. "Yes," I admitted.

"Because of what happened," he said knowingly.

"Yes."

He turned our hands and eased his fingers through mine, a question on his tongue when he said, "But you came out here."

"Against my better judgment," I conceded, earning a hushed laugh from him.

But the way he was looking at me was as if he could hear every single one of my thoughts. As if they echoed his own.

Because I can't seem to stay away from you. I can't stop thinking about you—wanting you.

"Tell me something about you," I begged when the connection between us pulled harder and harder, making my nerves jump in anticipation, and tried to ignore the way we'd both leaned closer. "Something you think I should know."

Reed sat back, blinking quickly as he pulled himself from the moment we'd nearly gotten trapped in again. "Something you should know?" He cleared his throat, searching around the porch before meeting my stare again. "Uh . . . I was engaged."

Reed didn't try to stop me when I pulled my hand back, but I felt his disappointment like a stake to my chest, amplifying my confusion and uneasiness at the revelation.

Not that I'd expected Reed to have been a monk, I clearly knew he hadn't been—given what I'd heard the first night I met him. But I'd never let anyone close enough to even push against one of my defenses, let alone slip past it, and Reed had been planning a wedding to someone.

"I knew her from Tampa—that's where I grew up. But we didn't get together until after I was a SEAL." Something like a smile crossed his face, but it was all irritation. "You know, because people hear *SEAL* and everything changes. I just hadn't realized that *then*."

His bitterness had me going still.

The reminder of how he'd reacted when I'd asked about him being a SEAL suddenly had a different meaning, and it made me want to protect my heart against him even more.

Because I saw the way Courtney reacted to him at the coffee shop, and it was ridiculous, he was right. But it went so much deeper for Reed than that—he was *hurt* by it. Still.

I nodded, my stare on the porch below the motionless swing. "I see."

"Yeah, I don't think you do," he said, voice rough and capturing my attention again. "Not if you're pulling away from me and already shutting me out. Emma, we broke up years ago."

"Why did you?"

"She was cheating on me." He shrugged. "She gave me the ring back almost as soon as I got stateside from one of my missions."

"All right, then I do understand," I argued. "Because I can hear your pain and bitterness when you talk about her. And if it had been up to you, you would be married right now."

"But I'm not," he said firmly. "Yeah, I'll admit, there's bitterness when it comes to her, but it's for more reasons than what happened between us. A lot is that I was completely blinded to her, and that pisses me off because I wasted years with her. Most of it goes back to my family." He leaned forward but was careful not to get in my space. "If you think I *miss* her or that I still *love* her? I can assure you, you're wrong."

"So easily," I murmured as my stare fell away again. "This is such a bad idea."

"You're about to stand up, please don't," he said quickly just as my muscles tensed to do exactly that.

Seconds passed in strained silence, but I never relaxed my body.

When he was sure I wasn't leaving, he asked, "What did

you mean by that? 'So easily,'" he clarified when I didn't respond, "what did you mean?"

"You," I finally said, voice soft. "You love someone enough to ask her to marry you, and then you no longer love her. You kissed me just weeks after I heard you having sex with someone else." My head shook quickly. "The way you move on and think and feel, it shifts so easily."

"Emma—" His head slanted, my name tripping up and coming out on a stilted breath when my stare shot to his. Almost as if he could physically see the way I'd already shut down, thinking of anything to say to make him leave.

Maybe my reaction was naïve, but I'd witnessed fleeting emotions through my mom. Husbands and boyfriends coming and going almost as fast as the seasons. The only emotions I'd ever experienced were fear and loathing.

Until Reed.

I was afraid enough of them. I wanted to run as it was.

I didn't want to let myself get caught up in the first real thing in my life only to find out it had just been another week . . . month . . . season for him.

"Before you go," Reed began, voice strained like he was trying so hard to keep his voice soft and even, "you should know that only two other people in this town know I used to be engaged—and that's because they were there for it." A huff of a laugh left him as he leaned forward, hands hanging between his legs. "Lala doesn't even know, and she knows too much about my life."

His head shifted my way, eyes searching me. "People don't know because it's in the past—there isn't a reason for them to. But *you*? I feel like you need to know the worst and most important parts of me."

"Why?"

"Why are you down here? Why did you tell me about the night with your mom and the stairs?" he challenged without hesitation. "Because I need to. Because you're different."

I wet my lips and tried to push deeper against the rope as he gave voice to my thoughts. Making them real.

"Having my heart broken and moving on from it wasn't *easy*," he continued. "The fact that I did means nothing because otherwise, I'd be the idiot still waiting around for someone who never actually loved me. As for the other night . . ." He forced out a heavy sigh and dropped his head to run his hands through his hair before sitting back and facing me. "It was a one-time thing, and it was a mistake because I'd already seen you." His deep voice dropped even lower and echoed with his regret. "I'd seen your disgust-fueled sneers and your scorn-filled glares, and I swear to God I started falling for you right then."

My stare dropped to my lap at his confession, my breaths short and uneven.

"I'm not faulting you for sleeping with someone the night you met me—or any night," I whispered, words trembling slightly. "You can sleep with whoever you want."

"I don't want to sleep with anyone else."

At his implication, fear unfurled in my belly and mixed with an exhilarating heat I was becoming alarmingly familiar with when it came to Reed Ryan. My lips parted to speak, but my mouth was suddenly too dry.

"If you think you'd ever be a *night*—someone I'd 'easily' move on from—Emma, you have to know how wrong you are." He held his hand out between us again but clenched it into a fist as if already knowing I wouldn't place mine there. "I wouldn't be here. I wouldn't be practically begging you to help me understand you."

I stared at his clenched hand as minutes came and went in tense silence. In all that time, I could've sworn Reed never took a breath as he waited to see what I would do.

After what felt like an eternity trapped in indecision where my heart was rooted in place and my mind was screaming at me to leave, I softly pleaded, "Tell me something you think I should know about you."

Reed's hand opened with a ragged exhale, and when I met his stare, his expression was pure relief. "Uh . . ." His head moved in faint shakes as he thought. "My family. We don't speak—haven't in years. But it's a story that spans my entire life, so I'll have to tell you on one of my days off."

I nodded, understanding that better than anyone probably could.

"My mom called herself a lover," I began, slipping my hand into his again. "I don't think she actually knew the meaning of the word. She got married and divorced at least once a year and had twice as many boyfriends. She'd leave them after robbing them blind, or they'd leave her for another woman." I swallowed back the shame that gathered in my throat and forced myself to hold Reed's stare. "The longest and most normal relationship I've ever witnessed lasted maybe five months. It was only because she'd landed a dealer, so he fed her addiction. He got tired of her eventually."

The way Reed was staring at me made me feel bare. As if he were looking into my soul and seeing the little glimpses of my life that I'd just told him. As if he'd realized what I'd carelessly revealed: that I'd never had a relationship. Letting it all help him piece and shape together what he already knew of me to get a more concrete idea of the girl sitting next to him.

"That wasn't love, that was people trying to fill voids," he said finally. "And that—" He'd been turning closer to me but stopped almost as soon as he began moving. "Can I touch you?"

I put a little pressure on his hand as if to remind him that he was.

His head slanted, his eyes searching mine earnestly. "Stop me," he offered softly as he reached forward with his free hand.

I watched, unable to move or speak as he rested his hand just above my knee. His tattooed fingers gently curling around me in a claim and a plea that had my chest shaking with a jagged exhale and my stomach dipping with want.

I felt like a traitor in my own body.

"This okay?"

My head bobbed quickly before I breathed out, "Yeah."

He waited another few seconds, studying my face and the way I was holding myself, before relaxing against the swing and continuing with what he'd been saying. "What you explained about your mom, that's the *easy shift* you're expecting, I'm getting it now. But that isn't what I want, and that isn't what this is. Give me a chance to show you that."

"It's dangerous to give chances," I said under my breath, memories and horrors ripping through my mind and sending a chill down my spine.

His head dipped, accepting the next piece I'd carelessly given him. When he responded, his tone was solemn. "I'm okay with fighting for it."

"I might just fight back."

A smile crept across his face at the warning, all amusement and unwavering interest. "I'm well aware of that, Emma Wade."

My lungs expanded so quickly they ached when he trailed the tips of his fingers across my palm before taking my hand in his. I wet my lips and struggled to clear my head when a simple touch had my thoughts and judgment clouded.

But there was just that moment. That touch.

There was just Reed and his presence that I was beginning to crave, steady and uncertain and good and terrifying. There were just his words and smirks that sent my heart into a frenzy.

A small smile of my own tugged at my mouth when Reed pushed against the porch, setting the swing into motion in a gentle sway.

Twisting to better face him, I studied his handsome face in the gray light of pre-dawn and said, "Tell me something you think I should know about you."

EIGHTEEN

EMMA

"Oh good, I was just about to call you."

I stilled with my hand on the door early that evening, so used to Lala's typical greeting being called out from the kitchen that I wasn't sure how to respond.

"Do you need to change?" she tossed out over her shoulder as she hurried to the kitchen from the entryway, fixing her hair as she did.

"For what?" I asked, finally managing to shut the door. "Is everything okay?"

"Didn't you hear?" She faced me when I followed her into the kitchen, hand on her chest and eyes closing as if trying to hold back some unfathomable emotion.

"Hear what? Are you okay?" I looked around as I listened for sounds of Nora. "Where's Nora?"

"At the neighbors'." Lala forced out a harsh breath, head shaking as she went back to packing up two large bags with food. "If you have to change, do it quickly. We have to go."

"I don't need to change," I said, not that I knew what I

needed to be dressed for because I didn't know what all that food meant.

"Then grab a bag, and let's go," Lala said, voice slightly frantic as she grabbed one, holding its weight carefully against her body.

I didn't say anything as I grabbed the second bag and followed her back outside to her old truck, noticing that the two ladies across the street were uncharacteristically quiet and somber as they watched from their chairs.

Taking the keys from me once I had the truck unlocked, Lala went around to the driver's side and got in without a word.

It wasn't until we had the food carefully placed in the truck and were driving away that I asked, "Lala, is everything okay?"

She tsked, her head shaking sadly. "The Allens," she finally said after another minute of silence. "They live just next door to Reed and Peter. Their—" She made a pained sort of sound and covered her mouth, tears streaming down her cheeks. "I just can't imagine."

I sat back in my seat and didn't try to ask anything else during the rest of the short drive. I let Lala be alone in her pain and thoughts, ones I knew I wouldn't have been able to share even if I'd known what was going on because I didn't know those people.

When she pulled up in front of the house beside Reed's, I looked at her, waiting for what she needed.

After wiping at her face, she blew out a steadying breath and carefully grabbed up one of the bags, carefully checking it over as she spoke. "I'm going to take this in and get it all ready for them so they won't have to worry about food," she said as if speaking the words to herself. "Take the other bag into Peter and Reed's. Get everything started, would you?"

I froze. "Wait, what?" I looked at the bag, head moving faintly. "I don't know—I don't cook, Lala."

"It's cooked. Just warm it up at three-fifty for a few minutes. It's Peter's favorite." Before I could object or maybe ask again what was happening, she reached out and touched my arm. "Emma, please. I'll be there after checking on the Allens and getting them settled with some food."

"Okay," I said softly and twisted around to pick up the remaining bag. Once she was getting out, I opened up my own door and followed the path to Reed's door.

Trying desperately not to think about the last time I'd been there and wondering what horrible thing had led to me being there then. Because I knew I wasn't supposed to be the person bringing food and comforting people.

That was Lala.

Not someone who was a virtual stranger.

The door swung open less than a minute after I knocked, revealing Peter. Hair wet and sticking out in every direction . . . shirtless.

I shifted my stare just past him as he said, "Reed isn't here."

Disappointment dipped in my stomach even though I'd already known he wouldn't be. "Yeah, I think I'm actually here for you." I cleared my throat and forced myself to meet his stare. "Lala sent me." I held out the bag awkwardly and hurried to explain, "With food."

He stepped back, letting me in, and shut the door behind me.

Putting me in a house alone with a man I didn't know.

"I'll be back," he said, giving me a tight-lipped smile as he started away from me. Turning to walk backward, he pointed off to the side. "Kitchen's back there."

Right.

Because I was supposed to be making something for him.

If Lala hadn't been so devastated, I would hate her for the position she'd put me in.

By the time I finally started walking toward the kitchen, I was shaking and on alert, watching for when Peter would return. Listening to every sound as I set the bag down on one of the counters and slowly began taking containers and dishes out. Looking at the displayed utensils and knife block as I looked around for the oven and turned it on.

"This isn't necessary," he said when he came back, making me jump. His steps too quiet to be natural for how tall and broad he was.

I whirled around to find him running his hands through his hair and looking over everything on the counter . . . wearing a shirt.

"Lala didn't need to go through the trouble, and she didn't need to send you here. I'm sorry she did." He gave me an apologetic look, then leaned up against the counter, folding his arms over his chest.

"It's fine."

Amusement left him on a huff at the clipped words, a smile slowly pulling at one side of his mouth. "Sounds like it."

"It is." I tried to sound assuring, but I was standing feet from a man I'd seen for maybe a minute before then. I'd never been alone with a man who wasn't Reed.

Not by choice, anyway.

It had every guard rising. It had every fear creeping to the surface until I was choking on them.

"You remind me of someone," Peter said, pushing from the counter and grabbing at a few of the containers to help me since I clearly didn't know what I was doing. "She's like my little sister, and she's the only part of Texas I miss."

"You're from Texas?"

He grunted in response, then groaned when he lifted the lid on the casserole. "Ah, Lala . . ."

"She said it was your favorite."

"It is," he said as he picked the dish up and took it over to set it in the oven. "She made it the first night I came here. Decided I was adopting your grandma and staying here forever right then."

A little smile shaped my lips as I closed the lid on the rice to keep it warm.

"Savannah," he said when he shut the oven, "that's her name."

I looked back at him, eyebrows drawn together.

"She's kind and sweet and caring, but if you cross her?" He made a face that was at once adoring and fearful. "Well, just don't cross her."

"The girl who's like your sister," I said in understanding.

He nodded.

"You said I remind you of her, but you don't know me."

A laugh broke free. "I can't get my guy to shut up about you."

As if just the mention of him had summoned him, the front door opened and shut, and Reed called out, "Forgot my keepers." Voice low and rough and sounding exhausted in a way that went so far past anything I'd been feeling from my sleepless nights and the tireless work at the store.

The heavy sound of his boots on the wood floors had my heart pounding and instincts rising to the surface.

When he cleared the hallway, my body went still—the same as his. The sight of him in uniform had my stomach twisting with disgust, all while something deeper yearned for him. Ached.

"Hey," he said slowly, looking between Peter and me, dark brows drawing together in confusion and question.

"Lala," Peter answered as he walked out of the kitchen, as if her name explained it all.

Reed waited until he'd disappeared before starting toward me, steps cautious and expression wary. When he was a handful of feet away, he said, "I'm gonna keep coming toward you until you tell me to stop."

I nodded, the movement jerky and rough as I watched him come closer, my body completely at war. Every defensive instinct thrashing, begging to be set free. But all I said was, "You might want to stop before you knock me over."

A ghost of a smile tugged at his mouth as he stopped directly in front of me. "Can't tell you how much I hate finding you in my house alone with my roommate," he said, words all a rough confession as he held his hand out between us. "But I needed this."

"I don't know what I'm doing here," I said honestly, slipping my trembling hand into his and melting against the counter when he lifted it to pass his lips across my palm exactly the way he'd done that morning as we were saying goodbye.

"Lala sent you over with dinner."

"But I don't know why." The words came out slow and unsure as I studied his eyes for the first time.

Flat and dull and filled with the same exhaustion I'd heard in his voice. Not at all matching the way he was looking at me as if he was trying to appear unaffected.

Peter had the same look when I'd forced myself to meet his stare.

"She's next door. She said she'd be here soon," I finished, then flinched from his grasp when the muffled sounds of people talking came through his earpiece, loud enough for me to hear.

The effect was immediate.

The instinct to run. To hide whatever shouldn't be seen. To protect a woman who had never protected me.

Alarm covered Reed's face before a devastating realization set in. His head dipped slowly, his hand coming up to grip at the back of his neck. "I have to go. I was just swinging by to grab something."

"Keepers," I whispered, recalling what he'd said when he walked in. Not that I had any idea what those were.

A muffled laugh left him, bemusement kissing his lips as if he couldn't understand how he'd forgotten them in the first place. "Yeah." He started stepping away but stopped, rocking back to face me. "Can I see you in the morning?"

My head moved in a mixture of a nod and a shake as I struggled to speak around everything choking me. "If you want. You seem . . ." My shoulders bunched up. "I don't know what happened, but something clearly did, or I wouldn't be standing here. Do you need to be here for Peter?" I searched his eyes again, my voice lowering. "Or just by yourself?"

Reed's voice was all strained gravel when he said, "I'd like to see you."

My chest ached at his veiled pain. At the words he didn't say but still hung between us as if he'd shouted them.

I need *to see you.*

"Okay."

"Yeah?" he asked, brow creasing as hope flickered in those gray eyes.

"Yeah, but I'll understand if something changes."

He let out something that might've sounded like a laugh if it wasn't so weighed down. "It won't," he said as he left the kitchen, the sound of his boots echoing in my mind and mocking me as he went.

I jolted away from the memories when a frantic knocking sounded on the door, my head snapping in the direction both guys had gone.

When neither appeared, I hesitantly started out of the kitchen and in that direction, hoping Lala was finally coming to help and maybe explain whatever was going on.

But when I opened the door, the woman on the other side wasn't Lala, and she looked just as surprised to see me as I was to see her. Cradling her swollen stomach and choking back sobs as she blinked up at me.

"Oh . . . um . . ." She forced a swallow, looking around her. "I'm sorry, I didn't mean to . . ."

I stepped away and called out for Reed.

The woman looked at me again, eyebrows twisting up with worry. "Is Peter not—*Peter*." A hiccupped sob escaped her as her stare caught on something past me.

I turned in time to see Peter falter in his steps, his expression falling before he was rushing for the door.

"What's wrong?" he demanded, stare darting all over the woman. Taking in everything about her before settling on her face, his hands hovering just over her body without actually coming in contact as if it was taking every effort not to touch her.

"What's wrong?" she asked in disbelief. "Are you okay? I just heard, and I can't—" Her head shook wildly as she pressed one hand to her mouth and placed the other to her stomach. "Oh God."

"Let's go sit down, yeah?"

She waved a hand at me. "I'm sorry, I didn't mean to interrupt."

"I'm no one," I said quickly from where I was stuck against the wall unless I wanted to touch Peter.

I didn't.

"This is Lala's granddaughter," Peter said without ever taking his eyes off the woman in the doorway, looking at her as if she placed the stars in the sky every night. As if that fact pained him.

Her eyes went wide as she turned to look at me, her mouth forming an O shape before her head snapped back at Reed's deep, soothing voice.

"Leah."

Her mouth trembled before another sob burst from deep within her. "Hey. Are you—"

"We're fine," Reed answered before she could continue. "You shouldn't be all worked up like this though, you need to be resting. How did you even get over here with this big guy in the way?" The question was all friendly affection as he passed his hand over her stomach and clearly worked as intended because she choked out a laugh and pushed him away.

"You jerk," she mumbled halfheartedly, eyes rolling and missing the way Peter was staring at her stomach.

At the exact spot Reed had touched.

Longing and jealousy burning deep before he forced his gaze away and swallowed forcefully.

"Hey."

I looked away, finding steel-gray eyes on me and the

sweetest invitation between us. Placing my hand into his without hesitation, a warm shudder moved down my spine when he lifted our hands and pressed his mouth to my palm.

"I'll wake you," he promised, voice soft and rough.

My head dipped on a delay when he started walking away, and I somehow managed to force out, "See you," before his fingers slipped from mine.

"Oh, this is very fun," Leah whispered, pulling my attention to where she had moved into the entryway to stand directly next to Peter, staring at me as if I were fascinating to her.

"Excuse me," I murmured and followed after Reed, calling his name and catching up to him halfway down the walkway.

He held up a hand and rocked back a step when I neared him, saying something into his mic too low for me to hear and then taking another step away as he seemed to listen to the response.

I didn't move.

I just waited, trying to block out everything that was happening as he muttered something else before closing the distance between us while reaching back to mess with something on his belt.

"You won't hear anything now."

My stare darted to his, awe moving through me and warming my chest at the gesture. At his obvious acceptance that I would tell him when I was ready even though the longing to understand swirled deep in his eyes.

I nodded in gratitude and blinked quickly, trying to remember why I'd followed him and why it was dangerous to let him take more and more of my heart. "Um . . ." I glanced back to the open doorway—to where Leah was crying all over again, and Peter was trying to comfort her without ever touching her—and gestured that way. "I feel like I shouldn't be here."

"Why?"

"Because everything about this feels wrong," I said adamantly. "Lala was meant to be here. Not me. It feels like I'm stepping somewhere I shouldn't. And people are crying, but you're saying everything's fine, and Peter's laughing and saying I remind him of a girl who's like his little sister."

Reed's stare drifted behind me for only a second before he jerked his chin in that direction. "You mean Leah?"

My mouth had been opened to continue but shut at the unexpected comment. "What? No. He said . . ." I pointed behind me, my head slanting. "You think he views Leah like a sister?"

"Yeah," he said without hesitation. "She's Nick's sister, which means she's basically our sister."

I pressed my mouth into a firm line as I remembered the way Peter had watched her and had been so careful not to touch her when Reed had touched her pregnant stomach so casually as if it had been nothing.

It would've meant something to Peter.

I cleared my throat. "Okay, but that isn't the point. Lala was clearly wrecked and so is Leah, but the two of you are acting like nothing happened. And whether or not something happened, I shouldn't be the one doing whatever it is Lala wanted me to because I don't know Peter."

"We're not acting like nothing happened. We're dealing," Reed said, voice grave. "We all have our own ways, and what you're seeing—laughing, joking, normalcy—is how Peter deals so he doesn't spiral. Leah coming over sobbing is going to make it a hell of a lot harder for him. If Lala does the same . . ." He shrugged.

I studied his eyes, watching how they seemed to dull in front of me, and wished I knew how to comfort him. That I had the *ability* to comfort him. "What exactly happened?" When he didn't answer, I said, "If you think I can't handle—"

"I know you can," he muttered, a deep ache weaving through his voice. "Emma, I haven't even scratched the surface with you, and I already know you can handle anything put in front of you. But you don't want to hear it from me—not right now."

I wrapped my arms around my waist as a sliver of unease wove through my confusion. "Okay."

"When we were overseas, we saw things we never imagined we'd come across. When things happen in the military or in our current line of work, they have to be categorized because, otherwise, there's no going on in that minute, and there's no surviving after it's over. So, you push it into a part of your brain, you continue doing your job, and you process it however you need to later so you don't lose yourself. And right now? I can give you the details of what happened, but that's all they'll be: Details. Because I need time before I start processing. Understand?"

I understood better than I probably should, and it made me hurt for him even more. For what he'd seen and whatever had taken place that day. "Yeah."

Appreciation swirled in those dulled eyes as he stepped back. "As much as I hate the thought of you in there with him, let him laugh. He'll process tonight, but he needs things to be normal today. If he doesn't have that? He's gonna be bad off . . . trust me."

"Of course. I'll—" My head moved in a mess of nods and shakes because I had no idea what I would do or say to ensure that happened. "Normal. He'll have normal."

“Thank you.” The words were weighed down with some emotion I couldn’t begin to fathom as he continued backward, his eyes shouting that he wanted to be closing the distance instead. “See you in the morning, Emma Wade.”

“Goodnight,” I whispered as he turned, hand already reaching back to turn on his radio again.

With a fortifying breath, I headed back into the house, opening the door as I went and letting out a relieved breath when I heard Lala’s voice coming from the kitchen area.

But the relief faded when I followed her voice and found her in front of the stove, heating up the rice and green beans as she spoke to Peter, tears falling freely down her and Leah’s cheeks.

Peter was standing there, stiff and stone-faced, with his arms folded over his chest.

He wasn’t even looking at Leah.

And I felt utterly lost right up until the moment Lala took the casserole dish from the oven, and Peter didn’t so much as move.

I walked into the kitchen, ignoring Lala’s questioning look, and went through cupboard after cupboard until I found the plates. Pulling four down, I set them onto the counter and then went about looking for silverware and cups.

“Emma, what are you doing?” Lala asked. “We are not inviting ourselves over for dinner—we are leaving Peter in peace.”

“You made enough to last them days,” I said matter-of-factly. “You’re already feeding them Thursday, and the chances of you feeding them tomorrow are high because, well . . . because you feed them constantly. So, the probability of the two of them getting through everything you made them is low, I'm starving, and I'm sure Peter won't mind having to share a meal with three women."

Lala's voice was all shocked mortification as Peter barked out a laugh. "Emma Wade, what in God's name has gotten into you?"

"Ah, Jesus," Peter sighed in amusement. "I'm adopting her too."

"Forgive her," Lala began, cutting a warning look my way. "Peter, honey, why don't you sit down, and I'll bring you a plate. Then we'll get out of your hair."

"No, y'all can stay." He placed a hand on his chest before gesturing to me, but his stare drifted to the woman at his side. "I'd love it if y'all stayed."

Leah looked from Peter to me, indecision playing out on her features as she cradled her stomach protectively.

"Unless you have to get home," he added, turning fully to Leah then, jealousy flaring before he could cover it. "You really should be resting anyway."

"No, I don't. I—you know how he is." She shrugged. "He works so hard, so he's always home late."

A muscle ticked in Peter's jaw and he grunted in response. When he spoke again, his voice was whispered gravel. "Then you should stay."

Her glassy gaze traveled all across his face as heat gathered in her cheeks. "Guess I'm staying."

I couldn't stop watching them from where I stood, slowly gathering everything into piles and moving the biscuits closer to the plates. It was like a bad car wreck you knew you didn't want to see but couldn't look away from.

"I'm not sure what's gotten into you this evening, but this is neither the time nor the place," Lala said in my ear. "You don't know what that boy's been through today."

"I'm very much aware of that," I said just as softly, turning to look at her so my voice wouldn't carry. "I might be the only person who doesn't know. But he needs this—he needs *us*."

"You do not know what—"

"Reed asked me to give him that, so that's what I'm doing."

Her eyes widened before blinking quickly. After long seconds, she released a weighed-down sigh and nodded. "He would know best."

I had no doubt of that, and I didn't want to let him or the people who meant the most to him down.

I turned and handed a plate to Leah before holding one out to Peter, determined to help him. "So, Texas, huh?" I said, forcing nonchalance as I went back to our earlier conversation. "I lived there for a little while."

"You did?" Peter and Lala asked at the same time.

Both Peter and Leah seemed taken aback by Lala's surprise, but I just hummed in response.

With another surprised look from Lala to me, Peter asked, "Where about?"

A soft laugh tumbled past my lips. "Quite a few places. Houston, San Antonio, Austin, and the Dallas-Fort Worth area. Always one of the smaller towns just outside the cities, and all in about three years." I gave him a knowing look. "We didn't stay anywhere long."

"I was a little over an hour from Dallas," he said after a moment, forcing away that look I'd seen so often from Reed, like he was trying to figure out my life from the little bit I'd given. "Small town—*microscopic*." He rolled his eyes. "Place has one traffic light. I hated it."

"And you ended up in a town so different," I said, sarcasm dripping from my lips and forcing another laugh from him.

"I told you . . . Lala fed me, and I was sold." He shrugged, holding out the hand with the plate while leading Leah toward the food with the other without actually touching her. "Colby can't get rid of me now."

Lala hummed in acknowledgment and pointed at the remaining plates, directing me to grab one. "Don't you underestimate the power of my food."

"I never have, I just said you feed people a lot," I reasoned as I stepped back, letting Leah and Peter grab their food first.

"You're the only person complaining about it," she added, pointing a serving spoon at me.

"I haven't been complaining, I've just—" I pressed my lips together when she lifted a blonde brow at me.

"I learned real quick that it's best to say 'yes, ma'am' and fill your plate with as much food as possible," Peter said from where he was doing exactly that.

The lightness of his tone and the adoring smile he tossed Lala's way before going back to his plate had relief barreling through me and a hint of a smile tugging at my own lips.

Catching Lala's eye, I offered her a thankful look for playing along despite her own worries and pain, then headed over to the stove. "Yes, ma'am."

NINETEEN

REED

My eyes stayed narrowed on the old truck parked in front of the house as I pulled into the driveway and got out of my own truck, steps hesitant and mind reeling as I headed around to the front of the house.

I hadn't heard from Rowe, not that I'd expected to. He knew I didn't talk when coming off of any bad situation, which made it hard when we were both dealing with something like we were then, since he needed to talk about everything *else*.

But I also hadn't heard from Emma—again, not that I'd expected to. Except Lala's truck was still there, and it was a little after four in the morning.

Glancing over my shoulder at the truck one last time, I turned to start up the porch and stopped when I saw her slowly rising from where she'd been on the top step. Blonde hair piled messily on her head, in a loose shirt and tiny shorts, much like she'd been the morning before, looking all kinds of hesitant.

I moved up onto the first step, bemusement slipping into

my voice even as a smile tugged at my mouth. "This isn't waking you up."

"I couldn't sleep," she explained. "I kept thinking about what you told me earlier—about how you all deal and then process." She twisted her fingers together in an uncharacteristically nervous gesture before pointing to me. "You never told me what *you* need . . . how you deal."

My head dipped in a slow nod before I climbed the rest of the steps and slowly reached out to her. "Unless you tell me 'no,' I'm about to kiss you."

Her eyes widened with a mixture of surprise and fear, but the word that left her was, "Okay."

Slipping my hand around her waist, I pulled her just close enough to lean in and press my mouth to hers, being careful not to touch her with my duty belt or any part of my uniform that would have her shutting down.

The kiss was soft and slow. Nothing more than a brush of my lips against hers and the faintest tease of her tongue against mine, but it was everything I needed.

"That," I said against her lips before placing another soft kiss there. "I needed that."

A whisper of a tremble moved through her, but instead of pulling back, she stayed in my arms, her mouth brushing mine when she spoke.

"What if I wasn't here?" From her tone, I knew she wasn't asking about right then. She meant at all—in Colby . . . in my life. Her eyes lifted to meet mine when she asked, "What would you need then?"

"To be alone."

She exhaled softly, nodding as she did. "Then I should go."

"I've been alone for the past twelve hours," I reminded

her as I stepped back, taking in the flush of her cheeks under the porch lights. "I was alone for a couple before that. And right now, I just want to be with you." Placing my hand out between us, I waited until she took it and pressed my mouth to the smooth skin of her palm.

"Sunrise?" she asked when I began leading her to the door, brows pulling together in question and curiosity, all as that fear lingered in her eyes.

I studied that look and the feel of her fingers wrapped up in mine. The way she clung to my hand with both of hers as she waited for me to respond, as if those touches were becoming easier for her. As if she wanted them as badly as I did when I knew how easily it could change with her.

How quickly she could shut down and push me away.

But right then, she was clinging. And I'd keep gently testing the boundaries with her as long as she did.

Sliding my key into the lock and opening the door, I pulled her with me as I spoke. "I need to change. Figured you wouldn't want to keep waiting outside by yourself while I do that."

"Oh. Yeah, I . . . I guess." The last two words were a strained whisper, her hands ripping from mine when I shut the door behind us and submerged us into darkness.

I quickly reached behind me, blindly searching for the light switch until the entryway light turned on above us. Revealing a blank stare and ice-cold exterior as she stood statue-still, arms folded beneath her chest and looking every bit the girl I'd first met.

Shit.

"Did you want to stay outside?"

Her eyes shifted my way before her head moved in the faintest shake. "I'm just staying here."

My lips parted to ask what it'd been that set her off—that set her *back*—but I just released a quick exhale and nodded as I started walking away. But after only a few steps, I turned back to her.

"I would never make you go somewhere you don't want to. I would never make you *do* something you don't want to. You understand that . . . right?"

Her silence was like a blunted dagger to my chest.

Swallowing past the shards of glass in my throat, I nodded and stepped away. "I'll be back."

I headed deeper into the house as my thoughts raced. Struggling to put together what little I knew of Emma with her very telling reaction just then. My mind rebelling against the probability even though my gut was screaming the signs were all there.

But I'd kill anyone who hurt her.

Once I was out of uniform and in a pair of athletic shorts, I grabbed a shirt, pulling it on as I left my room—and stopped when I caught sight of her.

Heart pounding out this fierce beat as I took her in. Head lowered and shoulders trembling with her heaving breaths. Every part of me wanted to pull her into my arms and be there for her. But I was terrified just stepping toward her would be the wrong thing.

Then again, I didn't know how to stay away from Emma Wade.

Just as I passed the kitchen area, she forced out a sharp breath and lifted her head. Spine straight and face fixed into an impassive mask until she realized I was there.

"Hey," I said softly, carefully searching her expression as panic tore across it. As if she was afraid of what I'd seen—as if she'd revealed too much.

"Why are you guys so quiet?"

Confusion slammed into me so quickly that I faltered for a moment when I met her in the entryway. "Not sure I know what you're talking about."

By the time she jerked her chin toward me, she was all fierce glares and cold words that were a clear warning I needed to tread carefully. "Peter doesn't make a sound. He kept appearing behind me. When you're in uniform, I know you're there because of your boots." Her hazel eyes darted to my bare feet before snapping back to mine. Her slender throat shifted with a forced swallow as she struggled with some memory I could only begin to guess at. "I hadn't realized how silent you are until just now."

"And that bothers you."

"I don't like that you can sneak up on me."

"I wouldn't do it intentionally," I said, honesty bleeding into the words.

"Except you just did," she ground out, gesturing down the long hall.

"Emma, I—" A rough breath fled from me as I glanced that way and then looked back to her. "Not *intentionally*. I'm always showing and telling you what I'm about to do . . . I wouldn't sneak up on you. But I can't exactly help how I walk."

"It's weird that you and Peter are both unnaturally silent."

"It's really not."

An irritated huff tumbled past her full lips. "I should go."

Fuck.

"Emma, don't—"

"No, because I came here to be here *for* you—not to do this. And I don't *want* to do this to you." Her stare found mine, pleading with me even through all that icy-cold exterior. "But I can't help it, and I'm sorry. So, I should go."

I placed my hand on the door just as hers wrapped around the handle, my voice soft and calm when her eyelids closed tight. "If we left each other every time you started throwing shields at me, we'd never see each other."

"Well, right now, I can feel it. I'm going to keep *throwing them,* as you call it. And after whatever you went through yesterday, you don't need that." Her eyes opened, a mess of emotions clashing within them as she pleaded, "Let me go."

"You want to go? Then go." I took my hand from the door, my voice lowering when I said, "But I told you I needed *you.* That I wanted to be with *you.* That means *this,* Emma. That means standing still even when you push." Keeping my stare on hers, I held out a hand between us. Sure she wouldn't take it yet, but wanting her to know the offer was always there, no matter how shaky the ground between us was. "Wanting you means wanting every part of you. It means being *right here* while you work through those fears and anger."

Her eyes went round with surprise and awe, transforming her face completely. Making her look so innocent and vulnerable in those seconds before her eyelids shut again, her body sagging back against the wall as a trembling breath left her. "I came here for you," she whispered. "To be here . . . to help you. I don't know . . ."

"You are."

"You're lying."

The corner of my mouth lifted. "Emma . . ." If only she knew how wrong she was.

Her being here was everything.

She'd come to me. She'd given me a little more of her, and

I craved those pieces I got each time I saw her. But for her to try to stop herself from pushing me away *for* me? That was huge.

Relief swept through me when her fingers trailed over my palm to curl around my hand. Bringing her hand up to my mouth, I kissed her palm and then interlaced our fingers as I let our hands fall.

"Why do you do that?" Her eyes met mine at her gentle question, her pinky trailing along my palm between our joined hands at my confusion.

An uneasy laugh crept up my throat. "Try to hold your hand?"

Her head listed, but her expression held hints of adoration and genuine curiosity within the remnants of her protective shield. "Kiss me . . . there."

Understanding wove through me as I reached down to grab her wrist. Bringing her hand up again, I placed her palm flat on my chest. After a few seconds, I pressed my hand harder against hers, putting the slightest bit of pressure there.

"I don't understand," she whispered.

"Touching you . . ." My head dipped as I remembered the way she'd shoved her palm against my chest the times I'd reached out for her during those first days. "I learned really quick that even grabbing your hand was such a mistake with you. So, when you give me your hand now? It feels like a gift every time because I know you could just as easily be using it to push me away."

"Oh," she breathed, those wide eyes staring at me with so much wonder and hesitation, as if she was afraid to believe me.

"Close your eyes."

That time, she only wavered for a second before closing her eyes, head slightly slanted as if she was listening to every movement.

Keeping her hand in mine, I lowered our arms and wrapped them around her back. My movements slow so she would know exactly what I was doing and could stop me at any time. Pressing our joined hands to the small of her back, I pulled her against my chest. Relishing in her soft inhale and the blush that crept up her cheeks.

"Neck," I whispered just before my fingers traced the soft slope of her neck, then trailed back until I was cradling her head in my hand. Eyes darting over her relaxed features and heart slamming against my chest at having her that close to me. "You're so beautiful."

A trembling breath danced along her full lips as she looked up at me—all surprise and incomprehension.

"Close."

Her head shook at the gentle demand, but a faint smile played on her lips when her eyelids slipped shut again.

Waiting until I thought I'd lose my mind if I didn't do something soon, I asked, "Are you afraid?"

"No." The answer was soft and immediate and seemed to surprise her.

"What do you feel?"

Her lips parted, but for a long time, nothing left them. "A lot of things," she finally admitted.

"Any of them bad?"

"No." Her eyes opened, her brows drawing together. "That doesn't mean they don't scare me."

I brushed my thumb along her jaw. "Yeah, I get that." Searching her eyes, I asked, "Now, looking at me, are you afraid?"

"No."

"Try to remember that," I gently begged. "I don't know what memories you're battling. Maybe one day, you'll tell me. But when they come up, try to remember this feeling. Know that I would never do anything to hurt you. I would never make you do anything you didn't want to," I said, going back to what happened when we'd first walked into the house. "I'll wear a fucking bell so I can't sneak up on you if it makes you feel better."

A shocked huff burst from her, her eyes rolling.

Pulling her even closer, I dropped my forehead to hers. "I'm not what your memories are forcing you to see," I said gravely. "I'm not whatever asshole you've dealt with in the past. And I'll remind you of that every time, but I can't do that if you walk away."

The hand wrapped in mine squeezed tighter. "You do have a problem with letting me walk away."

My mouth pulled up in a smirk at the veiled tease. "Emma, I'm gonna kiss you now."

Her head tilted up in response, her lips barely brushing against mine before I claimed her mouth, savoring the sound that rolled up her throat—all restrained need. Reveling in the way she seemed to fall into the kiss and me. The way she opened up a little more—handed me a little more of her trust—each time.

Reeling because I was falling for this guarded, maddening girl faster than should've been possible.

I wanted her secrets and whiplash temper. I craved her smiles that came so infrequently. I ached to have her on a primal level. And I would do anything to keep earning the small glimpses of who she really was—to get *her* all the time.

That freefall before deploying your chute . . . that's what Emma felt like.

Fast. Incredible. Like a shot of adrenaline to my heart.

She reached up with her free hand, gripping my shirt and pulling me closer when I deepened the kiss. Her moan getting caught somewhere between it all when I walked her back until she was pressed to the wall.

And just as quickly as she'd melted into me, she went still.

Shit.

Her hand flattened against my chest and pushed before I could step back. Sucking in broken breaths as her wide eyes dropped to the floor. Trembling hands straight out as if to keep me back when I was already against the other wall.

"I'm sorry."

A stunned breath burst from me at her apology. "What?"

"I'm sorry." Her voice was barely a whisper, her head shaking subtly. "I didn't—"

"Emma, you have nothing to apologize for. I know better." I *did,* but it was so easy to get wrapped up in her and forget that I needed to go slow with her.

"You know better," she echoed to herself, the words nothing more than self-deprecation. "Oh God, if that doesn't—why can't you see—"

"Don't."

Her stare snapped to mine and narrowed. "For so many reasons on my end, this can't work out. For so many on yours, you shouldn't want it to." Her hands lifted, encompassing us and the entryway. "Just these last few minutes are evidence enough of that, Reed."

"I don't agree."

"You need *solace,*" she said gravely. "I can't give you that."

"Believe me when I say I'd rather be here, figuring shit out with you, than doing anything else right now."

"Figuring . . . we're *not* figuring anything out," she said with a laugh that bordered on frustration. "If we were, you would realize what I'm saying is true."

"I think we're figuring things out just fine, and that scares you."

I watched as she tried to pull that shield around herself. But the hesitation billowing from her continued spilling through the cracks in her armor.

"You're . . ."—my head slanted as I tried to think of a way to describe her—"unlike anyone I've ever met. For so many reasons," I added, twisting her words back around on her. "The way you push me away now is not the same way you pushed me away those first days. There was so much hatred mixed in with your fear then. And this?" I lifted my shoulders. "This is just fear, Emma, and it isn't the same fear you first showed me. You're also *talking* to me about it instead of lashing out at me."

Her eyelids slowly shut on an exhale. "You say all that like it's simple, and it isn't."

"There isn't a whole lot about us that is simple, but that doesn't mean it isn't worth it."

"It won't be worth it," she said, voice trembling.

The corner of my mouth tipped up. "I love your lies."

Her shoulders sagged when she finally looked at me again, eyes begging me to agree with her.

"If you really believe that, why are you here?" I asked, knowing full well she couldn't stay away from me the same as I couldn't stay away from her. When her only response was a hopeless look, I gestured between us. "We've had this conversation before, and I know we'll have it again because whatever happened in your life is trying to make you stop *this* from happening. So, I'll gladly have this conversation with you as many times as it takes, knowing that each time will be a little easier until we don't have to have it at all."

"What if I can't give you what you want?"

My brows lifted at the unexpected question. "I want *you*, Emma."

Her head dipped in a nearly imperceptible nod as she repeated, "What if I can't give you what you want?"

The way her voice dipped and broke had my gaze dragging over her body, all long legs and subtle curves that were made for my hands. "Wanting to be with you and wanting your body are two separate things. But you should probably tell me if you're saving yourself for marriage, so I have a better idea of your boundaries."

Blood rushed to her cheeks as her stare darted to my face before falling away. "No, I—no. I'm not."

I studied her a while longer, the woman whose body and features were an intoxicating mixture of sex and innocence. Whose fierce expressions and sharp tongue could have any guy begging for mercy.

But that wasn't the real her.

"Are you a virgin?" I asked softly.

Her eyes met mine and narrowed in a look so cold, it had my heart faltering painfully. "No."

No more blush staining her cheeks.

None of the unease that accompanied the real Emma.

That one word was all ice and shields, and it shredded me because I *knew*. My gut screaming at me that I knew exactly what happened to her because I'd been *trained* to look for the signs.

"Emma . . ."

"I'm going to watch the sun rise," she said abruptly, yanking the door open before she'd finished speaking.

"Emma, wait." I took a step toward her, hand already reaching before I remembered to draw it back just as I was about to graze the skin of her arm.

And then the door was slamming shut in my face.

Fuck, fuck, fuck.

"Fuck," I ground out, hands curled into fists and a rage I'd never known racing through my veins at just the *thought* of someone touching her. Hurting her. Abusing her.

Raking my hands through my hair, I took a step away from the door and let my head fall back. My eyes closing as I dragged in deep breaths.

Trying to soothe that anger and calm my racing heart before I went after her, knowing it wouldn't help anything if I went outside and demanded she tell me what happened to her.

"What?" I ground out when I heard the floor shift behind me.

"I like her," Rowe said, voice subdued.

I let my arms fall like weights as my head dropped forward, bobbing a little in agreement as it did.

"See what you've been saying about her," he continued somberly.

Glancing over my shoulder, I narrowed my eyes at where he was leaning up against the wall. Arms folded over his chest and watching me carefully. "What do you mean?"

Rowe hesitated for so long that I eventually turned to fully look at him. "I like her," he repeated when I closed the distance between us. "She's actually pretty funny, and I appreciate the hell out of her for what she did for me tonight. But in the few hours she was here, it felt like there were two

Emmas. And one of those Emmas . . . I think you should be careful with her."

An irritated breath fled from me. "I fucking am." I gestured back to the door. "I'm always trying to be careful with her."

His head shook as I spoke. "No, man. Careful . . . because I think she'll hurt you worse than Sadie did."

I studied him for a while at the mention of my ex before taking a step back and shrugging. "You don't know her."

"Do you?" he challenged.

"Not nearly enough, but I'm getting there." My shoulders lifted. "Emma isn't the kind of person to spill out her life story. You have to earn it—and I am. A little bit at a time."

"Well, let me give you a little more," he said, tossing out a hand to gesture behind me. "I don't think she's ever been in a relationship. And I'm pretty fucking sure she isn't looking for one with you."

TWENTY

REED

A huff of amusement left me at Rowe's first bit of news. I'd gone still at the last. "What?"

"Leah asked how long y'all have been together."

"Shit," I muttered, already having an idea of how everything had gone after.

Rowe lifted his brows in agreement. "When Emma told her y'all weren't, Leah let her know exactly how wanted you are in town and that someone else was gonna try to steal you if Emma didn't get you off the market. Emma said, 'That's fine.'"

I nodded before my head began shaking. "Was she quiet?"

"What?"

"Emma . . . was she quiet? Did she seem uncomfortable?"

"Not then."

"Right, then I'm not surprised by her answer." I shrugged again. "It sounds like something she'd say. That's her getting on the defensive and blocking everyone else from knowing whatever she's thinking and feeling." I continued backward toward the door. "I appreciate you looking out, man, but I'm fine."

"She looked uncomfortable a lot of other times," he said before I could reach the door. "Like when Leah asked what brought her here, and Emma didn't really answer. So, Leah tried to figure it out and asked if it was a bad breakup. Emma seemed caught off-guard by the word *breakup* and fumbled over another answer. Then Leah about lost it when she found out Emma came from New York and asked a dozen questions, circling back around to what men there were like and how dating life must've been so different there."

I thought about the way Emma kissed me, all hesitation before igniting. The way she was slow to open up and quick to push me away.

None of those screamed she hadn't had a relationship before, but they were all bright signs of what she'd more than likely gone through.

"What'd she say?" I finally asked.

"Nothing," Rowe answered. "But she looked uncomfortable as hell and confused—like she wasn't sure how to answer something she didn't know anything about. So, she didn't. And all of that mixed with the last part of y'alls conversation I woke up to . . ." He unfolded his arms, holding them out to the sides before letting them fall. "I like her, Ryan. I really do. Just be careful."

I nodded as I reached back for the handle, pausing as I grasped it. "You good?"

He shrugged, his entire demeanor changing in an instant. "Yeah."

"You did everything right. There was no changing what happened."

"I know," he murmured, looking like he was going over it in his head, still trying to figure out how he *could've*.

"Kids hit hard," I said knowingly before forcing my voice into a tease as I pulled the door open. "You can always come watch the sun rise with us."

He huffed out a laugh, that heaviness disappearing from him as he pushed from the wall and turned for his room. "Such an idiot, Ryan."

Stepping out into the humid summer air, I shut the door behind me and was met with a pair of unreadable eyes, looking up at me from where she was sitting on the top step, legs stretched out in front of her and back pressed up against the railing.

"I left," she whispered, shame and apology dripping from the two words.

I held out my hand for her as I neared her, shrugging as I did. "You're right here."

A disheartened breath tumbled past her lips as she slipped her hand into mine and let me help her up.

"Sunrise?"

A pleading hum sounded in her throat when I passed my lips across her palm and then wrapped our joined hands around her back. "How's Peter?"

"He's good. Those situations are just a lot different than everything else."

Hesitation billowed from her as I began leading her down the porch steps and across the pathway. "Do you think you could tell me what happened?" Her hand tightened against mine as she hurried on. "If you still don't want to, that's fine. I understand."

"No, I can," I said as I climbed into the bed of Lala's truck and then reached back to help her up. "Our neighbors . . . their toddler died today. Walked right out of the house and into the street and got hit by a car."

She faltered in climbing over the tailgate, her eyes shifting to me before drifting to the neighboring house.

"We were getting ready to go work out when it happened. Peter was headed outside, I was still in my room, grabbing my stuff. By the time I got out here, Peter was already working on the kid. The Mom was . . ." I slanted my head, trying to get her screams and the way her child had looked out of my head as I pulled us both to sitting. "She was hysterical and trying to get to her son. So, I grabbed her and held her back while calling for an ambulance. But he was . . . he was gone."

"Oh my God," she whispered, voice hollow.

"Yeah," I murmured. "We've seen people mutilated and burned. I've held my friend's head together while we waited for a MEDEVAC. But, kids . . . kids hit differently, and they hit harder."

"Did he live?"

My brow furrowed at the question I was sure I'd already answered.

"Your friend," she clarified as she scooted closer to me.

"Oh." I leaned back against the cab of the truck and held out my arm for her. "No. We lost him a couple days later. But that is one of the days that haunts me the most," I admitted, breathing life to words I'd never told anyone. "Considering what we saw and did, I know I'm lucky that it doesn't happen often. But there are times those memories slip in and it feels like I'm right there again."

Understanding and empathy poured from her as she curled against my side, never saying anything about it. Not that I expected or wanted her to.

It was why I'd known she could handle anything I told her —because I already knew she'd seen so much in her life without knowing the specifics. And when you see horrors and experience devastation, you become numb to it, in a way. Even if it isn't the shit you're used to.

"Did Peter tell you to stay away from me?" she asked a while later as her body relaxed deeper into mine.

"What?"

A slow, exhausted breath teased her lips as she thought. "Over the night, he started watching me. And the way he was looking at me . . ." One of her shoulders lifted. "It was like he didn't trust me. I don't think I remind him of that girl in Texas anymore," she added, trying to joke and falling short.

"He actually told me he liked you . . . multiple times."

"Liar."

"I'm serious." I trailed my fingers along her shoulder as I admitted, "Doesn't mean he isn't worried about me."

Her silence tore at my heart.

It felt like she was taking what I'd said and handing it back to me as more proof of why we should stop before this could go any further.

"He was there when everything happened with my ex, and he went through worse. Peter's wife left him and made up a whole bunch of shit about him so he looked like an asshole—and he *still* did everything to make things work between them. So, he's just watching out because he doesn't want me to get hurt again."

"Peter was *married*?" she asked softly, a hint of shock weaving through the words.

"Yeah, they got divorced a few months before he moved here. And he's been here about two years, maybe more?"

Long seconds passed before her body shook with a muted

huff. "I just don't understand how people move on like this," she whispered, bringing up the conversation we'd had the morning before.

I ignored the implication because I didn't want to face that shield again when we'd already gotten through it. And, if Rowe was right—if Emma had never had a relationship—then she *couldn't* understand.

"Peter isn't moving on anytime soon," I said instead. "Guy was a fucking wreck when she left him. He hasn't so much as looked at another woman since."

If Emma hadn't been tucked so close to my side, I wouldn't have noticed the way she tensed at my last words.

Looking over at her, I searched her carefully masked features. "Emma?" At her responding hum, I pulled back to better see her. "What just happened?"

"What do you mean?"

I thought through my conversation with Rowe as I studied the girl beside me. "Did Peter say something to you?"

She looked at me then, a crease forming between her eyebrows. "He said a lot."

"Did he make a pass at you?" I clarified, doubt twisting the words.

Shock broke through her mask so quickly and faded into amusement. "I'm pretty sure he saw the 'Fuck Off' sign hanging above me that you've refused to notice."

A sharp laugh burst from me. "Trust me, I've seen it." I pulled her closer so she was leaning fully into me and away from the truck. "I also see when you take it down for me."

Her eyes flared, but her hand just pressed to where my heart was pounding out an unforgiving rhythm at having this moment and having her this close.

"But what happened with *you*," I said, refusing to let up.

"You went still when I said Peter hadn't looked at anyone else."

Emma's tongue darted out to wet her lips as her stare fell to where her hand rested on my chest. Lingering there as the silence between us formed and grew.

"Head," I whispered just before the tips of my fingers brushed across her temple. "You telling me what's going on up here is how we keep moving forward and figuring things out."

"I don't think it's for me to say," she finally said. "And if I'm wrong . . ."

"If it has to do with one of my best friends, I should probably know. Especially if it has you locking up on me."

"Reed . . ." She pressed her lips into a firm line, her eyes finally meeting mine again. With a fortifying breath, she said, "I've never cared about my reactions to anyone, especially men. But I hate what I keep doing to you and dragging you through. Sometimes it feels out of my control though."

I lowered my hand to cradle her neck as she skipped right past what I was asking about Rowe and started giving me more of herself instead.

"What happened inside . . ." Her head shook quickly. "I can't change that, and I don't know if it'll ever change. But I'm sorry for the way I reacted after."

"Don't," I said softly. "You have nothing to be sorry for." I searched her face, hesitation mixing with my anger and pain for whatever happened to her. "Can I ask something about it?"

Reluctance burst from her before she said, "Maybe."

"Was it being pressed up against the wall or being kissed?"

She didn't respond. Just stared at me as she seemed to fight those shields moving into place.

Before they could win out and fully block me from her thoughts, I asked, "You trust me to try something?"

"I don't want to trust you."

"Those lies, Emma," I whispered, my thumb tracing along her jaw.

She blew out a shaky breath, her eyelids slipping shut as she gave a reluctant nod.

"Need you to look at me."

"Coming from the man always telling me to close my eyes," she murmured as she gave me her attention.

A smirk tugged at my mouth. "They should be open this time because this will all be you." With one last sweep across her jaw, I told her, "I'm gonna move my hand lower."

Watching her eyes and feeling the slight weight of her body against mine, I slowly began moving my hand down her body. Over her shoulder and following the chills raising on her arms before dipping into her waist and settling on the flare of her hips. Taking note of the increasing rise and fall of her chest and the way her cheeks darkened.

"Thought you said this was me?" she asked, voice thin and raspy with desire.

"It's about to be," I assured her. "You wanna push me back, then push me back. We stop when you say to. Always." I searched her stare, making sure she understood I meant that. "But there's a change in you when I start taking control of things. So, why don't you control it?"

Her eyes widened, all confusion with a hint of fear.

"All of it."

Her chest shook against mine from where she was leaning against me and facing me. "I don't—what?"

"Still trust me?"

"I don't want to," she breathed, that time sounding more truth than lies.

"Do you?"

"Yes." The answer was immediate and so pure, it had me falling more and more for this girl.

I gave a gentle tug on her hip. "Then come here."

Uncertainty bled from her as she looked at my mouth and then shifted her body as if she was getting ready to kiss me. "That isn't really comfortable."

A rough laugh scraped up my throat. "Yeah, Emma, you need to move your legs."

I saw the moment she realized what I was trying to get her to do. The fear and hesitation and *innocence.*

And it hit me like a punch to the gut that Rowe might actually be right. But more than that, I was worried she'd never done *this*. Never experienced anything with a man that was voluntary.

I wanted to raze the earth, searching for whoever had hurt her. I wanted to apologize for whatever she'd gone through that had put this fear and hatred in her. I wanted to take it away.

Swallowing back my pain for her, I said, "You'll be in complete control. Anything we do or don't do will be determined by you. And you won't be trapped between me and another surface."

A whisper of awe and gratitude wove through everything else, but a minute came and went before she ever moved. Shakily shifting to her knees and moving one of her legs over me so she was straddling me.

Once she was steady, I released my hold on her and forced my hands to the truck bed when all I wanted was to keep holding her. Fill my hands with her curves and bring her closer to me.

But, Jesus Christ, the sight of her on her knees, staring at me with all the need coursing through my own veins reflected on her face and mixing with that curiosity and fear, was something I would never forget.

"What do I do?" she asked, voice trembling slightly.

"Whatever you want." I pressed harder against the truck to try to ignore my need for her as I said, "If you want to move back, you can. If you want to stay there, stay there. If you want—"

"I want you to do something," she breathed. Begged.

"This is you."

"Do something."

I had my hands in her hair and my mouth pressed to hers before the demand finished leaving her tongue. Pulling her closer and claiming her with my touch and lips as she settled onto my lap. A groan raking up my throat at the feel of her. Our shorts' thin material doing nothing to help my blatant need for her or the thought of how easy it would be to slip my hand between her thighs.

To feel her.

To make her moan. Tremble. Breathe my name.

A growl built in my chest and got lost in the kiss when she shifted, rocking against my hardening dick and gasping my name as if in answer to what I'd just been thinking.

And I about lost my goddamn mind because the sound of my name falling from her lips in that way was like a drug that I already wanted another hit of.

But then one of her hands drifted up my stomach to rest above my heart, and the feel of her palm on my chest was like a bucket of ice-cold water.

I pressed back against the truck, our mouths still brushing with each ragged breath as I searched her eyes—all open fear and want and confusion.

"You pushing?"

"What?" she asked, that confusion bleeding through for another moment before her eyes widened apologetically. "No. No, I just wanted to feel you." She pressed harder against the unruly pounding for emphasis.

Jesus Christ, this girl . . .

I slid one of my hands from her hair, my fingers passing over the pulse point in her neck before drifting lower and lower until I had my hand pressed firmly between her breasts. The wild thrashing of her heart slammed against my hand in time with my own as I held her defenseless stare.

This fierce woman with impenetrable walls and a sharp tongue.

This girl who was all uncomfortable gestures and whispered truths when those walls fell away.

This paradox who could drop me to my knees with her curious nature and vulnerability as she silently bared her gentle soul to me.

"Every part of you is so beautiful," I whispered as I was blasted with the realization that I was no longer falling for Emma Wade.

I'd fallen.

Thrown my heart in the ring somewhere along the way, knowing full well she might never add hers.

Wonder danced along her features at my words, as it had earlier. As if she truly didn't know she was beautiful. As if she couldn't comprehend that I craved her heart more than her body.

Her fingers curled against me, gently clinging as she asked, "You gonna kiss me now?" Voice all a whispered plea.

A smile ghosted across my face as I captured her mouth to do exactly that. Kissing her soft and slow. Faint brushes of my lips against hers and teasing her with my tongue.

Wholly different than before, but it had me aching for her just the same.

"Nope."

Emma jolted back at the loud voice, her heart racing against my hand in a new, desperate way as she looked around just as something landed in the bed of the truck.

"Jesus, Rowe," I snapped when Emma jerked again, trying to get away from the unexpected sound. "What the fuck?"

Emma's stare locked on the first bundle just as a second one landed in the bed of the truck without warning. Even looking in that direction, a little jolt went through her.

I shifted my arms around her back in a vain attempt to soothe her and bit out, "Fucking *stop*."

"Y'all stop," he said easily as another bundle thudded loudly in the truck. "You can't invite me to watch the sun rise and then make out the entire time."

"I—" A harsh breath left me. "Pretty sure you said you weren't coming."

"I think I said you were an idiot," he corrected as he pressed a hand onto the edge of the truck and hopped in.

Releasing a slow sigh and suppressing a groan, I let my head fall back to the window. "Peter's gonna watch the sun rise with us," I told Emma unnecessarily as she slid from my lap. Looking at Rowe, I spoke louder. "There's still a couple hours until it starts rising."

"And you're welcome," he said, not taking the hint as he chucked one of the bundled-up blankets at me. "Careful when you open that." Gently passing one to Emma, he nodded toward the large ball. "Same goes to you."

"What the hell?" I mumbled when a bunch of insulated travel mugs tumbled out of the blanket when I began unwrapping it.

"I told you to be careful," Rowe complained, kicking my foot.

"You *threw* the blankets into the truck," I reminded him as I righted them. "Why would I think all this shit was gonna fall out?"

He scoffed, the sound pure offense. "I put them in there. I knew they were safe."

"I'm afraid to open mine now," Emma muttered as she held the tightly packed bundle on her lap.

I took it from her, opening it slower than I had the one before, and caught the insulated tumbler that came rolling out.

"That's the creamer," Rowe said offhandedly as he finished unwrapping his blanket and held whatever had been in his close to his chest. "And this is mine."

I leaned forward. "Is that Lala's banana bread?"

The sound of foil opening stopped just as abruptly as it began. "No."

"Rowe . . ."

"I'm the one who made the fucking coffee." He waved a hand at where the travel mugs waited beside me. "Again . . . you're welcome."

"I can have that out of your hands before you try to open it again. You know I can."

He stared at me, all open challenge even though we both knew I was right. "If you wanted it, you shoulda brought it out here. Be thankful for what I did bring you

—look." He jerked his chin toward where Emma was grabbing up the creamer and one of the mugs. "She's not complaining."

"Because I already know you're going to share with me," Emma said softly as she popped the lid off her mug. "You're a Texas boy, which means your momma raised you better than to keep all that to yourself."

Her words were all slow and knowing. Her face faux innocence as a wicked little grin tugged at her mouth.

God damn, that girl was trouble.

"I don't like you anymore," Rowe said as he quickly opened the foil-wrapped loaf and took some before tossing it to me.

"Thank you," Emma responded, complete with one of those rare, genuine smiles as she finished pouring creamer into her coffee and putting the lid back on.

Once she was pressed against my side again, I held out the bread to her, but she just set the rest of the loaf between the three of us before coming back to my side with a slice in hand.

"He'll take the rest of it," I told her as I tossed one of the mugs to Rowe and then grabbed one for me.

"Then he takes the rest of it," she said with an easy shrug.

"I like her again."

Her shoulders shook with a muted laugh at Rowe's claim.

"So, New York and Texas," Rowe said around a mouthful of bread. "Where else did you live?"

"You lived in Texas?" I asked, mug suspended inches from my mouth.

Emma had been taking a breath to answer him but quickly released it as she looked up at me. "I lived everywhere, but, yeah . . ." Her shoulder bunched up against me.

"For a few years. It was the longest my mom and I stayed in a state."

I nodded, taking a sip of the hot coffee when she looked back at Rowe.

"Honestly, we lived almost everywhere," she said. "The only states we didn't live in were New York and the surrounding states there. It's one of the reasons I moved to New York."

"What was your favorite place?"

"New York," she answered him immediately.

He waved at her with his mug. "You chose there. What was your favorite place before that?"

A contemplative hum sounded in her chest as her head rested against my shoulder. As much as I loved how comfortable she was at that moment, I stayed still and silent, waiting to hear her answers. Wondering why it was so easy for Emma to answer him when I had to fight so hard for every answer from her.

It wasn't until their conversation continued that I realized the difference.

Rowe was staying away from hard, personal questions. He also wasn't threatening to Emma in any way.

He'd always been the easy-going guy who was quick to laugh—someone who made others feel relaxed with him. He didn't have any visible tattoos. He wasn't a cop.

And her heart wasn't on the line with him.

TWENTY-ONE

EMMA

I scrambled for my phone so quickly the next morning that I nearly knocked it off my bathroom counter when it vibrated with a new message.

Forcing myself to take a steadying breath, I glanced at the mirror one last time. Once I was satisfied that I didn't look like I'd just rolled out of bed, I hurried from the bathroom, a smile tugging at my lips as I opened the message and tapped out a response.

REED: *You want to watch the sun rise with me, Emma Wade?*

Me: *Stalker.*

GRIPPING THE RAILING, I quietly descended the stairs and held my breath. Silently praying the sounds of Lala in the kitchen didn't falter—that she wouldn't hear me.

I'd woken to her preparing for Thursday breakfast nearly half an hour before and hadn't been able to fall back asleep knowing my phone would be going off soon. So, I'd paced the length of my room a dozen times before realizing that Lala was *preparing* for Thursday breakfast.

That people would start showing up soon.

And I didn't want those private moments with Reed on display when they did. But just when I'd had the thought to meet him at his place again, I'd glanced around my room instead.

The panic and fear that had clawed at my chest had been immediate. The wraiths always waiting to remind me of every horrible nightmare in the form of a memory had rushed in until it felt like I couldn't breathe. Until I was contemplating ignoring Reed completely.

But then the previous morning flashed through my mind.

Reed's patience and understanding. The way he'd known what to give me, what to do, when I would've run without trying at all. The way he'd looked at me like I was everything and not a *thing* to destroy.

All of it slowly chased away the memories and made me want to try the way he'd tried so hard for me.

Once I reached the first floor, I sucked in another fortifying breath.

I can do this.

I *could* do it. It was just Reed and me in a room together. It was no different than when we were in the house alone or when we were mostly hidden in the dark of the early morning.

I refused to let my demons torment me simply because I was in a bedroom with Reed.

Being careful not to make a sound, I opened the front door, my heart doing all kinds of crazy things as soon as I saw him standing on the porch steps. Tattooed arms folded loosely across his chest. Devastatingly handsome smirk slowly stretching across his face when he saw me.

"Emma Wade," he said softly, then slanted his head in the direction of the swing. "Sunrise?"

"Uh . . ." I glanced behind me, toward the wall that separated the entryway from the kitchen, then looked back at him. "Can we watch it somewhere else?" At his confusion, I explained, "Lala's already making breakfast. People start showing up in about an hour."

"No shit?" he asked softly and moved down one of the steps. "You want to—" His expression slowly shifted to surprise and curiosity when I stepped back and opened the door wider in invitation.

"You can see the sunrise from my room."

Desire replaced everything else in an instant and had my stomach swirling with heat even as a sliver of fear raced down my spine. But he stood in place, unfolding one of his arms to rub at his jaw and shake his head firmly. "Emma, I can't go in your room."

I spared another quick look behind me. I didn't want Lala to know, but that was mostly because it wasn't her business, and I didn't want her to have any kind of gossip when she was about to see half of Colby. "Of course you can."

An animalistic smile flashed across his face. "Let me put it this way: You don't want me in your room. Not with where my mind just went. Not with what I want to do to you."

A stuttered exhale left me at his words, at their implication, but the memories didn't follow. The heat and the want were still there, as was the whisper of fear, but I was only overwhelmed by the need to feel his lips against mine again.

"I trust you." The horrifying truth fell from my tongue

like a dirty confession because the last thing I'd wanted was to trust him. To fall for him.

To get so deep that he had any chance of hurting me.

But I'd done that and more.

I was fairly certain I'd already begun giving him my heart, and I had no way of stopping it or getting it back.

He climbed the last couple steps and crossed the porch, movements slow and measured. As if he wasn't sure he'd heard me correctly, or maybe just giving me a chance to change my mind. But then he was stepping into the house and taking the door from me, eyes locked on mine.

"Say that again," he demanded.

"I trust you."

"I'm gonna kiss you," he said just as he pulled me against his chest and his mouth fell to mine. Tongue teasing the seam of my lips as he rested against the door and stumbled back with it when it shut the rest of the way.

A whispered curse left him on a rough laugh as he curled me closer.

"Emma, is that Reed again?" Lala called from the kitchen. "Are y'all staying inside today?"

I hurried to cover his mouth with my hand, eyes wide with warning.

Gripping my wrist, he pressed a kiss to my palm as he moved my hand away. "Yes, ma'am," he called back, smiling widely in response to my unamused glare. "Need any help?"

Her tsk could be heard from where we waited. "Now, you know I've got everything under control. Y'all make sure to grab something to eat before long."

"Yes, ma'am," he answered as he pushed from the door, walking me toward the stairs.

Just before we reached them, he released me and waited

until I was a couple steps away before following me up them. Being careful not to touch me or get too close when I'd just been in his arms.

And I was thankful for it.

"Hand," he whispered as soon as he was on the second floor with me. And then his fingers were easing through mine and he was turning me around, pulling me into his hold as his mouth found mine again.

"You gonna kiss me now?" I asked against the kiss, the corners of my mouth lifting in a teasing grin when he playfully tugged at my bottom lip before attacking the kiss with more passion than before.

Giving just as much as he demanded. Making my body tremble as that need for him built higher and higher. His fingers gripping me where he had my hand pinned to the small of my back, but the touch didn't scare me.

It felt carnal and tender. Desperate and adoring.

And I knew in the way he was holding me that he *had* me. That he would protect me instead of harm me.

"Trust me?" he asked as the bedroom door shut behind us.

I'd just begun nodding, already searching for his mouth again, when his hands dropped to my thighs and lifted me. The air ripped from my lungs, and my legs wrapped around him instinctively as he walked us through the room, never slowing as he knelt on the bed and lowered me. His lips capturing mine as he deftly turned us so I was positioned on top of him.

Never caging me in.

Never confining me.

Just stealing my breath and making my head spin and shaking my soul.

One of my hands moved up to his chest as I settled on top of him, to the unforgiving beating of his heart that was in sync with my own. A groan rolling up his throat and getting lost in the kiss as his fingers clenched tighter on my bare thighs, pressing me harder against him for a moment before his hands were moving.

Trailing up and up, the path all hesitance until I rocked against him. The feel of his hard length had heat unfurling in my belly and unease rolling down my spine as the first ice-cold finger brushed along the vault I kept the memories locked up in.

Oh God.

My breathing hitched when Reed's hands shifted beneath my shirt, lifting it as he continued higher and higher.

I slammed my eyelids shut and fought to keep the demons at bay. Struggled to know this was my choice and under my complete control. That it was *Reed.*

But they were there.

Mocking me as I was blasted with pieces from too many nights—flashing through my mind and blurring together like a horrifying collage.

"Emma."

"I can't," I choked out as if I'd been trying to get the words free, head moving in tight, quick shakes.

I wasn't sure when we'd stopped kissing or how many times Reed had said my name. Only that I was pushing against his chest and *shaking*. One of his hands was resting on top of mine while the other hovered in the air as if he wanted to touch my face and was afraid to.

Oh my God, I'm crying.

"Emma . . ." His gray eyes searched my face, pain and regret swirling there. "I'm so fucking sorry."

"I told—" A jolt went through me when a crash sounded from downstairs, everything from the past minutes making it hard for my mind to process what that meant until Reed was hissing a curse.

We scrambled off the bed and raced for the door. By the time I was starting down the stairs, Reed was already clearing the last chunk of the steps with a single jump and calling out Lala's name.

A heaving breath escaped me when her unconcerned response floated up from the kitchen, and I slowly backed up to the landing until I was pressed to the wall. Listening as Lala admonished Reed for worrying too much.

A soft laugh bubbled free when she said, "You don't see Emma running down here because a few pots fell."

By the time she finally let him go, I was sitting on the floor, going over what happened in the room. Trying to figure out what had gone wrong when everything had felt so right with him. And I couldn't help but wonder if I hadn't been met with all those haunting memories just minutes before Reed had shown, would I have still had the same reaction.

I studied his withdrawn expression as he climbed the steps, never taking his stare from me as he did. When he reached where I sat, I let him help me to standing and relaxed into his hold when he curled his free hand against my cheek and pressed his forehead to mine.

"Can we talk about it?"

"I don't want to." I wasn't sure I *could*. I was already so horrified by what he'd seen in the room.

He nodded against me after a moment. "Want me to go?"

"No," I admitted, even though he and I both knew I was always waiting for him to leave. Waiting for him to realize we couldn't work.

Leaning back, he passed his mouth across my forehead and then wrapped our joined hands around my back as he started toward my room again. Never saying anything until after we were in there and he was on the bed, propped up against the headboard.

"Tell me something about you," he said once I was seated beside him, bringing up our familiar request.

I bit back the impulse to turn the request right back around on him and thought for a long time before admitting, "I don't know how to do this—any of this. But I want it, and I hate that parts of you still terrify me and that I can't change that, just as I can't make you understand those parts."

"*Can't* make me understand?" he asked softly.

"*I* can't," I clarified, stare on the comforter as I waited for his reaction. When he just held out his hand, I let out a weighted breath and slipped my hand into his. "Tell me something you think I should know about you."

"These few hours with you aren't enough." His response was immediate and dripped with meaning.

He wanted more.

More time, more of this, just *more*.

"Tell me something about you."

"I hadn't realized that I couldn't breathe before you entered my life." The confession was softer than a whisper, but his hand tightened around mine once it finished leaving my lips.

"Emma . . ." My name was a revered breath. A prayer.

It had butterflies erupting in my belly and my heart racing like a stampede of wild horses.

My gaze shifted to him, that energy around us so charged and magnified from our revelations. "Tell me something you think I should know about you."

His brow furrowed as he searched my eyes, his free hand lifting slowly to my face and trailing along my jaw as he vowed, "I'll destroy whoever hurt you."

A shiver rolled down my spine at the low and threatening tenor of his voice, my head shaking subtly as I acknowledged, "It isn't that simple."

TWENTY-TWO

EMMA

A gasp ripped from me, my heart already racing and my body tensing as I was pulled from sleep.

The arm around me tightened, and I reacted.

Twisting and shoving my hand against the chest I was trapped against. Realizing too late where I was. Who I was next to.

Oh God.

Reed grabbed my wrist and wrenched my hand back as soon as it touched him, his eyes flying open and a fierce, terrifying look covering his face before he registered what was happening less than a second later. Chest pitching and muscles straining as he held me above him.

"Shit," he breathed, head falling back against my pillows before he gently released me and wrapped me in his arms. "Are you okay?"

"I'm sorry."

"Are you okay?" he repeated tightly.

"Yes." I listened to his thundering heart for a few

moments before saying, "Something woke me, and I—" I bit back the rest of the explanation. "I'm sorry."

"I grabbed you, and *you're* sorry."

"I hit you first."

A soft laugh rumbled in his chest, his hand making slow paths up and down my spine as we spoke, soothing me in that way he always seemed to. "I'll try to be prepared for that next time."

My stomach swirled with excitement and nervousness at the idea of *next time*. At the thought of *meaning* to fall asleep next to Reed. Because the last thing I remembered before freaking out on him was talking and waiting for the sun to finally come up.

My brow furrowed as I realized the room was lighter, and I turned my head, looking to the window. "We missed the—what time is it?"

I scrambled away from him, looking for my phone and finding Reed's where I'd been lying.

"I have to get ready," I said when I saw the time, a soft laugh breaking free when Reed grabbed the phone and tossed it aside before pulling me into his arms again.

"That time's wrong."

"Is that right?"

"By a few hours," he confirmed, a hopeful grin on his face that made him look younger and unreasonably adorable.

An amused hum sounded in my throat as the bed vibrated near my legs. "That's what woke me," I realized. "Your phone is vibrating."

"I don't care."

I lifted my hand to his chest, a deep breath leaving me at the feel of his steady heartbeat there. "Sunrise tomorrow?"

"I'll wake you," he promised as he placed one of his hands

over mine. "Tonight's my last shift for four days. Can I have more time with you while I'm off?"

The door opened before I could respond, quickly followed by Peter's voice. "Answer your fucking phone."

"Rowe, what the *fuck*?" Reed bit out as he turned, keeping his hand wrapped around mine.

He sent me a cheesy grin as he walked deeper into the room. "Morning, Emma."

"Hi, Peter."

Reed kicked Peter when he sat on the bed, but Peter just smacked Reed's leg and got comfortable. "Get up."

"Shoulda answered your phone," Peter said, unaffected.

Reed reached for his phone, only glancing at the lock screen long enough to swipe into his messages and tap into Peter's conversation.

Rowe: *Breakfast?*

Rowe: *I'm starving.*

Rowe: *Don't make me come up there. I missed sunrise with y'all.*

"LALA TOLD me where y'all were," Peter said when Reed dropped his phone between us with a sigh, grinning as if he was enjoying irritating Reed.

Reed's voice was deadpan when he asked, "And you took that as an invitation to join us?"

But I didn't hear the rest of their conversation.

I couldn't hear much of anything over the pounding in my ears. I couldn't focus on anything other than the way it felt like my stomach continued dropping as my mind raced.

Trying to understand words . . . trying to make them fit with what I knew about Reed.

Because another person had messaged him, and I'd had plenty of time to see it before Reed swiped away from it.

***Kira**: Please come home.*

"I HAVE TO GET READY," I said, getting off the bed as if in a daze as I thought of everything Reed had told me about his ex. Remembered the pain when he'd talked about her.

"Get out," Reed demanded as Peter asked me, "You're leaving? What about breakfast?"

"I have to go to work."

"You have breakfast without her every other day," Reed said as he got off the bed and started pushing Peter out of the room.

"Yeah, but I'm working, and I won't be able to eat with her tomorrow either."

"Jesus," Reed said on an incredulous huff. "*Leave.*" Once he got the door shut, he turned, confusion marring his features. "I'd apologize, but I don't know what the hell that was."

"I really have to get ready," I said when he started toward me. "I'm already late."

Reed's expression fell and his feet stilled. I wasn't sure if it was because he heard the lie or if, now that Peter wasn't in the room anymore, he could sense something was different. That I was struggling to hold myself together when my mind was coming up with a dozen reasons for the message.

Every one of them began with Reed's lies and a woman left waiting for him, broken and forgotten.

"You okay?" he asked carefully.

"I just should've been gone already, and I still have to shower."

"All right," he said after searching my face for a second longer. "I'll set an alarm tomorrow in case we fall asleep again." Gathering up his phone from my comforter, he looked at where I stood on the opposite side of my bed. Confusion and worry bleeding from him. "Can I kiss you?"

"Yeah." The answer came a beat too late, and his jaw flexed as if he were holding back his questions and concerns. I forced myself to move and tried to relax, but by the time Reed's hands curled around my cheeks, I was shaking from holding myself so tightly.

"Is it because he came in here?" he asked softly.

"What? No," I said quickly. "I just have to leave."

His forehead fell to mine, his fingers drifting down to tenderly curl around the sides of my neck. "I don't like this lie." The claim left his lips just before they pressed to my own.

The kiss was slow and pained and tasted like hesitation.

Or maybe that was my own.

Because there was a girl begging Reed to go *home*.

"Can I see you in the morning?"

My chest ached at the pain and uncertainty in his voice, but the shields forming around my heart kept me from doing anything more than nodding.

"Then, I'll wake you," he promised before pulling away and quickly leaving the room.

I sucked in a shuddering breath when the door closed behind him and stood in the pain and unknown for a little longer. Warring with myself over what I'd seen and what it could mean—that maybe I'd taken it out of context. But I already knew he didn't speak to his family, just as I knew how he sounded when he spoke about his ex.

And even if it wasn't her . . . it was someone.

That battle raged in my thoughts all through my shower and getting ready. By the time I was heading down the stairs, I was firmly in the middle of wanting to push Reed away and wanting to be brave and defenseless enough to just ask him who Kira was.

I waved to Nora and offered a forced smile for the people who were eating breakfast in the living room with her, then slipped between two uniformed men heading toward the tables with plates in hand as the front door opened to let in more first responders.

"Good morning," I murmured in return to whoever had said it, then hurried into the kitchen. "Morning, Lala."

She waved her spatula. "You want breakfast to go?"

"Oh . . . no. Thank you."

She turned and set a glare on me. "I asked if you wanted breakfast to go."

I eyed the empty containers next to her. "I believe my answer is *yes?*"

She smiled and turned back to the food. "I thought you might. Don't worry, I've got more than enough for Ms. Donna too." She held the containers out to me and said, "Fill those up full, don't go making me leave my station to do it for you."

I grabbed them and started turning for the food where it was laid out on the island. At the last second, I turned and hugged her. "Thank you, Lala."

"Go on now, get," she said, voice thick with emotion.

"I'll be back to help you with dinner tonight."

She scoffed and waved me off. "I've been doing this by myself just fine for years now, don't go worrying about getting back to me after a long day at work. Just help Ms. Donna, then come on home for some food."

I didn't answer because she and I both knew that I would end up helping her anyway—I just went over to fill up the containers. When two women started that way, talking and laughing, I stepped back, giving them time and space to get their food first.

"I can't believe it's finally happening for the two of y'all," one of the girls said, voice soft and wistful. "Every woman in town is probably grieving, even the married ones."

The one in uniform laughed but quickly quieted herself, looking around as if she was afraid of whoever might be listening. "We're not official or anything yet. Just having fun."

"Is that what they're calling it now?" The first snorted. "I call it him not taking calls or doing any kind of work during his shifts because you're keeping him all kinds of *occupied,*" the first said suggestively, complete with crude hand gestures, as the other tried to stop her.

"People will hear you."

"People already know, Hannah," the first went on, bumping the officer's shoulder. "You can't be sleeping with a guy like Reed Ryan and not have the town talking."

I went rigid.

My body felt cold.

My heart gave one painful thump before it and my lungs stalled.

I couldn't *breathe.*

"Lala."

I jolted at the booming voice and sucked in a ragged breath when it kickstarted my lungs.

I managed to force my stare from where it had been on the floor in time to see a bear of a man in uniform headed toward my grandma, arms opened wide, only to turn at the last second. Pointing toward the women who had just cracked the small part of my heart I'd unwillingly given Reed.

"Hannah, hold up, I need to talk to you."

I glanced between him and the women as he enveloped Lala in a big hug. After talking to her for a short second, he turned back to the women and pulled Hannah aside.

From where I stood, still rooted in place, I only heard the first few words from the man before they were out of hearing distance.

"Hey, I saw you at Reed's the other day when I . . ."

Oh God.

Oh God, oh God.

As soon as the first girl followed them with both their plates, I dropped the containers on the island and finally pushed away from the spot I'd been speared to, going straight to my grandma.

"Lala," I said, voice soft and sounding suspiciously like I might pass out or throw up.

She looked at me in alarm. "What is it?"

"The girl—" I licked my suddenly dry lips and shook my head, trying to get the text and conversations I'd just heard out of my mind. "The girl you said was trying to catch Reed's eye, the one you said would be good for him . . . what was her name?"

Her head listed and her eyes shifted around the kitchen, no doubt because she'd just been in there. "Well, I'm not sure why it matters now, but her name is Hannah."

All the shock and pain and denial built up inside me, forming a red-hot ball of anger in my chest. "She isn't trying to catch anything. They're well-acquainted with each other."

Before Lala could respond, I turned and left the kitchen, intent on running upstairs to get my purse and then leaving the house for the entire day, if at all possible.

But as soon as I took the turn out of the kitchen, I bumped off of a wall of muscle.

"Whoa, sorry about that." Hands came up around my arms to steady me, but I quickly maneuvered away from them.

I glanced up at the man who had just been in the kitchen, hugging Lala and talking to Hannah, and was hit with a flash from my past—from *that* night.

Standing in that exact spot as he'd pushed me into the kitchen, trying to get me away from where my mother had lain, just feet away from us. Taller, broader, and looking every bit a man rather than the teenage boy he'd been, but there was no doubt in my mind that this was Nick.

"Holy shit," he breathed. "You really are back."

I took a step away, trying to put distance between us, but he just continued staring at me as if he were looking at a ghost.

"Fuck, I, uh . . . wow. Last time—"

"We don't need to talk about that."

"Yeah, okay."

My stare darted around. Uncomfortable with this and uncomfortable with the knowledge that the other girl Reed was seeing was a dozen feet away from me.

I swallowed past my pain and focused on turning it into anger. "We really don't have to do this," I said when the silence between Nick and me stretched on even though his stare remained expectant.

Especially because I'm seconds from asking you to confirm what I overheard.

"Look, I'm sure seeing me is hard because of that night. Trust me, it's weird as fuck seeing you when all I can think about is your mom returning from the dead and cussing up a storm."

My chest pitched with a muted, pained laugh.

"But you being back changes things for a lot of people I care about, so I think it would be good for everyone if we tried to start over on a clean slate."

I didn't want a clean slate with him.

I didn't want anything from him.

He was a cop. He was Reed's best friend.

I just wanted to grab my bag and get out of there, but he was standing in my way of the stairs.

I glanced at him before quickly looking around us, nodding as I did. "For Lala and Nora," I clarified.

Hesitation and confusion swirled around him as he extended his hand. "I don't think we've met yet. I'm Nick Butler."

I stared at his hand for a long while, my body shaking and shaking and shaking from the morning and from an officer wanting me to take his hand for *anything*.

I forced my hand into his, holding myself rigidly as I did. "I'm—" I went absolutely still when what he'd said spun around in my mind. My head snapped up and my stare held his. "Did you say Nick *Butler*? Is your dad Ron Butler?"

His confusion intensified. Covering his face and dripping from his lips as he awkwardly shook my stiff hand. "Yes," he said, drawing out the word and making it sound like a question.

I ripped my hand away from his. "I have to go," I breathed and sidestepped him, backing away toward the front door.

I nearly ran to Lala's truck, forgetting my bag and not caring.

I didn't remember the drive to the bookstore.

I didn't remember what Donna said to me when I arrived.

All I could think of were the facts that Reed was seeing someone else and that someone was currently in Lala's house. Another girl was begging him to go home, and after the news of Hannah, I no longer had any idea who it could be. His best friend had witnessed the worst night of my life, and to make matters worse, Nick's brother-in-law—*Leah's* husband—had been one of the men trying to rape me my last night in New York.

If it weren't for Lala and Nora and Donna, if it weren't for the store, I would've driven out of Colby and never looked back.

I'D WANTED to linger at the store, but Donna had demanded we leave, saying one or both of us was going to pass out if we kept at it. From the look on her face, I knew she'd been trying to channel Lala. She'd failed, but it was adorable, nonetheless.

If I'd had the energy, I would've gone to the coffee shop or wandered around town, but Donna had been right. The day had been long, both so mentally and physically exhausting, that I barely had the strength to pull myself into Lala's truck and drive home.

When I arrived, I considered going straight to my room and falling asleep. But knowing Lala would worry if I didn't let her know that I'd made it back, I'd shuffled into the kitchen.

Disappointment dipped in my chest when I saw a pyramid of garlic bread stacked in the corner of the kitchen, only to quickly be overtaken by hurt-fueled relief.

The last thing I wanted was to spend the night wondering if Reed was going to stop by or not.

"Evening, Lala."

She took one look at me and her body sagged, but her face lit with joy. "Sit, I'll fix you a plate."

"No, no. I can get it in a bit." I glanced around the kitchen but couldn't seem to focus on anything. "What can I do?"

She pointed at the kitchen table with a wooden spoon. "You can sit your bottom down and tell me about the day."

A whimper escaped me. "Don't ever let me do this again. Cataloging an entire store worth of books is . . ."

"Rewarding?"

"It's driving me insane, Lala. I think I might literally be going crazy. Why did I think this was a good idea?"

She gave a little chuckle. "The end is in sight, Emma. You'll be done with this part by the end of the weekend, I have no doubt. Then it's maintaining the books, and that is a piece of cake compared to what you've done the last week and a half."

"Any kind of cake sounds good right about now," I murmured, nearly moaning at the thought.

"I noticed you left without food this morning," she said, disapproval weaving through her tone. "You best have eaten today."

"Donna grabbed salads for us for lunch," I said distractedly as my attention shifted to the bread again. "Sorry about this morning, I just . . . I'm sorry." I looked at Lala when she didn't respond and stilled when I saw her glare.

"A salad?" She looked pointedly behind me and snapped, "Sit down and let me feed you."

I lifted my hands in surrender. "I will get it."

"Christ Almighty," she mumbled under her breath. "Working all day and eats nothing but a damn salad." She snorted and shot me a look as I reached for a plate. "Bet it didn't even have any protein on it."

"It did," I said defensively.

She reached out to brush her hand against my cheek, then went back to the stove with a sigh. "I just worry about you. If I had my way—well . . ."

The air grew thick from the obvious turn in her thoughts and unspoken words.

If she had her way, she would've stopped my life from being what it had been.

"I know, Lala," I whispered softly, sadness weaving through the words.

I turned for the food, but my attention once again got snagged on the bread.

"He'll be back."

My head jerked in Lala's direction. "Hmm?"

"Reed," she said knowingly, then nodded toward the pyramid he built every week. "The nights he works, he drops off the bread before going in, but he always comes back for dinner."

I wanted to ask if he'd said anything.

If he'd asked about me. If he'd seemed concerned that I might know any of the things he was doing.

Then again, I didn't want to care.

"I don't want to be here when he comes back."

Lala dropped the wooden spoon into the pot and turned to fully face me. "After these mornings you've been sharing with him, I can't imagine why you wouldn't."

Because I knew.

I knew he had the power to break me, and he'd only had a fraction of my heart. I knew he was trouble. I knew he would be like every man I'd witnessed my mom with.

"It doesn't matter," I said softly.

"Help me understand why it doesn't."

"You don't need to understand," I said simply.

"Don't do this, Emma," she said as if preparing for a fight she knew would only continue to happen. "Don't let your past keep you from living life now. Don't let it stop you from having a future. Be the brave girl I know you are."

"I want nothing to do with Reed Ryan," I cried out, voice twisting painfully around his name. "Why is that so difficult for everyone to understand? I told you, Jesus, I *told you* that first night there was something about him, and I was right. I don't want him anywhere near me. Can you understand that?"

By the time I finished, I was trembling and my eyes were burning with tears I refused to shed over him. My chest jerked with my uneven breaths because this *hurt*, and I hated that I'd let myself fall.

Lala's stare bounced between me and something behind me, as it had when I'd first walked in. The kitchen table . . . she wanted me to go to it.

Only I had a feeling from her apologetic expression and the way her stare was continuously shifting back and forth that she was no longer just looking at the table.

I felt that intoxicating energy wrap around me. Trying to

comfort me when it was nothing but a reminder of the way I'd fallen. And then I felt *him*.

Felt his hurt and his anger weave through the inexplicable pull that was begging me to turn, begging me to look at him.

Holding my head high, I turned to face where he was standing with Nora and another officer. Once again, everything inside me recoiled when I saw him in uniform, but I locked it up tight.

Reed's wounded eyes were focused on me. His jaw was clenched tight, muscles working from the force there.

I didn't realize my hands had curled into fists until I felt the sting of pain from my nails.

"Why do you always say such mean things about my Reed?" Nora asked softly.

The officer next to them shifted uncomfortably, but I didn't look at either of them. I couldn't take my eyes from Reed.

The past came rushing to the surface as I stared at that man, and I let it.

I let it threaten to drown me. I let my demons wrap their arms around me and sink their claws into my skin. I let it all mix with every memory of Reed, with his patience and his smirks and his touch and our kisses until my knees shook from the force of the emotions building inside me.

Until I wanted to fall to the floor and *weep*. Because throughout it all, Reed continued standing apart from the rest, and something in me screamed that he always would.

But it didn't change anything. It didn't change that, all along, *he* had been the lie.

Lala made a sound of discontent. "Why don't the two of you go somewhere to—"

"You disgust me," I whispered, choking over the words.

Reed's head shifted in the faintest nod as if he were accepting my hate. As if he knew exactly *why* I was throwing all of it at him.

When I walked past him, he didn't say anything, and he didn't try to stop me. In those ruthless, endless moments, I knew I had finally succeeded in pushing him away.

And it shattered me.

TWENTY-THREE

REED

Garcia let out a slow breath from beside me. "So, that's the cop-hater?"

I didn't have it in me to shut him up. I couldn't wrap my mind around what just happened.

When I'd left Emma that morning, she'd started shutting down, yeah. But I'd thought it had to do with Rowe barging into her room because I had a feeling she didn't normally let people into rooms with her.

But *this*?

I didn't know how we'd gone from falling asleep with her in my arms after confessing just how much we meant to each other—all while dancing around those three words I was sure would have her pushing me away faster than anything had before—to *this*.

It didn't even feel like her shields. The pain in her voice and the tears in her eyes had felt more personal than anything before—and they terrified me as much as they hurt. Because that had been the real Emma saying she wanted nothing to do with me.

"Why is that one so mean to you?" Nora asked as she tugged at my hand. "I don't like her."

Lala stopped in front of me, face apologetic. "I'm sorry for that, I don't know what got into her tonight. Just give her time to come around."

A strangled laugh managed to escape me. I looked over to what I could see of the bottom of the staircase from where I was standing. I took a step back, head shaking. "Think she made herself perfectly clear."

"Now, don't say—"

"Lala, I've clearly been deluding myself into thinking something was happening . . . that something was going to. I don't know where everything got twisted and I went wrong—you know what? It doesn't matter."

From what I'd walked in on to the only words Emma actually spoke to me, not one part of it had sounded like her lies.

I dragged my free hand through my hair and blew out a harsh breath as I detangled myself from Nora. "I have to go."

Lala tried to stop me.

Nora and Garcia tried to follow me.

I didn't let any of them succeed.

I climbed into my patrol car and left, hoping the night ahead would clear my mind.

TWENTY-FOUR

EMMA

I held Lala's unreadable stare when she entered my room with a soft knock not long after I'd made it up there, waiting for what she would say.

If she would reprimand me. If she would demand I go apologize.

But all she said was, "He left."

I nodded against my pillow but didn't respond otherwise.

After a minute of us just watching each other, she pushed from the doorjamb and came to sit on my bed. "I may be old, but my mind isn't slowing yet."

"You're not old, Lala."

She huffed and twisted to face me. "I was trying to figure what could have possibly gotten into you as you were saying it, but I was too distracted by Reed showing up at the absolute wrong time that it stopped me from remembering what you said before leaving this morning." When I only stared at her, she explained, "About Hannah."

"I know what I said to you."

"Well, you were looking at me like you didn't remember.

Figured I'd help you along." I rolled my eyes, but she kept going. "What I'm gathering from this morning and tonight is that something happened with Hannah."

That pain pierced my chest and quickly pushed through my veins again, but I tried to force it away.

"So guarded," Lala whispered. "No way to live, Emma."

"They're together," I finally said. "Hannah and some other girl were talking about it in the kitchen this morning."

Lala leaned back, doubt on her face. "Now, I know what I told you. Hannah has been sweet on Reed for quite some time, but I've seen that boy around you. I know how he feels about you. And he isn't the kind to play around that way."

"Apparently, he is." A shaky smile lined my face. "I wanted to deny it, but then Nick said something to her about how he saw her at Reed's the other day."

"That could have meant anything." But even Lala looked disappointed, as if she didn't know what to do with the information I'd given her.

"It's for the best." Even as I spoke, I could hear the lie in my voice. "I should have known every instinct I had about Reed was right—was trying to tell me something. I should have known when I fell for him so fast that I was doing exactly what I was afraid of . . . following in Momma's footsteps."

"Emma, there's something that doesn't sit right with me about this. That boy is crazy about you. He was wrecked by what just happened downstairs."

An incredulous laugh left me. "He's perfect in your eyes. You'll never be able to believe that he could do something wrong."

"I told you, that boy is good to his soul." She held up a hand, stopping me from replying. "I know a thing or two about this. Everyone makes mistakes. No one is perfect—even Reed. He has his own things he needs to handle. But playing with a girl's heart? That isn't a mistake he would knowingly make."

"And if you're wrong?"

"I'll bust his tail right on out of Colby, but I know I'm not. Not about this." She settled deeper into the bed and released a weary sigh. "Your momma . . . she was a rebellious one. Always had been. We'd been at odds for a while, and she'd been getting into some things she shouldn't have. Hanging out with people she had no right being around. She never brought boys home, then one day, she did. This twenty-year-old man she wanted to show off. Rub in our faces because she knew we wouldn't approve."

I thought back to how old my mother had been when she had me and asked, "How old was she?"

Lala gave me a knowing look. "We had just celebrated her sixteenth birthday. Of course, we would've had our reservations with his age, but this man." Lala shuddered. "He'd just gotten out of jail for something or other. Was covered head to toe in vulgar and racist tattoos. And he was so high on something when he met us that he started throwing my dishes."

I was so embarrassed by the choices my mother made that my eyelids slipped shut. My mouth opened to automatically apologize, but the words never left my tongue.

There was no point, I knew that.

It happened before I was born.

Once again, another reflex from a lifetime with her. Of trying to clean up her messes as much as possible.

Lala nodded toward me. "You came along not even eight months later. None of us knew if he was the daddy or not. But the boys and men she'd been with at the time were all similar to him. Before she got pregnant, during the pregnancy, and—of course—after . . . she disappeared. All the time. We called the cops often to report it. After a while, we had to stop because we knew she was doing it for attention and was going to continue. She'd leave school or slip out in the middle of the night. Unless we wanted to chain ourselves to her, we couldn't prevent it."

She looked straight ahead, her eyes far away.

When nearly a minute passed, I wanted to beg her to continue but stayed silent. I didn't have any room to ask for information from anyone.

"I wondered so many times where I'd gone wrong with her," she finally said. "Eventually, I had to come to terms with the knowledge that we all make our own choices. If we didn't, who knows where you'd be."

The thought chilled me.

Fear had my stomach clenching.

Flashes of my life assaulted me, but I was quick to push them all away that time.

"After you were born, she left you with us and took off. Came back just before your second birthday. Next thing we knew, the both of you were gone." She cleared her throat, then did it again, her lips wavering. "That was the first time we called the cops on her in years . . . it was also the last. Your grandpa and I had no claim over you and had no way to prove anything she ever did."

"Lala." Her name was a breath. Shock filled every inch of me at the news. At how deep and real her fear of Nora being taken was.

I didn't know how to thank her for caring for me or apologize for the fear and heartbreak that must have caused.

I reached out and rested a hand on top of hers.

She glanced up and gave me a faint shrug. "But every year or two, the two of you showed up at my door because she'd run out of money. And every time, I asked for you back. I think she wouldn't give you to me because she knew I would give her money as long as you were with her. I knew where that money was going. I could see the drugs damaging her body. But . . . well, we all make mistakes. Enabling her was mine."

"You kept me alive."

She offered me a watery smile. "Do you see the differences, Emma? You may be here because you needed me. You may have fallen for a boy faster and harder than you ever expected—and he may have tattoos. But Reed is not those men, and you are not your mother, not in any way."

"That isn't what it feels like," I admitted softly.

"Maybe not now. Eventually, you'll let go of your fears, and you'll see." She brushed a hand across my cheek and stood. "I've got a kitchen to get back to. If you're not down there in five minutes to eat your fill, I'm sending whatever first responders are in my house up here to get you."

"Yes, ma'am," I said and watched her go.

Once she was gone, I sat up and focused on nothing other than breathing.

Not the pain or the anger or Reed Ryan.

Just breathing.

Just being.

TWENTY-FIVE

REED

I didn't have a fucking clue how I'd ended up there.

I'd been avoiding this place for over three years now. For most of that time, I'd been avoiding calls and texts from these people too, because they were the same over and over again.

Come home.

Come home.

Go home.

Home was the last place I wanted to go. *Home* no longer felt like the place I was sitting in front of. *Home* was a small town where I couldn't hide. *Home* was a girl with a fierce glare and a hard-to-come-by smile.

Apparently, I'd been wrong about it all.

As soon as my shift ended at four that morning, I'd showered, changed, gotten into my truck, and started driving.

No destination, no sunrises to watch with Emma, I'd just needed to go somewhere.

I'd needed to clear my head.

As I had three years ago, I'd realized not long after where

I was headed. It somehow only made me angrier, but I hadn't turned around.

Six hours later, I was sitting in front of my parents' house, glaring at it like the house alone was the source of all my anger.

I turned off the engine and stepped out of my truck, wondering why I was doing this. Why I was walking toward the front door. What the hell I was going to say to whoever answered.

When I was a few feet away, the door opened, and a man filled the frame.

Other than the gray peppering his black hair and the lines starting to show around his eyes, there wasn't a thing about him that set us apart.

From the build to the tattoos to the hardened stare to the way he stood, arms at his sides and hands fisted, prepared for anything.

Mirror image.

He jerked his chin at something behind me. "Your mom just left for Kira's."

I nodded.

"You gonna come in?"

"I don't know," I said honestly. "I don't know why I'm here."

He breathed out a huff that was a mixture of frustration and hurt. "Because this is your home, Reed." With that, he turned and walked away, leaving the door wide open.

After another minute of indecision, I followed him in.

I didn't need to wonder where he'd gone, I already knew where I would find him—in the kitchen making coffee. After, we'd move to the kitchen table and fight it out. It's what we'd always done.

Sure enough, coffee was just starting to brew, and he was pulling out a couple mugs when I entered the kitchen.

"Girls know you're back?" he asked without turning.

"I'm not back."

He twisted around and leaned against the counter, folding his arms over his chest as he did. "So, what are you?"

I lifted my shoulders. "Needed to go for a drive."

"Last time you did that, you didn't come home."

My brows rose knowingly. "This isn't the same situation."

"Then what is it? Because you've been gone for over three fucking years. The fact that you left after just coming home from the military *wrecked* your mom and your sisters. And now you don't talk to them at all. So, if you're here, it better start with a damn good apology."

A frustrated laugh rumbled in my chest. "Ah, Jesus . . . this is why I don't know why I'm here."

"Then go," he said carelessly. "Leave before your mom gets back and you wreck her all over again."

"I fucking left because of you," I snapped. "I left because this is all we do. We fight and fight, and nothing I did was ever good enough for you. As for the girls? First of all, Kennedy has no room to fucking talk, considering she moved to California. And all anyone ever says is, 'Come home. Come home. Come home.' That's all the messages consist of. No one's asked where I am, what I'm doing, or cared that I actually love where I ended up. So, yeah, I stopped responding."

"Nothing you did was good enough?" He gave me an incredulous look. "Are you serious, Reed?"

I just stared at him for a few moments, eyes wide and mouth open. "Dad . . . yeah. Every training, every scenario . . . once the girls got it, it was always *good job. Don't forget this. What would you do if this happened instead*? Me? You were so much harder on me, and I never seemed to get it right, even though I was twice as fast as the girls. *Do it again, Reed. Faster, Reed. Your family just died because you weren't fast enough, Reed. Do it again.*"

"I was pushing you."

"I was five years old," I shouted, spreading my arms out wide. "It was fucked up, and the thing is, you still don't realize it."

"Teaching my kids how to protect themselves . . . yeah." He shrugged. "Real fucked up."

"The fact that we had to do any of that at all," I said on an exasperated laugh. "Then I went away and got my ass handed to me anytime I came home because I didn't keep in touch while I was gone." I placed a hand on my chest. "For the guy who always taught us to protect our family, I thought not having contact with them while on highly secretive missions was a good way to protect them."

At that, his face turned to stone. No emotion, not a tick of his jaw, nothing.

Because he knew I was right.

"Even Sadie wasn't good enough—"

"She wasn't," he added coolly, but I continued as if he hadn't.

"But, for some goddamn reason, I always had to be okay with Kennedy and Kira's fucked-up relationships. Kennedy meets a random guy and gets married right out of high school? I had to be okay with it because no one else was on her side. He ups and disappears on her? I was pissed, but *you* told me I had to be okay with it. You told me to act like it never happened. Then, that last time I came home, not only is Kennedy off in California, married to some new guy with a kid. But her piece-of-shit ex is suddenly back and married to *Kira*, and everyone is just okay with it."

I still remembered that day.

Remembered the shock and utter confusion. The hurt and betrayal. The rage.

I gestured to my dad and said, "I about lost my mind, and you shoved *me* back and told me to take a walk. Me. No one had given me a warning about what I was walking into. No one had told me anything about him. And when I was trying to understand why he was standing there, why he was with *Kira*, what did you tell me?"

"You missed their weddings."

"You wanted me to apologize for it. What about no one cared to wait until I came home? No one even fucking told me they were happening?"

"You were told," he said with a scoff.

"No, I wasn't," I yelled, smacking my hand on the counter. "You think I wouldn't have been there? You think I would've missed seeing my sisters get married? Or that I would've missed Kennedy having a kid?"

"Kira just had twins a couple months ago. Why don't you tell me?"

All the air fled from my lungs so swiftly, so painfully, I wasn't sure I'd ever catch my breath again.

I stumbled back and then to the side, hand blindly searching for the counter again to support me. My head shook slowly as I opened my mouth to speak. To beg him to tell me he was lying, to ask if I had really done this to myself, to say *anything*, but no words came.

I turned and went to the table, falling roughly to one of the chairs there.

My elbows hit the hardwood and my head dropped into my hands.

Soon after, a mug was set in front of me, followed by the sound of my dad settling into one of the other chairs.

"In the eight years you were in the military, you only came home three times, Reed. Most of the time, it was radio silence from you. Your mom and I watched the news religiously because that was the only way we knew if you were alive. When anything happened to a SEAL team . . . fuck, Reed," he ground out, voice thick. "And half the time, we didn't know if you were stateside or there. I watched your mom and your sisters mourn you so many goddamn times, I lost count. What you were doing would've already had us worried for you, but you left everyone you loved in the dark, and that was a terrifying place to be. So, yeah, maybe when you finally showed up, the fear that always stayed with me lashed out at you."

A sharp laugh punched from me. "You're a hypocrite." I dropped my hands to look at him and leaned back in my chair. "I never thought anything of it, just that I was protecting my family in the only way I could. But what you just said?" I shrugged. "I get it now, what I was doing. And why wouldn't I? I learned from the best."

His brows set low over his eyes as if he was trying to figure out where I was going with this.

"Leaving everyone I loved in the dark." I nodded. "Yeah. Yeah, I can see how that would be hard for the people left behind. Then again, you used to leave everyone you loved in the dark. Without a word, without a way to get ahold of you, you'd vanish. I'm sure your family was terrified." I gave him a knowing look. "Weren't you sometimes gone for a year at a time?"

"I was an undercover detective in gangs, that's different. I had a cover that couldn't be blown."

"I was a SEAL. I was overseas on classified missions. I was at war." Each word was said slowly, carefully. "Tell me how that's different." I huffed bitterly. "Oh, wait, it's different because I didn't get caught. I didn't get my fiancée kidnapped and nearly killed on *two different occasions*. I didn't continue putting my family in danger."

His jaw tightened. "I had it under control."

"You mean after what happened to Mom the second time, right?" I asked meaningfully. "You could've gone anywhere. You and Mom could've gone *anywhere* and started over. We wouldn't have been *here*, where you'd done all that shit, growing up having to constantly look over our shoulders to make sure we weren't going to pay for everything you'd done."

"Everything I'd done." He laughed, but it was full of frustration. "I gave up my life and basically sold my soul so I could bring the filth out of their holes and put them in prison."

"Yeah, and you made sure we were prepared if any of them retaliated again by giving us the most fucked-up childhood."

"Tell me again how I ruined your childhood. Tell me that I was a shitty dad." He held his arms out and looked around. "Is that why you're here?"

"You were the best dad," I said softly. "I looked up to you —shit, you were my hero. It wasn't until I went into the Navy that I realized you and I were always fighting because, suddenly, we weren't. Because we weren't talking at all. Then I started hearing stories from other guys, stories about their childhoods, and I quickly found out that mine hadn't been normal. Nothing about it was." I roughed a hand over my jaw, my head shaking. "I wanted to be just like you . . . but I never measured up, and you stopped me at every turn."

Dad's mouth had formed a thin line as I spoke. At the last part, his eyes shot to mine.

"You and Uncle Mason are legends here. Even the shit you did that nearly got you fired only made the two of you more notorious. All I ever wanted was to be like you," I repeated. "But the second I mentioned becoming an officer, you shot it down. Every time I brought it up, you shot it down harder. 'Do something else with your life. Go to college and get a degree that puts you in an office somewhere,'" I mimicked him. "'You don't want to be known as Kash Ryan's kid.' Except I'd *always* been known as your kid. You trained us to escape life-or-death situations from the time we could walk because of it."

My dad's chest pitched with a defeated-sounding laugh. "First time you said that I was so damn proud." Before I had a chance to argue, he said, "Then you said, 'I'm gonna go undercover, just like you did.' Scared the shit out of me. And you were already the best at everything—better than my undercover trainees—at only thirteen. So, I knew whatever you went for when you grew up, you'd get it." He lifted his mug, a haunted kind of look washing over his face, his stare faraway. "And I couldn't let you live that life."

I knew stories from when he'd been undercover. He'd told them plenty of times as lessons, so I knew he and Uncle Mason had lived in ways that still haunted them. Just as I knew there were worse things they'd refused to tell us.

But that didn't change what I'd wanted or how he'd stopped me at every turn.

"Instead of tearing down my dream, why couldn't you

have tried to steer me away from *that* division?" I asked, voice soft and holding a hint of bitterness. "I was a kid, things change. I mean . . . sort of. I'm pretty sure I had a mohawk around that time too."

"You did," he said with a twitch of his lips.

"And I don't have one of those anymore." I let my hand fall heavily to the table. "Not that where I'm at has an undercover division, but even if it did, I like being on patrol."

Silence settled between us, heavy and filled with pain for long minutes before he finally said, "You didn't have to run away and abandon your family to be a cop."

I slanted a glare at him and reached for my mug. "You know that isn't why I left."

"Apparently, it's because of me, so might as well get it all out now since we're having the best conversation of my life," he said dryly.

"I told you," I murmured, "I was already reeling because Sadie left me. Then I came home to the twins and all their marriage surprises, and the first thing you did was make me feel like shit for not being there when I hadn't even known."

"You were told," he said, echoing his response from earlier.

I lifted my hands. "No, I—*when*? Who tried to tell me? Who tried to contact me? Because I fucking promise you, I would've been there."

"Both girls sent invitations. They called and texted for the weddings *and* when Kennedy got pregnant and had the baby."

"I never got anything," I said adamantly. "Never once. I —" Denial and regret slowly wound through me. "Radio silence," I said through shallow breaths.

Dad grunted in affirmation.

"But Sadie would've gotten the wedding invitations. She

would've told me that they'd gotten married while I was gone." My chest pitched as everything started adding up. "Except I came home to the news that she was leaving me."

"Still could've found time to tell you," Dad said. "Never did like her."

I shot him a look. "Yeah, and you reminded me of it any time she was mentioned. You were mad when we got engaged, and the day I came home and told you she'd left me, you said, 'I warned you about her.'" An irritated laugh crawled up my throat as I placed my hands on my chest. "I have to be okay with my sisters suddenly being married, one of them to the other's asshole ex, and I'm not supposed to ask questions. But I'm standing there, devastated because my fiancée left me, and that was all you could say?"

His head bounced in a faint nod. Sorrow and regret etched across his face.

"You and I nearly came to blows that night, Dad. I hadn't even been home for six hours. I'd left a huge chunk of my life behind, my heart had been ripped out, and my family had gone on with their lives like I didn't exist. Why the fuck would I have stayed?"

"You stay because we're family."

"Yeah, it didn't feel like my family anymore."

His jaw ticked in that way it always did when he was mad or hurting, but he just sat there, turning his mug in circles.

After minutes passed in uncomfortable silence, he asked, "You're happy in Colby?"

My chest heaved with a muted laugh. "Knew you'd track me."

"Had you flagged. Soon as you applied for a South Carolina license, it popped up. Right after, saw everything else you were applying for and knew you were going into the academy."

I sighed and sank lower in my chair. "Yeah, Dad. Really happy."

"No one knows who you are?"

I sucked in a quick breath through my teeth. "Small town, they all know who I am." I sent him a quick look before focusing on my coffee. "But no one wants to kill me because of my last name, so there's that."

"Got a girl?"

Flashes of wrath-filled glares and hesitant, earth-shattering kisses blasted through my mind. "Uh, no . . . I don't. That's why I'm here though."

I could feel his surprise from across the table, but he didn't ask.

"There've been girls, but there hasn't been anyone who's caught my eye since Sadie until a few weeks ago. And she hated me on sight."

My dad laughed, and I shot a cold look his way in response.

"This is unlike anything I've ever experienced. She looked at me like she hated me for even breathing, and I hadn't even met her. She was new in town, she didn't know me, so it didn't make sense. Skip forward a few, mostly hostile meetings, and she sees me in uniform for the first time." I curled my hand into a fist as I remembered that day on my porch. "Never seen that kind of hatred in someone."

"Shit," Dad said softly. "Why did she catch your eye again?"

I laughed sadly. "Well, she's fucking gorgeous, but she's the exact opposite of my type, so I have no idea. But there was always something there, something on her end that wouldn't let me leave it alone. Almost as if she was crushed that I was this person she hated. So I kept at it, slowly and cautiously because she could turn like that." I snapped my fingers. "But things were changing between us. *She* was changing. She was opening up, she was beginning to trust me, she was falling as hard as I did. It was . . . I don't know. We were *crawling*, but I was fine with that because she clearly needs to crawl. Then yesterday . . . I don't even know what happened. It all went to shit."

"You push her too fast?"

I breathed out something that edged on hysterical. "I don't know. The first time I kissed her was after a couple weeks—I told her I was going to while also telling her I wouldn't if she didn't want me to. And it's been steadily going from there. I always let her know what I'm gonna do because if I reach out to touch her when she's not expecting it, she goes on the defensive. She won't talk about it, but I'm positive she was sexually abused at some point—and I think it was recent. But then the way she reacts is like she grew up protecting herself, you know?"

Dad gave a hard nod.

"I just don't know from what. But from the little I've heard, her mom dragged her from place to place to place, never settling down. I don't know if they were ever homeless, but I have a feeling her mom put her in a lot of dangerous situations. Like, the type of shit you saw undercover."

"Might be why she hates cops," he said thoughtfully. "If she was in those situations, around those people, cops are the enemy. Growing up like that . . ."

"Yeah." I raked a hand through my hair and released a heavy sigh. "But now? She looks like she eats guys like me for breakfast. She can be fucking terrifying if she wants to be," I admitted, and my dad breathed a knowing laugh. "But when she lets go of that shield, everything about her is soft and gentle and fragile. She's hesitant when it comes to any kind of physical contact and she's . . ." I shrugged, trying to think of a way to explain Emma. "I don't know, everything about her is just addicting."

"So, what happened yesterday?"

My head shook as I thought back to Lala's kitchen. "Fuck if I know. I thought about it the entire drive here. I walked in on her raging about me to her grandma—saying she wanted nothing to do with me and didn't want me anywhere near her. When she realized I was there, she just looked at me with more contempt than ever while trying not to cry. Said, 'You disgust me,' and left."

"Jesus," Dad mumbled.

"The only thing I've been able to come up with is that morning. Early," I added. "I work nights, but she's gone nearly the entire day. So, we've spent a few hours together the last few mornings before she leaves for work. It, uh . . ." I swallowed uncomfortably. "She's been getting more comfortable with kissing me. Not that she was bad because, Jesus . . ." I forced out a quick breath. "But even with kissing, I could tell that she wanted to and was terrified to at the same time, but she was opening up and trusting me more and more each time. And I would never do anything she didn't want to, I would never do that to any woman, but I still know better than to take things any further with Emma without letting her know what I'm doing."

"Because you're crawling," Dad said knowingly.

"Right, but in that moment . . ."

"You're caught up," he supplied when I didn't continue.

"Right," I said, the word weighted and full of regret. "I

had my hands under her shirt, kinda lifting it, and she turned to absolute stone before she started *shaking*. Crying and saying, 'I can't,' over and over again like she had no idea she was even talking or that I was there with her."

Dad didn't say anything, but he didn't have to.

I explained everything that happened after, hoping my dad could make sense of what I couldn't. From our confessions to falling asleep to Rowe showing up and Emma shutting down before I left. "Then when I came back that night . . ." I shrugged.

"So, talk to her," Dad said easily, as if it were ever that simple with Emma.

My head shook widely. "I have tried so many times. I've gone back to her and I've stopped her when she tried pushing me away. But this was different. This wasn't because she hates cops or men. This was a you-and-I-are-done-forever kind of thing."

"Then let it go if she isn't worth it."

My body crumpled because Emma *was* worth it. She was worth everything.

"I think I fell in love with her the first time she told me off," I admitted softly.

After a moment, Dad sucked in a deep breath and sat forward to lean against the table. "I shouldn't have said what I did about Sadie," he began softly. "I should have supported you, but I could see what she did to you, and there was something about her that had me worried you would get trapped in that."

I lifted my hands slightly off the table before letting them smack down. "I clearly didn't."

"Reed, she wouldn't give you the time of day until you started training to be a SEAL. Then she was all about you and mostly about what you were. She brought it up every other sentence—she wouldn't even say your name, just called you *her SEAL*. It was weird. Not to mention, she moved out there to be near you as soon as the two of you started dating, and when we did see you, she was always with you. Which is fine, but she never left your side. She literally clung to you and wouldn't let you have a conversation without her. And things were always perfect in a way that seemed *wrong*. She was overly nice in a way that screamed *fake*, especially since we'd all known what she was like before you guys even started dating."

Amusement wove through my next breath because I'd never noticed before how much Courtney reminded me of Sadie.

Fake? Yeah, Dad wasn't wrong. Once Sadie and I had gotten together, she'd been overly nice to me, to my friends, to everyone.

I just hadn't noticed it until long after she'd handed me the ring I'd given her.

"Do you remember what I told you the day you and Sadie got engaged?" Dad asked.

"'Why?'" I recalled, annoyance dripping from the word. "'She isn't the one for you.'"

"I said you'd know when you met the one," he added when he realized I was finished. "That she'd hate you on sight. Drive you insane and trip up your heart. Make you want to punch things one minute and pull her into your arms the next."

I stilled as the memory tugged at my mind. As I realized what he was saying.

"Sadie wasn't any of those things," he said before admitting, "I could've handled it better though."

"You think?"

"Your mom didn't talk to me for two days. She was so sure you were gonna go elope without telling anyone because of me."

I just shook my head.

Sadie had brought up the idea more times than I could remember, but I'd never considered it. I wouldn't have considered anything without my family there.

One of the reasons I'd felt so betrayed by my sisters when I'd come home.

"This girl," he continued, "it's hard to see what it is about her that draws you in from what you've told me. But that says everything about why she's it for you. Says everything about why you're here and why you're so wrecked by a girl you're not even dating."

I gave him a blank look. "That doesn't make sense. You realize that, right?"

"Sadie was faking being perfect so that nothing would ever appear wrong with her or with your relationship, and everything about that *was* wrong. We could all see it, even if you couldn't at the time. But this girl? Everything is set against you two, you're wrong for each other in so many ways, but you're still fighting for her because a connection like that deserves to be fought for."

"Yeah, Dad, I think you missed the part where she doesn't want me in her life anymore."

"You've been talking to me for the first time in over three years, I haven't missed anything." As if he hadn't just taken a shot straight to my heart, he rubbed at his jaw and asked, "What happened between yesterday morning and last night?"

"Nothing, I hadn't even talked to her. She went to work. I went home and crashed and then started my next shift." I released a slow exhale and mumbled, "It wasn't even twelve hours, and I was asleep for most of it."

He looked at me solemnly and said, "I've been around a lot of different people in my career—women with trust issues and hatred built so deep inside them are no strangers to me. I've only ever needed to gain a sliver of trust to either help them or gain information, but I still know that it is a drawn-out process. It's half a step forward and two steps back. If this girl is really as guarded as you say, and you'd gotten to a point where she was opening up and trusting you, then she wouldn't have jumped back ten steps last night unless something happened."

I folded my arms over my chest and shrugged. "Other than what I told you, nothing happened."

"Then something happened to her."

My mind raced as I tried to think of anything that could've happened, but I came up with nothing.

Because it had been *me* she had been yelling about to Lala. *Me* she had been disgusted with. And I couldn't figure out what the hell I'd done.

"You gonna stick around, or are you headed back to fight for her again?"

"Who said I was going to?"

He huffed as he lifted his mug to take a long sip. "Your expression. The way you talk about her. You showing up here at all."

I didn't tell him he was right.

Every part of me was wondering why I wasn't in Colby trying to do exactly *that*. But there was still that small part that was hung up on the way it had all seemed so personal and final.

I cleared my throat and asked, "Kira really have twins?"

He dipped his head in a nod. "Almost three months ago."

"Then I'm gonna stick around for a couple days."

"Would you have stayed if she hadn't?"

"I don't know," I said honestly.

Things had ended on such bad terms between us all. After I'd left, it'd been strained for months before I'd stopped talking to them altogether. I still couldn't figure out why I'd driven here at all. Why I'd even sat at the damn table when things had immediately escalated, as they always did between us.

My dad gave a grunt as if he'd been expecting my answer, then stood from the table and grabbed his mug. After a step away, he said, "I *pushed* you to do something else because I never wanted you to glimpse the shit I lived through or the danger I put your mom and the three of you in. But I would've never stopped you. If you'd gone to the academy and applied here, I would've been just as proud of you as I've always been."

A flicker of doubt wove through me and faded when he continued.

"You were always more than enough, Reed. You always exceeded every expectation I had of you. I pushed you harder than the girls because I knew what it felt like to lose my entire world, and I never wanted you to experience that. I wanted you to have every tool to prevent that. I gave the girls what they needed to stay alive. I was giving you what you needed to protect your future family from the unimaginable."

I slanted my head in his direction when he faced me again.

Jaw tight.

Hands firmly gripping my mug.

Trying like hell to see things from his side when all I could remember was the constant training.

I knew how to escape cuffs and zip ties and the trunks of different types of cars as well as hotwiring them. I knew how to look at my surroundings and make almost anything into a weapon and use it, all because of the man standing in front of me.

And that was all by the time I was *five* . . . those were all things the girls knew too.

There had been so much more for me.

"When you came home . . ." He blew out a harsh breath and gave me a helpless look. "All we knew was that you hadn't come back for the girls, that you hadn't shown or said anything at all. You and I could've figured out why that happened *then* rather than waiting three years, but when one of us gets mad, the other follows. It's how we've always been."

"We're too alike," I murmured.

"You say that like it's a bad thing." The corner of his mouth tipped up in a smirk, but it quickly fell. "You're right though, we are. It's why I shoved you toward the door that day and told you to go for a walk. I knew exactly what you were going to do. I knew you were about to lose your shit and do something that would end up hurting Kira in the process."

I huffed. "I was gonna do what you should've done the second he showed back up."

"Her husband . . ." he said slowly, a little bit uncertainly, and then grimaced, "you're not all that different from him."

"I fucking doubt that."

He listed his head and said, "When Kennedy introduced

us to him after they were already married, I didn't know how to be mad because I was devastated for her."

Confusion slowly wound through me.

"Mason and I had just met him that afternoon at the department, and we'd told him to cut ties with any relationships and friendships."

"He was going undercover," I said under my breath as the realization hit me like a slug to the chest.

Dad nodded. "I couldn't tell Kennedy anything or even let on that I knew him. When he left to go undercover, it was hard to be mad at him when I knew the truth. When he got out of that division years later, he came back looking for her and fell for Kira—Kennedy was already dating the guy she's married to. I thought the whole thing was fucked up at first, but the girls are clearly with who they're meant to be with."

"He still a cop?"

He made a confirming sound in his throat. "Good one. But he isn't you." He headed into the kitchen, draining his mug as he went, then called out, "Let's go. Hope you don't like the shirt you're wearing."

"Where are we—wait, what?" I glanced at my shirt. "Why?"

He gave me a pointed look. "It's about to get covered in spit-up and your mom and sister's tears." A wry smile crossed his face. "Welcome home."

TWENTY-SIX

EMMA

Everything in me ached, my heart most of all. Everything groaned in protest when I attempted to move. I couldn't remember ever being more tired in my life. But I was happy despite it all. I had all this excited energy that made me want to keep going.

Made me want to do that *one last thing* every day.

Then again, I was sure if I stopped for even a minute, I would fall apart because there was a hole in my life in the shape of Reed Ryan. But, just two and a half weeks after being approved for the loan, the store looked brand new.

The windows were cleaned inside and out, then opened to let out the stale, musty smell. The carpet had been replaced and the wood polished. The walls were given a fresh coat of soft, gray paint that brightened up the place while also giving it a calming effect. And the lighting fixtures had all been replaced and updated.

I'd found a lady in town—who happened to *love* reading and also hadn't known there was a bookstore—who offered to make genre labels at an extremely discounted rate. Then, while the remodeled bathrooms had the finishing touches put on them, I'd taken Donna to a flower market and bought enough flowers to fill huge bouquets throughout the store. Those, combined with the essential oils set throughout, made it feel and smell like home.

At least, that's what both Donna and Lala said.

I wasn't sure what home was supposed to smell like—though, if I could choose a scent, it would've been books. Thousands upon thousands of books, waiting to bring comfort and safety.

The days our shipments of books came in, I'd considered walking out the door and never coming back. It had felt like we were drowning in a sea of boxes and books . . . but Donna hadn't been able to stop smiling, so I hadn't stopped moving until every book was cataloged and in its place.

Every reading chair.

Every children's bean bag lounger.

Every knickknack.

Nearly everything.

"I haven't seen this place look like this in . . ." Donna laughed, a soft, kind of hesitant sound. "Actually, I've never seen this place look quite like this."

My stare drifted to her, worry swirling through my stomach. "Is *this* good or bad?"

She'd had a say in all the changes and additions, not that she'd said no to any of my ideas, but this was her family's store. It needed to be perfect for her.

She looked around and sighed, her frail shoulders sagging with the exhale. "It's wonderful."

I glanced at Lala and tried to contain my smile when she just nodded approvingly at me.

Lala had come and gone every couple of days, watching

and giving her opinion. Snapping at me throughout it all when I'd climbed too high or rushed through the store, holding something she deemed too heavy while wearing the heels I refused to give up.

"This is where a certain man comes in handy. A certain Reed Ryan *man,"* she'd pointedly said too many times in the week since that devastating day.

Not that I'd ever responded or even let myself entertain thoughts of Reed while I was wrapped up in the store. I couldn't, and I refused to go down that road when I was soaking up all the warmth and excitement of the store nearly being finished with Donna.

It could wait until that night. It could wait until after the day was done and I was alone in my room to let the sorrow and the anger from Reed's betrayal and absence bleed out and consume me.

"Do you think people will come?" Donna asked, bringing me back to the store. Her tone was significantly different than just seconds before. Softer, uncertain.

"I'm sure of it," I said confidently. "It's the only store on this street—or any street around here—that has windows like these. Those alone make the store stand out. And we've been getting the word out that there's a bookstore here just by calling around, looking for help."

Donna didn't respond.

She just sat there, staring off, looking lost.

I dropped my forearms to the polished and decluttered checkout counter and caught her eye. "Your shop is beautiful. *You* and your soul are beautiful. And you have books to sell now," I said with a teasing grin. "They'll come. I promised you we'd pay off that loan within a year. That's what we're going to do."

She nodded, her expression showing equal parts joy and uncertainty. After a second, she scoffed. "Not with those doors, they won't."

A laugh bubbled free as I pushed from the counter.

Shooting Lala a secret smile, I said to Donna, "We'll see what we can do about the doors."

Lala dipped her head in a stealthy nod.

"I'll come, Ms. Donna," Nora called out as she came darting over from the children's section, cradling her stuffed puppy close to her side. "I'll be here every day, I promise, promise, promise!"

"See?" I gestured to Nora. "One customer, every day, guaranteed."

"And I'll bring my Reed," she said excitedly, pointedly ignoring me as she spoke to Donna.

My lungs forced out a pained breath. My heart ached and twisted. But I managed a smile and held up two fingers. "That makes two."

After everything had gone down with Reed, I'd been sure Nora would've been happy that Reed's attention had gone back to being solely on her. But her animosity toward me had only grown, and I hated that her ignoring me just then was the best interaction we'd had since the night she found out Reed and I kissed.

"Well, I'm famished," Lala said, casually pulling the conversation away from Reed. "How about we let this girl get her rest before she opens to the town next week?"

TWO HOURS LATER, we'd finished our early lunch and said goodbye for the weekend. After dropping Lala and Nora off at home, I ran to pick up Donna's first surprise and hurried back to the store in time to find the painters already at work.

Donna's second surprise.

Soon, the store would look as fresh on the outside as it did on the inside, with a deep gray exterior and bright white trim around the windows.

I watched as they scraped the old, chipped, green and red and gold paint off the outside for a few moments before unlocking the doors and hurrying in to set down my bag.

When I turned, a stuttered breath ripped from my lungs. Partly in surprise, partly in . . . God, just *Reed*.

Eight days.

It had been eight days since I'd read the text and found out about him and Hannah. Eight days since I'd seen him standing in Lala's kitchen—seen him at all. Nearly every moment had been spent at the store or running errands for it. The others had been spent hating myself for being stupid enough to fall for him. For missing him and wishing for my phone to go off in the early hours of the morning.

But none of that mattered.

Because it didn't change what he'd done. It didn't change that he'd made me want him only to shatter whatever had been between us that I'd been desperately trying to prevent.

I pressed a hand to my chest in a vain attempt to calm my thundering heart. But I had a feeling it would always beat erratically around Reed Ryan. "What the hell are you doing here?"

Reed's eyes had been scanning the store from where he stood near the doors but darted back to me when I spoke. His brow furrowed in a way that really wasn't fair. No man should look that good confused.

After a few seconds, he nodded. Just a slow dip of his

head as if something finally made sense to him. The creases in his forehead smoothed and the corner of his mouth tipped up in a smirk.

Sarcasm dripped heavily from his words when he said, “I’m gonna go, seeing as I’m not actually needed here.”

“I never said you were.”

The words were out before I could stop them.

The tone, all of it, I wished I could take it back. But pouring all my hatred on a man like Reed was as instinctive as breathing. I’d done it most of my life. And he’d done exactly what I’d feared he would.

He’d taken the small part of my heart I’d given him and thrown it away.

A sharp breath of a laugh left him as he reached for the door. “Noted.”

My chest wrenched watching him leave. I wanted to beg him to stay and demand to know why he’d turned out to be like every man I’d watched my mother with. Confess that I couldn’t stop thinking about him, even still . . .

But the pain from what he did burned deep, keeping the traitorous thoughts locked in my throat.

Reed paused with one of the doors cracked open. After a moment, he shut it and quickly erased half the distance between us, the muscles in his jaw straining under the force of the pressure he was putting on it.

When he stopped, all I could think of were the feet separating us.

How vast they seemed.

How small.

How much I wanted to cross them.

How badly I needed to place a barrier between us.

“What is it?” he demanded. “What happened? Because

I've been going out of my mind trying to figure you out and what I could've done to you."

A disbelieving huff tumbled from my lips. "Like you have to ask."

"Of course I have to fucking ask. Everything with you is locked up so damn tight, and I never know when or if you'll offer up a piece of yourself to me. Like this." He gestured to the store. "This is what you've been working on. What you wouldn't tell me about—what you *clearly* still don't want me knowing about."

I ground my jaw, the instinct to protect the store still so strong even though it was about to be revealed to the town and Reed was standing inside.

"From the first second you saw me, you looked at me like I disgusted you, *offended* you, and that was it. Your mind was made up. Then everything afterward just added to it." Frustration and confusion danced across his features, battling for dominance when he took a step closer.

My heart took off.

Wings fluttered in my stomach.

"But I was sure we were getting somewhere—that things were changing between us. Apparently, I had everything really fucking twisted because it blew up in my face. You looked at me like you genuinely hated me. Not my badge . . . *me.*"

I did.

I do. *I do. I had to.*

But with him there again, in front of me, all I could think of was how badly I wanted to feel his lips against mine again. Wondering what our next kiss would be like.

Soft or firm.

Comforting or unyielding.

He's with someone else.

He lied to you. He'll only hurt you more.

"And I cannot figure out why," he said sadly, then shook his head as if to clear it. Something like a laugh left him. "You know what, it doesn't matter. Because you made your point, and you're still making it. Goodbye, Emma."

My mouth opened . . . to stop him, to yell at him for what he did, to do *something*. But I forced myself to stand there, watching as he walked away, running his tattooed hands over his head as he did.

Every part of me felt like it was sinking to the floor once he was gone.

My shattering heart.

My twisting stomach.

My shoulders that suddenly felt so, so heavy.

But it was for the best. It had to be. I couldn't get trapped in Reed Ryan again.

Forcing out one excruciating breath after another, I blinked away the threat of tears and grabbed the book cart I'd left next to the counter that afternoon. Determined to push Reed from my mind and give my entire focus to readying the store for Donna. But my earlier excitement was long gone as I pushed the cart out to Lala's truck, and when I lowered the tailgate and got my first real look at the surprise, I paused.

"Oh, Emma, what did you get yourself into?" I murmured.

I should've known when it took two men to load them all into the truck that I wouldn't have been able to do it myself.

After another few seconds of hesitation, I steeled myself and reached in, grabbing for the first bubble-wrapped surprise.

"Jesus," I wheezed when I barely managed to move it an inch. Another tug and another rush of air, and I nearly collapsed on top of the pile. I pushed myself up on the tailgate, head lowered as I silently cursed tattooed men and heavy surprises.

"Need help?"

Heat raced across my skin. My chest pitched with my sudden inhale. I slowly looked to the side to see Reed standing there, eyes hard and jaw locked tight, colorful arms folded over his broad chest.

"I thought you were leaving." There was no bite behind my words, but it sounded like I couldn't catch my breath.

Stupid, fickle emotions.

His eyes darted from the bed of the truck to me. "Was. Then I saw you pull that cart out here." He cleared his throat, head slanting slightly. "Lala called earlier. Said she was here and needed a lot of help."

My eyelids slowly shut. The air left my lungs on a slow exhale. "Of course she did."

He made a frustrated sound in the back of his throat. "Don't think I've ever noticed this place before."

"No one has." I gave him a tight smile when I opened my eyes, then looked at the store. "But they will."

They had to.

I swallowed back the last of my pride and straightened as I turned to face Reed. "Yes."

His eyebrows lifted in question.

"I need your help."

Without a word or indication that he was going to, he leaned into the truck, lifted two of the frames from it, and set them on the cart.

Like they weighed nothing.

After making two trips to get all ten inside and spaced out on the floor, Reed looked at me curiously. "What are those?"

A smile pulled at my mouth that I couldn't contain if I tried.

I hurried over to my bag and pulled out the plans I'd drawn up and the knife I'd brought, ignoring Reed's amused expression when he saw what was in my hand. "I have a drill and hammer too. So, I'd be careful if I were you."

A laugh punched from his chest. Full, rich, and easily one of the best sounds I'd ever heard.

I ignored it.

The way it made my smile widen . . . the way it made my stomach flutter and chest expand . . .

I knelt down by the first frame with a calming breath and carefully cut through layer after layer of bubble wrap, then eased the covering off the picture. The air fled from my lungs when I stood and took it in, more perfect than I could've imagined.

"Who is that?" Reed was beside me, his voice gentle as he studied the picture on the floor.

I cleared my throat and gestured to the picture of a thirty-something Donna, sitting with her back to her husband's chest. Both wearing bright smiles and their best clothes.

Something about that picture, about them dressed to the nines but curled up together on the floor, had tugged at me the instant Donna showed it to me.

"That's Donna and her husband. All the pictures are of her, her parents and grandparents . . . this is her family's store."

Most were taken within the store. One was of the store-front when it first opened. Some were of the family all piled together. Another was of Donna laid out while her husband sat near her, reading aloud.

It might not have been what Donna was thinking of when she'd said she wanted art for the store, but from the pictures she'd shown me, this was so much more than a store. It was a place where two generations of her family had been raised.

And I hoped hanging these pictures would give it that extra, homey vibe.

Once they were all unwrapped, I stood back, trying not to let the emotions tightening my throat get the best of me.

"Now to hang them."

There was one for every divider between the floor-to-ceiling bookshelves. The one of the store when it first opened would go up behind the counter.

When Reed didn't respond, I looked over at him.

Heat and need raced through me at the look in his eyes—at the wonder on his face. As if keeping himself away from me was a constant struggle. As if all the energy swirling around us and through us was something he still felt.

But in an instant, the look was gone and replaced with a mask of indifference. He cleared his throat and looked at the pictures, voice cold and edged with frustration. "You planned on hanging these?"

"Yes. That's why I had them ordered."

His head shook, the movement all agitation. "No, I meant *you*. *You* were going to if I wasn't here."

I wondered again what I had been thinking getting frames like those, but I would figure out a way. I always had before.

"I still intend to," I said firmly. "You're more than welcome to leave."

"Jesus, Emma," he hissed. "Why?"

"Because I can handle this on my own," I said quickly.

"You brought them into the store, and I thank you for that. Now you want to leave, and I don't need your help anymore. So, go."

"No, *why*?" he shouted, his sorrow mixing with his plea. "Why are you doing this? What did I do?"

I sucked in a breath to yell at him but held it until I was calm.

Held it until all that pain and anger I'd felt when I heard those women talking poured out in my hushed declaration. "You know why."

"I told you, I don't," he said adamantly as I walked toward the counter, needing space from him, needing to breathe. "If you would just—"

"Stop pretending," I cried out as I whirled around on him. "Stop doing this!"

He lifted his arms out to his sides, his face utterly hopeless. "Doing *what*?"

"Hannah," I said through clenched teeth. "I know about Hannah, and I hate you for doing that to me. For pushing and pushing and weaving deeper into my life when I never wanted you there in the first place. Begging me for something I told you I didn't know how to give you."

I didn't realize I was crying until a sob ripped from my chest.

I dropped my head into my hands as shame and horror and embarrassment swirled through me like poison. Tears fell into my palms like tiny bombs that I couldn't stop no matter how hard I tried.

I continued back until I was pressed to the counter, a trembling mess of need and loathing and confusion, then slowly slid down to the floor, keeping my face buried in my hands.

"I found these," he murmured not long after.

"Why won't you leave?" I asked as I dragged my fingers across my cheeks and then let my hands fall to my lap.

"You say that a lot."

Another subdued sob climbed up my throat at his disappointed reminder. I glanced from the box of Kleenex beside me to where Reed stood a few feet from me, face set in frustration in a way that fascinated and terrified and intrigued me.

"Emma, I don't understand," he went on. "You already knew about Hannah."

"I can assure you, I did not. You would've never known any part of me, I never would've let you kiss me, I wouldn't have—" I quickly swallowed back the rest of the words that had nearly broken free.

I wouldn't have given you a piece of my heart.

Discomfort pulsed from him as he rubbed at his jaw. "You came to my house that first night we met, which you very clearly let me know about the next morning in the coffee shop."

My stomach churned and clenched. "That was—" I jolted when the heavy double doors opened and four guys came walking into the store.

I scrambled to standing, refusing Reed's hand when he offered it, my stare darting from them to the men working outside and back again.

"We're not open . . . yet." My words trailed off and ended on a breath when the men caught sight of us and one of them called out Reed's last name.

Nick.

Looking from him to the others, I nearly tripped over my

feet in my attempt to back away and slammed into the counter.

Because even though I'd only caught a glimpse of one of the other men before, I had no doubt he'd been standing beside Reed last Thursday night—the night everything had gone so horribly wrong.

"Cops," I rasped. "They're cops."

There.

Alone with me.

In the one place that had felt special and untainted to me just minutes before.

No, no, no.

Reed was in front of me in an instant, blocking them from my view. Concern and regret etched on his traitorous, deceitful face.

"Get away from me." I meant for it to come out harsh, but I wasn't sure he could even hear me.

"Emma, don't," he softly begged. "I asked for their help after Lala called me."

"You brought them here. You brought *them*."

"These are my friends. These are people I know and trust," he explained pleadingly.

"Get them out," I demanded, "and leave with them."

Reed reached for me when I started for the long hallway leading to the office, grasping my arm as I passed by. "Emma—" His fingers slipped away and his hands were already lifting in surrender when I twisted and shoved my hand against his chest.

The words, "Don't touch me," lashed out as instinctively as the defensive move and as cold as the glare I cast his way.

But when I reached the office, I heard his quick steps closing in on me. The door to the office slammed shut a few seconds after it should've, and I turned to find Reed in the room with me.

Hands fisted at his sides, body vibrating with barely concealed energy, looking like he was about to explode.

"Why won't you *leave*?"

"Because I love you," he said boldly and without reservation.

Taking another chunk of my heart.

As if I could afford to lose another part of it to him.

As if I weren't currently standing on a cliff, being dragged to the edge by demons, fighting not to fall.

"I love you, and we're never going to get anywhere if you keep pushing me back. If you don't let me in. If you keep hiding every goddamn piece of yourself from me." With each sentence, he took a step closer until he was in my space.

"I told you," I cried. "I told you, there is no getting past *you*. And you will not want me when you know where I come from. I cannot give you what you want."

"What if you're wrong?"

"How can I be wrong when all I see when I look at you is a lifetime of pain and fear and so much hate that burns so deep, I nearly choke on it?"

He rocked back a step.

Shock and pain and denial radiated from him and crept toward me.

"That's all you see?" he murmured so low I almost couldn't make out the words.

A sob broke free at the lie he so easily accepted.

My knees threatened to give.

But I forced myself to stand strong.

"Everything about you represents man after man that played a part in ruining my childhood. My life. You are everything I swore to get away from and never go near again." My words twisted with remorse when I offered them in the only version of truth I had left. "I look at you, and I want to hate you."

But I don't know how . . .

The words sat heavy on the tip of my tongue, begging to be freed, but I swallowed them back.

The corners of his mouth tipped up in a strained, wounded smile. "Still?"

My heart wrenched with shame and regret as I held his stare and kept my head high.

With a sharp nod, he started for the door.

Stop him.

Stop him.

Stop him.

A hard knock sounded on the door just as Reed gripped the handle. He opened it with so much force, I was sure the door would've smacked into the wall if he hadn't caught it with his shaking hand.

"Hey." A guy I had yet to see looked from Reed to me, then awkwardly glanced away when he realized he'd just walked in on something he shouldn't have. Slanting his head in my direction, he said, "There are some guys here with doors for you."

I replayed his words in my head a couple times before they finally registered. "*Oh.*"

With all the pain and lies and the storm of emotions and need begging me to take back everything I'd said, I'd managed to forget what was going on outside the office. The rest of Donna's surprises—new doors to seamlessly continue the flow between her beautiful bay windows was one of them.

"Right. Right . . . okay."

As soon as the guy walked away, I looked at Reed, but he was standing back, holding the door open wide and staring at the floor.

There were so many things I wanted to say. Things I wanted to confess and things I wanted to declare. But they all jumbled in my throat, choking me with the damage I'd already caused.

It's for the best.

If I thought it enough, maybe soon I would believe it.

With a defeated sigh, I walked from the office, stopping in the doorway when Reed spoke.

"That night you heard Hannah . . ." he began, voice like gravel, "that was the first and only time I've ever done anything with her."

A shuddering breath tore from me at the mention of her.

I hated that I wanted to believe him. That I wanted to believe the sincerity in his pained words when I'd heard the girls talking about it . . . when his best friend had confirmed it.

"She and a friend were talking about the two of you at Lala's—about the details of your 'relationship.'" I informed him before glancing over my shoulder to look at him. "Nick even said he saw her at your house *the other day*."

Reed just stared at me with a mixture of confusion and devastation that tore at my chest. After a while, a sad huff left him, one of his brows ticking up knowingly. "Rowe," he muttered as if everything finally made sense to him. "If you'd just told me that night, I could've explained everything then. I could've *fixed*—" His jaw ticked as his stare dragged away. "But I guess it doesn't matter, right?"

His name left me on a pained breath as the pieces of my heart I'd given him splintered.

His steel-gray eyes met mine. "You have people waiting for you."

I looked away before he could see the newly building tears and hurried away. My mind and heart so twisted up that I didn't even register the four men standing around the pictures and talking over the sketch I'd done as I passed them to head outside. So clouded with my pain and confusion that the men installing the doors had to repeat questions and simple statements multiple times.

But just before the doors were finished being installed, the fourth and final surprise was delivered and hung over the doorway. The sign, giving the bookstore its first, real name: Morrison's Books. And seeing it there helped ease some of my heartache and brought back my earlier joy for the store.

When I finally walked back in, half of the pictures were already hung, and they were even more perfect on the walls.

Reed glanced over his shoulder from where he stood with Nick beneath a ladder with a frame in hand, the smile falling from his face when he saw me there.

I'd done that. And nearly every part of me hated myself for it. The other parts had me walking away.

Without apologizing.

Without begging him to understand.

Without telling him somewhere beneath the fear, I'd fallen in love with him too.

TWENTY-SEVEN

REED

The five of us finished hanging the pictures not long after Emma had come back in. When the guys started heading for the door, I lingered, my stare drifting toward the hall Emma still hadn't reappeared from like a man drawn.

Fucking siren.

I needed to leave.

For both of us, I needed to head to my truck and do everything to avoid seeing her again. Especially after all the shit we'd already been through that day.

By far the worst encounter we'd had when I'd already thought nothing could top last week at Lala's. But I still felt myself being pulled toward her. Felt myself being called in that direction because I had lost my damn mind. Clearly.

"You coming?" Butler called out. "We're gonna grab some food."

I looked at the guys, then glanced at the painters still working out front.

I rocked back a step and nodded toward the hallway that

led to the office. "I'm going to let her know we're headed out."

Butler hesitated, looking like he either wanted to drag me out or stay behind with me. But a few seconds after the others left, he followed.

I waited until he was out the door before heading to the office, my steps slowing the closer I got. As if my brain and my heart and my body were all at war with wanting to go to her and wanting to avoid another fight.

Avoid hearing those words leave her lips again.

"Everything about you represents man after man that played a part in ruining my childhood. My life. I look at you, and I want to hate you."

I knocked on the office door as I opened it, my eyebrows drawing close when I found it empty. "Emma?" I called out as I shut the door and started back down the hall, stopping when I noticed a hidden set of stairs for the first time.

After glancing around the vacant hall, I climbed the narrow staircase and came out into a loft. Eyes quickly taking in the small end tables and the soft glow from the lamp on the opposite side of the room from where I stood. The couch that was positioned away from the large chairs that were situated on either side of a bookshelf and the most beautiful woman I'd ever seen. Heels discarded beside where she sat next to a tower of empty boxes while she pulled books from another.

My heart faltered under the love and pain that flooded me just from looking at her.

She stilled from reaching into the box, her back tensing just before she glanced over her shoulder. A ragged yet relieved breath escaping her when she saw me.

"Jesus, *how* are you so quiet?" she demanded breathlessly. "And what are you doing up here?"

"Sorry." I held my hands up in a calming gesture and rushed to continue before she could follow up with something similar to any of the things she'd said earlier. "We're done. Everyone's gone. I don't think you should be in here alone without locking the door since the painters are still outside."

She blinked quickly. "Right. Yeah . . . yeah, okay."

I nodded and stepped back. "Goodbye, Emma."

As soon as I began turning, she said, "About earlier—"

"We don't have to do this," I said with a laugh that revealed every ounce of my pain. "You explained yourself well enough. Seeing me is clearly something that bothers you. And I knew from night one—I did—but I just . . . fuck. There was something there that made me think that changed for you."

Her soft face crumpled. "Reed . . ."

"But it didn't. Now, this is a small town, so I can't make any promises, but I'll do what I can to make sure we don't cross paths again."

A shocked breath ripped from her and her chin trembled.

"Maybe that will make it easier for you." Pressing a hand to my chest, I forced out a huff. "It sure as hell will make it easier for me."

"Wait," she cried out when I turned. The sounds of her scrambling to follow filled the loft, but I needed to go.

I had to get out of there before I did something like pull her into my arms and try to remind her what we were like together. Show her I wasn't like every man she'd come across in her life.

Beg her to realize that I was different.

"Reed, *wait*," she pleaded, grabbing hold of one of my hands just a few steps from the top of the stairs.

I stopped as if I'd run into a wall the second her skin had touched mine, the contact like a shock straight to my system.

When she continued, her voice trembled. "Please . . ."

I glanced over my shoulder when she didn't go on, but her brows were drawn tight, her face pleading with me in a way that said it all.

Please don't go.

Please understand.

The same push and pull we'd been trapped in from that very first night, perfectly displayed in her eyes.

Turning, I gently pulled away from her, my own pain reflected on her face as she looked at her empty hand. "Tell me I'm the only one haunted by thoughts of you and me together, Emma. Tell me you don't want me."

Hesitation and need warred in her eyes.

That push and pull. Hurt and craving.

It was maddening.

But even before her lips parted, she looked as if just the thought of admitting the truth had her stripped. Exposed in a way she'd never been.

And that terrified her.

"Lie to me, Emma."

"I was wrong," she choked out as her hand pressed to her stomach. "I've been wrong. I was—God." A broken laugh that lacked all amusement fell from her lips. "I've been doing exactly what my grandma claimed I was: Projecting my life and my experiences onto you, and that wasn't fair to you. I know that, and I'm sorry. I'm sorry for hurting you, for what I said . . . for everything. I truly hate that *sorry* doesn't feel like nearly enough, but I *am* sorry."

"You've *been* doing that," I said, voice a soft murmur as I took in her pleading expression . . . the sorrow there. "I could handle that, Emma. I was there, trying to help you through that. But I can't help you *wanting* to hate me. And you seeing every man that ruined your childhood and life when you look at me? I can't stop that. I can't fight that."

Her jaw trembled, her beautiful face creasing as a lone tear slipped down her cheek. The sight of it tore through my chest, rough and jagged.

I swallowed past the tightness in my throat and tried not to let it show how this was breaking my heart. "So, goodbye, Emma."

Turning, I took the last steps to the stairs, feeling all her pain and longing explode behind me, amplifying my own.

"It's almost impossible for me to trust men," she said just as I'd taken the first step down. Voice soft and strained and shaky with a fear that had absolutely nothing to do with her hatred of men.

This fear? I felt it . . . it was different. It was the kind of fear that swirled in my chest like a poison each time she pushed me away.

And it stopped me in place.

"Even more, I don't trust any man with a badge or tattoos."

My head dropped, hanging low for a few moments before I turned to lean up against the wall. "I know that, Emma."

I watched as her entire spirit seemed to shudder as the walls she'd built around herself fell with a weighted breath. "Then why do I trust you? How can I be falling in love with you?"

TWENTY-EIGHT

EMMA

Reed's head snapped to the side, eyes piercing mine from where he waited at the top of the narrow staircase. Searching. Begging.

Guarded.

I'd done that too.

"I do want to hate you," I admitted. "I do, and I hate it even more that I can't. Your job—yes, Reed, I hate your job. But it . . . it goes so much deeper than hating what you are. Everything goes so much deeper than what you think. And even with it all, I can't help but hate when you aren't there. I ache when I push you away, and I feel alive when you're near me."

"But?" he asked after a moment, the word soft and filled with worry.

"But it's engrained in me," I admitted, my breaths turning shallow as I revealed things I'd sworn would never leave my lips again. "My mom was—I told you she wasn't much of a mom, but she wasn't a good person. She was a junkie, always looking for her next fix and the person who could supply it. I was only there for the ride because people felt bad for the child. People wanted to *help* the child. Some of the men she dated and married were into drugs, some weren't, but she somehow always found a man who was covered in tattoos."

Ice crept through my body, making me jerk with the sudden cold.

As if Reed could sense the change coming, he stepped back into the loft.

Slowly.

Hesitantly.

When I continued, my shamed revelation was soft and uneven. "She somehow always, *always* found a man who had a thing for little girls."

Reed's eyelids slowly slipped shut. His jaw flexed.

"If she was with a man at the time of being arrested, she told the officer that man was my guardian or father. The arresting officers never listened when I said they weren't—when I said what my mom's boyfriends and husbands were doing to me. And why would they?"

His eyes flashed open and narrowed in confusion. "They should have listened," Reed said adamantly. "They should've taken you away. Any cop knows better. Every claim is supposed to be looked into."

"*Supposed* to be." I nodded faintly. "But no one listened when it was my word over their friend's . . . their supervisor's."

Reed dragged a hand over his face as it paled with realization. "They were officers?"

"She went through a phase of dirty cops when I was young," I said through clenched teeth. "And I was *always* left with them—with all of her boyfriends and husbands. Left with assholes who wanted to 'play games' with me." A shudder ripped through my body as the haunting memories tore at my mind. "Like I didn't scream at them and fight until I was finally strong enough to protect myself when I was a teenager."

"Emma," Reed whispered as he staggered back a step until he bumped into the wall. His head shook slowly, and I could see it dripping from his expression. That look as if, of everything he'd imagined, he hadn't imagined *that*.

"But throughout my life with her, I had to protect my mom whenever cops showed because she either couldn't, or wouldn't, protect herself. I watched countless cops trade sex with her instead of arresting her. And as I got older, they started looking at me as if they expected it of me because I was her daughter."

At that, Reed went utterly still.

Unfocused stare on the floor near my feet.

Jaw clenched so tightly I thought it might shatter.

"Wherever we went, wherever we lived at the time, my mom gained a reputation with the worst kinds of people and law enforcement. There were always shady people coming to and from our RV, always illegal things happening inside. It wasn't difficult for a cop to come in and find something worthy of arrest, and I was an easy target because I was the one left to clean up while my mom went out or was passed out."

Pain and fury seeped between us in the tense quiet. "What happened?" Reed demanded after a while, eyes meeting mine.

"If my mom was there, she stepped in—mad that their focus was on me instead of her. If not . . ." My stare drifted as flashes burst through my mind, tormenting me. "My mom's boyfriends and husbands were no longer a problem, but when a cop comes onto you the way they did me, it's harder to turn them down . . . harder to fight them off. They threaten you with charges, like assault on an officer. Assault with a deadly weapon that you don't even have."

A huff burst from Reed—his lips twisted in a sneer.

"So, I figured out how to turn on their mics," I whispered, shame coating the confession even though I wasn't at all ashamed of what I'd done to protect myself. Maybe it was just that Reed now knew where I'd come from, what I'd grown up in, and I hated that he could see my demons.

For a long while, Reed just stood there, letting my past sink in and haunt his mind the way it still did mine.

"I want to find every one of them and put them in the ground." The declaration was said so low, I wasn't sure Reed meant to say it out loud at all. He lifted his head, grief and wrath lining his face. "Emma, I'm so fucking sorry. I'm sorry for what you went through and what happened to you. I'm sorry you had people who hurt you instead of helped you. I'm sorry they stole pieces of you until you were forced to harden and bury the rest. If I could, I would take it all away. If I could, I would make every one of those pieces of shit pay."

"I know."

"Lala . . . she said something the other day," he murmured, his head slanting subtly. "Said she couldn't imagine what had to have happened to bring you back to her." His eyes searched mine, silently vowing to somehow fix this. "This happen again? Recently?"

I sucked in a stilted breath, my head feeling all kinds of light as those wraiths swarmed me.

Wrapped their arms around me.

Held tight as their icy fingers trailed over my mind and down my spine.

"Different," I managed to say through my thin breaths.

I'd been saved before anything could truly happen. Yet, somehow, it'd been worse because it had been entirely unexpected. Because I'd foolishly thought I'd been respected by the person I worked for. Because, for once, I hadn't been Joslin Wade's daughter.

No dirty life surrounding me, bringing the foulest people and expectations.

I'd just been me.

I'd just been Emma.

Worse, because part of it was here, surrounded by the people I cared for and who cared for my family.

I moved to the couch, not sure how much longer I'd be able to stay standing, and sank heavily to it as I began telling Reed everything.

From when my mother took off for the last time to saving up to move and working my way up in Manhattan. How I'd fallen in love with the city and my job and how it'd felt like I found the life I was always meant to have. All up until that last night.

Cutting myself open wide and baring my soul in the most terrifying display of trust I'd ever made.

"They were laughing as they fought over who was going to go second and third and so on," I said, jaw shaking fiercely as I revealed that night.

Reed looked like he was made of stone as he listened.

Stare vacant. Every muscle tensed beneath his tattoos. One arm folded over his chest. The inked fingers of his other hand clenched into a tight fist against his mouth.

"They were holding me down because I'd been fighting too much, and my boss was undressing me and talking to me. Saying I needed to relax and do my job." I choked over the last word, my head shaking these tight, fast jerks as bile rose. "The strippers they'd hired came in just as he was reaching for his belt. A few of the guys chased them down when they bolted—I don't know what happened to them after that. The remaining guys panicked, and I ran."

At that, Reed's eyes shifted to me and his hand lowered. "Who are they?"

My body sagged with a heaving breath. I'd talked about so many people and hinted at more.

"Any of their names, I want them." When my head began shaking, his voice was all gravel and lethal intent as he begged, "Emma."

"What will it change?"

"It can't change what happened to you, but something needs to be done," he said firmly. "An officer abuses their badge? They need it taken away and to pay for whatever they did. Some asshole gets off on raping people—touching *children*? He deserves what's coming for him in prison. Someone touches *you*? Emma . . ."

I studied the pain and sorrow in his eyes as the grief in his voice slowly wrapped around me, trying to comfort me.

"I can't," I said softly.

"Emma—"

"No, Reed, you don't understand . . . I *can't*." I looked into his pleading expression for long moments before shrugging helplessly. "Boyfriends and husbands came and went so quickly with my mom. The only names I remember were near the end, and nothing happened with them. Nameplates on the officers she *didn't* date? That wasn't something I ever focused on."

He nodded after a moment, then said, "Your boss. His friends." The words prompting, expecting.

Defeat and anger pushed through me, mixing with the betrayal and pain from that night and the worry that came from having Jarrod Davis so close. "It doesn't matter."

"Yes, it does."

"I *can't,*" I cried out, my eyes burning with the threat of tears. "Reed, don't make me do this." When he started to protest, I stood up, trembling hands lifted in a silent plea for him to stop. "I've tried. I've done that before. I've put my trust in those kinds of people, and they stole a piece of my soul every time. Do not make me do this."

Reed rocked forward, only to stop. "Can I come to you?"

My chest shuddered with a ragged exhale when I realized just how far back I'd taken us.

When I nodded, he crossed the distance between us slowly, gray eyes searching me as if he were approaching a wild animal. "I'm not gonna make you do anything," he said softly. "I will *never* make you do anything you don't want to. Understand?"

"Yes."

I eyed the space he'd kept between us when he stopped as if he was forcing himself not to come any closer, then looked up at him, wanting to say so many things and not knowing how.

That I was sorry for everything.

That I was thankful he'd come closer rather than running.

That I was more terrified than I'd ever been because I'd just handed him every part of me. Every demon, every tattered piece of baggage, another chunk of my heart . . .

And I hated how vulnerable it all made me feel.

The urge to protect myself was so strong, but the fear of watching him walk away again was stronger.

"Thank you," he said reverently. "Thank you for trusting

me with what happened to you. If I could, I would take it all away. I would—God, Emma." He pressed a tattooed hand to his chest. "It's crushing me to know what you've been through. To know I can't help you because I only seem to hurt you."

"Reed—"

"I get it," he said quickly. "What you see when you look at me. Why you pushed me away so many times. I get it." A wounded laugh crawled from his chest. "I get it."

"Reed . . ."

A pained smile crossed his face. "It's like you said . . . you won't be able to get past what I am." He gestured to the side before his hand fell like a weight. "I love what I do. I've wanted to be a cop my entire life because my dad and uncle were my heroes growing up, and I wanted to be exactly like them. But even if I wasn't in this line of work, it's a part of me, Emma. It's in my family, it's in my blood, and that will remain a wall between us."

My head shook quickly but my voice was weak when I spoke. "I've wanted it to remain a wall between us, and I told you, I hated that it wasn't. That I was falling for you so easily despite the fact that you embody everything I've learned to fear. But that doesn't mean if you push past my defenses, they disappear. That doesn't mean they don't flare to life and suffocate me when, suddenly, I'm in a place alone with a handful of cops," I said pointedly.

Understanding and a lethal sort of calm settled over him, his dark brows pulling low over his eyes.

"I don't want a man who wears a badge and carries a gun. I don't want a man who is covered in tattoos. I didn't want a man at all." I shrugged because he'd known all those things from the beginning. "But for every reason I had to keep you away, there were more that had me dropping my guard with you. That had all those reservations slipping away. That doesn't mean I'm not haunted by things I never wanted anyone to know."

My tongue darted out to wet my lips as my stare fell to the floor between our feet, my body vibrating as I struggled to voice my fears. "I've never wanted to be touched by someone the way I want to be touched by you. And I want more. But what if every time is like that last morning? Because the only times I've been touched—" I swallowed thickly, my face crumpling when I looked at Reed.

His understanding shifted to sorrow before fading to nothing. Just *nothing*.

I nodded in acceptance and choked out, "I also told you there wouldn't be getting past what you learned about me."

"I want to destroy the people who hurt you," he ground out. "I want to erase what they did from your memory. I want to show you why you're *wrong*—why nothing you could tell me would make me want you any less. I want to show you what it's like to be adored and worshipped and loved. But right now, I feel like I'm dying because I don't know how much worse I've made it for you."

"You haven't."

Disbelief poured from him as he scrubbed a hand over his face.

"Who's Kira?" I asked, finally voicing the question that had swirled around and around for days.

His hand fell, his eyes narrowed on me at the abrupt change. "What?"

"Peter—" I swallowed thickly, my head shaking as I tried to explain, "When Peter showed up in my room, you looked at your phone to see his messages."

Reed nodded, the movement all hesitation as he waited.

"There was a message from her."

"'Come home?'" Reed asked, voice tight. When I nodded, he let out a huff that was all aggravation mixed with understanding. "That's why you shut down that morning . . . isn't it?" His stare bored into mine. "Next time, talk to me."

"Who is she?"

"She's my sister—one of. She's one of my sisters," he explained, sounding weighed down. "She sends that same text all the time, but that's a whole lot of shit we'll get into another day. Not today. Not after everything you just told me."

"*That*." My head bounced softly before shaking. "That is the only thing that can possibly be described as something you've made *worse* for me during these weeks. When I saw that message and heard Hannah talking, it felt like my initial assessment of you was being proven right, and it hurt." I pressed my hands to my chest. "Hurt more and hurt deeper than I ever could've expected, and I felt stupid. So stupid for letting myself fall. For ignoring every one of my principles. And I couldn't give you the chance to do it again."

"You still feel that way?"

My body seemed to crumple even though I didn't so much as flinch. "No. But my instinct was to push you away before you could do anything again. Today, my instinct was to push you away even though, deep down, I know you wouldn't have brought anyone here for any reason other than to help. My instinct will *be* to push you away . . . and now that you know where it comes from?"

"You keep saying shit like that as if what you endured could make me walk away," he said, voice grave. "But even before I knew what happened to you, remember that I've seen you react to a lifetime of pain. I've felt that push. There's a difference in what you're talking about and you forcing me out before I can touch your heart. Because I've felt that push too, and you made sure I knew it was absolute."

He took a step forward, still leaving a few feet between us that felt alive with the energy that always swirled around us, his jaw tense as he took me in. "*You* can make me walk, Emma, not your past. And if you hadn't noticed, I'm right here."

My heart was pure chaos as I studied Reed's distressed eyes. "What if it gets to be too much?"

"Gets?" A breath that edged on laughter left him. "Emma . . . you already frustrate the hell out of me." He held a hand between us, palm up. An invitation. "But I've never wanted to be frustrated by someone so badly in my life."

"Is that supposed to be a compliment?" I asked as I placed my hand in his slowly, tentatively. The tips of my fingers brushing across his palm before I gave him all of me. That wild pounding of my heart feeling like it just might escape my chest when one of his fingers curled, teasing the sensitive part of my wrist.

His eyes searched mine, the depth in them shouting that I should've known it was. "You have a shield that is as sharp as razors and as cold as ice, and it's infuriating because there's no getting through it. But watching you slip it off for even a minute?" His fingers slid up my forearm before slowly making the path back to my hand. "It's enough to bring me to my knees because I know that's you coming to me. That's you trusting me. Those seconds and minutes and hours are you giving me insights to you that I don't take for granted."

Oh.

Reed's voice softened to a whisper when he repeated,

"There's a difference in the way you push. I get that all of this is hard for you and new—I swear, I do. But you have to try to talk to me when shit like Kira's text or the Hannah bullshit happens." His throat shifted with a forced swallow as he studied me. "Emma, I'll help you come back every time you shut down and shut me out. But you push me away on a personal level? That's you retreating somewhere I can't follow."

I nodded slowly, my breath tumbling past my lips when he closed the last of the space and placed his forehead against mine.

"Thank you for trusting me with your pain," he said again, words washing across my lips and wrapping around my heart. "You didn't owe me any of your past, but I would've given anything to have it—to understand you."

A little shiver danced down my spine as one of the memories tried to break free, but I pushed it back and closed the box tightly, forcing myself to breathe. Let myself feel the comfort and warmth he was offering, and I'd been missing.

"I'm sorry for hurting you." The words slipped out unexpectedly and effortlessly. The truth of them filling the space around us and causing his hand to tighten on me for just a moment. "I'm sorry for the things I said." My head shook quickly against his as I confessed, "I hated thinking of you with her—with anyone else."

"I wish you would've talked to me," he said softly, an ache lingering in his words. "Hannah was sitting outside my house a couple weeks ago, waiting for me, wanting to talk about starting something between us." He placed a hand on his chest and quickly added, "I said no. I told her that night between us was a mistake, I even apologized to her for it. She was upset and started to leave, then asked if it was because of you. She'd heard about you and was clearly pissed there might be something between you and me. I didn't deny it, but I didn't confirm it either because you still had a ten-foot wall between us." He drew in a slow breath as the hand on his chest slipped around my back, holding me close. "Nick lives a few streets away from me. He told me he saw her waiting when he was driving home."

"Oh," I murmured as I thought back to that morning in a new light.

"Yeah. It all makes sense now though. Because Rowe was being weird as hell in your room, then he was waiting for me at the bottom of the stairs and kept looking up like he was expecting you to be there. He said, 'If I make it here in time for breakfast, I always bump into Hannah, which means she's probably on her way.'" Reed shrugged. "I don't give a fuck what Hannah does, so when I just stared at him, he told me that it had already made it to the fire department about Hannah and me."

My stare unfocused as jealousy roared to life in my stomach.

"I said something like, 'That took a while,' because that kind of news usually spreads around town as fast as it happens. People were talking about you and me before we even began," he explained. "Anyway, he looked disappointed as hell, but he just left without responding. I couldn't figure out why it was such a big deal because he'd already known about that night with her. I'd even told him that you'd heard her. But I didn't think much of it because she doesn't mean anything to me and then everything fell apart with you." He blew out an exhausted breath. "I'm starting to think what he'd heard—what I'd unknowingly confirmed—was that I was *still* sleeping with her."

"I should have talked to you," I said after absorbing his side of it all, the words laced with my regret. "But that isn't me—that isn't who I am. I don't trust or give chances or forgive easily. Still, after everything, you deserved that chance."

"Emma . . ."

Apologizing to a man had never been in my nature before Reed. If it had been anyone else, I wouldn't have bothered.

But I was sorry.

Sorry for blaming him for the days of pain and anger. Sorry for the things I'd said and assumed.

"Reed, I'm sorry."

The hand on my back tightened in response.

"I've missed you."

He pressed his forehead harder against mine for a moment, his eyelids squeezing tight before his eyes were boring into mine. "Tell me not to, and I won't. But—"

"Kiss me."

Reed's mouth was on mine in an instant.

Soft.

Sure.

A slow claiming of my heart and my soul.

Then he was cradling my neck and tilting my head back, deepening the kiss and stealing my breath in the most devastating way. Demanding everything I had to give while pouring out all his love and anger and desire and sorrow.

"I love you," he breathed against my lips. "I'm not going anywhere."

TWENTY-NINE

EMMA

"Oh good, you made it," Lala said from where she was standing just feet from the front door, casserole dish in hand. "Let's go. You won't need your bag."

My body sagged and ached for my bed after the physically exhausting week and emotionally exhausting day with Reed, but I just asked, "Where are we going this time?" as I dropped my bag inside the entryway and stepped back onto the porch.

"Next door—it's our monthly church potluck. Nora's already there, I just came back to grab this last one." She lifted the dish in explanation as she started down the steps. "I wasn't sure if you'd be home in time. Or home at all . . ."

"Because you tricked Reed and me into being at the same place again?" I asked bluntly.

She tsked, all feigned offense. "I would never do such an outrageous thing."

A weary smile tugged at my lips. "I'm thankful for it, Lala."

She stopped walking at that, hope and surprise lighting her features. "Is that so?"

I blew out a slow breath, shrugging nonchalantly as I did. "Of course. He got everything put up. The store's all ready now—all of Donna's surprises look great." At the tick of her eyebrow, I listed my head and conceded, "We needed that. Really, thank you."

She *hmphed* as she continued next door, but her smile grew as she asked, "Well then, where is this boy we've been missing so much?"

"He's working, and don't act like you haven't still seen him every day."

Lala studiously avoided responding but tsked again when we were walking up the path to the house. "When are you going to give up those heels?"

"Never."

"They're dragging."

"I'm exhausted, Lala," I reminded her, trying not to sound like I was falling asleep just answering the question.

"Bet you wouldn't be as exhausted if you wore sensible shoes," she muttered as she led the way up the porch.

I didn't respond, just fixed my expression into something I hoped looked a little more alive than I felt as I knocked on the door for her . . . only for my face to fall when Ron Butler answered.

I knew—I *should* have known from everything I'd been told.

I'd already known they lived next door. Lala *told* me she went to church with the Butlers.

How could I have missed putting it all together before then? What had Jarrod told him after I'd left the meeting? What had Ron put together from it?

His stare slid from me to Lala, features polite and not giving any indication that I'd *run* from his office just weeks before. "Come on in," he said fondly, taking the dish from her and scooting back to let us by.

Once she'd passed him, already chatting with the other people mingling inside, his eyes locked on me.

"Ms. Wade," he said, my name coming out in a soft, careful sort of way that had chills skating across my arms. "Good to see you again."

"You too," I murmured, caught off guard at the reaction and the way my mind was screaming to get away from him when there was nothing about the man that had given me pause before then.

"Emma!"

I turned, eyes widening when I saw Leah coming toward me, holding her swollen belly.

No, no, no . . .

"What are you doing here?" The demand was out of my mouth before I could remind myself to take a breath—to be kind. Because it wasn't Leah I was afraid of seeing.

It was the man I'd realized she was married to.

She gave an awkward little laugh as she gestured to the room we were in. "This is my parents' house. I live just next door."

Ice crept around my stomach. "You . . . you live next door?"

"Yeah." An uncomfortable smile pulled at the edges of her lips. "I wanted to tell you—you know, to come say 'hi' or something. But my brother thought you might need time." Her worried stare darted away as she mumbled, "He might've been right."

"No," I said quickly. "No, of course not. I'm sorry. I

just . . ." I fumbled for anything that might help me backtrack and gestured toward the door. "I'm so sorry. I haven't been sleeping well, and I've been working nonstop. I honestly think I might be asleep on my feet."

Her spirit brightened in an instant, a sweet laugh bubbling free. "You poor thing. My momma just finished brewing some coffee. Why don't you follow me?"

"Actually, is there a bathroom I can use?"

Hide in. Take a minute to collect myself. Breathe . . .

"Of course." She took my hand as if she'd known me forever and led me through the room and to the front of the hall. "Last door on the right." With a gentle squeeze of her fingers around mine, she said, "I'll get a mug ready for you," and started to release me only to tighten her grip.

When I looked back at her, her expression had changed entirely. Eyebrows drawn close together, eyes darting around us in worry, and a distant pain hidden deep in her eyes. "Thank you," she whispered as she stepped close. "So much."

"I don't . . ." My head slanted as confusion built.

"What you did for Peter." She pressed her lips together and looked around us as if checking to see who might be within hearing distance. "That was so kind. I can't thank you enough. Just . . ." She gave me another squeeze before pulling away. "Thank you."

I stood there for a moment, watching her waddle away as her obvious pain and love for another man made me ache for her. Made me ache for them both.

And then Ron caught my attention from where he was watching me from half a room away. In an instant, those chills returned as warning bells rang far too loudly even though he was laughing at what someone else was saying.

Once I was in the bathroom, I turned on the cold water and held my wrists beneath the faucet. Eyes shut as I focused on breathing. Telling myself repeatedly that I was being dramatic. My exhaustion was making me overreact because of who his son-in-law was.

That was all.

That's all, I mouthed as I shut off the water and let my hands drip-dry over the sink.

Determined to pull it together, I pushed from the counter and inhaled deeply, feeling my defenses form around me like armor as I left the bathroom.

The air rushed from my body, and I turned, already swinging for the person dragging me to the open doorway opposite where I'd been. But my first and second attempts were easily blocked as I came face to face with Jarrod Davis's unnerving grin.

"Ms. Wade," he whispered as his grip tightened on me.

"Let go," I said through gritted teeth.

"See, I can't do anything about you being just a couple houses away because there are eyes that see everything. But then you come to me—" He twisted his body and slammed me up against the doorframe with his hip when I tried to knee him. "Women have always thrown themselves at me, but ever since you . . . I've craved the way you fought."

"Fuck you."

"Yeah . . ." His grin widened. "I've been craving *this*."

"Touch me, and I'll kill you."

His eyes danced over my face, showing every bit of his enjoyment. "Ms. Wade, by the time I touch you, you'll be begging me to fuck you."

My stomach rolled and a tremor of fear ripped through me.

From the way his eyes flared, he felt it, and he was taking it the wrong way.

"You have a wife," I reminded him, voice all seething hatred as I fought harder against his unyielding hold. "A very pregnant wife who is in this house. I'm sure she'd love to know—"

"What?" he demanded, the unspoken warning lingering between us for a few seconds before he challenged, "Try me, Ms. Wade. Who do you think silenced those strippers? Who do you think destroyed all evidence of any of us being in the building that night?" He dipped his head closer and closer despite how I tried to get away from him. "Being me has its perks. Having Ron as my father-in-law has more."

I went still.

Horribly, sickeningly still.

"I told you, you can't touch me, but you and I both already know exactly how I can touch you."

I couldn't breathe.

I was shaking as flashes of that last night in Manhattan tore through my mind, and *I couldn't breathe*.

"I look forward to more of your defiance." His nose trailed up my cheek. "Even more, I look forward to when you submit."

"I will ruin you," I vowed, the threat weak.

His hushed laugh brushed against my skin. "Until next time, Ms. Wade," he whispered, leaving me trembling against the doorframe as I battled demons.

Once I managed to shut them away, I hurried out of the hall, my steps faltering when I entered the living room to twice the amount of people that had been there when I'd left for the restroom.

"Lala," I said when I found her, voice strained. "Lala, I have to go. I'm so sorry."

Her laughter from the group conversation she'd been in faded when she saw me. "Emma, what's wrong?"

"Nothing, I'm just—I'm tired. I'm so tired, I have to go," I repeated.

"Of course." Her head bobbed. "Of course, do you need us to come with you?"

"No," I said quickly. "I'm just gonna go to sleep. Have fun here. I'll see you tomorrow." The last words were a frail assurance as I backed away, already turning to go. Then I was out of the house and walking as quickly as I could without looking like I was running away.

But when I reached Lala's house next door, I didn't stop. I kept walking until there wasn't even a hint of my demons or memories or Jarrod Davis. Until my mind was blissfully blank and my feet ached.

Releasing a slow exhale, I slipped off my heels and gathered them in one of my hands as I finally looked around, trying to gather where I was.

My gaze caught on the cross-street sign a few yards ahead that was the last turn on the way to Reed's. I glanced that way before starting down the handful of houses that separated his house from me, never hesitating in knowing that was where I needed to go. The last time I'd wandered around after bumping into Jarrod, I'd ended up next to Donna's store—exactly where I needed to be. This was no different.

"Hey."

I glanced to the side as I neared the pathway leading up to the house, stopping when I saw Peter rounding his car with a small bag in hand. "Hi."

He pointed to the house. "Reed's working."

"Oh, I know. I can wait outside."

A snort left him as he met me at the porch, his brows drawing close. "Wait, did you . . . did you walk here?"

"Um . . ." I glanced down at my bare feet, my head slanting as I realized how odd that seemed now that I was standing there. "Yeah."

"You and Lala good?"

"Of course." I gave him an incredulous look. "I just started walking and ended up here."

He studied me for a moment before accepting my answer with a nod and heading up the steps. "You hungry?"

"Really, I can wait out here. I was planning on it."

"Okay, first, *no*. Second, I think Reed would kill me if I left you out here. Third, I'm starving. So, we either eat out here or in there. I vote in there, which means we're going in," he said with a cheesy grin as he unlocked the door.

"I guess we're going in," I murmured as I followed him.

"Does Reed even know you're here?" he asked as he took long steps through the front of the house to toss his bag into his room, expression equal parts expectant and concerned when he started back my way.

"No, I don't have my phone or anything." When the concern deepened, I reminded him, "Like I said, I just started walking and ended up here."

Peter nodded, stare drifting to the floor for a moment. "Is it going to be surprising to him that you're here?"

My mouth parted to once again tell him that I hadn't even known I was coming before I realized what he was really asking. The last he'd known, Reed and I weren't speaking.

"We talked today," I informed him. "Figured everything out and worked through a lot."

The corners of his mouth lifted. "Good." He started for

the kitchen and clapped his hands together. "All right . . . food. What do you want? Because I can really only make two things: Pasta and pancakes." He patted his flat stomach. "We like breakfast here."

"Then, there's your answer."

His hand lifted in a placating gesture. "Don't just let me have what I want—you have to eat too."

"I like breakfast," I said with a shrug.

I'd survived off dry sandwiches for most of my life. I liked most things.

"I knew I liked you," he called out as he moved deeper into the kitchen, already opening up cabinets and grabbing things.

I hung back, watching him for a minute before asking, "Did you need any help?"

"No, ma'am, you can just hang out."

I glanced around, feeling uncomfortable. Like there were layers of dirt and filth on me, and if I touched anything in their house, I would leave traces of my past and Jarrod.

"Emma."

I looked up and stilled when I found Peter watching me as if he could see straight through to my darkest secrets.

He pulled his phone from his pocket and held it out. "Do you need to call Reed?"

My head moved in slow shakes before moving faster. "No, of course not. I just—" An awkward huff burst from me.

"What? And for the love of God, don't say 'nothing,'" he added quickly, then shot me a look. "I was married, I know how women work."

I swallowed back that exact word and thought of every way to get out of explaining it when he was looking at me like he already knew what I was thinking. "Can we just forget about it?" I asked. "It's inappropriate and rude."

A soft laugh rolled up his throat as he leaned back against the counter, waiting expectantly. "I was in the military. You can't shock me."

I held his unwavering stare for a while longer before relenting, shame dripping from the whispered words. "I need a shower."

"Cool. We have two of those," he said indifferently, then jerked his chin toward the far end of the house. "Reed has one connected to his room."

"Peter, it's really—"

"Not a big deal," he said firmly, then started pulling out a large skillet from one of the cupboards. "Food will probably be ready about the time you're done. Grab some of Reed's clothes."

I stilled. "What?"

"Did you want to get back into your clothes after showering?" he asked slowly, uncertainly, then hurried to add, "You can. You can do whatever you want. But you can also borrow some of Reed's." He gestured off to the side. "You can even wash your clothes if you want, I don't care. Do whatever you need to."

"I'm just gonna go shower," I mumbled softly and hurried off in the direction I remembered Reed going the other morning.

Once I'd found my way to his room, I slowed, taking in his intoxicating scent and surprisingly tidy room. All masculine furniture and dark colors, the same as the rest of the house. A guitar was propped up in the corner, but that was the only personal touch. No pictures . . . nothing that would hint at the person who lived in that room.

Not that I had room to talk, but I also hadn't had a normal life.

Personal touches had been a luxury I could never afford to keep around.

Going back to the bedroom door, I locked it even though nothing about Peter gave even a hint of alarm. But neither had my boss or Ron Butler at first.

Heading for the attached bathroom, I paused next to the lone, tall dresser in his room. Contemplating Peter's suggestion for longer than was probably necessary before finally setting my shoes down beside it and opening the top drawer to search for something to wear.

By the time I was walking back out to where the smells of pancakes and bacon were filling the house, I was in a pair of Reed's athletic shorts and one of his shirts. The layers of grime had been washed away along with the feel of Jarrod's hands on me, and I'd fortified the walls in my mind.

"I texted Reed," Peter said before he ever turned around, as if he had superhuman hearing. "He wanted to know if you were okay." He grabbed a couple large plates and started for the table, catching my eye as he did.

"What'd you tell him?"

"What I knew so he could determine that on his own."

I nodded, watching as he set the food down and then went back to the kitchen. "Thank you for letting me shower. I know that was really—"

"Not a big deal," he reiterated.

"—inappropriate," I finished under my breath. I eyed the new bowls of food he set down, then glanced at the awaiting plates in front of two of the chairs. "Are more people coming?"

He snorted. "Told you I like breakfast." Grabbing a carton

of orange juice from the fridge, he came back and nodded to one of the chairs. "Sit."

I stepped closer, movements hesitant as I pulled back the chair opposite his. "Is this weird?"

His brows lifted as he watched me, seeming to wait for me. "Does it feel weird?" he asked, drawing out the question awkwardly and pulling a muted laugh from me.

"No, but I feel like it should. Being here alone with you, eating with you, when you're Reed's best friend and roommate."

Peter just shrugged. "Reed knows you're here. You still remind me of someone who is like my little sister. So, I'm good with not making it weird if you are."

After another second of contemplation, I sank into the chair, and he followed, groaning appreciatively as he did.

"Thank God, I'm so hungry."

"You don't need me here to eat," I said pointedly as I took one of the pancakes and pushed the plate toward him.

"Do you see how much I made?" he asked, tone deadpan.

"That isn't my fault, and you said you liked breakfast!"

He scoffed. "Yeah, but . . ." He looked pointedly at all the food littering the table. "Get to eating."

"Now you sound like Lala," I mumbled as I grabbed some of the eggs, hash browns, and mixed berries. "This is more than just pancakes, by the way."

"It's a package deal," he explained, waving a strip of bacon around to gesture to everything before passing the plate to me.

I hummed, all amused disbelief as I poured syrup over my pancake. "So, what would've been in the 'package deal' if I'd picked pasta?"

Peter let out a groan and said something that sounded like

best bread of your life around the bite he'd just taken, then launched into stories of his time in the military with Reed and Nick—all of which were heavily laced with humor. Most of them revolved around food, and, somehow, many ended with one of them comically naked, but the bond they had was evident in each one.

After listening to him talk for hours, I understood all too well why Reed and Peter had followed Nick back to Colby when they'd all gotten out of the military. They were family.

It also helped me understand why Reed viewed Leah as family and assumed Peter did too. But Peter didn't look at me or talk to me the way he did Leah. I was sure of it.

"I really appreciate it," Peter said when I finished putting the last of the dishes away. "But you didn't have to do that."

I shrugged and turned to lean against the sink. "You made everything."

"Yeah, but you're a guest," he said, repeating what he'd said multiple times when I'd started cleaning up. Only this time, the slow words faltered. "Hey, why don't you go crash?"

I looked over at him, my eyebrows drawing close. "What?"

"You look like you're about to fall over, and it's . . ."—he glanced at the oven before looking at me—"sort of late. Go crash."

"Here?"

"Were you planning on staying awake until Reed got home?" he asked a little uncertainly.

"I . . ." I blinked slowly because I hadn't thought that through. I'd just been planning on waiting outside.

"Reed also happens to have a bed," he said pointedly.

"I'm not going to sleep in his bed when he isn't here."

He gave me an incredulous look. “Why? I mean, you already took a shower here, and that’s super, fucking inappropriate.” A loud laugh left him when my mouth fell open in horror. “Kidding, Emma. Go to sleep.” When I wavered too long, he asked, “Would you feel better if I asked him?”

I narrowed my eyes and pushed from the sink in response, earning another laugh from him.

But when I passed him on the way to the hall leading to Reed’s room, I stopped. The question I’d been pondering for over a week pouring out as I turned back to face him.

“Do you love Leah?”

He slowly looked over his shoulder, everything about him different than it had been just seconds before. As if he was holding himself so tight so he wouldn’t react in ways he wasn’t supposed to—in ways he *couldn’t*—when it came to just hearing her name.

Clearing his throat, he gave a subtle nod. “We, uh . . . we all do.”

“No, are you in love with her?”

“She’s married.” His answer was immediate and filled with a horrible mixture of pain and loathing.

“That isn’t what I asked.”

His jaw worked for a while before he muttered, “I won’t answer that.”

I nodded, accepting the truth he’d given me within his non-answer. “I’m not going to tell Reed, I just . . .”

Just what, *Emma?*

Because I didn’t need to be interfering in people’s personal lives. I didn’t need to be revealing what was waiting to fall from my tongue—that wasn’t what I did with people before Reed, and I wasn’t going to start then.

I hadn’t even told Reed about Jarrod.

But I also saw the way Leah looked at Peter, how she looked just talking about him . . . and I knew how kind she was to complete strangers. How unsuspecting she was when it came to her disgusting husband—to her marriage.

"She shouldn't be in the marriage she's in." The air rushed from my lungs at stepping over a line that shouldn't be crossed.

"Yeah, you don't have to tell me that," Peter ground out. "Her husband's an asshole."

My head shook because I could hear in his tone that whatever Peter knew about her husband, it wasn't what I knew. "Peter, he is not a good man," I confessed on a reluctant breath.

He pushed from the counter and twisted to face me, a crease forming between his eyebrows as he studied me.

I started backward, raising my hands apologetically for what I'd already said.

"Emma—"

"Goodnight," I said quickly.

"Emma, what do you know?" he demanded, *begged*, as he started after me.

"That's all. I shouldn't have said anything," I stammered as my steps quickened. "Please stop following me!"

He stopped as if he'd run into a wall, hands slightly lifted at his sides to show he wasn't moving. "Emma, *please*."

"It's like you said—he's an asshole. That's all," I said through clenched teeth, body shaking slightly as I regretted ever saying a word. "I'm going to bed. Do not follow me."

"I'm not gonna follow you," he assured me. "Just tell me if he's hurting her."

I reared back, caught off guard by the thought. "No. I mean . . . I wouldn't know. You know her better than I do."

He nodded, some relief seeming to ease his rigid stance as he put more distance between us. "I'm sorry for . . ." He gestured to me, then gripped at the back of his neck. "Sorry. Goodnight."

"Goodnight," I mumbled as I hurried to Reed's room, locking the door behind me and sagging against it as regret and shame wove through me.

THIRTY

REED

I quietly stepped through my room, eyes having already adjusted to the dark from the house, and stopped at the foot of my bed when I saw her there.

In my bed.

The sight of her did crazy things to my heart. Like she *belonged* there. Like I would do anything to come home every morning to her waiting for me the way she was then.

I rounded the bed, a little smile tugging at the corner of my mouth when I saw her heels placed carelessly next to my dresser, and carefully eased myself onto the edge of the bed beside her. Prepared for when she would wake.

Her reaction.

Her shoving palms.

I could've changed first to make this easier, but if we were ever going to survive, we had to make it through her haunting past. The uniform I was wearing was one of them, I already knew. But this was bigger: Being woken in the middle of the night to find someone else there.

It was why I'd just had to pick my own lock—not that I'd

been surprised. Rowe had called to let me know he'd scared Emma. So, I'd been expecting a locked door at the very least.

"Emma," I whispered as I trailed my finger down her jaw. Quickly catching her hands in mine when they shot out in front of her and then easing them to my chest so she could still feel me. "It's me."

A shuddering breath left her, her body sagging against the bed and hands relaxing beneath mine. But seconds later, her hands went rigid. "Are you in uniform?"

"Yeah. Do you think you could help me with something?" I lifted one of her hands and passed my mouth across her palm. "You have to get out of bed for it." When her hesitation bled through the dark, I asked, "Trust me?"

Her hand relaxed in mine. "Yes."

With another kiss to her palm, I stood from the bed and walked across the room to turn on the light, warning her just before I did. A groan building in my chest when I turned and saw her stumble adorably out of the bed.

In my clothes.

"Jesus," I muttered.

She stopped, blinking quickly against the light and then dropping her head to see what I was looking at. "Oh, I'm sorry. I—"

"Don't." My head shook. "Don't be sorry." I just hadn't thought it was possible to want her more than I already did until that moment.

And I needed a clear head for what we were about to do.

Forcing my stare away, I glanced to the bathroom only for my attention to drag back to her as I said, "Uh . . . closet. We have to go to the closet." I suppressed another groan and headed to the walk-in closet attached to the bathroom.

When she followed me in, her eyes fell on everything in

there, taking it all in before focusing on me—making sure not to look at my uniform. "What do you need help with?"

Holding my hand out for her, I waited until she took it and then stepped back to where my empty shelves and hooks waited. "I want you to see that what I'm wearing can't hurt you," I said softly. "That it's just objects and clothes."

Emma's expression shifted from confusion to worry in an instant. "What?"

"I want you to take off my uniform."

"No." Horror dripped from the small word, her eyes widening with a terror I couldn't begin to understand.

"Trust me."

"I—" A stuttered breath heaved from her and her tongue darted out to wet her lips.

"Hey," I breathed, curling my hand around hers and pulling her closer. "I can't take away what happened to you—no matter how much I want to. But I can try to change what you see when you see *me* like this. I can try to give you other memories." Placing her hand on my chest, I waited until her eyes met mine and repeated, "What I'm wearing can't hurt you. Let me show you that."

"Okay." The word was a reluctant whisper, but she pulled her hand from mine and reached for the buckle on my duty belt like she knew from experience that it needed to go.

And I fucking hated it for her.

I stilled her hands before she could reach it and said, "Radio first."

"Oh," she said numbly, looking for where it was attached to the belt and me.

"It's already turned off, you won't hear anything," I assured her as I showed her what to do and where to place it to charge without actually touching anything.

She nodded as I spoke, stare focused on her trembling hands and what she was doing. Once she was looking at my duty belt again, she stopped, glassy eyes taking in everything still attached to it. "Um . . ."

"All that stays on," I said gently, then pointed out the keepers that held the belt in place. "There's a few of them."

Once those were on a shelf and she was placing the heavy belt on the waiting hooks, she turned back to me just as the first tear slipped free and ripped at my soul.

"Cheek," I whispered as I lifted my hand and cradled her face in my palm, wiping at the tear and searching her eyes.

She sucked in a deep breath and leaned harder against me.

"You're so strong." I wrapped my other arm around her waist and lowered my forehead to hers. "I love you. I love you, I'm sorry."

Her head shook against mine before nodding fiercely, and then she was pressing her lips to mine. The kiss a soft, tentative claim of her own. "How do I take this off?" she asked, touching the camera on my chest.

"Pull it."

She gasped when the strong magnet finally released, a startled laugh dancing on her lips that I leaned in to taste.

"Just an object," I repeated against the kiss as she blindly placed it on one of the shelves.

Her fingers wove through my short hair, her eyelids squeezing tight for a few moments before she stole one last, slow kiss, then cautiously asked, "Now what?"

I walked her through the rest, letting her do every part of it and watching as her eyes cleared and her shaking gradually ceased. The entire process taking a hell of a lot longer than I'd meant for it to as our kisses came more and more frequently. Lingering and heating until I had my hands filled with her, and she was dropping my Kevlar vest on the floor.

"I don't think that's where I was supposed to put it," she breathed against my mouth, whimpering when I caught her bottom lip between my teeth.

"I don't give a fuck." A growl raked up my throat and my head dropped back when her fingers went to the top of my pants. "Jesus Christ, Emma, you need to stop."

"You said—"

"I know what I said, but if we're gonna stop, then I need you to stop."

She looked at me, all wide, passionate eyes as she carefully resumed undoing my pants.

"Emma . . ."

"It's just clothes," she whispered as she let them fall around my ankles, tossing my words back at me. But this was different.

The slight hitch in her voice, the waver of fear and wonder and *need* said this had changed to something else.

"We don't have to do this," I said as she reached for the hem of my undershirt. "We don't have to do anything."

"Kiss me."

My mouth was on hers before the words finished leaving her, claiming her and pouring every ounce of my soul into that kiss. All demanding lips and teasing tongues and nipping teeth as I grabbed the back of my shirt and finished taking it off for her.

The muscles in my stomach twitched and tensed as she lightly ran her fingers down my skin, my cock aching when she stopped at the band of my boxer briefs—trailing along the edge before tentatively dipping just inside.

"I want you." Her head lowered to my chest. "I want to try."

I pressed my fingers under her chin to lift her head. "We don't have to do this."

"I want to. I want to with you."

I studied her features, all that need and desire and fear, before lifting one of her hands so she could feel the absolute chaos she was inflicting on my heart.

Keeping her hand there, I slowly started walking her backward, out of the closet, never taking my stare off hers. "You push at any time, we stop," I assured her.

"I trust you."

I captured her lips, pulling her closer and turning her in my arms until her back was to my chest. Tilting her head back, I took and took and took from her until she fully relaxed. Falling into me and that kiss in a way that made me want to do anything to always be worthy of the trust she was giving me.

"I love you." It was a breath, a vow, all wrapped up in awe for the girl in my arms. "Now, open your eyes."

Once she was looking at me, I gently turned her head so she was facing forward and looking at our reflection in the bathroom mirrors.

"I'm in control of this," I said, teasing the slope of her neck with my teeth. "So, I want you watching. Seeing what we look like together and how fucking beautiful you are. Seeing how your body responds to me when it's something you *want*." I trailed my hands lower with each sentence until I was gripping the top of my shorts she was wearing.

Her eyes met mine in the mirror, wide with all that fear even as her cheeks flooded with heat.

"Pushing?"

"No."

Holding her stare, I placed slow, open-mouthed kisses down her neck and across her shoulder as I lifted the shirt she was wearing until my arm was banded around her waist, leaving her stomach exposed. My thumb brushed across her smooth skin as I gently eased the shorts lower until I was teasing where she was already bared for me and the material was one move from slipping past her hips.

The material fell and she slowly stepped out of it, eyes locked on mine in a show of trust that threatened to bring me to my knees.

I trailed my fingers along her stomach, watching her reaction as I went lower and lower and dipped between her thighs. A groan raking up my throat when I slid my fingers between her slick folds and pressed into her heat.

"Fuck," I muttered as I pressed my forehead to her shoulder, fighting the impulse to get lost in her when I knew I needed to be watching and feeling every response from her. But, Jesus, just the feel of her gripping my fingers was enough to make me forget my name.

I looked up as a tremor ripped through her body, but her expression had me continuing as I slowly pumped my fingers in and out of her. Giving her time to simply feel me before I slid them back through her folds and teased her clit. Holding her tight as half a dozen emotions flitted across her face before pleasure overtook them all. Building her up higher and watching this beautiful girl let herself experience what had been stolen from her.

Lifting one of her hands, she slid her fingers around the back of my neck, gripping tight.

"Pushing?"

Her head moved in quick, faint shakes as she tilted it back

and pulled me closer. Capturing my mouth in a fevered kiss when I eased my fingers inside her again.

I stepped back until I was pressed to the wall, releasing her waist and grasping her chin to lift her head higher, deepening the kiss as she began trembling. Gripping my fingers tight as I brought her closer and closer until she was arched against me and my name was tumbling from her lips on a plea.

I pressed my thumb to her clit, sending her spiraling. Shattering against me. Her lips parting with a breath of a moan and her fingers digging into my neck, branding me as I worked her through her first orgasm and into a second.

"Oh God," she cried out as her body shook from the force of it. Her head fell back to my chest and her pleasure-filled gaze weakly found mine in the reflection as I slowly brought her down and removed my fingers.

"Fucking beautiful."

The corners of her mouth lifted in an exhausted smile before falling. And then my groan was filling the room when she reached behind her, trailing her fingers over where my aching cock was pressed firmly against her ass.

"Emma," I said through clenched teeth, my eyelids shutting and my hands gripping her hips in warning when she reached the band of my boxer briefs. "Emma—*fuck*," I ground out when she teased the head of my cock as she pushed the material down.

Trailing my mouth up her neck, I forced my eyes open to watch her as I whispered in her ear, "You sure you want this?"

"I trust you."

Releasing her hip, I brought my hand to her jaw and tilted her head back so I could search her eyes. "Do you want this?"

I asked, the question coming out a harsh demand when her fingers wrapped around my length and stroked up.

Her throat shifted beneath my hand with a forced swallow, but her voice and eyes were clear when she said, "I want you."

"Need you to tell me what you want before I take this somewhere you don't want to go."

"Everything." She leaned up to press a faint kiss to my lips. "I want everything with you."

I captured her mouth and turned her around, holding her close as I walked her out of the bathroom and into my room, never pausing until we were standing just beside the bed.

"Push," I reminded her as I lifted my shirt off her body and lowered her onto the bed. Maybe *demanded* because I was terrified of hurting her . . . of ruining this gift—this trust—she was handing me.

"I know." Her hazel eyes softened when I passed my mouth across her palm and placed it against my fiercely racing heart for a moment before pushing off the bed.

My movements coming to a halt when I got my first full look at her.

"Do you have any idea what you do to me, Emma Wade?" I asked, voice soft and rough with the emotion that washed over me just looking at her because I loved her in a way I'd never loved anyone.

And she was there. Every shield stripped. Vulnerabilities laid bare. So damn beautiful it made my heart falter.

Her cheeks filled with heat, wonder and disbelief danced across her features for a moment before she cracked a grin and said, "I frustrate you."

A breath of a laugh left me as I grabbed a condom and tore open the wrapper, a surge of primal need racing through my veins at the shock she struggled to hide when I finished removing my boxer briefs.

"I, uh . . ." She stared unabashedly as I knelt onto the bed, slowly pumping myself as I watched that blush creep all the way down to her chest.

"You challenge and surprise me," I told her as I rolled the condom on. "You consume me."

Her stare darted to mine at the confession, a mixture of emotions flashing through them as I settled between her legs.

"You pushing?" I asked softly and covered her hand with my own when she placed it on my chest.

"I trust you," she whispered, her eyes filling with tears. "I love you."

Her claim could've stopped the world with the way it stopped my heart and stalled my lungs for those next seconds.

And then I was capturing her lips and tasting the remnants of her words as I slid my cock against her slick folds, pressing against her entrance and feeling the way she shook beneath me in anticipation.

I wanted to bury myself in her. Lose myself in the way she felt.

But I forced myself to grip the comforter, listening to every hitched breath and feeling the pressure against my chest as I slowly began easing inside her. Shallowly rocking and going a little deeper each time and trying not to lose my goddamn mind because she felt like heaven, and I wanted more.

"Fuck," I ground out, my teeth scraping along her jaw as I bottomed out and forced a whimper from her. And I knew I could've stayed there, her words echoing in my mind and her silent show of trust and love pressing against my chest, wrapped up in her, for-fucking-ever.

With a soft kiss to the same spot, I pushed up to hover over her and slowly pulled out before driving back in. The movements coming faster and faster until Emma's breaths were uneven and her eyelids were fluttering shut. Letting herself feel me and experience *this* without her fears and memories forcing their way between us. Losing myself in her a little more with each passing minute until I was gritting my teeth and fighting the fast-building pleasure.

I swallowed her surprised gasp when I lowered myself to her and switched our positions. "You're in control," I said against the kiss. "So, control it."

Her wide eyes bounced quickly between mine, her head shaking as she looked at me. "I don't know what to do."

"Yes, you do," I assured her.

Gripping her hips, I gently guided her, a groan breaking free at the feel of the new position. At the feel of her weight on me as she continued, the rocking of her hips pure hesitation until my hands began moving over her body—searching and teasing and learning. Kneading her breasts and torturing her nipples with my tongue and teeth until she was sitting back. Looking like an intoxicating mixture of sin and innocence as she began riding me. Hands pressed firmly to my chest, eyes heavy-lidded and full lips parted with her rough breaths. Threatening to send me over the edge as pleasure gathered at the base of my spine.

But I needed her there with me.

Reaching between our bodies, I circled my fingers around her clit again and again and again before focusing on the bud.

"Reed," she cried out, her walls clenching around me like a vise as she fell apart around me and forced me into my own orgasm. These weeks of hostility and pain and love magnifying the pleasure that barreled through me until all I saw, all I knew, was Emma.

Tremors rolled through her body and transferred into my own for long moments until she went lax above me. Easing onto my chest and resting her ear where her hands had been as her arms fell limply to my sides.

I trailed my fingers up and down her spine as I held her close, measuring her deep breaths, broken up every now and then by an errant shudder as we both came down. Lingering in the silence and the feel of each other.

"You okay?"

"I feel like I shouldn't be," she said after a while. "It feels wrong that I am." Putting her chin on my chest, she looked at me, eyebrows drawn close. "Does that upset you?"

"Me?" A soft huff left me. "No. And don't worry about me. However you feel when it comes to physical stuff is how *you feel*. It's not for me to have a say in."

Her stare drifted to the side as she weighed whatever was on her mind.

"Just say it."

"What if the next time's different?" Her eyes met mine again, worry seeping into them. "What if, the next time, I can't?"

"Then we won't," I assured her.

"You say that like it's simple."

"It is," I said firmly. "You know I want you—that isn't new, and it won't ever change. But this doesn't change what I know you need. It doesn't create expectations. You push, we stop. Always. Understand?"

Her eyelids slowly shut as she nodded and then rolled her

head to the side again, a deep, contented sigh leaving her as she did. "I didn't know you played guitar."

A soft laugh rumbled in my chest at the unexpected change. "Guess what? I play guitar."

She scoffed and pressed up to fold her arms over my chest and stare down at me. "Tell me something you think I should know about you."

I glanced over to where my dad's old guitar sat propped up in the corner before looking back at her. "My dad played and sang—"

"In a band?" she asked, surprise weaving through her expression.

"No," I said quickly as I pushed back so I was propped up against the pillows, careful not to shift her. "He's a cop."

"Oh, I think . . . I think I knew that," she muttered, trying to blink away the instinctive animosity that had been quick to surge forward.

I resumed trailing my fingers up and down her spine, trying to help soothe her. "I always wanted to be just like him, so I learned to play. I can't sing like him though. That's his," I said, slanting my head toward the corner.

"Will you play something?" Her eyes lit at the idea.

"There's actually something I need to talk to you about—it isn't bad," I hurried to assure her when that light dimmed and was replaced with a look I was beginning to know too well from her. "I forgot all about talking to you about it before I went to work yesterday. By the time I remembered, Rowe was texting me that you were here, and I didn't want to bring it up to you when I had a feeling there was something wrong." My brow furrowed at the memory. "Was there something wrong?"

"Can you finish what you're saying?" she pleaded in a hollow tone.

"I have to go to Florida today—home." I gripped her hips as I explained, "My parents are having an anniversary party that I promised I'd be there for. I have to leave . . ."—I glanced at the clock on the bedside table—"soon."

"Oh." She started pushing off me. "Why didn't you tell me before? I wouldn't have—"

"Will you come with me?"

Emma stilled, her eyes widening as she stared at me as if trying to make sure she'd heard me correctly. "What?"

"To Florida. Will you come with me?"

"To your parents'," she said slowly. "To their anniversary party." When I started responding, she shook her head. "Reed, I can't meet your parents."

"Why?"

She sat back, grabbing at the comforter and pulling it up to cover her bare chest as she floundered for her response. "Because it's soon, isn't it?" Her head shook. "I don't know how these things work, but isn't it soon? And I have the store opening next week. And they don't even know I exist."

"Trust me, they do." At her wide-eyed shock, I asked, "Where do you think I went last week?"

"Oh my God, what did you tell them?"

I leaned forward and cradled her face in my palm. "They know I love you. They know you pushed me away and they both thought I was an idiot for not being *here* trying to get you back. The rest?" I shrugged. "Emma, if you don't want to go, I won't make you go. But I can have you back for the store's opening, and I don't give a shit if anyone thinks what we do is too soon." At her hesitation, I said, "You opened up dark pasts and gave me all of you yesterday. Going home with me? That's the best way I can give you all of me."

She watched me for a long time before asking, "When are we leaving?"

A smile stretched across my face as I grabbed one of her hands and pressed a kiss to her palm. "As soon as we get in my truck."

Her expression fell. "Wait, what? We're driving?"

"It takes a little less than six hours to drive there," I explained as I climbed off the bed, bringing her with me as I headed for the shower. "Takes a lot more than that to get to an airport and fly there."

"But you—when was the last time you slept?"

That smile grew as I stopped and pulled her in for a slow kiss. "We used to have to stay awake for days at a time for missions. I'm fine. Are you?"

"I don't know. I've never met parents, and I wasn't expecting to meet yours because you said you didn't speak to them."

"I'll explain all that on the way," I said as I turned on the shower. "Don't worry, I think they already like you more than they like me."

"They haven't met me," she muttered, earning a scoffing laugh from me.

"You haven't met *them*."

THIRTY-ONE

EMMA

My mouth fell open as an audible breath escaped me, all shock and disbelief.

"I know," Reed said as he took a turn into a neighborhood that afternoon. "A lot to wrap your mind around."

That was an understatement.

After he'd taken a quick shower and tossed some things into a backpack, Reed had driven me to Lala's to grab what I needed and leave a note for her and Nora, and then we'd left. We'd been on the road within half an hour from deciding I was going with him.

To meet his parents.

We were just minutes away, and I still couldn't figure out why I'd agreed. I had no experience with this and didn't know anyone who'd gone through this sort of thing, but it felt weird to be meeting his parents when just twenty-four hours before, Reed and I hadn't been speaking.

At the same time, I didn't want to be anywhere else. I'd missed him, and I loved hearing about his life and his family—as unbelievable as it all sounded. The stories that helped explain *Reed*—the man who looked like heartbreak and had a gentle soul.

"So, *Kennedy's* husband disappeared," I said, the words coming out slow as I tried to put the story together in my mind. "And the next time you saw him, he was married to *Kira*—her identical twin."

"Right," Reed said as he took another turn.

"And the reason he disappeared was because your dad sent him undercover . . ."

"My dad and uncle Mason train people to go undercover," he corrected. "Rhys was already going, they just trained him."

I nodded as I fixed the story in my mind before my head shook quickly. "And Kennedy's just okay with this?"

"According to the rest of my family," he said with a shrug, then gave me a look like he thought it was crazy. "I haven't talked to her in years."

"Is she going to be there this weekend?"

"No," he muttered, sounding like that bothered him. "She and her husband live in California." He made an uncomfortable sound as he pulled up in front of a house. "Looks like you're about to meet everyone else though."

I looked around at the cars lining the driveway. "I thought their party was tonight?"

"It is." He jerked his chin in the direction I'd just been looking. "But those all belong to my family."

"And they're all cops?" I asked, breaths getting shallow now that we were here, and I was about to face them all.

Reed's gray stare focused on me as he held out a hand between us. "I would not have asked you to come with me if they weren't *good*. You are safe with me, and you are safe with them."

"Your dad taught you how to escape impossible situations after enduring psychological torture among a lot of other weird and disturbing things."

An amused huff bled from him. "I know. But after what I told you happened to my mom, can you really blame him?"

"You do."

He shrugged. "I resented him for it because I thought I was never good enough. But I can't help but think I would've done the same thing."

"You're going to make your future kids put together a disassembled rifle and fire at a target while you choke them out?" I asked dryly.

One side of his face scrunched up adorably. "Okay, no. I already told you a lot of it was fucked up."

A hum of acknowledgment sounded in my throat and ended on a soft inhale when he lifted my hand to press a kiss to my palm.

"But he did what he thought he had to. He made me who I am. I was a fucking good SEAL because of him, and if anyone ever comes after you?" His stare slowly searched my face, his voice lowering gravely. "They won't be able to get close enough to touch you."

I nodded and tried not to think about the things he didn't know.

The people.

"Ready for this?"

"No," I answered honestly, already reaching into the back seat for my bag. "But I won't ever be ready, so we should probably just go in."

His laugh followed me out of the truck, his expression all amusement and assurance as he rounded the front and reached out to take my bag. "It's gonna be great."

I let out a slow breath when he took my hand in his, my head listing as a thought came to mind. "If you're supposed to be this badass, or whatever," I began and elbowed his side when he scoffed, "why have I been able to hit you?"

His hand squeezed mine. "Each time, I could see I'd done something I shouldn't have. I was already backing away from you. All defenses down," he said seriously, but when he continued, a hint of amusement wove through his tone. "If you were the slightest bit of a threat, you never would've been able to touch me."

I believed it.

The morning we'd accidentally fallen asleep in my bed flashed through my mind as he opened the front door and led me inside. Reed's expression when I'd woken him had been terrifying in that second before he'd realized it was me. A chilling sort of calm beneath the lethal look in his eyes.

"Ready?" he asked again as the front door shut heavily behind us.

I sucked in a steeling breath and ran my hand over my uneasy stomach, the action bringing a smile to his face.

"I have no doubt they're gonna love you," he said before the sound of fast-approaching steps had him looking away, his expression filling with disbelief and wonder. "Holy shit."

I glanced in that direction in time to pull my hand from his and step away as a woman launched herself at him, her excited cry filling the entryway when Reed caught her and held her close.

"The fuck are you doing here?" he asked when he set her on her feet, keeping one hand on her shoulder and offering his hand to me in invitation.

"What do you mean?" She wiped at the tears slipping

down her cheeks, and it was then I realized how much they looked alike.

All dark hair and littered with tattoos, but her eyes were dark blue where Reed's were like steel.

"Dad said you weren't going to be here," Reed explained as he looked at me. "Emma, this is Kennedy."

"California-Kennedy," I said, realizing exactly why Reed had been so surprised.

A wicked grin lit up her face. "That would be me," she said before whirling around at the sound of the toddler running up behind her. Bending to scoop him into her arms and smiling warmly at the man who followed closely behind.

"Jesus," Reed muttered, voice thick as Kennedy stepped close to show off the little boy while reaching back to touch the large, tattooed man. "This is my husband. Liam, this is Reed and *Emma*, right?"

I offered a small smile of acknowledgment and tried to blend into the wall as the guys said their greetings. Wishing more than anything that I would've stayed in South Carolina.

Reed hadn't *talked* to this sister in years.

He hadn't seen her in longer.

He was meeting her husband and son for the first time . . . I shouldn't be there for that.

"And this is Chase," Kennedy announced, all affection as she pressed her nose to the blond-haired, blue-eyed boy. "Can you say 'hi' to your uncle Reed?"

"What's up, little man?" Reed asked, holding out his fist.

The boy gave a cheesy grin, showing all his little teeth as he gave an overenthusiastic fist-bump.

Reed gave a soft laugh, his voice tight when he said, "I would've been there."

"Dad told me," Kennedy said, all saddened understanding, then gestured into the house with her head. "Come on, Mom and Dad were just getting everything ready for lunch. And what do you mean he said I wouldn't be here?" She gave him a bemused look. "Why else would *you* be here?"

Reed grabbed our bags from where he'd dropped them and waited until I slipped my hand into his before following after them. "For their anniversary party."

Kennedy's brows lifted. "Their what?"

"Their—" Reed stopped walking, his tone dropping low. "There isn't a party tonight, is there?" When Kennedy tried to swallow back a laugh, he hissed, "Asshole."

As we passed through the living room, he set our bags on one of the couches and pulled me into his arms, his eyes searching mine as he brought our joined hands up to his chest.

"You got quiet," he said softly. "I can see those shields starting to form and I can see what you're thinking." Placing my palm flat against where his heart was beating strong and steady, he leaned closer until his forehead was pressed to mine. "You should absolutely be here. I wouldn't want to be here with anyone else, and I wouldn't want to be here without you."

Swallowing back all the reasons why he *should* be there without me, I simply nodded and let him lead me into the kitchen.

And went still when I nearly ran into a wall of muscles and tribal tattoos and *oh my God.*

The man didn't need an introduction or a uniform for me to know he was a cop. Everything about him screamed it.

And he was easily the most terrifying man I'd ever seen.

His stare darted over me, quickly assessing as he took a

careful step away and offered me a comforting smile that in no way comforted me.

"Emma, this is my uncle Mason," Reed said between calling out something to someone across the kitchen.

I nodded shakily and forced out something that might've resembled a greeting before I was excitedly greeted by Mason's wife and then released to continue meeting more people.

"Breathe," Reed said in my ear. "I swear to you, no one in here would ever think of hurting you."

"He was terrifying," I admitted, unable to keep the words in.

A scoffing laugh climbed up Reed's throat. "Yeah, he looks it. Fucking teddy bear, though. Just wait." He placed a reassuring hand on the small of my back and jerked his chin to where Kennedy's identical twin was sitting at the table, holding one of her newborn babies. "Let's finish introducing you to everyone."

"We're having a party?" Reed's mom yelled as we were walking over so I could meet her and her husband. Her wide eyes slowly shifted to where her husband was leaned up against the kitchen island, trying to hide his smile.

"That's what Reed said," Kennedy explained, waving her hand in our direction.

"That's what Dad told me," Reed argued. "That's why we're here."

Their dad's face scrunched up on one side, the exact way Reed's did, and their mom smacked his shoulder. "Logan Kash Ryan," she snapped, "is there something I need to be aware of?"

A breath of a laugh left him as he held out a hand toward

Reed. "I didn't know if he'd show up if I just said Kennedy was coming."

"Wow," Kennedy said dryly. "Thanks, Dad."

"Fuck you, old man," Reed said, grabbing a carrot from the counter and launching it at his face. But his dad caught it and threw it back.

"You're here, aren't you?" his dad challenged, a grin shaping his lips and mesmerizing me for a moment because it was like looking into the future with Reed.

Other than the years separating them, they were remarkably identical, down to their expressions and how they held themselves.

I jerked into Reed's side when a foam ball went soaring just past my face, then turned to find Mason with a large toy gun aimed at the kitchen. Eyes wide as he pointed at a sleeping infant, trying to pin it on him.

Reed's chest shook against me as he pulled me close. "Did I mention he's also a child?"

"Can we be clear that I don't need to prepare for a party tonight?" Reed's mom asked.

"No party, Sour Patch." Her husband winked when she glared at him, then turned to me, dipping his head in a nod. "I'm Kash, by the way. We've heard a lot about you."

"And we're really glad you're here. My husband just likes to make things difficult," Reed's mom said with an irritated sigh even though the corner of her mouth kept lifting with affection. "I'm Rachel." She placed a hand to her chest before gesturing to me with it. "Really . . . we're so glad you decided to come. Sorry we're not more normal."

A breathless laugh left me because I wouldn't know what normal was if it was placed directly in front of me. "You guys are fine," I hurried to say and watched another foam ball go soaring past me, landing in the pile of food.

"For the love of God, Mason," Rachel snapped. "I'm not making pancakes. Get over it."

Kash lifted his hands, looking past me. "What do you want from me? I tried."

I drew in a quick breath as things started making more sense. "Pancakes," I muttered. "I see where it comes from."

A rumble of assent sounded in Reed's throat as he pressed his mouth to my shoulder. "You hungry?"

"Starving, and that all looks so good." My gaze darted over the different bread, meats, cheeses, and vegetables laid out to make sandwiches, reminding me so much of Lala.

When Kash called out for everyone to eat, Mason asked, "So, Emma, how's our Reed treating you?"

My lips parted, and I desperately prayed that I didn't look as flushed as I felt as that early morning in Reed's bed flashed through my mind.

"Because we could kill him for you, you know," Mason went on, forcing a stunned laugh from me and effectively pushing away all thoughts of that morning. "Hide the body. No one would ever know."

"Jesus." Reed rolled his eyes, a wicked grin tugging at his mouth as he looked over his shoulder. "You could try."

Another foam ball sailed past us in response.

"Could I use your restroom?" I asked Rachel to get out of responding.

She gave me a look as if she thought I was funny for even asking. "Of course. There's one right next to Reed's old room —Reed, show her where you're staying. Let her get settled before she's forced to deal with us."

"Oh, that isn't what I—"

"Honey, did you somehow miss the middle-aged man shooting NERF balls because I won't make pancakes or my husband who lied about a party to get my son home?"

"I got him here," Kash said, feigning offense.

She sighed, her eyes rolling. "And the fighting hasn't even started yet."

My gaze drifted from Reed back to his mom in time to see her point from Kash to Reed.

"These two," she explained. "They can't be around each other long without fighting. And with Kennedy here . . ." Her brows lifted. "She's just like them, and they all fuel each other. One of them says something, and the others go off."

"She talks about us like we're a bad thing," Kennedy said from where she was setting her toddler up with food.

"And that's our cue," Reed said as he slipped his fingers through mine.

Rachel just winked as he led me from the kitchen, stopping to grab our bags on our way through the house to his bedroom that was so similar to the one in Colby—all masculine furniture and colors and unreasonably tidy.

"This is us," he said as he set down our bags on the edge of the bed.

My stomach dipped. "We're sharing a room?"

Reed stilled, his eyes taking me in, gauging my reaction. "Unless you don't want to?"

"But this is your parents' house. Isn't that . . . I don't know." I shrugged helplessly. "I don't know how these things work."

A breath of a laugh tumbled past his lips as he stepped back to close the door, his eyes narrowing playfully as he reached for me. "If my parents want you to sleep in another room, they'll make a point of saying it, and it'll be because they don't like you. Trust me."

"You realize I'm going to be worrying over them telling me to sleep in another room now," I said as I let him pull me into his arms. "Right?"

His responding laugh was rich and full and had a warm shiver moving down my spine.

"Oh my God, Reed," I hissed softly when he stepped back and fell onto the bed with me still cradled against his chest. "We can't—"

He silenced me with his mouth to mine, his lips moving soft and sure before he gave me the faintest tease of his tongue against my own.

"Gonna kiss you now, Emma," he muttered before capturing my mouth again. Kissing me until I was leaning into him and forgetting the world outside that room.

Until my legs were tangled up in his, and his hands were in my hair.

Until the only thing that mattered was Reed.

Every touch was slow as we undressed and he eased me on top of him. His strong hands gently guiding my movements between reverently learning the curves of my body.

Every thrust of his hips was powerful yet somehow still so tender when he rolled us over and settled between my legs again. Kissing me as if he needed me to breathe, and stealing all my breaths in return.

Every look was a silent claim and vow, slowly taking the rest of my heart until I knew I'd fallen for Reed Ryan in an eternal, irrevocable way.

THIRTY-TWO

REED

I woke to palms shoving me away, the fear exploding from her sliding over my skin like a disease as I fought the reactive instinct to being woken that way.

Gripping her hands and flattening her palms against my chest instead, I said, “Emma, it’s me,” as she whispered, “Oh God.”

I searched out the horrified gaze that matched her tone, her head shaking in apology.

“I’m sorry.”

“It’s fine.” I curled one of my hands around both of hers and slowly reached up to cradle her cheek in my palm. “Babe, it’s fine.”

Her chest shook with a ragged exhale before she lowered herself onto me. “Maybe I should just offer to sleep in another room,” she tried to joke and then stilled. “Oh God, how am I supposed to face your family?”

“What do you mean?” I asked as I wrapped my arm around her to trail my fingers up and down her back.

“They’re going to know what we’ve been doing in here.”

She sat up a little, looking around. "How long have we even been back here?" She inhaled quickly when I rolled us to the side so I could grab one of our phones off the floor, her eyes wide with shock when I settled back against the bed. "Thanks for the warning."

My lips twitched into a smirk that had her fighting her own smile. Glancing at her phone, I noted the time and then breathed out a laugh when I saw the message she'd just received a minute before.

Lala: Make sure you're feedin' that poor boy for me.

"We must've just fallen asleep—we only got to my parents' about forty-five minutes ago," I told her. "But I think I know what woke you." Turning the phone so she could see it, I watched as her eyes rolled before she dropped her forehead to my chest.

"Oh, Lala," she muttered before sitting back and shifting away from me. "That doesn't answer how I'm supposed to face your family. What are they going to think?"

"I don't give a fuck what they think."

"I do."

My eyebrows lifted, my grin widening. "Is that right?" Wrapping my arms around her waist again, I pulled her back to me. "The girl who doesn't care what anyone thinks cares about *my* family's thoughts?"

Her eyes narrowed for long moments before she conceded with a sigh. "Don't go reading anything into it," she muttered, but the ghost of a smile crossing her face offset it.

"Wouldn't dream of it."

A disbelieving hum sounded in her throat as she sat up, reaching for my hands to pull me off the bed with her. "Bathroom?" she asked once she was dressed again and stepping into her heels.

I watched as she rose a handful of inches, bringing her nearly eye level with me, a smirk tugging at the corner of my mouth when she sighed contentedly. "You comfortable like that?"

Her eyebrows lifted in question until I glanced down. "Not you too," she murmured. "Lala says something about my shoes every day."

"Just asking a question, Emma."

"As comfortable as I was in your clothes," she said, some of that shield slipping in as she turned and opened the door, leaving my room before I had the chance to stop her.

My eyelids shut as a curse slipped free.

After dragging in a steadying breath, I followed her out into the hall. Propping up against the wall with my arms folded over my chest and my head rested back.

"I don't know what Lala says, and I don't care what you wear," I began once she'd left the bathroom and met me where I was waiting halfway down the hall. "It was a question because they don't *look* comfortable, yet you seem like you're comfortable in them."

Her head bobbed a few times. When she spoke, her tone was soft and repentant. "Like I said . . . as comfortable as I was in your clothes."

"All I know is how much I liked seeing you in them."

"Is that right?" Amusement and mischief danced in her eyes and abruptly faded to shock when we exited the hallway. "What . . ." she whispered, steps slowing as she took in the scene in front of us.

A huff pushed from my chest as I listened to the razzing and watched my sisters' husbands trying to escape multiple zip ties and duct tape.

"What is going on?" Emma asked.

"They're escaping—*trying* to," I said, then gave her an unapologetic look. "This is my family. I tried to warn you."

"Dad, I thought you trained him," Kira complained, pointing to where her husband, Rhys, was still struggling.

My dad and uncle just raised their hands as if Rhys' ability to escape his current predicament hadn't been their responsibility.

Kennedy was on the floor next to Liam, trying to coach him through what to do.

"Cheating," I called out, gesturing to her.

"Fuck you, you would know!" she yelled back.

"Someone's still bitter."

She flipped me off.

"Cheating?" Emma asked softly, drawing out the word.

"Kennedy's always been mad that I've been able to get out so fast."

"Of this," Emma said doubtfully, gesturing to where the guys were in the middle of the living room—all the furniture having been pushed back to make room.

A rumble of assent built in my chest and turned into a rough laugh when Rhys managed to break through the tie keeping his bound hands and feet connected behind his back.

"You can get out of that?" she asked, voice still skeptical.

I glanced at her, a smirk slowly creeping across my face. "Did you not listen to the stories I told you on the way here?"

"Yeah, but there was never anything about being . . . hog-tied," she sputtered.

"This is nothing. This is more of a long-running family challenge than training." I slanted my head toward the living room. "Obviously."

Her gaze fell to my arms, studying and gauging before slowly drifting over the rest of my body.

"Are you checking me out, Emma Wade?"

Those eyes snapped back to mine and narrowed. "I'm just trying to figure out *how* it's possible."

"Ouch . . ."

A playful huff tumbled past her lips as her stare caught on my arms again. "You're well-aware that isn't what I meant. But the blond one," she said, looking back at the guys.

"Liam," I offered, never taking my eyes off her.

"Right. He's a lot bigger than the other guy—I mean . . . the other guy is really big too," she hurried to add.

"Are you checking out my sisters' husbands, Emma Wade?" I asked, voice all mischief with a hint of jealousy.

"I am not," she hissed, color rising to her cheeks as she turned so she was facing me fully. "I'm never going to be able to look at them again without worrying I'm checking them out."

My next laugh was sharper, fuller, and only built when she pushed her hand into my side. "Liam looks stronger," I admitted as I wrapped my arm around her. "But that won't give him the advantage. The girls can get out of them too. You just need to know *how* to break a zip tie—breaking the one connecting your hands to your feet is what makes it difficult."

I looked over when Kennedy bit out a curse to see Rhys free just as Liam was reaching for the duct tape binding his ankles together.

"Dad?" Kira asked, looking at him expectantly, but he and Uncle Mason were trying not to laugh.

My mom smacked his shoulder and glanced at the phone in his hand, answering, "Just under ten minutes."

"Is that bad?" Rhys asked from where he was sitting with his arms resting on his knees, looking exhausted.

"In general, or compared to when we were six?" Kennedy asked, laughing when Liam glared at her. Turning her stare on me, she gestured to the open living room. "Let's go, small-town."

My eyebrows lifted. "You don't want to do that."

"No?"

"I could get out of that three times over and still have time to watch you break free."

A wicked grin slid across her face. "What about between you and the old guys in the corner?"

Uncle Mason looked behind them as if there'd be a couple old men standing there. Challenge lighting up his expression when he realized she was talking about him and my dad.

"I understand if you're scared," Dad said with a shrug, already handing his phone to Mom.

"Scared you'll break a hip," I shot back easily, squeezing Emma closer to me before slipping away.

They were twice my age, but that didn't mean shit.

They'd trained all of us and still did plenty of daily training that kept them at military levels.

"Emma, honey, did you want to eat now?" Mom asked. "This will be over as soon as it begins."

"I wouldn't be so sure," Kennedy muttered.

"I'll wait," Emma said, voice hesitant.

I glared at Kennedy as I passed her. "I don't trust you."

She just lifted the zip ties and duct tape as if she had no idea what I was talking about.

Jerking my head toward Dad and Uncle Mason, I said, "Since you like to cheat . . . do theirs first."

A scoff left her as she went between the two of them, securely wrapping their ankles and then tying their hands, making sure the zip tie wasn't so loose they could slip out but wasn't so tight they could easily break free. Then loosely bound their hands and feet behind their backs.

"Satisfied?" she sneered as she turned to me.

I responded by lowering myself to the floor on my stomach, emptying my head of everything else other than the sound of the tape and how many times she was wrapping it. The feel of the ties—

"Cheating," I snapped when a second pair of ties went around my wrists.

"Just evening out the playing field," she said, sounding all kinds of proud of herself.

"I'll still get out," I said when she used two ties to connect my hands to my feet.

"Oh, I know." She knelt beside me, sliding one of her arms beneath my throat. "You know, my father-in-law owns a gym."

"That's great," I muttered as I took in her position and tried to anticipate what she was about to do.

"He trains MMA fighters."

I lifted my head higher and tried to move away when she curled her arm around my neck.

"I've gotten really good at my chokehold," she hinted wryly.

My dad barked out a laugh.

"Get him, Kenz," Uncle Mason called out.

"Let's see if you can get out before you lose consciousness," she said as if she were betting on the fact that I wouldn't.

"Wait, *what?*" Emma whispered, sounding horrified.

Liam waved us off. "I've learned to just go with it."

"But—"

"Babe." I waited until her wide stare shifted back to me, a small grin lifting at the corner of my mouth. "Trust me."

"All right," my mom called out, "in three, two, one . . ."

I sent Emma a wink just as Kennedy's hold tightened around my neck.

THIRTY-THREE

EMMA

"You need to sleep," I said to Reed that night as I took in his heavy-lidded eyes.

His stare shifted to me, the corners of his mouth lifting in a tired smile. "Yeah, I think I'm done."

Between the extreme and dangerous competitions that had continued well into the night, more extended family coming and going, arguments that were over as quickly as they began, and the laughter and food that never seemed to end, the day had been full. It had also been easy to get caught up in Reed's family and their obvious love for each other. Easy to see how everything about the man beneath the tattoos and uniform drew me in.

Reed pulled me closer on the outdoor lounge chair we were sharing, his voice dropping lower. "Think I can take you to bed?"

"Please," I said with a sigh, then glanced pointedly at where Kennedy and her husband were whispering not far from us—everyone else having already left. "Is it okay with you if we go?"

A mixture of irritation, disgust, and amusement darted across his face. "I'd rather not have to see them make out again."

As if on cue, Liam stood up and pulled Kennedy with him, holding her around the waist as if she were a rag doll. "Goodnight," he called out to us, all smiles as she cussed him up and down between her laughter.

"Fucking fantastic," Reed muttered. "Their room is close to ours."

A snort left me, causing me to laugh harder, then harder still when Reed glared at me. "I'm sorry, it isn't funny."

"All right, we need to get you to bed," he said, easily maneuvering me so I was standing.

"Says the guy who hasn't slept in days."

"I got a few minutes earlier," he said as he stood and pulled me into his arms. "And I'm also used to it."

I hummed some kind of assent as I let my forehead fall to his neck. My heart skipping and my head emptying of all thought when Reed grabbed one of my hands and brought it up to his chest, placing my palm against the steady pounding there as he began moving us. Slowly rocking to the soft music playing through the outdoor speakers and stealing my heart all over again as one song bled into the next.

His hand curled around mine as the other pressed to the small of my back, keeping me close to him in a way that was all subtle possession.

And I wanted it.

The way he waited for me to come to him, then held me close as if he wouldn't let me go. The comfort and safety I felt in his arms, the love wrapping around us, I wanted it forever.

Hours later, and the realization still had undiluted fear clawing at my chest.

"You okay?" he asked, his mouth grazing my cheek.

I hadn't noticed we'd stopped moving—that *I'd* stopped us—until then.

"I'm terrified," I admitted when every instinct was screaming at me to pull away from him. To leave.

His hands curled tighter. "Of what?"

"You," I whispered, my stare on our joined hands against his chest when he shifted away. "What you do to me and how badly I want this."

The corners of my lips lifted when his heart beat harder and faster beneath my palm in response.

"See what you do to me?" he asked, his voice dipping when he confessed, "When I look at you, I see the rest of my life."

My heart pounded out an unforgiving beat as a lifetime of watching empty promises play out had doubt weaving through my thoughts. "Don't say things you don't mean."

Reed's brows lowered as the hand on my back pressed me even closer. "So there's no confusion," he began, tone a low rumble, "I love you more than should be possible. I see our future when we're on the porch swing or when I listen to you walking up the stairs. I see my *wife* when I look at you." His mouth brushed across mine when his words pulled a stuttered breath from me. "That's how badly I want this."

The admission had a terrible effect on my heart and my mind. Joy and love clashing with fears and vows until my breaths were coming out quick and shallow.

"We are not your mom and every guy you watched her with," he said, sensing where my panic was coming from.

"But you . . . you can't know that," I said around the

wraiths gripping at my throat. "Just yesterday, we weren't even speaking. And it's soon. Isn't all of this too soon?"

Understanding and patience poured from him as he let me release my fears. "We weren't speaking because of a misunderstanding," he said gently. "And, Emma, people fight. But us? We're going to be different because you have walls and a hard time trusting anyone, including yourself. What matters is that you and I end up right here." He pressed me closer in emphasis.

"It's soon," I whispered, knowing the argument was weak, even against my own feelings.

"I'm not dragging you to a church, Emma," he teased, his smile flashing in the dark.

Amusement bled from me on a breath as my forehead fell to his shoulder, a deep sigh leaving me and taking most of my worries when he began moving us to the music again.

"Tell me how badly you want this," he begged soon after, voice soft as he spoke into my ear.

"Forever," I said without hesitation.

He pressed his head harder to mine as he continued swaying us. "It's a little soon to be saying things like that."

His rich laugh filled my world when I pushed against him, and then he was pulling me close again and stealing a kiss as my own laugh lingered on my lips.

"Gonna take you to bed now and hold you in my arms as I fall asleep," he said, all traces of laughter fading. "I'm gonna be there whenever you wake up, afraid of who's next to you. And one day, I'm gonna marry you."

My heart faltered before taking off in a desperate sprint for the man it belonged to. Wanting everything he'd so plainly laid out through all the fear. "Okay," I managed to whisper.

A hint of a smile played on his lips as he echoed, "Okay."

Turning me, he tucked me against his side and led me into the house, slowing to turn off the music and lights as we slowly made our way through the house.

"You have the tidiest rooms," I said once we were both back in his room after getting ready for bed, still marveling over how much his old room looked like the one he currently lived in. "There's nothing out of place. You only have what's needed. There are no personal touches."

I turned when Reed didn't respond to see him leaning up against the closed door, watching me with gentle amusement.

"Don't get me wrong, I don't have many things either. I moved everything I own into one room at Lala's, but I didn't have the family you do. I didn't have that kind of love."

He dipped his head, then looked pointedly around his room. "It's like this for a reason."

Reed pushed from the door and moved to his dresser, tugging on the top drawer just enough so it wasn't perfectly seated in place anymore. Continuing through his room, he went to his nightstand and opened the drawer there before quickly shutting it.

"The stories I told you on the way here?" he asked as he walked back to where he'd originally been. "Now, walking in, I can glance around the room and know someone was in here. There aren't personal things because if someone comes in, I don't want them to have something to use against me—like my family."

I hummed in acknowledgment and looked around again. "You're worried about that in Colby?"

"Not really. But I was trained my entire life to be prepared for it, and my dad's undercover work put a huge target on us when his cover got blown."

"I can't imagine what that must've been like," I muttered, then turned to face him. "I couldn't understand it when you first told me everything, but after meeting your family . . . I get it—what your dad did." I shrugged. "He did everything he could to protect you because he loves you." My stare fell as old memories pushed to the surface. "I spent half my life protecting my mom from drugs and every kind of asshole imaginable, and I hated her. If I'd loved her, I might've gone to extremes like your dad."

"It wasn't your job to protect her."

A huff fell from my lips as I stepped out of my heels and went to the bed. Once I had my toiletry bag put away and was digging through my overnight bag to find something to sleep in since I'd just shoved a bunch of random things in there that morning, I said, "I started running when I moved to New York. In a sense, I'd been running my entire life. And once I finally moved there, I had the strongest urge to stay there while running from everything." Another laugh tumbled free, my head shaking. "That sounds stupid."

"No, it doesn't," Reed said, gently urging me to continue.

I put whatever I'd managed to grab back in my bag and faced him again. "I've never felt so free as when I'm running. I mean . . . I think I almost passed out the first few times," I admitted, earning a soft laugh from him.

"But even on the days I can't outrun my past, it's like there's a layer between everything that happened and me. Like it can't actually touch me. And it's . . ."—I floundered for the right words when nothing seemed to be enough—"freeing and calming. And I feel strong and confident and like I'm not that scared girl in an RV."

Reed's face creased with sorrow and a subtle fury when my voice dipped and twisted at the end.

"You asked if I was comfortable in heels, and I am." I lifted one of my shoulders. "As ridiculous as it sounds, that's exactly how I feel when I'm wearing heels."

"Nothing can touch you," he said, understanding wrapping around the words. Pushing from the door again, he erased the distance between us, pulling the shirt he'd changed into off his body as he did. "You're strong and confident no matter what you wear."

I looked at the material he was holding out to me, my stare drifting back to him as my fingers gently curled around it. "What's this?"

"You said you're as comfortable in your heels as you were in my clothes." He lifted a brow meaningfully, his stare falling to my cheeks when they filled with heat.

"Thank you," I whispered, my gaze lingering when he backed away with a brush of his fingers across my hip and started tidying up the room as if he hadn't just given me something priceless.

Or maybe he just understood I needed room to breathe after he went and spoke to my soul that way.

I slipped into the shirt as I undressed and put away my other clothes, a soft sigh leaving me when the thin cotton of Reed's shirt felt like warmth and familiarity as it slid over my skin.

It was ridiculous, really, that a shirt could mean so much. Or that I could find comfort being surrounded in Reed's scent when all of this was so new.

"I see my wife *when I look at you."*

So new. So early.

But this connection between us felt more real than anything I'd ever experienced.

My stare drifted to where Reed was waiting next to the bed, wearing an indescribable expression as he stared at the floor. Arms folded over his bare chest and being entirely distracting from his gunmetal eyes and his too-handsome face to his perfectly muscled body covered in colorful designs.

I flipped off the main light, leaving the room still lit under the glow of the lamp he'd turned on. "What are you thinking?"

His gaze flickered to me, his brow furrowing. "There's something I want to tell you."

I gave him a questioning look, the corner of my mouth twitching into a playful smirk. "I thought you weren't going to drag me off to a church."

His chest shook with a muted laugh. "Yeah, I'm not." Pulling the covers back, he nodded to the bed and gently pleaded, "Come on."

I paused next to the side of the bed when he got in, unease starting to creep into my stomach as I wondered what could be weighing so heavily on his mind. "Should I be worried?"

"No," he said quickly. "I'd figured you would've already been told, but I don't think you have. And I just think it's something you should know."

After another moment of hesitation, I slid in next to him but didn't go to where he held out his arm for me. I turned so I was facing him and sat with my legs crossed and back straight, preparing for whatever he was about to tell me.

"Emma," he said softly as he held out his hand between us, "it isn't bad. It'll just explain some things."

"So explain," I said as I placed my hand in his.

He nodded, his eyes darting over my face as if he could sense I was already preparing to put my shields in place. "You said you thought Lala and I were in some fucked-up family thing to raise Nora," he began, then gave me a pointed look. "Again . . . your assumption was disgusting. She's like my grandma—she's like *everyone's* grandma."

"Right, I don't actually think you're in some kind of relationship with my grandma," I said dryly.

"Progress," he teased, a small smirk pulling at his mouth when I squeezed his hand in response. When he continued, his voice dropped into something more somber. "But the reason I'm there every day . . . Nora . . . I told you, I'd die for her." His throat shifted with a forced swallow, his head bobbing slowly. "That little girl grabbed my heart and fit herself inside there right about the second she grabbed my hand and claimed I was hers. Then when Lala had her stroke, Nora lost it."

It felt like I was holding my breath as I listened to Reed speak. Clinging to every word and every emotion as he offered me parts of my family I hadn't been there for and gave me what clearly meant the world to him.

"She stayed curled in a ball, screaming. If anyone tried to go near her, she'd scream louder." His gaze shifted to meet mine as he emphasized, "Shrieking like she was in pain, or something."

"Even with you?"

His head listed. "No, I was the only one who could calm her. But even after I'd have her calm for a while, she'd lose it if I tried to leave, so I stayed. Took care of her until even after Lala came back from the hospital."

Gratitude bled from me, but I waited, wondering what it was Reed thought I needed to know.

"About a month later, Lala had me come over. Nick's dad was there—he's a lawyer."

I went still at the casual mention of Ron Butler but struggled to relax before Reed could notice as he went on.

"He's been helping Lala with all of Nora's legal things since your mom left her."

"Wait." I sat back, head shaking a little. "What legal things?"

"Getting custody and things like that."

A stunned breath fled from me. "I didn't think Lala had custody—she told me she's afraid my mom's going to come back for Nora."

"She is," he said with a hint of a shrug. "She's worried Joslin will just *take* her. But Lala made sure to do everything to get custody of Nora."

An uneasy breath left me as I realized there had been no point in any of the research I'd done. And if I'd never scheduled the meeting at Butler and Davis, I wouldn't have bumped into Jarrod Davis. I wouldn't have realized we were in the same town.

Then again, I'd unknowingly walked into the Butlers' house where Jarrod was waiting just the night before.

"Why do you look like that's a bad thing?"

"It's a great thing," I said on a breath. "When I first got here, I was researching how to get Lala custody so my mom couldn't do exactly that, but I kept running into all these blocks." I lifted a shoulder. "The way Lala talked about it, I hadn't known she'd already done everything."

He curled his hand around mine when I eased it back into his.

"But what you're saying . . . I guess it makes sense." I searched his curious stare and said, "Apparently, my mom left me with Lala and my grandpa too, not that I knew any of this until recently. When I was two, she came back and took me. Lala said there'd been nothing they could do."

A grunt rumbled in Reed's chest, all sorrow and pain and frustration.

"I'd be there anyway," he said after a moment, "checking on them—checking on Nora and just being there for her. But it's important for me to be active and a constant in her life because Nora's mine."

I blinked slowly, unable to process the words that had just left him. "Excuse me?"

"After the stroke, Lala was afraid of what would happen to Nora if anything were to happen like that again . . . with a worse outcome. And of everyone, your grandma trusts me with Nora because Nora trusts me."

"So, she just gave her to you?" I asked incredulously.

His head slanted in the beginnings of a shake as he explained, "If I were to only get custody of her in the event of Lala's death, Nora would go into the system while everything was settled legally. Lala didn't want that to happen, especially after she found out how Nora reacted to everyone when Lala was in the hospital. And she didn't want us to both be guardians of her because that would have its own complications later."

"So, she just gave her to you?" I repeated, the words coming out clipped.

"Have you met your grandma?" he asked, the words all a breathless laugh. "She said she'd give me a couple days to think about it, but that Ron was already there, getting all the paperwork ready. And she'd rather have it taken care of before she had to start dinner."

"Of course she did," I mumbled, rubbing at my temple with my free hand before asking, "What'd you say?"

"I left." His chest pitched with strained amusement. "I went for a run to clear my head and then came back and asked what I had to do."

I watched him for a long time before the question swirling around in my mind finally slipped free. "Why?"

"I love that girl, Emma," he said softly. "I'd do anything for her."

"But . . ." My stare fell to my lap as a forced breath broke free. "You didn't have to—you shouldn't have let Lala push you into that. Nora isn't your responsibility."

"She is."

"But she wasn't," I argued as my gaze drifted back to his. "You didn't have to do this."

"I know," he said easily.

My head shook as I continued struggling to wrap my head around this. "I don't understand—you have full custody?" When Reed dipped his head in a nod, I asked, "But she lives with Lala."

"Nora doesn't know."

My brows lifted in surprise.

"Lala didn't want to unnecessarily upset her, she wanted to keep Nora's life how it was, and I agreed. So, this is all in place in the event something bad happens. Hopefully, nothing will, and it's just something we can explain to her when she's older."

"But what about doctors and school and things like that? If you're her guardian—"

"I've already signed everything I need to," he answered

with a shrug. "Lala can take her to and from school and to checkups. If she has to go to the hospital, I'll be there. But I'd probably be there anyway." A heavy sigh left him when I lowered myself onto the pillows. After turning off the lamp, he rested his head near mine. "You're mad."

"I'm not."

"You're shutting down."

"I'm not trying to," I assured him and reached out to thread my fingers through his. "Just thinking."

His eyes searched mine in the dark, questioning and prompting.

"I'm grateful that Nora has a legal guardian who isn't my mom," I said, voice soft as I tried to get out my jumbled thoughts. "I'm shocked . . . I don't think that's a big enough word. But I can't believe a twenty-nine-year-old man would willingly take custody of a six-year-old, who he isn't even related to."

"She was four at the time," he mumbled and breathed out a laugh that was all a rough whisper when I pushed against his stomach.

"And I guess there's just that part of me that rebels against the idea of a man having custody of her," I said, the words full of horrors and shame. "Every instinct in me wants to keep her from men, and yet . . ."

"I will protect her with my life," Reed vowed gravely.

"I know," I said confidently. "I know you would never hurt her. It's just a deep-rooted reaction . . . some horrors are hard to shake."

He pressed his forehead to mine as he lifted our joined hands to his chest. "Hopefully, her life will continue as it is. Living with Lala while I come and go simply as one of her favorite people. But if it ever comes down to it, she'll never be displaced. She'll be protected. She'll be safe. All right?"

I nodded. "Thank you."

For telling me.

For loving my family.

For protecting us all.

He brushed his mouth across mine in response, leaving me wrapped up in all that comfort and security as I finally let my eyes close.

THIRTY-FOUR

EMMA

"When are you coming back?" I heard Nora ask the next day as I slipped back into the room from showering and dressing. Reed had coaxed me out of bed early by promising a sunrise and then had tried to kill me by taking me for the hardest run of my life on the beach.

Reed's stare shifted to me, slowly devouring me before he glanced back to his screen. "Tonight or tomorrow." He cleared his throat and gave her one of those easy smiles. "So, I'll probably see you tomorrow."

"Are you bringing that one back with you?"

Reed's expression shifted to a mixture of patience and reprimand. "You can't keep calling her that, Nora. Her name's Emma, and she's your sister."

"I just wanted to know if you're bringing her back because she left me too."

"We didn't leave you. I talked to you about this—my family is here. We came to see them for a couple days."

Nora was silent for a while, and I pressed up against the

wall. Content to let them finish their conversation. "Do you love her more than you love me?"

"I love her differently," he said with a soft shake of his head. "I don't love either of you more."

"Can I tell you a secret?" she asked, her voice getting louder even though she was clearly trying to whisper.

Reed's eyes lit with amusement as he waited.

"I think she loves you differently too."

"Oh yeah?"

"Yeah, because she's been extra sad lately, and I heard my Lala say so," Nora whispered, then continued in a normal tone. "Is she your girlfriend now?"

His gaze drifted to me again, studying me with a fierce intensity that made my heart race. "She's something," he finally answered.

Lala's voice sounded from far away, and Nora sighed. "My Lala said I have to go get ready for church now."

"Then you better listen to her so you can get all fancy."

"The fanciest," Nora said on an excited gasp. "I have to go!" The pounding of her feet could be heard before she yelled, "Bye, my Reed!" and then the phone was being shuffled around.

"That child, I swear," Lala said with an affectionate laugh.

"Your head hurt?" Reed asked, eyebrows pulling together as he gestured to his temple.

"You and your obsessive worrying. Can't even let an old woman rub at her head," she mumbled, pure annoyance.

"Just making sure you're all right."

"I'm just fine," she said with a scoff. "Now go on and get. Have yourself a good time and make sure my granddaughter's feeding you."

"He's eating, Lala," I called out from my spot, my eyes rolling.

"Don't you go sassing me on the Lord's day," she shot back.

I just rolled my eyes again, forcing a laugh from Reed.

"Bye, Lala," he said before ending the call, dropping his phone to the bed with a weighted sigh and dragging a hand through his hair.

"What's wrong?"

He blew out another slow breath and stood, offering me a smile that didn't reach his eyes. "I haven't missed a Sunday with Nora in a couple years."

Surprise pulsed through me as I got a glimpse of just how much Nora meant to him.

It was one thing to hear him say it—words could always be just that: words. But it was another to witness the impact their being apart had on Reed.

"We can go," I offered softly. "Be back in time for dinner, and you can read to her then."

He was already shaking his head before I finished.

"After the years apart, I need this weekend with my family. And this is good for Nora. She needs to have things change up on her every now and then to push her out of her comfort zone."

"But you don't like it," I said in understanding.

A huff left him, all saddened amusement. "No. No, I don't." A crease formed between his eyebrows when he stopped in front of me. "You're surprised by that."

I slid my hand into his when he offered it, shoulders lifting. "I just don't think I was paying attention before."

A grunt rumbled in his chest. "Think you've been

shielding and pushing," he claimed as he leaned in, keeping his lips an inch from my own.

"You just have me all figured out, don't you?"

The corner of his mouth twitched as his eyes searched mine. "I don't think I'll ever have you figured out, but that's one of the things I love about you." He captured my lips for a slow, teasing kiss that had my belly dipping with heat and my head getting all kinds of light as I pulled him closer only to have him reverse our positions so he was against the wall. Bringing me closer and gripping me as if he never wanted to let go.

A groan rolled up his throat and did amazing things to my body when I pressed the tips of my fingers beneath his shirt, tracing the ridges of his muscled stomach down to the top of the shorts he was wearing.

"Bed," he said against the kiss, the word a plea and a demand and a question.

Always a question. Always an invitation.

Always my choice.

But before I could respond in any way or even move in that direction, someone slapped against the bedroom door and yelled, "Breakfast!"

"Fuck off," Reed called out before capturing my lips with his again in a kiss that instantly had my knees going weak. All fierce possession and need and desire.

The drumming on the door resumed even louder as the feminine voice said, "You never see your family. Make babies when you're back home!"

I staggered away from Reed so quickly that I nearly tripped over myself.

He hissed a curse as he caught and steadied me, annoyance coloring his expression when the drumming turned into incessant banging. "Jesus, Kennedy, we get it," he said as he swung the door open to her wicked grin. "Fuck you."

She placed a hand on her chest and clicked her tongue, feigning adoration. "Well, isn't that just the sweetest? Good morning to you too." Her other hand shot out, and Reed's entire body jolted as Kennedy yelled, "Tag!" over Reed's curses and then took off running.

I stood there for a few seconds after Reed had scrambled after her, shouting threats throughout the house, unable to wrap my head around what had just gone down in front of me or the noise I'd heard.

But by the time I found them and their family in the kitchen, Mason was laughing, Kash was trying to mediate between Reed and Liam, and Reed had Kennedy in a choke-hold as she struggled to get away.

My blood turned to ice and my body swayed as frigid fingers trailed down my spine, breaking every lock I had on the memories that haunted me.

THIRTY-FIVE

REED

"She can get out of it," my dad said, trying to reason with Liam.

"I know she can," he bit out, "but why the hell does he even have her in one, and why is he saying he's going to kill her?"

"She—*fuck*," I yelled just as another jolt of electricity hit me, seizing my muscles. "Fucking drop it."

Uncle Mason started laughing even louder, and soon, my dad joined in.

Scrubbing a hand over his face, Dad gestured to where I had my sister in a chokehold but spoke to Liam. "I'd say she deserves it."

"Drop it," I demanded through gritted teeth, my breaths sharp and heavy. "Drop it."

"I'll knock you the fuck out if you put my wife to sleep," Liam said in a threatening tone.

Kennedy continued struggling and trying to twist in my hold, intent on breaking free.

"What is going on?" Mom asked when she and my aunt

came in, weighed down with bags of food, looking equally shocked and worried and annoyed.

"She keeps tasing him," my uncle said, smiling as if it were the funniest thing in the world.

Mom's expression deadpanned. "Kennedy, drop the taser right now."

"God damnit," I snapped when she hit me again. Every muscle locking up for a few seconds before I was able to relax them.

"Let her go," Liam said when I tightened my arms around her neck, words all a dark warning as he stepped closer.

Just as Kennedy started trying to twist again, I knocked out her knee and shoved her forward, grabbing the taser from her loosened grip when she tried to steady herself as she staggered away.

Her laughter filled the kitchen as she bent at the waist, trying to drag in air. "I could've gotten out," she said, smile wide and mischievous when she slanted her head to the side.

"Bullshit," I said irritably, then held up the taser. "What the hell?"

She straightened, hands on her hips as she struggled to catch her breath. "Um . . . the last time we played tag, I seem to remember you using a metal meat mallet." She gave me a look as if I should've remembered.

I watched her, brows lifting as if she'd lost her mind. "Kennedy, we were kids. I can't even remember when that was."

"That isn't my fault. That mallet hurt like a bitch. I had a horrifically epic bruise that I had to hide from Mom for a week because of it."

Mom lifted her hands and turned to Dad. "Wait, *me*? Did you know about their extreme tag?"

Dad looked at Uncle Mason and then to the floor, fighting a smile and choking on a laugh.

"Logan Kash Ryan," she said, all shock and frustration. "A *meat mallet?*"

Dad just shrugged and turned to her. "I didn't know about that one."

"In Reed's defense, I think Kira used Dad's expandable ASP right before that," Kennedy said as if she were helping the situation.

Dad pointed to her. "I may have given Kira that." When Mom looked like she was going to start yelling, he tried to laugh it off. "They were playing tag!"

"That is not playing tag." She gestured to me. "*That* is not playing tag," she said and then released a heavy sigh. "Poor Emma probably thinks we're insane."

"I've warned her," I mumbled, then pointed at Kennedy with the taser. "I'm getting you back."

"Reed."

I looked at my dad to see both him and Mason looking at something behind me. The way they'd straightened and sobered, staring ahead as if they were being careful about the way they were even breathing, had every sense heightening and my heart rate slowing. But then I turned, and my stomach dropped when I saw her.

All ice and shields as she stood there, tall and still, face utterly unreadable except for the demons dancing in her eyes.

And I knew . . . I knew in an instant what I'd done.

What she was seeing. What I'd brought back for her.

"Emma," I whispered as I started closing the distance between us. Gauging her reaction the closer I came, my chest aching at the subtle way she shifted from me when I was within a few feet of her. "Emma, I'm sorry."

"Why?"

"Because I can see what this is doing to you," I said, voice soft as I led her into the living room and further from the kitchen.

"I'm fine."

My jaw flexed at the lie. "Emma—"

"Are you okay?" she asked, stopping me from continuing.

"You can't even look at me. No, I'm not okay."

Her hazel eyes shifted to me, a gut-wrenching mixture of horror and numbness filling them as she forced herself to hold my stare.

"I'm not whatever you're seeing."

Her body sagged the slightest bit.

"Emma, I am not those men."

"I know," she whispered, the words sounding pained as they scraped up her throat.

When I held my hand out to her, she rocked forward and fell into my chest instead. Head pressed to my shoulder and a stuttered breath leaving her when I wrapped my arms around her.

And I was floored.

By that moment and her trust. By the changes in her as she slipped off the shield for me. For *us*.

"She was trying to get away," she said, soft and shamed.

I brushed the tips of my fingers up and down her back in a soothing trail. "She could've tapped out, Emma. It wasn't like that—I would never hurt her."

"I know." A shudder rolled through her body. "And I know it's just how your family is—I watched all of you together yesterday. This just . . ."

"Brought things back," I offered when she didn't go on.

She didn't respond, but the deep sigh that left her when she leaned away was answer enough.

"Emma, I'm sorry."

"Stop . . . please stop." She gave me a look as if she was desperately trying to ignore whatever nightmares were slowly destroying her mind, and it tore at my soul. "I know you aren't them, Reed." Her stare darted over me. "Are you okay?"

"I don't know," I said honestly.

"Physically."

I pressed my hand to the small of her back, pulling her closer as my head dipped in a delayed nod because that was the least of my worries. "Yeah, I'm fine."

"Reed, they found her," my dad said, voice closing in on where we stood.

Anticipation and a hint of worry pounded through my veins before I narrowed in on the crease forming between Emma's brows as she looked from him to me.

"Found who?"

"Shit," I hissed, hand sliding to her waist as I twisted to see my dad. Holding my hand up for him to wait, I focused on Emma. "I didn't get a chance to talk to you because of the whole taser thing. But when you were in the shower, I asked my dad to see if one of their guys could try finding your mom."

Her expression fell before going utterly, heartbreakingly blank.

"I can't do that," I hurried to explain. "I can get in trouble if I just go looking up someone for no reason. Dad and Uncle Mason have people who can do this—people they trust implicitly."

"You asked them to find my mom," she said, voice a clear warning that every shield was about to slip into place.

And I was fucking terrified that I'd made a grave mistake. At the same time . . . "Emma, Lala and I are constantly worried she's going to come back. *You* were worried. It'd help if we knew where she was and had someone watching to see if she starts making her way back to us."

Her head moved in the faintest nod before shaking. Voice cold when she said, "I want nothing to do with her—I don't want *anyone* to have anything to do with her. She's toxic, whether she's physically near you or not. Look what she's done to Lala."

She pressed her lips tightly together, and I could practically hear the words she refused to give voice to.

Look what she did to me.

I released a heavy exhale and moved my hand into hers. "All right," I conceded. "All right, tell me you don't want to know, and that'll be the end of it. I'll have my dad tell his guy to stop tracking her, and we won't find out, I swear to you."

Emma sucked in a breath, and I knew from the look in her eyes that she was about to take that offer. That all her years of rebuilding herself had her wanting to stay on a path far from her mom's reach.

But at the last second, her stare slid to my dad, and she asked, "Where is she?"

I studied her for a second longer and then looked at where he was watching me, as if waiting to make sure I thought Emma could handle whatever the news was.

With a nod, he handed Emma his phone as he spoke. "Montana state prison. Serving a ten-year sentence as of six months ago for her second conviction of aggravated robbery."

Emma studied the details and mugshots on the phone for

a few moments, her hands trembling before the rest of her body joined in too. And then she was leaning into me as she gave the phone back to my dad, a pained breath tumbling free when I wrapped her in my arms.

"She looks terrible," she said when my dad slipped away. Her voice twisting and dipping as if some distant part that would never let go still felt responsible for her mom—felt at fault for her mom's current state.

"Over twenty years of her lifestyle would be hard on anyone." When she just nodded against my chest, I begged, "Tell me something about you."

A soft huff fled from her. "I'm glad that she can't get to me or Nora or Lala . . . that she can't get to you. That she can't poison our lives. And I don't know if I should feel bad about that, but I don't." Hesitation built between us for a few moments before she admitted, "I hate that I feel bad for her."

"You took care of her for over half your life," I said understandingly. "And no matter what she did, she's still your mom."

"Yeah," she whispered, then pulled slightly from my hold when Kennedy and Chase came rushing through the room.

"Ignore us, ignore us! We aren't here," Kennedy called out as she scooped up her laughing son and started back toward the kitchen.

"We should probably get back in there," Emma said, her eyes a mixture of pain and love and gratitude.

Curling my hand around her cheek, I lowered my forehead to hers. "I love you."

She rested her hand on my chest in response, her head nodding against mine.

"How was your run this morning, Emma?" my mom

asked when we got back into the kitchen from where she and my aunt were setting out the food they'd brought.

"It was good," Emma answered, clearing her throat and offering a smile that only hinted at everything we'd just gone through. "My legs feel like Jell-O though, I'd never run on the beach before."

Liam grunted in agreement, but he was all smiles when he said, "Brutal."

Kennedy flipped him off and then used her middle finger to point at him. "I'm pretty sure this one was born running on the beach. He's always trying to make me go with him."

"You might like it," he said with a grin that said he knew she wouldn't. "Chase loves it."

"Chase also used to like eating sand," she argued before blowing a raspberry on the little boy in question.

I stepped back to where my dad and uncle were talking—their stares shifting to Emma . . . studying. Assessing. Worrying.

"She okay?" Dad asked once I was beside them.

I dipped my head in response.

"You can see the way she reacts to being near men she doesn't know," Uncle Mason began, tone low, and my dad grunted in agreement. "Looks at them and shifts away. It goes along with the way she reacted to you keeping Kenz in that chokehold."

"That's a fear that comes from trauma," Dad finished for him.

I swallowed thickly, trying to push past the guilt that was quick to build from being the one to bring all those demons back. "Yeah, I know."

"Do you?" he asked doubtfully, considering I hadn't

known much of anything the last time he and I had talked about Emma.

"She told me," I said through the gravel in my throat. "She told me everything."

"That's a trust that isn't given lightly," my uncle said, and I just nodded because I was more than well aware of that.

Dad made another one of those agreeing grunts. "It's easy to see she trusts you though." His stare shifted to me, the corner of his mouth ticking up in a look that was all sympathy and encouragement. "Your mom and I like her." My uncle smacked him, and Dad rolled his eyes as he amended, "We *all* like her."

"We're here," Kira called out just as the front door opened.

Dad grabbed my shoulder before heading over to greet them as my uncle went to steal food from the kitchen.

"Why do you have this face?" Kira asked when she reached me, kissing my cheek and handing me one of her babies so she could continue greeting everyone.

"What face?"

"Like horrible things are happening." Her voice dipped lower. "Don't say trouble in paradise, I really like this one."

"Kennedy decided to play tag and kept tasing me," I said, giving her the first thing I could think of and avoiding the rest.

Her soft laugh trailed behind her as she left me, going from person to person.

"Look at you with a baby," Kennedy said when she came up beside me a few minutes later.

A grunt rumbled in my chest as I thought about the little girl my family didn't know about.

"You notice you can hold a baby, and Emma doesn't freak

out and demand children?" she asked on a whisper. "Night and day, those two."

"Think the idea of kids scares the shit out of her," I said just as softly.

She seemed to think about that for a moment before asking, "Does that bother you?"

Before I even had time to think about my answer, Kira spoke up as if picking up on Kennedy's thoughts from across the room.

"Has anyone else noticed that Emma is perfectly fine being away from Reed?" she asked, then looked at where Emma had moved into the kitchen to continue talking to my mom and aunt. "You've been really refreshing in every way . . . but this particular thing?" Her eyes rolled. "Sadie would've been attached to him like a monkey and would've thrown a fit if he ever left her side."

"Kira," I snapped, a deep sigh slipping free when Emma looked at me in question.

Kira's eyes widened in surprise and apprehension as she glanced around when everyone went silent and then settled on me. "Oh my God. I'm sorry, I didn't—I thought she—" She pressed her mouth into a firm line, sorrow bleeding from her.

"She doesn't know you were engaged?" Kennedy asked loudly, always the blunt one.

"Jesus, *yes*, she knows. That doesn't mean Sadie needs to be brought up or that Kira needs to compare them."

"Um, *one*," Kennedy went on, gesturing between her, Liam, Kira, and Rhys, "our entire lives are the ex-files. *Two*, why wouldn't she be brought up? Sadie was the *worst*."

"Kennedy, I swear to God," I began, but Dad cut me off.

"Kenz, unless you want me to hold you while Reed tases you, I'd stop talking."

My stomach churned and my lungs ached when I looked over to see Emma standing in quiet discomfort, vacant stare on the floor.

"God damnit," I breathed as my head fell back to the wall.

This day couldn't get any worse.

THIRTY-SIX

EMMA

She had a name now.

She had a name, and from what little Kira had said, I had a feeling she was my opposite. Someone who would've never pushed Reed away but clung to him. Someone who would've never shielded him from her life and probably willingly gave all her thoughts and affection to him.

His family hadn't liked her, that much was clear, but Reed had loved her.

And I was nothing like her.

I couldn't figure out why that was bothering me so much, but I was stuck on that thought still, even after we'd finished breakfast and were still gathered around the table. Everyone having their own conversations that constantly morphed as new people were pulled in.

"What's going on in that head of yours?" Reed asked, voice nothing more than a breath that seemed to force my thoughts free.

"I'm the opposite of her."

His brows were raised when I risked a glance at him.

"Sadie?" When I simply nodded, his head slanted in denial. "Whatever you're coming up with about that, I assure you, you're wrong."

"Am I?"

The way he looked at me would've been answer enough, all searing gazes that warmed every part of me and touched my soul, but he still continued. "If you think I'm with you because of *anything* to do with her . . ."—his head moved in slow shakes as he leaned closer—"Emma, I wasn't looking for her opposite. I wasn't looking for *anyone* when you crashed into my life."

"Is that what I did?" I asked, the words holding a hint of playfulness.

He rumbled in both response and amusement, then pointedly glanced around the table before settling on me. "My family talks about her because they hated her from day one, and she caused a lot of tension between us. But she's my past, and I'm fucking glad to keep her there." His eyes searched mine, waiting until I conceded with a soft sigh. "All right?"

"Yeah."

"Besides," he went on, the corner of his mouth ticking up mischievously, "she had nothing on you—she didn't frustrate the hell out of me."

I pushed at his side, a small smile crossing my face when he pressed his lips to my forehead.

"So, you're from South Carolina, Emma?" Rachel asked, pulling me from my little bubble with Reed into whatever conversation she was having with her husband and Rhys.

"Um, no," I said, pushing away any lingering thoughts of Reed's ex. "My grandma is—she's been in that house since before my mom was born, but I'm from everywhere. I've lived in almost every state."

Rachel's eyes widened with surprise and wonder and excitement. "What was that like?"

A huff tumbled past my lips because it hadn't been nearly as amazing as it could've been. "Unsettling," I answered honestly. "Half the time, I woke up not remembering what city or state we were in."

"Oh, that's so sad," she murmured, but I shrugged it off because it had been the least-sad part of my life. "So, were you homeschooled? Or did you get to experience new schools with each new place?"

My smile fixed on my face when it felt like everything else about me fell. "I didn't have any schooling," I admitted, embarrassment flooding me when I felt Reed go still beside me. But I struggled to grasp and hold onto my waning confidence. "I got my GED after I moved to New York when I was twenty-one, but everything else, I either taught myself or learned from watching other people."

Rachel nodded, but her smile was softer and the pity in her eyes was unmistakable. "That's very incredible," she said. "I feel like you've had the most interesting and exciting life of us all."

"Mom," Reed began, but Kash spoke over him. "Do you plan on staying in Colby?"

"Um . . ." I hesitated as a disgusting, creep of a man and a lifetime of running urged me to keep moving while everything else begged me to stay.

Reed slowly looked over at me when I took too long to answer. Jaw tight and a whisper of panic in his eyes.

"I plan to," I hurried to say, my attention shifting from Reed to his dad, "I do. I think it's just hard for my soul to stop feeling so restless when going there was an impulsive decision. But I accidentally fell into a job there that I love, and then there's—" I glanced at Reed again, my words getting all jumbled up. "I plan to."

Questions swirled in his eyes, but he held them back, waiting for when we were alone.

"Oh, what job?" Rachel asked, all excited interest again.

"It's this . . ." My stare drifted from her back to Reed when he pulled his phone from his pocket to see messages lighting up his lock screen.

Butler: *Where are you?*

Butler: *Answer your phone.*

Rowe: *911*

"It's this bookstore," I said slowly, unease winding through my body and squeezing my chest when Reed pushed his chair back and stood, already calling Peter as he stalked off. When I continued, the excitement over the store was weighed down by my worry for whatever was happening back in Colby. "It looked abandoned and looted when I found it a few weeks ago. But the owner is the sweetest woman, and it's been in her family for generations, so I helped her get a loan and renovate it. It looks incredible—like a completely different store—and it reopens tomorrow."

"What an incredible gift you've given that woman by helping her," Rachel said. "I would love to see it and check out this town my son loves so much."

"We have to go," Reed said as he came storming back into the kitchen, face tight and fiercely terrifying. "Now."

I was so taken aback by his expression that I just sat there, watching as he reached out for me.

"Come on," he said as he helped me up.

"What's going on?"

"Go pack," he demanded, voice soft and dark and stare refusing to meet mine.

"Tell me—"

"Emma," he said through clenched teeth. *Begged*.

I studied the sharp lines of his jaw for another second before hurrying through the house to his room. Throwing things into my bag as quickly as I could and then rushing to pack for him.

Once I had all of our things, I grabbed the bags and turned just as he came into the room. "I got your stuff."

"Let's go," he said with a nod as he took the bags from me.

"What about your family?"

"They understand."

My heart was racing, and I didn't even know what was happening. My stomach twisting up until I felt sick because I'd never seen Reed this way. And it had me equal parts terrified for what I would find out and wanting to comfort him.

But he was rushing me from the house, barely giving me the chance to say goodbye to the majority of his family where they lingered in the living room, watching with ranging looks of sorrow.

"Emma, it was wonderful meeting you," Rachel said from where she and Kash were waiting next to Reed's truck.

I tried to smile, but I wasn't sure I succeeded. "Thank you for letting me crash your family weekend."

"Of course." She wrapped her arms around me, squeezing me tight. "Come back anytime." Offering me a worried smile when she pulled back, she whispered, "Thank you for making my boy happy."

I nodded and then turned to say goodbye to her husband before Reed was ushering me into the passenger side of his truck.

By the time he climbed into the driver's seat, my chest was tight, and I was struggling to pull in air as the weight of Reed's urgency and fear started to fully settle over me.

"Reed, what is going on?" I softly pleaded as he tore away from the house, knuckles straining from his tight grip on the steering wheel. "What did Peter say?"

It wasn't until we were out of the neighborhood that Reed finally spoke. Voice detached as he accelerated well past the speed limit. "Lala and Nora were in a wreck."

WE'D MADE the trip back to Colby in five hours.

Nora had a broken arm and a couple cracked ribs. Reed lost his mind when we'd arrived and been told they'd sedated her because she'd been screaming and thrashing—unable to see reason that she'd only been hurting herself more.

Lala still hadn't regained consciousness but had managed to escape any broken bones even though she was bruised all over.

From what people on the scene had said, Lala had flown through a red light on the way back from church. Never slowing and seeming to go much faster than the speed limit before another truck had T-boned them.

"My Emma?"

My heart stalled before racing at the soft, uncertain voice that was claiming I was hers. I looked up from where I'd been researching on my phone, scanning all over Nora's small body in the big hospital bed. "Yeah, Nora?"

"Is my Lala going to be okay?"

The assurance was on the tip of my tongue—anything to soothe her when she seemed so fragile, but I swallowed it back. Glancing over to where Reed stood just a couple feet away, exhaustion dripping from him, I whispered, "I don't know. But I hope so."

Reed's stare shifted to me, his head dipping in a small nod just as the door opened.

"Ms. Wade?"

I turned to see Lala's doctor glance from the file in his hand to me expectantly. "Yes?"

He stepped back out of the room, holding the door open. "Let's talk in the hall."

"Come on, Tanner," Reed said, voice like gravel.

The doctor grimaced. "You aren't family, Reed. I'm sorry."

My mouth parted to tell the doctor it was fine—whatever he was going to tell me, he could say in front of Reed since I would just relay all the information to him anyway. Besides, Reed was more family to Lala than I was. But I thought about the little girl behind me and stepped toward the doctor instead, glancing at Reed over my shoulder as I did.

"I'll be right back," I whispered and let my stare slide to Nora meaningfully.

He nodded and released a heavy exhale as he sank to the chair next to her bed.

I closed the door behind me as I followed the doctor into the hall, my knotted stomach sinking when the doctor gave me a look he'd clearly practiced.

Folding my arms around my waist, I drew myself up tall

and tried to hold myself together when it felt like that simple look already had me crumbling. "Is she awake?"

"Just a few minutes ago." His lips twitched, a slight hint of encouragement tilting them when I sighed in relief. "But we've been running tests and scans, and I've spoken with some of her other doctors." He cleared his throat and took another few steps away from Nora's room, his voice lowering when I followed him. "I know you haven't been here long, Ms. Wade, but are you aware your grandmother had a stroke a couple Christmases ago?"

I nodded, my stomach knotting tighter and tighter. "Did she have another one? Is that what happened today?"

"No," he said quickly, but there was no assurance in his voice. "But when she was here for the stroke, we found a mass on her brain during one of her scans, so I referred her to an Oncologist."

I stilled.

My heart felt like it was beating so hard and so loud that it was drowning out every other sound.

"I just spoke with that doctor . . . your grandmother refused a biopsy after the first meeting and hasn't seen her since." He cleared his throat and said, "We ran the same scans and tests, and the mass has grown and multiplied."

"She has brain cancer?" I asked, the words coming out slow and sounding so confused because it didn't make sense.

The doctor hesitated. "I can't say for certain, but the tumors seem to be very aggressive."

My head shook, unable to accept it even though I knew in my gut because *Lala* knew. She'd known all along. "But she's . . . she's so strong. She's constantly going and cooking for people."

"I'm sorry," was all he said. "I'm hoping you'll be able to

convince her that a biopsy is needed so she can start receiving the necessary treatment. It looks like your grandmother had a seizure today while driving, and that is a common symptom of brain tumors. She could have more in the future."

I nodded at the warning and concern in his words.

"However, your grandmother is . . . a very strong-willed woman," he said after a moment of thought, an affectionate laugh leaving him. "As her closest family, I need you to be aware of what's going on with her so you can best take care of her. Things like driving, being alone, and going up and down stairs . . . she can't do those anymore. Well . . ."—he gave me a meaningful look—"she can, and I have no doubt she'll try since she's adamant she's capable of doing all those things and more. But it isn't safe for her or others anymore."

"I understand," I muttered and looked across the hall. "Can I see her?"

"Of course, but we would like to keep her here overnight. I think Reed should be able to take Miss Nora home soon though."

"Thank you," I said as I started for Lala's door. My steps slow and heavy as the weight of the news pulled at me.

By the time I slipped into her room, I was a confusing mixture of struggling not to cry and half-formed shields.

I looked over her bruised face and arm, my chest aching as I went to the side of her bed so I could grab her good hand.

She tsked before I reached her. "Don't you come in here like you're walking into my funeral," she said, voice weak but still managing to hold plenty of that Lala bite.

The corners of my mouth tilted up even as my throat tightened with tears. "Hi, Lala."

She finally opened her eyes, only looking at me for a moment before letting them shut again with a deep sigh. "Nora?"

"Reed has her, and she'll be fine."

Her jaw trembled and she sucked in an unsteady breath when I slipped my hand around hers. "Well, my truck probably looks worse than me."

"Lala—"

"That poor beast has been with me forever."

"Lala—"

"Enough of this nonsense. Let's get me on out of here before I go out of my mind." She opened her eyes and looked around. "Nothing to do in a place like this."

"I wish I'd come back sooner," I said before she could try to stop me. "I wish I'd been here for so many reasons, but I hate that I missed all those years I could've had with you."

"I am still alive," she admonished, complete with a weakened scoff.

"I know you are, and I'm incredibly thankful for that," I said gently. "But why didn't you get the biopsy done, Lala?"

Her expression fell and her stare drifted away from me, her voice nothing more than a tremor when she said, "Don't let that silly doctor fill your head with nonsense."

"You wouldn't have made sure Reed had custody of Nora if it were nonsense," I said confidently. "I figured out that much, but I can't figure out why you refused the biopsy."

"Well, it's my right not to have one."

I pulled my hand from hers, my voice rising and cracking with my pain. "Lala, that's bullshit. You wouldn't just leave something like that up to fate when you have Nora."

"I chose what I did for her," she snapped, then let out an aching breath, her eyes filled with tears as my own slipped down my cheeks. "With where it was located and the size of it, that specialist doctor said it needed to be removed—the entire thing. Said if I left it alone, the stroke I had was just the beginning, but that I probably had five years, if not more. Surgery . . . she said the surgery was a very complicated one and suggested chemo instead." Lala slanted her head. "I'm not living my last years that way, and I'm not putting Nora through that."

"So, you'd rather her watch you go through this?" I asked shakily.

"I don't need you criticizing my decisions. I've made them, and that's that."

"It doesn't have to be. You can still change your mind."

"I'm not going to," she said definitively. "Now, get me out of here."

I studied her for a while as the tears continued falling. "They're keeping you overnight." When she scoffed, I reminded her, "Lala, you were just in a major accident because you had a seizure, and you were unconscious for almost eight hours. You *just* woke up."

"And I'm fit as a fiddle."

"No, you're stubborn because you're a Wade." When she turned her exhausted but irritated stare on me, I repeated, "I wish I'd come back sooner."

Her tears finally fell as she weakly squeezed my fingers. "Me too, child."

"Now, I know you like bossing me around, but I'm telling you that you're staying here and you're going to rest. And whatever the doctors and nurses say, try not to sass them too much."

A huff of a laugh left her.

"Reed and I will take Nora home, and I'll be back tomorrow, all right?"

"Well," she said with a muted sigh, "seems I don't have much of a choice."

"That's right." I leaned over her bed to kiss her cheek, my voice cracking as I said, "Bye, Lala."

"Walking right on back out of here like it's my damn funeral," she tsked, pulling a soft laugh from me that did nothing to ease the intense aching in my soul.

"Emma."

I looked up as I shut the door behind me, and that pain seemed to fall away when I saw Reed standing outside Nora's room. All worry and exhaustion playing across his face as he started toward me.

"She awake?" he asked at the same time I slipped my hand into his and asked, "What's going on with Nora?"

"They're getting her ready to discharge her," he answered, then pulled me into his arms. "Is Lala awake?"

My head bobbed quickly before I let it fall to his chest as I desperately tried to swallow back the building sob.

His hands clenched around me tighter, gripping me with the fear we'd been sitting in all day, silently begging me to tell him what was happening with the woman I'd just left.

"Did you know?" I asked around the glass in my throat. "About Lala—did you know?"

He leaned back, one of his hands shifting to lift my chin so he could search my eyes. "What are you talking about?"

"When she asked you to take custody of Nora . . . did she say why?"

Confusion poured from Reed. "What? Yeah, babe, I told you last night. She wanted—"

"No." My head shook, stopping him from continuing because I could already see in his eyes and the way he was speaking that he didn't know. "She had a seizure today. But that and her stroke . . . it's because she has tumors on her brain."

Reed's confusion slowly melted away to shock and denial.

"After her stroke, they found a mass. Today . . . the doctor said it's grown and multiplied aggressively. She refused chemo and the surgery to have the original mass removed."

After long seconds of silence, Reed released me and stepped back to lean against the wall. "It wasn't a just-in-case thing," he muttered, then clarified, "Nora."

"I don't think so."

His eyelids shut and a deep sigh left him. "Does she know if it's cancer?"

"She doesn't. But after the stroke, the Oncologist said she could have at least five years as she was." I hesitated and fought the newly-building tears. "But if it's aggressive and if it's spread the way this doctor said . . ." When Reed nodded, I asked, "If you'd known, would you have made a different choice with Nora?"

"No." His eyes were glassy when they opened. Roughing a hand through his hair, he let out another deep sigh and pushed from the wall. "This fucking day." He glanced at Nora's room and then turned to me, reaching out for me and teasing my hip with the tips of his fingers. "Can you see how they're doing with Nora? I'm gonna check in with Lala before we go."

"Of course."

I watched him go for only a moment before hurrying off to the door a few rooms down, peeking my head in and offering Nora a smile when I found her very obviously ignoring the nurse who was helping her.

"Good timing, sis," the nurse called out, trying to be excited for Nora. "We're all unhooked and dressed and ready to go!"

Nora's eyes shifted from the nurse back to me, her little face scrunched up with apprehension from being around a person she didn't know.

The nurse handed me a stack of papers as she began explaining everything she'd apparently already told Reed, using her hands wildly as she spoke. "But if something seems off, just bring her right on back. Sound good?"

"Sounds good, thank you."

"But what about my Lala?" Nora asked when the nurse left.

"I just saw her," I said as I gently helped Nora off the bed, minding her arm and side and wincing when she did. "She's awake and wanting to go home, but the doctor's going to keep her here tonight."

I saw it hit Nora in an instant. The utter look of fear and being lost within her exhaustion—and it shattered something inside me.

"You're coming home with Reed and me," I said quickly, dropping to a crouch to be on her level. "Then hopefully tomorrow, Lala will come home."

"My Reed?" Nora asked, shaking out of her panic just as quickly as it had consumed her. "I get to go home with my Reed?" When I hummed in confirmation, she put her good hand in mine. "Okay, let's go."

I stared at the tiny fingers in mine, my heart swelling as I straightened and led her from the room just as Reed was coming down the hall.

A smile broke across his face when he saw us. "There's my favorite girl. You ready to go?"

Nora bounced and cried out when she landed.

"Be careful," Reed and I admonished at the same time, but her excitement shone through her pain.

"My Emma said I get to go home with you tonight!"

"Yeah, but if you keep jumping around and hurting yourself, we're all gonna have to stay here," he said gently. When Nora went comically still at my side, Reed jerked his head in the direction of the exit. "Let's get out of here. We have a surprise for you."

I widened my eyes at him because I knew absolutely nothing of a surprise, but he just offered me a warm smile as he lifted my hand to press a kiss to my palm.

"When I look at you . . ." he whispered, the incomplete thought holding so much meaning and making my spirit soar in the midst of all this worry.

"Forever," I vowed.

THIRTY-SEVEN

EMMA

"Long day." Reed's deep voice met me a second before his arms curled around me. Pulling me against his chest and holding me like he needed me to keep standing.

"Longest," I agreed as I turned and rested my head against his shoulder, my hand finding the steady beating of his heart as we stood in his kitchen late that night.

I thought the *surprise* he'd mentioned to Nora had been a booster seat for his truck that was already in place and ready to go when we'd left the hospital—thanks to Leah and Peter. But then Reed had driven us back to his house instead of Lala's, where they'd been waiting along with Nick and his wife, Jenn.

Almost all of Nora's favorite people, ready to welcome her to a new place and make her feel completely at home.

They'd had Nora's favorite dinner ready and had turned Peter's room into something out of a fairytale, complete with some of Nora's stuffed animals and clothes from Lala's.

I'd been stunned by the love that poured from the house and the sense of family weaving through those friends, so different and somehow so similar to what I'd just witnessed in Florida.

And instead of that flare of unwelcome resentment I'd become used to, I'd been so thankful Nora had their love and support—that she would continue having it no matter what happened to Lala—that I'd nearly been brought to my knees in gratitude.

"Did you check on Nora?"

Reed's acknowledgment rumbled against my ear. "Out."

I sucked in a shocked gasp when his hands curled around my hips and lifted me onto the counter I'd just finished cleaning. "Thanks for the warning," I muttered against his playful smirk before falling into the kiss.

All soft and teasing with an underlying tone of carnal need.

I pulled back slightly when Leah's laugh reminded me we weren't alone yet, and Reed groaned, his forehead dropping to my collarbone.

"Think if we go to bed, they'll notice?"

I glanced over to where she was talking animatedly to her brother and sister-in-law while Peter sat, fully absorbed in each word she said, and decided against answering that. "Where's Peter sleeping tonight?" I asked instead.

"Couch."

A sound of discontent crept up my throat. "That isn't fair to him. You should've let us go back to Lala's."

A soft laugh left him as he leaned back to look at me. "If you knew any of the places we've slept over the years, you'd know he's gonna be great on the couch. And it was his idea anyway—I told them to give Nora my room."

I nodded and slid my hand up his chest to wrap my arms loosely around his neck, contemplating talking to him about what I'd been thinking of ever since the doctor and nurses described Nora's meltdown that day.

"Something's going on in that head of yours," he mumbled softly, pulling me closer to the edge of the counter and him.

My lips parted, but I just studied him for a moment before glancing over to where his friends were at the table. "I wanted to talk to you about something, but I don't know how you're going to take it," I said as I looked back at Reed.

His dark brows knitted together as he waited.

"Because I could be wrong and crossing the line and offending—"

"Just say it," he said gently. "If you are, we can deal with all that once I know what's going on."

My tongue darted out to wet my lips, my stomach swirling with nervousness as I thought about what I'd been told and what I'd read while we were waiting in the hospital.

"You told me about Nora," I began. "You explained her learning delay and how she was when we first met, and you explained more last night, but I don't think I fully understood until today when the nurses and doctor were describing it. And then I kept thinking about what I've seen —how she avoids so many people and how she reacts to the people she doesn't trust. How she gets possessive over the ones she does. So, I started researching it while we were waiting for her to be released today."

I searched Reed's gray eyes for any sign that I was stepping into a place I shouldn't, but he was just watching me. Seeming to expect something as he waited.

"Reed, I think she might be on the spectrum," I said softly, my body tensing as I waited for his reaction.

But he just dipped his head and mumbled, "Yeah, I know."

I sat there in stunned silence for a moment before asking, "What?"

He let out a heavy sigh, his hands moving down my thighs and then back up to my hips. "I did the same thing after the first time I saw her break down. Researching . . . looking into it further when everything pointed to it. Started watching her more closely when I started doubting myself because there are days when nothing even hints at it, but she had a lot of the signs."

"Why didn't you say anything before?"

His face did that adorable scrunching thing, all hesitant apologies before he explained, "Again, it's something I figured Lala would've mentioned, but it also isn't something we really talk about because she's just Nora." He lifted one of his hands off me in a helpless kind of shrug. "But Lala and I got her into therapy to help with her speech and social skills. And we help her in the ways that we can—getting her around other people and encouraging her to talk to them, like on Thursdays and at church. And other little pushes to get her out of her comfort zone . . .

"If Nora had her way, I would be there every day at the exact same time. And I'm there because I wouldn't miss that time with her, but I don't show up at the same time, and I don't stay the same amount of time each day. It drove her crazy at first, but she's used to it now."

"Helping her be okay with change and the unexpected," I said in understanding, and he dipped his head before slanting it to the side.

"Now, why did you think you were going to be crossing a line?"

My shoulders sagged a little. "Because what if I was wrong? And it isn't exactly my place."

"She's your sister."

"I don't really know her," I argued. "And the two of you are . . . well, you're everything to each other."

A hum of understanding and agreement sounded in his throat. "She's your sister," he repeated resolutely.

"That's weird, isn't it?" I mumbled, earning a rough laugh from him.

"It's been weird," he countered before capturing my lips for a brief kiss. "Just talk to me. It's easier and safer for us than you keeping things in your head."

I let my fingers trail forward to his jaw before kissing him again, letting that be my response since there were still things he didn't know.

"You're quickly becoming everything to me," he said against my lips, sending my heart into a beautiful sort of chaos.

"Reed—"

He sighed in irritation when someone loudly cleared their throat behind him.

"I mean, we can leave if you want," Nick said, smirking when I peeked out around Reed's shoulder.

"Night," Reed called back, coughing out a laugh when I smacked his stomach.

Jenn rolled her eyes from beside Nick. "We actually are leaving. I didn't realize what time it was, and *some of us*"—she cast an annoyed look at all the boys—"have to work in the morning."

Nick just smiled and pulled her against his side. "I told her she could come work our schedules."

"I like working nine-to-five," she said as she cupped her

hand around his neck. "I would just maybe like it more if Mondays weren't included."

"But then Tuesday would be Monday," Reed argued, and Nick held out an arm toward him.

"Exactly. Thank you. Glad I'm not the only one who understands that."

"If you don't want Mondays on a Monday, your best bet is to come work with us," Reed added.

"Like I said." Nick smirked victoriously. "Don't we need a dispatcher?"

Reed shrugged. "We could use a new one."

"Done," Nick said. "Application in tomorrow."

Jenn just sighed and focused on me as she gestured between them. "This is what you're getting into. Think really hard before—" Her feigned warning cut off into laughter when Nick dug his fingers into her sides.

I glanced over to see Peter desperately trying not to look at where Leah was smiling softly, cheeks red with heat, stare bouncing all around—the same way it'd been all night. The two dancing around each other and pretending they weren't stealing glances or that the tension in the room didn't grow each time Peter side-stepped her to avoid touching her.

She tensed, eyes widening with obvious worry when Nick tapped her arm.

"You heading out?"

Her head bobbed. "Yeah, um—yes." She pointed behind her and cleared her throat. "I'm just going to use the bathroom first."

"Want us to wait?" he asked, pausing when he and Jenn had started stepping away.

"No, go on ahead. I'm right behind you." Leah grabbed his hand and squeezed it. "I'll see you soon."

"Let us know you got home."

Leah scoffed at Nick's demand as she walked away and sarcastically mumbled, "Okay, Dad."

Nick gave Reed a frustrated look as he and Jenn slowly began walking away. "She isn't even supposed to be driving right now."

"This is Leah we're talking about," Reed tried to reason, "she'll probably drive herself to the hospital."

Nick sighed heavily as if he'd been worrying about that before he and Jenn called out their goodnights.

I awkwardly waved goodbye to them but didn't move from my place at the edge of the kitchen as Reed walked them out. Once they were out of my line of sight, I glanced to my side to see Peter with his head down and to the side, looking over his shoulder.

"You have to stop," I mumbled under my breath, knowing he could hear me.

The breath he'd been taking paused before he sucked it in quickly and shifted his head toward me, shame clouding his eyes.

"I don't know you well, but the guy who's been here tonight isn't you. You've barely spoken five words, and they had to have noticed," I continued in the same whispered tone. "They're going to notice *why* soon."

His head bobbed slowly. "Yes." When my brow furrowed, he said, "Yes, I'm in love with her."

My chest ached at the pain in his confession, my words twisting when I said, "I know, but you can't be."

His expression creased. "You think I want this?" His stare snapped to the side and he forced out a deep breath as his features smoothed just before the front door closed.

A few seconds later, Reed rounded the corner, silent and handsome as ever.

That smirk doing dangerous things to my body as he pulled me close and pressed a faint kiss to my neck. "Can I take you to bed now?"

An exhausted hum sounded in my throat, but I said, "I need to rinse off first. I smell like the hospital."

One of his hands curled tight, all possession and need just as Leah came back.

"Is there anything else I can do before I leave?" she asked, stopping near Peter.

"And Leah's still here," I said helpfully, a soft laugh tumbling past my lips when Reed mumbled a curse as if he'd completely forgotten.

"No," Reed said, turning but keeping me in his arms. "You guys did so much. And, Leah . . . you did way more than you should've. You need to be resting."

"So everyone keeps telling me."

"Because your doctor told you to," Reed reminded her.

She swept her hands over her stomach and smiled adoringly. "There's no resting anymore anyway. I can't get comfortable, and he wakes up whenever I'm ready to sleep." A tired laugh left her as her fingers trailed higher up on her belly. "On cue."

"Getting you ready for when he's here," Reed teased, and Leah gave him an irritated look.

"Maybe I'll make you come take the night shift since you're already awake."

"You have a husband for that," he shot back just as easily, his words making my lungs stall and sending Peter back another step from Leah. "Speaking of, where's he been all day? Not that I wanted to see him."

Leah shrugged. “Big case—you know how it is. He—”

“Works so hard,” Reed finished for her, sounding annoyed and earning an eye roll from her.

“Be kind.”

“That’s my middle name,” he said sarcastically, a soft laugh rumbling from him when she scoffed.

“Did you want to feel him kick?”

I looked at Reed when he curled his fingers tighter against me for a brief second, then over to see Leah watching me. “What?”

“Did you want to feel him kick?” she asked again, her tone inviting and her face curious, and it was only then that I realized I’d been staring at her stomach as they’d bantered. “It’s fine, I really don’t mind.”

I didn’t move from Reed’s side. “I . . .” My head shook slightly. “I’ve never, um . . .”

Her eyes brightened. “Really? Oh, you have to!”

I pressed harder against Reed for a moment before cautiously stepping forward to meet her when she approached us, hand outstretched for mine. Hesitation curling through me as she grabbed my fingers and pressed them all too firmly against her belly, excited stare on mine as if she were waiting for something.

Just as I was about to step away and avoid touching her stomach ever again, I sucked in a gasp when something hit my palm.

A soft giggle left Leah as she pressed my hand harder, voice all affection as she whispered, “There he is.”

I tensed when another two bumps pressed against me in rapid succession. “Oh my God, that’s incredible.”

“Right?”

After another few nudges to my hand, I pulled away and stepped back to Reed's side. "Thank you for that."

She looked at me as if my gratitude were the funniest thing. "Of course." With another sigh, she turned, her stare lingering on Peter before falling to the floor as another blush crept over her cheeks. "I guess I should—whoa!"

"What's wrong?" Peter demanded, stepping closer.

A breathless laugh left her. "Nothing, he just started going crazy. Feel this," she said, reaching for Peter even when he shifted away.

"It's a baby, not a bomb," Reed teased.

Peter's jaw ticked, but he took another step back until he was pressed to the counter.

"He's never been this wild—you have to feel this," Leah said as she managed to take hold of his hand and press it to her stomach.

The tension mounting all night came to a tangible high as soon as Peter's large hand curled around her stomach. As if the excitement over what was happening in her body had Leah forgetting the dance they'd been in until that moment, and then she realized they were there.

Invisible line crossed.

Touching each other and closer than they'd allowed themselves to be.

His stare lingered on where he was touching her for long moments until he brought his other hand up to cradle her belly, his eyes shifting to meet hers in a moment so intimate that it made me hurt for them.

Reed went still beside me for long seconds before asking, "Leah, you need a ride home?" The low tone of his voice snapping Leah and Peter out of the moment they'd fallen into and forcing the two apart.

Peter pressed back against the counter, hands gripping the edge so tightly his knuckles turned white instantly as Leah stepped away.

"Um . . . no," she said, looking partly dazed and a whole lot horrified. "No, I'm fine." She smoothed back her hair, stare darting all around as she forced a smile. "But I should go. Let me know if you need any help with Nora."

I looked up to see Reed's glare set on Peter and offered, "I'll walk her out." Hurrying after her when she seemed intent on running from the house as fast as her pregnant belly allowed.

"I'm not a bad person," she whispered when I caught up to her at the door, her eyes filled with tears. "I'm not—I wouldn't—"

"I know," I said, trying to assure her even though I didn't know her nearly well enough to say that.

However, I was sure Peter would do anything to prevent it.

"I'm so sorry," she said, her voice strained as I followed her onto the porch. "Please don't think of me like this."

"Like what?" I gestured to the door with a nod. "We were just feeling your baby kick."

Her face creased and she nodded because we all knew that moment had been so much more than that for them. "Goodnight, Emma."

"Goodnight. Get home safe."

I waited until she was in her car to walk back into the house. The tension thicker than when I'd left it, the guys in the exact positions they'd been in, neither speaking. Reed looked ready to unleash a day's worth of worries and fears on Peter, while his friend looked sick.

"I think we should go to bed," I said as I neared Reed. "You guys can talk in the morning."

He watched Peter for a moment longer before reaching for me and pulling me close to his side as we left the kitchen.

"Reed—"

"She's married," Reed snapped, turning on Peter as if he'd been waiting for him to make the first move. "And that's Butler's sister. She's like our sister."

"No, she's like *your* sister," Peter fired back, pushing from the counter and gesturing to himself. "And I know she's married. I fucking know that. But her husband's an asshole."

"That doesn't matter," Reed said on a laugh that was pure frustration. "We're all aware he's a piece of shit, but that doesn't mean anything because Leah's *married* to him, Rowe. For some unknown fucking reason, she likes him, and they're about to have a kid—as you just witnessed."

Peter looked like he was about to concede before his attention shifted to me. "Emma—"

"Don't bring her into this," Reed said in low warning.

"You said Jarrod wasn't a good man," Peter went on. "You said Leah shouldn't be in the marriage she's in. Why?" His expression alone was desperate and pleading, but it felt like ice was being shoved through my veins when Reed turned to look at me.

THIRTY-EIGHT

EMMA

"You knew about this?" He lifted a hand and pointed to Peter. "Wait, what he just asked . . . why would you say that and how do you even know Jarrod?"

"I don't," I said weakly. "Not really."

"Lie," Reed mumbled, the word sounding at once wary and wounded.

"I'm not." I tried to meet his stare but couldn't hold it as I fought back every memory tied to the man in question. "I hardly know him."

"You don't know Jarrod, but you'd say that to Rowe about him?" Reed asked in disbelief. "You have a hard time grasping how anyone can move on after a relationship, but you'll talk to my best friend about why he should have an affair with someone?"

My head jerked back at the accusation. "I said something I shouldn't have because other peoples' relationships aren't my business, whether it's Leah's marriage or the way she and Peter are very clearly trying *not* to feel about each other. But I never once told Peter to have an affair with her," I said, offense weaving through my tone.

"Which I'm not," Peter added. "I don't touch her. I keep my distance."

"And you'll continue to," Reed said definitively.

Peter nodded, contradicting the words that left him. "She shouldn't be with him."

"We all know that. But until the day Leah decides not to be and makes it legal, there's nothing you can do." Reed's voice dripped with hidden command and effectively ended their conversation.

He reached for me, but I stepped past him and walked up to where Peter was staring at the floor, gripping the back of his neck.

"Thank you for everything you did for Nora," I whispered when I was a step away.

His head bobbed. "Anything."

I tried for the easy physical contact Reed's family and friends all effortlessly had, but my hand shook, and I nearly brought it back to my side a handful of times before I finally placed it on his shoulder.

"I'm sorry," I murmured, voice even softer than before. "I'm sorry you're hurting."

"Why'd you say it?" he begged.

"I wish I never had."

His hand fell and he glanced up at me, a strained smile on his face. "That isn't an answer."

"Yes, it is. I'm sorry it isn't the one you want, but it's all I can give you." Turning, I walked from the kitchen and past Reed, heading for his room without him.

But he was there, following silently even though I felt his storm of emotions like a weight pressing against me.

"You honestly think I would've told *anyone* to have an affair?" I hissed when he shut the door behind us, not bothering to look at him as I stepped out of my heels on my way to where our bags from this weekend were.

"You knew, and you didn't tell me."

"How did you not know?" I demanded as I furiously searched for clothes to wear. Once I had them out, I turned on him as I pulled my hair into a messy knot on top of my head before pointing to the door. "The times I've seen them, it's been exactly *that*. All night tonight, it was *that*."

Reed's head shifted back, shaking slightly as if he couldn't believe it—as if it was bothering him that he'd missed it. "If Butler finds out—"

"Don't you think Peter's beating himself up enough?" I grabbed my clothes off the bed on my way to his bathroom, my steps coming to a jarring halt when Reed spoke.

"How do you know Jarrod?"

"I told you, I don't," I said softly as the memory of Jarrod's hands on my body had me all the more eager to get to the shower.

"And you're lying."

I thought for a moment, trying to think of anything to say to ease his curiosity and worries, and finally continued walking away without saying anything at all.

Once I was under the warm spray of the shower, I closed my eyes and released a heavy breath as I focused on forcing away the wraiths releasing memories that were better left locked away.

When the shaking in my bones settled and my breathing eased, I finally opened my eyes in time to see Reed walk into the bathroom, pulling his shirt over his head as he did.

I twisted away and covered my chest instinctively, even

though he'd already seen every part of me. But there was something different about standing there, waiting for him this way that was a territory all on its own. And it had my heart racing as I watched him shed the last of his clothes, leaving all those long muscles and decorated skin exposed to me in the most devastating way.

His eyes searched mine as he stepped into the shower, all question and carnal need. "I'm gonna touch you."

My eyebrows lifted at the question posed as a statement, and I fumbled over a nod.

His hands slid over my slick hips, pulling my back to his chest and forcing a stuttered breath from me at the feel of him pressed to me.

"Pushing?" he asked as his mouth brushed along my shoulder.

I tried to swallow, but my throat had gone so dry as heat and need flared in my body. "No," I managed to say.

With another kiss to my shoulder, he reached past me for the soap and rubbed it between his palms. Once his hands were on me, slowly and tenderly washing my stomach and hips, he asked, "What are you keeping from me, Emma?"

My eyelids had closed from the intoxicating feel of his hands slipping over me and his length pressing against my butt but snapped open again at the question.

And despite how hard I'd tried to shut the box, Jarrod's words slipped free.

"Who do you think silenced those strippers? Who do you think destroyed all evidence of any of us being in the building that night? Being me has its perks. Having Ron as my father-in-law has more. I told you, you can't touch me."

Forcing it away and fortifying the walls on my mind, I softly pleaded, "Can we forget this for tonight?"

"Emma—"

"Today has been so long and emotionally draining," I said as I placed a hand over his. "The last few days have all been exhausting in one way or another, even though I had such a great time with your family. But I'm worn out. I need you and I need sleep, so please . . . just not tonight."

"That isn't helping ease any of the thoughts going through my head on how you might know him."

"I told you, I don't."

Jarrod was just a man who tried to have his way with me once and who I'd, unfortunately, run into twice more.

There was nothing I truly knew about him other than he was a disgusting excuse for a man.

"I don't like this lie."

"I don't like talking about someone else when you're holding me this way."

Other than the sound of the water surrounding us, silence met me for a while before he sighed. "Then not tonight," he conceded, but I knew in his tone that Jarrod was something Reed didn't plan to drop.

"Tell me something you think I should know about you," I pleaded when the following silence got to be too much.

"I like the way you fit in my life," he said after a moment and finally began washing my body again, his hands cupping my breasts and lightly teasing my nipples when I arched against him. "My family, my friends . . . everywhere." His mouth brushed across my shoulder as one of his hands drifted up my chest, his fingers gently teasing the slope of my neck. "I feel possessive over you in ways that would probably scare you."

My chest shook with the impact of his confession. "You want to possess me?"

"No," he said immediately, voice rough and dripping with sex. "I want to fuck the pain from your past until there are no more demons lingering in your eyes. Until all you see and feel and crave is me."

Warmth pooled low in my belly and desire raced through my veins. My heart hammering recklessly as he pressed his hand between my breasts to feel the frantic beating.

"I want to show you how worthy you are to be loved, and I want to be the one who gets to love you." The hand at my neck crept higher, curling around my jaw to tilt my head back until I was looking into his darkened eyes. His mouth a breath from mine when he said, "I want to brand my name on your soul because you're already burned into mine."

He lingered there, waiting for my reaction.

Clearly refraining himself from what he wanted and expecting that push.

"You're shaking," he whispered.

I nodded slightly, my lips faintly brushing against his. "Because it does scare me," I admitted before saying, "But I want it all."

His mouth captured mine as he turned me in his arms, moving us until my back was against the shower wall. Pulling me closer and pressing every soft curve of my body to every hard line of his. Shielding me from the spray of water and caging me in with his large frame.

Trapping me.

My breathing hitched and my hands quickly moved to his chest as memories broke free, but before I could react, he met me there.

Holding my hands close to his chest and gripping them tight. His voice all rough comfort as he spoke through the kiss. "I've got you. You're safe." His mouth moved to my jaw and down my neck as my chest rose and fell wildly. "I'm the one here with you, Emma," he said into my ear before nipping the soft skin beneath it. "Not them."

I closed my eyes tight, my head shaking as I struggled to fight against what was so quick to overwhelm me.

"I love you," he breathed before lifting one of my trembling hands to press his mouth to my palm.

My next breath came out ragged and broken because I could feel his love surrounding me, and I wanted to embrace it and this time with him. But I couldn't figure out a way through the nightmare being caged against a hard surface put me in.

Surprise and need bled from me on a fractured whimper, my eyelids flying open when Reed's mouth caressed the underside of my breast to see him lowering to his knees in front of me.

I was so dazed by the sight of this man on his knees and the look of absolute desire in his gunmetal eyes that I just stood there, shaking with all my demons as his hands moved up my thighs to grip my hips and then slowly worked back down.

Oh God.

"What do you feel?" he asked as he gently pushed my legs farther apart, his hold firm and somehow gentle at the same time.

"You."

He placed a kiss to the inside of my thigh, sending a tremor through my core. "What do you see?"

"Everything," I answered honestly.

I saw every man who'd taken advantage of me, made up into a blur. I saw Manhattan.

Most of all, I saw Reed.

His head slanted. "It's just you and me." With another kiss to the inside of my thigh, he whispered, "Push," before he set his mouth on me. His tongue slipping through my folds and flicking against my clit and making my knees go weak.

"Oh God," I whispered as I reached for the adjacent wall with one hand and gripped at his hair with the other.

He made the path again and again, slowly tormenting me and making the world fade away when his stare met mine for a brief moment. All desire and love with a hint of all that trouble I'd always known he was.

And then he let go of the leash he'd been keeping himself on.

Devouring me until it was all I could do to stay standing. Pressing a finger inside me as he brought me higher and higher with his tongue and teeth and lips. My stomach curling with heat when he added a second, fucking me until my body was buzzing. Winding me up until I was standing on the edge and trying not to fall.

And then he curled his fingers and sucked my clit into his mouth, and I was lost.

Floating in a sea of stars as pleasure coursed through my veins for immeasurable moments until I came crashing back to Reed as he stood and pulled me close. His tall, hard body forming to mine and humming with an energy that was all wicked pleasure, waiting to be set free.

"What do you see?" he begged, his mouth hovering over mine.

"You."

The corner of his mouth ticked up before he captured mine for a slow, brief kiss, tugging on my bottom lip as he released me.

Grabbing my hands in his, he slid them up his slick abdomen until they were pressed firmly to his chest. A silent offer and demand to push if I needed to. Then his fingers were sliding past my hips and gripping my legs as he lifted me and settled between my thighs.

"Gonna fuck you now, Emma," he rumbled, voice pure sin and doing dangerous things to me.

Dangerous things that I was sure I would never get enough of as he slowly inched inside me. My lips parting at the feel of him stretching and filling me so wholly until he was fully seated. Again and again, filling me only to leave me. Making me breathless with the agonizing torture until he slammed into me with one long thrust. His mouth falling to mine to swallow my cry as he set a harsh rhythm that had that knot of heated pleasure in my belly forming and my body trembling as I struggled to hold on to his wet skin.

He held me tenderly, fingers gripping and clinging to me as if I were something to be worshipped.

He kissed me until I was his air, and he was mine. Both demanding more from the other and giving just as much.

He fucked me roughly, savagely, as if he'd never get enough.

The contradicting combination made my head spin in the most exhilarating way. And while he fucked me, there were no icy fingers trailing down my spine. There were no taunting demons. There were no memories.

It was just Reed, claiming me until I fell apart around him.

His mouth tore from mine with a curse as he drove harder still. Prolonging my orgasm as he thrust with abandon, losing all sense of rhythm. His muscles bunching and tightening beneath my fingertips until he went still as he found his release inside me.

His chest and shoulders heaved with ragged breaths as he continued holding me in his arms. Tremors rolling through his body and transferring to my own as I let my head rest against the wall I was pinned to, never taking my eyes off him as I slid one of my hands from around his neck to feel the unruly pounding of his heart.

"Reed, I love you."

His stare lifted to mine, all wonder and disbelief. "For the rest of my life, I'll never get tired of hearing those words from you," he said softly, then leaned forward to capture my lips. "Burned into my goddamn soul."

THIRTY-NINE

REED

"Where are you going?"

Rowe barked out a laugh, and Emma's shoulders sagged as she turned to face me early the next morning, muttering, "Damn it," under her breath.

My brows lifted at that, but then her stare skated over my bare chest. Her cheeks heating and the corners of her mouth twitching when her gaze met mine.

And, fuck me, that's when I finally noticed what she was wearing: Skin-tight jeans and one of my shirts, knotted high on her hip to keep it fitted to her body. My blood pounded through my veins at the sight of her, all primal satisfaction in that simple claim.

"I told her she looked like she was doing the walk of shame," Rowe said as he leaned back against the kitchen counter and lifted his mug.

Emma scoffed and shot him a glare before setting down the heels she'd been carrying and stepping into them. "I was trying to be quiet so you could finally sleep."

My head slanted when I stopped a few feet from her.

Sometime earlier, I'd woken to her hands slamming into my chest as she'd scrambled away, breaths harsh and eyes vacant and frantic.

After I'd calmed her and pulled her back into my arms, I'd whispered with her in the dark until sleep claimed me again. Considering there hadn't been any more pushes and I'd just woken alone, I was assuming she'd slipped out of bed soon after.

"There a reason you didn't want me to know you were going?"

"Because you don't ever sleep," she said, all exasperation as if she'd just had this conversation.

From Rowe's smirk, she probably had.

"You haven't gotten much sleep recently either."

"Right, but I have to go," she said, glancing at her phone. "The bookstore's reopening is in less than an hour, and I have things to do before then."

"Shit," I mumbled and scrubbed my hands over my face. With the wreck and everything we'd found out about Lala, I'd completely forgotten. "All right, let me put a shirt on." I'd turned to head back to my room but stopped at her genuine confusion.

"Okay? But I'm leaving."

"Did you want me to drive you? I mean, unless you wanted to take my truck."

Surprise lit her expression. "What? No, of course not. I have a car coming."

"Why?"

She gave me a look as if she couldn't understand the problem and then glanced at her phone again. "So I wouldn't have to walk?"

Rowe coughed out a laugh and tried to cover it by drinking his coffee.

"We have cars here," I said slowly. "Why would you have walked?"

"Because they aren't mine." Some of that girl I'd first met bled free. Fierce expression and tone, daring me to keep challenging her.

And, Christ, I wanted to.

But then she said, "And you need to be here for Nora."

"I'll take you," Rowe offered.

I nodded toward him in agreement and added, "Or you can just take my truck." Each word coming out low and firm to emphasize how ridiculous this conversation was.

"Or I can go get in the car that just showed up, and you can be okay with it." Her brow ticked up as she grabbed her purse, and then she was walking from the house without another word.

"Have I mentioned I like her?" Rowe asked once the door shut.

I heaved a sigh and jogged after her, leaving the front door open wide as I called out her name and cleared the porch.

She turned in time for me to cradle her face in my hands and crush my mouth to hers. The kiss hard and just as fierce as the girl I was holding.

"You're infuriating," I growled against her lips.

A ghost of a smile crossed her face before she pressed her mouth to mine again. "You're welcome."

A rumbling laugh built in my chest. "I love you."

She inhaled quickly, her eyes dancing when she looked at me. "You still can't drive me."

"Doesn't mean I don't love you."

She pressed her hand to my chest, her next smile wide and unrestrained. "I'll see you later."

"Congratulations on the store."

Excitement burst from her when she pulled away, the tips of her fingers lingering on my chest as long as possible. "Try to get more sleep."

I just stepped back and watched her go, knowing sleep would be impossible without her.

A couple nights with her in my arms, and I was ruined for anything less.

"DAMN, what did this place used to be?" Rowe asked that afternoon when we walked into Morrison's Books with Nora.

"Apparently, this bookstore."

"No shit?" I gave him a look, and he cringed. His stare darting to where Nora was trying to disappear into my side. "No way? I never even knew this was here."

I lifted my eyebrows in agreement. "Same. Emma said it looked forgotten inside and out. What she described . . . *shit*."

Rowe shoved my shoulder and then went still when his stare followed my line of sight to the person I'd just noticed.

Nora gasped from beside me and bounced on her toes. "My Leah!"

"Don't even think about it," I said in low warning to my friend.

"Man, I didn't do anything. I *haven't* done anything."

"And we're keeping it that way," I muttered as Leah disappeared down another row without noticing us.

"Can we go talk to my Leah?" Nora asked and tugged on my hand. "I want to tell her that my Peter made me pancakes and now we're going to get burgers! But no pickles and no onions. I don't like those. Maybe she can come with us?" she rambled quickly.

"I don't—"

"What are you guys doing here?"

I turned at the sound of Emma's voice, surprise lighting up her face as she looked at us. "Hey."

"Hi." Amusement danced in her eyes before concern wove through them when she focused on Nora. "How are you feeling today?"

"Good!" she said excitedly. "But not really that good because I hurt in lots of places. But my Peter made me pancakes this morning, and now we're going to get burgers."

"We wanted to swing by here first," I said, stopping the rest of her repeated ramble. "Check out how things were going and maybe look for some Fancy Nancy." I drew out the last words, making them sound like a question and earning a gasp from Nora.

Mischief tugged at Emma's mouth, her eyes bright as she glanced between the three of us. "I think I saw some books with that title in the children's section. However . . . there's something I wanted to show you first." She scanned the store for a moment before whispering, "Follow me."

"Stop," I warned softly when we started after her, Rowe lagging behind and cautiously glancing over his shoulder.

"Jarrod is here," he muttered beneath his breath before falling into step with us.

I didn't bother reminding him that was Leah's husband—he already knew. Besides, from the way Rowe's stare darted curiously over Emma, his thoughts had gone to the same place as mine:

How did she know him?

I gave her last night because we'd had a hell of a weekend and a shitstorm of a day, and I'd give her this time while she was at the store. But once I got her back tonight, I wasn't letting it go.

"The secret room?" Nora asked on a soft gasp when Emma led us to the hidden staircase in the hall. "But my Lala said I couldn't go up there."

"That's because it wasn't finished yet," Emma said over her shoulder, looking so at ease and taking my damn breath away with the gentle smile touching her lips. "But I know she's okay with you being up there now."

Nora still looked at me in question first, and then it was all I could do to make her take the stairs slowly when she tried to make a mad dash up them.

"Wow," she said loudly once she stepped into the loft. "My Reed, look! You can see the whole store and all the people from up here." Her bright laugh followed soon after when Rowe fell heavily onto the couch. "That isn't for you, my Peter."

"This is definitely for me," he argued with a strained smile.

"How's it been so far?" I asked as I stepped up beside where Emma was watching them, suppressing a laugh when Nora tried to squeeze onto the couch next to Rowe.

"Incredible," she breathed, eyes bright as she moved closer to my side. "Already this morning, the store's brought in more than it has in the last three years." At my shock, she conceded, "Granted, Donna hasn't had much business these last years. But, still huge, and she's been on cloud nine all day. And we've had multiple people ask if we're planning on doing certain things—like Mommy and Me mornings and book clubs. Which, we weren't, but I'm going to look into it now."

"That's amazing," I said on a stunned breath. "You're amazing for doing all this."

She let out a disbelieving huff. "Anyone could've done this." When I started to argue, she stepped away and said, "Hey, Nora, I wanted to tell you something."

Nora popped up from where she'd been trying to push Rowe and then jumped from the couch, hissing and grabbing at her side even as she darted over to where we stood.

Emma went into a crouch, somehow managing to balance on her high-as-fuck heels as she looked directly at Nora. Excitement slipping into something darker—shadowed. Something I couldn't accurately begin to describe, but it had me going still.

As if every part of me that was connected to Emma knew I needed to hear whatever she was about to share. Already knew the words about to leave her mouth were going to make me ache for her.

"You know, when I was growing up, I didn't have anyone who read with me," Emma began, lips trembling.

"Like my Reed?" Nora asked hesitantly, seeming to sense the gravity of what Emma was telling her.

Emma nodded. "And I didn't get to go to school like you do, so no one taught me how to read either."

"Oh," Nora said sadly. "Maybe my Reed can teach you. He helps me, and so does my Lala."

A shaky laugh left Emma. "I actually know how to read now—I taught myself. Every time we moved somewhere new, I found a library or a bookstore like this one. And a lot of days, I'd stay there all day long because it didn't cost anything to hide in the corner with a book."

My chest wrenched, but I forced my outward appearance to remain unchanged as she painted more of her past, helping me understand her that much more . . . like why it was so hard for her to accept help.

She'd spent most of her life trying to erase her mom's debt, and everything she had—including basic skills that should've been taught to her—she'd attained on her own. All while taking care of her mom and defending herself from the pieces of shit lingering around.

"Did you read Fancy Nancy?" Nora asked.

"Fancy Nancy wasn't around when I was doing that, but I think if she were, I probably would've liked her as much as you do."

Nora lit up, just the slightest mention of the character and books making her so damn excited.

"But Ms. Donna gave me this loft to do with as I wanted, and since it's quite a corner, I thought I'd make it *your* corner for when you come visit." She tilted her head and pointed to the bookshelf beside her, drawing Nora's attention there—and mine.

And my heart fucking stopped.

"Fancy Nancy!" Nora cried out and darted past Emma, dropping to her knees and letting her good hand flutter over the completely stocked shelves as if she was afraid to touch the books.

By the time I was able to look at Emma again, she was straightening from her crouch, a gentle smile touching her face that fell to worry when she glanced my way.

"When did you do this?" I asked, throat thick with emotion that built and built. Something I couldn't understand because this was all new territory.

"Last week," she mumbled warily. "That's what I was doing when you came up here."

I blinked slowly, trying to comprehend as I looked back to where Nora was still only studying the books—not touching them. "You did this for her?"

Her stare darted over to where Rowe was trying to make himself invisible and then back to me. "I know you buy her the books, and I'm not trying to take that away from you. I just thought she might also want them—"

I pressed my mouth to hers, silencing her apologetic ramble and swallowing her shock of surprise. "I fucking love you," I whispered against her lips before kissing her again.

"You're not mad?"

"Are you kidding?" I pressed my forehead to hers for a few seconds before pulling back, keeping my hand on her waist. "This is everything to her. No, I'm not mad."

Relief fled from her on an exhale. "When I bought them, I didn't know if I'd ever be able to show it to her. But I wanted it in case Lala brought her—speaking of, have you heard from her?"

"Yeah, she called just as we were headed over here." The corner of my mouth lifted as I told her, "She tried to guilt me into getting her out of the hospital—saying you're leaving her in there."

"I am not," she said defensively even as a breath of a laugh slipped free because it was such a Lala thing to say. "I talked to her doctor about an hour ago. He said they're hoping she can come home tonight . . . unless she has another seizure."

I curled my fingers tighter against her waist at the worry that flashed through her eyes. "Let's hope she doesn't. But we're gonna head over there after lunch to check on her."

She nodded after a moment and whispered, "Okay."

"She'll be home soon, bossing people around and getting in their business, and back in the kitchen for Thursdays in no time," I said, trying to soothe her worries. "All right?"

A brief smile touched her lips. "If she were anyone else, I might not believe you." Letting her fingers trail over my chest, she stepped away, her entire demeanor shifting back to excitement. "I almost forgot," she said under her breath, "I got something for Nora."

I gestured to the bookshelf as I turned to watch her take a step back toward the stairs. "More than the books?"

"Well, Donna and I thought the loft needed to feel more like *hers*," Emma explained softly so her voice wouldn't carry to Nora. "It's a large, princess castle tent to relax and read in that has twinkle lights and big star lights. It's very fancy."

Wonder tugged at my chest as a smile stole across my face. "I'm never going to be able to get her out of there."

She rolled her eyes, looking all playful and light. "I'll be right back, it's in the office."

I watched her go, my heart racing the way it always did around her and twisting up because she was doing things for Nora. She'd *been* doing them even when Nora wanted nothing to do with her.

"Can I look at one, my Reed?" Nora asked, voice all reverence as she continued looking over what seemed to be every Fancy Nancy book ever made.

"Go for it," I managed to say, gravel scratching up my words as I watched her carefully select one of her favorites and sit back with it right there in front of the shelf.

"Ryan, what the hell?" Rowe asked when he came up beside me. Shock and horror practically bursting from him and filling the open space. "What kind of life did she have?"

My head shook, but I didn't look away from Nora.

"I knew she moved a lot, but . . ."

"Can't do this, man," I murmured low enough for the conversation to stay between us. "Not my story."

Rowe was silent for more than a minute as we watched the little girl read the book to herself, mostly from memory. "Did you know?"

I released a slow breath. "Every day, I find out something new that tears at a piece of my soul." Sparing him a glance, I muttered, "That wasn't the worst. By far."

Worry and sorrow bled from him, but he just stood still and silent beside me for a while before asking, "Have I mentioned I like her?"

A huff left me, and I rubbed my hand over my chest. Skin suddenly feeling too tight for my body.

"I like her," he said resolutely, then mumbled, "Look what she did for the kid." Awe wrapping around the words as Nora finished the book and put it back in the same place before searching out another.

A smile broke free only to falter when I realized Nora had already finished a book, and Emma still wasn't back.

If she'd just been running to the office and back, that trip would've taken a minute.

"You good?"

I glanced over to see Rowe staring at where I was still rubbing at my chest. Hadn't even realized I was until then.

"Emma should've been back," I muttered, crossing the loft to look out over the store. Gaze shifting from person to person in quick succession before I was moving back across the space to where Rowe was waiting.

Years of working together on missions had him on high alert, but the guy was always so at ease that you'd never know anything was wrong unless you knew his tells. The way his head slightly dipped and slanted, listening for threats. Eyes trained on the only entrance to where we were, daring someone to come through it.

All so subtle while he stood there with a smirk and his arms folded casually across his chest.

"She out there?" he asked, feigning indifference. When I shook my head, he shrugged. "She could've gotten a call—maybe for Lala?"

My head continued to shake. "Feel like I'm crawling out of my skin," I said as I backed up to the stairs, attention shifting to where Nora held the second book on her lap, completely unconcerned.

Rowe casually positioned himself between her and the doorway, silently letting me know he had her, and that was all I needed to go hurrying down the stairs.

Taking a step out of the hallway and into the store, I made a quick sweep to see if she might be there, but there was nothing. Just people walking throughout, oblivious to the feeling creeping across my body and growing stronger when I turned and moved down the long hall.

My steps slowed to a stop when I slipped up to the office and heard the deep, unmistakable tenor of a man seeping out of the cracked-open door.

Taunting.

Demanding.

Pressing up against the door, I glanced through the crack just large enough to show the back of a man . . . and Emma, pinned between him and the wall.

FORTY

REED

Rage exploded in my veins, but I forced myself to take a breath. To remember every second of training I'd endured so I wouldn't put her at risk.

Pulling my gun from the holster hidden beneath my shirt, I chambered a round and slowly leaned against the door, letting it open enough for me to step through as the man spoke.

"I think it's me who's going to be doing the ruining, Ms. Wade."

"Fuck you," she breathed, voice twisting around the words. "Fuck you, fuck you, *fuck you.*" She thrashed against him, and he laughed as he pressed her harder against the wall.

"That's the idea," he said as I edged around the desk, giving me a clear view of him for a moment when he pressed his nose to her neck and breathed her in, nearly causing me to stumble and forget fucking *everything* because someone was touching her.

Not just someone—Jarrod fucking Davis.

But I somehow managed to keep each step quick and careful.

Silent.

Still, I fought to keep my stare on him when it kept drawing back to Emma. Checking her, making sure she wasn't hurt and getting stuck on the absolute terror in her eyes. Haunted and familiar . . . the steel she normally wore like armor shaking, struggling to remain in place.

"Rot in Hell," she seethed and looked up at him, her face falling when she saw me there.

"Get the fuck away from her," I demanded as I pressed the gun to the base of his spine and gripped his shoulder, digging my fingers into the pressure point there and walking him back when he arched away from her. "You okay?"

Emma just stared at us, expression vacant, chest pitching wildly.

"Babe, I need an answer."

Her head moved in a mess of nods and shakes as she blinked away whatever she was seeing.

Jarrod hissed when I dug my fingers into the spot behind his collarbone even harder. "You're making a mistake."

"That right?" I asked through clenched teeth. "Except you were touching someone who isn't yours. Someone who clearly didn't want to be touched."

He roughed out a low laugh. "That's just her game, the little tease."

I twisted and flung him back into the desk, punching him before he managed to catch himself on it.

"Reed!" Emma cried out, horrified.

Jarrod held a hand to his face, blood pouring free from his nose, and yelled, "I can destroy you like that." Snapping his fingers. "Do you know who I am?"

"I don't give a shit who you are. You touched my girl."

He smiled through the blood and sneered, "You're very focused on that. Or is that how it is with you? Touch it, it's yours?" His stare shifted behind me. "If that's the case, she was mine first."

I hesitated, waiting for Emma to deny what Jarrod had said, then slowly placed my other hand back on the gun, securing my hold as I aimed at his stomach. My own clenching with unease.

"You can't shoot me," he seethed, "but I'm going to enjoy ruining your career and your life. You small-town, worthless excuse for a boy with a toy gun. I will slowly tear you down until you are nothing."

"Is that right?" I asked with a soft twitch of my lips. Letting all the panic and fear coming from behind me wrap around me, I lowered my voice to something softer, more comforting. "Emma, now's the time to tell me how you know him."

"Oh, we just go way back. Isn't that right, darlin'?" Jarrod asked as he swiped at his face and more blood pooled out.

"It's going to be a very painful and slow death if I shoot you now," I said in low warning. "I'd stop talking if I were you."

"The oath you took to get your badge protects me from that."

A smirk slowly stole across my face. "My family has a reputation for conveniently forgetting the law when necessary. From what Emma said about you before and what I just walked in on . . . I'm still figuring out if this is one of those *necessary* situations. And I'll gladly lose my badge if it is."

I stepped back and to the side, keeping my gun level and

stare on Jarrod as I did until I could see Emma out of the corner of my eye.

Still back against the wall. Arms wrapped around herself.

"Emma, how do you know him?"

Jarrod's eyes narrowed in obvious warning and challenge as they shifted to her.

"Babe," I softly begged when a minute came and went in thick silence.

"Shit—*what?*" Rowe hissed when he stepped into the office, taking everything in.

"Nora," I demanded without taking my stare from the man leaning against the desk.

"She's with . . ." Rowe gestured to Jarrod, an irritated huff tumbling free as he positioned himself so he could better look at Jarrod while still guarding the door. "She's with Leah—who was looking for you, by the way."

When Jarrod rolled his eyes, Rowe rocked forward, hands curling into fists when he forced himself to move back a step instead.

"This might be your only chance," I mumbled.

Rowe's head snapped up, his surprise filling the room.

"He had Emma pinned against the wall," I explained as Emma muttered my name in a soft plea for me to stop. "She clearly didn't want him in here with her."

Rowe was erasing the distance between him and Jarrod before I'd finished explaining. Grabbing the collar of his shirt when Jarrod stumbled over himself to get away and pulling him closer to deliver a hit to his jaw.

"You know exactly what that was for," Rowe ground out.

"Reed, stop him," Emma begged as Rowe continued.

"This? This is for the way you treat Leah." The next

punch sent Jarrod sprawling onto the floor, his grating laugh mixed with his panting breaths.

"Tell me," Jarrod said, spitting blood onto the carpet before glaring up at Rowe, "the baby she's carrying . . . is it mine?" He smirked even though it looked like it caused him more pain. "Because you've been drooling over her like a starved dog since you showed up in this town."

"Some of us know when to keep our hands to ourselves."

"I doubt that," Jarrod goaded as I glanced back at Emma.

Brows drawing together and a fist clenching my stomach when she looked between Jarrod and Rowe as if she didn't know what to do—didn't know how to stop what was happening.

"How do you know him?" I asked, searching those hazel eyes when they dragged to me, pleading with me to end this.

"Reed, just let him go."

Unease snaked through my veins as those demons continued dragging her back. "Emma, I saw you—I'm looking at you now."

Her head moved in quick, tight jerks. "You need to let him go."

My shoulders sagged when tears gathered in her eyes, but I forced myself to relax my stance and holster my gun.

Jarrod coughed out a laugh. "What was that you were saying about her being yours?"

I faced him again, but not before I saw the way Emma's expression creased with pain and disgust at his words. "Have you forgotten you're married?"

He huffed out a pained wheeze. "Leah knows her place."

"Peter," Emma cried out when he charged Jarrod again.

Chest heaving and hand clenched into a tight fist as he stared Jarrod down with pure rage.

"I need you to go," Emma said, voice trembling.

I jerked my head at the mess of a man in front of me. "You heard her."

"Reed," she choked out. "Reed, I need you and Peter to go."

A horrible mixture of ice and fire washed through me, stealing the air from my lungs and crushing my heart as I stood there. Every warning sign flashing. Every protective instinct locking me in place.

Triumph and pleasure and desire flashed across Jarrod's expression before he glanced my way and mocked, "You heard her."

"Reed—"

"I can't," I breathed, head shaking for a moment before I looked at Emma again. "I can't leave you with him."

"I need you to." When I didn't move, she straightened herself and tried pulling all that steel and ice around herself as she ground out, "I don't want you here, can't you understand that?"

But her eyes told me something else.

Gave me all that pain and sorrow and a fear that was so different from what haunted her while begging me to trust her.

Confusion swam through me as I studied her, but I just gave her the slightest dip of my head and muttered, "That's what you really want?" Giving me another moment to try to figure out what I was missing.

"Get out," she demanded, all venom wrapping around her sorrow.

I nodded more exaggeratedly and stepped back, holding her stare for a second longer before turning.

Rowe scoffed out a sound that was all disbelief and not at

all him. Whatever Emma was trying to tell me, he saw it too. "Are you serious? You're gonna leave her with this asshole?"

I let my glare slide to Jarrod before stalking toward the door, not responding as I slipped out into the hall and took a few thundering steps away before silently moving back to the doorway just as Rowe slammed the door and took his place beside me against the wall.

"It didn't latch," he said under his breath, then made a little motion as if wiggling a doorknob. "I held on."

I nodded, then strained to listen.

"What the hell is going on?"

"I have no idea," I answered, closing my eyes to better focus on the muted sounds coming from the room. "But if I try to kill him . . . don't stop me."

A dark, dark rage seeped out from my friend even as he scoffed. "I'll be right there beside you."

FORTY-ONE

EMMA

"Reconsidering, Ms. Wade?" Jarrod asked once the door slammed shut, removing his button-down shirt to use as a towel for the blood smeared all over his face.

"You can't take Nora from him," I said, picking up where we'd been when Reed had come in earlier, voice nothing more than a trembling breath as he edged closer again.

That charming grin that was so, so cruel was back as if he hadn't just taken all those punches. "Actually, I can," he said easily. "See, Ron did all the paperwork, which means I have access to the paperwork. Some changes here and there, and what do you know?" He lifted out the hand not holding his shirt. "Your boyfriend no longer has custody." He stepped closer, his voice dropping lower. "No one has custody . . . imagine that."

"You can't—"

"You keep saying that," he said with a laugh that was all frustration as he tossed his shirt aside. "I've already shown you what I can do, Ms. Wade. I assure you, the next step will be child's play. And after this?" He waved to his face. "I won't just take away his custody, I'll make good on the rest—he'll no longer have a career."

"Reed hasn't done—" I slammed my hands against his chest when he ran his fingers down my arm, a strangled cry working up my throat when he gripped my wrists to the point of pain. "He hasn't done anything," I cried softly, pleadingly.

"But he's the key to everything." He pressed his body to mine, smiling when I tried leaning away. "He currently has what I want, and he has a lot to lose. And I can't imagine you'd want him to lose his career and that adorable little girl."

Of course I didn't.

I would do almost anything to protect Reed and Nora from this—*almost*. Giving Jarrod what he wanted wasn't one of those things.

"I see you trying to figure a way around this, but I will get what I want. Soon. Ron ensured that."

I looked up at him as I tried to get out of his hold, my silent question lingering in the small space between us.

"He got your mother's police records and gave them to me. He also came up with the ingenious idea of creating a record for you . . . based off hers."

My stomach dropped and shock had me frozen in place.

"How would that look on your boyfriend while his career is also being destroyed? His drug-addicted, prostitute girlfriend, dragging him down," Jarrod taunted. "How would that look on your precious grandmother? Unable to face the town's judgment because both her daughter and granddaughter turned out the same way." He dipped down, a wicked grin crossing his face. "How would it look when you try to get custody of Nora?"

A breath that was all horror and pain and sorrow for what I was about to do to the people I'd come to know left me when I asked, "What do you want from me?"

A victorious smirk met me as he leaned in closer. "Good girl."

"What do you want from me?" I asked again.

He stepped away, eyes devouring me as he reached for his belt. "I want you to beg me to fuck you."

My head moved in a mess of nods as I reached for my phone that I'd slipped into my front pocket during the commotion with Reed and Peter.

"I think—" I choked out a relieved cry when I saw it was still recording. "I think I'll just tell you, once again, to rot in Hell."

Jarrod looked at once terrified and terrifying. "What are you doing?" he asked softly, his voice warning me to answer carefully.

"You're no longer untouchable," I muttered as I stopped the video and slid the phone into my back pocket. I started walking quickly away, a cry ripping from my throat when he lunged forward and yanked me back.

"You stupid bitch," he seethed as he held me close with one arm and searched for my pocket with the other hand as Reed and Peter came rushing in. Shouting things at Jarrod as Reed pulled me from Jarrod's grasp and held me close.

"I've got you," he breathed, stare quickly searching me.

"Manhattan," I choked out, and Reed's eyebrows drew together in confusion. "He's my boss's friend. I know him from that night in Manhattan."

Reed went still against me as a dark wrath seeped from him and spilled into the room. "Rowe," he said softly, the tenor sending chills up my spine. "Take Emma out of here."

"Reed, please," I whispered softly, my head shaking.

But his gray eyes were all dark intent. "Baby, he *touched* you. Those demons in your eyes are from him." He dipped his head closer, his mouth passing across my jaw and lingering when he said, "You can't ask me to let that go."

"If it can ruin your life . . . yes, I can."

He pressed another soft kiss there before saying, "Rowe." The name nothing less than a command.

I pulled away from Reed reluctantly when Peter appeared beside me and let him lead me out of the office and into the hallway.

"You okay?" Peter asked once the door was firmly shut behind us and he was leading me away. "Did he hurt you?"

I tried looking back when I heard raised voices, but Peter kept me going forward. "Uh . . . no, not really."

Peter stopped us at the entrance of the hidden staircase and seemed to search me the way Reed had—as if looking for any injuries. "You said 'Manhattan.'" When I looked up at him in surprise, he slanted his head down the hall. "What happened there?"

My gaze drifted to the floor as that night burst through my mind and mixed with everything that had happened since. Reaching back to touch my phone, I released a weighted sigh once I was sure it was still there, and muttered, "Something that's going to hurt a lot of people."

FORTY-TWO

REED

I sat on the opposite side of a table from one of our detectives and my chief that afternoon, both of them wearing identical expressions of disappointment and frustration.

My chief sighed and lifted his hands out in front of him as if I'd literally tied them. "I can't help you here, Reed."

The detective grunted. "Davis already has his father-in-law with him, and they're going for your badge and a civil suit for the unprovoked assault." He glanced at Chief and made a face. "They're trying to go for a higher charge because you're an ex-SEAL—saying you're lethal."

I snorted. "He would've been dead if I'd wanted him that way."

"This isn't a joke," Chief said.

"I'm aware," I muttered and glanced to the door, knowing Emma was somewhere in one of the other rooms.

I'd backed Jarrod into the corner of the office, delivering hit after hit to his chest and torso as I'd seethed over what he'd done to Emma before knocking him out cold.

If I'd known I'd still end up here, I would've taken my time. Tortured him because that night was sure as fuck still torturing her. Given him back to Rowe to finish off. Anything to satisfy this wrath still coursing through me, knowing *he* was one of the men from that night.

"And I wouldn't exactly call it unprovoked," I continued, looking back at them. "He tried to rape her about a month ago. When I walked in, he had her pinned to the wall, and she was trying to get away from him." I watched as the detective wrote something down. "He's lucky I didn't shoot him."

"You're not helping, Reed," he mumbled as he continued writing, then sighed as his focus returned to me. "Will the people in that room back your story?"

I hesitated for a while before slanting my head. "Probably not," I admitted. "Peter Rowe came in a few minutes later, and he doesn't know about what happened to Emma. Emma . . ." My stare darted to the door again as everything ached to get to her. "I doubt she's saying a word—she doesn't trust cops."

His brow lifted and he shared a look with Chief. "This . . . Emma Wade . . . is your girlfriend, correct?" When I nodded, he asked, "Is she aware you're an officer?"

"It caused a lot of tension, trust me. But it would honestly shock the hell out of me if she so much as says 'hi' to whoever's in the room with her. She's had a shitty life, and police officers were usually at the center of it."

We all looked at the door when a knock sounded just before it opened, and then one of the other detectives was poking his head in to say, "Need a word," to the one talking with me. When he stepped back far enough to hold the door open, I saw Butler standing in the hall. Arms folded tightly over his chest and looking anxious as hell.

Once he caught my stare, he dipped his head. Silently letting me know he was there—no matter what.

Chief sighed and took the empty seat once the door closed. "This doesn't look good for you, Reed."

"I know," I said softly.

"If no one's going to corroborate your story. If your girlfriend isn't going to talk. If they're saying you assaulted without provocation, and his face looks ten shades of busted up—the same as your knuckles." He clicked his tongue. "Your side is sound, but not when the woman it all happened to won't validate it."

I grunted in understanding.

In the middle of Rowe helping me drag Jarrod out of the bookstore, trying to calm a frantic Leah, and driving over here with a waking Jarrod to get everything out of the way that we already knew was coming, Emma had whispered twisted confessions.

Telling me how she hadn't known a thing about Jarrod when he'd shown up that night with her boss and others—including where he was from. How horrified she'd been when she stumbled upon him in Colby. How he'd cornered her last week and what he'd wanted her to beg for . . .

I'd nearly stopped my truck to beat the shit out of him again as silent rage had exploded from me, and it was physically draining to sit in that room when I didn't feel nearly done with him.

"I'd still do it again," I murmured. "Just to give him a moment of the pain she's been living in."

Chief's head bobbed as he leaned across the table. "I get it—I do. If that happened to my wife, I'd be right there, doing and thinking and saying the same things. But since you're refusing a lawyer, let me tell you that saying shit like that is going to land you in prison."

I nodded as my mind raced, continuously pulling back to Emma and Nora and what was going to happen to them until the door opened a few minutes later.

"You are free to go, Reed," the detective said, looking like he was glad to be saying it when I was too shocked to believe that I was hearing him correctly.

"What?"

"Get on out of here unless you've formed an attachment to this room."

I stood, confusion weaving through me as I moved toward the door. "What happened?"

He lifted his brows. "Seems you're about to have the hell shocked out of you because your girlfriend thought it best to talk." He gestured down the hall. "I'll let her explain."

I started for the doorway but paused just outside it when he continued.

"I didn't know you had kids, Reed."

"You have kids?" Chief asked, looking more surprised than I'd been to be released.

"I—" I faltered in my response because Nora *wasn't* mine, but she'd felt like it for longer than I'd had custody of her. "It's complicated," I finally said. "I have custody of a six-year-old, who happens to be Emma's sister. Why did she come up?"

"Sounds complicated," the detective agreed with a soft laugh, then gestured down the hall again. "But I think I better let your girlfriend explain this one."

Worry crept through my veins and urged me out of the room even though the detective hadn't seemed like anything was wrong.

"What happened?" Butler asked, falling into step beside me.

"I don't know. Did something happen to Nora?"

He slipped his phone out of his pocket. "I don't have anything from Jenn or Leah."

That eased my worries only slightly as we moved through the hallways faster and faster until we spilled out into the large entrance where Rowe waited beside a girl of ice and steel.

Emma was standing so tall with a look similar to the one she'd worn the first few times I'd seen her. Arms folded beneath her chest and radiating a warning for people to stay far away. All of which broke the instant she saw me.

Her chest caving and her shoulders slumping as she staggered forward before running into my arms.

I held her close, absorbing her shudders as she eased one of her hands between us to rest it against my chest.

"I'm so sorry," she whispered, words warped with the tears she was fighting.

"Don't," I said just as softly. "You have nothing to be sorry for." Cradling one of her cheeks in my palm, I leaned back to search her eyes. "You okay?"

She nodded against my hand, but the tremors rolling through her and that haunting look in her eyes said differently.

"What'd you tell the detective?" My continued surprise at the shift in the last few minutes wove through the question. "Because it changed everything."

"Leah's in labor," Butler said, smacking at my shoulder and already heading for the doors as he brought his phone to his ear.

"Is she okay?" Rowe asked, voice more frantic than it should've been.

Thankfully, Butler didn't notice. He just glanced back at Rowe with a look as if he should know better. "After everything that happened with her husband today? Fucking doubt it, man—*hey,*" he said into the phone. "Where are you?"

He rested his back against the door to open it, listening to whatever was being said on the phone as Rowe went out the door beside him, already set on getting to Leah.

"We're on our way," Butler said, nodding to me as he stepped outside.

"Was that Jenn?" I asked as I slipped outside with Emma's hand firmly in mine.

Butler nodded. "They're already at the hospital. Nora's with them," he added as soon as my mouth opened to ask.

I gave him a grateful smile and pulled Emma closer to ask, "You want me to take you home, or do you want to come with us?"

Her hand squeezed mine, those walls nothing but rubble on the ground as insecurities and vulnerabilities bled free. "These are your friends—your family. I shouldn't be there. I can find a way home."

"You should absolutely be there," I said softly. "I want you with me always, Emma."

Her hazel eyes met mine, all hesitation as she gave a slight nod. "Then I want to be with you. Besides, I still haven't heard from Lala. I need to check on her."

I pulled up our joined hands and turned hers over to press my mouth to her palm. "Then that's what we're going to do."

ALL HELL BROKE LOOSE at the hospital.

The strain of having left Leah when she'd been a sobbing mess only to find her screaming in pain had broken Rowe when we'd arrived.

He'd pushed through Butler and Jenn to get to her, whispering soothing words while apologizing for shit that he'd had no part in. Butler had lost it right about the second he'd seen what we'd all been blinded to for so long. Yelling and pulling Rowe away from Leah and out of the room, throwing a punch as soon as they'd crossed the threshold. Demanding to know what was going on between him and his sister and throwing another punch before Rowe could begin to explain.

I didn't blame him. But the stress of it all had been too much for Leah and the baby—setting off alarms on her monitor and snapping them out of it long before security had gotten there. Still, none of us were allowed to see Leah anymore. And there'd been a thick layer of tension between everyone ever since.

Tension that had grown when Emma and I had taken Nora to the other side of the hospital to see Lala—only to find out Lala had another seizure and was going to have to stay for a couple more days at least.

Nora hadn't said a word since. Emma and I were struggling to hide our grief over the doctor's grim news. My best friends looked ready to explode. And it only got worse . . .

"What?" Butler's mom cried out, standing and looking all around her as she held her phone to her ear. "What do you mean—okay, yes. I'll be right there."

"What's wrong?" Butler asked.

"Your father was arrested while helping Jarrod," she responded, sounding blindsided as she whispered, "This can't happen," to herself repeatedly while searching for her bag.

"Who was that, and what'd they say?"

"It was your father," she answered, voice trembling now. "He's being charged with tampering with evidence."

A sharp huff left Butler. "He *what?*"

"I don't—" Her head shook quickly. "I have to go. He said he needs me there."

"I'll go with you."

"No," she said and pointed to Butler, motioning for him to sit back down. "One of us needs to be here for your sister."

He watched her go, looking torn and helpless before he sat and mumbled, "What the fuck?"

Jenn rubbed at his back, whispering something to him as he roughed out a strained laugh.

"My dad might suck as a dad, but he wouldn't do anything illegal." He gestured to me. "And what the hell is going on with this day?"

I forced my expression to remain neutral when it hit me and glanced at Emma in time to see Rowe do the same, as if he'd just made the same connection.

But she was sitting on the opposite side of Nora. Eyes wide and lips firmly pressed together. Chest hitching with ragged breaths. Looking like she was already spiraling.

"Emma," I said softly, and reached behind the chairs to brush her shaking shoulder with the tips of my fingers.

She jolted but didn't respond.

"Emma, what'd you say?"

Her body shook with a ragged inhale and her stare drifted toward me even though she continued facing straight ahead as she confessed, "The truth."

I gripped her shoulder in an attempt to comfort her and looked back to where Butler was slowly getting more aggravated. "I'm sorry, man."

"It's bullshit," he mumbled, eyes narrowing. "Jarrod? Yeah, I get it. Guy's a fucking asshole. But my dad?"

I swallowed thickly and tried to keep my tone calm when I reminded him, "Butler, you know they aren't going to arrest him without any kind of proof."

Suspicion and betrayal stole across his face. "Excuse me?"

"I'm sorry all this shit's happening to your family—I am. But you know they wouldn't."

"You're saying my dad's been tampering with evidence?" he asked, tone warning me not to respond.

"I'm just—"

A laugh that was pure betrayal left him. "One of my best friends is having an affair with my sister."

"Not," Rowe bit out as Butler continued.

"The other is accusing my dad of this shit?" One of his brows ticked up. "Are *you* the one who said something, Ryan? Because you were just in there with plenty of time to talk when the person you should've been talking to is *me*."

"I did it."

My stomach dropped at the soft voice that came from the girl near me.

Butler looked over at Emma, blinking slowly as if he hadn't heard her correctly.

When she spoke again, her voice was stronger and held a hint of that steel, all wrapped up in sorrow. "I'm so sorry, Nick. I didn't want this."

Butler just stared at her in complete disbelief for a few moments before looking at me. "Did you know this?"

"No," Emma answered for me. "I didn't want anyone to know. If I had my way, no one would know still."

"Know what?" Jenn asked when Butler looked back to Emma on a delay.

"Yeah, enlighten us," Butler said, voice nothing but a warning growl. "I find it really fucking hilarious that all this shit started happening once you came back to town." His stare slid back to me. "I told you to stay away from her."

"That's enough," I warned darkly.

"None of this was happening before her," he shouted, flinging an arm out to gesture to where Emma was sitting, still as stone.

"He needs to stop being mean to my Emma," Nora whispered from where she was tucked against my side, curled into a tight ball.

"I know," I mumbled softly to her and then directed my attention back to my best friend. "Just because it came to a head with her doesn't mean it wasn't happening before her. I know you're upset, but you're pushing all your anger on the wrong person, and you're pushing me to a breaking point."

He worked his jaw, his eyes narrowed on me for a while before they snapped to Emma. "I want to know what you said. What you *supposedly* know."

"You don't owe him anything," I said when I looked over and saw her hardened exterior being torn away by all those demons.

When minutes came and went in strained silence, Butler huffed. "Look, I am the first to say that my dad isn't the best guy in the world—he and I have our own shit that goes back as far as I can remember. But I *know* he wouldn't do this. That guy is by the book—both legally and biblically."

Emma looked at me then, her eyes glassy with unshed tears as she struggled to hold herself together.

With a shaky inhale, she bent down to Nora and whispered, "Cover your ears."

When she was satisfied that Nora was doing her best to block out what was around us, she twisted in her chair to face me better, even as she reached behind her for her bag.

"When you and Peter came in today, I—well, I was horrified and scared and so many things," she began, her head bouncing in a faint nod. "But I grabbed my phone and started the video before putting it in my front pocket."

My brows rose in surprise when she brought her phone in front of her and began swiping across the screen. "You recorded it?"

"That's why I needed you to leave," she explained, her voice twisting. "I needed him to repeat at least some of what he'd been saying, and I knew that was my only chance to get it." Her throat shifted with a forced swallow. "To get any kind of proof of who he really is because he makes sure there isn't any."

Her stare darted to the side where Butler and Jenn sat before falling back to her phone.

Once she had a video waiting on it, her eyes lifted to mine. "Manhattan . . . Reed, when he cornered me last week, he said he made that entire night disappear—*destroyed* all evidence of it. That he silenced the strippers that had shown." Her head shook quickly. "I don't know in what way, but he said being him had perks, and having Ron as his father-in-law had more."

"Shit," I hissed and looked down at the phone when she handed it to me.

"I showed the detective that video. I told him about

Manhattan and what Jarrod said—they were already requesting records of that night when they let me go." Tapping Nora's shoulder, she leaned close and said, "Let's go for a walk."

"Where are you going?" I asked when she stood and grabbed her purse.

A tear slipped free, and she quickly brushed it away. "I can't be here when you tell them about Manhattan. And she shouldn't be here for that video."

"Can we walk to find French fries?" Nora asked as she grabbed up Emma's hand. "I'm hungry, and fries sound so, so good."

"Fries, huh?" Emma said with a strained huff as she led her away. "We can try to make that happen."

I watched them leave over my shoulder before facing where Rowe, Butler, and Jenn were watching me expectantly.

"What's on that phone?" Butler asked, voice almost wary.

"Today," I said around the jagged rock forming in my throat because this wasn't my story to tell. These were Emma's demons, and I hated the thought of anyone else getting a glimpse of them. "But I need to tell you something first."

FORTY-THREE

REED

We all sat there after the recording ended. Not speaking or moving as time passed around us.

He was going to take Nora from me.

"Jesus," Butler said a while later and sat back, dragging his hands over his face.

"He was going to take Nora from me." My voice was detached as I gripped Emma's phone in my hand. "He was going to take her just to force Emma into fucking him," I snapped, standing and pacing away. Turning, I set my glare on Butler. "They were going to give her a fucking record."

Butler's head slowly shook, his face twisted in a mixture of rage and disbelief.

"All because—" I gritted my teeth and stalked closer, my voice lowering. "All because he wasn't able to rape her. All because he wanted her to *beg* for it. And you tried to make Emma feel like shit for finally saying something?"

"Man, I didn't know. How the hell was I supposed to know?"

"None of us knew, but you're the only one who doubted her," I shouted.

"That's my dad," he shot back. "What if it'd been your dad or yours?" He gestured to Rowe. "None of us have good relationships with our parents, but neither of you would've accepted that shit."

My head shook quickly even as I agreed, "You're right. I probably wouldn't have." Holding his stare, I shrugged. "But if my dad had already been arrested? I would've had to face the fact that there was proof somewhere. There's proof now—more than what's in this video."

"When Ryan and I went back into the office, Emma said she knew Jarrod from 'that night in Manhattan,'" Rowe began from where he'd moved to be closer so we could all watch the video. "I got her out of the office and asked what happened there, and all she said was, 'something that's going to hurt a lot of people.'" Rowe gestured to where I was still gripping the phone. "She didn't want this getting out because she knew what it was going to do to you and Leah and your mom." His stare met Butler and he huffed sadly. "You heard what she said at the end. 'You're no longer untouchable.' She wanted to stop Jarrod and save herself and Ryan from what he planned to do. She used it to keep Ryan from going to jail. And you just ripped into her like she set out to fucking destroy your family."

"It's a hard day for you—we get it," I said softly. "But do you have any idea how fucking hard today has been for Emma?" I set my glare on him as I sank back into the chair I'd pulled up to form our little circle, but he was staring at the floor. "I'm sorry for what you're going through, but she didn't deserve the shit you said."

He nodded slowly. "I'll talk to her when she comes back—

apologize," he said softly, remorsefully, but still didn't look up until Rowe stood with a determined sigh.

"Where are you going?" I asked when he pushed his chair back to where it'd originally been.

He hesitated before facing us, his steps slow and his smile strained. And for a moment, he just stood there seeming to weigh whatever was on his mind before shrugging like he no longer cared about the consequences. "Right now, Leah's in that room all alone. Honestly, we all know Jarrod wouldn't have been here for her anyway, and she probably knows it too. But your sister is also hurting and about to have a baby, and she's *alone*."

"She's alone because the staff kicked us out," Butler said, his tone holding a hint of his earlier warning.

"Yeah, I don't care. Unless Leah tells me to leave, they can say whatever they want." Rowe pressed a hand to his chest and released a strained laugh as he looked between us. "I've never touched your sister—I swear to God, I haven't. But I'm in love with her, and I'm not letting her go through this alone."

With that, he turned and left.

"This fucking day," Butler ground out as he sat forward and scrubbed his hands over his face. Resting his forearms on his knees, he slanted a questioning look in my direction. "Did you know about them?"

"Not until last night," I admitted. "Lost it about the same as you did—Emma had to calm me down."

"Last night?" he asked, the question almost a demand as he straightened. "We were all together last night."

I lifted my head in the beginnings of a nod. "After you left, the baby started kicking. Leah had Emma feel it and then said the baby was freaking out and told Rowe he had to feel it. She basically grabbed his hand and forced him to. As soon as he did . . ." My chest pitched with amusement. "It was like some kind of bomb went off in the house, stealing all the sound and focusing all the energy on the two of them. They were just standing there, but when I hinted that Leah needed to go, they jumped apart like I'd caught them in bed or something."

Butler looked even more pissed than before. "So, this isn't just him?" he asked, confirming what he'd already figured but was clearly hoping he'd been wrong about.

"Apparently not. Emma couldn't figure out how I hadn't noticed before."

"It is painfully obvious," Jenn said from where she'd been silently sitting ever since I'd begun telling them about Manhattan.

Butler's eyes went wide as he twisted to look at his wife. "*What?*"

"The way they look at each other, the way they can hardly speak to each other when other people are near . . ." She lifted a shoulder. "It's just so obvious."

"And you didn't think to say anything?" Butler asked, sounding hurt that she'd kept something from him.

"Honestly, I just wanted to see your sister happy." Jenn's eyes lifted to meet mine before falling back to her lap. And after a few steadying breaths, she turned her body toward Butler's. "I know things about your dad and Jarrod—things that weren't in that video."

Butler and I went still.

Butler looked like he was one more piece of news from breaking down.

I was ready for another reason to find Jarrod and tear into him again.

"When we first started dating, they used to say things to me—things that I tried to brush off. But as time went on, it continued and started bothering me more and more."

"Like what?" Butler demanded.

Jenn's tongue darted out to wet her lips, her chest caving. "Just about the way I looked. The way you seemed to be happy—as if *I* knew how to keep you happy. And how they were always ready to *properly* welcome me into the family—if I thought I could handle them."

"They *what*?" he snapped. "My fucking dad? And you didn't say anything?"

"It's your dad," she tried to explain, her voice twisting as if she'd had no choice but to live with what was happening. "You already had such a bad relationship with him and hated Jarrod. We almost never see them because of that, so I just tried to ignore it when we did see them."

"You don't fucking ignore that, Jenn. You're my wife. You tell me this shit, and I take care of it."

Her head bobbed before shaking. "It's just words."

"It isn't," Butler argued coldly, but Jenn continued.

"It's nothing compared to what Emma went through, but I'll back her up on anything that I can," she said, looking at me again. "And I think Leah might too, at least on part of it." She wrung her hands together as she tried to calm her shaky breaths. "Leah came to me when she found out she was pregnant. She couldn't stop crying—she was absolutely devastated. Even though she never said it, I knew it was because she was worried about what Peter would think when he found out."

"Jesus, how did we not know this when everyone else did?" Butler asked, eyelids shutting as he pinched the bridge of his nose.

"She'd said things to me before—asked me things," Jenn said uneasily. "Nick, she said I was lucky that you hadn't turned out like your dad, and she asked if every day was like living in a fairytale." A soft laugh left her, but it was warped. "I'd laughed then, even though I was and *am* deliriously happy with you, because she genuinely seemed to want to know, and I couldn't understand until she started spilling everything about her marriage to Jarrod."

For long seconds, Jenn just sat there as if she was remembering.

Neither Butler nor I said a word as we waited.

"She asked if we had sex often." Jenn's cheeks heated with embarrassment as she quickly continued. "I didn't know what to say because it's your sister, and we had never talked about that stuff. But then she told me that she *has* to have sex with Jarrod three times a week, no exceptions."

"This isn't something I want to know," Butler groaned.

"And he gets to have sex with at least one other woman a week," Jenn finished, and I choked out a cough as Butler's eyes grew wide.

"What?" I asked, sure I'd misunderstood.

"She said the first time he'd come home smelling like another woman, he didn't even deny it, and she lost it. Screaming at him and saying she was going to divorce him. She went to your parents' house because he wouldn't leave theirs." Jenn sucked in a deep breath and looked between us. "That's when your dad told her that's what she has to let Jarrod do to be happy."

"What the fuck?" Butler whispered.

"Apparently, that's how your parents' marriage is too," Jenn explained. "Leah knew that was ridiculous, so I asked why she didn't just leave him like she'd threatened to that night, and she said, 'I can't. I made the mistake in marrying him, and it's one I have to live with.'"

"That's bullshit."

"I know," she said to her husband. "I tried telling her that, and we've had similar conversations when no one else is around, but she says something along those lines every time. Which is why . . ." She let out a ragged breath and gestured off in the direction of Leah's room. "When Peter moved here, and I noticed the way she was looking at him, I didn't say anything to you. And when Peter started looking at her the same way a few months later, I decided to keep it to myself because your sister deserves that."

Butler's head shook. "No, you needed to tell me this—*all* of it. We don't keep things from each other, and you definitely don't keep things about my family from me. Especially if they're doing them to you. And, yeah, Leah absolutely deserves to be happy and deserves someone who isn't Jarrod, but not that way."

Jenn made a face. "Nick, she and I talked about it again when you and I got back from our honeymoon because I'd noticed that it was getting harder for her and Peter to stay away from each other. She said, 'There's nothing I can. I need to continue filling my role as Jarrod's wife. Leaving him? Well, there is no leaving a man like him—just ask my mom.'"

Butler looked horrified. "What the fuck, Jenn?"

"I'm sorry," she said quickly. "I'm so sorry. But she was adamant that I couldn't tell anyone—especially you. He doesn't hurt her, I made sure of it. She's just trapped. She and your mom are trapped."

"You should've told me," he said firmly.

I stood and grabbed the back of my chair to put it in place, giving them time to work through what Jenn had just shared as I went in search of my girls even though I didn't have a clue where to start.

But I needed to walk.

I needed time to process everything I'd learned since Emma and I had come back from Florida barely twenty-four hours before.

Lala. Rowe and Leah. Jarrod and what exactly he meant to Emma. What he'd been threatening her with just so he could have what doesn't belong to him. And all the other bullshit that had just come pouring out.

I could've lost Nora . . .

From the wreck. Because of Jarrod and his manipulations. Because of my need to physically destroy Emma's demons . . .

I lowered my head and drove a hand through my hair as I stumbled back to a wall. My chest twisting up and my lungs aching at the thought of losing that little girl who had captured my heart and become my entire world as if she were my own flesh and blood.

I dropped my head back to the wall and released a pained breath when my phone vibrated in my pocket. My gaze automatically swept the hall and caught on the long, horizontal windows in front of me, leading to a room filled with newborns as I pulled my phone from my pocket.

DAD: *Checking in again. Want to know you made it back all right. Your mom's worried about you and Emma's grandma and sister.*

I'D MEANT to text him back a dozen times yesterday and had kept forgetting to with everything going on. But as I went to respond, I glanced back at the long windows and then over to the man in front of them, staring at one of the bassinets with overwhelming love and joy pouring from him. And for a second, I envied him and the life he was going to have with his child.

Nora was legally mine, but I had to leave her in another house every day. I had to hide my role in Nora's life from nearly everyone—including my family. And they were missing out on knowing this amazing little girl. And I fucking hated when people referred to her as just Lala's granddaughter or Emma's sister when my soul screamed that she was my kid.

Deleting the two letters I'd managed to type, I tapped on my dad's name and called him.

"You good?" he asked as soon as he answered.

I nodded tightly as I paced in a small circle. "Sorry for not responding, it's been busy here. Emma's grandma had a seizure while they were driving and went through a red light. They got T-boned. She had another seizure this afternoon. Apparently, she has brain tumors, and she's known it for a long time, just been hiding it from everyone."

"Shit," Dad hissed, then mumbled something away from the phone and then my mom was there with him.

"How's Emma handling that?" she asked.

I thought back to the pain in her eyes this afternoon and sighed. "Pretty wrecked."

"And her sister?"

My heart raced and my throat tightened to the point I was sure I wouldn't be able to speak when I tried. "Cracked ribs and a broken arm," I managed to choke out. "But that's why I'm calling. Nora, Emma's sister . . . there's something I need to tell you about her."

FORTY-FOUR

EMMA

"What do you think my Leah's baby's name will be?" Nora asked that night as I turned off her bedroom light. Well, Peter's bedroom that was still fully decked out for Nora since she would be staying there for the unforeseeable future.

By the time we'd finally gotten back to Reed's from the hospital, it had been so late. Reed and Nora had made a game plan for bath time and bed, but before we'd made it inside the house, his phone had begun ringing and had only continued. People wanting to know what exactly had gone down this afternoon, and others needing stories verified from both of us—mainly Reed.

So, I'd fumbled through bath time even though helping a child bathe was a foreign concept to me since I couldn't remember my mom ever bathing me—it was just another thing I'd figured out on my own when I was younger than Nora. Add on the cast that absolutely could not get wet, and I'd felt lost. But we'd made it through, and I'd gotten her in her pajamas and tucked in just as her eyelids started drooping.

"I'm not sure," I said as I walked over to the bed. "I'm sure naming a baby is very difficult. She might have to think about it for a while."

Nora tilted her head on the pillow as she thought about that. "Do you think my Peter will help her name the baby?"

My brows lifted in surprise that even Nora had noticed the connection between the two. Then again, Leah hadn't let Peter leave her side once he'd gone back to her—not that he'd tried to.

He'd been there for the delivery. He'd been standing by her side, pride and love pouring from him, when we'd been allowed to see Leah and the baby. He was staying there with her tonight . . .

I'd pulled Reed from the room before he could voice his displeasure at that news.

"Probably not," I said with a little smile. "It's Leah's baby, so I'm sure she'll name him."

Nora's eyes seemed more alert as she considered that before saying, "Well, his name can only have four letters."

A soft laugh bubbled free. "Is that right?"

She nodded quickly as she sat up. "Yeah. Four."

"And why is that?" I asked with veiled amusement.

The expression on her face was pure Wade sass, and it was all I could do to hold back my next laugh. "My Lala's name has four letters—same with my Reed. My name has four letters, and so does yours. So does my Nick's and my Jenn's and my Leah's." She sighed heavily and said, "My Peter's doesn't, but 'Pete' is short for Peter . . . did you know that?"

I stared at her in stunned surprise for a moment before stammering, "I-I did."

She nodded again. "So, he can have four if he wants. But my Reed calls him 'Rowe,' and my Lala spelled that for me, and that's four letters too. Did you know that?" Before I could respond, she went on. "And guess what, my Emma?"

"What?"

"Our last name has four letters. My Reed has a last name that also has four letters—do you know what it is?"

"Ryan," I answered softly.

The soft glow from her nightlight perfectly showed the excitement dancing across her face. "So, see? That's how I know we're all supposed to be together. That's how I know we were all supposed to find each other."

A mixture of awe and adoration wove through me at the innocence behind her logic—at her absolute assuredness. And for a while, I just stood there watching her wait for my reaction.

"I think that's beautiful, Nora," I finally managed, unable to see it any other way and wishing I could see the world the way she did. Offering her a little smile, I shrugged. "I guess we'll just have to see what she names her baby. But until then, it's bedtime."

She heaved a sigh and shifted back down onto the pillows. "My Emma?" she began hesitantly as I pulled the comforter around her again.

"Hmm?"

"I think my Lala might be really sick."

I stilled from where I'd been straightening and loosed a breath, warring on what to say. But I'd never been one to sugarcoat things—even with Nora in those first days of meeting her. And I couldn't imagine that lying to her now would help anything.

"Yeah, I think you're right," I whispered as I sank down to sit on the edge of the bed.

"She says she's tired a lot—that she needs to rest. And I think her head hurts her. Sometimes, she stops walking and touches her head for a while before saying she's ready to walk again. Sometimes, she sits down and holds it before going to lay down again."

My brows drew close as I tried to remember Lala doing any of the things Nora was telling me. "When does she do this?"

"When my Reed isn't there," she said matter-of-factly. "And never *ever* on Thursdays when she's cooking."

When no one's around to notice, I realized as my chest panged with sorrow and guilt for not knowing. For not being here before now to take care of Lala when she so clearly needed it.

"I didn't know," I murmured and then squeezed her good hand. "But it's important that I do, so thank you for telling me."

She squeezed my hand tighter. "Is she going to leave me?"

I sat there with her hand in mine, my throat closing up as I thought of that bossy, opinionated woman who had been a safe haven for me for so many years. Who had kept me alive.

When the doctor had spoken with Lala and me this afternoon, I'd struggled to keep my composure while I'd slowly shattered inside at the news: With Lala still refusing any type of surgery or treatment, the Oncologist was now giving her just two months, and I was told to expect a sharp decline now that it had begun.

I'd been given information for hospice care while Lala had

scoffed and told me to get her out of the damn hospital—she had baking to do.

I'd managed to fake smiles and fight the burning in my eyes while Nora and Reed had visited with her—well, Reed had. Nora had sat there, staring at the floor. But when we'd eventually gotten back to the maternity ward in the hospital and Reed had pulled me off to the side to find out what the doctor said, my pain and tears had slipped free.

Clearing my throat, I looked into Nora's wide eyes and said, "At some point, everyone has to leave. But I know she would never want to leave you, and for right now, she's still here." I leaned forward to tuck some of her hair behind her ear and lowered my voice. "I can't imagine how much it will hurt when she has to go, but you won't be alone when she does. You'll have so many people here for you—Reed, most importantly."

"And you? I'll have you?"

I hesitated for only a moment before answering truthfully. "Absolutely. Now go to sleep—we have a big day at the bookstore tomorrow."

Excitement replaced the sadness on her face in an instant, and she shut her eyes so tight that her face scrunched up.

A soft laugh left me as I stood from the bed. "Goodnight, Nora."

"Night, my Emma," she whispered when I turned to leave—and nearly missed a step when I saw the man leaning in the doorframe.

Tall and dark with a look on that sinfully handsome face that had my stomach swirling with heat and my heart threatening to escape my chest.

His eyes followed me until I was beside him, and then his

tattooed hand was on my hip, stopping me from going any farther as he slipped past me into the room.

Bending over the bed, he murmured a few words to Nora and then earned a soft laugh when he tickled her comforter-covered feet as he pushed away.

As I watched him, I was hit with the same indescribable feeling I'd been experiencing throughout the day.

Tugging at my chest and stealing the air from my lungs. Making the world slow and terrifying me with how fiercely I craved more of it.

But then Reed had his fingers pressed to my stomach and was guiding me back as he closed the door behind us, and the feeling faded away as something else settled low in my belly. All white-hot need to be wrapped up in this man. To be loved and worshipped by him.

"Rest of my fucking life," he murmured as we turned the corner to head toward the hallway leading to Reed's room. His hand slid around my waist and he pulled my body close. "Exactly what I see when I look at you."

"Even after today?" My tongue darted out to wet my lips as I thought about his rage that had flooded the room and my fear when I'd found out Ron and Jarrod were trying to press charges against him. "Even after I hurt people you consider your family? When I almost got Nora taken from you?" I asked, my voice twisting on the last.

"*You* didn't do those things," he said firmly. "But after today?" He grabbed up one of my hands and placed it on his chest so I could feel the fierce pounding of his heart. "Emma, more than ever, I want you in my life."

Wings took flight in my stomach at his claim, making me feel light and dizzy and like I was falling impossibly more in love with him.

"But I frustrate you," I murmured, the reminder a soft tease wrapped in the deepest question—because I still couldn't grasp what was happening between us. Couldn't understand how I could want Reed this way and how he could say these things when it was so soon.

But I felt it just the same . . .

"Oh, babe, you do," he said with a wicked smirk as he dipped his head to brush a kiss across my lips. "And you terrify me and surprise me and just about make me lose all sense of reason with how badly I crave you." He captured my mouth in another brief kiss as he closed his bedroom door behind us, locking it as he went.

"I want sunrises with you, and I want to spend my days earning more of your story," he said softly, his deep voice sending a flash of chills across my body. "I want to walk into a room and have my heart stolen by you all over again by something as simple as watching you put Nora to bed."

"Reed." His name left me on an unsteady breath as that same indescribable feeling overwhelmed me again. Only now, in Reed's arms, everything became perfectly clear.

That feeling tugging at my chest and stealing my breath was a love so pure and whole that it was rocking the ground I'd stood on for so long. A love that went beyond what I already felt for Reed.

This was a claiming of souls. It was protection and selflessness. It was support and devotion.

And I never wanted it to end.

"I have a lot of baggage," I whispered, studying my fingers as I curled my hand against his chest, "and it's all so bad." My gaze flickered up to his. "Reed, I know what you said last night, but there's a possibility those demons will always be there."

"Then I'll spend forever chasing them away," he vowed without hesitation.

"I can't promise a day will ever come when I'm not afraid of who I'm waking up next to." I swallowed thickly. "I can't promise old fears won't pull me back and make me hesitate or shut down and push you away."

One of his hands lifted to cradle my neck as he subtly nodded.

"But I told you I want forever with you, and I do. You branded your name on my soul, and there's no coming back from that."

He pressed his mouth to mine in a feather-soft kiss that made my body tingle and come alive as he gently pulled my shirt higher and higher until it was going over my head and falling to the floor.

"I love you," he whispered against my lips as I stepped out of my shoes at the same time his fingers fell to my pants.

"I know." I pulled at his shirt until he took it off for me, then wove my hands through his hair and pulled him close, whimpering against the force of the next kiss. "And I'm in love with you."

A rumble of approval and need sounded in his chest as he lifted me into his arms and took the last steps to lay me on the center of his bed.

Kissing and kissing me until I was breathless before sitting back, his mouth making a trail down my chest and stomach as he finished unzipping my pants and started dragging them and my underwear down my legs.

"Emma." My name was a demand and a plea as my clothes fell to the floor. "We can do this for the rest of our lives, and I'll always stop whenever you push. Understand?"

"I'm not pushing."

"Understand?"

I nodded weakly as he took his time spreading my legs and curling over me so he was holding himself up with one arm. "I understand—oh God." The words left me on a whisper when he trailed his fingers over where I was aching for him before sliding one inside me. And then another.

He captured my mouth again, the kiss soft yet demanding and matching the way he was moving his fingers inside me. Fucking me slowly, thoroughly, while giving me teasing brushes against my clit until I was writhing beneath him. Trying to get closer to his touch and that promised abyss.

Taking my bottom lip between his teeth, he slowly released it before moving down my body. Fingers effortlessly playing me and pulling breathless moans from me until he leaned forward to taste me.

A cry tumbled past my lips and I reached for him, gripping at his hair and holding tight as he devoured me. Torturing me in the sweetest way. Alternating between soft licks and flattening his tongue against me and pulling my clit into his mouth. His fingers moving harder and deeper before letting off until it was all nothing more than the faintest touch and brush of his lips, over and over, and I was left swaying on that ledge.

My body strung so tight.

Begging for that fall.

"Reed," I breathed. Pleaded.

His eyes met mine. The sight and feel of his lips twitching with that wicked smirk had a shiver ripping through me.

He pressed a gentle kiss to my clit, drawing out the moment and my need until I was on the edge of begging him again. And then he sucked my clit into his mouth and curled his fingers inside me, hitting that spot as I broke apart with a breathless moan.

Pleasure coursed through my body as I fell.

Fell into him.

Fell into that sea of stars.

Fell into this place where nothing mattered more than this moment or Reed.

"I need you," I breathed, gripping at his shoulders and trying to pull him closer.

With a teasing kiss to the inside of my thigh, he removed his fingers and let me move him up my body until his denim-covered hips were between my legs. "You have me," he said, dipping his head to kiss me quickly. "Forever."

I reached for the button on his jeans, fingers trembling as I leaned up to kiss him again. Our movements almost frantic as we tore at the remainder of his clothes. But then he was pushing inside me as my legs curled around his hips, and I was crying out as he found and kept a punishing rhythm.

Building me up all over again, higher and higher, until I was buzzing.

And I was enraptured. Fully and completely in him.

In the way he loved me. In the way his muscles rolled and twitched as he fucked me. In the designs that began at his knuckles, swept up to the base of his neck, and crept across his chest and torso. In how beautiful he was beneath that sinfully handsome exterior.

"I love you."

The roll of his hips slowed to a stop as he curled his body around mine. Dipping so close that his mouth brushed across mine when he spoke. "Rest of my life, right there." He kissed me gently. "Right here."

Everything shifted with our confessions.

The urgency from before faded as we took our time exploring and learning each other's bodies. Touches and kisses softer as I focused on the parts of his body that had whispered curses escaping his lips, and he lingered on the places that made my eyes roll back. Bringing me to highs I'd never imagined possible as the controlled movements of his hips shattered every barrier and pushed us over that edge.

Falling together.

Dancing in that sea of stars.

Wrapped up in all that love and trust and everything that was us . . . forever.

FORTY-FIVE

EMMA

"I'm going to marry you, Emma Wade," Reed said the next morning, voice still husky from sleep even though we'd been up for a while. "I'm going to make you my wife."

We'd woken the same way we had the other mornings—with my palms firmly planted against his chest as tremors rocked through me. His own horrors and training flashing through his eyes before he'd wrapped me up tight and whispered that I was safe until my shaking had subsided.

And then I was clinging to him and kissing him, begging Reed to do exactly what he'd promised—erase the past.

We'd come together in a clash of fevered kisses and desperate hands. All frenzied passion that had chased away the lingering memories and still rivaled the beauty of what we'd shared the night before.

The way he'd looked at me as if there was no one else in his world. The way his hands had moved over me, gripping and worshipping and showing me how much he needed me in those simple yet vital touches. The way *I love you* had scraped up his throat as if he couldn't contain the words.

I could've lived in that moment with him forever.

But I had a feeling no matter how we came together, I would always feel that way because it was Reed, and he'd taken hold of me. Heart, body, and soul.

We hadn't moved as we'd come down from the highs of our time together, just continued laying in the afterglow. But his declaration had my fingers stilling for a moment before I resumed running them through his hair.

"Then do it."

He quickly looked up from where his face had been partially buried in my chest, shock written across his features. "What?"

"You keep saying you're going to marry me." I held his stare and whispered, "Do it."

Excitement and disbelief and love poured from him as he pushed up onto his hands so he was caging me to the bed. "Told you I wouldn't drag you off to a church, but right now, I'm kinda reconsidering that."

I fought a smile as my stomach filled with dozens of fluttering wings. Forcing myself to take a calming breath, I considered his words for a while before shaking my head. "Do we need a church?" At his surprise, I hurried to explain, "I've never been in a church before, and it just . . . I don't know. It doesn't feel like us when I think about it." My eyebrows drew close. "Is that wrong?"

His head slanted in answer and encouragement. "What feels like us?" he asked, his deep voice wrapping around my heart.

I only had to think for a moment before the answer tumbled free. "Sunrises."

His lips twitched into a hint of a smile. "I think we can find one of those." Lifting one of his hands from the bed, he curled it around my cheek as his eyes bored into mine. "You really want this?"

"I want you."

"You already have me."

I nodded before shaking my head. "I want all of you the same way you demand all of me."

The need and excitement pouring from him danced across my skin when he asked, "When can I marry you?"

I hesitated, my stare drifting to the sun-lit windows. "Not today."

He passed his thumb across my lip, gently tilting my face back to his. Comfort and love swirling in his steel-gray eyes as he studied me. "When?"

I thought for a while before finally saying, "Marry me on a day where there's no sorrow or pain or anger." I lifted one of my hands to his chest to feel the fierce pounding there as I continued. "Marry me when it's only sunrises and easy days followed by long nights wrapped up in each other. Marry me when we can't go another day without belonging to each other."

He pressed his lips to mine, the kiss soft and slow and doing dangerous, dangerous things to my heart.

"Marry me then," I whispered. "Keep me forever."

He smiled against the kiss and shifted to settle between my thighs, his lips moving to my ear as he vowed, "Rest of my fucking life."

My eyelids fluttered shut and a whimper fell from my lips when his thumbs brushed across my nipples at the same moment he nipped at the base of my neck.

"I have to get ready for work," I mumbled halfheartedly.

"Then go get ready," he muttered against my neck as he made another pass across the hardened peaks.

A moan caught in my throat when he rocked against me, my legs curling around his hips involuntarily.

"Are you fucking kidding?" he growled when the doorbell chimed through the house. After a moment, he pushed from the bed and started grabbing at the pile of clothes we'd left on the floor the night before. "We're finishing this."

"I'll be right here," I said, fighting a smile at his growing frustration.

When the doorbell sounded again, he hurried to step into his jeans as he unlocked and flung open the door. Charging from the room and snapping, "Swear to God, if that woke Nora . . ."

I pushed up onto my elbows, biting at my bottom lip to hide my amusement. Then slowly slipped out of bed and grabbed my underwear. I was just pulling on Reed's shirt and tiptoeing out of the room and down the hall when Reed answered the door to voices I definitely hadn't expected to hear.

Scrambling back to the room, I hurried into my jeans as Reed's shock floated to me from the front of the house.

"What . . ." he said slowly as if he couldn't figure out how they were at his door. "What the hell are you guys doing here?"

"What do you mean? And why are you being so rude?" his mom asked. "How about something more along the lines of, 'Hey, Mom and Dad! This is the place I've been hiding away at for years. Come in and let me show you around.'"

"At least I give you coffee when you show up," his dad said.

"I just . . . I mean—what the fuck?" Reed stammered. "You couldn't have told me you were coming?"

"We did," Rachel said just as I stumbled into the living room from the hallway. "Oh, Emma, hi!"

"Hi," I said uneasily and hoped I didn't look like I'd literally just crawled out of bed with their son. "So good to see you again."

"See?" Rachel said with a scoff, gesturing to me.

Reed groaned and dragged a hand over his face. "I *am* happy to see you. I'm just surprised. I don't know why you didn't say anything when I was talking to you yesterday."

Rachel twisted to glare at where Kash stood with his arms folded across his chest.

"Don't give me that look, Sour Patch," he said with a shrug. "I told him we were gonna have to come meet this little girl he's been keeping from us."

"You didn't say *today*," Reed said with a frustrated laugh.

"Okay, first, you need to learn to clarify," Rachel said, pointing at Kash before putting her attention on Reed. "Second . . . by the way, Reed, we're stopping off in Savannah for the night and then continuing to your place first thing in the morning. *Surprise*—we're here!"

Another one of those laughs built in Reed's chest as she continued.

"Third, you've kept this from us for years. You really think we're just gonna let more time go by before we meet our granddaughter?"

Reed held his arms out. "I told you the situation. She doesn't live with me—she's only here right now because Lala's in the hospital," he explained, dropping his voice to a whisper.

Rachel gasped. "She's here?"

"Yes, and she's probably awake now because you kept ringing the doorbell." He held up a hand as if to stop

Rachel's excitement. "And like I told you: She doesn't know. You're gonna freak her out if you try to grandparent her when she thinks I'm just Reed."

"*Her* Reed," I added, earning a dry look from him. "Her *favorite* person."

The expression that took over his face tugged at my chest because I knew she was his too. I knew Nora was so much more than some child he had custody of—he loved her like his own.

"We agreed," he said softly, voice twisting. "Lala and I agreed not to change her life unless it was absolutely necessary."

"It's about to be necessary," I told him as my own sadness wove deep. "You know it is . . . Nora does too."

"But it shouldn't be," he said adamantly. "I should've known. I should've seen something was wrong. I should've forced her to get treatment years ago so we wouldn't be going through this."

I stepped up to his side and slipped my hand into his. "I know how much she means to you . . . how much she means to this entire town. And you have no idea how grateful I am that you've all been there for her—you especially." The pain weaving through my body matched the grief in his eyes, and when I spoke again, my voice wrenched with the emotions I was struggling to keep in check. "But this is *Lala*. She doesn't listen to anyone, even though everyone else better listen to her."

A strained laugh left him even as he shook his head. "What if Nora hates me when she finds out?"

"I don't think she could ever hate you," I said softly and gripped his hand tighter, trying to take on all his worries and pain. "But if you aren't ready to tell her yet, then don't. Just keep taking it day by day the way you are now. You'll know when you're both ready to talk about it."

He loosed a slow breath and let his forehead fall to mine, resting there for a moment before muttering, "Okay."

"I know you're hurting, but don't question yourself with Nora. If anyone knows what's best for her, it's you. That's why Lala chose you."

He wrapped our joined hands around my back and pressed me closer for a few moments before shifting away a fraction to look at where his parents stood, hunched close together. Seeming to have a hushed argument.

"Absolutely not," Rachel hissed before Kash covered her mouth with a hand and sent us a wide grin.

"Two things," he began as Rachel rolled her eyes, "where's the best place to get pancakes around here? Where's the closest hotel? And I thought you had a roommate."

"That's three things," Reed argued. "Better question: How did you know where I live?"

Kash sent him a dry look that made him look identical to Reed. "Really?"

"You're still tracking me?"

Kash just continued unapologetically staring at Reed before asking, "Pancakes?"

Rachel sighed and looked at me. "We don't have to get pancakes."

"How dare you," Kash whispered, all offense that had her fighting a laugh as she elbowed him.

"I actually have to get to work," I said a little hesitantly.

"The bookstore," Rachel said, her eyes brightening. "How did the opening go?"

An uncomfortable hum sounded in my throat as I looked

to Reed for help. When he just rubbed at the back of his neck, I said, "Well, it, um . . . it was actually fantastic. So much better than we thought it would be."

At their obvious confusion and curiosity, Reed said, "I'll explain later. And I actually get pancakes with Butler and Rowe on Tuesday mornings anyway—not sure if they'll be there because things are . . . I'll just explain all that later. A lot of shit's gone down since we got home."

Kash's teasing mood disappeared as he seemed to pick up on the tension rolling across Reed's skin. "On top of the wreck and Emma's grandma being sick?" When Reed nodded, Kash studied him for a while before asking, "Everything good?"

Reed sucked in a breath at the sound of an interior door opening and shifted so he could see the girl slowly emerging from the small hallway. Looking at once wary of the two strangers and ready to burst from excitement at getting to spend another day with Reed.

"There's my girl," Reed whispered, and a small smile cracked through Nora's unease as she quickly darted around Reed's parents and rushed to his side. Grabbing hold of his free hand and burrowing into his leg as she stared at Kash and Rachel, who were already completely enamored with the sight of them together, given their expressions.

Reed gripped me tight before releasing me and crouching down next to her. "Nora, these are my parents. They wanted to come visit."

Nora studied them with that intensity of hers—seeming to look right into their souls to determine their true purpose for being there while assessing if they were people she could trust—before turning to Reed. Lowering her voice to a whisper we could all hear when she said, "I heard my Lala say you don't talk to your parents . . ."

The question in her statement was clear and settled heavily in the room.

Reed let out a stilted breath as his stare darted to Rachel and Kash. "Right," he murmured, focusing on Nora again, "and that's been hard. But I've been going to see them recently, remember?" His voice dropped lower as he assured her, "They're good people. They're *my* people."

Her eyes widened at the claim and then drifted to me for confirmation—a move that stunned me. I still couldn't wrap my mind around the shift in her trust.

But I nodded, excitement building in my chest as a thought occurred to me. "You know . . . Reed's parents' names are Kash and Rachel. *Rach* is short for Rachel." I held up four fingers and whispered, "That's four letters for both of them."

Nora's mouth popped open wide as she looked over at them, studying them in a new light, and Reed glanced over his shoulder as he stood, all adoring bemusement on his face as he studied me.

"Has she never mentioned the four-letter thing to you?" I asked softly, and he shook his head.

"You'll have to tell me later."

"Oh, I think she should tell you. It's—" I pressed a hand to my warming chest and let him pull me against his side. "It's such a Nora way of looking at the world, and it's beautiful."

His stare danced over my face, all love and wonder, before darting to the side when Nora stepped up to his parents.

"My name is Nora," she said confidently. "Have you ever been to Paris? Do you like French things?"

Rachel let out a soft laugh. "Do croissants count?"

"Yes!" Nora said, all excitement. "I like croissants the best."

"But how do you feel about pancakes?"

"Oh my God, Kash," Rachel whispered, her eyes rolling.

"Crêpes are French pancakes, and I think I would love those." Nora stepped closer and whispered, "But my Lala and my Reed don't know how to make those, so we just eat regular pancakes and make them fancy."

A soft smile tugged at the corner of my mouth as Reed's parents asked all about Nora's cast—the Eiffel Tower Reed had drawn and French words I'd looked up and written. Quickly falling in love with her as she excitedly explained about Fancy Nancy and her love for all things French and fancy. All while Reed looked on with an expression that said this moment was something he never wanted to forget.

Tilting his head toward me, he passed his lips across my jaw and then brought them to my ear, pressing me close to his side as he whispered, "Rest of my life. Right here."

EPILOGUE

REED

"My Reed!" Nora said excitedly as she raced toward me.

I caught her up in my arms and hushed her, but the smile on my face had hers growing even wider. "Look how beautiful you are!" I said, keeping my voice soft to remind her we needed to be quiet.

"But am I fancy?" she asked quietly, leaning back to show off her dress and jewelry my sisters and mom had no doubt spoiled her with.

"The fanciest."

She wiggled in my hold, her excitement growing. "Do you think my Emma knows?"

I made a face that earned a soft giggle from her. "No way, but she's about to." Setting her on her feet, I nodded in the direction of where my family and friends had changed the living room into a salon and dressing room. "Go hang out with everyone."

She hurried back to where mine and Butler's moms were doing their hair, and Kennedy looked over at me from where she was talking to Kira, Leah, and Jenn.

"I know," I whispered when she tapped on her bare wrist.

"The guys are almost done out back," she informed me as if that would hurry me.

"That isn't going to change when the sun rises."

"No, but you gave them forever, and you're leaving us no time," Jenn argued, and the other three nodded in agreement.

I just rolled my eyes, the smile on my face only continuing to grow as I made my way upstairs and to the bedroom.

The past nine months had been a roller coaster.

Once Lala was released from the hospital, I'd moved into the Wade house with Emma to be with her during the few hours we had when both of us weren't working, and to make the transition of caring for Lala and Nora easier.

I'd figured out a new routine where Nora was the center of it all and solely *mine*. Not that she'd been fazed when I'd told her what she truly was to me. She'd simply smiled and grabbed my hand, saying, "I know." And that had been that.

And we'd tried to give Lala her freedom until that decline we'd been warned about happened . . . and were absolutely destroyed when it did. Just as the doctor had said, it was fast and drastic.

We were lucky to have five months with her before she passed, but the wake she left behind had rocked the entire town. I wasn't sure any of us started truly moving on from it until a month later when Nora made a sign and put it in the front yard, saying our house was open for First Responder Thursday again.

Not that we'd known until the first person had shown.

Emma and I had scrambled to start cooking and hadn't stopped the entire day, Rowe and Leah coming over with groceries and to help when we'd run out. It was the lightest any of us had felt in a long time as we'd told stories of Lala and joked, wondering how in the hell she'd been able to do all that on her own when four of us had struggled.

Thursdays had continued since, and we'd found a groove —whoever was actually cooking at the time since Butler, Rowe, and I were never on the same schedule, and the girls had their own thing going on with the bookstore.

Emma and Donna had quickly realized they couldn't continue pulling thirteen-hour days by themselves with how busy the store was, even more with us needing to split our time between work and taking care of Lala and Nora.

But Donna had been hesitant to hire anyone else since Emma was the first person to work in the store who wasn't family. It'd been hard for her to imagine straying further from the *family* part of the store even though she was the only one left.

"Family doesn't always mean blood," I'd told Emma one night, voice soft in the dark of the room. "Butler, Rowe, and I . . . we're family. And Lala . . . it's different with Butler because he grew up with her, but I have more of a connection with her than my own grandparents. Rowe would say the same. And Nora?"

"She's yours," Emma had whispered.

"She is absolutely mine," I'd agreed, then said, "Blood has nothing to do with it—with any of them."

Emma had pushed up on an elbow to look down at me, her expression soft and adoring even as she'd said, "I'm understanding that more and more, but I don't think Donna has anyone like that either."

"No, but we do. You've already given Donna her store back, you can give her a new family." At Emma's confusion, I'd lifted a shoulder. "There's Jenn."

"But she loves her job," Emma had said. "Wasn't she just telling us that last week?"

"No, she hates her job. She just likes the hours." Excitement had slowly lit Emma's face as the idea took hold, so I'd continued. "Leah and her mom are going to need income now. Leah will need some time because of the baby . . . but in a couple months?"

"I'll see what Donna thinks," she'd said softly, but no less enthusiastically. "But I have a feeling she's going to love the thought of it."

SHE HAD.

Within a week, Jenn was working there. Soon after, Mrs. Butler and Leah were too.

Nothing was ever set in their schedules, but somehow, there were always at least two of them at opening and closing. With all of them coming and going and effortlessly switching whenever one of them needed to leave. The guys and I didn't understand it, but it worked for them, and Donna said it truly felt like family—everyone working to constantly make the store better while helping each other.

And Emma was happy.

That was all that mattered to me.

Ron and Jarrod had recently been sentenced and were going to prison for a long damn time. Emma's old boss and a couple of the other guys that had been there that night didn't get nearly as long, but it was still something.

And it was over.

Leah and her mom's worries that Jarrod and Ron would be released—since no one knew how they would react to the women divorcing them. Rowe and Leah having to suppress what they felt for each other—not that Butler and I hadn't given Rowe shit for it when they'd moved in together.

Emma's unwarranted guilt for hurting and breaking up the Butler family . . . the way she'd fought against her shields each time she was questioned and had to take part in the trials . . . it was all over.

Now, it was our time.

I crawled onto the bed, lifting the shirt she was wearing just enough to press my mouth to the small bump growing between her hips, then moved farther up her body until I was caging her in.

"Emma Wade," I whispered against her lips, then passed a soft kiss across them. "Wake up."

She stretched beneath me, one of her hands slowly coming up to rest against my chest. "Sunrise?" she asked, voice soft and groggy.

"Only sunrise," I whispered, a smile tugging at my mouth when she blinked until she could keep her eyes on me.

"What?"

"Only sunrises and easy days," I said, recalling her words from all those months and heartache ago. "Only long nights wrapped up in each other."

She inhaled quickly, her eyes widening when she realized what I was saying.

"No pain. No anger. No sorrow."

"Reed . . ." Her stare darted over me, just now realizing how I was dressed. "Oh my God."

"I can't go another day without you being my wife."

A soft laugh tumbled free when she looked back up at me, smile all unrestrained joy. "Then marry me."

I dipped down to steal another kiss just as someone began pounding on the door, causing Emma to jolt beneath me.

"You already made a baby," Kennedy yelled. "We need to get her ready."

"Was that one of your sisters?"

An irritated huff slipped free as I nodded. "My family flew in last night," I said unapologetically. "They're all waiting for you downstairs."

"All of them?" she asked, eyebrows lifting in surprise.

"Leah and Jenn too."

I nipped at her jaw when her surprise deepened and then sat back. "Sunrise is in an hour. I'll see you out back."

"Wait, out back? What?"

"You said no to a church," I explained. "This is where you first started trusting me. This is where you started loving me. This is where I first started seeing you as my future." I lifted a shoulder and leaned over her again. "This house is us."

A soft sigh slipped past her lips, her fingers playing with one of the buttons on my black button-down. "It is, and it couldn't be more perfect."

Cradling her neck in my palm, I searched her hazel eyes. Letting all my love for her overwhelm me for a while before whispering, "Gonna marry you now, Emma."

"And then forever?"

"Babe . . ." I passed my mouth across hers. "We're already living our forever."

THE END

Want to see how the Ryan family got started? Check out the *Forgiving Lies* novels from Molly McAdams!

Forgiving Lies

Deceiving Lies

Trusting Liam

Coming soon . . .

From *New York Times* bestselling author, Molly McAdams, comes a new, captivating series that follows five girls sharing a house in the heart of Hollywood who all have secret lives of their own. From following passions, to loving freely, to working scandalous careers, the Secrets in L.A. series is filled with excitement, romance, and lies.

ACKNOWLEDGMENTS

Cory—As always, thank you for being my constant support. Everything I do is possible because of you. I love you!

Molly and Amy—A massive thank you for the never-ending support and encouragement. Your friendships mean the world to me. I don't know what I would do without the two of you.

Molly's Monsters—Y'all are literally the best group on Facebook. This story would've never happened if it weren't for you and that incredibly epic thread. Without y'all, Reed would've remained "the missing Ryan brother" and #HesOverseas. Even though I have loved every shirt and sign and petition made for him, I truly hope you've enjoyed his story.

Eric, Letitia, & Shannon—Thank you, thank you, thank you for making this book what it is! From the photo to the cover to the edits . . . you're all such rock stars!

ABOUT THE AUTHOR

Molly grew up in California but now lives in the oh-so-amazing state of Texas with her husband, daughter, and fur baby. When she's not diving into the world of her characters, some of her hobbies include hiking, snowboarding, traveling, and long walks on the beach . . . which roughly translates to being a homebody and dishing out movie quotes with her hubby. She has a weakness for crude-humored movies and loves curling up in a fluffy blanket during a thunderstorm . . . or under one in a bathtub if there are tornados. That way she can pretend they aren't really happening.

Printed in Great Britain
by Amazon

69218338R00324

Afronauci

W serii ukazały się ostatnio:
Dariusz Rosiak *Ziarno i krew. Podróż śladami bliskowschodnich chrześcijan*
Piotr Lipiński *Bicia nie trzeba było ich uczyć. Proces Humera i oficerów śledczych Urzędu Bezpieczeństwa* (wyd. 2 popr. i rozszerz.)
Paweł Smoleński *Zielone migdały, czyli po co światu Kurdowie*
Wolfgang Bauer *Przez morze. Z Syryjczykami do Europy*
Cezary Łazarewicz *Żeby nie było śladów. Sprawa Grzegorza Przemyka*
Elizabeth Pisani *Indonezja itd. Studium nieprawdopodobnego narodu*
Beata Szady *Ulica mnie woła. Życiorysy z Limy*
Rana Dasgupta *Delhi. Stolica ze złota i snu*
Ed Vulliamy *Wojna umarła, niech żyje wojna. Bośniackie rozrachunki* (wyd. 2)
Andrzej Brzeziecki, Małgorzata Nocuń *Armenia. Karawany śmierci*
Katarzyna Kwiatkowska-Moskalewicz *Zabić smoka. Ukraińskie rewolucje*
Anna Sulińska *Wniebowzięte. O stewardesach w PRL-u*
Anjan Sundaran *Złe wieści. Ostatni niezależni dziennikarze w Rwandzie*
Ilona Wiśniewska *Hen. Na północy Norwegii*
Mur. 12 kawałków o Berlinie pod red. Agnieszki Wójcińskiej (wyd. 2 zmienione)
Iza Klementowska *Szkielet białego słonia*
Piotr Nesterowicz *Każdy został człowiekiem*
Dariusz Rosiak *Żar. Oddech Afryki* (wyd. 2 zmienione)
Anna Mateja *Serce pasowało. Opowieść o polskiej transplantologii*
Linda Polman *Karawana kryzysu. Za kulisami przemysłu pomocy humanitarnej* (wyd. 2)
Scott Carney *Czerwony rynek. Na tropie handlarzy organów, złodziei kości, producentów krwi i porywaczy dzieci* (wyd. 2)
Misha Glenny *Nemezis. O człowieku z faweli i bitwie o Rio*
Adam Hochschild *Lustro o północy. Śladami Wielkiego Treku*
Kate Brown *Plutopia. Atomowe miasta i nieznane katastrofy nuklearne*
Drauzio Varella *Klawisze*
Piotr Lipiński *Cyrankiewicz. Wieczny premier*
Mariusz Szczygieł *Gottland* (wyd. 3 zmienione)
Maciej Czarnecki *Dzieci Norwegii. O państwie (nad)opiekuńczym*
Zbigniew Parafianowicz, Michał Potocki *Kryształowy fortepian. Zdrady i zwycięstwa Petra Poroszenki*
Paweł Smoleński *Wieje szarkijja. Beduini z pustyni Negew*
Albert Jawłowski *Milczący lama. Buriacja na pograniczu światów*
Lidia Pańków *Bloki w słońcu. Mała historia Ursynowa Północnego* (wyd. 2)
Mariusz Szczygieł *Niedziela, która zdarzyła się w środę* (wyd. 3)
Aneta Prymaka-Oniszk *Bieżeństwo 1915. Zapomniani uchodźcy* (wyd. 2)
Wojciech Górecki *Toast za przodków* (wyd. 2)
Jonathan Schell *Prawdziwa wojna. Wietnam w ogniu*
Wojciech Górecki *Planeta Kaukaz* (wyd. 3)
Janine di Giovanni *Tamtego ranka, kiedy po nas przyszli. Depesze z Syrii*
Wolfgang Bauer *Porwane. Boko Haram i terror w sercu Afryki*
Wojciech Górecki *Abchazja* (wyd. 2)

W serii ukażą się m.in.:
Anna Pamuła *Polacos. Chajka płynie do Kostaryki*
Paweł Smoleński *Pochówek dla rezuna* (wyd. 3)

Bartek Sabela

Afronauci

Z Zambii na Księżyc

wydawnictwo czarne

Wołowiec 2017

Projekt okładki Agnieszka Pasierska / Pracownia Papierówka
Projekt układu typograficznego Robert Oleś / d2d.pl
Fotografia na okładce © by Bartek Sabela

Redakcja Tomasz Zając
Korekta Iwona Łaskawiec / d2d.pl, Katarzyna Rycko / d2d.pl
Redakcja techniczna Robert Oleś / d2d.pl
Skład pismami Warnock Pro i Futura Małgorzata Poździk / d2d.pl

Książkę wydrukowano na papierze Ecco-Book Cream 70 g/m², vol. 2,0, dystrybuowanym przez firmę Antalis Sp. z o.o.

ISBN 978-83-8049-460-2

Rodzicom

Nie jestem Afrykaninem dlatego, że urodziłem się w Afryce, lecz dlatego, że Afryka urodziła się we mnie.

Kwame Nkrumah (tłum. Bartek Sabela)

Jakaż inteligentna istota, jakie istnienie zdolne do emocjonalnych uniesień może patrzeć na postrzępiony, srebrzysty sierp Księżyca drżący na błękitnym niebie nawet poprzez najsłabszy z teleskopów i nie zostać uderzonym w bezgranicznie przyjemny sposób, nie poczuć się odciętym od mozołu ziemskiej codzienności i przeniesionym daleko na ten pierwszy z przystanków niebiańskich podróży? Jaka wrażliwa dusza mogłaby spoglądać na lśniącego Jowisza z jego czterema satelitami lub na wspaniałego Saturna otoczonego tajemniczymi pierścieniami, lub na podwójną gwiazdę mieniącą się odcieniami purpury i szafiru pośród bezkresu nocy i nie być ogarnięta poczuciem zachwytu? Tak, w rzeczy samej, jeśli ludzkość – od skromnych rolników na polach i strudzonych pracowników w miastach, przez nauczycieli, ludzi zamożnych, którzy wspięli się na szczyty sławy i bogactwa, po nawet najbardziej frywolne kobiety – jeśli oni wszyscy byliby świadomi, jak głęboka, wewnętrzna rozkosz czeka na wpatrujących się w niebo, wtedy Francja, więcej, cała Europa wypełniłaby się teleskopami, a nie bagnetami, skutkiem czego byłaby powszechna szczęśliwość i pokój.

Camille Flammarion (tłum. Bartek Sabela)

Część I

1

Siedzi naprzeciwko mnie. Wyprostowany, jakby na baczność, trochę jak uczeń w szkolnej ławce, skarcony przez nauczyciela. Ubrany w dwurzędową marynarkę, spod której wystaje zszarzała koszula z obgryzionym kołnierzykiem, ściśnięta mocno kolorowym krawatem. Ta ciemnozielona marynarka, o kilka numerów za duża, z rękawami, które gdy wstanie, sięgają mu niemal do kolan, z błyszczącymi guzikami i z mozaiką plam, to jego jedyne odświętne ubranie. Do kościoła, do fotografii czy na ważne spotkanie, jak to dziś. Zresztą ubiera się tak zawsze, gdy się spotykamy. Do tego wkłada ogromne spodnie w prążki i za duże, koślawe, skórzane kamasze. Tak, można by powiedzieć, że wygląda śmiesznie, nawet komicznie, jak bohater kreskówki albo filmu. Jego dłonie z długimi, smukłymi palcami spoczywają nieruchomo na udach, ledwo wystając z rękawów marynarki. Jej połami mógłby się zawinąć ze dwa razy. Galowej prezencji dopełniają medale dyndające w klapie. Dwa błyskające krążki jakiegoś taniego metalu, jeden mniejszy, drugi większy, z kawałkiem materiału w kolorach zambijskiej flagi. Duma. I honor.

Siedzi nieruchomo na plastikowym krześle pod ścianą i patrzy w okno, przez które wpada do pokoju melodia niedzielnego, leniwego poranka. Świergot ptaków, szelest drzew, uporczywe bzyczenie grubych much. Jakiś wrzask dzieciaków grających w piłkę lub klakson auta przedzierającego się przez gęste uliczki sąsiedztwa. Żółta firanka w pasiaste wzory popychana podmuchami październikowego wiatru wydyma się czasami jak wielki żagiel i wtedy przysłania mi na chwilę jego postać. Patrzę na niego długie minuty. Jego czarna twarz zwrócona w stronę okna łapie promienie światła. Rozmawiamy już którąś godzinę w tym pokoju, ale teraz, w tej ciszy, wszystko nagle się zatrzymało. Widzę tę scenę jak w jakimś zwolnionym filmie. Nagromadzenie sekund, minut, powolnych, niewypełnionych żadnym działaniem, żadnym wydarzeniem czy słowem. Jedynie odległym wspomnieniem, cichą emocją, starczą reminiscencją. Może marzeniem. Lub ciekawością. Rozglądam się po pokoju, by nie naruszyć tej kruchej chwili refleksji. Po jego niebieskich ścianach, brudnych, ulepionych, ulanych, oskrobanych, z lamperią z olejnej farby. Po podłodze przykrytej ceratą w czarno-białe geometryczne wzory niczym podłoga w pałacu lub bogatej kamienicy. Patrzę na stary telewizor stojący na drewnianym stoliku i na stertę pozwijanych kabli rozpaczliwie próbujących doprowadzić do niego prąd. Myślę, że te sterty gazet, papierów i zapisków przykrytych koronkowym obrusem to może być całe jego życie. Całe życie. Dalej za nim kalendarz, aktualny, z galopującym rumakiem, a ponad nim ulotka z ostatnich wyborów. Zerka z niej na tę naszą scenę Edgar Chagwa Lungu – wygląda sympatycznie, ponoć dobry z niego prezydent, choć ulica mówi, że ma złych doradców i pije. Nic nadzwyczajnego w Afryce. Patrzę na drzwi z dykty, w których ktoś wykopał dziurę, na brudne koszule wiszące na tychże drzwiach i na kołyszącą się nad nami lampę, która dawno nie miała w sobie żarówki. Chwilę dalej spotykam swój własny wzrok, odbity w dużym lustrze w ozdobnej, krzywej ramie, dziwnie niepasującej do tego pokoju. Obok niego kilka dokumentów, plakatów przyklejonych do ściany srebrną taśmą niczym w pokoju zbuntowanego nastolatka. A w rogu tego przedziwnego pomieszczenia, z ikony w iście bizantyjskim stylu patrzy na nas Najwyższy. Z rozłożoną księgą, złocistą aureolą, dobrotliwym uśmiechem i uniesioną w geście błogosławieństwa (lub ostrzeżenia?) dłonią.

On teraz uśmiecha się nieznacznie. Wielkie czarne usta odsłaniają spore żółte zęby. Może coś sobie przypomniał? Albo roześmiał się w duchu? Psychologowie twierdzą, że wraz z wiekiem maleje emocjonalne nasycenie naszych wspomnień, zwłaszcza negatywnych. Blakną, płowieją, toną. Na wierzchu unoszą się te pozytywne, miłe, może nawet lekko przylukrowane, wyidealizowane i oszlifowane czasem. Zresztą w pewnym momencie już trudno określić, co naprawdę się wydarzyło, a co dopisała nasza wyobraźnia. Ale choć logika wskazywałaby inaczej, z jakiegoś względu ludzie po sześćdziesiątce lepiej pamiętają wydarzenia z okresu, gdy mieli od dziesięciu do trzydziestu lat. Taki sprytny mechanizm pozwalający nam w jesieni życia bardziej optymistycznie spojrzeć na nasze dotychczasowe dokonania, sięgnąć nostalgicznie do czasów młodości, odnaleźć zapomniane szuflady wspomnień.

– Ojciec zmarł 4 marca 1989 roku w lokalnym szpitalu. – Ożywia się nagle, odwraca od okna, śmieje. – Ale zanim umarł, powiedział do lekarzy: „Wy, doktorzy i pielęgniarki, nie znacie się na nauce! Nic o niej nie wiecie!". Krzyczał: „Idźcie się douczyć, bo nie umieliście mnie wyleczyć! Jestem bohaterem, bojownikiem o wolność i naukowcem! A teraz odchodzę, bo naukowiec nigdy nie umiera, on tylko odchodzi!".

10 marca na pierwszych stronach zambijskich gazet można było znaleźć takie tytuły: „Bohater pochowany" albo: „Wojownik odszedł na spoczynek". Dziennik „Times of Zambia" pisał: „Dźwięk trąb, salwy z broni palnej oraz płomienne przemówienia prezydenta Kaundy i przewodniczącego South West Africa People's Organization Sama Nujomy żegnały weterana walki o wolność pułkownika Edwarda Mukukę Nkoloso, który wczoraj odszedł na wieczny spoczynek". W „Daily Mail" artykuł zaczynał się słowami: „Prezydent Kaunda poprowadził wczoraj kondukt żałobny tysięcy ludzi na pogrzebie weterana, polityka, aktywisty, pułkownika Mukuki Nkoloso na cmentarzu Leopards Hill". Na zdjęciu w „Times of Zambia" elegancka trumna wynoszona jest właśnie z katedry Świętego Krzyża w Lusace. Na schodach

kościoła dziesiątki wojskowych oficjeli w ciemnych okularach i galowych mundurach, za nimi przedstawiciele rządu, premier, ministrowie, zagraniczni goście oraz kościelni dygnitarze.

„To wielka strata nie tylko dla Zambii, ale i dla całej Afryki. Jak bardzo bym pragnął, by on nadal żył i mógł zobaczyć niepodległość Namibii, która nadejdzie nieuchronnie. Mówię temu wielkiemu synowi Afryki, że walka trwa nadal, a zwycięstwo jest pewne!" – przemawiał nad grobem pułkownika Nkoloso Sam Nujoma, wznosząc wysoko zaciśniętą pięść w symbolicznym geście znanym na całym kontynencie. Rok później został pierwszym prezydentem wolnej Namibii.

„Daily Mail" zilustrował artykuł zdjęciem, na którym grupa wojskowych składa do grobu trumnę przykrytą zambijską flagą. W tle, po charakterystycznych białych włosach, można rozpoznać prezydenta Zambii Kennetha Kaundę. Zaraz weźmie garść ziemi, by wrzucić ją do grobu, a chwilę potem zaintonuje swoją ulubioną pieśń:

Tiyende pamodzi ndim'tima umo
A yuthi tiye Limbo moyo
Tiyende pamodzi ndim'tima umo
A yuthi tiye Limbo moyo
Tiyende pamodzi ndim'tima umo
Tioloke Limpopo ndim'tima umo
Comex Tiyende, Limbo Moyo
Tioloke Limpopo ndim'tima umo
Comex Tiyende, Limbo moyo
Tiyende pamodzi ndim'tima umo

Śpiewano ją w Zambii w czasach walki o niepodległość, w latach sześćdziesiątych i pod koniec lat pięćdziesiątych XX wieku. To nie jest hymn – podniosły, smutny. To po prostu piosenka – wesoła, skoczna. Kaunda często sam grał ją na gitarze, niektórzy nawet mówią, że ją skomponował. Dziennikarze będący tego dnia na cmentarzu opisali prezydenta jako wyjątkowo zasmuconego i przygnębionego. Ponoć kilkakrotnie wybuchał płaczem.

Wtedy prosił zgromadzonych, by śpiewali *Tiyende pamodzi*, bo tylko to przynosiło mu ulgę.

Żegnano przyjaciela, opłakiwano członka rodziny, oddawano honor partyzantowi, wojownikowi, wspominano polityka, członka rządzącej partii United National Independence Party (UNIP).

Ale nikt nie żegnał naukowca.

2

Ale to dopiero później. Najpierw była fotografia. A właściwie cały cykl kwadratowych, kolorowych zdjęć, które przykuły przypadkiem moją uwagę. Na nich na poły baśniowa, na poły realna wizja kosmicznych podróży. Te fotografie śmiało mogłyby być ilustracjami *Bajek robotów* Stanisława Lema. Na jednej z nich astronauta we wzorzystym stroju i szklanej bańce na głowie przytula się czule do słonia. Na innej ta sama postać przedziera się dziarsko przez wysokie afrykańskie zarośla. Na jeszcze innej widać marzycielsko zamyślonego czarnego chłopca, który siedzi w obskurnym pokoju. Do odrapanych ścian poprzylepiane są świecące gwiazdki. Na biurku, przed chłopcem, stoi papierowa rakieta kosmiczna.

Seria fotografii, pięknie wydana w postaci książki-albumu, nosiła tytuł *Afronauts*. „W 1964 roku zambijski nauczyciel Edward Mukuka Nkoloso postanowił wyszkolić pierwszą afrykańską załogę, która poleci w Kosmos" – zaczynał się krótki opis zdjęć. Byłem pewien, że to fotoreportaż. Że bohaterami zdjęć są osoby, które faktycznie były zaangażowane w te intrygujące i zupełnie nieznane mi wydarzenia sprzed kilkudziesięciu lat. Że to taka podróż w czasie, barwna retrospekcja, w której biorą udział ci sami ludzie, którzy pół wieku temu rzekomo wpadli na tak śmiały pomysł. Nie wiem, dlaczego tak pomyślałem, ale wydawało mi się to zupełnie naturalne. Skontaktowałem się z autorką zdjęć, hiszpańską fotografką Cristiną de Middel. Ku swojemu rozczarowaniu dowiedziałem się, że zdjęcia zostały zaaranżowane w Europie z udziałem przyjaciół i znajomych autorki, a sama de Middel nigdy nawet nie pojechała do Zambii.

3

Obawiałem się, że go po prostu nie znajdę. Że mimo wielu tygodni, które miałem spędzić w Lusace jesienią 2015 i wiosną 2016 roku, nie odszukam go w gęstwie drobnych ulic i uliczek wyglądających na mapie jak potłuczona szyba samochodowa. Ale odnalazłem go już pierwszego dnia, zupełnie przypadkiem, w dwumilionowym afrykańskim mieście, choć wiedziałem jedynie, jak wygląda i że nazywa się tak samo jak ojciec, Edward Mukuka Nkoloso.

– Wiem, gdzie mieszka syn tego człowieka. Chcesz pojechać? – usłyszałem. Szczęście przybrało niespodziewanie postać tęgiego mężczyzny, który zza mych pleców patrzył na to samo zdjęcie w Archiwach Narodowych w Lusace. Był na nim Edward Mukuka Nkoloso, roześmiany, w ekscentrycznym stroju, obok poważnego, ubranego w garnitur Kennetha Kaundy.

Chwilę później byliśmy gdzieś na południu miasta. Skręciliśmy w uliczkę, na której wrak spalonego auta zawalał przejazd. Na drutach wysokiego napięcia dyndały powiązane sznurówkami dziecięce buty. Sądząc po ilości, to ulubiona rozrywka tutejszych dzieciaków. Człowiek, który mnie tu przywiózł, wskazał na jedno z domostw. Ledwo je było widać zza rozrośniętych krzaków i ogrodzenia z trzciny. Przed domem stał mały sklepik sklecony z dykty i blachy, na nim widniał duży czarny napis „*Thanks Be To God*". Dzięki Bogu można tu kupić coca-colę, jabłka, ryż. Za skrzypiącą stalową bramą było niewielkie, zarośnięte podwórko, na którym walały się resztki jedzenia, śmieci i góra obierków po kukurydzy. Kilka kur uciekło przed nami w popłochu. W cieniu jednego z drzew siedziała stara kobieta, której z początku zupełnie nie zauważyłem. Jej popękana, brunatna skóra stapiała się z korą drzewa, a ostre cienie południowego słońca rozmazywały kształty zawiniętej w barwną chustę postaci. Tylko delikatny ruch ręką i ciche słowa powitania zwróciły moją uwagę. A więc to był dom człowieka, którego szukałem. Zapukaliśmy. Raz, drugi, piąty. W końcu dał się słyszeć szczęk zamka i stalowe drzwi lekko się uchyliły, a w ciemnym wnętrzu dostrzegłem zarys czarnej twarzy i oczy mrużące się od ostrego światła. Od razu wiedziałem, że to on. Człowiek, który mnie przywiózł, wymienił z nim kilka zdań w języku bemba. Nic nie rozumiałem, ale od razu było jasne, że coś jest nie tak. On sprawiał wrażenie zdenerwowanego, wręcz urażonego. Wyłapałem pojedyncze słowa, zapewne celowo wypowiedziane po angielsku. *Europe, white, not nice, not good, no time.* Mężczyźni coś sobie tłumaczyli, ale on potrząsnął głową w geście niezadowolenia i powoli przymknął drzwi, chowając się w mroku domu. Na mnie w ogóle nie patrzył. Jego wzrok był wbity w ziemię. Desperacko włączyłem się do konwersacji w nadziei, że bezpośrednia rozmowa coś zmieni. Wytłumaczyłem, kim jestem i po co przyjechałem, ale odpowiedź była krótka:

– Nawet w Europie nie przychodzi się do czyjegoś domu bez zapowiedzi. Nie chcę tu żadnych białych dziennikarzy, proszę opuścić mój dom.

Dopiero w hotelu uświadomiłem sobie, że nie miałem pojęcia, gdzie byłem. W swym niedowierzaniu z powodu nagłego, przedwczesnego spotkania i rozczarowany jego przebiegiem, nie zanotowałem ulicy, nie zapytałem o nazwę osiedla. Wiedziałem tylko tyle, że to najprawdopodobniej Chilenje. Dom, w którym byłem, wyglądał na taki sam jak tysiące innych, które mijałem po drodze. Spojrzałem na mapę i rozpaczliwie próbowałem sobie przypomnieć, jak jechaliśmy, gdzie skręcaliśmy. Na próżno.

Chilenje to ogromna część południa Lusaki. Cała wypełniona małymi domami, poszatkowana krótkimi uliczkami. Zacząłem przeglądać notatnik i wydzwaniać pod wszystkie lokalne numery, jakie udało mi się zdobyć jeszcze w Polsce. Do ludzi, którzy mogli pomóc, załatwić, sprawdzić. Odebrała tylko jedna osoba.

4

Cuthbert Kolala zjawia się nagle. Przerażona recepcjonistka puka do mojego pokoju i mówi, że mam gościa. Zamykając za sobą drzwi, na krótką chwilę się zatrzymuje i dodaje, że ów gość jest bardzo dziwny, przestraszyła się go. Nie wiem, kogo się spodziewać. Owszem, rozmawiałem z panem Kolalą wcześniej przez telefon. Kilkakrotnie nawet, ale nie jestem pewien, czy się w ogóle zrozumieliśmy przez skrzeczące połączenie między kontynentami, gdy dzwoniłem do niego przed przyjazdem. A teraz on siedzi na kanapie w holu skromnego hotelu w Lusace. Witam go serdecznie, ściskamy sobie dłonie, pozdrawiamy się, by rozładować wiszącą w powietrzu niepewną atmosferę. On powściągliwy, niezbyt wylewny, żeby nie powiedzieć: oschły. Siadamy obok siebie. Zapada długa cisza. Zastanawiam się, który z nas – ja jako przybysz czy on jako gospodarz i starszy człowiek – powinien ją naruszyć. Zaczynam. Mówię, że cieszę się, że udało nam się spotkać. Ale on nie słucha, patrzy tylko przed siebie. Czuję, że moje słowa przelatują obojętnie obok jego uszu.

– Wierzysz w Boga? – pyta w końcu stanowczym głosem. W tym pytaniu nie ma choćby cienia życzliwości. Pyta jak zniecierpliwiony urzędnik na godzinę przed zamknięciem biura. – Zanim zaczniemy rozmawiać, powiedz, czy wierzysz w Boga.

Dopiero teraz nawiązuje ze mną kontakt wzrokowy. Świdruje mnie swoimi przekrwionymi, wyłupiastymi oczami, gotowy wyłapać każde zawahanie, każdy fałsz. Co ma odpowiedzieć w takiej sytuacji człowiek, któremu do Kościoła jest dalej niż z Warszawy do Lusaki? Wiem, że od mojej odpowiedzi zależy bardzo dużo, być może wszystko. Wspinam się więc szybko na wyżyny dyplomacji i stosunków międzynarodowych, bo domyślam się, że zwykłe „tak" wypowiedziane bez przekonania może nie wystarczyć. Zastanawia mnie tylko, o jakim Bogu on mówi. Katolickim? Protestanckim? Może jeszcze o jakimś innym, nieznanym mi?

– Oczywiście. Jestem katolikiem z dziada pradziada. Jan Paweł II był z Polski.

Nieładnie kłamać. Zwłaszcza w sprawach tak zasadniczych jak wiara, ale czuję, że w obecnej sytuacji nie mam wyjścia. Szczera odpowiedź mogłaby zakończyć moją pracę w Zambii. Zresztą, na uspokojenie tłumaczę sobie od razu, że Bóg a Kościół to dwie różne sprawy i w zasadzie nie mam powodów do wyrzutów sumienia. Sroga twarz pana Kolali zaczyna lekko się rozluźniać, rysuje się na niej poczucie ulgi, które udziela się także mnie. Wszystko wygląda na to, że trafiłem, wierzę w odpowiedniego Boga.

– To pomódl się ze mną teraz.

Prosi, byśmy stanęli naprzeciw siebie i złapali się za ręce. Egzotyka tej niespodziewanej sytuacji wręcz mnie uwodzi. To jak jakiś rytuał inicjacyjny, przepustka konieczna, by zrozumieć ten świat. On zaczyna. Dziękuje, wzywa, prosi, zaklina, wyraża wdzięczność i uwielbienie. Jest teraz niczym ksiądz Bashobora z Ugandy, który na Stadionie Narodowym przemawiał do tysięcy wiernych. Kiedy trzeba – spokojny, delikatny, wyważony. Ale potrafi tupnąć, uderzyć ręką w stół, dać upust pasji, dać się porwać emocjom. Uznaję, że lepiej będzie, jak zamknę oczy. I jak chwycę pana Kolalę mocniej za dłonie. On kontynuuje, niesiony falami natchnienia jak dziewiętnastowieczny poeta. Mówi o długiej walce, więzieniu, krzywdzie. A najwięcej o Bogu, któremu wszystko zawdzięcza. Ze słów wynika, że Jego sprawką jest także moja obecność w Zambii. To chyba dobrze. Czuję się w obowiązku dorzucić do naszej modlitwy kilka skromnych wersów. Korzystając z pauzy, zaczynam improwizować po polsku ekumeniczną modlitwę, łączącą wszystkie wersy *Aniele Boży, stróżu mój, Ojcze nasz, Zdrowaś Maryjo,* jakie pamiętam z koszmarnie odległych lekcji religii. Im więcej mówię o Bogu, o Janie Pawle II, tym lepiej. Im więcej wyrazów typu „ojczyzna", „naród" (te celowo wypowiadam po angielsku), tym mocniej trzymamy się za ręce. Widzę, że momentalnie kiełkuje w nim ziarno zaufania, być może nawet jakiejś drobnej sympatii. Czarna twarz rozpromienia się, gdy padają słowa „Polska", „Zambia". Hotelowy pokój pęka w szwach od patosu. On cieszy się, po chwili wyrzuca swoje i moje ręce w górę, podskakuje, macha rękoma i przybija mi zamaszystą piątkę jak w hiphopowych teledyskach. Zapewnia, że we wszystkim pomoże, wszystko załatwi. I że tylko on potrafi namówić człowieka, którego szukam, na rozmowę.

– Amen! – mówi. Nie jest to zwykłe „amen", ciche, wstydliwe i smutne. To „amen" afrykańskie, przeciągłe, głośne, egzaltowane. Z akcentem na „a", pełne nadziei i wypełnione wiarą aż po brzegi.

Następnego dnia przyjeżdża punktualnie o siedemnastej, dokładnie tak, jak się umówiliśmy. Ubrany paradnie – garnitur, spodnie w kant, biała koszula, buty na obcasie i białe skarpetki. Niczym Michael Jackson, gdy jeszcze był czarny. Pod pachą skórzany neseser wypchany dokumentami. Zaczynamy oczywiście od modlitwy. Modlitwa stanie się punktem obowiązkowym każdego naszego spotkania. Czasami będziemy ją powtarzać kilka razy dziennie w rozmaitych okolicznościach: w aucie, stojąc w korku, w budynku rządowym, czekając na spotkanie, w supermarkecie, pochylając się nad talerzem frytek. Gdy już siedzimy rozluźnieni, gotowi do rozmów o naszej pracy, on, jakby od niechcenia, przypadkiem pyta, jakiego jestem wyznania. Byłem przekonany, że mamy to już wyjaśnione, ale przypominam, że katolik, że Jan Paweł II i że Polska. W odpowiedzi słyszę, że on jest wyznania mojżeszowego, to stara wiara, fundament wiary. Dopiero teraz zauważam, że jego czarną głowę przykrywa jarmułka wyszywana w dawidowe gwiazdy.

– Przez czterdzieści lat żyłem jak ślepiec – wyznaje Cuthbert Kolala. – Nie znałem za bardzo Starego Testamentu. A tam jest wszystko. To tak, jakby zapomnieć o swoich rodzicach, o swoim pochodzeniu. Naszym pochodzeniem jest Bóg Izraela, a sam Izrael to najwspanialszy kraj. Kiedyś mój przyjaciel zaprosił mnie na spotkanie. I już nigdy nie wróciłem do anglikanizmu. Teraz jestem żydem.

Pytam go, czy był w Izraelu. Nie był. Kładzie na stole swojego starego laptopa. Włącza go, zaczyna czegoś szukać.

– Chciałbym zobaczyć teraz minę Welensky'ego*. Czarnuch, który umie obsługiwać komputer! Założę się, że skurwiel zadzwoniłby prosto do królowej! – Znów ma iskry w oczach, jak wtedy, gdy ponosi go modlitwa. – Ten komputer to jest to, o co walczyliśmy.

Po paru minutach na ekranie pojawia się niebieski pulpit zawalony dokumentami i zdjęciami. Kolala twierdzi, że w tym laptopie ma wszystko, co mu potrzebne, czyli Stary i – ku mojemu zdziwieniu – także Nowy Testament. Z nieskrywaną dumą włącza program o nazwie e-Sword. The Sword of the LORD with an Electronic Edge. *Star Wars*, myślę sobie. Potem czytam na stronie producenta, że aplikację pobrało już ponad trzydzieści pięć milionów ludzi w dwustu trzydziestu pięciu krajach świata. Można dzięki niej studiować Biblię w różnych językach, przeszukiwać, porównywać wersje ewangelii, psalmów, przypowieści, listów, wersów. Pan Kolala tymczasem, wciąż rozprawiając o Bogu, wyciąga z reklamówki kilka kartek. Z namaszczeniem rozkłada na stole parę pożółkłych zdjęć. Jedno z Kennethem Kaundą, stare, czarno-białe, pewnie z lat siedemdziesiątych. Drugie już kolorowe. Widać na nim jakąś uroczystość, świtę dostojników z orderami. Pokazuje palcem siebie – stoi tuż za Levym Mwanawasą, ówczesnym prezydentem Zambii, i niedaleko Paula Kagamego, prezydenta Rwandy. Z kieszeni marynarki wyjmuje ordery, kładzie obok zdjęć. Jest w tym wszystkim bezczelnie pewny siebie.

* Sir Raphael „Roy" Welensky – rodezyjski polityk, w latach 1956–1963 premier Federacji Afryki Centralnej, w której skład wchodziła Rodezja Północna, dziś Zambia. Zwolennik segregacji rasowej i supremacji białych osadników (wszystkie przypisy pochodzą od autora).

Ale jednocześnie nie potrafi zagrać tak dobrze, bym nie wyczuł kompleksów skrywanych za fasadą politycznych osiągnięć i życiowych sukcesów. Teraz sięga po telefon, kieruje ekran w moją stronę i bez słowa pokazuje listę kontaktów. Pyta, czy chcę do kogoś zadzwonić, może do prezydenta albo któregoś ministra?

– Do prezydenta lepiej nie – prostuje szybko. – KK* ma już dziewięćdziesiąt jeden lat i zapewne śpi o tej porze, nieładnie byłoby go budzić.

Ale dzwoni na pokaz do jednego z ważnych polityków, którego imię i nazwisko – Sikota Wina – w tym momencie jeszcze nic mi nie mówi. Rozmawia z nim jak ze starym kumplem, zerkając co chwila w moją stronę, czy na pewno podziwiam. Skończywszy rozmowę, wyjmuje z papierów swoje CV. Curriculum vitae bojownika o wolność. Mówią w Zambii o nich Freedom Fighters. Czyli weterani ruchów narodowowyzwoleńczych z lat pięćdziesiątych i początku sześćdziesiątych. Przerzucając kartki, pan Kolala pokazuje mi, co, gdzie, jak, z kim, ile, w którym więzieniu i dlaczego. Od czasu do czasu pyta się, czy teraz widzę, z kim mam do czynienia.

Prosi mnie, bym wziął kartkę, długopis i pisał to, co on podyktuje. Na skrawku papieru spisujemy kontrakt, w którym w bardzo formalnych, wyniosłych, acz pokracznie brzmiących słowach ja jako „szef" zobowiązuję się do współpracy z nim, zatrudnionym na stanowisku *Research Assistant*. Warunki, cele, terminy zostają określone szczegółowo jak między dwoma brytyjskimi dżentelmenami. Dochodzimy do kwestii wynagrodzenia. Proponuję dwieście pięćdziesiąt dolarów, próbując wyczytać w oczach błysk radości albo grymas rozczarowania. Jednak to drugie. Pyta, czy to za jeden wywiad, czy za całą pracę, i kręci głową zawiedziony, choć pieniądze, które proponuję, to dość pokaźna suma w Zambii, dla wielu doskonała miesięczna pensja. Chodzi przecież jedynie o pomoc w dotarciu do kilku osób. W końcu mówi, usprawiedliwiając swoją zgodę:

* KK – tak pieszczotliwie Zambijczycy nazywają swojego byłego prezydenta Kennetha Kaundę.

– OK. To jest kwota podyktowana przez Boga, nie mogę się nie zgodzić.

Zresztą wszystko według pana Kolali jest podyktowane przez samego Boga. Obawiam się tylko, jaką cenę Bóg zasugeruje jutro za auto pana Kolali, bo ów wielokrotnie podkreślał, że auto to odrębna sprawa. Też staram się wspominać o Bogu jak najczęściej, widzę, że wtedy rozmowa lepiej nam się klei, nawiązujemy nić porozumienia. Poza tym Bóg może być argumentem ostatecznym, z którym dyskutować nie wypada. Zatem podpis. Pan Kolala mówi, że jestem zesłany przez Wszechmogącego. Że jedynie On mógł to zrobić. Amen.

– Mukuka Nkoloso jest nieufny, zbyt wielu ludzi próbowało go oszukać – zaczyna ni stąd, ni zowąd pan Kolala. – Będzie mówił tylko przy mnie. O jego ojcu nikt dziś nie pamięta, a on żyje w nędzy. Ale jak pojedziemy razem, to będzie chciał rozmawiać.

Nie wierzę. Od samego początku czuję, że pan Kolala nie jest szczery i po prostu gra ze mną jak sprzedawca na targu. Ale załóżmy, że to prawda. Zatem druga próba. Znów Chilenje, znów uliczka, czerwony sklepik i podwórko. Warkot trzydziestoletniego białego forda ze sportowym wydechem płoszy wszystkie okoliczne psy, koty i kury. Nawet dzieciaki nieruchomieją, gdy parkujemy tego starego grata pod sklepikiem. Pan Kolala jednak czyni cuda. Mukuka Nkoloso, który kilka dni wcześniej wyprosił mnie z domu, już od progu wita nas z otwartymi ramionami, uśmiechnięty i życzliwy. Wygłasza formalne powitanie, jakby trenował całą noc:

– Witamy pana w domu rodziny Nkoloso w Lusace. Ja, Mukuka Nkoloso, doktor – pauza – głowa tego domu, pierworodny syn bohatera – pauza – bojownika o wolność, wyzwoliciela Afryki. Stoję w imieniu jego, ale także innych kombatantów. Jestem zaszczycony, że będę mógł panu przekazać informacje!

Chwilę później jedziemy w trójkę białym fordem przez ulice Lusaki. Kolala oczywiście w jarmułce, Nkoloso w bejsbolówce z napisem „JESUS".

– Ci ludzie, z którymi przyjechałeś za pierwszym razem, to żadni przyjaciele – wyjaśnia Mukuka Nkoloso sytuację sprzed kilku dni, gestykulując swoimi długimi palcami. – To zwykła policja. A ja policji nie lubię. Węszą, szpiegują, chcieliby wszystko wiedzieć. Co Nkoloso robi? A kto Nkoloso odwiedza? A o czym Nkoloso opowiada?

Hałas starego forda nie daje dalej rozmawiać, wyłapuję tylko strzępki słów, i tak trudnych do zrozumienia, bo wymawianych z bardzo silnym afrykańskim akcentem. Patrzę na Mukukę Nkoloso z tylnego siedzenia. Od razu jakoś podskórnie go lubię. W przeciwieństwie do pana Kolali. Jest w nim coś szczerego, radosnego, naiwnego i przepełnionego wiarą. Coś, co widziałem na zdjęciach jego ojca.

*

Przez następne tygodnie bywam w jego domu wiele razy. Czasem z panem Kolalą, czasem sam, zaznajomiony z ulicami, zapoznany ze ścieżkami, oswojony z miejskim transportem. W zasadzie każde nasze spotkanie wygląda tak samo. Dość formalnie. Syn Mukuki Nkoloso nie rozmawia. On „przekazuje informacje" prowadzony jakimś dziwnym poczuciem obowiązku i lojalności wobec ojca. Trochę jak wojskowy. Co nie znaczy, że mówi oschle i bez emocji. Wydarzenia, czas i postacie w jego opowieściach stanowią jedynie luźne elementy, które dowolnie łączy, przeplata, ugniata niczym ciasto. Czasami mam wrażenie, że słucham jakiegoś wewnętrznego strumienia świadomości rodem z *Ulissesa*. Syn Mukuki Nkoloso odgrywa dialogi, buduje sceny, kreśli postacie, a wątki i dygresje mnoży bez opamiętania. Moje pytania mu raczej przeszkadzają, niż pomagają. Siedzimy zawsze na tych samych krzesłach w tym samym ciemnym, lepkim wnętrzu jego domu. Czasami do pokoju wkradają się jego dzieci lub wnuki, których nie potrafię zliczyć, i przycupnąwszy gdzieś z boku, słuchają razem ze mną o człowieku, który chciał lecieć na Księżyc.

5

Jadąc z Kasamy w Prowincji Północnej prosto na zachód drogą krajową M3 w kierunku Demokratycznej Republiki Konga po prawie dwustu kilometrach dojedziemy do miasta Luwingu. Dwadzieścia kilometrów na południowy wschód od niego jest osada Mucheleka, a w jej okolicy wioska Dismas. To chyba tu w 1919 lub, jak mówią inni, w 1924 roku na świat przyszedł Edward Mukuka Nkoloso, syn Marthy Kusangwy Nkoloso i Dismasa Kadambwe Nkoloso. Ojciec nadał dziecku afrykańskie imię Mukuka i poprzedził anglosaskim Edward. Edward był synem pierworodnym młodej pary, więc dodatkowo dostał też imię Festus, wywodzące się od słowa oznaczającego „święto", „festiwal". Podobnie jak jego ojciec i podobnie jak jego dziadek. Cała linia pierworodnych mężczyzn. Martha i Dismas wychowywali syna w wierze katolickiej, charakterystycznej dla Prowincji Północnej opanowanej przez plemiona Bemba, które już dawno przyjęły chrześcijaństwo.

Mukuka Nkoloso, syn Edwarda, który opowiada mi historię rodziny, mówi, że dziadek Dismas był kucharzem w armii, gotował „dla tych wszystkich dużych ludzi". Był bardzo posłuszny i lojalny. Dismas walczył na „trzech wojnach światowych", podkreśla syn Mukuki Nkoloso. Tej pierwszej i drugiej, które dla nas są oczywiste. I trzeciej – o wyzwolenie Afryki. Syn Dismasa i Marthy poszedł do szkoły, gdzie ukończył gładko szóstą, siódmą, ósmą, a także dziewiątą, dziesiątą, jedenastą i dwunastą klasę. Katolickie wychowanie zainspirowało go, by kontynuować naukę w seminarium. Studiował teologię, chciał zostać pastorem.

Syn Mukuki Nkoloso przygotował specjalnie dla mnie kartkę, na której lekko koślawym pismem zebrał informacje o swoim ojcu. Życiorys zaczyna się pytaniem: „Kim jest Edward Festus Mukuka Nkoloso?". Odpowiedź: „Edward Festus Mukuka Nkoloso to muntu wafita – Czarny Człowiek, Prawdziwy Syn Afrykańskiej Ziemi. Pierwszy zambijski afronauta, prawnik, naukowiec, pierwszy Afrykanin, który odkrył Marsa, Księżyc i gwiazdy".

Młody Nkoloso nie zdążył jednak zostać pastorem. We wrześniu 1939 roku imperium brytyjskie ogłosiło nabór do wojska we wszystkich swoich zamorskich koloniach, również w Rodezji Północnej, dzisiejszej Zambii. Studenci, silni mężczyźni, jak Mukuka Nkoloso, byli dla kolonialnej armii najcenniejszym łupem. Jednak dla czarnych mieszkańców Afryki, pomnych doświadczeń I wojny światowej, perspektywa udziału w nowym konflikcie nie wydawała się zbyt atrakcyjna. Brytyjczycy, podobnie jak dwadzieścia lat wcześniej, obiecywali dużo. Plakaty kuszące dobrym żołdem, możliwością zobaczenia świata i przede wszystkim służbą w słusznej sprawie zalały kontynent. Podobne pojawiły się również w Indiach, Birmie, Australii, Kanadzie i wielu mniejszych zakątkach kolonialnego imperium. Od Kairu po Kapsztad latały samoloty zrzucające ulotki, a armia organizowała festyny, parady wojskowe i koncerty muzyczne, zachęcając czarnych mężczyzn, by sprawdzili, czy są prawdziwymi wojownikami. „Imperium potrzebuje ludzi!", krzyczał plakat z dumnym lwem stojącym na skale. Zapewniał, że z pomocą młodych lwów stare lwy pokonają wroga. „Zapisz się!" Inny przedstawiał sielankową wizję służby wojskowej: „Zobacz świat i dostań za to godziwą zapłatę". Jeszcze inny plakat pokazywał siedmiu mężczyzn o różnych kolorach skóry kroczących pod jedną, brytyjską flagą. Nie wiedzieć czemu ten z najciemniejszą skórą stał w ostatnim rzędzie, ledwo wystając zza Hindusa w turbanie i pięciu białych na pierwszym planie. Ale napis pod grafiką głosił: „Razem!". Tym, którzy nie do końca byli przekonani o sensie udziału w nie swojej, odległej wojnie, dawano do przeczytania *Mein Kampf*, zwłaszcza fragmenty, gdzie autor w klarowny sposób wykłada swe poglądy na temat czarnej rasy. Zresztą wojna trwała w Afryce już od 1935 roku, gdy włoskie wojska najechały niepodległą Etiopię, graniczącą z koloniami brytyjskimi. Cesarz Hajle Syllasje musiał szukać schronienia w Londynie. Tymczasem wojenne miesiące uciekały szybko, podobnie jak brytyjscy żołnierze z plaż Dunkierki czy miast Afryki Północnej. W im większych opałach znajdowało się imperium, tym większe były obietnice. W końcu koloniom obiecano coś, co kusiło znacznie bardziej niż „zwiedzanie świata", pieniądze i wątpliwa chwała. Wolność.

W tym czasie w telewizji i w kinach na Wyspach Brytyjskich pokazywano propagandowe filmy przedstawiające wspaniałych, umięśnionych czarnoskórych mężczyzn, którzy „uznali, że flaga Union Jack to symbol, pod którym warto żyć i za który warto umierać". Wielu z nich, wbrew zapewnieniom narratora, nie było jednak ochotnikami. Brytyjczycy wcielali młodych Afrykanów, w większości niepiśmiennych, do kolonialnych jednostek często siłą lub podstępem, umiejętnie wykorzystując władzę starszyzn plemiennych. Lokalni wodzowie zostali zmuszeni, by oddać dziesięciu najwyższych i najzdrowszych mężczyzn ze swoich wiosek. Pod koniec wojny Brytyjczycy werbowali nowych rekrutów wprost ze szkół. Rankiem przed zajęciami oficer wchodził do szkoły ze specjalną, długą linijką i zabierał wszystkich, którzy byli odpowiedniego wzrostu. Wielu z tych chłopaków nie dostało nawet szansy, by pożegnać się ze swoimi rodzinami. Wprost ze szkół zabierani byli do koszar w Lusace i Livingstone, a potem dalej na fronty II wojny.

W ciągu sześciu lat wojny do walki z państwami Osi stanęło na wezwanie królowej ponad milion czarnych mieszkańców Afryki*. Przed biurami werbunkowymi ustawiały się długie kolejki

* Martin Plaut, *The Africans who fought in WWII*, http://news.bbc.co.uk/2/hi/8344170.stm, dostęp: 1.12.2016.

mężczyzn, często bez butów i porządnego ubrania, niedożywionych i chorych. Brytyjczycy nie byli jedynymi, którzy werbowali żołnierzy w swoich koloniach. Za Francję biło się blisko dwieście tysięcy mieszkańców Maroka, Algierii, Senegalu, Sudanu Francuskiego, Górnej Wolty, Wybrzeża Kości Słoniowej, Dahomeju, Czadu, Nigru. Za Belgię – dwadzieścia cztery tysiące Kongijczyków. Czarnoskórzy walczyli również po drugiej stronie. Włochy Mussoliniego zwerbowały ponad sześćdziesiąt tysięcy Libijczyków, Somalijczyków, Etiopczyków, Erytrejczyków. W wielu rejonach Afryki czarnoskórzy żołnierze walczyli przeciw sobie w zupełnie nie swojej wojnie za kraje, które odmawiały im podstawowych praw w ich własnych domach.

– Ojciec chciał być księdzem, ale powiedzieli mu: „Najpierw pójdziesz na wojnę, a jak wrócisz, to zrobisz, co zechcesz". No to pojechał – opowiada powoli syn Mukuki Nkoloso. – Dostał buty, mundur, broń. Pożegnał się z rodziną i wsiadł na statek gdzieś na wschodnim wybrzeżu. Na statkach śpiewali piosenki wojskowe. Ojciec mówił, że mu się podobało. Może dlatego, że wcześniej był harcerzem. Miał dobre pomysły. Został przydzielony do jednostki rozpoznania, żeby sprawdzać, z której strony nadchodzą wrogowie.

Większość mieszkańców brytyjskich posiadłości zasiliło formacje kolonialne utworzone wiele lat wcześniej, jeszcze przed I wojną światową. Setki tysięcy ludzi z zachodniej Afryki (Gambia, Sierra Leone, Nigeria, Złote Wybrzeże, Kamerun Brytyjski) walczyło w szeregach jednostki West African Frontier Force rzuconej do walk w Somalii, Etiopii i Afryce Północnej. Na afrykańskich frontach bili się także czarni żołnierze King's African Rifles, formacji złożonej z mieszkańców Ugandy, Kenii, Tanganiki, Niasy, obu Rodezji, Afryki Południowej i Południowo-Zachodniej. Początkowo Brytyjczycy zakładali, że wojska kolonialne będą używane jedynie do walk na terenie samej Afryki. Ale szybko zmienili zdanie. Wkrótce askarysi (tak nazywano czarnych żołnierzy) umierali za imperium również w samej Europie, na wyspach Pacyfiku i w południowo-wschodniej Azji. Ponad sto tysięcy czarnych mężczyzn, z czego połowa Nigeryjczyków, walczyło w Birmie. Burma Boys wraz z batalionami z Indii przez trzy lata bronili kolonii przed atakami Japończyków w najdłuższej lądowej kampanii, jaką przeprowadziło imperium w II wojnie światowej. Dlatego w wielu afrykańskich stolicach, w tym w Lusace, znajdzie się zawsze Burma Street.

Nastoletni Mukuka Nkoloso służył w 1 batalionie pułku Rodezji Północnej i wraz z nim wkrótce został przeniesiony najpierw do Afryki Północnej, gdzie pod dowództwem generała Montgomery'ego tropił Lisa Pustyni, a potem na ciężki front w Birmie. W ustach syna wojenne historie Mukuki Nkoloso brzmią prawie jak baśń. Gdy opowiada o ojcu, widzę w nim coś delikatnego. Mówi tak, jakbym słyszał kilkuletniego dzieciaka. Koloryzuje, owszem, ale co z tego.

– Tata zauważył ich stopy i już wiedział, że zaczaili się w okolicy. „Musicie patrzeć na drzewa – powiedział do swoich kolegów – ci ludzie są bardzo sprytni". Potrafili się ukrywać na drzewach, myślałeś, że to ptak, a to był japoński żołnierz! Jak szedłeś, to oni brali cię z zaskoczenia z tych drzew. Kiedyś złapali tatę i innych naszych żołnierzy. Tata spytał się tych Japończyków: „Dlaczego walczycie z nami?". „Chcemy podbić cały świat, my, Japończycy, chcemy władzy, bo nie mamy zamiaru podporządkowywać się temu wszystkiemu! A ty kim jesteś?" „Ja jestem muntu wafita", odpowiedział tata. „Skąd?" „Pochodzę z Chambeshi"*. To na północy.

Wojenna tułaczka askarysów trwała długo. Wielu z nich przez lata wojny służyło na różnych frontach i kontynentach. Ale z końcem 1945 roku porty w Mombasie, Lagos, Durbanie, Takoradi zaczęły zapełniać się wojskowymi transportowcami. Na niewielu czekały rodziny, większości ludzi nie było bowiem stać na to, by przyjechać do odległych portów i witać synów, mężów, ojców. Lokalne władze rzadko organizowały też oficjalne powitania. Demobilizacja trwała blisko dwa lata, ostatni czarni

* Region w Prowincji Północnej Zambii.

żołnierze wrócili do domów dopiero w 1947 roku. Pamiętali, co im obiecało imperium brytyjskie.

– A potem wojna się skończyła. I ojciec mówi temu Montgomery'emu, bo Montgomery lubił ojca: „My, czarni, umieraliśmy za was tysiącami! Obiecaliście nam, że jeśli pomożemy wam walczyć z faszyzmem, to oddacie nam nasz kraj". „Tak, tak, wiemy, oczywiście", odpowiedział Montgomery. Ale Brytyjczycy nagle zmienili zdanie, po prostu ich oszukali. No to tata i ci wszyscy ludzie rozeszli się do swoich miejsc, bo co mieli zrobić.

Nie wiem, czy Edward Mukuka Nkoloso faktycznie kiedykolwiek rozmawiał z marszałkiem Montgomerym. Nie wiem też, czy wojenne przygody Edwarda Mukuki Nkoloso wyglądały tak, jak opowiada je syn. Ale chyba nie ma to żadnego znaczenia. Powrót dla askarysów był często dużym rozczarowaniem. Wojenni bohaterowie wracali do krajów, w których nadal byli obywatelami drugiej kategorii. Szybko okazało się, że nie ma dla nich ani pracy, ani domów, a przywiezione z wojny pieniądze starczają na bardzo krótko. Ich wojenny wysiłek nie został w żaden sposób doceniony. Politycy w Londynie dobrze zdawali sobie sprawę z zagrożenia, jakim są setki tysięcy powracających bitnych mężczyzn. Brytyjczycy szybko zmienili zdanie co do obiecanej niepodległości. Wykończone wojną imperium potrzebowało teraz ludzi do pracy i surowców, które zapewnić mogły tylko kolonie. Mężczyźni, którzy jeszcze niedawno walczyli na froncie, teraz zostali rzuceni do katorżniczej pracy w kopalniach węgla, złota, miedzi. W lutym 1948 roku grupa czarnych weteranów ze Złotego Wybrzeża wyszła na ulice Akry, by wręczyć swoje żądania przedstawicielom władzy. Ta odpowiedziała ogniem.

Przed wojną zabicie białego człowieka czy spanie z białą kobietą było dla przeciętnego Afrykanina czymś zupełnie niewyobrażalnym. W Zambii krąży anegdota o pewnym młodzieńcu, który zastrzeliwszy białego człowieka, nie mógł uwierzyć w to, co zrobił. Biegał po wiosce na przemian przerażony i dumny, krzycząc: „*I killed a white man!*". Tymczasem w wojennych okopach wszyscy okazywali się równie bezbronni wobec śmierci. Wojna pokazała Afrykanom, że biały umiera dokładnie tak samo jak każdy czarny. Wracający z wojny askarysi odczarowali białego człowieka, odarli go z szat fałszywej wyższości. Wojsko wprowadzało również nową hierarchię, liczoną nie kolorem skóry, lecz belkami i gwiazdkami na pagonach. Czarny mógł mieć wyższy stopień wojskowy niż biały. To dlaczego, wracając do domu, miałby mu nadal usługiwać i kłaniać się w pas?

Oprócz wojennego doświadczenia i niewielkich pieniędzy afrykańscy żołnierze przywieźli z wojny coś jeszcze. Przez lata konfliktu mieli okazję poznać swoich braci nie tylko z innych zakątków Afryki, lecz także tych z Ameryki czy Europy. Ci, którzy walczyli w Birmie, zetknęli się z filozofią Mahatmy Gandhiego.

Nadzieję i inspirację narodom pod panowaniem imperium dawały również wydarzenia na świecie i w samej Afryce. W 1945 roku wybory w Wielkiej Brytanii wygrała Partia Pracy, której lider Clement Attlee już przed wojną mówił o potrzebie przyznania niepodległości koloniom brytyjskim. W tym samym roku została powołana Organizacja Narodów Zjednoczonych, ufundowana na hasłach wolności, praw człowieka i prawa do samostanowienia, w które wtedy jeszcze wierzono. Dwa lata później Gandhi bezkrwawo poprowadził Indie ku niepodległości. Na Czarnym Lądzie zaczęło być coraz głośniej o pewnym nauczycielu imieniem Kwame Nkrumah, który głosił idee panafrykanizmu i mówił o wolności dla Złotego Wybrzeża oraz całej Afryki.

Zamiast wolności Edward Mukuka Nkoloso dostał tymczasem medal Africa Star, ładny, z brązu, ze wstążką opracowaną ponoć przez króla Jerzego VI. Nkoloso wrócił do swojej wioski z medalem na piersi, stopniem sierżanta i bez grosza przy duszy. Czarnym weteranom II wojny władze brytyjskie odmówiły bowiem przyznania rent.

– Matka i ojciec powiedzieli mu: „Chyba lepiej, żebyś się ożenił, Mukuka, bo pomysł, żeby zostać księdzem, nie jest dobry. Ożeń się, Mukuka, znajdź sobie jakąś miłą żonę" – opowiada mi syn Mukuki Nkoloso. Siedzimy w trójkę, wraz z panem Kolalą. Nkoloso nieufnie patrzy w migające światełko rejestratora dźwięku, który postawiłem na stole. Długo zajęło mi przekonanie go, że to niezbędne urządzenie. Nawet umowę musieliśmy podpisać. – A on jako żołnierz po wojnie… wiesz… więc kobiety przychodziły. Ale Mukuka wybrał siostrę zakonną, Susan! „Chyba się ożenię z zakonnicą", powiedział ojcu i matce. „Z zakonnicą?" No ale zorganizowali wszystko. Matka musiała się wystarać o specjalne pozwolenia. Pobrali się w czterdziestym którymś, po wojnie w każdym razie. W czterdziestym szóstym chyba.

Seminarium faktycznie wydawało się już odległym pomysłem. Ale chęć nauczania, nie Słowa Bożego, tylko przedmiotów ścisłych, zmotywowała Edwarda Mukukę Nkoloso do przeprowadzki pod Lusakę, do Chalimbany. Nie mając wyższego wykształcenia, zapisał się na kurs dla nauczycieli i wkrótce zaczął nauczać w miejscowej szkole podstawowej. W wolnych chwilach pisywał artykuły do gazety „Mutende News" i „Nshila Magazine", czasami dorabiał jako tłumacz dla lokalnej administracji. Oprócz angielskiego na wojnie nauczył się kilku innych języków, ponoć znał nawet łacinę. Już rok po ślubie narodził się pierwszy syn państwa Nkoloso. Ojciec nadał mu swoje imię.

Wygląda na to, że Mukuka Nkoloso spełniał się jako nauczyciel. Objął nawet stanowisko dyrektora, i to po jakimś białym, lecz szybko został zwolniony. Zbyt dużo mówił o wolności, co nie mieściło się w ramach brytyjskiego sylabusa. Wyrzucony z pracy, próbował otworzyć własną szkołę, w której mógłby nauczać uwielbianej fizyki, matematyki oraz religii w swój własny, autorski sposób. Kolonialne władze nową placówkę jednak szybko zamknęły, a krnąbrny nauczyciel został znów przeniesiony. Lusaka, potem Prowincja Północna, a w końcu Ndola w Prowincji Pasa Miedzionośnego. Zawód nauczyciela, wrodzone nieposłuszeństwo i nonkonformizm rzucały rodzinę po całym kraju.

– I tu zaczęła się polityka! – mówi syn Mukuki Nkoloso.

6

Pas Miedzionośny, jedna z dziesięciu prowincji Zambii, w latach pięćdziesiątych XX wieku był gorącym miejscem. Nagromadzenie kopalni miedzi, uranu, cynku, ołowiu, srebra spowodowało również nagromadzenie wyzysku, krzywdy i dyskryminacji. Intensywna eksploatacja Pasa Miedzionośnego zaczęła się w latach dwudziestych. Belgowie odkryli ogromne złoża miedzi w Katandze – południowo-wschodniej prowincji swojego Konga, wciśniętej w przedziwny, ale typowy dla kolonialnej topografii sposób między tereny brytyjskiej Rodezji. Wkrótce okazało się, że podziemne bogactwo nie zna kolonialnych granic i pokłady miedzi występują także po stronie brytyjskiej, na terenach administrowanych przez Brytyjską Kompanię Południowoafrykańską, których jeszcze wtedy nie nazywano Rodezją Północną. Pierwsza kopalnia została otwarta w 1916 roku w Kabwe. Kilka lat później senna, rolnicza do tej pory prowincja zakwitła dziesiątkami kopalni od Ndoli na południu do Chililabombwe na północy. Nowe dziury w ziemi powstawały w zastraszającym tempie. Administracja kolonii, która od 1924 roku formalnie nazywała się Rodezją Północną i była protektoratem Królestwa Wielkiej Brytanii, zbudowała linię kolejową łączącą kopalnie ze stolicą w Livingstone. Do pracy w kopalniach brytyjska administracja ściągała czarnych pracowników z całej kolonii. Najwięcej przyjeżdżało tych z północnego wschodu, z plemion Bemba. W 1927 roku kopalnie zatrudniały ponad osiem tysięcy czarnych pracowników. Trzy lata później już trzydzieści dwa tysiące. I garstkę białych, tych z maszynami do pisania, którzy zarządzali wydobyciem, i tych z karabinami, którzy pilnowali czarnych. Pas Miedzionośny w ciągu dziesięciu lat stał się nowym centrum gospodarczym kolonii. Przeciętna płaca czarnego górnika była od trzydziestu do czterdziestu razy niższa niż białego. Czarni wykonywali pracę, ale to biali dostawali pieniądze. Ndola, Kitwe, Chingola, Luanshya stały się miastami, w których krystalizował się brytyjski kolonializm i segregacja rasowa. Akcja spowodowała jednak reakcję. Miasta Pasa stały się tym samym kolebką zambijskich ruchów niepodległościowych.

Już na początku lat trzydziestych powstały pierwsze organizacje upominające się o prawa czarnej ludności. Native Welfare Society otworzyło swoje biura w Livingstone, Lusace i miastach Pasa. Na zebraniach organizacji krytykowano kolonialne porządki i mówiono o potrzebie dostępu czarnych do dobrodziejstw przyniesionych przez europejską cywilizację. Kiedy wiosną 1935 roku brytyjskie władze ogłosiły zamiar wprowadzenia podwyżki podatków, w odpowiedzi w Nkanie (dziś dzielnica Kitwe) na drzwiach baraków, w których mieszkali czarni górnicy, pojawiały się napisane w bemba ulotki: „Słuchajcie tego wszyscy, wy, którzy mieszkacie w tym kraju! Wiecie, jak przez nich cierpimy! Wiecie, jak nas oszukują, aresztują, gdy nie pracujemy, prześladują nas i wsadzają do więzień, gdy nie płacimy podatków! Ci, którzy umieją czytać, niech mówią swym kolegom, by 29 kwietnia nie przyszli do pracy! Bóg będzie z nami!". W maju, ku zaskoczeniu białej administracji, większość czarnych pracowników nie stawiała się na szychtach. Kopalnie Pasa Miedzionośnego stanęły na tydzień, a na ulicach górniczych miast wybuchły zamieszki, czarni atakowali biura kopalń, domagając się uczciwych pensji. Pięć lat później, w marcu 1940 roku, strajki znów objęły cały Pas Miedzionośny. Czarni robotnicy opuścili szyby, wyszli z podziemnych tuneli, porzucili młoty i wiertarki.

Tymczasem wojna potrzebuje surowców. Naprzeciw robotników stanęły oddziały kolonialnej policji i wojska. Padły strzały.

Do nieposłuszeństwa i walki o swoje prawa czarnych robotników inspirował też nowy ruch religijny o tajemniczej nazwie Strażnica. Jego liderzy, czarni i biali, w większości dobrze wykształceni, często również pracujący dla kolonialnej administracji, mówili o równości i o palącej potrzebie walki z szatanem, który jest wszechobecny na ziemi. Dowodem na jego istnienie była powszechna niesprawiedliwość. Wieszczyli, że szatan zostanie pokonany w bitwie zwanej Armagedonem, która przyniesie nowy ład na świecie. Ale inaczej niż dotychczas w ich kazaniach szatan nie był utożsamiany z czarami, zabobonami i wiejskimi gusłami. Szatan uosabiał dla nich kolonialny porządek wraz z jego prawami, władzą i niesprawiedliwością. Na tajnych spotkaniach organizowanych w czarnych osiedlach, w domach, na zapleczach sklepów czy kopalń można było usłyszeć następujące kazania: „Biali, którzy teraz są pierwszymi, będą ostatnimi, a czarni, którzy teraz są ostatnimi, będę wkrótce pierwszymi!". Członkowie, a nawet założyciele Native Welfare Society tłumnie dołączyli do komórek Strażnicy. Działalność polityczna zyskała teraz wymiar również religijny. Kolonialny system to nie była tylko niesprawiedliwość, dyskryminacja, rasizm. To było coś znacznie więcej. Zło. W najczystszej postaci. Co bardziej radykalni liderzy nowego ruchu, jak Joseph Sibakwe, dodawali otwarcie, że wcieleniem szatana był król Jerzy v. Sibakwe obiecywał, że upadek kolonializmu przyniesie niebo na ziemi, bo tym samym raz na zawsze zostanie pokonany szatan. Sibakwe zapewniał też, że posiada tajemnicze księgi, które przez lata celowo były ukrywane przed czarnymi, by trzymać ich w niewiedzy. Przypominał o potrzebie edukacji i głosił, że już wkrótce dotychczasowe ofiary będą sądzić swoich katów, a całe cywilizacyjne dobrodziejstwo europejskiej kolonizacji za sprawą Jezusa zostanie przekazane w ręce Afrykanów. W nowym królestwie to Afrykanie, a nie Europejczycy mieli zasiąść najbliżej Jehowy i Jego Świadków. Choć sam Joseph Sibakwe został aresztowany, skazany i wypędzony z Pasa, władza, jaką mieli nad czarnymi przedstawiciele brytyjskiej administracji, zdawała się niczym w porównaniu z duchową potęgą, jaką dysponowali prorocy Strażnicy. Do końca lat pięćdziesiątych Strażnica, której oficjalna nazwa od 1931 roku brzmi Świadkowie Jehowy, miała w Pasie Miedzionośnym tysiące aktywnych pastorów i dziesiątki tysięcy wiernych wyznawców. Więcej niż Kościół katolicki i Kościół protestancki. Wieszczony przez samozwańczych proroków Armagedon, którym najpierw miała być I, a potem II wojna światowa, jednak nie nadszedł. Wbrew obietnicom Strażnicy szatan nadal mieszkał na ziemi i miał się bardzo dobrze.

W 1945 roku władze Rodezji Północnej zgodziły się na utworzenie African Representative Council (ARC), organizacji, która miała reprezentować interesy czarnej ludności przy rządzie Rodezji Północnej. Dwóch reprezentantów ARC dostało nawet prawo zasiadania w Radzie Legislacyjnej (jednej z dwóch izb parlamentu, drugą była Rada Wykonawcza) jako członkowie nieoficjalni. Pod koniec lat czterdziestych za przyzwoleniem Rady Legislacyjnej Rodezji Północnej, obawiającej się bardziej radykalnych ruchów, powstał pierwszy związek zawodowy – African Mineworkers' Union (AMU), na razie jeszcze kontrolowany przez białych. Pierwsze zebrania AMU pomagał organizować młody, zdolny pracownik biurowy kopalni Nchanga w mieście Chingola – Kenneth Kaunda.

Równolegle z prorokami Strażnicy hasła wolności i równouprawnienia głosiły świeckie organizacje skupione wokół Native Welfare Society. W połowie lat czterdziestych rozrzucone po całej Rodezji i nieskoordynowane w działaniu grupy połączyły się w Federation of African Societies, w 1948 roku przekształciły się w Northern Rhodesia Congress, a trzy lata później w Northern Rhodesian African National Congress (ANC) pod przewodnictwem Harry'ego Nkumbuli, jednego z niewielu czarnych w tym czasie posiadających wyższe wykształcenie. Rodezyjski ANC, pierwsza partia polityczna reprezentująca interesy czarnej ludności w kraju, czerpał inspirację wprost z Afryki Południowej, gdzie partia o tej samej nazwie działała już od 1923 roku.

– I tu zaczęła się polityka – powtarza syn Mukuki Nkoloso. Mówi coraz szybciej, a im szybciej, tym ciszej, im z kolei ciszej, tym więcej głosek nie wypowiada w ogóle. Czasami używa słów, którym nadał swoje własne, znane tylko jemu znaczenie, równie często tworzy autorskie konstrukcje gramatyczne. Często wtrąca też słowa z bemba. Jego *African English* jest trudny do zrozumienia. Czasem aż zastanawiam się w myślach, czy to aby na pewno angielski. – Czarni nie mieli nawet przerwy na lunch. Gdy biali nauczyciele szli jeść, czarni musieli po prostu czekać. Ale ojciec się tym nie przejmował. Któregoś dnia poprosił mamę, by przyniosła do szkoły jedzenie dla niego i kolegów. „Przecież my też musimy jeść!", wołał. Moja mama przyniosła im wszystkim obiad, trochę nshimy* z warzywami, kurczaka. Wtedy pojawili się biali i oznajmili: „Czarnuchom nie wolno jeść!". Ojciec wstał i odparł na to, że od dzisiaj wolno, że właśnie mają lunch, więc prosi, żeby się odsunęli i nie przeszkadzali im w jedzeniu. Ale tamci swoje, że czarni nie mają lunchu. Na to ojciec spytał jednego z nich: „A kim ty jesteś?". „Brytyjczykiem!", odpowiedział białas. A wtedy ojciec: „Czy to nie wam pomagaliśmy walczyć z Hitlerem? Byłeś na wojnie?". „Byłem". „A znasz króla Jerzego VI?" I wyciągnął z kieszeni ten swój medal. Biały zamilkł, a ojciec kontynuował: „Nic nie wiesz o wojnie, byłeś szeregowcem, więc zostaw nas w spokoju, bo właśnie jemy obiad. To, co robicie, nazywa się rasizm. A my jesteśmy równi! Pijesz wodę?". „Tak". „Oddychasz powietrzem?" „Tak". „Widzisz słońce?" „Widzę". „Otóż to, ja też". Ojciec tak właśnie z nimi rozmawiał. A na koniec powiedział mu: „Wiesz, kim jestem? Jestem Edward Mukuka Nkoloso, muntu wafita".

Jakiś czas później równie zdolny, co wygadany Edward Mukuka Nkoloso zaangażował się w działalność polityczną i dostał miejsce w African Urban Advisory Council** w Ndoli. Zdobył

* Tradycyjna potrawa w wielu krajach Afryki, przygotowywana z kaszy kukurydzianej.

** Nieznaczące instytucje doradcze składające się z czarnej ludności, powołane w miastach Pasa Miedzionośnego po strajkach z połowy lat trzydziestych.

również dobrą pracę w dużej firmie farmaceutycznej Lever Brothers. Wysłano go nawet na szkolenie do Salisbury (obecnie Harare), stolicy Rodezji Południowej. Po powrocie do Ndoli otrzymał posadę w marketingu, a do dyspozycji motorynkę i rower. Był przedstawicielem handlowym, sprzedawał leki czarnym, bo jak powszechnie twierdzono, choć nie byli równi białym, to równie często chorowali, a zatem musieli kupować leki, zwłaszcza ci, którzy pracowali pod ziemią. Nkoloso jeździł więc po kopalniach, fabrykach, które w Pasie stały jedna koło drugiej. Był w tym dobry, łatwo nawiązywał kontakty, umiał rozmawiać i doradzać. Dolega ci to i to, proszę, ten specyfik na pewno pomoże. Czujesz się tak i tak? Najlepsze będzie to. Kaszel? Mamy świetny syrop! A na przeziębienie najlepiej te pastylki. Pracował dużo, zarabiał jak na czarnego sporo, miał ambicje, by żyć tak jak biali i jeść to, co oni.

– Ale markety były tylko dla białych! – tłumacz mi syn Mukuki Nkoloso. – Raz sprzedawca zatrzymał go w drzwiach i powiedział: „Wynocha, dla czarnuchów jest okno z tyłu sklepu". To ojciec mu na to: „W takim razie daj mi łóżko przez to okno! I materac. I nowy rower". Stać go było. Wybuchła awantura, ale ojciec w końcu wszedł do sklepu, wziął, co chciał, i powiedział do sprzedawcy, kładąc plik banknotów: „Przyjmij pieniądze, dobry człowieku, reszty wydawać nie musisz".

Dzieci syna Mukuki Nkoloso, które słuchają tych opowieści wraz ze mną, wybuchają teraz śmiechem i klaszczą w ręce.

– Zaraz po nim inni czarni, którzy stali przed sklepem i się bali, zaczęli wchodzić, a sprzedawca musiał wezwać policję!

Gdzieś w 1956 roku Edward Mukuka Nkoloso wtargnął siłą do biura kolonialnego komisarza powiatowego w Ndoli i w niewybrednych słowach zaczął się domagać wyjaśnień, dlaczego kolonialne władze ekshumują cmentarz w jednej z dzielnic Ndoli mimo wyraźnego sprzeciwu czarnej ludności, dla której relokacja zwłok była profanacją. W Afryce ze śmiercią nie ma żartów, a szczątki przodków to relikwie. Nkoloso już wcześniej zabierał głos w tej sprawie w African Urban Advisory Council i zdobył dzięki temu ogromne poparcie rady i jeszcze większe zwykłych mieszkańców górniczego miasta. Tak otwarte przeciwstawianie się białym było wtedy nadal zachowaniem niespotykanym, graniczącym z niepoczytalnością.

Nkoloso został zwolniony z pracy w firmie farmaceutycznej i wyrzucony ze szkoły, w której nauczał, za zorganizowanie protestu uczniów i nauczycieli przed biurem kolonialnego kuratora oświaty. Co więcej, zbiegło się to z nowymi manifestacjami górników zrzeszonych w African Mineworkers' Union. Nkoloso, choć nie był członkiem związków zawodowych, wkrótce został aresztowany wraz z siedemdziesięcioma innymi osobami i trafił przed sąd. Ponoć pytany o dane osobowe, odpowiadał, że jest księciem Imperium Bemba, mężem księżnej Susan Nkoloso. A ku frustracji sędziów na pytania odpowiadał po łacinie. Lub po francusku. Niemniej incydent z komisarzem powiatu spowodował, że Edward Mukuka Nkoloso został wyrzucony z Ndoli i przeniesiony siłą z powrotem do Prowincji Północnej do swojej rodzinnej okolicy, Luwingu. Zgodnie z nowym prawem nie mógł jej opuszczać i znajdował się pod nadzorem lokalnego wodza Shimumbiego, otwarcie kolaborującego z Brytyjczykami. To ponoć po tym pierwszym spotkaniu z sądem Nkoloso zaczął nosić tradycyjną kolorową afrykańską togę. I drewnianą włócznię przy boku.

Nie mogąc się przemieszczać, Edward Mukuka Nkoloso, będący już wtedy szefem miejscowego oddziału African National Congress, skierował działania przeciw lokalnej administracji. Na prowincji Brytyjczycy sprawowali władzę za pomocą instytucji zwanych Native Authorities, które w założeniu miały dbać o interesy lokalnych społeczności. W ich skład wchodzili miejscowi mieszkańcy oraz przede wszystkim wodzowie wiosek. W praktyce jednak Native Authorities nie dysponowały ani większą władzą, ani pieniędzmi, a skorumpowani wodzowie stanowili po prostu przedłużenie kolonialnej władzy. Stosunki z Shimumbim od samego przyjazdu do Luwingu nie układały się najlepiej. Swoją otwartą współpracą z kolonialistami wódz budził niechęć nie tylko zbuntowanego Mukuki Nkoloso, lecz także większości miejscowych. Rozniosło się, że to Nkoloso inspiruje ludzi do nieposłuszeństwa, podżega do buntu, mówi, że wódz Shimumbi sprzedał kraj Europejczykom. Sam Nkoloso otwarcie nie okazywał wodzowi należnego szacunku i zachęcał do tego innych. Na spotkaniach i w publicznych wystąpieniach namawiał do niepłacenia należnych podatków i nierespektowania rozkazów wodza. Więcej, zamiast tego proponował ludziom, by pieniądze przekazywali na działania ANC, a słuchali jego. Pod wpływem Mukuki Nkoloso ludzie zaczęli bojkotować sklepy prowadzone przez Europejczyków, odmawiali pracy dla białych i ich instytucji. Nkoloso podburzał również przeciwko lokalnej misji katolickiej, znanej z wspierania władz. Sabotował też system edukacji, przekonując ludzi, by nie posyłali dzieci do misyjnej szkoły. Po kilku miesiącach pobytu Mukuki Nkoloso w Luwingu autorytet wodza, a tym samym kolonialnych władz został tak nadszarpnięty, że nieuchronnie zbliżała się konfrontacja. Nawet młodzi chłopcy nie szanowali wodza, ludzie nie ustępowali mu miejsca na spotkaniach Native Authority, niektórzy zwracali się do niego na „ty", pomijając oficjalny tytuł. Zniewaga była potężna. Tymczasem biura ANC wyrastały w wioskach jak grzyby po deszczu, trudno było znaleźć ludzi, którzy nie popieraliby nowej partii. Za ANC stanęło również wielu okolicznych wodzów, lecz nie Shimumbi.

Każdego lata na rozległych równinach Prowincji Północnej wypalano trawy. Było to zadanie lokalnych władz, ludzi podległych wodzowi. Ale w 1957 roku, niby przypadkiem, oprócz połaci rudych traw zapłonęły też stodoły, spiżarnie, domy i ogrody mieszkańców wspierających Mukukę Nkoloso i ANC. W okolicy pojawiły się uzbrojone patrole kolonialnych służb, szukające charakterystycznego mężczyzny. Pod koniec sierpnia Edward Mukuka Nkoloso napisał do swojego przełożonego w ANC: „Z przykrością donoszę, że członkowie wszystkich okolicznych oddziałów ANC są aresztowani [...]. Moje biuro jest nadal w drodze, ukrywamy się w buszu, policja, donosiciele i inne uzbrojone służby ścigają wszystkich członków ANC".

Brytyjczycy wydali nakaz aresztowania i list gończy za Mukuką Nkoloso, a do Luwingu zjechały konwoje land roverów z uzbrojonymi funkcjonariuszami. Tymczasem setki miejscowych wyszły bronić swojej nowej partii. Tańczyli, śpiewali, wykrzykiwali poparcie dla Mukuki Nkoloso i groźby pod adresem kolonialnych władz i wodza Shimumbiego. Wkrótce podniosły się zaciśnięte pięści, poleciały pierwsze kamienie, w ruch poszły pałki, łopaty, co kto miał pod ręką. Polała się krew, a land rovery wypełniły się aresztowanymi. Brytyjczycy szybko złapali ojca i wuja Mukuki Nkoloso i zmusili ich do zeznań. Wkrótce nad brzegiem rzeki jeden z patroli otoczył samego Mukukę Nkoloso. Policjanci skuli mu ręce, związali nogi. Dla pewności przywiązali mu jeszcze do pleców jego ciężki rower. Tak by na pewno nie wygrał z nurtem.

Ale wygrał. Edward Mukuka Nkoloso z rowerem na plecach nie utonął. Przed krokodylami szamoczące się ciało dostrzegły dwie czarne kobiety, które robiły właśnie pranie w wodach rzeki. Nie dane mu było jednak uciec. Pobitego i mokrego policjanci zawieźli wpierw do misji katolickiej w Lwenie. Tam zebrali ponad setkę dzieci uczących się w misyjnej szkole. Większość ich rodzin sympatyzowała z ANC, a same dzieciaki znały Mukukę Nkoloso. „To jest właśnie wasz Kongres – powiedział komisarz powiatowy, pan Walsch – a teraz go zwyzywajcie, oplujcie, pobijcie".

Edward Mukuka Nkoloso następnie trafił do domu wodza Shimumbiego, który przez cały czas zamieszek siedział ze strzelbą na tarasie. A w domu wodza, jak wiadomo, można było więcej niż w katolickiej szkole. W ruch poszły pałki, buty, nożyczki. Na drewnianej podłodze pojawiła się krew. Ktoś szepnął Edwardowi Mukuce do ucha: „Zdechniesz".

Syn Mukuki Nkoloso wstaje teraz z krzesła i idzie do drugiego pokoju. Po chwili wraca, trzymając w ręku dwie fotografie. Na jednej z nich trzech mężczyzn. Ten w środku jest czarny, ma na sobie podarte łachmany, stoi boso. Na twarzy widać wycieńczenie, a potargane włosy sugerują wielodniowy brud. Z szyi zwisa mu rozchełstany krawat. Mukuka Nkoloso sprawia wrażenie, jakby ledwo trzymał się na nogach, ciężkie od zmęczenia, spuchnięte od ciosów powieki ledwo odsłaniają oczy, w których widać ślad rezygnacji. Może dlatego ci dwaj pozostali trzymają go, jakby pokazywali upolowaną zdobycz. Ci dwaj są rzecz jasna biali. To rodezyjscy policjanci w fikuśnych kolonialnych strojach, z białymi korkowymi hełmami, krótkimi spodenkami, grubymi skarpetami do kolan i klamrami podkreślającymi mundurową dystynkcję. Są wyżsi, dostojni, a ich twarze zdobią precyzyjnie wystrzyżone wąsy. Wyglądają zupełnie niedorzecznie, prawie jak grupa cyrkowców zrzucona z jakiegoś powodu w środek afrykańskiego buszu. Bije od nich poczucie wyższości, przekonanie o brytyjskiej supremacji. Trzymają zmaltretowanego więźnia na długość wyciągniętej ręki, jakby nie chcieli się nim pobrudzić. Zdjęcie zrobiono 4 września 1957 roku.

A potem znów wybuchły zamieszki i karano tych, którzy sympatyzowali z ANC i Mukuką Nkoloso. On sam po wyroku sądu trafił na półtora roku do więzienia. Kilka lat później Nkoloso przywoływał pobyt w więzieniu z typowym dla siebie dystansem. W wywiadzie dla jednej z gazet mówił tak: „Wspominam ten czas z dumą, zwłaszcza dzień, gdy na mojej piersi żołnierze wyryli pinezką litery PG, Prison Graduate".

Kilka tygodni po zajściach w Luwingu Edward Mukuka Nkoloso napisał zażalenie do powiatowego komisarza sprawiedliwości. Kilkustronicowy list zakończył słowami: „Proszę, nasza policja nie może siać postrachu wśród obywateli, dokonując tak okrutnych i bezwzględnych ataków na bezbronne kobiety i mężczyzn. Wszakże to właśnie policja w Wielkiej Brytanii jest dla nas wzorem do naśladowania w przestrzeganiu prawa i porządku. To wyjątkowo nieludzkie próbować kogoś zabić tylko dlatego, że jest liderem Kongresu".

I dalej: „Nie przeczę, że jeśli uczyniłbym coś złego, to powinienem zostać aresztowany, ale nadal podtrzymuję, że nie dopuściłem się przestępstw wobec Native Authorities, za które władze mnie ukarały w tak brutalny i niegodziwy sposób. *Justitia et Pax Regina Britannia Fiat ruat Caelum.* Proszę, niech sprawiedliwość i pokój w imię Królowej Brytyjskiej zostaną dokonane, choćby niebiosa miały runąć".

Ale jest jeszcze coś. Coś, czego nie znalazłem w dokumentach archiwalnych, a co opowiedział syn Mukuki Nkoloso. To mogło być tak:

Pobitego i zmęczonego Edwarda Mukukę przyprowadzono do rodzinnej chaty w wiosce ojca. Zamęt. Krzyk. Kłęby pyłu poderwane z klepiska. Przerażenie. Brytyjscy policjanci chcieli aresztować pozostałych członków rodziny. Wrzaski, lamenty. Przepychanka. Ciotka Edwarda Mukuki, Pauline Nseko, uderzyła w twarz jednego z Brytyjczyków. W Zambii ciotka to druga matka. Sam Edward Mukuka mówił o niej w wywiadach właśnie jak o matce. Jakiś dzieciak podbiegł do policjanta i rzucił mu w oczy garść piachu z papryką chili – prymitywna, lecz niezawodna broń. Znów krzyk, teraz po angielsku, ze wściekłością i serią przekleństw. Padł strzał. Może przypadkowy, może wymierzony. Ciotka Mukuki Nkoloso osunęła się na podłogę chaty. Na jego oczach. Rana nie była jednak śmiertelna, Pauline Nseko przeżyła i wraz z mężem oraz ojcem Edwarda Mukuki została aresztowana i trafiła do więzienia. Zmarła dopiero kilka dni później. W raportach władz kolonialnych można przeczytać, że z przyczyn naturalnych. Ale rodzina mówi co innego.

Kilka miesięcy po zamieszkach w Luwingu Kenneth Kaunda opublikował książkę zatytułowaną *Dominion status for Central Africa?*. W jednym z rozdziałów przytoczył wiele wydarzeń z życia Edwarda Mukuki. Napisał też tak: „Nie uważam, bym poświęcił zbyt dużo miejsca przypadkowi Mukuki Nkoloso. W jego historii bowiem można znaleźć zasadniczą przyczynę niechęci Afrykanów do brytyjskich władz kolonialnych; zasadniczą przyczynę przekonania, że sprawiedliwość w stosunkach między Afrykanami a białą społecznością nie istnieje. W skrócie, ta historia to typowy przykład tego, czego Afrykanie doświadczają coraz częściej od 1952 roku".

7

Dwadzieścia jeden tysięcy białych. Bogatych, uprzywilejowanych, sytych, czystych, trzymających władzę. Ponad półtora miliona czarnych. Biednych, upokorzonych, głodnych, brudnych, pozbawionych praw na swojej własnej ziemi. Zmuszonych, by ustępować miejsca w autobusie, schodzić z chodnika, gdy idzie biały, kupować jedzenie przez okno na zapleczu sklepu, a na poczcie stać w oddzielnej kolejce. To Rodezja Północna w 1945 roku. Zakończona wojna pogrążyła świat w kryzysie gospodarczym. Wzrosty cen odczuwalne były również w Afryce i pogłębiły i tak ogromne nierówności społeczne. Czarni w zasadzie nie mieli dostępu do wyższej edukacji. W 1948 roku w szkołach ponadpodstawowych uczyło się jedynie stu trzydziestu czarnych studentów. Program szkolnictwa był skonstruowany tak, by utrudniać czarnym zdobycie wykształcenia. Kolonializm brytyjski stawał się coraz bardziej opresyjny. Biali reprezentanci zajmowali wszystkie miejsca zarówno w Radzie Legislacyjnej, jak i Radzie Wykonawczej, organach władzy kolonialnej. Prawo skonstruowano tak, że by móc zostać członkiem Rady Legislacyjnej, trzeba było być obywatelem Wielkiej Brytanii i wykazać odpowiednie dochody w funtach brytyjskich lub być posiadaczem nieruchomości. By zminimalizować prawdopodobieństwo buntu, prawo zakazywało czarnym posiadania broni palnej. Wśród białych zaś broń była powszechna, a kary za jej ewentualne nadużycie w stosunku do czarnego niewielkie. Władze wręcz zachęcały osadników do posiadania strzelby, sztucera lub choćby rewolweru.

Ale w Rodezji Północnej i tak było lepiej niż w Południowej, dzisiejszym Zimbabwe. Populacja białych osadników była tam ponad dwukrotnie większa niż na Północy i dwudziestokrotnie większa niż w Niasie (obecne Malawi) przy zbliżonej liczbie czarnych mieszkańców. Tam czarni nie mieli żadnych praw, nie istniały żadne partie polityczne czy związki zawodowe reprezentujące czarnych, a biali cieszyli się pełnią władzy. Wielu białych z Północy od lat zazdrościło Rodezyjczykom z Południa i podnosiło idee scalenia trzech brytyjskich kolonii regionu – obu Rodezji i Niasy – w jedną potężną Federację Afryki Centralnej z nową konstytucją i systemem segregacji rasowej na wzór tego, jaki obowiązywał w Rodezji Południowej. Nikt nie miał wątpliwości, że bogatsza, bardziej rozwinięta Rodezja Południowa miałaby odgrywać dominującą rolę w federacji, zarówno pod względem politycznym, jak i ekonomicznym, a scalenie kolonii na wiele lat odsunęłoby jakiekolwiek marzenia czarnych o równości. Rodezyjczykom z Południa federacja również była na rękę ze względu na dostęp do bogactw Pasa Miedzionośnego.

Z początku rząd Wielkiej Brytanii nie był przychylny tym pomysłom, mając na względzie opinię międzynarodową i rosnące w siłę związki zawodowe Rodezji Północnej. Zagorzałymi orędownikami federacji byli Godfrey Huggins, wieloletni premier Rodezji Południowej, i przewodniczący Rady Legislacyjnej Rodezji Północnej sir Roy Welensky, syn polskiego Żyda z Wilna. Wizja federacji spędzała sen z oczu czarnym politykom skupionym wokół African National Congress.

Obawę czarnej ludności, oprócz ewentualności pogorszenia ich statusu i praw, budziła kwestia własności ziemi. Na początku lat pięćdziesiątych blisko sześćdziesiąt procent terytorium Rodezji Północnej stanowiły tereny wydzielone jako Native Trust*.

* Robert E. Baldwin, *Economic development and export growth: a study of Northern Rhodesia 1920–1960*, Berkeley 1966.

Biali nie mogli się na nich osiedlać i choć formalnie pozostawały one pod władzą kolonii, w praktyce należały do wodzów plemion i miejscowej ludności. Do wyłącznej dyspozycji białych osadników pozostawało jedynie 5,6 procent ziemi. Terytorium Rodezji Południowej podzielone było natomiast sprawiedliwie, po połowie, między białych i czarnych*. Z tym że czarnych było dwadzieścia razy więcej niż białych. Wraz z powstaniem federacji spora część Native Trust Rodezji Północnej miała być przekształcona w Crown Land (ziemię dla europejskich osadników), by zaspokoić potrzeby białych z Południa.

Opór wobec federacyjnych planów jednoczył wszystkich – plemiennych wodzów, którzy nierzadko stanowili przedłużenie kolonialnej administracji, związki zawodowe i organizacje Native Welfare Societies, czarnych pastorów różnych wyznań – wokół kampanii zorganizowanej przez ANC. Harry Nkumbula na zebraniach wygłaszał płomienne przemowy, demonstracyjnie darł projekt federacji i wzywał do ogólnokrajowego strajku (strajk jednak się nie odbył, bo górnicy dostali podwyżki). Gazeta „The Freedom Newsletter" wydawana w miastach Pasa Miedzionośnego nawoływała do buntu. W dystrykcie Chinsali grupa młodych nauczycieli – Kenneth Kaunda, Simon Kapwepwe, Robert Kapasa Makasa – jeździła na rowerach po okolicznych wsiach, zachęcając do wspierania ANC. W czerwcu 1953 roku Elżbieta II została koronowana na królową Wielkiej Brytanii i Irlandii Północnej. Lecz w Rodezji Północnej uroczystości zbojkotowali przedstawiciele czarnej ludności, a pomniki upamiętniające koronację stały się celem ataku czarnej młodzieży.

Za pomysłem federacji według Zambijczyków stał rzecz jasna sam szatan. Przybrany we flagę Union Jack – co do tego nikt nie miał wątpliwości. Od Lusaki przez Kitwe po Chinsali na północy można było usłyszeć też, że na ziemię powrócili *banyama*. A *banyama* to postacie z plemiennych mitów, paskudne i wyjątkowo

* Reginald Austin, *Racism and apartheid in southern Africa: Rhodesia*, Paris 1975.

przerażające, bo zwykłe żywić się i handlować ludzkim mięsem. Przed *banyama*, szatanem i czarami można się było bronić tylko w jeden sposób. W Lusace, pierwszy raz w historii, czarna ludność zorganizowała dwudniową „modlitwę narodową".

Niespodziewanie dla Europejczyków Zambijczycy wykorzystali idee chrześcijaństwa, by walczyć o niepodległość. Biblia naucza przecież, że wszyscy są równi, dlaczego więc jedna rasa miałaby być wyższa ponad drugą? Zambijscy nacjonaliści zwracali uwagę, że w chrześcijaństwie nie ma miejsca na wykorzystywanie ludzi. Kenneth Kaunda w swojej książce *Zambia Shall Be Free* potępił misjonarzy i władze kolonialne za to, że nie praktykowali chrześcijaństwa w sposób, który przyniósłby równość rasową. Krytykował ich za to, że nie żyli tak, jak nauczali. Chrześcijaństwo stworzyło również płaszczyznę porozumienia i wsparcia między skolonizowanymi narodami.

Mimo wysiłków politycznych, setek zebrań, wieców, modlitw i egzorcyzmów od 1 sierpnia 1953 roku Rodezja Południowa, Rodezja Północna i Niasa decyzją królewskiego rządu połączyły się w Federację Afryki Centralnej z Godfreyem Hugginsem na stanowisku premiera. Huggins, kawaler wielu orderów i tytułów brytyjskiego imperium, kilka miesięcy po nominacji na stanowisko mówił: „Nie można oczekiwać od Europejczyków, by stali w jednej kolejce z brudnymi ludźmi, na przykład ze starą *mfazi* (czarną kobietą) z dzieciakiem na plecach, które płacze, rzyga i robi bałagan. To chyba oczywiste dla wszystkich, że system, który wypracowaliśmy w Rodezji Południowej, jest najbardziej satysfakcjonujący dla obu stron i nie ma możliwości jego zmiany, dopóki szanowni przywódcy afrykańskiej ludności nie umyją choć trochę swoich braci. Wtedy zobaczymy, co możemy zrobić".

8

W latach pięćdziesiątych główny zakład karny Federacji – więzienie w Salisbury – gościł nadzwyczaj wielu niepokornych czarnych. Małe cele aresztu na długie miesiące stały się domem dla prawie wszystkich członków przyszłego rządu niepodległej już Zambii. Nader aktywna w działaniach była grupa nauczycieli z Chinsali w Prowincji Północnej, z Kennethem Kaundą na czele. W połowie lat pięćdziesiątych Kaunda wraz ze swoimi stronnikami przeniósł się z dalekiej północy do centralnie położonej Lusaki, z której znacznie bliżej zarówno do miast Pasa Miedzionośnego, jak i do Livingstone. Niewielki dom Kaundy pod adresem Chilenje 280 na południowych przedmieściach Lusaki stał się kwaterą główną antykolonialnej konspiracji. Kenneth Kaunda, Simon Kapwepwe, bracia Arthur i Sikota Winowie, Alexander Grey Zulu, Reuben Kamanga, Mainza Chona posiadali już wizję przyszłego państwa, choć nie mieli jeszcze odpowiedniej dla niego nazwy. Rodezja kojarzyła się wyjątkowo źle, choćby ze względu na Cecila Rhodesa – twórcę kolonialnego systemu ekspansji i eksploatacji, założyciela Brytyjskiej Kompanii Południowoafrykańskiej, człowieka znienawidzonego przez czarnych. Przywódcy przyszłego państwa sięgnęli zatem do czasów przedkolonialnych, gdy ziemie te odwiedzali pierwsi Portugalczycy. Wtedy o tych rejonach mówiło się Zambezia. Od rzeki Zambezi, rzeki Boga. Simon Kapwepwe zaproponował wersję krótszą i milszą dla ucha: Zambia.

Pod koniec lat pięćdziesiątych słowo „Zambia" pobudzało wyobraźnię. O Zambii mówiło się od Mongu na zachodzie po Chipatę na wschodzie i Kasamę na północy. Zambia przemawiała nie tylko do wąskiego grona polityków i wykształconych ludzi, lecz także do rzeszy wieśniaków, biedaków, górników i służących.

W 1958 roku sir Arthur Benson, gubernator Rodezji Północnej, rozpoczął pracę nad nową konstytucją kolonii. Zaproponował, by czarnym mieszkańcom przyznać osiem z dwudziestu dwóch miejsc w Radzie Legislacyjnej. Dla Harry'ego Nkumbuli, szefa ANC, było to rozwiązanie warte zaakceptowania. Dla ludzi Kennetha Kaundy to była zniewaga i przekreślenie szans na wolność. Pod koniec 1958 roku doszło w ANC do rozłamu i powstała nowa partia, bardziej radykalna w planach niż lekko ospały i tracący wigor ANC, a jej liderem został Kenneth Kaunda. Za przykładem Kaundy ANC opuściły rzesze członków rozczarowanych polityką Nkumbuli. Założyli oni Zambia African National Congress (ZANC) – niewielka zmiana w nazwie była ogromną różnicą w planach i aspiracjach. Nie chodziło już tylko o obronę praw czarnych. Teraz celem stała się niepodległa Zambia, wyzwolona spod władania kolonialnego szatana, Zambia, która była obietnicą raju na ziemi, zarówno w sensie metaforycznym, jak i dosłownym. ZANC został zdelegalizowany przez władze kolonialne już w marcu 1959 roku, a Kaunda i jego współpracownicy trafiali do aresztów z długimi wyrokami więzienia. Edward Mukuka Nkoloso, który do tej pory prowadził własną, spontaniczną walkę z kolonializmem, w więzieniu w Salisbury spotkał polityków z pierwszej linii.

Nie wiem, czemu Mukuka Nkoloso trafił do więzienia w Salisbury. Jego syn nie potrafił odpowiedzieć. Czy już wtedy był ważnym działaczem ZANC? Czy powodem były kolejne akty brawurowego sprzeciwu i braku pokory? Nie ulega wątpliwości, że był już dobrze znany kolonialnym władzom i mógł być uznawany za jednego z najbardziej aktywnych nacjonalistów. Życiorys Nkoloso pełen jest dziur, których już raczej nigdy nie wypełnią fakty i dokumenty. Zresztą w Afryce fakty nie są najważniejsze. Nie wiem też, kiedy Edward Mukuka Nkoloso poznał osobiście Kennetha Kaundę. Może właśnie wtedy, w więzieniu, jak twierdzi jego syn? A może znacznie wcześniej, w Ndoli, gdzie Kaunda bywał regularnie? A może jeszcze wcześniej, w czasach gdy oboje byli nauczycielami w Prowincji Północnej? Chinsali, rodzinne miasto Kaundy, i Luwingu jak na warunki afrykańskie leżą blisko siebie.

– Któregoś dnia – opowiada syn Mukuki Nkoloso – pod prysznicem jakiś inny osadzony, wskazując na Kaundę, spytał tatę, czy wie, kim jest ten człowiek. W tym więzieniu siedzieli przecież też ludzie z Rodezji Południowej i z Niasy, nie wszyscy znali czarnych polityków z sąsiednich krajów. „Oczywiście! – odparł ojciec. – To jest nasz król! Lider ZANC z Rodezji Północnej". Na co tamten mówi: „Ma ciężkie życie tutaj, Brytole właśnie mu wylali na głowę wiadro ze szczynami". Następnym razem, gdy przyszli biali strażnicy, ojciec już miał gotowe wiadro i bez wahania wylał swoją urynę na jednego z oficerów.

Pobili go za to i przenieśli do więzienia w Lusace. Bezkompromisowość w stosunku do spraw wolności i godności osobistej zjednywała mu jednak coraz więcej przyjaciół. Edward Mukuka Nkoloso, podobnie jak Kenneth Kaunda i wielu innych, opuścił więzienie na początku 1960 roku.

Na wychodzącego z więzienia Kennetha Kaundę czekały tysiące ludzi. Kaunda pozdrawiał ich gestem zwanym *chisokone*. Było to uniesione w górę ramię i trzęsąca się dłoń. Znak, że kolonializm się rozsypuje. W odpowiedzi zgromadzeni krzyczeli: „Zambia! *Butungwa!* (wolność), *Tekele!* (niepodległość)". Kaunda stał się męczennikiem, mesjaszem zbawienia, pod jego stopami kruszyło się Zło kolonializmu, był „Mojżeszem prowadzącym swój lud przez ziemie faraona, by domagać się praw dla większości, które zesłał Bóg" – pisała nowa, partyjna gazeta „Voice of UNIP". Bo na Kaundę, oprócz rzeszy zwolenników, czekała też założona w miejsce zdelegalizowanego ZANC nowa partia – United National Independence Party.

Utworzyli ją jego współpracownicy, ci, którzy pozostali na wolności, i ci, którzy otrzymali krótsze wyroki. Kaunda, doceniający siłę prostych słów, ukuł slogan *„Freedom NOW"*, od którego Federacja Afryki Centralnej nieuchronnie zaczęła się trząść w posadach.

9

Sikota Wina przyjmuje mnie w swoim domu na przedmieściach Lusaki. Stalową bramę odsuwa ubrany w łachmany odźwierny. Czekamy dłuższą chwilę, zanim poprowadzi nas przez aleję ogrodu w kierunku rozłożystego budynku. Siadamy w niewielkim pokoju, który równie dobrze mógłby być salą muzealną. Tyle przeróżnych zbiorów nie ma nawet zambijskie Muzeum Narodowe. Z różowych ścian pokoju patrzą na mnie wszelkie osobistości afrykańskie, prezydenci, premierzy, biskupi różnych wyznań, przy stołach, na stadionach, przed mikrofonami, oprawieni w złote ramy. Wśród tych prominentów, trochę jak wśród drzew sawanny, kryją się tu i ówdzie wypchane głowy zwierząt – to gazela, to jakiś egzotyczny ptak. Zakłopotany, nie wiem, gdzie usiąść, żeby nie poruszyć jakiegoś obrazu, nie zbić wazy czy pucharu. Z szaf, półek, pomocników i sekretarzyków zerkają figurki afrykańskich bóstw, uwiecznione w ciemnym, twardym drewnie, ze wszelkimi atrybutami swej afrykańskości – wielkimi stopami, obfitymi piersiami, wydatnymi penisami i wiszącymi uszami. Do tego gdzieniegdzie jakieś zegary, stare zestawy do herbaty zapewne z jakiegoś arabskiego kraju, proporce egzotycznych klubów piłkarskich, srebrne tace, kieliszki, dziwne instrumenty muzyczne, bębny, grzechotki, zestawy świeczników czy stada porcelanowych łabędzi.

– To żona, uwielbiała kolekcjonować przeróżne rzeczy – tłumaczy Sikota Wina, widząc, że nie mogę oderwać wzroku od tych osobliwych zbiorów. Wskazuje na duże zdjęcie starszej, pięknej kobiety wiszące we wnęce ściany. – To ona. – Teraz dostrzegam, że jest razem z nim na większości fotografii. Patrzę z powrotem na stojącego przede mną potężnego mężczyznę i od razu wiem, że jego żona nie żyje.

Pokój, w którym przebywamy, w istocie jest salą muzealną. Zastygły w nim wspomnienia pozbierane z całego domu, z całego życia, usunięte, by nie zadręczały samotnej codzienności, nie łzawiły oczu, nie ściskały serca. Sikota Wina wżenił się w ród królewski. Nakatindi była księżniczką, wnuczką króla Lewaniki, wodza plemion Lozi zamieszkujących Barotseland' region we wschodniej części Zambii. Lewanika był prawdziwym afrykańskim królem, szanowanym zarówno przez czarnych, jak i białych. Mówi się, że był władcą mądrym i sprawiedliwym. Zwalczał niewolnictwo i czary, był przychylny chrześcijańskim misjom, choć sam nigdy nowej wiary nie przyjął. W 1902 roku został zaproszony na koronację króla Edwarda VII, gdzie traktowany był jako równorzędny monarcha. Dostąpił nawet osobistej audiencji u brytyjskiego władcy i jego rodziny. Znalazłem jego zdjęcia. Jedno z 1886 roku, gdzie Lewanika wraz ze swoją żoną siedzą w kucki przed chatą, on goły, jedynie z kijem w ręku i lamparcią skórą u nóg. Drugie zostało zrobione szesnaście lat później w Londynie. Lewanika pozuje na nim w królewskich, bogato wyszywanych szatach, z cylindrem w jednej i szablą w drugiej ręce.

Siadam na kanapie, równie różowej, co ściany. Tuż za moimi plecami szczerzy się w moją stronę naturalnej wielkości wypchany wielki kot, lew, tygrys czy inny lampart. Drugi, taki sam, przechadza się po niskim parapecie, uchwycony w pozie sugerującej polowanie. Księżna Nakatindi lubiła polowania. Sikota Wina rozsiada się obok mnie w ogromnym skórzanym fotelu. Pasuje do tego wnętrza i do tych zwierząt. Wielki, zwalisty typ z naturalnie zatroskanym wyrazem twarzy i spadającą powieką jednego oka.

– Po skończeniu liceum pojechałem na studia do RPA – opowiada osiemdziesięcioletni Sikota Wina, weteran zambijskiej polityki, jeden z trzech obok Kennetha Kaundy i Alexandra Greya Zulu najważniejszych żyjących polityków ówczesnej UNIP. – Na uniwersytet dla Afrykanów, ten sam, na którym studiował Mandela i wielu innych. W drodze do RPA wydarzyły się ciekawe rzeczy. Na jednej ze stacji wyskoczyłem z pociągu, by kupić paczkę papierosów. Nie wiedziałem, że jesteśmy już w RPA. Stałem przed kontuarem z pieniędzmi w ręku, a biały sprzedawca patrzył na mnie z pogardą i ciągle obsługiwał tylko białych. Usłyszałem gwizdek pociągu. Sprzedawca spytał mnie, czy to mój pociąg. Odpowiedziałem, że tak, ale chcę kupić papierosy. On znów mnie zignorował, a pociąg już powoli ruszał ze stacji. „Czy to twój pociąg, czarny chłopaku?" „Tak, mój, ale chcę papierosy!" On wziął paczkę, rzucił na ziemię i zaśmiał się: „No to goń go!". Udało mi się, zdołałem się uczepić któregoś z wagonów, wskoczyłem na pierwsze stopnie schodów. I wtedy przybiegł biały konduktor i zaczął mnie bić pałką po rękach, bym puścił barierki. Okładał mnie tak, że spadłem i sturlałem się z nasypu kolejowego. Na szczęście dałem radę szybko wstać i dogoniłem ostatni wagon. Wskoczyłem do niego i znów zobaczyłem nad sobą tego konduktora. Stał nade mną z pałką. „Wiesz, dlaczego nie pozwoliłem ci wsiąść do tamtego wagonu?", spytał. Nie miałem pojęcia. „Bo to jest wagon jadalniany dla białych! I żaden czarny pies nie może tam wchodzić, zwłaszcza gdy biali jedzą lunch!" Mogłem zginąć pod tym cholernym pociągiem tylko dlatego, że białasy jadły lunch. Zacząłem studia, pierwszy rok, drugi, zaangażowałem się w politykę w RPA. Nigdy nie poznałem osobiście Mandeli, choć śledziłem wszystko, co robił. Ten uniwersytet był wtedy w tej części Afryki jedynym miejscem, w którym czarni mogli studiować. Spotkali się tam wszyscy przyszli przywódcy i rewolucjoniści. Cały przyszły pierwszy gabinet RPA tam był. Ja studiowałem historię sztuki. *Makbeta* znałem na pamięć. W ogóle Szekspir był tu bardzo popularny.

Oczywiście to wszystko ani trochę nie przygotowywało nas do życia i pracy, bo czarni wówczas pracowali w kopalniach lub na farmach. Ale właśnie wtedy wprowadzono w Afryce Południowej słynny Bantu Education Act, którym rozdzielono programy nauczania dla białych i czarnych. Czarni mieli się przygotowywać do prac, które będą w przyszłości wykonywać, a nie uczyć o rewolucji francuskiej czy innych takich głupotach. To był pięćdziesiąty trzeci rok. Czarni studenci zaczęli się buntować, nie mogliśmy przecież się na to zgodzić. Któregoś ranka na teren kampusu uniwersyteckiego wtargnęła policja. W głośnikach usłyszeliśmy, że zajęcia zostają odwołane, szkoła zamknięta, wszystkie książki mają niezwłocznie zostać zwrócone do biblioteki, a studenci mają opuścić kampus. Zrobiłem beznadziejnie głupi błąd, zostawiłem w pokoju dokumenty, które czytałem nocami: jakieś manifesty komunistyczne, zapiski z procesu Jomo Kenyatty, przemówienia Kwame Nkrumaha. Oczywiście znaleźli to. Moje studia się skończyły, musiałem uciekać z Afryki Południowej. Wróciłem do Rodezji i zająłem się polityką.

Sikota Wina wraz z bratem Arthurem był jednym z najbliższych współpracowników Kennetha Kaundy, choć pochodzili z odległego, położonego na zachodzie Rodezji Północnej Mongu. Na początku lat sześćdziesiątych, gdy powstała UNIP, Sikota Wina został dyrektorem działu Publicity and International Affairs. Sam mówi, że był człowiekiem od propagandy.

– Edward Mukuka Nkoloso wszedł do mojego biura – zmienia temat Sikota Wina – i powiedział, że to, co go martwi, to brak ochrony najważniejszych osób w UNIP. Mówił, że dokądkolwiek idziemy, ja, Kapwepwe czy Kaunda, Brytyjczycy nas obserwują i śledzą. Przyznał, że najbardziej martwi się o KK, i poprosił, bym mianował go jego osobistym ochroniarzem. Dodał, że ludzi do pomocy zbierze i wyszkoli sam i będzie odpowiedzialny za bezpieczeństwo KK, gdziekolwiek ten się pokaże. Odparłem, że to dobry pomysł. Nie byliśmy pewni, co zrobią biali. Nkoloso został więc osobistym ochroniarzem KK.

Niewiele osób działających w UNIP miało jakiekolwiek doświadczenie wojskowe. Pięć lat na frontach II wojny światowej czyniło z Edwarda Mukuki Nkoloso niemal eksperta na tym polu. On sam podszedł do zadania niezwykle poważnie. Zebrał grupę młodych ludzi, wyszkolił ich w zakresie samoobrony i posługiwania się bronią. Nie palną, tej nie posiadano. Za to każdy doskonale nauczył się strzelać z procy i celnie rzucać kamieniami. Powstałe grupy młodych bojowników nazwał Action Groups. W jego zamyśle miały one służyć nie tylko do ochrony osobistej członków UNIP, z Kaundą w szczególności, lecz także do podejmowania zaczepnych działań w stosunku do Brytyjczyków. Jako człowiek odpowiedzialny za ochronę Nkoloso organizował też rytuały inicjacyjne dla młodych obrońców UNIP. Legitymację, kawałek papieru, można było przecież podrobić, a Brytyjczycy mieli swoich szpiegów i donosicieli również wśród czarnych. Ale nikt nie mógł sfałszować aktu chrztu. Nkoloso, niedoszły ksiądz i wtedy jeszcze gorliwy katolik, został więc Janem Chrzcicielem młodzieżówek UNIP.

„Przyrzekam bronić kierownictwa UNIP i ludności Zambii oraz walczyć o odzyskanie naszej ziemi z rąk brytyjskich imperialistów, tak mi dopomóż Bóg! Zwycięstwo lub śmierć!" – deklarował adept, stojąc po pas w wodach rzeczki Chunga, która zmieniała się na chwilę w Jordan.

„W imię Ojca i Syna, i Ducha Świętego. Amen! W imieniu prezydenta Kennetha Kaundy i najwyższych władz UNIP przyjmuję cię do naszej organizacji! Amen!" – odpowiadał Mukuka Nkoloso, polewając głowę delikwenta wodą.

Nkoloso stał się bliskim przyjacielem Kaundy. Wyróżniał się umiejętnościami, sposobem mówienia i ekscentrycznym wyglądem. W czasach, gdy większość czarnych polityków ubierała się, wzorem Europejczyków, w normalne garnitury, jego można było zobaczyć odzianego w tradycyjne afrykańskie kolorowe stroje lub skóry zwierząt, z plemienną biżuterią na rękach i włócznią w dłoni. Nosił też bujne, nigdy nieuczesane i nieprzycinane włosy – na znak żałoby po ciotce zamordowanej przez Brytyjczyków. Wiązał je opaską z jej sukienki.

– Zawsze nalegał, by stać przy boku KK z tą swoją włócznią – przypomina sobie Sikota Wina. – My się z tego śmialiśmy, pytaliśmy: „Mukuka, a ilu kolonialistów zabijesz tą dzidą?". Gdy ktoś chciał go odsunąć od Kaundy, wzburzony krzyczał, że jest „*chief security guard*". Ale to wszystko miało przecież jakiś wymiar symboliczny.

10

Tego hałasu nie da się z niczym pomylić. Około dziewiątej rano stary, zdezelowany ford z zamontowanym dla zabawy sportowym wydechem parkuje na podjeździe mojego hostelu. Wysiada z niego pan Kolala, jak zawsze paradnie ubrany, kręci młynka palcem wskazującym i żartuje, że helikopter przyleciał. Dziś dla odmiany jest kowbojem. Kapelusz, koszula ze skórzanymi przeszyciami i buty rodem z dobrego westernu. Cały w bieli. Wraz ze swoim białym rumakiem tworzą w tych brunatnych, zakurzonych okolicznościach wyjątkowo egzotyczny zestaw. Pan Kolala zawsze stawia auto tak, by podczas ruszania miało z górki. Wsiadamy, on grzebie pod stacyjką, szukając trzech magicznych kabli i modląc się do Boga, by dał upragnioną iskrę. Gdy Wszechmogący jest łaskawy dla naszego auta, pan Kolala odwdzięcza mu się głośnym „*Thank you, Lord!*". Jeśli nie, to znak, że Bóg ma dla nas inne plany na dzisiaj.

Chwilę później płyniemy fordem przez posępną topografię spalonych, rozgrzanych do czerwoności ulic Lusaki, przez krajobraz zbudowany z asfaltu i czerwonej, jakby przesiąkniętej krwią, afrykańskiej ziemi. Auto pana Kolali oprócz wielu oczywistych zalet ma też pewne wady. Z jakiegoś powodu część spalin zamiast na zewnątrz trafia prosto do kabiny. Nurzamy się więc w oparach przetrawionego diesla, nurkujemy w kłębach dymu palonych na ulicach śmieci, obłokach brunatnego pyłu podrywanych porannym wiatrem, w gęstniejącym hałasie klaksonów, krzyków, silników i cykad zlewającym się w jedną, nieznośną, wiercącą dziurę w głowie miejską kakofonię. Auto pana Kolali nie ma tablic rejestracyjnych. Odkręcił je w geście protestu, jemu wolno, bo przecież walczył o ten kraj. Zamiast tablic mamy za to menorę na szybie i napis „*Standing with Israel*". Ale stary ford jest autem religijnie synkretycznym, podobnie jak jego właściciel, i menora z tyłu nie przeszkadza, by na przedniej szybie umieścić napis „*This car is protected by the blood of Jesus*". Zresztą tu każdy samochód, autobus czy rower manifestuje wiarę swojego właściciela. Z haseł na pojazdach w Lusace można by uszyć całą świętą księgę niejednej religii. Wersy, wezwania, cytaty. Stary autobus na poboczu krzyczy „*Believe in Jesus and you will have eternal life!*". Z drugiej strony taksówka odpowiada „*Work like a slave to live like a king!*". Jednym z bardziej popularnych aut w Zambii jest Toyota Noah (Noe), wielkie auto mogące pomieścić nawet bardzo dużą rodzinę. Prawdziwa arka.

Brak tablic rejestracyjnych daje nam niewątpliwą przewagę w tym mieście. Korki mijamy bezpardonowo, jadąc poboczem, nieczuli na zawiść mijanych kierowców. Gdy ktoś da wyraz swojemu oburzeniu, pan Kolala wyjmie legitymację albo jakiś order, machnie ręką i rzuci z pogardą, że jemu wolno, bo jest przecież Freedom Fighter. Sunąc po szerokich ulicach tego piekielnego miasta, mijamy powoli sprzedawców, którzy niczym matadorzy z rozpostartymi koszulami, spodniami, sukienkami stoją na środku jezdni i czekają na nadjeżdżające niechybnie auta. Są jak myśliwi zaganiający zdobycz. Gdy tylko jednemu uda się zatrzymać auto, to od razu podlatują inni. Oczywiście najgorzej jest przy skrzyżowaniach, gdzie przeciągające się czerwone światło stwarza naturalną okazję do polowania. Wychudzeni sprzedawcy z bogatą ofertą wszystkiego, co może ci być w tej chwili potrzebne: paski do spodni, okulary, koszulki, artykuły spożywcze i owoce, piłki nożne czy doładowania do telefonów. Na rękach dźwigają też asortyment dla bardziej wymagających: węże ogrodowe, portfele, dmuchane kaczki tudzież mapy Zambii do powieszenia na ścianie lub rzeczy tak egzotyczne i niezrozumiałe w tym kontekście jak na przykład plakaty z anatomią człowieka lub psa. Tak czy inaczej, najlepiej sprzedaje się po prostu woda. Sprzedawcy kuszą oszronionymi butelkami niczym z reklamy coca-coli. Ale woda to zakup wysokiego ryzyka. Większość butelek jest fałszowana, napełniana ponownie wodą z kranu i oklejana folijką dla niepoznaki. Tylko pływające na jej powierzchni drobiny kurzu i wszelakiego życia widoczne pod światło zdradzają podstęp. Ale nierzadko można trafić na butelkę, po której już na pierwszy rzut oka widać, że przeszła przez wiele spoconych zambijskich rąk, dotknęła wielu spragnionych czarnych ust.

Ten handel na jezdniach to zderzenie dwóch równoległych światów. Jeden symbolizują biedni, przykurzeni ludzie siedzący na krawężniku w starych klapkach i umorusanych dresach (najlepiej z Bobem Marleyem lub Marcusem Garveyem), bujający się w rytm reggae lub zambijskiego popu puszczonego z telefonu. Próbują zarobić drobne pieniądze, sprzedając cokolwiek, co wpadnie im w ręce. Sprzedają temu drugiemu światu – ludziom w autach, w większości wielkich, terenowych, błyszczących. Toyoty, nissany, land rovery, jeepy, często prawie nowe, płyną na kontenerowcach z Japonii do tanzańskiego portu Dar es-Salaam, skąd potem rozjeżdżają się po krajach tej części Afryki. Dar es-Salaam to chyba najlepsze miejsce na świecie, by kupić terenówkę. Część z nich, te najbardziej luksusowe, to własność białych mieszkających w bogatych osiedlach. Ale nie tylko. Auto to symbol statusu, chyba ważniejszy niż dom, więc czarnoskórzy mieszkańcy równie chętnie kupują ogromne auta. Tylko od czasu do czasu w to ekskluzywne towarzystwo z napędem 4×4 wmiesza się jakiś połatany gruchot z dziesiątką dzieciaków na pace albo bus, z którego wystawać będą kończyny tych, co wsiadali ostatni.

Na chodnikach kwitną inne gałęzie ulicznego handlu, te, które wymagają trochę więcej czasu niż zmiana światła z czerwonego na zielone. Na rozłożonych kocach, pledach, trzcinowych matach najlepiej sprzedaje się, oprócz ładowarek do telefonów, Biblia. Różne wydania, formaty, okładki. Wersje katolickie, protestanckie. Do tego do kompletu plakat z Jezusem w kolorowej aureoli i z hasłem o miłości lub zbawieniu – wielki jak plakaty z Michaelem Jacksonem, Guns N' Roses czy Metallicą, które wieszało się za dzieciaka na drzwiach pokoju.

Zainteresowaniem cieszą się również kolorowe książki – poradniki, jak zmieniać swoje życie, jak uwierzyć w siebie, jak osiągać cele, jak stać się bogatym. Poradnik na każdą sytuację życiową, każdą bolączkę. Można by pomyśleć, że współczesna Afryka potrzebuje coachingu jak chleba. Z okładek tych książek patrzą na mnie uśmiechnięci, ogoleni, pięknie ubrani, pachnący mydłem i perfumami ludzie sfotografowani w pozach jednoznacznie sugerujących sukces. I to sukces, który jest na wyciągnięcie ręki. Ciekawe, że zawsze są biali. Te białe twarze spoglądają na tabuny czarnych twarzy, z których większości nigdy nie będzie stać, by kupić jakąkolwiek książkę. I mówią im, jak mają żyć.

Prawie codziennie przemierzam długie ulice Lusaki, także na piechotę. Chodzę po bogatych osiedlach zamieszkanych przez potomków białych kolonizatorów, gdzie ulice zdobione są pasmami kwitnących jakarand, które zasypują asfalt opadłymi fioletowymi kwiatami. Domów tutaj nie widać. Wszystkie skryte są za potężnymi murami, które zwieńczone są zawsze drutami pod napięciem i koronką z tłuczonych butelek. Nawet ładnie to wygląda, gdy zapomni się o jej funkcji. Zwłaszcza o zachodzie słońca, kiedy światło przebija się przez powbijane na sztorc kolorowe szkło, wypełniając wnętrze ulicy refleksami. Tu jest cisza, jest i spokój, przerywany jedynie szumem SUV-ów wyjeżdżających zza stalowych bram. Te masywne mury służą również jako powierzchnie reklamowe. Zdobią je malowane ręcznie ogłoszenia produktów, usług, hoteli. Ale to enklawy dostatku w morzu nędzy i upokorzenia.

Kilka ulic dalej luksus rozpływa się, znika z każdym metrem i niemal bezszwowo przechodzi w niekończące się osiedla biedy – slumsy dzielnic Matero, Chilenje czy Kamwala. Barwne jakarandy i bugenwille znikają przed kotłującym się kłębowiskiem ostrych agaw. Murowane ogrodzenia zamieniają się w płoty z dykty, trzciny, skrawków blachy, znika też asfalt. Beton wypiera błotna cegła lub szary pustak. Szkło ustępuje miejsca folii. Kamień ucieka przed blachą falistą i azbestem. Zapach kwitnących drzew rozpływa się w woni stęchlizny. Jedyną wspólną cechą dzielnic tego miasta pozostaje rdzawoczerwona ziemia. Nawet powierzchnie reklamowe murów i parkanów służą tu innemu nadawcy. Napisy w stylu „*Jesus saves*", „*God bless you*" zapełniają to, co niezarośnięte przez krzaki i bluszcze. I te plakaty. Są wszędzie, na przystankach, słupach, znakach drogowych, nawet na wielkich billboardach. Zerwane walają się po ulicach, przyklejają do aut i ludzi. Zapraszają na zgromadzenia, wspólne modlitwy i żale za grzechy. Obiecują oświecenie, kuszą zbawieniem i życiem wiecznym. Zwołują na stadiony na spotkanie z Nim. Wzywają do krucjat i zachęcają do poszukiwania cudów. Moje ulubione są te z pewnym białym pastorem rodem z dawnych Prus Wschodnich, który z jakiegoś względu upodobał sobie Czarną Afrykę jako miejsce głoszenia ewangelii. Nazywają go „kombajnem Boga", na swojej stronie internetowej twierdzi, że osobiście nauczał ponad sto dwadzieścia milionów ludzi, a kolejne siedemdziesiąt dwa miliony „prowadził w modlitwie zbawienia" (cokolwiek to oznacza). A teraz po raz pierwszy będzie głosił Słowo Boże na Stadionie Niepodległości w Lusace. Podwójna gratka, bo nie sam, lecz ze swoim wiernym uczniem, równie białym jak on. Zapraszają na wspólną czterodniową „krucjatę Ewangelii" i obiecują, że każdy z uczestników otrzyma błogosławieństwo od Boga (w cenie biletu?). Ostatniego dnia imprezy na stadionie i w jego okolicach gromadzi się ponad dwieście pięćdziesiąt tysięcy Zambijczyków.

– Przed 1964 rokiem w Zambii wszyscy byliśmy anglikanami albo katolikami – tłumaczy mi Cuthbert Kolala, gdy suniemy przez Burma Road w kierunku domu syna Mukuki

Nkoloso. – Wtedy kafar* nie mógł zostać pastorem czy biskupem. A teraz każdy może. I to się Bogu podoba!

Liczne wspólnoty religijne zaczęły wyrastać jak grzyby po deszczu po uzyskaniu przez Zambię niepodległości w 1964 roku. Wcześniej o rząd czarnych dusz walczyły głównie misje katolickie i protestanckie. Areną tych zmagań przez długie lata była Prowincja Północna, okolice Kasamy, Chinsali, serce ziem zamieszkanych przez ludy Bemba. Pod koniec XIX wieku, dwadzieścia lat po Livingstonie, na te tereny dotarł pewien starszy człowiek z długą brodą, ubrany w białe szaty. Biskup Dupont był misjonarzem katolickiego zgromadzenia Ojców Białych. Ze względu na porywcze usposobienie miejscowa ludność nazywała przybysza „*moto moto*" – co w języku bemba znaczy „ogień". W rzeczy samej katolicki płomień ogarnął szybko wioski Prowincji Północnej, ale już wkrótce w ślad za Ojcami Białymi przybyli misjonarze z protestanckiego Kościoła Szkocji. Misje katolickie i protestanckie prześcigały się w budowaniu nowych szkół, domów i kościołów. I w zbieraniu datków. Placówki często wyrastały jedna obok drugiej jak konkurujące ze sobą sklepy. Chrześcijanie głosili ewangelię i zwalczali lokalne wierzenia, przed wszystkim wiarę w czary. Misjonarze mówili o obecności szatana i powszechności grzechu, nawoływali do nawrócenia i porzucenia pogańskich przekonań. Ale wielu Bemba pojęcia grzechu i szatana utożsamiało właśnie z czarami. Idee chrześcijaństwa natrafiły na wieki lokalnej kultury i uwarunkowań, o których europejscy misjonarze nie mieli bladego pojęcia. Głosząc potrzebę walki ze złem, którą tubylcy rozumieli jako walkę z czarami, misjonarze jednocześnie krytykowali narzędzia do walki z nimi, pozbawiali Bemba możliwości obrony, uzurpując ją wyłącznie dla samych siebie. Wpadli tym samym nieświadomie we własne sidła – wielu Bemba zaczęło uważać misjonarzy, zwłaszcza tych katolickich ze zgromadzenia Ojców Białych, za czarowników.

* Obraźliwe określenie stosowane przez Brytyjczyków pod adresem czarnoskórych mieszkańców Zambii.

Powstało naturalne zapotrzebowanie na ruchy religijne tworzone przez samych czarnych, łączące w sobie tradycyjne wierzenia z nową, chrześcijańską wiarą. W latach trzydziestych do zmagań o dusze włączyły się zatem ruchy rdzennej ludności. Konkurencja rosła. Z Malawi na tereny północnej Zambii przybyli „czyściciele czarów" – Bamuchape. Członkowie sekty jeździli po wioskach i przekonywali, że dysponują niezawodnym lekarstwem na czary. By identyfikować czarowników, używali lustra. Gdy niecny delikwent został zdemaskowany, zmuszano go do wypicia specjalnej mikstury. Wmawiano czarownikom, że od tej pory, jeśli tylko spróbują czarować, obecna w ich ciele substancja spowoduje, że spuchną i umrą w boleściach. Za niewielką opłatą „czyściciele" sprzedawali również domowe środki do walki z czarami, a nawet eliksiry, dzięki którym posiadacz stawał się odporny na rozkazy kolonialnych władz. W ten sposób Bamuchape wkrótce „oczyścili z czarów" większość północnej Zambii. W krótkim czasie ruch Bamuchape stał się na tyle potężny, że konkurował o władzę dusz z Kościołami katolickim i protestanckim, a misje katolickie zabroniły członkom ruchu wstępu na swoje tereny. W rewanżu Bamuchape oskarżyli księży katolickich o praktykowanie czarów.

Podczas pobytu w Zambii miałem okazję porozmawiać z doktorem Walimą Kalusą, wykładowcą historii na University of Zambia, autorem książek na temat wierzeń i religii w Zambii.

– Czary powinny być rozumiane jako dyskurs, przez który ludzie organizowali swoje stosunki społeczne – twierdzi doktor – jako narzędzie harmonizowania społecznych relacji. Przeważnie jednak są postrzegane jako zło. Kogo uważa się za złą osobę, tego zazwyczaj oskarża się właśnie o praktykowanie czarów. Lecz czary mają różne aspekty. Najczęściej związane są ze złem i stają się przyczyną problemów. Ale jednocześnie czary mogą być źródłem dobroczynnej mocy. Możesz używać czarów na przykład, by wygrać mecz w piłkę nożną. Niektóre drużyny z Afryki zwracają się do czarowników, by zapewnić sobie sukces na boisku. Niektórzy ludzie odwiedzają szamanów, by zapewnić sobie szczęście na egzaminach naukowych lub dostać pracę w banku. To się zdarza. Wielu z tych ludzi to osoby bardzo dobrze wykształcone, z doktoratami wspaniałych uczelni zagranicznych. Czary były również używane jako narzędzie w walce z kolonializmem. Edward Mukuka Nkoloso przekonywał innych nacjonalistów, że skoro brytyjscy kolonialiści są tak potężni militarnie, to jedyna droga, by ich pokonać, to właśnie czary. Argumentował, że nacjonaliści powinni skorzystać z pomocy potężnego *nganga*, czarownika, by zniszczyć kolonializm. Bo czary są źródłem mocy i władzy, tak jak obecnie chrześcijaństwo.

Do walki z wszechobecnym złem, czarami i kolonializmem w latach pięćdziesiątych stanął kolejny nowy ruch religijno-społeczny. Kościół Lumpa, prowadzony w Prowincji Północnej przez charyzmatyczną Alice Lenshinę, już w 1958 roku miał więcej członków niż Kościoły katolicki i protestancki razem wzięte. Lenshina, urodzona jako Alice Mulenga Lubusha w 1920 roku, ogłosiła się prorokiem po tym, jak zachorowała na malarię mózgową. Twierdziła, że podczas śpiączki spotkała Jezusa Chrystusa, a on powierzył jej stworzenie nowego Kościoła, który powróciłby do źródeł wiary i odnalazł utracone wartości. Lenshina w języku bemba znaczy „królowa". Z głoszonymi przez królową radykalnymi ideami w samej Prowincji Północnej identyfikowało się około stu tysięcy ludzi. Wyznawcy Kościoła odrzucali jakiekolwiek zwierzchnictwo – i to duchowe, i świeckie, kolonialne czy nacjonalistyczne – potępiali spożywanie alkoholu, poligamię, odrzucali władzę plemiennych wodzów, a przede wszystkim walczyli z czarami i europejskimi misjami katolickimi. Wkrótce stworzyli zamknięte enklawy wyjęte spod kontroli władz, w tym największą w rodzinnej wiosce Lenshiny, którą nazywano Syjonem. Popularność sekty Alice Lenshiny i głoszone przez nią anarchistyczne i marksistowskie poglądy spowodowały, że wkrótce Kościół Lumpa stał się poważną konkurencją i zagrożeniem zarówno dla kolonialnych władz, jak i dla walczących z Brytyjczykami nacjonalistycznych ugrupowań. Na przełomie lat pięćdziesiątych i sześćdziesiątych Lenshina miała setki tysięcy zwolenników już nie tylko na rodzimej północy, lecz także w miastach Pasa Miedzionośnego i samej Lusace, a jej Kościół dysponował pokaźnym budżetem z datków wiernych. W Syjonie rozpoczęto budowę okazałej murowanej świątyni, która architekturę zawdzięczała „boskiej inspiracji"*. Alice Lenshina ogłosiła, że w Zambii powstanie „Nowe Jeruzalem". Trzynawowy budynek wielkością dorównywał katolickim katedrom, a inauguracyjną mszę miał odprawić sam Jezus Chrystus.

Kościołów przeróżnych wyznań jest w Lusace mnóstwo. Nie wiem, czy ktokolwiek zna ich liczbę. Czasami aż zastanawiam się, skąd biorą parafian, w końcu Lusaka to nie Szanghaj, ma niespełna dwa miliony mieszkańców. Mniej lub bardziej okazałe budynki sakralne można zobaczyć niemal na każdym rogu. Mam wrażenie, że każdy, kto dysponuje garażem bądź większym domem, może się nazwać pastorem i założyć swoją własną denominację chrześcijaństwa katolickiego, protestanckiego lub jeszcze jakiegoś innego, synkretycznego. Wystarczy zrobić plakat ze swoją podobizną, najlepiej w towarzystwie uśmiechniętej, krągłej żony, dodać trochę ciepłych kolorów i ładny napis. Dobrze robi umieszczenie gdzieś postaci Jezusa z wyciągniętą dłonią lub zambijskiej flagi. Można też wydrukować ulotki lub gazetki i zatrudnić kilku nastolatków, by rozdawały je na ulicach. W tym kanale promocji i kontaktu z klientem bezsprzecznie mistrzami są świadkowie Jehowy. Nie ma dnia, żebym na ulicy nie spotkał kogoś, kto będzie mnie zachęcał do przeczytania „Strażnicy" i do rozmowy o Bogu. Można też zainwestować w inne formy religijnego marketingu. Na przykład postawić w centrum miasta „namiot modlitwy" lub zapłacić taksówkarzowi za okazały baner na drzwiach auta. Domyślam się, że najtrudniejsze w zakładaniu własnego Kościoła w Zambii musi być wymyślenie nowej

* Złośliwi twierdzili jednak, że do złudzenia przypomina kościół pobliskiej misji katolickiej.

nazwy. Takiej, która jeszcze nie została zajęta przez konkurencję, przecież liczba kombinacji słów takich jak „Bóg", „Jezus", „ewangelia", „przymierze", „serce", „miłość", „światło", „cud", „nowy" czy „wieczny" jest w końcu ograniczona.

*

Nie lubię tego miasta. Męczy mnie, dusi spalinami, przytłacza milionem krzyków i dźwięków, przyprawia o świdrujący ból głowy. Nie umiem go polubić. Zwłaszcza centrum i tych kilku ulic do niego prowadzących, obsadzonych tu i ówdzie przez pomnikowe rządowe gmachy i siedziby międzynarodowych korporacji w architekturze betonowego brutalizmu lat sześćdziesiątych i siedemdziesiątych, nadszarpniętego czasem, okaleczonego niedbalstwem, takiego z powybijanymi szybami, pourywanymi kawałkami elewacji i dyndającymi na wietrze szyldami reklam. Centrum dawnej Rodezji Północnej wyznaczone skrzyżowaniem dwóch głównych ulic kolonii – Great East Road, biegnącej z Mongu na zachodzie do Chipata na wschodzie, oraz Great North Road łączącej Livingstone z miastami Pasa Miedzionośnego. Na skrzyżowaniu tych dróg powstała Lusaka. Cairo Road to część arterii północnej. Te ponure symbole potęgi – władzy bądź pieniądza – wyrastają bezpośrednio ze świata zbudowanego z dykty, tektury, szmat, świata podpartego kijem, związanego sznurkiem, utopionego w śmieciach, umazanego gównem. Takie to organiczne, bezwzględne i w jakiś sposób naturalne w zasadzie. Jak drzewa z torfu. Z jednego z wieżowców całe miasto błogosławi wielka reklama Samsunga. Widać ją zewsząd, zawsze jest na horyzoncie, bliższym lub dalszym. Można by pomyśleć, że Lusaka sponsorowana jest przez Samsunga. Te kilka wieżowców Cairo Road stoi tuż obok biedamarketów, setek, może tysięcy prowizorycznych wiat handlowych rozstawionych wzdłuż torów kolejowych, pod wiaduktem Independence Avenue. Część z tych bud stoi prawie na torach. Każdego dnia o zachodzie słońca w ten tłum ludzi i produktów wjeżdża pociąg relacji Lusaka–Livingstone. Sapiąc, świszcząc syrenami, przedziera się przez kolorowe kłębowisko, które zasklepia się tuż za ostatnim wagonem. Jak Mojżesz przez Morze Czerwone.

Pierwszy deszcz tego roku, tej pory deszczowej, łapie mnie pewnego popołudnia pod wiaduktem na rogu Church Road. Jeszcze niewielki, trochę nieśmiały, ale już z piorunami i stalowogranatowymi chmurami, które wyglądają, jakby miały zmieść to miasto z powierzchni ziemi. Siedzę na torach wraz z kilkoma dzieciakami niosącymi na głowach wielkie torby plastikowych butelek. Są większe niż one same. Patrzymy na mokre, błyszczące tory, które wiją się, rozjeżdżają, odbijają na bocznice, spotykają ponownie. Obok jakaś rodzina oraz kilku bezdomnych. Za chwilę ma jechać pociąg, do którego burt przyczepią się kurczowo i dojadą do swoich odległych przedmieść. Te tory biegnące wzdłuż zatłoczonej Cairo Road, za linią zabudowy, to jakaś antyteza samej ulicy, jej alter ego. Jest tu zadziwiająco cicho. Można powoli obserwować życie rozłożone na części pierwsze. Jest w tym miejscu coś bardzo prawdziwego, jakaś surowa, czasami brutalna nagość, która umyka na hałaśliwej Cairo Road. I ziemia ma tutaj inny kolor. Nie jest czerwona, jest żółta, jakby składała się z samego piasku, czasami umazanego i tłustego od czarnych kolejowych smarów wielkich lokomotyw i wagonów towarowych. Dla jednych to szlak transportowy. Z jakiegoś powodu ludzie wolą chodzić po torach niż po biegnącej obok ścieżce czy oddalonej o sto metrów Cairo Road. Sam wolę iść torami, bo zachęcają do rozmyślania, obserwowania. Chodzimy więc po tych torach jak jacyś pielgrzymi, jakby na ich końcu było coś, co może dawać nadzieję. Jest w nich jakaś zmaterializowana linia czasu, obietnica przyszłości i wspomnienie przeszłości, odliczane precyzyjnie każdym podkładem kolejowym, klatka po klatce, sekunda po sekundzie. W tych rozjeżdżających i zjeżdżających się na powrót stalowych torach jest jakaś metafora czasu i przestrzeni.

Dla innych to miejsce pracy, drobnego handlu. Marne targowisko za trzecim wiaduktem jest zatłoczone przez cały dzień, mam wrażenie, że tu mieści się właściwe centrum tego miasta.

Są też dzieci, dla których tory to place zabaw lub miejsce zbierania puszek czy plastikowych butelek. Dla jeszcze innych trzy wiadukty przecinające tory to miejsce schronienia, ucieczki, a nawet zamieszkania, w podłych budach kleconych z kartonów i wszystkiego, co udało się znaleźć na śmietnikach. Są też ci, dla których tory są miejscem palenia skrętów, ćpania, wąchania kleju i ostatecznie umierania. Docierają tu do ostatniego podkładu kolejowego. Leżą na torach, siedzą na nasypach, czasami z narkotycznego letargu wyrwie ich przejeżdżająca drezyna. Bo pociągów jest niewiele, jeden, czasami dwa dziennie, w Zambii są tylko trzy linie kolejowe.

Lubię patrzeć na to miejsce z góry, z wiaduktu Great East Road. Wtedy widać je na tle całego miasta, wielkich reklam Toyoty, Samsunga, Barclaysa i ogłoszeń o „krucjacie Ewangelii". I wielkiego centrum handlowego, które przypomina o swojej obecności głośną muzyką. Te centra brytyjskich sieci handlowych, powiew zachodniego świata, rozrzucone są po Lusace jak rodzynki w cieście, każde jedno ogromne jak warszawska Arkadia. Gdy pytam się mieszkańców Lusaki, co ciekawego można zobaczyć w ich mieście, wielu odpowiada: *„Have you seen Levy Center?* Oh, you should!"*. Nawet dla Europejczyka cena kawy jest tu zaskoczeniem. Kogo stać na zakupy w tych wypucowanych butikach, kto kupuje w tych błyszczących marketach, przed wejściem do których pan w mundurku podaje ci specjalną chusteczkę, byś mógł sobie zdezynfekować ręce i uchwyt wózka? Na parkingu pod Manda Hill, Levy Center czy East Park trudno znaleźć wolne miejsce. Wytworny market Food Lover's kusi górami błyszczących owoców, ułożonymi według kolorów, ekskluzywną, delikatnie gazowaną wodą w eleganckiej buteleczce i całym wyborem świeżo wypieczonych bułeczek, ciast, ciasteczek i kanapek. Widzę, że młody chłopak podający mi struclę z jabłkami wielkości bochenka chleba patrzy na nią tęsknym, wymownym wzrokiem maskowanym usilnie uprzejmym „*Thank you, sir*". To wszystko

* Levy Center – wielka galeria handlowa w samym centrum Lusaki.

jest banalne i oczywiste w Afryce, połowie Azji, w ogóle w połowie świata. Ale nadal tego nie rozumiem. Zresztą, te cholerne galerie handlowe stają się moim azylem. Błogosławię je w duszy. Uciekam do nich desperacko kilka razy dziennie, ratując się przed brudem, tłokiem i skwarem ulicy. One przyjmują mnie w swoje klimatyzowane ramiona, a ja za tę chwilę wytchnienia chętnie zapłacę pieniądze, które wielu Zambijczykom starczają na tydzień. Pierwsze, co robię, to biegnę do kibla zmyć z rąk te dziesiątki spoconych uścisków i tłusty brud banknotów. Potem kawa i ciastko. I jeszcze raz do kibla, jakbym musiał się przygotować na ponowne starcie z ulicami tego miasta.

Tymi torami – idąc za pociągiem dalej na południe – można dojść do rozległego osiedla Misisi. Choć *„compound"* – słowo, którego używa się w Zambii na określenie takich miejsc – nie oznacza wcale osiedla. *Compound* to bardziej getto. Nagromadzenie ludzi, domów. I skrajnej nędzy. Do Misisi nikt nie chodzi ulicą, choć ta biegnie tuż obok. Wszyscy idą właśnie torami. Wśród wysokich, brzęczących cykadami traw i gór śmieci duszących odorem. Nawet stragany po drodze do Misisi stoją przy torach, tak jakby to one były główną arterią komunikacyjną, a nie pobliska ulica. Może dlatego, że to biegnący prosto kolejowy nasyp, a nie meandrująca ulica wyznacza granicę tnącą południową część miasta na dwie części. Po stronie wschodniej jest Kamwala, jedna z pierwszych czarnych dzielnic Lusaki, z wydzielonymi ortogonalnie uliczkami, niewielkimi prostokątnymi działkami i małymi domkami. Przypomina nasze pracownicze ogródki działkowe. Nieuważny obserwator mógłby nazwać Kamwalę osiedlem slumsów, którym w istocie jest, choć zapewne żaden z mieszkańców Lusaki by jej tak nie określił. Mógłby, gdyby nie odwrócił się za siebie i nie spojrzał na rozciągające się po drugiej stronie torów Misisi. Wtedy doszedłby do wniosku, że Kamwala to jednak oaza dobrobytu, bogate osiedle o przestrzennym rozkładzie, uporządkowane i zadbane. Miejsce, w którym domy mają adresy, a posesje ogrodzenia. Za torami rozciąga się bowiem urbanistyczno-ludzka dżungla, labirynt bez ulic, bez wydzielonych działek, bez nazw i numerów, miasto w mieście, chaos wewnątrz i tak bezładnej struktury. Lusaka jest zresztą pełna takich enklaw. Misisi widziane z góry przypomina jednorodną kolonię bakterii albo innych miniaturowych istot, gęsto upchanych, pączkujących spontanicznie w każdym kierunku, wypełniających każdy metr kwadratowy wolnej przestrzeni, pulsującą drobnymi, chaotycznymi ruchami. Na tej samej powierzchni, na której po drugiej stronie torów stoi jeden niewielki skądinąd dom, w Misisi stoją cztery budynki, pięć, czasami sześć, z błotnej cegły i trzciny lub szarego pustaka. Gęsto upakowane jak komórki w tkance, stykające się dachami, ścianami, zaglądające sobie wzajemnie w tysiące małych okien i drzwi. Za tymi drzwiami, w ciemnym, zatęchłym wnętrzu, dzieje się życie, którego nie jestem sobie w stanie wyobrazić. Czasami przejścia między domami są tak wąskie, że trzeba iść bokiem, uważając, żeby nie zawadzić głową o blaszany dach. Misisi to jedno z tych miejsc, które rządzi się swoimi prawami. Prawami tworzonymi w społecznościach skrajnie biednych i wykluczonych. Choć do centrum jest może piętnaście minut na piechotę, policja raczej się tu nie zapuszcza, biali omijają osiedle szerokim łukiem, a drogę w tej plątaninie potrafią odnaleźć tylko miejscowi.

Przechodzę przez targ węglowy, jakbym w jednej chwili zstąpił w głębokie otchłanie piekieł. Czarna ziemia, czarne stragany, czarne twarze patrzące nieufnym wzrokiem, czarne długie ręce przekładające bryły węgla i sięgające po czarne banknoty. I czarny dym. Misisi nieustannie płonie. Stertami śmieci i górami węgla. Zwłaszcza tu, na targu. Dym przyćmiewa nawet zachodzące słońce, sprawia, że jego promienie z trudem przedzierają się przez czarne obłoki, obrysowując ludzi i kształty. Co chwilę z kłębów dymu wyłaniają się przeróżne postacie. Jakby cienie. Kobiety z koszami na głowach, mężczyźni pchający wyładowane po brzegi taczki, grupy młodych chłopaków w kapturach, czasami bose dzieciaki goniące piłkę lub wychudzony pies. Ten węgiel to podstawa egzystencji. W każdym z tych tysięcy domów gotuje się na węglowych fajerkach, wokół których siedzą kobiety skrobiące kukurydzę czy pojedyncze warzywa. Świat jak z ponurej wizji przyszłości, w której nadrzędnym dobrem jest paliwo i złom. W centrum targu węglowego stoi wielka ciężarówka, znacznie większa niż każdy z okolicznych budynków. Jej gigantyczna naczepa jest cała ze złomu. Każdego dnia lokalni zbieracze przymocowują do tej konstrukcji kolejne znalezione elementy: stalową kratę, starą pralkę, samochodowe drzwi, maskę lub rurę wydechową. Albo beczkę po oleju, zlew kuchenny czy dziurawy garnek. Tony stalowego złomu z każdym dniem formują się w kształt naczepy tira, setki niepotrzebnych stalowych gratów zamykają się samorzutnie w ogromny prostopadłościan. Nic nie wystaje, nic nie wisi. Pościągane pasami, podoginane, pospawane przez chudych zbieraczy. Spontaniczna konstrukcja ze stali i rdzy, którą z powodzeniem można by wystawić na jakiejś poważnej wystawie sztuki współczesnej. Gdy zbieracze doczepią już ostatni znaleziony drut, ostatnią felgę czy blachę falistą, samochód ruszy z ciężkim stalowym chrzęstem niczym czołg albo parowóz. Wróci niebawem z pustą naczepą gotową przyjąć kolejne samochodowe wraki i wysłużone do granic możliwości sprzęty domowe. Wtedy zacznie się od nowa. Ale jest jeszcze coś. Wzdłuż północnego krańca Misisi, dokładnie ponad targiem węglowym, biegnie sieć wysokiego napięcia. Wielkie słupy otoczone dymem wyłaniające się z wieczornego światła wyglądają jak armia robotów z wysokobudżetowego filmu science fiction. Kroczą ponad domami spowitymi kurzem, ponad autami, ponad głowami, dźwigając na kratownicowych ramionach dziesiątki bzyczących napięciem kabli.

Zagłębiam się między kolejne ulice i zakamarki, czuję się, jakbym schodził na kolejne poziomy piekieł. Na szczęście ponad blaszanymi dachami, dociśniętymi kamieniami, by nie odleciały, ciągle widzę reklamę Samsunga na jednym z wieżowców przy Cairo Road. Jest dla mnie jak latarnia morska. Gdy spojrzę potem na Misisi z lotu cyfrowego ptaka za pomocą Google Maps, ze zdumieniem stwierdzę, że ledwie wszedłem w tę dzielnicę. Byłem raptem na brzegu, ledwie co dotknąłem, zaledwie spróbowałem. Tylko zanurzyłem nogi w tym morzu, tylko stałem na brzegu, bojąc się fal. Nic nie widziałem. A może jednak widziałem już wszystko?

Krążę tak po Lusace niemal każdego dnia. Sprawdzam miejsca, zdarzenia, szukam ludzi. Składam puzzle historii, która zaciągnęła mnie do Zambii. Uświadamiam sobie, że gdyby nie te wydarzenia sprzed ponad pięćdziesięciu lat, pewnie nigdy bym nie przyjechał do tego kraju. Zatem przypadek w zasadzie. Albo plan Stwórcy, jak twierdzi pan Kolala, który od pierwszego dnia uważa mnie za bożego posłańca.

*

Wiedziałem, że pan Kolala któregoś dnia podsunie kartkę z kwotą za użytkowanie swojego luksusowego auta. Tak by wyrównać niedosyt spowodowany „ceną podyktowaną przez Boga" za jego usługi. I podsunął. Dwieście dolarów za dzień plus paliwo. Odsunąłem ją z powrotem w jego stronę bez słowa.

– OK, zapomnijmy o tym – odrzekł tyleż zdezorientowany, co rozczarowany.

11

„Zawsze was prosiłem, byście byli cierpliwi i nastawieni pokojowo w swych myślach, słowach i działaniach. Ale teraz usuwam jedno z tych szlachetnych słów z mojego słownika i jest nim »cierpliwość«. Welensky nie chciał być cierpliwy i dostał to, czego pragnął. My, którzy wykazujemy się cierpliwością, zostaliśmy pominięci. Obawiam się, jeśli się ze mną zgodzicie, że musimy działać" – mówił KK w czerwcu 1961 roku.

Słowa KK były reakcją na manipulacje, jakich dopuścił się sir Roy Welensky przy tworzeniu nowej konstytucji Federacji Afryki Centralnej. Po wyjściu KK i pozostałych czarnych liderów z więzień UNIP szturmem zdobyła poparcie, już nie tylko wśród elit, ludzi wykształconych i młodych. W ciągu kilku miesięcy od stycznia 1960 roku UNIP urosła do potęgi, której kolonialne władze nie mogły już dłużej ignorować, a jej członków zamykać w więzieniach. Do końca 1960 roku wolnością cieszyła się już prawie cała Afryka Północna, Zachodnia i Wschodnia. Europejskie kolonie utrzymywały się jeszcze tylko w Afryce Południowej. Z opuszczeniem swoich posiadłości nadal zwlekały Portugalia, Hiszpania i Wielka Brytania. W samym imperium coraz głośniej słychać było głosy liderów Partii Pracy wzywające rząd do ostatecznego rozstania się z koloniami. Zresztą, nawet część brytyjskich posiadłości, tych mniej znaczących, jak Sudan, Somali Brytyjskie czy Złote Wybrzeże, uzyskała już niepodległość. Ale Federacja to inny przypadek. Tożsamość kolonialna i związki z imperium były tu (zwłaszcza w Rodezji Południowej) znacznie silniejsze, głos białych osadników bardziej doniosły, a ziemia bogatsza. Niemniej Niasa, część Federacji, od 1958 roku tonęła w chaosie. Nyasaland African Congress pod przywództwem Hastingsa Bandy, który potem dał się poznać jako niezwykle ekscentryczny prezydent niepodległego już Malawi, rozpoczął kampanię obywatelskiego nieposłuszeństwa wobec władz. W odpowiedzi władze wprowadziły stan wyjątkowy, a na ulicach Lilongwe i Blantyre od kul policji zaczęli ginąć ludzie. Z początkiem 1960 roku na tereny Federacji przybywali przedstawiciele specjalnie powołanej przez rząd w Londynie komisji, której celem było zbadanie sytuacji w koloniach i nakreślenie planu na najbliższą przyszłość. Raport komisji Moncktona, ku zdziwieniu królewskiego rządu, jednoznacznie wskazał na potrzebę głębokich reform konstytucji oraz najszybszego dopuszczenia czarnej większości do władzy. Alternatywą było jedynie użycie siły. Wściekły sir Roy Welensky odrzucił raport, nazywając go gwoździem do trumny Federacji. Kenneth Kaunda miał więc mocną pozycję, gdy został zaproszony do wzięcia udziału w pracach nad nową konstytucją. Dla wszystkich było jasne, że musiała ona dopuścić rządy czarnej większości. Tak się jednak nie stało. W czerwcu 1961 roku do już uzgodnionego tekstu sir Roy Welensky, desperacko próbując uratować Federację, zakulisowo wprowadził zapisy uniemożliwiające czarnym zdobycie większości w parlamencie.

– KK zawsze powtarzał, że nasza walka będzie bezkrwawa, pokojowa. Bez użycia przemocy. Ale wkrótce stało się dla nas jasne, że administracja kolonialna nie jest gotowa na takie przekazanie władzy – wspomina Sikota Wina. – W Londynie zorganizowano konferencję na temat przyszłości Federacji. Kaunda zwrócił się bezpośrednio do Brytyjczyków: „Jeśli Wielka Brytania i premier Federacji sir Roy Welensky będą kontynuowali działania mające na celu przeszkodzenie dążeniom czarnej ludności Rodezji Północnej do samostanowienia, wybuchnie masowe powstanie, przy którym rebelia Mau Mau w Kenii wyda się niczym więcej niż dziecięcym piknikiem!". Następnego dnia KK dzwoni do mnie rano, żebym szybko przyszedł do jego pokoju. A tam na stole czekały już rozłożone wszystkie te gazety. „Daily Telegraph", „Times", „The Observer", wszyscy trąbili, że Kaunda grozi buntem!

Gorące wystąpienie Kennetha Kaundy w czerwcu 1961 roku, które wszyscy odebrali jako wezwanie do powstania, podsumowała jedna z kobiet, Mama Chola, w tych słowach: „To będzie prawdziwy taniec! Zaprosimy Europejczyków, zaprosimy Afrykanów! Kury, psy, wszystkie boskie stworzenia dołączą do naszego tańca, nawet Królowa będzie tańczyć naszą cza-czę!".

– Tak się zaczęło, *enough is enough*. Tak naprawdę Cza-cza była pierwszym stopniem naszego planu. Nastąpiłyby jeszcze cztery kolejne etapy, gdyby pierwszy nie przekonał Brytyjczyków. Na szczęście nie musieliśmy ich wprowadzać w życie. Rodezja popadłaby w kompletny chaos. Nie powiem ci o nich – śmieje się Wina, wymieniając porozumiewawcze spojrzenie z panem Kolalą. – Umówiliśmy się z KK, że jeśli nie zostaną zrealizowane, to pozostaną na zawsze tajemnicą.

O tych tajemniczych kolejnych stopniach słyszę często od różnych osób, ale żadna nie chce mi zdradzić, jakie byłyby scenariusze działania, gdyby buntowniczy „taniec" nie przyniósł rezultatów. Ponoć plan działania został rozpisany w czarnym notesie, który Kaunda miał ze sobą na każdym spotkaniu. Ale on sam zaprzeczał i twierdził, że Cza-cza była tylko w jego głowie.

*

Pierwsze zapłonęły dokumenty. Ludzie oddawali je z ulgą, z poczuciem wyzwolenia z ucisku, z poczuciem wyzwolenia spod władzy Zła. Także dlatego, że ich posiadanie było podstawą do opodatkowania na rzecz znienawidzonej Federacji. Całe worki, kartony, taczki *chitupas* – kolonialnych dowodów osobistych – lądowały na stosach, ku uciesze tańczących wokół ludzi. Bo *chitupas* nie wystarczyło po prostu wyrzucić, podrzeć. Należało je oddać płomieniom. Brytyjska flaga paliła się niezwykle szybko, a ogień przynosił poczucie oczyszczenia i wolności niczym w trakcie szamańskich rytuałów. Walka toczyła się również na płaszczyźnie symbolicznej, gdzie religia mieszała się z czarami i wierzeniami. We wsiach i miastach organizowano symboliczne pogrzeby. Do ziemi składano kukły sir Roya Welensky'ego, w trumnach zamykano symbole Federacji. W miejsce zniszczonych *chitupas* ludzie od razu dostawali legitymacje członkowskie UNIP, a podatki, które do tej pory oddawali władzom, płacili ochoczo skarbnikom partii. Legitymacje UNIP rozdawane w miejsce kolonialnych dowodów były jednak czymś więcej niż tylko symbolem przynależności do organizacji. Były nową formą identyfikacji z jeszcze nieistniejącym, ale wymarzonym państwem, manifestacją chęci i dążeń, opisywały tożsamość nowego, wolnego czarnego człowieka. Palenie kolonialnych dowodów stało się bezprecedensowym aktem buntu i wyraźnym sygnałem dla sir Roya Welensky'ego.

Edward Mukuka Nkoloso od początku twierdził, że Brytyjczycy nie oddadzą tak łatwo władzy i że prędzej czy później trzeba będzie ich zmusić siłą. Namawiał do tego Kaundę, ale lider UNIP, będący młodym, acz rozważnym politykiem, nie był przekonany do paramilitarnych pomysłów swojego nowego przyjaciela. „Słuchaj, Mukuka, wiem, że byłeś w armii, i wiem, że wiesz, o czym mówisz, ale nasza walka będzie pokojowa – powtarzał KK ku rozczarowaniu Mukuki Nkoloso. – Taka jak w Indiach. W Zambii nie będziemy przelewać krwi ani białych, ani czarnych".

Kaunda nie chciał tworzenia przy UNIP formacji partyzanckich. Uważał, że mogłoby to jedynie zaszkodzić wizerunkowi partii i jej działaniom. Nkoloso, choć w zupełności posłuszny decyzjom swojego szefa, prezydenta, króla, postanowił jednak na wszelki wypadek podjąć pewne działania.

– Gdyby nie to, że KK miał inną wizję naszej walki, Nkoloso był naprawdę gotowy to robić, stworzyć regularne grupy partyzanckie z chłopaków z Matero i innych przedmieść – tłumaczy Sikota Wina. – Powtarzał często, że gdyby miał swoją drużynę, podkładałby bomby w domach białych. Ale KK właśnie tego chciał uniknąć. Nkoloso mimo to potajemnie szkolił młodych chłopaków, nawet zorganizował jakieś pojedyncze ataki na białe farmy i akcje, które miały napędzić białym stracha.

Action Groups, które Nkoloso stworzył jako formę straży przybocznej Kennetha Kaundy, przerodziły się w regularną młodzieżówkę UNIP balansującą na krawędzi polityki i bijatyki. Edward Mukuka Nkoloso zgromadził wokół siebie grupę wiernych chłopaków, którzy podobnie jak on uważali, że Brytyjczykom trzeba pomóc opuścić Zambię. Wprowadził wojskowy dryl, dyscyplinę i rytuały inicjacyjne z pogranicza chrześcijaństwa i afrykańskiego szamanizmu. Nazywał swoje młodociane oddziały, chyba bardziej dla żartu niż na poważnie, Zambia Police. W 1988 roku magazyn „ZMagazine" opublikował niewielki wywiad z Edwardem Mukuką Nkoloso, który właśnie został awansowany przez Kennetha Kaundę na stopień pułkownika. Ze zdjęcia ilustrującego artykuł patrzy na nas poważny, dystyngowany dygnitarz wojskowy z medalami na piersi, rzucający groźnym spojrzeniem spod wojskowej czapki z daszkiem. Tak wspomina swoich wychowanków: „Nasza młodzież wtedy to byli ludzie, którzy bez problemu mogli przebiec siedem mil. Byli silni, odporni na uderzenia. Kiedyś zorganizowaliśmy specjalny post, by hartować ducha i prosić Boga, by dał nam jak najszybciej wolność. Pod koniec tego postu byliśmy tak wygłodniali, że gdy jeden z nas złapał węża, to zjedliśmy go na surowo!".

Nkoloso mówi też o jednej z bardziej spektakularnych akcji swojej młodzieżówki: „Poszliśmy do kostnicy i przekupiliśmy strażnika. Daliśmy mu pięć funtów i przekonaliśmy go, by wydał nam ciało jakiejś białej kobiety. Potem zabiliśmy kozę, usmarowaliśmy tego trupa we krwi i zanieśliśmy do hotelu Ridgeway. A wtedy to było miejsce tylko dla białych. Udało nam się odciąć prąd i weszliśmy do hotelowej restauracji, gdzie białasy akurat jadły kolację, popijały wino, śmiały się. Rzuciliśmy tego trupa na podłogę i krzyknąłem do nich: »Białasy, wasz czas się kończy! Zabiliśmy żonę Welensky'ego i was też wkrótce dopadniemy!«.

Biali pouciekali w popłochu, a my spokojnie dopiliśmy ich piwa i wina".

Syn pułkownika dopowiada:

– Bo on ciągle coś kombinował, planował. Na przykład konstruował domowe bomby. Z butelek po piwie, benzyny, którą kradli z aut białych, parafiny, kawałków sznura. Podkładali te bomby w różnych miejscach, głównie nocami, w sklepach, na ulicach.

„*One boy, one road! / One man, one block! / One car, one bomb! / One man, one stone! / One man, one vote!*" – śpiewali młodzi z bojówek Edwarda Mukuki Nkoloso i wielu innych, które powstawały ochoczo w całej Rodezji Północnej. Tych wyrostków, często bosych, niemających nawet dziesięciu lat, nazywano „Dziećmi Zambii". Lub „Dziećmi Kaundy". Sam KK miał później powiedzieć, że „UNIP jest matką, a naród jej dzieckiem".

Zapłonęły szkoły, symbole kolonialnego wychowania i dyscypliny. Zapłonęły mosty i budynki publiczne, elementy obcej infrastruktury. Zapłonęły sklepy białych, symbole codziennej dyskryminacji i segregacji rasowej. Zapłonęły również budynki misji, zwłaszcza tych katolickich, które podejrzewano o współpracę z władzami i czary. I domy białych, ale także czarnych, którzy pozostawali obojętni i nie identyfikowali się z działaniami UNIP. W odpowiedzi płomienie ogarnęły wioski czarnych, którzy wspierali nową partię. Ogień trawił pola i magazyny żywności. Władze tłumaczyły, że przyczyną tak wielu pożarów w zbuntowanych wioskach są prymitywne kuchnie.

Choć sama Cza-cza to lato 1961 roku, niepokoje trwały w miastach Rodezji już od początku 1960 roku. Sytuacja nieuchronnie zaczęła wymykać się spod kontroli. Miesiące, w których czarni zaprosili białych do Cza-czy, przynosiły coraz więcej ofiar. Wbrew założeniom Kennetha Kaundy na ulicach Lusaki, Ndoli, Kasamy, Kitwe rozlała się zarówno czarna, jak i biała krew. Już w maju 1960 roku doszło do brutalnego zabójstwa na tle rasowym. Lilian Burton, biała kobieta, wracała autem wraz ze swoimi dwiema córkami z Ndoli na swoją farmę. Była postacią znaną nie tylko w Rodezji, ale i nawet Londynie. Samochód został zatrzymany na drodze przez grupę czarnych mężczyzn uzbrojonych w kije i kamienie. Wybili szyby, do środka wlali benzynę. Lilian Burton oraz jej córki, pięcio- i dwunastoletnia, wydostały się z płonącego auta, ale nie udało im się daleko uciec. Kobieta wraz z dziećmi została znaleziona martwa kilka godzin później na skraju lasu. Na sprawców zorganizowano obławę sięgającą nawet za granicę z Kongiem. Czterech czarnych mężczyzn zostało złapanych i kilka miesięcy później, po burzliwym procesie, zawisło na szubienicy. Wszyscy byli powiązani z UNIP.

Gazeta rządowa „White Paper" tak podsumowywała wydarzenia lata 1961 roku: „Nie ma wątpliwości, że przyczyną tych zamieszek jest niezadowolenie związane z planami zmiany konstytucji przez rząd brytyjski. Gdy negocjacje nie doprowadziły do osiągnięcia celów UNIP, do głosu doszli adwokaci przemocy. Działacze partii, zwłaszcza na niższych szczeblach, przejęli inicjatywę i wykorzystali okazję, by wzniecać przemoc, zwłaszcza w Prowincji Północnej i Luapula. O udziale partii w zamieszkach świadczy duża liczba jej członków i zwolenników, którzy zostali aresztowani w trakcie rozruchów".

„Voice of UNIP" ripostował w dramatycznym, propagandowym tonie: „Jeśli chodzi o przemoc, to stanowczo odrzucamy twierdzenie, jakoby Afrykanie uciekali się do przemocy. W ciągu całych tych tragicznych wydarzeń nie słyszeliśmy ani o jednym przypadku, żeby czarny podniósł choćby palec na białego – informatora czy jakiegokolwiek członka służb bezpieczeństwa. Przeciwnie, to właśnie służby bezpieczeństwa są odpowiedzialne za śmierć ponad pięćdziesięciu bezbronnych Afrykanów. To służby bezpieczeństwa nadal dopuszczają się brutalnych pobić i tortur. Tysiące rodzin zostało zmuszonych do ucieczki do lasów w strachu przed tymi służbami. To są służby bezpieczeństwa? O czyje bezpieczeństwo one dbają? W wyniku ich barbarzyńskich działań tysiące ludzi mogą umrzeć z głodu. Setki ludzi pozostaną do końca życia kalekami. Tysiące dziewic zostało skalanych, tysiące kobiet zostało pobitych w majestacie prawa".

Ale Cza-cza to nie było to samo co rebelia Mau Mau w Kenii. Choć zambijscy Freedom Fighters lubią przedstawiać lato 1961 roku jako „totalną wojnę", prawda jest inna. Jeśli mierzyć skalę wydarzeń liczbą ofiar (co oczywiście nie jest miarodajne i może być krzywdzące), to Cza-cza była raczej niewielką bitwą niż wojną czy powstaniem, jak lubią ją nazywać weterani. W zamieszkach zginęło jedynie dwadzieścia parę osób, choć około trzech tysięcy zostało aresztowanych, z czego większość trafiła do więzień.

W języku bemba jest pewne słowo. Wtedy było na ustach wszystkich, tych młodych z kamieniami w rękach i tych starszych stojących przed tłumami. Dziś tak nazywa się zambijska waluta, wiele ulic, placów czy budynków. *Kwacha* oznacza świt.

Część II

12

„Chcemy polecieć na Księżyc! – mówił dumnym i zdecydowanym głosem prezydent John Kennedy w duszne popołudnie 12 września 1962 roku. – Chcemy polecieć na Księżyc! – powtórzył raz jeszcze, a fala oklasków przetoczyła się przez trybuny Stadionu Rice w Houston. – Chcemy polecieć na Księżyc jeszcze w tej dekadzie oraz podjąć inne wyzwania nie dlatego, że są one proste, ale właśnie dlatego, że są trudne, ponieważ to osiągnięcie będzie miarą naszych najlepszych energii i umiejętności, ponieważ to wyzwanie jest tym, które chcemy podjąć, którego nie chcemy odkładać i w którym zamierzamy zwyciężyć, podobnie zresztą jak w innych. [...] Kosmos na nas czeka, a my zamierzamy się tam wybrać. Czekają na nas także Księżyc i planety oraz nowe możliwości rozwoju wiedzy i pokoju na świecie. A zatem prosimy Boga o błogosławieństwo, wyruszając w tę najbardziej niebezpieczną, ryzykowną i największą przygodę, na którą kiedykolwiek zdecydował się człowiek".

JFK opuszczał mównicę nagradzany gromkimi brawami tysięcy ludzi zgromadzonych na stadionie.

Ale sytuacja nie przedstawiała się zbyt dobrze i wszyscy oficjele polityczni i wojskowi stojący za prezydentem doskonale zdawali sobie z tego sprawę. Stany Zjednoczone ewidentnie zostawały w tyle, przegrywały wyścig w Kosmos, którego stawką było technologiczne i militarne panowanie nad światem. Od siedmiu lat amerykański program kosmiczny był pasmem porażek. 29 lipca 1955 roku rzecznik prasowy Białego Domu ogłosił, że w ciągu dwóch lat USA zamierzają umieścić na orbicie ziemskiej pierwszego satelitę. ZSRR podjął rękawicę cztery dni później, ogłaszając podobne zamiary w „najbliższej przyszłości". Naprzeciw sobie stanęło dwóch genialnych konstruktorów – czterdziestoośmioletni Siergiej Korolow oraz pięć lat młodszy Wernher von Braun, który jeszcze dziesięć lat wcześniej konstruował rakiety V-2 dla zupełnie innego szefa. Już pierwsze zawody Amerykanie wraz ze swoim niemieckim inżynierem przegrali z kretesem. Zespół Korolowa, ku trwodze Amerykanów, skonstruował i z powodzeniem odpalił 21 sierpnia 1957 roku pierwszą międzykontynentalną rakietę balistyczną. Trzydziestoczterometrowy olbrzym o kodzie R-7 Siemiorka miał zasięg dziesięciu tysięcy kilometrów, co wystarczało, by dolecieć do Nowego Jorku czy Florydy. Niespełna dwa miesiące później zmodyfikowana wersja Siemiorki wyniosła na orbitę pierwszego w historii ludzkości sztucznego satelitę. 4 października prawie równo o północy czasu moskiewskiego, po dziewięćdziesięciu pięciu minutach od startu, rosyjski Sputnik nadał swój pierwszy sygnał na Ziemię. Przez następne dwadzieścia dwa dni powtarzane co sekundę „bip, bip, bip" było powodem do dumy od Berlina Wschodniego po Kamczatkę. I do zmartwień od Nowego Jorku po San Francisco. W amerykańskich miastach wybuchła panika. Władze zaczęły budować schrony przeciwatomowe, a ludzie uzbrojeni w lornetki i lunety z trwogą i niedowierzaniem patrzyli w niebo, szukając sunącego po niebie punktu. Miesiąc później na pokładzie Sputnika 2 w Kosmos w straceńczej misji wystartował niewielki kundel o imieniu Łajka. Zwierzę z nadmiaru emocji padło po siedmiu godzinach lotu (co ujawniono dopiero w 2002 roku), ale jego truchełko szybowało ponad Ziemią zgodnie z planem przez następne dziesięć dni. Łajka nie była pierwszym kosmonautą. Przed nią w 1947 roku na pokładzie rakiety V-2 pofrunęły w Kosmos muszki owocówki.

Desperacko próbując strzelić Rosjanom kontaktową bramkę, 6 grudnia Amerykanie wystrzelili nie do końca przygotowaną rakietę Vanguard TV3. Rakieta spłonęła, rozpaczliwie próbując oderwać się od Ziemi, ku trwodze milionów Amerykanów zgromadzonych przed telewizorami i radości Nikity Chruszczowa po drugiej stronie globu. Chruszczow nie szczędził sobie okazji do żartów, proponując rosyjską pomoc „dla zacofanych technologicznie krajów". Gazety na całym świecie prześcigały się w wymyślaniu odpowiedniej nazwy dla amerykańskiego nielota: Flopnik, Dudnik, Kaputnik.

31 stycznia 1958 roku Amerykanom w końcu udało się umieścić na orbicie ziemskiej pierwszego satelitę. Explorer 1 w przeciwieństwie do kulistych Sputników miał kształt cygara długości niespełna dwóch metrów. Dwa miesiące później na orbicie ziemskiej znalazł się już kolejny sztuczny satelita – amerykański Vanguard 1, pierwszy satelita wyposażony w baterie słoneczne. Choć łączność z urządzeniem utracono w 1964 roku, Vanguard nadal znajduje się gdzieś na orbicie, będąc najstarszym sztucznym satelitą Ziemi. Niepowodzeniem skończyły się jednak śmiałe próby umieszczenia na orbicie księżycowej sond Pioneer 1 i 2, które miały wykonać pierwsze zdjęcia powierzchni Srebrnego Globu. Prezydent Eisenhower, zaniepokojony rosyjską przewagą w kosmicznym wyścigu, powołał w lipcu 1958 roku National Aeronautics and Space Administration – NASA. Pod koniec 1958 roku USA wysłały satelitę SCORE, z którego na Ziemię popłynęły pierwsze słowa nadane z Kosmosu – życzenia świąteczne nagrane przez prezydenta Dwighta Eisenhowera.

Od 1959 roku z kosmodromów w Bajkonurze (Kazachstan) i na przylądku Canaveral (Floryda) kolejne modele coraz potężniejszych rakiet z coraz to bardziej wymyślnymi sondami na pokładach startowały niemal każdego miesiąca. Wyścig kosmiczny nabrał zawrotnego tempa. W styczniu 1959 roku zespół Korolowa znów mógł otwierać szampana. Albo wódkę. Rosjanom udało się umieścić w Kosmosie pierwszego satelitę okołosłonecznego. Choć niezupełnie taki był plan. Łuna 1 miała dolecieć do Księżyca i zderzyć się z jego powierzchnią. Zamiast tego zawisła gdzieś na orbicie w pół drogi między Ziemią a Marsem. Tak czy inaczej, srebrna kula z wąsami, o wadze trzystu sześćdziesięciu jeden kilogramów to pierwszy obiekt, któremu nadano drugą prędkość kosmiczną i który wydostał się poza grawitacyjne oddziaływanie Ziemi oraz dotarł w pobliże Srebrnego Globu. W trakcie drogi na Księżyc Łuna 1 odkryła zjawisko wiatru słonecznego.

Amerykanie nie pozostali dłużni i w lutym wystrzelili w Kosmos pierwszego satelitę z urządzeniami do pomiarów meteo. Ważący niespełna dziesięć kilogramów Vanguard 2 krąży nad Ziemią do dzisiaj. Przez następny rok Amerykanie wystrzelili w Kosmos dziesięć rakiet Thor-Agena z satelitami Discoverer o kolejnych numerach porządkowych. Tylko połowa z nich dotarła na orbitę. W Kosmos poleciał również satelita Explorer 6, który przysłał pierwsze zdjęcie Ziemi widzianej z Kosmosu. Lecz końcówka 1959 roku należała zdecydowanie do Rosjan. Sonda Łuna 2 to pierwszy obiekt, któremu udało się dotrzeć na powierzchnię Księżyca. Rozbiła się gdzieś w okolicy księżycowego Morza Deszczów, wysypując z siebie kilkadziesiąt stalowych tabliczek z napisem „Wrzesień 1959, Związek Socjalistycznych Republik Radzieckich". Miesiąc później nad Księżyc nadleciała siostrzana sonda Łuna 3, wyposażona w aparat fotograficzny. Przesłała na Ziemię siedemnaście zdjęć. Po raz pierwszy człowiek mógł obejrzeć niewidoczną stronę Księżyca.

Amerykanie zrewanżowali się, wysyłając pierwszego satelitę meteorologicznego, a w czerwcu 1960 roku pierwszego satelitę szpiegowskiego. Obiekt o nazwie GRAB przez dwadzieścia dwa dni fotografował Ziemię, zwłaszcza gdy przelatywał nad ZSRR i Chinami. W sierpniu na orbitę trafiała sonda Discoverer 13. To pierwszy obiekt, który w nienaruszonym stanie udaje się sprowadzić z orbity z powrotem na Ziemię.

19 sierpnia 1960 roku na pokładzie statku Korabl-Sputnik 2 w Kosmos poleciały dwa psy, Biełka i Striełka, czterdzieści myszy, dwa szczury i grupa owadów, roślin i grzybów. Cała wycieczka po dobie spędzonej w Kosmosie wróciła bezpiecznie na Ziemię. Rok później kosmopies Striełka dorobił się grupki szczeniąt, z których jedno Nikita Chruszczow dał w prezencie Jacqueline

Kennedy. Puszynka, tak nazywał się pies, wkrótce nawiązała gorący romans z psem Kennedych i wydała na świat cały miot zimnowojennych szczeniaków. Po śmierci Striełka i Biełka zostały elegancko wypchane i do dziś jeżdżą po muzeach i szkołach całej Rosji, przyćmiewając sławą Łajkę. Zanim w przestrzeń pozaziemską udał się pierwszy *homo sapiens*, Rosjanie wysłali w Kosmos trzy kolejne psie misje.

W 1961 roku Rosjanie sięgnęli jeszcze dalej. W lutym w Kosmos wystartowała potężna, beczkowata w kształcie sonda Wenera 1, obierając kurs na Wenus. Po trzech miesiącach doleciała do planety. Niestety łączność z sondą urwała się tuż przed zbliżeniem z Wenus.

Niektórzy twierdzą, że Jurij Gagarin wcale nie był pierwszym człowiekiem, który poleciał w Kosmos. Był tylko pierwszym, który z niego powrócił. Mówi się, że zanim ZSRR odtrąbił wiekopomny sukces, oprócz psów w Kosmosie ginęli również ludzie. W niedoskonałych kombinezonach, niedopracowanych kapsułach, skazani na samotną śmierć w lodowatych, czarnych otchłaniach. Ku chwale socjalistycznych republik, z CCCP na prymitywnych hełmach. Ich niknący, słabnący, drżący ze strachu głos można usłyszeć na nagraniach. Czy są prawdziwe? Ilu? Jak się nazywali? Czy nadal krążą gdzieś na orbicie? Czy są jednym z tych punktów mknących jednostajną prędkością przez nocne niebo? Ile razy otoczyli już naszą Ziemię? Niemniej 12 kwietnia 1961 roku kończy się pierwszy etap kosmicznego wyścigu. Na mecie pierwsi meldują się Rosjanie. Dwudziestosiedmioletni Jurij Gagarin zapisał się w tomach encyklopedii jako pierwszy kosmonauta, a jego słynne „pojechali" wypowiedziane w momencie startu weszło do popkultury krajów bloku wschodniego. W ciągu godziny i czterdziestu ośmiu minut Gagarin zamknięty w stalowej kuli o średnicy nieco ponad dwóch metrów okrążył Ziemię, przelatując nad Syberią, Kamczatką, Oceanem Spokojnym, Ziemią Ognistą, Oceanem Atlantyckim i Afryką. Wylądował na polu, tysiąc pięćset kilometrów na zachód od Bajkonuru, ku zdziwieniu okolicznych wieśniaków. Okładki magazynów, pierwsze strony gazet na całym świecie zapełniły się zdjęciami Gagarina. Wostok 1 z Gagarinem na pokładzie był dwudziestą czwartą rakietą wysłaną w Kosmos przez ZSRR. Tylko połowa misji zakończyła się sukcesem. Trzy tygodnie później Alan Shepard przeszedł do historii jako pierwszy Amerykanin w Kosmosie. Shepard trafił na okładkę magazynu „Time". Zresztą temat wyścigu kosmicznego zdobił pierwsze strony tygodnika już regularnie od połowy lat pięćdziesiątych. Amerykanie, w odróżnieniu od Rosjan, swoich kosmicznych pilotów nazywali astronautami. Bo *astra*, czyli gwiazdy, to przecież dalej niż Kosmos, który umownie zaczyna się już sto kilometrów nad powierzchnią Ziemi. Misja Sheparda trwała jednak zaledwie piętnaście minut. Astronauta osiągnął wysokość niespełna dwustu kilometrów i wrócił na Ziemię, nie dotarłszy na orbitę.

Przegrawszy pierwszy etap kosmicznego wyścigu, prezydent John Kennedy zalicytował wysoko. Teraz Księżyc.

13

– Mukuka Nkoloso przyszedł do mojego biura – zaczyna cichym, ledwo słyszalnym głosem Sikota Wina. Widzę, że wspomnienia o Nkoloso sprawiają mu radość. – Stanął w drzwiach, zastanowił się chwilę i powiedział: „Sikota, nie uważasz, że my też byśmy mogli dokonać tego, co robią teraz biali?". „O co dokładnie ci chodzi", spytałem. „No o ten cały wyścig kosmiczny", odparł. Roześmiałem się głośno. Nigdy by mi to nie przyszło do głowy! Owszem, słyszałem o tym, że Amerykanie próbują wysłać człowieka na Księżyc. Powiedziałem mu: „Nie wydaje ci się, Mukuka, że my tutaj mamy wiele ważniejszych spraw na głowie niż lądowanie na Księżycu? Na przykład musimy wyzwolić nasz kraj! Wycieczka na Księżyc może poczekać?". Nie wyglądał na przekonanego, wręcz przeciwnie. Powtarzał: „Nie, nie, musimy pokazać białasom, że my też potrafimy, że możemy to zrobić tutaj, w Lusace!". Spytałem zatem, gdzie chce zacząć, bo byłem przekonany, że żartuje. A on mi na to: „Właśnie dlatego do ciebie przychodzę, Sikota, jeśli się zgodzisz, to zacząłbym trenować ludzi tu, na wzgórzu".

Biuro UNIP, w którym pracował Sikota Wina, znajdowało się wtedy w czarnej dzielnicy Matero. Za nim wyrastało niewielkie, porośnięte buszem wzniesienie.

– On naprawdę wierzył, że to jest możliwe – mówi Sikota Wina. – To dawało nadzieję. Jego przesłanie było bardzo proste i porywające: możemy robić wszystko to, co biali, nawet tu, w Zambii. Z Lusaki do Ameryki. Z Lusaki nawet na Księżyc.

*

Znalazłem to wzgórze. Zresztą jedyne w okolicy Lusaki. Wszędzie dokoła płasko po horyzont, a pośrodku dzielnicy Matero ni stąd, ni zowąd wzgórze. Niewielkie, choć w tym krajobrazie wystarczająco wyraźne. Lusaka była przez lata miastem dla białych. Zbudowano ją na początku XX wieku i wkrótce przejęła od Livingstone funkcję stolicy Rodezji Północnej. Z czasem Brytyjczycy pozwolili czarnym osiedlać się w mieście, ale z początku wyłącznie na odległych północno-wschodnich rubieżach. Tak powstało Matero, całe czarne, całe zastawione małymi chatami z dachami z blachy falistej. Szybko zaludniło się, rozrosło się, wypączkowały z niego dzielnice jeszcze większej biedy, jak George, Chunga czy Lilanda. Matero to morze afrykańskich slumsów z jedyną falą, jaką jest wzgórze Chingwele Hill, również gęsto porośnięte małymi domkami. Naturalną koleją rzeczy Matero stało się matecznikiem czarnego ruchu oporu. Tu mieszkała większość działaczy i polityków, tu siedzibę miały partie i organizacje tworzone przez czarnych, tu nie zaglądała kolonialna policja. U podnóża Chingwele Hill, w domu jak wszystkie inne dokoła, znajdowało się również biuro UNIP.

Z Chingwele Hill Lusaka wygląda niemal ładnie. Zwłaszcza o zachodzie słońca, które powoli chowa się za domami na krańcu wzgórza. Niemal malowniczo, niemal urokliwie. Gęsta roślinność przysłania hektary czarnej biedy, rozpuszczony we mgle horyzont rysuje się linią wieżowców Cairo Road, a odległy szum miasta zdaje się miłą melodią kończącego się dnia. Nawet ptaki słychać na Chingwele Hill. Zresztą z zachodzącym słońcem wszystko wygląda ładnie. Nawet pobliskie wysypisko śmieci nabiera intensywnych kolorów, a rozsypujący się Stadion Niepodległości, szczerzący się pustymi betonowymi trybunami, zyskuje romantyczny wdzięk. Chingwele Hill to takie miejsce, w które przychodzi się, gdy nie ma co robić. Wtedy można posiedzieć na murku, w cieniu potężnych, zardzewiałych zbiorników wody pogapić się na miasto. Albo wypić kilka piw, wypalić jointa i pogadać z kumplami. Lub umówić się na randkę z dziewczyną z sąsiedztwa. Krajobraz zmusza do refleksji. Na chwilę można znaleźć się ponad brudem Lusaki, a jednocześnie nie tracić jej z oczu. Taka zmiana perspektywy, chwilowe oddalenie, ale nie zerwanie. Chingwele Hill musiało być świadkiem wielu wspaniałych momentów, nagłych uniesień, wybuchów emocji. Zapewne miłości, pewnie nierzadko też zazdrości czy nienawiści. Pewnie kilka osób dostąpiło tu oświecenia, bo ludzie przychodzą się tu modlić, jak młody człowiek stojący nieopodal mnie, który w modlitewnym szale wyrzuca z siebie prośby i przyrzeczenia. Domyślam się, że na Chingwele Hill zrodziło się również wiele małych i wielkich pomysłów. Tych codziennych, zwykłych, i tych poważnych, na całe życie.

– Czego tu szukasz?

W moją stronę zmierza postawny mężczyzna z pobliskiego domu. Wcale nie wygląda na przyjaźnie usposobionego. Dziś Matero to wylęgarnia przestępców, zła okolica.

– Wiesz, że z tego wzgórza, tu, gdzie mieszkasz, miała polecieć rakieta? – odpowiadam.

Facet przystaje.

– W Kosmos – dodaję – na Księżyc.

Facet zatrzymuje się i zawraca do domu.

Nie wiem, gdzie Mukuka Nkoloso wpadł na swój pomysł. Ale lubię sobie myśleć, że wydarzyło się to właśnie na Chingwele Hill. Bo Księżyc z Lusaki jest blisko. Teraz właśnie wstaje, żegnając umykające słońce. Zachęca, zaprasza, kusi, by po niego sięgnąć, usiąść na jego krawędzi i spojrzeć z góry na tonące w coraz dłuższych cieniach miasto. Zwłaszcza dziś, gdy jest w pełni, i to tej niezwykłej, bo znajduje się w perygeum, czyli najbliżej Ziemi. Wielki jak dynia, jak ogromna bombka na choince. Wstaje na zachodzie, zawadza o dachy i kominy, przedziera się przez drzewa i wieżowce Cairo Road. Jest niewiele dalej niż na wyciągnięcie ręki. A dziś w wyjątkowym towarzystwie. Nad nim Uran, a po przeciwległej stronie nieba na spotkanie wybiegają kolejno Wenus, Mars i Jowisz. Wysoko w zenicie wszystkich wita Orion, z niezwykle jasnym Rigelem u dołu szaty. Orion mierzy łukiem w nadbiegającego Byka, któremu w oku błyska gwiazda Aldebaran. Na szczęście wojownik ma przy sobie wiernego Wielkiego Psa, z Syriuszem, najjaśniejszą gwiazdą na niebie, niczym mokrym psim nosem. Wszyscy oni, tak jak ja, przyszli podziwiać Księżyc. Dziś widać każdy krater, każdą górę, każde wypełnione pyłem morze. Jakie piękne nazwy mają księżycowe morza. Morze Przesileń, Żyzności, Jasności, Nektaru, Chmur, Deszczów. Jakby nazwy te nadawała jakaś inna, nieziemska cywilizacja. I tylko jeden Ocean Burz, groźny, złowrogi, tak dla równowagi. Dlaczego Księżyc się nie obraca, czemu pokazuje nam tylko swoją jedną stronę? Czy jego niewidoczna strona pokryta jest morzami Zmartwień, Głodu, Zawiści i Cierpienia?

Mukuka Nkoloso nie był pierwszym Afrykaninem, którego fascynował Księżyc – rozpalał on wyobraźnię afrykańskich ludów od dawna. Ponoć ludzie z dynastii Rozwi, plemienia Szona, zamieszkujący tereny dzisiejszego wschodniego Zimbabwe, w swojej ambicji i brawurze chcieli sięgnąć po niego i zdjąć go z nieba. Pyszny książę Chirisamhuru, syn króla, by przypodobać się ojcu, rozkazał zbudować ogromną wieżę na jednym z okolicznych wzgórz. Księżyc, w języku Rozwi *Ndiro Chena*, miał być podarkiem dla króla i zastąpić talerz używany przy szamańskich rytuałach. Plany pokrzyżowało zazdrosne Słońce, które spaliło drewnianą konstrukcję.

Bemba wierzą, że ich przodkowie przyszli z nieba, z Kosmosu. Mukulumpe Mubemba, potężny wojownik, był wodzem plemienia Luba zamieszkującego tereny południowo-wschodniego Konga, rejony dzisiejszej prowincji Katanga. Pewnego dnia na dwór Mukulumpe dotarła wiadomość, że w okolicznych lasach widziano piękną kobietę o uszach wielkich i cienkich niczym u słonia. Mukulumpe, nie czekając ani chwili, sam ruszył na spotkanie nieznajomej. Gdy stanęli naprzeciw siebie, kobieta wypowiedziała swoje imię: Mumbi Mukasa. Na pytanie, skąd pochodzi, wskazała na niebo i dodała, że jest królową Klanu Krokodyli. Mukulumpe od razu zakochał się w kobiecie o wielkich uszach, a ona wkrótce urodziła mu trzech synów: Katongo, Chiti, Nkole, i córkę Chilufyę. Boskie pochodzenie matki intrygowało synów do tego stopnia, że gdy dorośli, postanowili zbudować wielką wieżę, by ich matka mogła wrócić do swojego niebiańskiego domu. Niestety, ogromna budowla runęła z wielkim hukiem i pogrzebała w ruinach wielu poddanych wodza. Mukulumpe był wściekły. Wygnał żonę z domu, a niepokorne dzieci kazał uwięzić w wieży. Jednak Katongo, Chiti, Nkole i Chilufya uciekli przed gniewem ojca i po długiej tułaczce osiedlili się na rozległych równinach nad rzeką Chambeshi w dzisiejszej Zambii. Doprowadził ich tam tajemniczy mędrzec Luchele Nganga, którego skóra była zupełnie biała. (Katoliccy misjonarze, którzy przybyli na ziemie Bemba kilkaset lat później, usłyszawszy tę legendę, tłumaczyli tubylcom, że Luchele Nganga był zapewne pierwszym Europejczykiem, wysłannikiem nowego boga. W ten podstępny sposób udało im się wykorzystać legendę, by zbudować własny autorytet). Luchele był wędrownym prorokiem, któremu niektóre podania również przypisują niebiańskie pochodzenie. Chiti wkrótce spotkał piękną kobietę, Chilimbulu, której skóra pokryta była niezwykłymi tatuażami. Miłość półboskiego Chitiego do autochtonki Chilimbulu w symboliczny sposób połączyła wędrowców Klanu Krokodyli i tubylców. Niestety płomienne uczucie stało się zgubą dla kochanków. Chilimbulu bowiem była żoną lokalnego myśliwego o imieniu Mwase, który odkrywszy gorący romans, w porywie złości zabił Chitiego zatrutą strzałą. To nie skończyło spirali miłości, zazdrości i śmierci. Nkole wkrótce pomścił śmierć brata, zabijając Mwase oraz jego urodziwą żonę. Zachował jednak piękną, pokrytą tatuażami skórę Chilimbulu, która uwiodła jego brata. Ta skóra stała się najświętszą królewską relikwią Klanu Krokodyli – *babenye* – zapewniającą żyzność ziemi i płodność ludzi. Jej posiadanie było oznaką władzy każdego przyszłego wodza, który od tej pory będzie nosił imię Chitimukulu – Wielkie Drzewo. Miejsce w którym zostali pochowani Chiti, Mwase, Chilimbulu, a potem także Nkole – Mwalule – gdzieś w rejonie dzisiejszego Chinsali, było odtąd duchowym centrum ludu Bemba. Półboscy Chiti i Nkole stali się częścią ziemi, na którą przybyli. Ich pochówek w metaforyczny sposób połączył niebiański Klan Krokodyli z powrotem z ziemią. Duchy zstąpiły na ziemski padół, boski pierwiastek dotknął mokrej, brudnej ziemi. W ten sposób Klan Krokodyli otrzymał duchową legitymację, by władać ziemią i niebem ponad nią.

Wieś, w której urodził się Edward Mukuka Nkoloso, leży w samym sercu dawnego królestwa Bemba. Nkoloso zapewne znał legendę o Klanie Krokodyli i jego półboskich założycielach. Czy była dla niego inspiracją? Czy jak Chiti, Nkole, Katongo i Chilufya zapragnął w śmiały i bluźnierczy sposób wrócić do miejsca, z którego przybyli jego praprzodkowie? W jednym z wywiadów mówił: „Chcę stąd uciec. Zbyt wiele pokoleń umarło już na tej ziemi. Ja chcę spocząć tam".

Gdy stoję na Chingwele Hill, znów mam przed oczami rycinę z dziewiętnastowiecznej *L'Atmosphère: Météorologie Populaire* francuskiego astronoma Camille'a Flammariona. Obraz, choć wcale nie pochodzi ze średniowiecza i najpewniej jest dziełem autora książki, ilustruje ten fragment tekstu: „Pewien misjonarz z czasów średniowiecza mówi nam, że w jednej ze swych podróży w poszukiwaniu ziemskiego raju dotarł do horyzontu, gdzie spotykały się ze sobą ziemia i niebo. Odkrył tam pewne miejsce, gdzie nie były one ze sobą połączone, i zgiąwszy się wpół, przeszedł pod sklepieniem niebios".

Czy ta dziura była pomyłką, niedoróbką boskiego krawca, który zapomniał w tym miejscu zszyć niebiosa z ziemskim padołem? Czy jednak szansą, przejściem pozostawionym celowo, by kiedyś mógł je odnaleźć jakiś niestrudzony naukowiec? Może ta szczelina znajdowała się właśnie tu, w Lusace?

Domyślam się, że Mukuka Nkoloso nigdy nie słyszał o Flammarionie, nigdy też nie czytał jego dzieł. Ale ponoć można go było zobaczyć, jak w nocy stoi sam na Chingwele Hill, zupełnie jak średniowieczny astronom, który właśnie doszedł do krańców świata i nieśmiało wystawia głowę poza niebiańskie sklepienie, by w zachwycie i strachu spojrzeć na kosmiczną maszynerię. Ludzie mówią, że czasami unosił włócznię i celował ostrzem w Księżyc. A potem brał zamach i z całych sił ciskał nią w Srebrny Glob. Gdy ktoś go wtedy zapytał, co robi, odpowiadał: „Spójrz na to drzewo. Ponieważ je widzę, mogę do niego dojść. Tak samo jest z Księżycem".

14

Pod koniec 1964 roku do Lusaki przyjechała ekipa z brytyjskiej telewizji ITN. Kolonialna administracja opuściła Rodezję Północną ledwie miesiąc wcześniej. Dziennikarze znaleźli Edwarda Mukukę Nkoloso, o którym ulica dużo wtedy mówiła, na opuszczonej farmie kilka kilometrów od miasta, w dzielnicy Chunga. Oglądałem ten krótki materiał filmowy ITN już dziesiątki razy. Pięć minut i czterdzieści sekund. I tysiąc lat świetlnych. Większa część nagrania jest bez dźwięku, więc lubię sobie puścić do tego *Space Oddity* Davida Bowiego. Choć Bowie nagrał utwór kilka lat później, w 1969 roku, trudno o lepszy obraz do tych słów i o lepszą muzykę do tego obrazu.

Ground Control to Major Tom,
Ground Control to Major Tom,
Take your protein pills and put your helmet on.

Mukuka Nkoloso stoi pośrodku niewielkiego placu. W tle drzewa, jakieś zabudowania, volkswagen garbus i grupka ludzi wykonujących jakieś ćwiczenia. Nkoloso ubrany elegancko, spodnie w kant i krawat. Na ramiona ma zarzuconą wyszywaną togę, zupełnie jak sędzia wysokiego sądu lub średniowieczny monarcha. Do tego stalowy hełm z siatką, pewnie jeszcze z czasów II wojny światowej. Udziela właśnie wywiadu białemu dziennikarzowi.

„Panie Nkoloso, czy to jest miejsce, z którego odpali pan swoją rakietę? I gdzie ona się teraz znajduje?"

„Tak, to jest to miejsce, a moja rakieta jest tuż za nami" – mówi Nkoloso bez cienia ironii czy zawahania. Odpowiada pewny siebie, z powagą wskazując na stojące z tyłu obiekty, kształtem przypominające beczki. Jeden z nich jest podłużny jak wielka łuska od pocisku z wykrojonym okrągłym otworem.

„A jak nazywa się pańska organizacja?" – dopytuje grzecznie dziennikarz.

„Moja organizacja to Narodowa Akademia Nauki, Badań Kosmicznych i Filozofii".

„A jaką pozycję zajmuje pan w tej organizacji?"

„Jestem dyrektorem generalnym badań kosmicznych i filozofii" – odpowiada dumnie Nkoloso i uśmiecha się, ukazując swoje braki w uzębieniu.

Ground Control to Major Tom
Commencing countdown, engines on
Check ignition and may God's love be with you.

„A kiedy odpali pan swoją pierwszą rakietę i dokąd pan ją wyśle?"

„Rakieta wystartuje z Lusaki i poleci prosto na Księżyc, wszystko zależy od tego, ile dostanę pieniędzy. Jeśli będziemy mieli odpowiednie finansowanie, to wydarzy się to w bardzo niedługim czasie, nawet w połowie 1965 roku. Jeśli nie, to będziemy musieli poczekać trochę dłużej".

Ten, Nine, Eight, Seven, Six, Five,
Four, Three, Two, One, Liftoff

„A jak pan sądzi, jaka będzie reakcja Rosji i Ameryki, gdy dowiedzą się, że Zambia przyłącza się do wyścigu kosmicznego?" – indaguje dziennikarz.

„O, na pewno będą zaskoczeni! Oni nie doceniają środków, jakimi dysponujemy, i naszej inteligencji. Jestem pewny, że ich doganiamy".

„Czy prezydent Kaunda wydał pozwolenie na pański projekt i czy rząd Zambii go zaaprobował?"

„Jeszcze nie, ale interesują się tym, co robię, bo to jest nowatorskie w tym kraju" – tłumaczy zupełnie niewzruszony Mukuka Nkoloso.

This is Ground Control to Major Tom
You've really made the grade
And the papers want to know whose shirts you wear.
Now it's time to leave the capsule if you dare.

Kilku młodych chłopaków, może po piętnaście–siedemnaście lat, siedzi boso w krótkich spodenkach na ziemi. Nad nimi rozpostarty transparent z koślawym napisem „Zambian Space Academy". Młodzież wykonuje posłusznie jakieś ćwiczenia fizyczne, macha rękoma. Ktoś wszedł na beczkę i przygląda się grupie. Cięcie. Ćwiczenia pokazuje dyrektor, który teraz buja się, siedząc na trawie. Coś mówi, coś tłumaczy, rozkłada szeroko ręce. W tle rakieta, ta sama, którą pokazywał wcześniej. Cięcie. Mukuka Nkoloso siedzi na trawie wraz z resztą grupy. Dyrektor ubrany w mundur wojskowy i wojskowe buty. W rękach trzyma książkę, pokazuje zdjęcia, objaśnia. Zbliżenie na książkę. Na ilustracjach planety, niebo, teleskop.

This is Major Tom to Ground Control
I'm stepping through the door
And I'm floating in a most peculiar way
And the stars look very different today.

Dyrektor Nkoloso tyłem do kamery, na zboczu niewielkiego wzgórza. Ręka uniesiona w górę, toga przerzucona przez ramię powiewa na wietrze. Powyżej niego dwóch chłopaków trzyma stalową beczkę, taką, w jakich transportuje się ropę naftową. W środku beczki jeden z nastolatków. Dyrektor daje znak, beczka wraz z delikwentem w jej środku zaczyna się swobodnie toczyć w dół zbocza, aż łapią ją chłopcy stojący u podnóża. Cięcie. Dyrektor maszeruje, trzymając przed sobą jakiś znak, może godło lub sztandar. Za nim wszyscy idą posłusznie gęsiego, najpierw młoda dziewczyna, a potem rząd młodzieńców.

For here
Am I sitting in a tin can.
Far above the world,
Planet Earth is blue,
And there's nothing I can do

Dyrektor Nkoloso poprawia hełm, zarzuca togę i staje na baczność przed rakietą. Podbiega do niego grupa nastolatków, kładą beczkową rakietę na ziemi. Jeden z nich szybciutko, wytrenowanym ruchem, wskakuje do środka. Nie mieści się w rakiecie cały, wystaje mu głowa, którą dyrektor trzyma w rękach. Cięcie. Teraz wszyscy razem podnoszą rakietę wraz z pilotem, unoszą ponad głowy (jakby świętowali jego urodziny) i potrząsają to w lewo, to w prawo.

Though I'm past one hundred thousand miles
I'm feeling very still,
And I think my spaceship knows which way to go.
Tell my wife I love her very much
She knows.

Dyrektor Nkoloso siedzi na huśtawce zawieszonej na gałęzi drzewa. Wokół niego chłopcy. Zaczynają go bujać. Mocniej. Mocniej. Jeszcze mocniej. On zadowolony, uśmiechnięty, znów coś mówi, coś tłumaczy. Cięcie. Teraz na huśtawce dziewczyna. Jej sukienka podnosi się i opada w rytm ruchów huśtawki. Cięcie. Dwóch chłopaków na brzegu rzeki. Trzeci nastolatek, z hełmem na głowie, siedzi w beczce. Beczka kołysze się wypychana powoli na głębszą wodę.

Ground Control to Major Tom
Your circuit's dead, there's something wrong.
Can you hear me, Major Tom?
Can you hear me, Major Tom?

Dziewiątka nastolatków, w tym dziewczyna, stoją w rządku. Za nimi znów napis „Zambian Space Academy", jakiś budynek w tle. Przed nimi dyrektor Nkoloso. Apel. Albo odprawa. Padają komendy. Nie, to ćwiczenia. Znów komenda. Wszyscy skaczą, ręce uniesione w górę, klaskają, robią pajacyki. Dziennikarz o urodzie aż nadto brytyjskiej odwraca się w stronę kamery i komentuje z londyńskim akcentem:

„A więc tutaj, na opuszczonej farmie niedaleko Lusaki, mamy młodą grupę przyszłych astronautów, którzy bawią się w dołączenie Zambii do wyścigu kosmicznego. Jednak dla większości Zambijczyków ci ludzie to po prostu banda głupków. I po tym, co miałem okazję dziś zobaczyć, muszę się z tym zgodzić".

Cięcie.

15

Lepię postać Edwarda Mukuki Nkoloso z różnych kawałków, pozszywanych, połączonych, posklejanych. Układam ją z opowieści syna, wspomnień kilku ludzi. Powoli naświetlam zdjęcie. Z każdą rozmową pojawiają się na nim kolejne cienie, pierwsze kształty, w końcu widać zarys postaci. Lecz mimo mijających tygodni ten obraz nadal pełen jest dziur. Nie mogę być pewien dat ani miejsc, wypowiedzianych słów. Czasami nie mam możliwości potwierdzić kolejności chronologicznej ani przyczynowo-skutkowej. Afryka. Tu czasoprzestrzeń ma inną gęstość, jakby miała zupełnie inną konstrukcję, ulepiona była z innych cząsteczek. Czas chyba nie jest tu czymś linearnym. Ani ciągłym. Liczyłem na to, że wiele z tych dziur uda się uzupełnić dzięki dokumentom znalezionym w muzeach, archiwach czy ministerstwach. W końcu Nkoloso był osobą publiczną, znaną, a papier pamięta lepiej niż ludzie. Ale może z drugiej strony to właśnie cały urok tej postaci i tej historii? Że jest niedopowiedziana, pozostawia wiele miejsca na pytania i domysły?

Archiwa Narodowe

Pierwszy strzał, trochę na oślep – Archiwa Narodowe. Domyślam się, że Zambia w jakiś sposób pamięta o tak barwnej postaci. Idę na piechotę z północnych dzielnic, przemierzając po raz pierwszy ulice nieznanego mi jeszcze miasta. Betonowy budynek Archiwów na południu Lusaki wygląda zresztą, jakby sam właśnie przybył z Kosmosu. Nieodparcie przypomina jakiś latający spodek lub lądownik księżycowy, który w wyniku błędu pilota osiadł zupełnie w innym miejscu, niż planowano. Paradne wejście z podcieniem jak otwarta rampa, po której miałby wyjechać na tę dziwną planetę kosmiczny łazik, dalej zimny, kamienny kontuar, a za nim dwie panie w białych fartuchach rozprawiają o pogodzie, wpatrując się z nadzieją w niedziałający wiatrak. Październik, miesiąc największych upałów, czas cierpienia i oczekiwania na zbawienne deszcze. W tle czytelnia, trochę taka jak w szkole podstawowej, może w liceum. Pytam śmiało o Edwarda Mukukę Nkoloso, pewny, że za chwilę otworzą się przede mną niezliczone księgi i katalogi, z szaf wysypią się dokumenty i akta, a stalowe szuflady poczęstują mnie bogatą kolekcją zdjęć. Słychać stukanie w klawiaturę, wertowanie kartek podręcznych indeksów. Pachnie starym, pożółkłym papierem i kurzem, któremu nagle przerwano odwieczny sen na grzbietach grubych katalogów.

– Nie ma. Nie ma żadnych dokumentów o tym człowieku. A kim on w ogóle był? – mówi zdziwiona kobieta o przeuroczej, bujnej fryzurze w stylu lat pięćdziesiątych.

– Astronautą. To znaczy chciał nim być.

Pani za kontuarem wybałusza swoje wielkie czarne oczy. Sam czuję, jak komicznie to brzmi w tych okolicznościach.

– Tu, w Zambii? – pyta z niedowierzaniem.

– No tak. Może niech pani spróbuje poszukać hasła „Zambijski Program Kosmiczny".

Chwila oczekiwania, znów żółte strony zapisane wyblakłym, rozpływającym się maszynopisem, indeksy pokryte pyłem, jakbym był pierwszym, który z nich korzysta. Ale żadna kartka nie skrywa szukanych słów.

– Też nic. W ogóle pierwszy raz słyszę o tej historii. Ale jak pan mi kupi zimną fantę, to jeszcze poszukamy.

Wracam po chwili z butelką pomarańczowego nektaru dla każdej z pań z nadzieją, że sprawi ona cuda.

– To może „Zambijska Akademia Kosmiczna"?

Kobieta, ożywiona kolejnymi łykami zimnej fanty, znów wertuje hasła w papierowych katalogach. Przed naszymi oczami przelatują daty, nazwiska, miejscowości.

– Nie, też nic.

– Może „Księżyc"? Lub „rakieta"? „Wyścig kosmiczny"?

Jak to? Człowiek, który na początku lat sześćdziesiątych chciał lecieć na Księżyc, był przyjacielem prezydenta i bohaterem żegnanym z państwowymi honorami, nie zapisał się w państwowym archiwum nawet jedną marną kartką? Choćby katalogiem zdjęć, szufladą wyblakłych wspomnień, kartonem pamiątek lub honorową wzmianką?

– Nkoloso... Nkoloso... – zastanawia się druga kobieta. – A czy to nie jest ten człowiek, który zawsze chodził z włócznią?

– Tak! – wykrzykuję uradowany, że łapiemy jakiś trop.

– On jest na jednym zdjęciu. W holu, na dole, w gablocie.

Na czarno-białej fotografii Edward Mukuka Nkoloso przemawia do ludzi zgromadzonych przed budynkiem. Rozkłada ręce w geście zwycięstwa, radości, wytchnienia. Ubrany w znoszony wojskowy mundur, w lewej ręce trzyma potężną, rzeźbioną, wrzecionowatą włócznię. Za nim stoi Kenneth Kaunda, a z boku biały fotograf próbuje złapać najlepszy kadr tej chwili. Doniosły moment. Sześćdziesiąty trzeci? Sześćdziesiąty czwarty? Podpis pod zdjęciem mówi jedynie: „Mukuka Nkoloso, bojownik o wolność i wierny stronnik dra Kaundy i UNIP". Nic więcej.

– Ona na pewno jest w Archiwach – zaręcza za każdym razem syn Mukuki Nkoloso, gdy pytam, co się stało z rakietą, którą skonstruował jego tata. – Tylko nie mogą ci pokazać, bo to tajne rzeczy. Wszystkie te wynalazki są tam, w specjalnych skrzyniach, ale nie pokazują ich nikomu. To trochę tak jak z przechowywaniem pieniędzy w banku: nie możesz ich zobaczyć, jak pójdziesz do Bank of Zambia, to ci ich przecież nie pokażą, ale one tam są, budują za nie drogi albo robią wybory prezydenckie. Jeśli pogadasz z dyrektorem, to może ci pozwoli. A jak nie, to musisz się zwrócić o pozwolenie do ministerstwa. Wszystko, co związane z programem kosmicznym, jest tam, tak samo jak łuki, dzidy i siekiery. Rakieta też jest. Oni cię oszukują w tych archiwach i muzeach. To wszystko tam jest, są papiery i dokumenty, nawet ubrania, togi, zdjęcia.

Syn Mukuki Nkoloso przez lata był pracownikiem Archiwów Narodowych. Tym bardziej nie wiem, jak mam traktować jego słowa. Często podaje mi nazwiska konkretnych osób, z którymi należy rozmawiać, bo oni coś wiedzą. Mówi na przykład:

– Idź do pana Chulu, taki wysoki, starszy, on będzie wiedział, bo pracuje tam długo, albo do pani Winnie Bandy, ona też wie. Bo ci wszyscy inni to młoda gwardia i nawet nie wiedzą, co mają w tych kartonach.

Ale nie wiedzą. Ani pan Chulu, ani pani Banda, ani kilka innych osób. Za każdym razem zapewnienia syna Mukuki Nkoloso rozpływają się, gdy tylko przekraczam progi Archiwów. Przed wyjazdem do Zambii pewien znajomy życzył mi, bym spotkał tam jak najwięcej wariatów. Tych zawieszonych w nieokreślonej przestrzeni między rzeczywistością a szaleństwem, między możliwościami a marzeniem, między rozpaczą a wiarą. Tak, chyba przyjechałem tutaj szukać właśnie takich wariatów. Bo jak inaczej nazwać Edwarda Mukukę Nkoloso, który chciał w sześćdziesiątym czwartym lecieć z Lusaki na Księżyc? Udało się, znalazłem wariatów, myślę za każdym razem, gdy rozmawiam z jego synem i panem Kolalą. To, co mówi syn Mukuki Nkoloso, rzadko znajduje pokrycie w rzeczywistości. Niemniej chcę mu wierzyć. W tej historii jest coś, czego nie potrafię zrozumieć, coś, co porusza się na zupełnie innych, afrykańskich płaszczyznach, nieuchwytnych dla człowieka ze świata kartezjańskiego racjonalizmu, coś z pogranicza czarów i wierzeń zderzonych z obezwładniającą wizją. Czasami wydaje mi się, że Edward Mukuka wcale nie musiał lecieć w Kosmos. Był tam, być może nawet bardziej niż Gagarin, Shepard i Armstrong. Przecież sam lot, sam odcisk stopy w księżycowym pyle, to tylko jakiś *grande finale* – spełniający, ale i unicestwiający ideę. Może ta idea jest lotem w nieznane znacznie bardziej niż sam fizyczny akt jej realizacji?

– Zostaw to Bogu – komentuje Cuthbert Kolala stanowczym głosem, ale już po chwili wpada w swój religijno-polityczny szał. – Pokaż mi tych, którzy mówili, że nie ma tych informacji w Archiwach! Pokaż! Oni już są zwolnieni! Oni już nie pracują! Jutro idziemy do dyrektora!

Chodzę do betonowego budynku Archiwów Narodowych co kilka dni. Pytam o wskazane przez syna Mukuki Nkoloso osoby, dokumenty, fotografie. Zamawiam roczniki gazet i magazynów. „Northern News", „Mutende News", „Central African Mail", „Nshila Magazine", „DRUM Magazine", „Panafrican Political Magazine". Zmęczony archiwista w białym fartuchu, niczym doktor na dyżurze, przywozi wózkiem kolejne sterty zakurzonych tomów. Wiele z tych tytułów to dzienniki. Zamawiając jeden rocznik, dostaję ponad trzysta wielostronicowych egzemplarzy. Te stare gazety drukowane w ogromnych formatach, za którymi swobodnie można było się ukryć i pogrążyć w słupkach, szpaltach, nagłówkach na całe dnie, leżą przede mną i odkrywają tajemnice sprzed pół wieku. Ale zazwyczaj nie te, których szukam. Niektóre arkusze cienkiego gazetowego papieru są tak delikatne, że rozpadają mi się w rękach. Ciekawi mnie, czy jestem pierwszym, który je ogląda od tych pięćdziesięciu lat. Najciekawsze są reklamy. Oszczędne, posługujące się zamiast zdjęć wysmakowaną grafiką, jednym kolorem, kształtem czy miłym, a nie krzykliwym hasłem. Te same marki co dzisiaj, a w jakże innej oprawie. Na łamach „Nshila Magazine" pasta Signal chwali się „przełomowymi czerwonymi paskami" i zapewnia o swojej skuteczności szerokim uśmiechem czarnego mężczyzny. Ze stron „Northern News" Schweppes zachęca do spróbowania oranżady z „prawdziwych pomarańczy". Jedna plama ładnego żółtego koloru pomiędzy szpaltami czarnego druku robi piorunujące wrażenie. Niezwykłą popularnością cieszą się skarpetki Cromwell, nylonowe, prążkowane, odpowiednie zarówno do pracy, jak i na weekend poza miastem. Fred Coates, zambijski biały zapaśnik wagi najwyraźniej ciężkiej, poleca owsiankę Energy Porridge, która „wymaga jedynie gorącej wody". Coates, o twarzy rasowego rozbójnika, pozuje do zdjęcia we włochatych majtkach w cętki, jakby zrobionych ze skóry geparda. Pan Frederick Mukwesha, gwiazda futbolu, zapewnia z kolei, że jego pieniądze najlepiej czują się w banku Barclays.

Czasami któryś z pracowników coś sobie przypomni. Że gdzieś widział albo ktoś kiedyś coś mu mówił, a tamten znał, a inny był. Urywki historii rozerwanej na strzępy przez lata. Zdarza się, że trafię na jakiś trop, na zdjęcie czy zdanie o człowieku, którego szukam. Najczęściej są to zdjęcia Kennetha Kaundy, na które jego wierny stronnik załapał się przy okazji, zawsze z włócznią przy boku, ubrany w fantazyjny strój. Wraz z kolejnymi wizytami znajduję jakieś pojedyncze dokumenty dotyczące Mukuki Nkoloso, jego korespondencję czy notatki ze spotkań. Ale nigdy nie są one związane z Akademią Kosmiczną. O tej w oficjalnych dokumentach nie ma ani słowa. A w latach sześćdziesiątych dużo pisało się o kosmicznym wyścigu nawet tu, w Zambii. Gagarin, potem Shepard, chwilę później John Glenn, Gemini, Atlas Agena, Mariner, zdjęcia, ilustracje, rysunki i wielkie tytuły z wykrzyknikami i znakami zapytania. W 1965 roku „Nshila Magazine" wspomina obszernie o amerykańskiej misji Mariner IV, która w założeniu ma przelecieć tuż obok Marsa. Autor artykułu pyta, czy na Czerwonej Planecie jest życie, i ostrzega Marsjan, że my, Ziemianie, nadciągamy. Na następnej stronie znajduję komentarz do tych wydarzeń: „Czy podbój Kosmosu ma jakiekolwiek znaczenie dla niewyedukowanego mieszkańca Zambii? [...] Czy nauka o Kosmosie może być w ogóle traktowana poważnie w Zambii? [...] Ludzie potrzebują lepszego jedzenia, lepszych domów, lepszego dostępu do edukacji i służby zdrowia. Do tej pory wiedza, jaką uzyskaliśmy w trakcie podboju Kosmosu, nie została użyta dla dobra ludzkości. Centralnym punktem wszelkiej aktywności człowieka powinien być sam człowiek. Tymczasem kosmiczne plany okazały się jedynie sposobem na wzbudzanie strachu na Zachodzie lub Wschodzie. Kraje mniej rozwinięte nie czerpią z tego żadnych korzyści. Przepaść między biednymi i bogatymi nadal się pogłębia. Jeśli wiedza związana z podbojem Kosmosu nie jest wykorzystywana dla dobra człowieka, to przestaje być w jakikolwiek sposób użyteczna. To nie jest wyścig, do którego Zambia chciałaby się przyłączyć".

A jednak chciała. Może nie tyle Zambia, ile jeden Zambijczyk. O tym jednak żadna z gazet nie pisze.

Muzeum Narodowe

Wejście do ciężkiego, modernistycznego gmachu zagradza ogromny posąg. Wyłania się z ziemi, powstaje z chodnika, nabiera kształtu, oblekając swoją stalową konstrukcję szatą z setek kawałków błyszczącej w południowym słońcu blachy połączonych grubym spawem. Czarny Człowiek z Żelaza. Ciężki, przysadzisty, ostro ciosany, jakby budził się do życia, powstawał z bagna, które jeszcze trzyma jego nogi. Ale pierś już dumnie wypięta, wydatne murzyńskie usta zwarte, wzrok rzuca wyzwanie przyszłości, a zaciśnięta, przesadnie duża dłoń trzyma włócznię. W pierwszej chwili myślę, że inspiracją dla rzeźbiarza musiał być właśnie Edward Mukuka Nkoloso.

Kustosz muzeum, w garniturze błyszczącym jak blacha posągu, ozdobionym finezyjnie krawatem z Kaczorem Daffym, wita mnie, jedynego gościa muzeum, w przepastnej sali tylko gdzieniegdzie upstrzonej jakąś gablotą, zdjęciem czy zabytkową figurką. Pytam o Edwarda Mukukę Nkoloso.

– Kiedyś była o nim wystawa nawet – odpowiada cichym, matowym głosem typowym dla wszystkich muzealników, niezależnie od długości i szerokości geograficznej. – To znaczy tylko jedna tablica – prostuje, jakby zmieszany – ale zdjęliśmy, bo to była tymczasowa wystawa. Były też te ich stroje i... no bo – widzę wyraźne zakłopotanie w gestach kustosza – pan Nkoloso... on trochę... w pewnym momencie – zbliża wskazujący palec do skroni – on myślał, że jest astronautą, że poleci w Kosmos.

Gdzie jest teraz tablica, wie jedynie pewna kobieta, która przebywa na urlopie. Wielki, pusty gmach muzeum to część kompleksu rządowych budynków w centrum miasta. Zachodzę tam, gdy tylko jestem w okolicy, i za każdym razem słyszę od kustosza ze śmiesznym krawatem, że pani archiwistki wciąż nie ma. W końcu wraca. Na moje pytanie uśmiecha się z politowaniem, ale i pewną życzliwością. Zarządza wielkie poszukiwania, choć, jak na wstępie zaznacza, pewnie się nie uda. Pracownicy ubierają się posłusznie w białe fartuchy i przedzierają przez sterty kartonów kryjących stare ekspozycje o tematyce od flory i fauny terenów Zambii, przez konstrukcję afrykańskiej chaty, po życiorys Kennetha Kaundy. Po kilku godzinach poszukiwań wychodzę z muzeum z jednym zdjęciem.

Archiwum UNIP

Moja taksówka zatrzymuje się wzdłuż długiego murowanego ogrodzenia przy Sheki-Sheki Road, na północ od centrum Lusaki. Wszyscy mówią, że właśnie tu siedzibę ma UNIP. Wcześniej biuro partii znajdowało się w dzielnicy Matero, a na początku w domu Kennetha Kaundy. Zamknięte. Nie ma nikogo, jedynie odźwierny informuje, że partia to już nie tutaj, że przeniosła się do centrum, gdzieś niedaleko Cairo Road, a tu został tylko dumny napis „United National Independence Party" i logo z pochodnią płonącą ogniem w zambijskich barwach. I kilka pudeł z dokumentami, których jeszcze nie zdążyli zabrać. Bo UNIP dzisiaj to już ledwie wspomnienie. W ostatnich wyborach UNIP, z Tilyenjim Kaundą, synem Kennetha, na czele, zdobyła poparcie na poziomie pół procent i nie weszła do parlamentu. Sam Tilyenji Kaunda wystawiony przez partię jako kandydat na prezydenta uzyskał raptem jeden procent głosów.

Nikt więc nie wie dziś nawet, gdzie jest biuro UNIP. W latach sześćdziesiątych każdy potrafił wskazać mały dom w Matero. Pytam taksówkarzy, policjantów, ochroniarzy w bankach, sklepikarzy, zwykłych przechodniów i nikt nie potrafi odpowiedzieć.

Nawet kierowca taksówki jest zaskoczony i zaczął to traktować jako osobiste wyzwanie. Jeżdżę po centrum dobrą godzinę, zanim znajduję zapuszczony budynek gdzieś przy Freedom Way. Puste, ciemne korytarze, długie schody na pierwsze piętro, ściany obite drewnianą płytą. Nawet wiatraki u sufitu stoją nieruchomo, jakby nie miały już siły mielić gęstego, lepkiego od październikowych upałów powietrza. Jest i pracownik biura partii za jedynym biurkiem. I jego szczera odpowiedź rozwiewająca wszelkie nadzieje.

– Jesteśmy, jak pan widzi, w trakcie przeprowadzki. Całe archiwa zostały spakowane do pudeł. Ale powiem panu szczerze, że i tak nic tam pan nie znajdzie. – Po chwili namysłu dodaje: – No chyba że o KK, no to będzie.

David Kaunda National Technical High School

– Jest nawet kółko tematyczne, nazywa się Space Club. W DK High School, a to niedaleko stąd, przejdziesz na skróty przez szpital UTH, to na jego tyłach. Oni będą widzieć, bo oni się interesują. Młodzież i nauczyciele – zapewnia syn Mukuki Nkoloso.

Ubrani w mundurki uczniowie czekają przed salą. Siedzą na baczność, rękoma trzymając złożone na kolanach podręczniki. Wchodzę do pokoju nauczycielskiego, w którym krzesła przypięte są do stołu grubym łańcuchem zapiętym tu i ówdzie na kłódki. Przy stole, długim na wiele metrów, siedzi tylko jeden nauczyciel i od razu podoba mu się moje pytanie.

– Bo wie pan, to niezwykła sprawa! Ja też mam na imię Mukuka! To zupełnie jak ten człowiek, który pana interesuje. A do tego na nazwisko mam Kennedy! Jak JFK!

Wracając z DK High School, przechodzę przez teren szpitala UTH, by zaoszczędzić sobie drogi do centrum. Gubię się między oddziałami ogromnego ceglanego gmachu, między łącznikami, przejściami, podwórzami. Te wszystkie przestrzenie wypełnione są ludźmi. A w zasadzie wyłącznie kobietami, młodszymi, starszymi, a także takimi, których wiek bardzo trudno rozpoznać.

Tych jest właśnie najwięcej. Długimi ramionami obejmują swoje śpiące dzieci. Bo prawie każda z nich ma przy sobie co najmniej jedno. Niektóre próbują te dzieci karmić suchymi, wyciągniętymi piersiami, w których dawno nie było pokarmu. Siedzą na krawężnikach, leżą na trawniku, opierają się o mury szpitalnych bloków. W ciszy.

Zambia National Broadcasting Corporation

– Ooo, w Kosmos? Niesłychane! – Oczy młodej kobiety robią się ogromne, a jej trzepoczące rzęsy powodują niemal odczuwalny ruch powietrza. Przestaje nawet piłować paznokcie. – Z Lusaki? Na Księżyc?

– A potem na Marsa – dopowiadam.

Choć ZNBC powstało dopiero w 1987 roku, jest w prostej linii spadkobiercą Central African Broadcasting Station, instytucji założonej przez władze kolonialne jeszcze w latach czterdziestych. Pierwszy nadajnik radiowy zainstalowano w Lusace w 1941 roku. Emitowano z niego głównie audycje nawołujące czarnych, by wstępowali do wojska w obronie imperium. W 1966 roku CABS przemianowano na dumne Zambia Broadcasting Corporation, a potem na ZNBC, które dziś ma trzy kanały telewizyjne, trzy radiowe i nadaje w języku angielskim i kilku językach afrykańskich. Tak czy inaczej, kilkadziesiąt lat historii zapisanej na magnetycznych taśmach. Zastanawiam się, czy któraś z tysięcy kaset VHS, miniDV, 8 mm leżących jedna obok drugiej na tych regałach, półkach, w kartonach poustawianych jeden na drugim kryje to, czego szukam. Jeśli nie wideo, to może chociaż audio? A więc któraś ze szpul magnetofonowych? Albo jedna z klisz, jeden z milionów slajdów zamkniętych w plastikowych ramkach? Czy w ogóle ktokolwiek jest w stanie powiedzieć, co kryją te rolki? Ktoś kiedyś obejrzał te wszystkie obrazy, wysłuchał tych wszystkich dźwięków? Czy gdzieś na tych kilometrach taśm jest Edward Mukuka Nkoloso i jego kosmiczne marzenie?

– Zadzwonimy do pana, jak coś znajdziemy – obiecuje entuzjastycznie kobieta wśród taśm, a ja już wiem, że jej obietnica jest tylko uprzejmością.

„Times of Zambia"

Stary „Times of Zambia" ma format małego dwuosobowego namiotu. Teraz już nie ma takich gazet. Można się nim przykryć przed deszczem wraz z całą rodziną, skutecznie schować przed niepożądanym wzrokiem, zapakować weń udziec byka, a kilkoma numerami wytapetować całe mieszkanie. To dziennik, najpoważniejsza gazeta w Zambii, wychodząca nieprzerwanie od lat czterdziestych, choć kiedyś pod nazwą „The Copperbelt Times", a potem jako „Northern News". Każdy miesiąc to około trzydziestu numerów – jeden katalog w grubej, czarnej, sztywnej okładce. Cztery katalogi stanowią już ciężar, który trudno podnieść. Licząc od lat pięćdziesiątych i zakładając regularność archiwizacji, w pokoju, w którym jestem, znajduje się blisko osiemset katalogów z poszczególnych lat i miesięcy, poukładanych w kilkanaście stert wyższych od człowieka. Oczywiście mogę zawęzić poszukiwania do określonych lat, czasami nawet do miesięcy. Ale jedynie niewielka część katalogów jest w jakikolwiek sposób podpisana. Te starsze lubią leżeć najbliżej podłogi.

– W Zambii mamy kulturę przekazu ustnego – wyjaśnia ktoś życzliwy – raczej nie dba się u nas o dokumenty. Tu się opowiada. Ale możemy dać ogłoszenie, że szukasz informacji na ten temat, zwłaszcza tych osób z Akademii Kosmicznej. Może ktoś ich zna, ktoś się zgłosi? Gazeta dociera do całej Zambii, czasami ludzie się znajdują.

Na ogłoszenie w „Times of Zambia" odpowiada jedna osoba:

– Znasz wymienione w ogłoszeniu osoby? – pytam ją.

– Nie. Ale podoba mi się ten Nkoloso!

MUVI Television

Największa prywatna telewizja w Zambii. Medialne imperium wyrastające tuż nieopodal kompleksu telewizji publicznej. Zostaję zaproszony do śniadaniówki *Breakfast with the Boys* prowadzonej przez lokalnych celebrytów. Sofa, stolik z samochodowej opony, zestaw do minigolfa i kilka potężnych kamer celujących prosto we mnie. Przyzwyczajony do poziomu polskich programów śniadaniowych ze zdziwieniem odkrywam, że rozmowa na żywo trwa już ponad pół godziny. Z jeszcze większym zdumieniem przyjmuję fakt, że nie toczy się wokół tego, co lokalne gwiazdy robiły w weekend. W ogóle nie toczy się wokół nich, lecz wokół zaproszonego gościa. Oni ją jedynie prowadzą. I to w sposób ciekawy, umiejętny, elokwentny, gdy trzeba – z poczuciem humoru, gdy trzeba – z powagą. Najbardziej zaskakuje mnie, że traktują mnie jak równoważnego partnera do rozmowy, a nie jako scenografię do własnego występu.

– Dlaczego ktoś z kraju tak odległego jak Polska interesuje się kawałkiem naszej historii i człowiekiem, o którym niestety nawet my sami zapomnieliśmy? – pytają prowadzący.

Na koniec programu odczytuję nazwiska osób, których poszukuję, by złożyć w całość moją kosmiczną odyseję. Ktokolwiek widział, ktokolwiek wie. Przecież oprócz syna Mukuki Nkoloso w Akademii było ich jeszcze jedenastu. Lista nazwisk płynie w Zambię za pośrednictwem kabli i białych talerzy. Godfrey Mwango. Martha Mwamba. Ruben Simwenga. Bracia Wilfred i John Chikoti. Mathews Mambwe. Paul Chewe. Devison Bambo Miti. Samson Mwanga. Deusdedit Chewe. Victoria Chiti. To imiona kosmicznych kadetów Edwarda Mukuki Nkoloso. Nikt nie odpowiada.

Daję też ogłoszenia w portalach społecznościowych, zapisuję się do zambijskich grup na Facebooku. Wynajduję ludzi o nazwiskach osób, których szukam, piszę do nich, lecz większość nie zadaje sobie trudu, by odpowiedzieć. Czasami konwersacja kończy się, gdy tylko zaczynam o coś prosić. Nawet osoby, z którymi wielokrotnie rozmawiam, będąc w Lusace, gdy kontaktuję się z nimi z Polski, po prostu nie odpisują. Również dziennikarze, ludzie wykształceni, posługujący się każdego dnia komputerem i telefonem. Kontakt, mimo uprzejmych zapewnień o chęci pomocy, urywa się, gdy wyjeżdżam z Zambii. Wielu obiecało mi wsparcie w poszukiwaniu pozostałych osób związanych z Akademią. W Lusace twierdzili, że wiedzą, że znają, że słyszeli, że na pewno znajdą. Będąc na miejscu, miałem środki nacisku upierdliwego reportera – mogłem przychodzić wiele razy do tej samej instytucji, czekać godzinami na danego człowieka, jak nie tu, to tam, próbować kontaktu przez jego znajomych czy rodzinę. Mogłem przypilnować, by ktoś na pewno sięgnął do szuflady, by ktoś inny wykonał przy mnie telefon, jeszcze ktoś inny, by znalazł zdjęcie czy artykuł. Z Warszawy mogę jedynie dzwonić i pisać. Wiem, że część osób, których szukam, już zapewne nie żyje, ale ktoś ponoć nadal mieszka w Lusace, ktoś inny w Kasamie, jeszcze inny gdzieś w Mozambiku. Tak twierdzi syn Mukuki Nkoloso. Ale niełatwo znaleźć człowieka pamiętającego wydarzenia sprzed pięćdziesięciu lat w kraju, w którym w latach dziewięćdziesiątych jedna czwarta społeczeństwa była zarażona HIV, a średnia długość życia ledwo przekraczała czterdzieści lat.

„Dzień dobry! Czy znasz Godfreya Mwango (piszę do osoby o tym samym nazwisku)? Jestem pisarzem z Polski, pracuję nad tematem, w którym pan Mwango mógłby mi bardzo pomóc".

Odpowiedź przychodzi po miesiącu: „Jakim tematem"?

„Piszę książkę o Edwardzie Mukuce Nkoloso. Pan Mwango był jego bliskim przyjacielem".

„Czy znasz pana Mwango osobiście?"

„Nie. Staram się go znaleźć od wielu miesięcy. Jesteś jego rodziną?"

„Być może. Tylko nie wiem, o jakiego pana Mwango chodzi. Znam ich wielu".

„Godfrey Mwango, którego szukam, powinien mieć około 73, 74 lat. Pracował z Mukuką Nkoloso w Liberation Center, a wcześniej był członkiem Zambijskiej Akademii Kosmicznej".

„To raczej nie pomogę. Chyba że podasz mi więcej szczegółów.
„A znasz wielu Godfreyów Mwango w tym właśnie wieku?”
„Być może to mój ojciec, jego bracia, jego kuzyni? Może sąsiedzi? Może znajomi z kościoła?”
„Oni wszyscy nazywają się Godfrey Mwango i mają 74 lata???”
„Tak”.
„A możesz ich chociaż zapytać?”
Odpowiedzi już nie dostałem.

16

Na YouTubie można znaleźć krótki dokument o Mukuce Nkoloso, zrobiony dla afrykańskiego oddziału chińskiej telewizji – CCTV Africa. Tak, Chiny mają już swoją telewizję w Afryce. Film kończy się serią wywiadów z młodymi Zambijczykami. Mówią o swoim podziwie, zachwycie i szacunku dla śmiałych pomysłów Edwarda Mukuki Nkoloso. Mówią, że jest wzorem do naśladowania, niektórzy sugerują, że gdyby nie brak funduszy, jego pomysły mogłyby zostać zrealizowane. Na podstawie filmu można odnieść wrażenie, że Nkoloso to postać dobrze znana przeciętnemu Zambijczykowi, nie wspominając o tych bardziej wykształconych. Szukam w szkołach, instytucjach, pytam w urzędach i na ulicach. Rozmawiam z młodymi i ze starszymi. Nie udaje mi się znaleźć takich osób. Zambijski Program Kosmiczny nic im nie mówi, a pytający o niego biały człowiek z odległego kraju jest większą egzotyką niż same kosmiczne plany Edwarda Mukuki Nkoloso. Jedni reagują śmiechem, drudzy zdziwieniem, jeszcze inni uważają, że żartuję, próbuję ich nabrać. Gdy opowiadam o rakiecie i podróży na Księżyc z Lusaki, otwierają szeroko oczy i usta, niektórzy pukają się w głowę. Zaledwie kilka osób w ogóle zna jego nazwisko, zazwyczaj bardziej w kontekście walki o niepodległość. Ci, którzy słyszeli o kosmicznej historii, traktują ją niezupełnie serio. Są też tacy, którzy wpadają w zakłopotanie, wstydzą się, marzenie Mukuki Nkoloso uważają za wariactwo, a jego samego za człowieka niespełna rozumu. Osoby, które znały Edwarda Mukukę Nkoloso z tamtych lat, wspominają z kolei jego kosmiczny epizod raczej z politowaniem niż podziwem. Szybko zmieniają temat, wolą rozmawiać o walce o niepodległość, o Kaundzie i brytyjskiej fladze, którą opuszczano z masztów. Do takich należą głównie byli politycy UNIP. Niektórzy utrzymują, że nie pamiętają, inni, jak generał Kingsley Chinkuli*, że nie są odpowiednimi osobami, by udzielać takich informacji. Cuthbert Kolala to jedna z tych osób, które wyrażają się o Mukuce Nkoloso i jego planach z dużym, może ironicznym, a nawet przesadnym szacunkiem. Czasami zastanawiam się, czy ze mnie nie żartuje, czy naprawdę myśli tak, jak mówi, czy jedynie przybiera taką pozę, bo uznał to za stosowne. W końcu mamy spisany kontrakt, jest moim *Research Assistant* i dostaje za to pieniądze. A może on też jest z tej kategorii wariatów jak Mukuka Nkoloso i jego syn? Kolala twierdzi przy każdej okazji, że Mukuka Nkoloso był geniuszem i że gdyby Amerykanie nie wykradli mu jego technologii, z pewnością to jeden z jego kosmicznych kadetów, a nie Neil Armstrong byłby pierwszym człowiekiem na Księżycu.

– Amerykanie skopiowali to wszystko! Doktor Nkoloso był tak wyjątkowy, że gdyby tylko dali mu pieniądze i materiały, dziś żylibyśmy w innym świecie, a on siedziałby na Księżycu! Miał wspaniały umysł i marzenie, w które inni nie wierzyli. Wiesz, gdy widziałem, jak wymyślił ćwiczenie z beczką... ja widziałem, że on rozmawiał z Bogiem, mówił „Boże, pomóż mi w tej wielkiej misji!".

Ale nawet Cuthbert Kolala nie bardzo może zrozumieć moje zainteresowanie Zambijskim Programem Kosmicznym. Wielokrotnie pyta, czemu to dla mnie aż tak ważne, zdaje się zmieszany i lekko zawstydzony, gdy indaguję jego kolegów, weteranów niepodległościowych zmagań, o rakietę Mukuki Nkoloso, a nie

* Gen. Kingsley Chinkuli – minister obrony narodowej i głównodowodzący zambijskiej armii w latach siedemdziesiątych.

o trudy wyzwoleńczej walki. Ma zupełnie inną wizję tego, co ja chcę zrobić. Wszem wobec rozpowiada, że piszę książkę o Freedom Fighters, między innymi oczywiście o nim. W każdej instytucji, do której wchodzimy, przedstawia mnie jako wielkiego pisarza z Europy, który przyjechał udokumentować historię walki Zambijczyków o niepodległość, i zawsze zaznacza, że z nim już przeprowadziłem wywiad. Zapewnia też, że książka zostanie przetłumaczona na angielski i będzie dostępna również w Zambii. Na początku staram się to prostować, ale szybko dochodzę do wniosku, że nie ma to jednak sensu. Niech każdy z nas ma swoje wyobrażenie naszej pracy.

Sam nie wiem, czemu aż tak bardzo fascynuje mnie ta historia. Dziwnym zbiegiem okoliczności okazuje się, że Edward Mukuka Nkoloso urodził się tego samego dnia co ja. 2 lutego. Nie wierzę w takie rzeczy, do astrologii podchodzę z dystansem. Niemniej czasami historia ta wydaje mi się dość zwykła, nawet banalna, innymi razy aż mnie ściska, gdy o niej myślę. Jest coś wzruszającego w tej naiwnej, prostej wierze w wielkie rzeczy, nieograniczonej okolicznościami, trudnościami, niebiorącej pod uwagę możliwości technicznych i finansowych. Marzenie samo w sobie, czyste, wykrystalizowane, leżące bardzo blisko szaleństwa. Czarny człowiek zrzuca kajdany i od razu leci w Kosmos. Edward Mukuka Nkoloso śmiało mógłby dopisać linijkę do słynnego przemówienia Martina Luthera Kinga.

Jest w tej historii też coś czysto dziecięcego. Czasami myślę, że jest jak scenariusz romantycznego filmu dla wytwórni Disneya. A jednak kosmiczna wycieczka nie była pomysłem dziesięciolatka, lecz człowieka mocno osadzonego w rzeczywistości, byłego wojskowego i aktywnego polityka UNIP. Sam, gdy byłem mały, uwielbiałem wyobrażać sobie Kosmos. Wyobrażać, niekoniecznie obserwować. Dostałem od rodziców książkę, która wydawała mi się ogromna jak cały Wszechświat. Były tam planety, gwiazdy, komety, mgławice i kosmiczne obłoki, Droga Mleczna, kratery na Księżycu i kosmiczne sondy. Moim ulubionym znaczkiem pocztowym w kolekcji, którą dostałem od ojca chrzestnego, był ten z kosmonautami. Nie pamiętam, czy rosyjskimi, czy amerykańskimi. Pamiętam tylko tę czarną przestrzeń za postacią w grubym skafandrze i wielką owalną szybę hełmu, w której wszystko się odbijało i zakrzywiało. Na któreś urodziny w domu pojawił się też plastikowy łazik księżycowy radzieckiej produkcji, który buczał, warczał, migał zielonym światełkiem, kręcił w kółko plastikową anteną i zawsze jechał w innym kierunku, niż chciałem. Mniej więcej w tym samym czasie, miałem może siedem lat, czyli pod koniec lat osiemdziesiątych, dostałem na Gwiazdkę kupiony za ciężko zarobione pieniądze, wystany w długiej peweksowskiej kolejce zestaw Lego. Kosmos. Najprawdziwszy. Granatowe klocki układały się w statki kosmiczne, rakiety i księżycowe bazy, a ludziki miały na plecach butle z tlenem i hełmy z małą ruchomą szybką. W przerwach w składaniu klocków oglądałem *Sondę,* gdzie panowie Kurek i Kamiński zgłębiali tajemnice mikro- i makrokosmosu. Dobrze pamiętam czołówkę programu – ze statkiem kosmicznym o dziwacznym kształcie lecącym w ciemne, rozgwieżdżone otchłanie przy akompaniamencie dramatycznej muzyki. O dziwo, nigdy nie byłem fanem *Gwiezdnych wojen*. Do dziś nie widziałem żadnej części pierwotnej trylogii i żadnego z następnych sequeli i prequeli. Nie bawił mnie też Pi i Sigma, szyty zbyt grubymi nićmi, zbyt naiwny i niedorzeczny. Nie opuszczałem za to żadnego odcinka *Star Treka* i marzyłem, żeby kiedyś na pokładzie statku Enterprise osiągnąć prędkość warp. Gapiłem się także w okrągłą mapę nieba i choć kompletnie nic z niej nie rozumiałem, to zapamiętywałem nazwy i kształty. Pierwszą swoją dziewczynę poderwałem na to, że potrafiłem pokazać na niebie gwiazdozbiór Kasjopei. Nie tam Wielki Wóz, to potrafił każdy. Ale Kasjopea – pięć ułożonych w zygzak gwiazd mitycznej królowej Etiopii – czyniła cuda. A potem na balkonie na siódmym piętrze bloku z wielkiej płyty na łódzkich Bałutach stanęła mała plastikowa luneta. Nie pamiętam, co było przez nią widać, możliwe nawet, że niewiele, bo potem przez długie lata zbieraliśmy się z tatą, by w końcu kupić lepszą. Już nie lunetę, tylko teleskop.

Przeglądaliśmy katalogi, jeździliśmy po sklepach, planowaliśmy wypady na otwarte pola, niezanieczyszczone świetlnym szumem wielkiego miasta. Nigdy go nie kupiliśmy, choć przez lata wielokrotnie wracaliśmy do tego pomysłu. Teleskop kupiłem dopiero dwadzieścia lat później, w prezencie na sześćdziesiąte urodziny taty. Wielki, profesjonalny, prawie tak wysoki jak on sam, tak żeby dało się przezeń dojrzeć to, co tata pokazywał mi w książkach. Zawsze marzył o takim teleskopie i tym marzeniem zaraził również mnie. Ale mimo że popłakał się, gdy otwierał wielkie pudło, przez ostatnie kilka lat udało nam się usiąść na balkonie zaledwie raz, na krótką chwilę.

„Poprosiłem pilota, by się zatrzymał tak, bym mógł wysiąść i przejść się po chmurach – tak Edward Mukuka Nkoloso wspominał w jednym z wywiadów swój pierwszy lot samolotem, zapewne podczas wojny. – Odmówił. Ale ja wtedy podjąłem decyzję, że kiedyś polecę w przestworza".

Jak Edward Mukuka Nkoloso wyobrażał sobie Kosmos? Jakie obrazy rysowały mu się w głowie, gdy patrzył w niebo? Co myślał, gdy celował swoją włócznią w tarczę Księżyca? I przede wszystkim, co opowiadał swoim nastoletnim, bosonogim kadetom, z których żaden nigdy nie oglądał *Sondy*, *Star Treka*, nie bawił się kosmicznym zestawem Lego ani nie miał plakatu z mapą nieba na ścianie swego pokoju? Co mówił im o gwiazdach, jak przedstawiał planety? Jak oceniał możliwości techniczne i środki, którymi dysponował? Chciałbym tego posłuchać, siedzieć wraz z nimi wśród suchych traw afrykańskiego buszu w Zambii początku lat sześćdziesiątych i słuchać o Kosmosie. O tym, że wkrótce ktoś z nich poleci na Księżyc, gdzieś, gdzie nie był jeszcze żaden człowiek. Pierwszym będzie Zambijczyk. Martha Mwamba? A może Godfrey Mwango? Albo Ruben Simwenga? Lub syn dyrektora, Mukuka? Może jednak wszyscy, jeden po drugim, i wtedy spotkają się na Księżycu, zatkną tam zieloną, zambijską flagę z orłem? Niczym wycieczka francuskich naukowców z niemego filmu *Le Voyage Dans La Lune* Georges'a Mélièsa z 1902 roku. Jak będzie wyglądał lot kosmiczny? Czy długo będzie trwał? Dłużej niż autem z Lusaki do Livingstone lub Kitwe? Co czuli ci ludzie, gdy patrzyli na Księżyc, leżąc wśród traw, w ciszy afrykańskiej nocy, wypełnionej cykaniem grubych świerszczy? Czy bali się tej podróży w nieznane? Co myśleli o Księżycu? Jaki im się wydawał? Jak wyobrażali sobie pierwszy krok na jego powierzchni? Jaki Księżyc jest w dotyku? Jaki ma zapach, kolor? Czy zastaną tam jakieś istoty? I czy będzie stamtąd widać Ziemię i Lusakę? Jakie nadzieje wiązali z tą podróżą? Czy ich wyobraźnia rozpalona obrazami rysowanymi przez dyrektora Nkoloso była gotowa udźwignąć rozczarowanie i porażkę? Te pytania można by mnożyć w nieskończoność. Czy nie poczuli się zawiedzeni i oszukani, gdy jednak żaden z nich nie poleciał w Kosmos?

17

– Myślisz, że to wszystko było na poważnie? – pytam Sikotę Winę.

– Tak, sądzę, że Nkoloso traktował to bardzo serio. Myślę, że on czuł się niezwykle ograniczony realiami kolonializmu, może stąd to pragnienie wyrwania się, przesuwania granic, zgłębiania przestrzeni, w których nikt jeszcze nie był.

W starym „Nshila Magazine", który teraz już nie jest wydawany, znalazłem zdjęcie. Sześćdziesiąty trzeci, może początek sześćdziesiątego czwartego roku. Delegacja UNIP wybiera się do Londynu, Kaunda macha na pożegnanie ręką, zmierzając w kierunku samolotu. Przy jego boku uśmiechnięty Mukuka Nkoloso, jak zawsze odstający ubiorem i fryzurą od innych polityków. Ale nie strój jest tutaj najważniejszy ani włócznia, tylko podpis pod zdjęciem. Redaktor artykułu określił Mukukę Nkoloso mianem *„the space-man"*.

Nie jestem pewny, kiedy Nkoloso zaczął snuć plany podboju Kosmosu. Niektórzy twierdzą, że dopiero w 1964 roku, inni, że dwa lata wcześniej, jeszcze inni, że pod koniec lat pięćdziesiątych. Ale najbardziej prawdopodobną datą zdaje się rok 1963, gdy ferwor Cza-czy już opadł, a obie strony zaczęły sobie zdawać sprawę, że wkrótce musi dojść do jakiegoś rozwiązania politycznego.

– My mu na początku nie wierzyliśmy. Ale potem on to tak pięknie objaśniał, że przekonał nas, że jesteśmy kadetami, afronautami – rozmarza się syn Mukuki Nkoloso. – Tak nas nazywał. Zrozumieliśmy, o co mu chodziło. Bo mogliśmy dojść bardzo daleko. Gdy on tłumaczył, wszyscy siedzieli cicho i słuchali. Czasami siedzieliśmy całymi dniami i nawet nikt nie czuł się głodny, bo go słuchaliśmy. „Jesteście głodni?" „Nie". „Nie? Ale musicie jeść, inaczej nie będziecie się mogli skoncentrować!" On był bardzo miły i radosny, prosty i bardzo wyrozumiały. Naprawdę zależało mu, żeby nam przekazać wiedzę i rozbudzić w nas to zainteresowanie. Chciał, byśmy byli wolni, byśmy mieli wolność edukacji, myślenia, poruszania się. Większość studentów pochodziła z Matero, niektórzy z dalszych osiedli. Zresztą kto chciał, ten mógł do nas przyjść. I przychodzili, a on opowiadał o tym, co chce zrobić. A my jako uczniowie byliśmy bardzo szczęśliwi. Choć było wiele osób, które go nie rozumiały. Pytali, jak ten człowiek chce dotrzeć na Księżyc. Byli ignorantami. Tata im odpowiadał wtedy: „Jeśli ptak może latać, to czemu my nie możemy?". Ktoś na to, że nie, to niemożliwe, bo nie mamy skrzydeł, nie mamy tego, nie mamy tamtego. „Nie! Macie za to coś więcej! – I pokazywał palcem swoją głowę. – Macie mózgi, które dostaliście od Boga!"

18

– Nie bałeś się? – pytam.

– Lecieć na Księżyc? Nie, nie bałem się. Ciągle o tym czytałem, o tym, co robią Amerykanie. Nawet dziś się tym interesuję, lubię czytać o Kosmosie, ale dziś już gazety nie piszą o sprawach nauki. Mnie bardzo ciekawiły te ciemne miejsca na Księżycu. Gdy byłem mały, mama i tata opowiadali mi, że te ciemne miejsca to futro królika. Mamy tu taką historię, w Zimbabwe też ją mają. Że te kształty na Księżycu to królik, który w jakiś sposób się tam dostał i nie może się stamtąd ruszyć, nie może wrócić. Jak się przyjrzysz, to one przypominają królika. Pytałem rodziców, co on tam robi, ten królik, po co tam poszedł. Marzyłem, by polecieć do tego królika i zobaczyć, dlaczego on tam utknął. No ale potem, jak te Armstrongi tam poleciały, to się okazało, że to nie królik. Tylko kaniony, doliny. Ale wtedy tego nie wiedzieliśmy, więc bardzo chciałem na Księżyc, żeby zobaczyć, jak tam jest, czy tak samo jak na Ziemi, czy inaczej. I jak daleko jest do Słońca. Czy Księżyc i Słońce to sąsiedzi? Nie wiedzieliśmy nic o innych planetach. Widzieliśmy tylko Księżyc, Słońce i gwiazdy. Te gwiazdy zdawały się niezmiernie daleko, ale Księżyc i Słońce jednak dość blisko. Ciekawiło mnie, czy z Księżyca da się przeskoczyć na Słońce. Więc kiedy nadeszła ta okazja z Mukuką Nkoloso, nie wahałem się ani chwili.

Devison Bambo Miti był jednym z kadetów Zambijskiej Akademii Kosmicznej. Spotyka się ze mną w kawiarni w galerii handlowej. Choć proponowałem, że przyjadę do niego do domu, z jakiegoś powodu się nie zgodził. Chciałem zobaczyć, jak mieszka niedoszły astronauta, ale on najwidoczniej nie chciał pokazać. Zatem galeria. Na spotkanie pan Miti spóźnił się kilka godzin, ale ja już byłem przyzwyczajony do tego, że czas to rzecz bardzo względna. A może lepiej powiedzieć: osobista. Wszystko zaczęło się od słów syna Mukuki Nkoloso, który drapiąc się w głowę, powiedział, że pan Miti był kiedyś urzędnikiem w jednym z rządowych budynków. Złapałem trop. Znalezienie pana Mitiego zajęło mi wiele dni, jeszcze więcej telefonów i przemierzonych kilometrów. Zatem czekałem cierpliwie, dzwoniąc do niego co jakiś czas i słysząc te same zapewnienia, że niedługo będzie. Chodziłem dokoła galerii, sprawdzając, czy aby na pewno to samo wejście, ten sam budynek, bo miałem świadomość, że jeśli się miniemy, następnej okazji może już nie być.

– Mieszkałem w Matero, większość kadetów była stamtąd – mówi cichym, zmęczonym głosem pan Miti. Czasami z trudem go rozumiem, jego słowa giną w kawiarnianym gwarze, a ja muszę wytężać słuch, by je złapać, nim przepadną. – Wielu pochodziło z mojej szkoły, kilku z innej, Matero Boys. Miałem wtedy szesnaście lat. Któregoś dnia Mukuka Nkoloso przyszedł do naszej szkoły i rozmawiał z dyrektorem. A potem zrobił apel. Ustawiliśmy się wszyscy w rzędzie. Mukuka Nkoloso oświadczył, że zbiera ochotników do budowy rakiety kosmicznej! Wszyscy słyszeliśmy o tym, że Amerykanie już latają w Kosmos, gazety o tym pisały. Bardzo mnie interesowało, no to od razu podniosłem rękę. Myślałem sobie, że on pewnie był w USA, w Miami, że widział to wszystko. Bardzo chciałem zobaczyć, jak buduje się rakietę. I bardzo chciałem polecieć na Księżyc, zobaczyć, jak wygląda. I jak Ziemia wygląda z Księżyca. Marzyło mi się, żeby zobaczyć, jak daleko jest do Słońca, a przecież Księżyc musiał być trochę bliżej Słońca niż Ziemia. Nie wiedziałem, że Słońce jest aż tak daleko.

Devison Bambo Miti w swojej opowieści wciąż wspomina o Apollo 11, który miał być inspiracją dla dążeń Mukuki Nkoloso. Zapewne myli go z rosyjskim Sputnikiem lub amerykańskim Explorerem, Apollo 11 to dopiero rok 1969. Ale gazety w Rodezji Północnej, a potem niepodległej Zambii śledziły rozwój wyścigu na Księżyc zaskakująco precyzyjnie. Są pełne zdjęć rakiet i astronautów. Pojawiały się nawet komiksy i ilustrowane kosmiczne historyjki. Ponoć to właśnie z komiksu Edward Mukuka Nkoloso wziął pomysł, by zmierzyć się z Kosmosem. Próbuję sobie wyobrazić, czym pojęcie lotu w Kosmos musiało być pięćdziesiąt lat temu dla mieszkańców Zambii. Nkoloso w jakiś sposób przełożył koncepcję lotu kosmicznego na warunki afrykańskie, ubrał ją w lokalne realia, symbolikę, wpasował w narrację walki o wolność. Bo jeśli oni mogą, to czemu my nie możemy? Wydaje mi się, że ta sama odwaga, zuchwałość, która pozwoliła mu konfrontować się z białymi w tak otwarty sposób, była siłą napędową jego kosmicznych planów. Lot w Kosmos to tak, jak uderzyć białego w twarz.

– Ja wtedy sprzedawałem gazety, więc miałem to wszystko na bieżąco – ciągnie dalej Devison Bambo Miti. – A Nkoloso był tu znany, bo był szefem młodzieżówki UNIP. Bardzo się interesowałem rakietami, więc gdy powiedział, że będziemy budować taką, co poleci w Kosmos, to od razu przystąpiłem. No bo zawsze chciałem zbudować rakietę! Ufałem mu dlatego, że był wojskowym, wierzyłem, że wojskowy to człowiek zdyscyplinowany. A do tego był naukowcem, tak o sobie mówił. Był zafascynowany Księżycem i tymi wszystkimi rakietami, co wtedy latały. Więc jak tylko kończyłem szkołę koło szesnastej, to szedłem do Nkoloso, tam zawsze było co robić. A byli tacy, ci starsi, Mwango, Simwenga, Mwamba, którzy nie chodzili już do szkoły, nie mieli nic do robienia, więc siedzieli tam cały czas. Mieliśmy dużo treningu wojskowego, maszerowanie, dyscyplina. Bo Nkoloso trochę też szkolił nas jako młodzieżówkę UNIP. By bronić naszej partii, jeśli zajdzie taka potrzeba. Ale Księżyc był najważniejszy. On miał trochę książek o Kosmosie. Opowiadał nam to, co sam wiedział, i mówił o tym, co robili Amerykanie. A my byliśmy tym wszystkim niesamowicie podekscytowani. Nie mieliśmy nawet teleskopu. Poza tym po co teleskop, przecież Księżyc widać każdej nocy gołym okiem! Czasami nasze zajęcia w Akademii przeciągały się do późnej nocy, zwłaszcza gdy Księżyc wstawał wcześnie. Wtedy siadaliśmy na trawie, a on nam o nim opowiadał.

19

– Ta sama siła, która sprawia, że włócznia spada na ziemię i wbija się w ciało zwierzęcia, albo jak rąbiesz drzewo, to ta sama siła, która sprawia, że siekiera się wbija, to jest ta sama siła, która może nas zaprowadzić na Księżyc. Grawitacja. – Syn Mukuki Nkoloso tłumaczy mi właśnie zjawisko grawitacji. Tym razem wystawiliśmy plastikowe krzesła przed dom. Siedzimy w cieniu blachy falistej i patrzymy na biegające po podwórku kury.

– Tak samo z psem. Nawet jeśli ma jedno oko, to jeśli położysz mu nshimę z kurczakiem, to tym jednym okiem on trafi do jedzenia. – Siedzący obok Cuthbert Kolala cmoka z zachwytem i prawdziwym przejęciem.

– Albo z kotem, co miauczy. Widzisz po tym, jak się zachowuje, jak chodzi, że nic nie jadł, że chce mu się jeść. Tata to wszystko analizował. Ptak leci z jednego drzewa na drugie. Małpa skacze z jednej gałęzi na drugą. Orzeł leci i łapie rybę swoimi szponami. A my nie możemy tego zrobić? Jeśli ptak lata, to my też możemy! On był filozofem, naukowcem-filozofem. Czasami, gdy już wszyscy spaliśmy, można go było zobaczyć, jak czyta. Po prostu czyta i notuje. A rano tylko obmywał twarz wodą i zaczynaliśmy zajęcia.

Wieść o kosmicznych ambicjach osoby, o której i tak ciągle było słychać, niosła się przez Lusakę błyskawicznie i szybko przyciągnęła uwagę lokalnych mediów. Na opuszczoną farmę w dzielnicy Matero nieopodal Chingwele Hill zaczęli zjeżdżać dziennikarze. Już w styczniu 1964 roku „DRUM Magazine" – południowoafrykański tygodnik adresowany głównie do czarnej ludności – poświęcił trzy strony na obszerny, ilustrowany reportaż z kosmicznej bazy. Na pierwszej stronie Edward Mukuka Nkoloso, stojący dumnie na stalowej drabinie, takiej z osłoną dokoła, jakich używa się do wchodzenia na kominy czy anteny. Domyślam się, że fotografia musiała zostać zrobiona na Chingwele Hill. Do dziś stoją tam potężne zbiorniki wody dla miasta. Wprawny fotograf skadrował zdjęcie tak, że można odnieść wrażenie, że drabina prowadzi do samego nieba. Albo że jest częścią jakiejś kosmicznej instalacji. Artykuł nosi tytuł *The Black Astronaut of Zambia* i otwiera go taki manifest dyrektora Nkoloso: „Nasz statek kosmiczny, Cyklop I, wzniesie się w kierunku głębokich, bezdennych przestrzeni, daleko poza epicykle siódmego nieba*. Nasi potomkowie, czarni naukowcy, nie ustaną w eksplorowaniu niebiańskich nieskończoności, aż będziemy kontrolować całą przestrzeń kosmiczną".

Dalej czytamy: „Edward Mukuka Nkoloso, założyciel i dyrektor generalny Narodowej Akademii Nauki, Badań Kosmicznych i Filozofii, wycelował włócznię w Księżyc i wyjaśnił swoje plany, by polecieć tam z Lusaki we własnej rakiecie. Pan Nkoloso przemierzał właśnie miejsce, z którego w przyszłości odpali rakietę. To Chingwele Hill, piaszczyste wzgórze z widokiem na miasto. Za nim podążał jego wierny pomocnik Samuel Makonde**, niosąc drewnianą włócznię i teczkę. Obecnie wzgórze zabudowane jest zbiornikami na wodę.

– I to jest właśnie kłopot – powiedział człowiek, który w porywach romantyzmu lubi się nazywać Czarnym Astronautą. – Nie

* Mukuka Nkoloso mierzył zatem wysoko. Musiał znać lub przynajmniej słyszeć o kosmologii żydowskiej lub islamskiej. To w nich funkcjonuje termin siódmego nieba, tego, w którym Żydzi umieścili Jahwe, a muzułmanie Allaha. Koncepcja wywodzi się z kosmologii starożytnej Mezopotamii, pojawia się również w mitologii hinduskiej.

** Żadna z osób, z którymi rozmawiałem, w tym syn Mukuki Nkoloso, nie przypomina sobie jednak Samuela Makondego.

mam jak odpalić rakiety, to wszystko bardzo przeszkadza. Zawiadomiłem już Radę Miasta, by usunęli te zbiorniki, ale się nie zgodzili. Pewnie boją się mojej rakiety.

Pan Nkoloso jest wyróżniającą się postacią z kolorową peleryną, nieobciętymi, potarganymi włosami i zębami prawdziwego wojownika. Włosów nie obcina w żałobie po swojej ciotce, która zginęła trzy lata temu podczas zamieszek w Prowincji Północnej. Peleryna natomiast to oficjalny strój urzędowy Akademii Nauki, której motto głosi: »Dokądkolwiek prowadzi przeznaczenie i chwała człowieka, tam zawsze będziemy«.

Akademia zajmuje połowę małego budynku, usytuowanego wśród zabudowań osiedla Matero, tuż pod piaszczystym wzgórzem. Pomieszczenia dzieli z National Rate and Rentpayers Association, którego dyrektorem jest również pan Nkoloso.

To tu, za skrzypiącymi drewnianymi drzwiami, znajduje się centrum dowodzenia najmniejszego i najmłodszego uczestnika kosmicznego wyścigu – operacji »Cyklop«. W przeciwieństwie do potężnych rywali, jak Ameryka i Rosja, załoga operacji »Cyklop« (nazwanej tak od psa pana Nkoloso) chętnie dzieli się swoimi sekretami.

– W rzeczy samej – mówi Nkoloso – zamierzam poprosić Amerykanów i Rosjan, by przyjechali i przetestowali moją rakietę, zanim wyślę w niej w Kosmos mojego kuzyna.

Kuzyn pana Nkoloso to młody chłopak, John Chikoti, jeden z dwunastu kosmicznych studentów, którzy aktualnie przechodzą intensywne ćwiczenia.

– Uczę ich astrofizyki, aerodynamiki, kosmologii i astrologii – mówi dyrektor, zasiadając za biurkiem Akademii. Na jego pelerynie przypięty jest mały aluminiowy znaczek w kształcie rakiety. Za jego plecami wisi kalendarz z hasłem »Kosmos pomaga ludzkości« wydany przez American Information Service. Na ścianie wiszą również wycinki z gazet, a obok stoi szafka wypełniona książkami o różnej tematyce, niezbędnymi w pracy badawczej: *1936 Rocznik Rolniczy*, *Kreskówki ze stempla*, *Historia kolei żelaznej na południu*.

Bukiet ziół w butelce i egzemplarz manifestu Akademii zdobią biurko dyrektora. »Załoga Czarnych Synów Niebios – głosi manifest – wykona plany Akademii i wyśle człowieka na Księżyc w przyszłym roku«.

Zdaje się jednak, że Akademii brakuje wyposażenia technicznego. Gdzie na przykład jest rakieta?

– Otóż to – mówi pan Nkoloso i wyjaśnia, że w związku z bezkompromisowym podejściem Rady Miasta do kwestii zbiorników wodnych baza rakietowa operacji »Cyklop« została przeniesiona około sześciu mil dalej, do tajnego ośrodka w dolinie Chungi.

Dyrektor generalny twierdzi, że udało się już zbudować kapsułę wysokości sześciu stóp i kuzyn Chikoti z powodzeniem się w niej mieści.

– Huśtaliśmy go dokoła w tej kapsule – opowiada Nkoloso – a on krzyczał: »Wujku, czy ja zginę?«. Ale zapewniłem go, że nie ma się czego bać. Powiedziałem mu, żeby miał wiarę w swego wuja, bo jesteśmy z jednej krwi. I zwyciężymy!

I kuzyn Chikoti przeżył.

– Moi uczniowie ślubowali śmierć – wyjaśnia pan Nkoloso i odwołuje się do manifestu Akademii, w którym jest napisane: »Wyrzekną się pragnienia, by pozostać na Ziemi, i złożą przysięgę przed Mukuką Nkoloso, i po wsze czasy wyprą się przynależności do tej planety«. Czynię ich nieśmiertelnymi. Sprawiam, że wspinają się na wzgórza, skaczą i biegają wiele mil. Jeżdżę za nimi w ambulansie Akademii i zbieram tych, którzy zemdleją. Huśtam ich też na linach, które w odpowiednim momencie przecinam. To trening grawitacyjny.

Wspinają się także na zbiorniki wodne. Ten rygorystyczny trening nie spodobał się jednak matkom niektórych młodszych studentów. To właśnie między innymi dlatego dyrektor woli, by uczniami Akademii byli członkowie jego rodziny.

Oprócz prośby wystosowanej do Rady Miasta, dotyczącej usunięcia zbiorników wody, pan Nkoloso zwrócił się również o pomoc do UNESCO.

– Szacuję, że potrzebujemy jakieś siedem i pół miliona funtów brytyjskich.

Dużym kłopotem technicznym jest napęd. Odbyło się już próbne odpalenie kapsuły Cyklop I przy użyciu afrykańskiego systemu napędowego (systemu Mukwa opracowanego na podstawie procy). Statek wzniósł się na wysokość około dziesięciu stóp.

– Teraz prowadzę badania nad nowymi możliwościami – wyjaśnia pan Nkoloso. – Interesuje mnie zwłaszcza teoria Diokletesa. Był on starożytnym Grekiem, który poleciał w kierunku Słońca*.

Samotny orzeł krążył wysoko ponad Akademią Nauki.

– Widzisz? – krzyknął Nkoloso. – Bardzo dokładnie studiuję lot ptaków i ryb, tak, ryb również.

Dyrektor generalny wygląda teraz na rozmarzonego.

– Ludzie twierdzą, że jestem szalony. Ale zobaczą. Jeśli człowiek może dostrzec gwiazdy swoimi oczami, to na pewno może też do nich dotrzeć. Pragnę stąd uciec. Zbyt wiele pokoleń umarło już na tej ziemi. Ja chcę spocząć tam – powiedział, ponownie celując włócznią w Księżyc".

* Panu Nkoloso chodziło zapewne o Dedala, ojca Ikara. Lub o Dioklesa, starożytnego matematyka, ten jednak nigdy nie poleciał w stronę Słońca.

20

Pewnego dnia przychodzę do Mukuki Nkoloso pokazać mu wszystkie materiały, jakie znalazłem o jego ojcu przez ostatnie miesiące. Siadamy na plastikowych krzesłach, chwilę rozmawiamy, potem wyciągam laptopa i stawiam przed nami. On woła swoje liczne dzieci, które siadają dokoła nas. Jedynie żona nie chce dołączyć, obserwuje mnie zawsze nieufnym wzrokiem, w którym wydaje mi się, że dostrzegam nutę pogardy. Kosmiczne przygody jej męża najwidoczniej nie robią na niej większego wrażenia. Puszczam film archiwalny ITN. Syn Mukuki Nkoloso mruży oczy i przysuwa komputer bliżej siebie. Długim palcem wodzi po ekranie. Przez chwilę zdaje mi się, że nie rozpoznaje tych obrazów. A na pewno widzi je po raz pierwszy. Puszczam raz jeszcze. I jeszcze.

– Tak, to mój ojciec – mówi w końcu, tak jakby nie był pewny. – A to chyba Godfrey Mwango w tej rakiecie! – Po chwili napływają kolejne obrazy. – To wszystko tam w dolinie Chungi, w ukrytym miejscu, na farmie nieopodal miejskiego wysypiska śmieci. To tam ćwiczyliśmy. Tam mieliśmy rzeczkę Chunga i takie wzgórze, obok stadionu, na którym prowadzili ćwiczenia z beczkami. Dolina była zaciszna, było słychać śpiewające ptaki, nikt nie przeszkadzał. Dlatego wybrał to miejsce. Tata opowiadał o Kosmosie, o planetach. Czasami polecał różne książki, w których można było czytać o gwiazdach. Mówił o pieniądzach, o imperializmie, kapitalizmie. Bo imperialiści wierzyli tylko w pieniądz. Opowiadał o tym marksizmie. Wiesz, Karol Marks. Mówił także o Sokratesie i innych filozofach. Pieniądze są ważne, materializm jest częścią życia, ale jest też człowiek, który musi być ważniejszy, tak mówił. Poza tym ktoś musiał to wszystko stworzyć. Bóg stworzył ziemię i niebo. I ptaki, ryby, oceany, więc Bóg jest wielki. A my? My zostaliśmy stworzeni na jego obraz. Zatem musimy wykorzystywać zdolności, które nam dał. A dał ręce, stopy, oczy, nawet jak ma się jedno, tak jak jego pies, to i tak trzeba go używać.

Czarno-biały, kilkuminutowy film ITN leci zapętlony na laptopie. To ciekawe zderzenie. Obcy człowiek z innego kontynentu odtwarza starszemu Afrykaninowi na ekranie kawałek jego młodości, o której przecież nie może mieć zielonego pojęcia. Dla Afrykanina to konfrontacja tego, co zapamiętane, choć pewnie zniekształcone, ale za to bogate w emocje, z suchym dokumentalnym obrazem. Być może właśnie burzę mu jakieś wyobrażenia? Nie, chyba jednak nie. On zerka na ekran od czasu do czasu i wtedy wysypują się kolejne słowa.

– W Akademii zajęcia odbywały się codziennie. Uczyliśmy się o niebie, planetach, gwiazdach i o Księżycu. Ojcu zależało, by wszyscy dobrze zrozumieli. Nie żeby oblali, tylko żeby się nauczyli. Nie było innych nauczycieli, uczył nas wyłącznie ojciec. Do tego codziennie biegi z przeszkodami, ćwiczenia, przysiady. Nazywali nas zambijskimi afronautami. Wybrano chłopaków i kobiety, wśród nich Marthę Mwambę. Dwunastu kadetów jak dwunastu apostołów w Biblii. Wchodziliśmy na wzgórze, wskakiwaliśmy do wielkiego bębna i puszczali nas z górki. Egzaminował nas mój ojciec, czasami był jeszcze lekarz, jego znajomy. „I jak się czujesz?" „W porządku!" „To dobrze, zdałeś!" Ale jeśli okazało się, że nie jesteś wystarczająco wysportowany, to nie mogłeś brać udziału w dalszych ćwiczeniach. Trzeba było sturlać się z tej góry dwadzieścia razy! Zresztą najpierw do tego bębna włożyli kota, żeby zobaczyć, czy da radę. Koty radziły sobie najlepiej, najgorzej szło kurom. Jak się okazało, że kot przeżył, to wsadzili

Marthę. Dobrze! Potem Godfreya. Też dobrze! Potem Rubena. Też zdał! Potem Mathews Mambwego. Też dobrze! Spróbować mógł każdy, nawet dzieciaki ze szkoły. Ale niektórzy się bali, inni nie dawali rady.

Potem pokazuję mu kilkadziesiąt stron przyszłej książki. Ciąg liter przelatujący na ekranie robi na nim spore wrażenie, zwłaszcza gdy gdzieniegdzie widzi imię i nazwisko swojego ojca.

– Mieliśmy specjalne mundury i inne rzeczy – śmieje się Nkoloso. – Wyglądaliśmy trochę jak Niemcy na wojnie. Jak kierowcy czołgów albo piloci. Mieliśmy nawet hełmy, dla ochrony. To wszystko jest w archiwach, nie wiem, dlaczego ci nie pokazali. Te zajęcia były codziennie. Czasami mieliśmy także zajęcia nocne. No i w nocy, gdy ludzie już spali, o północy, tak do drugiej rano. No i oczywiście to wszystko była tajemnica. Tata nie chciał, żeby ktokolwiek wiedział, tylko astronauci byli wtajemniczeni. Niektórzy nocowali w Akademii, zostawali na cały tydzień i wracali do domu dopiero na weekend. A potem w niedzielę, po kościele, przyjeżdżali z powrotem do Akademii. *Full time!* A jeśli ktoś opuszczał zajęcia, to dyrektor go zawieszał, no bo program gonił, inni już byli w przodzie. On nauczał, robił egzaminy. Byliśmy podzieleni na grupy. A, B, C i D. Jak ktoś odstawał, to lądował w grupie D. Częścią tego wszystkiego było też uczestnictwo w zamieszkach! Robiliśmy bomby, niszczyliśmy mosty, budowaliśmy barykady na ulicach, atakowaliśmy sklepy i biura administracji Welensky'ego. Kradliśmy jedzenie z magazynów. Albo je wymuszaliśmy. Czasami nawet w maskach. Jak ktoś nie chciał dać, no to *one, two, three* i miał wybite szyby. Mąkę, olej, podstawowe rzeczy, rozdawaliśmy rodzinom. Bo to była także akademia ruchu oporu. Matka płakała, jak ojciec mnie wziął do tej swojej Akademii, nie podobało jej się to.

21

Cuthbert Kolala dziś znów niezwykle elegancki, wytworny. Połowa października, najgorętszy miesiąc roku, a on w pełnym galowym rynsztunku – z garniturem, koszulą i wełnianym swetrem. Słońce świeci pod kątem dziewięćdziesięciu stopni. Wypala dziurę w głowie, topi asfalt, rozgrzewa do czerwoności brunatną ziemię, jakby chciało spalić to miasto, przez które znów toczymy się starym fordem. Dobrze, że to nasze auto jest chociaż białe. Dziś ford jakoś wyjątkowo głośny i kapryśny, śmiejemy się, że ten stary rupieć to właśnie rakieta Edwarda Mukuki Nkoloso, której na próżno szukam w muzeach i archiwach. Po zachowaniu Kolali wyczuwam, że ta niedziela nie będzie zwykłym dniem. Zatrzymujemy się przy jakimś budynku, on wybiega, z kimś rozmawia, coś załatwia, po chwili wsiada znów do auta i uradowany wręcza mi kopertę.

– Otwórz, zobacz, pójdziesz dzisiaj ze mną.

Wyciągam z koperty kartonik z orzełkiem na froncie i pozłacanym brzegiem dokoła. Zaproszenie. Zaprasza Jego Ekscelencja Edgar Chagwa Lungu, Prezydent Republiki Zambii, wraz z Pierwszą Damą Esther Lungu. Na Narodowy Dzień Żalu za Grzechy, Postu i Modlitwy. Pan Prezydent informuje mnie też uprzejmie, że uroczystość odbędzie się na stadionie dziś o godzinie czternastej i że obowiązuje „strój narodowy, garnitur lub mundur". Zaznacza, że rankiem przed uroczystością zachęca się uczestników do wzięcia udziału w mszy świętej w stosownym dla swojego wyznania kościele. Na dole zaproszenia znajduję jeszcze ciekawe hasło: „Budujemy fundamenty silnej Zambii, odnajdując Przebaczenie, Skruchę, Współczucie oraz Miłość w Bogu".

Cuthbert, widząc moje zakłopotanie pomieszane z brakiem zrozumienia, wręcza mi jeszcze broszurę pokaźnego formatu z programem uroczystości, bym mógł się zapoznać i zachwycić. Program ma dziesięć stron. Po raz pierwszy do narodowej modlitwy wzywał Kenneth Kaunda pół wieku temu. Miała ona uratować Zambijczyków przed powołaniem Federacji Afryki Centralnej. Modły najwidoczniej nie zostały wysłuchane. Przez następne dziesięciolecia zambijski naród do modlitwy wzywano wielokrotnie, gdy tylko kraj stawał w obliczu kryzysu politycznego, społecznego lub gospodarczego. Tym razem przyczynkiem do modłów jest bezlitosna, na wskroś materialistyczna, ani trochę nie uduchowiona ekonomia. W ciągu ostatnich miesięcy ceny miedzi, której sprzedaż generuje siedemdziesiąt procent przychodów państwa, lecą na łeb na szyję ze względu na zmniejszone zapotrzebowanie Chin, głównego partnera gospodarczego Zambii. Miedź ciągnie za sobą kwachę, która zamiast świtać w glorii poranka, nurkuje w najciemniejsze otchłanie walutowej impotencji. Od początku roku kwacha straciła w stosunku do dolara czterdzieści pięć procent swojej wartości. Jak na złość, kryzys gospodarczy idzie w parze z kaprysami natury. W Zambii od miesięcy nie spadła kropla deszczu. Zamiast pory deszczowej jest nieznośny, niedający wytchnienia upał. Poziom wody w największym zbiorniku retencyjnym kraju – jeziorze Kariba – zrobił się tak niski, że hydroelektrownia nie jest w stanie produkować wystarczającej ilości prądu. Od kilku tygodni Zambijczycy spędzają wieczory przy świecach lub w hałasie przydomowych, benzynowych generatorów prądu. W wielu miastach prąd wyłączany jest dzielnicami – w dni parzyste jedna część, w nieparzyste druga, a rozpiski dostaw energii wiszą na słupach ogłoszeniowych. Brak prądu to również brak poczucia bezpieczeństwa, bo większość ogrodzeń w bogatszych okolicach wieńczą druty pod napięciem. Przeciągająca się susza i wybryk chińskiej gospodarki odbijają się na kosztach życia. Ceny żywności zaskakują Zambijczyków każdego dnia, gdy idą po zakupy.

O Dniu Modlitwy trąbią od kilku dni gazety. „Daily Mail" pisze: „Po raz kolejny Zambia tworzy historię, gdy jej obywatele zbierają się do wspólnej modlitwy, postu oraz żalu za grzechy i proszą Boga o przewodnictwo na drodze rozwoju". Można także przeczytać, że prezydent Lungu, zwołując Dzień Modlitwy, bierze przykład z najznamienitszych przywódców świata, takich jak George Washington czy Abraham Lincoln. Obok, w ramce, cytat ze Starego Testamentu, Księga Daniela 9:17–19: „Teraz zaś, Boże nasz, wysłuchaj modlitwy Twojego sługi i jego błagań i rozjaśnij swe oblicze nad świątynią, która leży zniszczona – ze względu na Ciebie, Panie! Nakłoń, mój Boże, swego ucha i wysłuchaj! Otwórz swe oczy i zobacz nasze spustoszenie i miasto, nad którym wzywano Twego imienia. Albowiem zanosimy swe modlitwy do Ciebie, opierając się nie na naszej sprawiedliwości, ale ufni w Twoje wielkie miłosierdzie. Usłysz, Panie! Odpuść, Panie! Panie, miej na uwadze i działaj niezwłocznie, przez wzgląd na siebie samego, mój Boże! Bo Twojego imienia wzywano nad Twym miastem i nad Twym narodem"*. Na prośbę prezydenta zostają odwołane wszelkie imprezy, kluby sportowe wstrzymują rozgrywki, właściciele barów i restauracji wywieszają w drzwiach kartki z napisem „zamknięte". Naród idzie stanąć przed obliczem Boga i prosić o łaskę.

Tekst w „Daily Mail" ilustruje zdjęcie prezydenta kibicującego narodowej reprezentacji w meczu z Mozambikiem, który odbył się dzień wcześniej. Zambijczycy właśnie strzelili trzecią bramkę. Lungu w kowbojskim kapeluszu i piłkarskim szaliku w barwach zambijskiej flagi klaszcze w dłonie.

(Gdy chodzę ulicami miast, niezależnie, czy to Lusaka, Livingstone, czy zabite dechami Chirundu na granicy z Zimbabwe, ludzie wołają za mną, machają do mnie rękoma. W autobusach,

* Cytaty z Pisma Świętego za Biblią Tysiąclecia.

na przystankach, na targowiskach podchodzą do mnie, robią sobie ze mną zdjęcia telefonami komórkowymi. Z początku myślę, że to ze względu na mój wzrost, że to po prostu oznaka zaciekawienia, sympatii, jak w każdym innym afrykańskim czy azjatyckim kraju. Powód tak żywego zainteresowania moją osobą wyjaśnia mi dopiero pewien człowiek, którego spotykam pod wiaduktem w centrum Lusaki. Niesie kolorową piłkę dla swojego siedmioletniego syna. Mówi, że to dlatego, że wyglądam jak pewien Francuz, były trener narodowej reprezentacji, z którym Chipolopolo* zdobyli w 2012 roku Puchar Narodów Afryki. Kupuję od niego tę piłkę i proszę, by powiedział synowi, że to prezent ode mnie. Że dziś pod wiaduktem przy Church Road jego ojciec spotkał Hervé Renarda).

Modlitwa i futbol są fundamentem tego kraju.

Z zaproszeniem w ręku studiuję program Dnia Modlitwy, podczas gdy nasz ford mozolnie przedziera się przez zatłoczoną Chachacha Road, torując sobie drogę przez setki ludzi, dziesiątki małych busów i góry śmieci. Town Center Market, targowisko i dworzec autobusowy w jednym, to jądro ciasności tego miasta. Zagęszczenie ludzi, tych biegających, krzyczących zza swoich małych straganów, gestykulujących, tych siedzących na chodnikach, tych śpiących na ulicy, osiąga tu kulminację. Nasycenie smrodu spoconych ciał, suszonych, miniaturowych rybek kapenta i spalin dziesiątków wiekowych silników diesla, potęgowanych rozgrzanym, blaszanym zadaszeniem, wierci nozdrza, dusi, przyprawia o zawroty głowy. Miasto osiąga tu nieprawdopodobną wręcz konsystencję. Town Center Market jest niczym czarna dziura, Lusaka zapada się tutaj sama w sobie i osiąga masę absolutną. Ludzie, auta, towary i zapachy mieszają się w jedną, zwartą, pulsującą substancję, rozciągliwą gumę, bezkształtną plazmę. Ciało doskonale czarne. Co chwilę z tej tętniącej masy, w dźwięku klaksonów i krzyków,

* Nazwa reprezentacji narodowej Zambii. Chipolopolo znaczy miedziany pocisk. To nazwa obowiązująca od niedawna. Za czasów rządów Kaundy reprezentację nazywano KK 11.

wydostaje się jakiś bus, mniejszy lub większy, wypełniony po brzegi ciałami, który pojedzie w kierunku Chilenje, Mutendere czy Chelston. Te nazwy, powtarzane uporczywie przez stojących w progu autobusowych drzwi naganiaczy, rezonują w mojej głowie niczym uderzenia młota. Zawiesistość, gęstość tego miejsca obezwładnia, wysysa energię. Za każdym razem opuszczam to miejsce zmęczony, mokry od potu, wciśnięty między kilkunastu innych pasażerów płacących kilka monet zmotoryzowanemu Charonowi, by przewiózł ich z tego piekła w stronę spokojnych przedmieść.

Ktoś puka w karoserię naszego auta, stojącego teraz w korku bardziej między ludźmi niż autami. Za szybą widzę okrągłą czarną twarz z przekrwionymi oczami, poruszające się szybko grube usta i rękę skierowaną ku niebu. Nie ustępuje, macha, coś pokazuje, jakby ogarnięty euforią lub szaleństwem. Otwieram z trudem szybę, do auta wlatuje podmuch żaru i ulicznego smrodu. Teraz widzę, że on nie jest jedyny. Całe Town Center Market patrzy w niebo. Niektórzy z niedowierzaniem, inni z radością, jeszcze inni z przerażeniem. Ludzie wychodzą spod blaszanych wiat dworca, oniemiali wysiadają z busów i taksówek.

Bo nad Lusaką dziś zdarzył się cud. Dziś, w dniu, w którym cały naród będzie się modlił o upragniony wzrost gospodarczy, Bóg dał znak i zesłał nad to ciemne miasto światłość. Jest samo południe, słońce w zenicie, a wokół niego niebotycznych rozmiarów tęcza. Nie zwykła, nieśmiała, półkolista, nietrwała, ginąca po krótkiej chwili w krajobrazie. Ta jest ogromna, wyraźna i okrągła, jakby była odrysowana bożym cyrklem. Wypełnia pół nieba, rozświetla obłoki i przez ponad godzinę otacza słońce kolorowym welonem. To boska aureola jak ta otaczająca głowy świętych. Nimb łaski, blask nadziei. Lusaka w glorii.

„Bóg jest Bogiem cudów i jeśli Go poprosimy, to On nas pobłogosławi i kwacha odzyska swoją dawną siłę, a ceny dóbr znów spadną" – powie następnego dnia w wywiadzie dla Agence France Presse biskup Simon Chihana, przewodniczący International Fellowship of Christian Churches w Zambii.

Tereny Showgrounds przy Great East Road wypełnione są po brzegi. Showgrounds to taki trochę stadion, trochę park, miejsce, w którym organizuje się miejskie imprezy, zawody sportowe, koncerty. Albo modlitwy. Zielono-czerwono-żółty tłum ludzi ściąga z najdalszych dzielnic, mimo uporczywego upału. Jestem gościem uprzywilejowanym. Jako zagraniczny dziennikarz piszący o Zambii oraz przyjaciel obwieszonego orderami Cuthberta Kolali siedzę w loży dla VIP-ów nieopodal głównej mównicy przystrojonej godłem kraju. Wokół mnie w większości starsi ludzie, wielu z nich z odznakami, w mundurach, garniturach. Dalej dostojnicy kościelni różnych wyznań, jedni w białych, inni w czarnych, jeszcze inni w purpurowych szatach. Bo narodowa modlitwa jest modlitwą religijnie synkretyczną, chrześcijańsko-judaistyczną. Za duchownymi rzędy zajmowane przez generalicję wojskową oraz rząd i *entourage* prezydenta Lungu. Na razie czekają puste. Najważniejszym przywilejem loży vipowskiej, oprócz miejsca siedzącego, jest zadaszenie. Z ratującego życie cienia patrzę ze współczuciem na tysiące ludzi – mężczyzn, kobiet, dzieci i starców – którzy stoją na płycie boiska jak na skwierczącej patelni. Z tłumu czarnych głów tu i ówdzie wystają transparenty z napisem *„Let Us Pray!"* lub *„Jesus is Alive!"*. Gdzieniegdzie też proporce, szaliki, tablice z nazwami odległych prowincji, z których przybyli. Niektórzy musieli jechać cały dzień lub dwa dni. Atmosfera zupełnie jak na koncercie jakiejś gwiazdy pokroju Rolling Stonesów albo U2. Koloru dodają liczne zielone, zambijskie flagi. Ku mojemu zaskoczeniu wśród tłumu dostrzegam również dużą flagę Izraela.

Nastrój oczekiwania, nadziei i ogólnej, bardzo wyraźnej radości. Czekamy na przyjazd głównych gości. Zerkam na program. Najpierw pojawią się członkowie korpusu dyplomatycznego, potem liderzy partii politycznych, wiceministrowie. Po nich na stadion przybędą członkowie rządu wraz z władzami miasta stołecznego, następnie przewodniczący Zgromadzenia Narodowego. Na końcu podjadą limuzyny z byłymi prezydentami Kennethem Kaundą i Rupiahem Bandą. Jako ostatni zaszczyci nas obecnością Edgar Chagwa Lungu wraz z Pierwszą Damą. By zająć dobre miejsca, niektórzy przyszli na stadion już rano. Stoją wytrwale od wielu godzin, niektórzy mdleją, inni ratują się rozdawaną wodą w butelkach. Będą tak stać do wieczora. Ciężar narodowej winy najwyraźniej jest sporych rozmiarów, a zaplanowana pokuta musi być wymierna. Modlitwa będzie bowiem trwać sześć godzin.

Znów zerkam na rozpiskę, by nie dać się zanadto zaskoczyć rozwojowi wydarzeń. A więc najpierw wysłuchamy modlitwy otwarcia oraz zaśpiewamy hymn państwowy w wykonaniu Chóru Świętego Ignacego. Potem przywitanie, kilka przemówień i wstęp do głównej modlitwy. Następnie posłuchamy kilku czytań z wybranych fragmentów Biblii. Będzie Święty Mateusz dla wielbicieli Nowego Testamentu i Święty Jonasz dla zwolenników Starego. Dalej wyznanie wiary w trzech odmianach w wykonaniu trzech duchownych różnych Kościołów. Na koniec homilia. To tytułem wstępu.

Lecz najpierw koncert. Dzień Modlitwy to nie jest przepełniona smutkiem stypa. Tu nikt nie będzie się zamartwiał czy udręczał. Nie będzie przeciągliwych dźwięków kościelnych organów. Nie będzie frasobliwych chórów i boleściwych hymnów. Będzie za to muzyka. Gitary, perkusja, bębny. Będą tańce. Będą okrzyki, spazmy radości i religijnej ekstazy.

Scena wypełnia się muzykami, instrumentami. Na estradę wchodzą też zwykli ludzie, każdy, kto ma ochotę. Nawet Cuthbert Kolala podryguje do afrykańskich rytmów, potrząsając swoimi medalami. Pod sceną, z której płyną gorliwe muzyczne dziękczynienia w kierunku Boga i Jezusa, tańczy osobliwa para: obszerna czarna kobieta w kolorowych afrykańskich chustach, zapewne matka kilkanaściorga dzieci, oraz muzułmanin w powłóczystej dżalabii i czerwonej kefii na głowie.

– Czy nie jesteście dumni, że urodziliście się w Zambii? Czy nie cieszycie się, że jesteście Zambijczykami? BBC traci właśnie wspaniały materiał! CNN powinna tu być! Al-Dżazira powinna tu być! – wykrzykuje biskup otwierający uroczystość.

– Alleluja! – odpowiada tłum, witając pierwszego wykonawcę.

– To nie jest zebranie polityczne! – zaczyna inny z biskupów, gdy cichną dźwięki instrumentów i głosy artystów. – To nie jest zebranie żadnej partii politycznej! To jest zebranie eklezjastyczne! Ale to na wezwanie prezydenta Lungu niewierni nawrócili się i stali się wierzący! Jesteśmy bezgranicznie wdzięczni Bogu, albowiem teraz szatan, nasz wróg, zostanie pokonany! Zostanie wyrzucony raz na zawsze z Zambii! – mówi kategorycznym głosem.

– Tak! – odpowiadają tysiące zgromadzonych.

– Szatan nie należy do Zambii!

– Nie!

– Szatan nie jest obywatelem tego kraju!

– Nie! Nie! Nie!

– Szatan nie ma dowodu osobistego Zambii!

– Nie! Nie! Nie!

– Szatan nie ma adresu w Zambii!

– Nie!

– I przez autorytet, który został mi dany wolą Boga, jako biskup przysięgam wam, że zanim skończymy dziś nasze spotkanie, szatan zostanie wygnany do najdalszych głębin piekła! Tam skąd przyszedł! A my nie zawahamy się nazwać go po imieniu! *Enough is enough!*

– Alleluja!

– Módlmy się! Nasze spotkanie dziś albo nas umocni, albo złamie. Ale jestem święcie przekonany, że od tej chwili Zambię czekają lepsze czasy!

– Amen!

– Gdy jutro rano wstaniemy, będziemy śpiewać i tańczyć! Radość Boga będzie naszą siłą! Nasz Niebiański Ojciec, nasz kochający Bóg, Jahwe, który panuje nad wszystkim. Niewzruszony Wzruszyciel! Bóg, który jest żywym Bogiem w świecie umarłych. W imieniu tych wszystkich, którzy tu przyszli, w imieniu tego prezydenta i jego całego gabinetu szukamy Jego oblicza! Publicznie, bez wstydu. Otwarcie, nie ukrywając się. Deklarujemy naszą wiarę, że to Ty jesteś naszym Bogiem i w Tobie pokładamy naszą nadzieję! Ci, który wierzą w złotego cielca, niech w niego wierzą. Ale my dziś dokonujemy wyboru, niczym Jozue. Cała Zambia za pośrednictwem swojego prezydenta wstaje i dumnie deklaruje, że będzie służyć Bogu! I będzie mu służyć dobrze! Boże, modlimy się do Ciebie w wierze, że gdy stoimy tu przed Tobą, Ty słuchasz naszych modłów. W imię tego, co uczynił Twój syn, Jezus Chrystus, który stał się człowiekiem i został ukrzyżowany, i umarł za zbawienie Zambii i każdego, kto żyje w Zambii i w Ciebie wierzy!

Ktoś puka mnie w ramię. W rzędzie za mną siedzi ekipa dziennikarzy z miejscowej radiostacji. Pytają, czy jako obcokrajowiec mógłbym udzielić wywiadu, proszą, bym porównał wiarę w Zambii z tą w Polsce. Jestem w kropce, brodzę w płytkich, dyplomatycznych zdaniach. Wierzyć znaczy tu coś zupełnie innego niż w Europie. Coś, czego ja nie pojmuję. Coś, co wydaje nam się śmieszne, godne pożałowania, wstydliwe i zupełnie niewspółczesne. I bardzo łatwe do dyskredytowania. Staram się nie oceniać, ale jest to trudne. Nie wiem, czym jest afrykańska religijność. Nie rozumiem jej, choć mnie fascynuje. Siedzę wśród ludzi, którzy są przekonani o tym, że Bóg jest obecny. Każdego dnia. Można go o coś poprosić, można z nim rozmawiać jak z członkiem rodziny, jak z najlepszym przyjacielem. A on może wysłuchać i – jeśli zechce – zmienić rzeczywistość. Nikt z tych tysięcy ludzi nie ma co do tego najmniejszych wątpliwości. Najmniejszych. Jeśli wiara przenosi góry, to ta zgromadzona tutaj mogłaby ruszyć całe kontynenty. Siedząc na trybunach, odnoszę wrażenie, że to jest ten sam rodzaj wiary, który prezentował Edward Mukuka Nkoloso. Tak, polecimy na Księżyc, nawet na Marsa. Nadal tam lecimy.

Jednocześnie w jakiś sposób im zazdroszczę. Może to dlatego też tak fascynuje mnie historia absurdalnego lotu na Księżyc. To musi być piękne żyć w takim przeświadczeniu. Rozglądając się dokoła, nie widzę przed sobą ludzi smutnych, zmartwionych czy pogrążonych w zadumie.

Jakiś czas później rozmawiam o tym z doktorem Walimą Kalusą z University of Zambia.

– Wielu Zambijczyków – komentuje – zwłaszcza tych skrajnie biednych, wierzy, że ekonomiczne zbawienie nie zależy od polityków w parlamencie, lecz od łaski samego Boga. Dlatego ludzie dosłownie proszą Boga o rozwiązanie ich problemów ekonomicznych. Proszą o bardzo konkretne, przyziemne rzeczy. Wielu wierzy, że jedyną siłą sprawczą, która może rozwiązać ich problemy, jest wyłącznie Bóg. Bóg jest jedyną odpowiedzią. Przed nadejściem chrześcijaństwa ludzie modlili się do duchów i przodków w bardzo bezpośredni sposób zawsze, gdy potrzebowali ich pomocy. Szedłeś polować, to modliłeś się do duchów o udane polowanie. To przekonanie przetrwało w afrykańskim chrześcijaństwie. Dziś zamiast prosić przodków, prosisz Boga. Bo te idee nie umarły, zostały wciągnięte do chrześcijaństwa, dlatego modlitwy Zambijczyków potrafią być tak bezpośrednie. Te wszystkie hasła, które widzisz na ulicach, na autach, to afrykański sposób wyrażania wiary. Chrześcijaństwo to już religia afrykańska, połączyło się z naszą kulturą! Chrześcijaństwo zostało przyniesione i narzucone przez Europejczyków, ale Afrykanie je przeformułowali. Przekomponowali tak, by pasowało do afrykańskich wierzeń, tradycji i mitów. To już nie jest obca religia. Zreinterpretowaliśmy ją tak, by była nasza. I nie jest już chrześcijaństwem europejskim. Gdy Europejczycy przynieśli chrześcijaństwo, myśleli, że Afrykanie przyjmą je na europejskich warunkach, że będą je rozumieć w ten sam sposób jak europejscy misjonarze. Ale tak się nie stało. Gdy chrześcijaństwo znalazło się w afrykańskim kontekście, uległo głębokim zmianom. By dać prosty przykład: misjonarze myśleli, że gdy Afrykanie przyjmą chrześcijaństwo, to rozstaną się ze swoimi tradycyjnymi wierzeniami i czarami. Bo przecież czary to bzdury, zabobony, niesłuszna wiara. Ale tak się nie stało. Ludzie nadal wierzą w czary, nawet ci bardzo oddani chrześcijanie. Co więcej, ludzie używają chrześcijaństwa przeciw złym czarom! Pójdź do zielonoświątkowców, zobaczysz. Wiara w czary istnieje nadal, a chrześcijaństwo stało się dodatkowym narzędziem, by walczyć z czarami. Afrykanie używają chrześcijaństwa w sposób, który Europejczykom nawet by nie przyszedł do głowy. A to dlatego, że chrześcijaństwo jest rozumiane przez Afrykanów w sposób, który tworzy dla nich kulturową logikę zupełnie niezrozumiałą dla Europejczyków.

– Oczywiście wstąpiłeś do nieba – przemawia tymczasem dalej biskup na stadionie – a teraz siedzisz po prawicy Ojca naszego, Boga Ojca. Prosimy Cię, Boże, bądź łaskaw nachylić swe ucho i wysłuchaj nas! A gdy słuchasz teraz naszych modlitw, my, wierni słudzy, oferujemy Ci nasze dusze! I gdy będziemy Ci służyć, ucz nas, że Zambia zawsze powinna być na pierwszym miejscu. Nie nasze kieszenie! Zambia! Nie nasze domy! Nie nasze auta! Nie nasze rzeczy! Ucz nas, byśmy nigdy nie zapomnieli, że na pierwszym miejscu zawsze powinna być Zambia! Pamiętaj o swoim prawdziwym i niepodzielnym Kościele w Zambii. Naznaczonym Twoją krwią. Krwią, która służy, krwią, która oczyszcza, krwią, która chroni, krwią, która jest dobrym świadectwem. Umacniaj Zambię i jej przywódców, powiększaj ją i utrzymuj w pokoju. Uchroń ją od złych duchów, niech nasza modlitwa sprawi, że bramy piekieł zostaną zamknięte. Że nigdy nie zapanują nad naszym narodem, nad naszym rządem, nad naszym prezydentem, nad naszymi wodzami!

Modlitw będzie pięćdziesiąt. W pięciu godzinnych blokach po dziesięć. Każdy zestaw modłów zakończą wspólne wyznanie wiary i krótka przerwa. Naród modlić się będzie pod przewodnictwem biskupów, pastorów, wielebnych różnych Kościołów, ale również wodzów i plemiennych królów. Każdy z nich poprowadzi jedną modlitwę w zadanej intencji. Pomodlimy się zatem za łaskę i bożą uwagę. Za powodzenie dzisiejszej ceremonii uświęconej krwią Jezusa oraz o to, by Bóg usunął wszelkie przeszkody, które mogą stanąć nam dziś na drodze. Wzniesiemy modły za to, by narodowa modlitwa została wysłuchana i by wrogowie przebaczenia, miłości i skruchy w tym nie przeszkodzili. Wyznamy grzechy i odprawimy pokutę za występne miłowanie ołtarzy Zła.

Będziemy prosić Boga, by wzmocnił jedność narodu i pomógł utrzymać dobre relacje między zambijskimi plemionami. Pomodlimy się także za kobiety i dzieci oraz za młodzież, by nie schodziła na nieprawą drogę, trzymała się z dala od nałogów i niecnych pokus. I za miłość, by panowała w naszych rodzinach. Wyrzekniemy się domowej przemocy i potępimy wszelkie konszachty ze Złym.

– Jesteśmy tu dziś, by się modlić! Za grzechy naszych ojców. Albowiem zbudowali ołtarze, ołtarze grzechu! Modlili się, lecz nie do Boga! A dziś to pokolenie, które nie chce dźwigać winy ojców, woła: nie! My się modlimy! – wykrzykuje duchowny. – By każdy ołtarz grzechu został obrócony w pył! W imię Chrystusa! Bo po to tu przyszliśmy. By odwrócić się od naszych grzechów. Bo jeśli wszyscy jesteśmy grzesznikami, to ten dzień jest dla nas ważny. Przyszliśmy tu stanąć przed Jego obliczem i modlić się, i odwrócić od grzechu! A nadejdzie zbawienie! Nastanie nowy kraj, nowa Zambia!

– Amen!

– Zambia, którą wszyscy będą podziwiać. A gdy odwracamy się od grzechu, to następuje czas skruchy. Skrucha to powiedzieć: „Panie, zgrzeszyłem, proszę, wybacz mi!". A Bóg odpowie: „Podejdź do Mnie, ukoję twój ból". Albowiem Bóg jest nowym początkiem! Więc dziś zwrócimy się do Niego, a On nam przebaczy. Nasza ziemia dozna przebaczenia i oczyszczenia. Zambia dostąpi przebaczenia! Jesteśmy tu nie po to, by wywyższyć człowieka. Niech żaden człowiek nie przypisuje sobie chwały. Tylko Bogu należy się tu chwała! Nawet prezydentowi się ona nie należy, tylko Bogu! Tylko Bóg, tylko Jahwe zasługuje na wywyższenie! On wyznacza nowy kierunek temu krajowi. Bo nadchodzi skrucha, będzie przebaczenie i oczyszczenie. Ci, którzy postępowali niecnie, muszą się zmienić. Urzędnicy, którzy byli nieuczciwi, muszą się zmienić! Po tej modlitwie nie możesz pozostać nieuczciwy, musisz się zmienić!

– Tak! Tak! Tak! – Na słowa o nieuczciwych urzędnikach na stadionie wybucha euforia.

– Ktoś mnie spytał, co będzie po osiemnastym października. Odpowiedziałem: „Chwała". Będziemy świętować dzieło Boże. Ci, którzy w to wątpią, niech wątpią. To sprawy duchowe, oni tego nie rozumieją. Jahwe wznosi ten kraj na wyższy poziom. Niech Bóg błogosławi Zambię! Niech Bóg zamieszka w Zambii!

– Amen!

– Mój Boże, mój Boże! Gdybyśmy żyli w czasach biblijnych, jestem pewny, że ten dzień zostałby odnotowany na stronicach Biblii! Gdyby to były te czasy, Zambia z pewnością znalazłaby się w Biblii! Ale może tego po prostu nie zauważyliśmy, muszę sięgnąć do mojej Biblii, sądzę, że Zambia jest już w Piśmie Świętym! O Boże, nigdy nie byłem tak dumny z tego, że jestem Zambijczykiem! O Boże, gdy kiedyś wyjadę za granicę, będę z dumą mówił moim zambijskim akcentem! I będę nim mówił również, gdy wrócę. Nie powiem: *„Hey man, yo, what's up, how ya doin"*. Wrócę i powiem: „Alleluja!".

W końcu wzniesiemy modły za polityczną jedność narodu i jego duchową odnowę. Poprosimy Boga, by otoczył Zambię troską i opieką, taką, na jaką zasługują szczególne, wybrane narody.

– Ojcze, błogosław Izrael! Błogosław Jeruzalem! Ziemię Boga żywego! – przemawia Jego Wysokość Wódz Chipepo. – Dziękujemy Ci, Boże, że pozwoliłeś zesłać naszego ambasadora do Izraela. Drzwi się otworzyły, łaska płynie, ponieważ w końcu połączyliśmy się z Izraelem, pierworodnym synem Boga. Zambia jest jego drugim synem! Alleluja, Zambia! Dziś wszyscy zmieniliśmy imię. Od dziś jesteśmy Bożymi wybrańcami. Nasze nowe imię to Boża Łaska!

– Nasze nowe imię to Boża Łaska!

– A teraz wznieście do nieba prawą dłoń! Wszyscy! Niech każdy Zambijczyk i każdy przybysz tu obecny wzniesie dłoń i wyzna swoje grzechy! Te, które skrywacie przed żonami, mężami i dziećmi. Przyznajcie się! W imię Jezusa Chrystusa! Inaczej nie dostąpicie łaski Bożej! A teraz skierujcie swe ręce w stronę naszego prezydenta! Chwalmy naszego prezydenta! Także jego imię to Boża Łaska. Niech zawsze będzie otoczony tą Łaską, gdy odwiedza nasze wioski, gdy wyjeżdża za granicę, gdy spotyka się z innymi przywódcami, gdy pojedzie do Anglii, by spotkać się z królową. Teraz zapanował niebiański porządek. Bo Bóg jest tutaj z nami. Jezus Chrystus jest z nami. Duch Święty jest z nami! Wszyscy tu są, tu w Zambii! Niebiosa się otworzyły. A my od teraz cieszmy się niebem na ziemi! Albowiem Bóg wie, jak pięknym i bogatym krajem jest Zambia. Zawsze gdy królowie Izraela byli skorumpowani i źli, Izrael upadał. Zawsze gdy królowie postępowali zgodnie z Bożą wolą, Izrael rozkwitał. W imieniu całego narodu, w imieniu wodzów plemion chcemy Cię, Boże, prosić, byś zstąpił do naszych wiosek, albowiem one należą do Ciebie. Każde nasze królestwo należy do Ciebie! Tak by Zambia była krajem dostatnim. Błogosław wody, słońce i księżyc, które są ponad nami. Odkryj dla nas ukryte surowce naturalne, by twój naród mógł się rozwijać!

– Amen!

Następnie zapewnimy Boga, że w akcie dziękczynienia wzniesiemy w zambijskim narodzie największe boskie ołtarze ku Jego chwale. Ale modlić będziemy się również za rzeczy bardziej przyziemne, wręcz materialne. By górnictwo przynosiło jak największe zyski Skarbowi Państwa, a pora deszczowa przyniosła zbawienne deszcze, które zapewnią rozkwit rolnictwu. I by te deszcze nie zakończyły się powodziami. By gospodarka przezwyciężyła kryzys. By dług narodowy zmalał, a waluta umocniła się w stosunku do dolara. By telewizja, radio, gazety były zawsze świadkami bożej prawdy.

– Słyszę dźwięk obfitości! – zaczyna płomiennie kolejny z biskupów. Na stadionie krzyki, wuwuzele, trąby, gwizdy. – Czy możemy wszyscy unieść ręce i prosić Boga o przebaczenie? Cokolwiek złego uczyniliśmy, prośmy o przebaczenie i niech deszcze w końcu spadną na tę ziemię! Mój Boże i Ojcze, jako naród przychodzimy przed Twe oblicze i prosimy o przebaczenie, odwracamy się od grzechu i modlimy! Przebacz nam i uzdrów tę ziemie! Otwórz niebiosa! Otwórz niebiosa! Otwórz niebiosa! I niech pada deszcz! W imię Jezusa Chrystusa! Albowiem jeśli przyjdziesz w skrusze i modlitwie, On będzie mógł uczynić cuda. Da jesienny i wiosenny deszcz jednocześnie. Prośmy o to! Niech Bóg napełni Karibę! Niech Bóg napełni Zambezi! Niech Bóg napełni Kafue*! Tak by zakręciły się wszystkie turbiny hydroelektrowni i przyniosły ręką Boga ulgę wszystkim tym, którzy cierpią z powodu braku prądu! W imię Chrystusa! Wołajmy: Ojcze!

– Ojcze!

– Boże Abrahama! Izaaka i Jakuba! W imię Jezusa, usłysz nas! Jako naród Zambii! Ześlij nam deszcz! Rozstąp niebiosa! Niech spadnie deszcz! Niech pada! Niech leje! Niech leje! Jeśli jesteście tu ze mną, krzyczcie wniebogłosy, niech Bóg nas usłyszy!

Kolejne godziny modłów, stopionych słońcem w jeden niekończący się ciąg religijnych uniesień na najwyższych amplitudach. Zastanawiam się, jak długo ci ludzie mogliby się modlić. Trzeci blok modlitw rozpoczniemy od wyznania grzechów i skruchy w imieniu całego Kościoła w Zambii. Pomodlimy się za jego jedność i pozytywny wkład w rozwój zambijskiego narodu oraz o to, by głoszone przez niego nauki stały zawsze w zgodzie ze Słowem Bożym. Odmówimy modlitwę przeciw praktykom okultystycznym, a następnie uderzymy się w pierś w żalu za grzechy naszych przodków. Wyrzekniemy się korupcji, złośliwości, nienawiści i zazdrości. Dalej będziemy prosić Boga o zmniejszenie ubóstwa, o redukcję bezrobocia i poprawę warunków pracy tych, którzy ją mają. Pomodlimy się za cały sektor usług, za mniejsze i większe przedsiębiorstwa i ich udane inwestycje oraz za tych, którzy zakończyli życie zawodowe, by żyło im się jak najlepiej na rentach i emeryturach. Będziemy również modlić się za wszystkich wodzów i członków królewskich rodów oraz za pokój i patriotyzm, by trwały jak najdłużej. Na koniec pomodlimy się w intencji prac nad nową konstytucją, za powodzenie debat trwających obecnie w parlamencie i za wynik zbliżającego się referendum.

* Rzeka płynąca przez Demokratyczną Republikę Konga i Zambię.

Żaden z przemawiających nie omieszka wspomnieć o dzisiejszej tęczy jako o cudzie i dowodzie na to, że Bóg otacza Zambię swą opieką. Niestety zmierzch złapie nas gdzieś przy końcu trzeciego zestawu modlitw i za równie wiele rzeczy nie zdążymy się pomodlić. Obszerny program Narodowego Dnia Żalu za Grzechy, Postu i Modlitwy przerósł możliwości czasowe i z zaplanowanych pięciu bloków modlitewnych do zmroku udaje się zrealizować jedynie trzy. Czyli trzydzieści modlitw. Kolejnych dwadzieścia pozostanie jedynie na papierze. Nie pomodlimy się za urzędującego prezydenta i jego małżonkę. Jak i za wszystkich byłych prezydentów i ich małżonki. Nie starczy czasu na modlitwę za przywódców partii politycznych. Bóg nie usłyszy modłów za dobre prawodawstwo i sprawne sądownictwo. Nie pomodlimy się też za wybory parlamentarne w 2016 roku i ich pokojowy przebieg. Ani za liderów biznesu, zarówno tych w firmach prywatnych, jak i państwowych, a także pracowników licznych organizacji non profit i agencji pomocy humanitarnej. Modlitwą nie wesprzemy niestety członków organizacji międzynarodowych obecnych w Zambii ani dyplomatów innych krajów. Bez narodowej modlitwy będzie musiał sobie również poradzić sektor opieki zdrowotnej, zwłaszcza na polu sprawnej dystrybucji leków oraz niełatwej walki z HIV i AIDS. Nie zdążymy też podziękować Bogu za jego szczególną opiekę i za to, że Zambia jest krajem chrześcijańskim.

Nie starczy czasu na modlitwę o dobrobyt przyszłych pokoleń. I o to, by wszystko to, o co się modlimy, zostało przypieczętowane krwią Jezusa. Nie pomodlimy się o to, by Zambia na zawsze pozostała krajem chrześcijańskim, wolnym od złych występków, w szczególności takich jak seksualna niemoralność, aborcja czy morderstwo. Nie poprosimy Boga, by pomógł nam odnaleźć nowe złoża surowców mineralnych i byśmy mogli je wykorzystać dla dobra narodu. Bóg nie będzie miał szansy wysłuchać naszych modłów o zesłanie miłości, tak byśmy mogli nawzajem się szanować i inspirować do boskich działań, zamiast oczerniać i szkalować. Nie zwrócimy się do Wszechmogącego o pomoc w konstruktywnej, a nie destruktywnej debacie społecznej. Nie usłyszy On również próśb, by zesłał mądrość na naszych liderów, zwłaszcza tych odpowiedzialnych za dystrybucję dóbr i bogactw, by czynili to sprawiedliwie. I by żywność była dzielona uczciwie i się nie marnowała. Do boskich uszu nie dotrą również modły o to, by Zambia była wzorem dla całego świata we wszystkich aspektach życia. Zwłaszcza w bogobojności i pobożności.

Słońce zachodzi powoli za wypełnione ludźmi trybuny, dając upragnioną ulgę tysiącom tych, którzy nie załapali się na cień vipowskiej loży. Po ostatniej modlitwie, na którą pozwolił nieubłagany czas, biskup prowadzący zebranie zapowiada przemówienie prezydenta, cytując wersy Starego Testamentu:

Oto mój Sługa, którego podtrzymuję.
Wybrany mój, w którym mam upodobanie.
Sprawiłem, że Duch mój na Nim spoczął;
On przyniesie narodom Prawo.
Nie będzie wołał ni podnosił głosu,
nie da słyszeć krzyku swego na dworze.
Nie złamie trzciny nadłamanej,
nie zagasi knotka o nikłym płomyku.
On niezachwianie przyniesie Prawo.
Nie zniechęci się ani nie załamie,
aż utrwali Prawo na ziemi,
a Jego pouczenia wyczekują wyspy.
Tak mówi Pan Bóg,
który stworzył i rozpiął niebo,
rozpostarł ziemię wraz z jej plonami,
dał ludziom na niej dech ożywczy
i tchnienie tym, co po niej chodzą.
„Ja, Pan, powołałem Cię słusznie,
ująłem Cię za rękę i ukształtowałem,
ustanowiłem Cię przymierzem dla ludzi,
światłością dla narodów,
abyś otworzył oczy niewidomym,
ażebyś z zamknięcia wypuścił jeńców,
z więzienia tych, co mieszkają w ciemności.

Ja, któremu na imię jest Jahwe,
chwały mojej nie odstąpię innemu
ani czci mojej bożkom.
Pierwsze wydarzenia oto już nadeszły,
nowe zaś Ja zapowiadam,
zanim się rozwiną,
wam je ogłaszam"*.

Lecz to nie Lungu jest postacią, na którą wszyscy dziś czekają. Zanim obecny prezydent pojawi się na scenie, za mównicę wchodzi zgarbiony starzec o nad wyraz charakterystycznej twarzy i dobrotliwym spojrzeniu. Ledwo wspina się na stopnie, podtrzymywany przez funkcjonariuszy prezydenckiej ochrony. Jest jednym z ostatnich afrykańskich przywódców pamiętających falę afrykańskiej wolności lat sześćdziesiątych. Nie żyją Kwame Nkrumah, Sekou Touré, dawno odeszli Julius Nyerere, Milton Obote czy Jomo Kenyatta. KK żyje. Ma dziewięćdziesiąt dwa lata i niektórzy mówią, że jest nieśmiertelny. Choć już w 1972 roku zdelegalizował opozycyjne partie**, wprowadzając system jednopartyjny, a potem rządy autorytarne***, choć znany był z sympatii do takich ludzi jak Josip Broz-Tito, Nicolae Ceaușescu i Saddam Husajn, choć swoimi rządami doprowadził stosunkowo bogatą Zambię na skraj bankructwa, Kenneth Kaunda nadal jest bożyszczem narodu. Niektórzy nazywają go nawet afrykańskim Gandhim. Może dlatego, że mimo tak wielu błędów w dwudziestosiedmioletnich rządach nigdy nie stał się jednak krwawym, bezwzględnym dyktatorem, jakich Afryka była i jest pełna. W 1991 roku zaakceptował wyniki wyborów i jako jeden z niewielu afrykańskich przywódców pokojowo, bez rozlewu krwi, oddał władzę, a kilka lat później w ogóle wycofał

* Księga Izajasza 42,1–9.

** W tym United Progressive Party założoną przez swego dawnego, wiernego kompana z czasów walki o niepodległość, Simona Kapwepwego.

*** Oparte na kulcie jednostki oraz na doktrynie „zambijskiego humanizmu" próbującej połączyć idee socjalizmu, scentralizowanego państwa i gospodarki planowanej z tradycyjnymi wartościami afrykańskimi, takimi jak życie we wspólnocie, zaufanie, lojalność.

się z polityki. To na niego wszyscy czekają. Ludzie opuszczają trybuny, biegną w stronę vipowskiej loży, kto ma, wyjmuje aparat, telefon. KK witany jest gromkimi brawami, wzniesionymi w górę flagami i szalikami. Euforia. KK drżącą ręką przybliża mikrofon do ust. Wygłasza raptem jedno zdanie. Jego słaby, zachrypnięty głos z trudem przedziera się do publiczności:

– Niech Bóg Wszechmogący błogosławi cię – zwraca się do obecnego prezydenta – i prowadzi we wszystkim, co myślisz i robisz dla twojego kraju i twojego ludu. Amen.

Owacja na stojąco, oklaski, dźwięki plastikowych trąbek i zagubione pośród tego zgiełku słowa „amen" i „alleluja". Po KK za mównicą pojawia się Rupiah Banda, czwarty prezydent Zambii, rządzący krajem od 2008 do 2011 roku. Drugi prezydent Frederick Chiluba nie żyje. Trzeci, Levy Mwanawasa, i piąty, Michael Sata, zmarli, sprawując urząd. Szóstym prezydentem, pełniącym funkcję jedynie kilka miesięcy, został Guy Scott. Biały. Precedens w postkolonialnej historii Afryki. Lecz jego nie ma dziś w honorowej loży. Rupiah Banda zaczyna od hasła, które zna każdy Zambijczyk:

– *One Zambia!*

– *One Nation!* – odpowiada tłum.

– Kościół dokonał dziś czegoś niezwykłego. Wszyscy jesteśmy z tego dumni. I prosimy Boga, by nadal pomagał rozwiązywać problemy, które staną przed tym młodym człowiekiem*. Jeśli będziecie kontynuować to, co zrobiliście dziś, to jest przyszłość dla Zambii!

Teraz prezydent Edgar Chagwa Lungu, wysoki, szczupły mężczyzna z niezwykle wydatnym uzębieniem, wśród oklasków zajmuje miejsce za mównicą. Mówi z silnym, afrykańskim, bulgoczącym, trudnym do zrozumienia akcentem. Dziękuje Bogu i ludziom. Wspomina Jakuba, Abrahama, Izajasza. Gdy cytuje wersy Biblii, tłum szaleje, wykrzykując każde słowo. Mówi o trudnościach, które napotkał kraj. Zapewnia jednak, że jeśli

* Edgar Chagwa Lungu miał wtedy 59 lat.

wyznamy nasze grzechy, Bóg z pewnością okaże miłosierdzie. Sam bije się w pierś, żałując za przewinienia i niedopatrzenia. Mówi o potrzebie zmiany i odrodzenia w każdym Zambijczyku. Bo Zambia zawsze powinna być na pierwszym miejscu. Wychwala kraj i jego bogate ziemie. Mówi o potrzebie dialogu i współpracy, rozprawia o miłości, tej Bożej i tej człowieczej. Oraz rzecz jasna o samym Wszechmogącym i jego wiernym, zambijskim narodzie. Zapewnia, że z bożą pomocą sprosta wyzwaniom i nie zawiedzie zaufania, jakim obdarzył go jego lud. Bo z bożą pomocą wszystko jest możliwe. Z Bogiem porażka nie jest przecież możliwa. Przysięga też, że już wkrótce mieszkańcy Zambii odczują wzrost gospodarczy. (Przez tłumy ludzi przetacza się westchnienie ulgi). W geście dziękczynienia Lungu ogłasza, że Narodowy Dzień Żalu za Grzechy, Postu i Modlitwy będzie od tej pory organizowany corocznie, po wsze czasy. 18 października, na kilka dni przed Dniem Niepodległości. Tłum spija każde słowo z ust prezydenta z coraz głębszym uniesieniem. Ekstaza. Gdyby dziś zorganizowano wybory, dostałby zapewne sto procent głosów. Na koniec Edgar Chagwa Lungu deklaruje solennie z poczuciem dobrze wykonanej pracy, że od teraz Zambia jest już wolna od sił Złego.

Edgar Chagwa Lungu oraz Kenneth Kaunda biorą w ręce dwa białe gołębie i na znak zakończenia Narodowego Dnia Żalu za Grzechy, Postu i Modlitwy wyrzucają je w powietrze. Te, oszalałe od nagłej wolności, zdezorientowane błyskami fleszy i ogłuszającym wiwatem publiczności, długo obijają się o scenę i blaszany dach, zanim w końcu znajdują drogę ku przestworzom.

To KK jest powodem mojej obecności na dniu modlitwy. Cuthbert Kolala powiedział, że dziś będzie szansa na rozmowę z byłym prezydentem. Staram się o to od wielu dni. Tymczasem KK znika wśród rosłych ochroniarzy, pozdrawiając wielbicieli wzniesioną dłonią. Po chwili widzę, jak długa czarna limuzyna rusza powoli spod vipowskiej loży. Przedzieramy się przez tłumy ludzi, dziennikarzy i ochroniarzy, goniąc za odjeżdżającym autem. Cuthbert Kolala uparcie zapewnia, że spotkanie jest umówione. Że KK zgodził się na rozmowę i będzie na nas czekał w swoim domu na przedmieściach Lusaki. Ufam, że Cuthbert wie, gdzie mieszka KK. Przed stadionem zablokowane ulice, cała Great East Road stoi w gigantycznym ludzko-samochodowym korku. Biegniemy w boczne uliczki w poszukiwaniu taksówki z kierowcą, który znałby odległy adres. W końcu jest. Wydostanie się z Lusaki zajmuje nam godzinę. Kolejną godzinę błądzimy po ciemnych peryferiach miasta, pytając o drogę coraz rzadziej spotykanych ludzi. Szybko zauważam, że ani Kolala, ani taksówkarz nie mają bladego pojęcia, gdzie jest dom KK. W końcu nasze auto zatrzymuje się przed masywną bramą posiadłości gdzieś na opustoszałych wzgórzach, na południowy wschód od Lusaki. Czekamy. Ochroniarz. Portier. Telefon. Rozmowy. Brama się otwiera, auto parkuje na podjeździe okazałej, rozświetlonej willi. Wita nas młody człowiek w garniturze. Przedstawia się jako wnuk Kennetha Kaundy i jego asystent.

– Przykro mi, ale dzień był męczący dla niego. Doktor Kaunda już śpi. Proszę przyjść jutro do biura, na pewno znajdzie dla pana czas.

Ale nie znalazł, choć pod biurem w dzielnicy Kabulonga czekałem od dziewiątej rano. Co jakiś czas otrzymywałem telefon od asystenta z informacją, że sprawy się trochę przedłużają, ale za godzinę na pewno uda się spotkać. Ani za godzinę, ani za dwie, ani za siedem. Spotkanie z Kennethem Kaundą było dla mnie niezwykle ważne, czułem, że bez wywiadu z prezydentem historia Akademii Kosmicznej Mukuki Nkoloso jest niekompletna. Wielu powtarzało mi, że Kaunda zapewne będzie najlepszym źródłem informacji, bo Nkoloso był jego bliskim przyjacielem. Od wszystkich słyszałem: „*Go to KK, he will tell you!*" albo „*You should see KK! He knows everything!*". O szesnastej asystent prezydenta, z którym tego dnia wymieniłem już kilkanaście telefonów, poinformował mnie, że Kaunda jednak nie znajdzie dla mnie czasu.

Zastanawia mnie stosunek Kennetha Kaundy do Edwarda Mukuki Nkoloso. Kaunda kreował się na polityka nowoczesnego, wyważonego, prawdziwego współczesnego męża stanu, który może być partnerem dla prezydentów i premierów zachodnich państw. Dobrze odnajdywał się na salonach, dbał o prezencję, zawsze nienagannie ubrany. Tymczasem w Zambii lubił się pokazywać w towarzystwie człowieka z włócznią, ubranego w lamparcie skóry, z potarganymi włosami spiętymi kawałkiem sznurka. W dodatku prowadzącym badania kosmiczne. Edward Mukuka Nkoloso na pierwszy rzut oka potwierdzał wszelkie negatywne stereotypy o Afryce i jej przywódcach, którym Kaunda chciał zaprzeczyć. Wielu polityków w UNIP żywiło niechęć do Mukuki Nkoloso i starało się go odsunąć na boczny tor. Jednak przez wiele lat Kaunda go chronił i trzymał blisko siebie, zapewniając pozycję poza oficjalną rządową i partyjną hierarchią. Tolerancja zmieszana z wyrachowaniem? Może po prostu sympatia? Byłem bardzo ciekawy, co Kaunda powiedziałby na temat swojego ekscentrycznego towarzysza. Miałem nadzieję na długie wspomnienia, przeplatane śmiechem i wzruszeniami.

Kilka miesięcy później Kenneth Kaunda udzielił wywiadu zambijskiej pisarce Namwali Serpell. Umówienie spotkania zajęło jej pół godziny. Spytany o Edwarda Mukukę Nkoloso, Kenneth Kaunda odpowiadał krótko, zdawkowo. Na pytanie o Akademię roześmiał się: „Tak, on był aktywnym człowiekiem, tak, dość aktywnym".

22

– Mój ojciec dożył niepodległej Zambii – opowiada Cuthbert Kolala któregoś popołudnia. Siedzimy na tarasie hostelu, w którym mieszkam. Zaczyna się najprzyjemniejsza część dnia. Resztki słońca przedzierają się przez pióropusze palmowych drzew, zbliżająca się noc powoduje lekki ruch powietrza. Niestety ten błogi spokój trwać będzie tylko chwilę, już niedługo powietrze wypełni zgraja uporczywych komarów, które zmuszą nas, by szczelnie zakryć każdą wystającą część ciała i wysmarować się specyfikiem o słodkim i mdłym zapachu. – Poszedłem do moich rodziców i krzyknąłem: „A nie mówiłem!". Płakali i tańczyli ze szczęścia, ojciec nosił mnie na plecach. Ten dzień był piękny i radosny. Dostaliśmy nową falę energii, by pracować razem. Ludzie tańczyli, śpiewali, biegali w kółko. Jakby niebo spadło na ziemię. To było jak sen, który się spełnił. Sądzę, że Bóg był tam z nami i tańczył. Cały ból, który nam towarzyszył przez lata, zniknął z dnia na dzień. Patrzyliśmy, jak opuszczali Union Jacka, i baliśmy się, że to tylko na chwilę, że zaraz podniosą z powrotem. Ale nie podnieśli. Opuszczali na dobre! Na jego miejsce wjeżdżała nasza flaga. Ludzie mdleli. A potem przyjechała królowa. Do Afryki, wyobrażasz sobie? Ona tu nigdy wcześniej nie była. W sumie cieszyliśmy się, że przyjechała.

Ale królowa wcale nie przyjechała do Zambii. Cuthbert Kolala, jak i kilka innych osób, które dzieliły się wspomnieniami z tego dnia, źle pamięta. Do Lusaki w imieniu królowej Elżbiety II przybyła Jej Królewska Wysokość Księżniczka Królewska Maria Windsor. Wielu zapamiętało ją jednak jako królową. To ona wręczyła Kennethowi Kaundzie symbole konstytucyjnej niepodległości. Prawdziwa królowa kazała na siebie czekać jeszcze wiele lat. Przyjechała do Zambii dopiero w 1979 roku.

Choć nie tak spektakularna, jak ją opisują weterani, Cza-cza zniweczyła zakulisowe starania Roya Welensky'ego, by do nowej konstytucji wprowadzić zapisy uniemożliwiające czarnym przejęcie władzy. Pod koniec 1962 roku członkowie UNIP, w niełatwej koalicji z resztkami ANC Harry'ego Nkumbuli, weszli do Rady Legislacyjnej i utworzyli pierwszy w historii Rodezji Północnej rząd czarnej większości. Rok później, dzięki staraniom czarnych polityków z Rodezji Północnej, ale również wzrastającej niechęci białych z Rodezji Południowej i topniejącemu poparciu w Londynie, Federacja Afryki Centralnej została rozwiązana. W styczniu 1964 roku nowe wybory wyniosły do władzy UNIP, już bez kłopotliwego ANC i bez wiszącego widma federacji. Kenneth Kaunda został premierem rządu, a droga do niepodległości była prosta i szeroka. Pozostał mu do rozwiązania jeden niespodziewany problem – rosnący w siłę, bezczelnie anarchistyczny i kwestionujący jego przywództwo Kościół Lumpa Alice Lenshiny. Król bowiem może być tylko jeden. Latem 1964 roku premier Kaunda wysłał dwa tysiące uzbrojonych żołnierzy w rejon Prowincji Północnej. W wyniku strzelaniny zginęło ponad tysiąc wyznawców Lenshiny, kolejne piętnaście tysięcy musiało uciekać do Konga. Sama Lenshina spędziła następne dziesięć lat w więzieniu. Choć Syjon Alice Lenshiny wraz z budynkiem Nowego Jeruzalem został doszczętnie zniszczony, a Kościół Lumpa zdelegalizowany, jego wyznawcy nadal żyją poza granicami Zambii. Człowiek, którego ludzie nazywają afrykańskim Gandhim, ma na rękach krew ponad tysiąca niewinnych osób. Kenneth Kaunda nie lubi w wywiadach odpowiadać na pytania dotyczące tych dni, a lokalni dziennikarze nie lubią ich zadawać.

Niemniej 24 października 1964 roku do Lusaki przybyli goście z ponad sześćdziesięciu państw świata oraz przedstawiciele wielu instytucji i organizacji międzynarodowych. Dwuosobową reprezentację na obchodach miała nawet Polska. By pomieścić setki delegatów oraz tysiące Zambijczyków, zbudowano nowy stadion, dziś zwany Stadionem Niepodległości. Betonowe trybuny nie stanęły w centrum miasta czy wśród bogatych białych przedmieść. Wyrosły tuż u podnóża Chingwele Hill, w czarnej dzielnicy Matero, tam gdzie przez lata siedzibę miała UNIP. I tam gdzie Edward Mukuka Nkoloso prowadził swoje kosmiczne badania.

Ludzie zapamiętali płomienne przemowy, tłumy na trybunach i wielkie godło nowego kraju: z czarno-białymi pasami, ogromnym orłem i z napisem „*One Zambia, One Nation*". Wciąż pamiętają setki tancerzy Ngoni z Prowincji Wschodniej, w barwnych tradycyjnych strojach i maskach, z tarczami i dzidami. I ludzi poprzebieranych za różne zwierzęta – krokodyle, słonie. Pamiętają także występy gimnastyczne i parady młodzieży, śpiewy i wystrzały w powietrze. Oprócz księżniczki Marii Windsor Brytyjczycy przysłali również trzy działa kalibru 105 milimetrów, by niepodległościowy salut mógł odpowiednio głośno wybrzmieć. Ludzie wspominają także wielki znicz z miedzianej blachy, otoczony zambijskimi orłami, który stanął na szczycie Chingwele Hill. Dzień i noc buchał z niego kilkumetrowy płomień, było go widać z każdego miejsca w Lusace. Pamiętają też moment, gdy Kaunda odpalał od niego dziesiątki pochodni, które zaniosły „ogień niepodległości" do każdego zambijskiego miasta. Wspominają wielki amerykański kabriolet Chrysler Imperial, którym KK jeździł po Lusace i pozdrawiał ludzi. I tysiące gardeł krzyczących „*kwacha*", gdy równo o północy czerwono-zielono-czarno-pomarańczowa flaga zastąpiła brytyjskiego Union Jacka.

Mnie najbardziej porusza zdjęcie, które znalazłem w Archiwach Narodowych. Kenneth Kaunda tańczy na nim z Jej Królewską Wysokością Księżniczką Królewską Marią Windsor. On niezwykle czarny, ona arystokratycznie, brytyjsko biała, z koroną we włosach i naszyjnikiem z pereł. On jeszcze trzy lata wcześniej gnił w brytyjskim więzieniu, oblewany moczem strażników, bity i poniżany. Ona, członek rodziny królewskiej, dystyngowana, wyniosła, dumna.

23

– Pierwszą rakietę tata zbudował z mukwy – opowiada syn Mukuki Nkoloso, rysując w powietrzu kształt rakiety. – To najmocniejsze drewno na świecie, robi się z niego na przykład rękojeści karabinów. A nas Bóg pobłogosławił i w Zambii mamy tego drewna bardzo dużo. Drugą rakietę tata zrobił z azbestu. Potem zaczął eksperymenty z beczkami, metalowymi i mocnymi. Takimi jakich się używa do transportu paliw.

– Spójrz na ten wspaniały pomysł, by użyć arkuszy blachy! – wtrąca Cuthbert Kolala. – I to był pomysł czarnego! Daleko przed białymi! To było coś!

– Tata chciał odpalić rakietę w Dzień Niepodległości, by pokazać światu, że możemy to zrobić, by pokazać tym *prophets of doom*, tym imperialistom, co potrafimy! By rzucić im wyzwanie, tym faszystom, tym wielkim siłom zła. Chodziło o to, by przestraszyć białych. I pokazać im, że my też znamy naukę i że już odkryliśmy gwiazdy i Marsa – kontynuuje syn Mukuki Nkoloso.

Cuthbert Kolala wybucha krótkim śmiechem.

– Że mamy takie rzeczy jak teleskop. I to wszystko ładnie wyszło!

Stare plastikowe krzesło, na którym siedzę, nagle pęka z trzaskiem, a ja ze swoim dyktafonem ląduję na podłodze. Cuthbert Kolala zrywa się nagle jak rażony piorunem.

– Odejdź, siło nieczysta! Wracaj, skąd przyszedłeś! – Wymachuje rękoma, w jego oczach znów pojawia się obłęd. Dopiero po chwili, zbierając się z podłogi, orientuję się, że nie mówi do mnie, lecz do Złego. Bierze rękoma powietrze i wyrzuca je za drzwi, tak jakby wypraszał wyimaginowanego, bardzo nieproszonego gościa. – Szatan chce przeszkodzić w tym, co robimy! Widzisz, czyha na ciebie, bo robisz dobrą rzecz!

Miałem nadzieję, że znajdę tę rakietę, że stary grat, któremu nigdy nie było dane wznieść się w przestworza, znalazł jakieś wygodne lądowisko w szopie, garażu czy zapomnianym magazynie. Na początku byłem nawet przekonany, że syn Mukuki Nkoloso musi ją ukrywać gdzieś w swoim gospodarstwie, przysypaną stertą kukurydzy, przykrytą szmatami, trochę jak zabawkę z dzieciństwa, trochę jak skarb. A może trzyma ją muzeum lub jakieś zapomniane archiwum? Niektórzy, w tym syn Mukuki Nkoloso, twierdzili, że ona gdzieś jest. Chodziłem, szukałem, pytałem. Pięknie byłoby ją znaleźć, nawet jeśli okazałaby się niczym więcej niż blaszaną beczką. Lecz nie. Prototyp pierwszej afrykańskiej rakiety kosmicznej przepadł zupełnie bez wieści.

Devison Bambo Miti opowiada mi kilka dni później:

– Parę miesięcy przed uroczystościami, gdy już pewne było, że niepodległość nadejdzie, Nkoloso przedstawił nam ten pomysł z budową rakiety. On ogromnie pragnął, żeby odpalić ją właśnie w ten dzień, podczas uroczystości. Już wiele miesięcy wcześniej ćwiczyliśmy paradowanie i maszerowanie. Ja chodziłem wtedy do Chingwele Primary School. Przy szkole były takie pola, to tam budowaliśmy tę rakietę. Moi rodzice myśleli, że Akademia była częścią zajęć szkolnych. A to Mukuka Nkoloso wszystko wymyślał. My tylko pomagaliśmy: przynieś to, tamto. Byliśmy dumni, że jesteśmy studentami Mukuki Nkoloso, to było wyróżnienie, chcieliśmy być naukowcami tak jak on. Potem Mukuka Nkoloso zakupił tę wielką beczkę. Już nie pamiętam, co tam zainstalowaliśmy. Bo my tę rakietę budowaliśmy ze wszystkiego, co znaleźliśmy: o, weź to, o, zobacz, tamto też się przyda – dodaje po chwili namysłu Miti. – No ale przecież tak się nie da zbudować prawdziwej rakiety. Ale gdyby były pieniądze, to pewnie nawiązalibyśmy kontakt z NASA. Być może dziś byśmy mówili o takiej instytucji tu, w Zambii. Ale rząd mu nie pomógł. To była główna przyczyna porażki. Oni nie traktowali kwestii lotu w Kosmos poważnie. Uważali Mukukę Nkoloso za szalonego naukowca. Gdyby było inaczej, dziś mielibyśmy swoje satelity tak jak inne kraje – mówi z prawdziwym żalem pan Miti. Po chwili wraca do tematu: – Rakietę wnieśliśmy na wzgórze na sam koniec, tuż przed Dniem Niepodległości. Nkoloso nazwał ją D-Kalu 1, od Davida Kaundy*, pierwszego prezydenta. Ale w ostatniej chwili to właśnie KK nie wyraził zgody na odpalenie rakiety w ciągu dnia, podczas uroczystości. Dowiedzieliśmy się o tym dopiero na stadionie. Nkoloso był bardzo rozczarowany. Cóż, za dnia nie mogliśmy, ale mogliśmy w nocy. No i tego dwudziestego czwartego, to była niedziela, weszliśmy na Chingwele Hill, gdzie czekała już nasza beczka. Odpaliliśmy naszą rakietę tuż po północy, po tych wszystkich fajerwerkach i balonach, które poleciały w powietrze podczas głównych uroczystości. Były trzy ładunki wybuchowe, tak, trzy, pamiętam. Wszyscy tam byliśmy, cała nasza grupa, na galowo, w mundurach i hełmach. Z naszywkami z Księżycem. To była poważna sprawa! I ona pofrunęła na jakieś osiemset stóp! Oczywiście bez nikogo w środku. Leciała i leciała! Taką rakietę zrobiliśmy!

Syn Mukuki Nkoloso twierdzi nawet, że w odpalonej rakiecie była Martha Mwamba, że to był pierwszy lot „Siostry Niebios". Choć gdy spytałem, jak wylądowała i czy nic jej się nie stało, nie odpowiedział.

Ale nie wszyscy pamiętają ten dzień tak jak syn Mukuki Nkoloso i Devison Bambo Miti. Niektórzy, zwłaszcza politycy UNIP, twierdzą, że żadnej rakiety nie odpalono. Że, owszem, Mukuka Nkoloso wystawił coś na wzgórzu, ale tajemnicze urządzenie nigdy nie wzniosło się w powietrze.

* Kenneth Kaunda miał na drugie imię David. Było to również imię jego ojca.

– Za dnia więcej ludzi mogłoby zobaczyć naszą rakietę – ciągnie dalej pan Miti. – A tak to tylko garstka osób widziała ogień, no bo w nocy rakiety przecież nie widać. Podczas uroczystości nad stadionem fruwały takie duże balony z napisem „Zambia" i z mapą kraju. Może się bali, że rakieta w nie wleci. Ale i tak byliśmy szczęśliwi, jak poleciała w powietrze, skakaliśmy, klaskaliśmy. Nigdy nie zapomnę startu tej rakiety. To było piękne, szkoda, że żaden z nas nie miał kamery. Dwa tygodnie temu był mały artykuł w „Daily Mail" o Mukuce Nkoloso. Od czasu do czasu ktoś o nim przypomni. Rozmawiałem o nim z kimś niedawno. A potem, ni stąd, ni zowąd, dzwonisz do mnie ty. Co za zbieg okoliczności!

Kilka dni po uroczystości tygodnik „Time" tak pisał o nowym państwie: „Wśród ponad 3 600 000 ludzi rozrzuconych po powierzchni większej niż Teksas Zambia ma jedynie 1500 absolwentów szkół średnich, mniej niż setkę absolwentów uczelni wyższych, w tym czterech doktorów, dziesięciu prawników i żadnego inżyniera. [...] Po tym, jak został proklamowany na prezydenta nowego narodu, Kaunda zwrócił się do tłumów i przedstawił swoją wizję wolnej i pokojowej Zambii, »gdzie ludzie wszystkich plemion, ras, religii i opinii politycznych będą mogli żyć w szczęściu i harmonii«. Podczas obchodów niepodległości tylko jeden Zambijczyk zdawał się nie podzielać panującego entuzjazmu. To Edward Mukuka Nkoloso, nauczyciel szkoły podstawowej i dyrektor Narodowej Akademii Nauki, Badań Kosmicznych i Filozofii, który twierdził, że uroczystości kolidowały z jego kosmicznym programem mającym na celu pokonać USA i Związek Radziecki w wyścigu na Księżyc. Mukuka Nkoloso trenuje dwunastu zambijskich astronautów, w tym szesnastoletnią, krągłą dziewczynę – turla ich w beczce po oleju dookoła drzewa i uczy chodzić na rękach, »w jedyny sposób, w jaki ludzie mogą chodzić na Księżycu«".

W listopadzie afrykański „DRUM" wypuścił specjalny numer magazynu poświęcony nowemu afrykańskiemu państwu. Z okładki do czytelników uśmiechał się Kenneth Kaunda. Ale na czterdziestej piątej stronie znajdziemy coś znacznie ciekawszego. Artykuł zaczyna się odręcznym rysunkiem autorstwa Edwarda Mukuki Nkoloso. Na nim wszelkie atrybuty nowoczesności – futurystyczne wieżowce wyrastające spomiędzy mostów, estakad i autostrad, między nimi jakieś kopulaste kształty, przypominające obserwatoria kosmiczne, wieże zwieńczone czymś, co przywodzi na myśl latający spodek, wycelowane w niebo anteny satelitarne, a z tyłu, za tym wszystkim, mknie w przestworza beczkowata rakieta. Miasto trochę jak z *Metropolis* Fritza Langa. Podoba mi się ten rysunek. Jest jak odpowiedź na temat „Miasto przyszłości" na zajęciach z plastyki w szkole podstawowej. Zgrabnie narysowany, zwłaszcza jak na kogoś, kto nie miał żadnego wykształcenia w tym kierunku. Tym miastem jest Lusaka. Stolica Zambii na początku lat sześćdziesiątych jest niezwykle daleka od tej wizji. Nie powstały nawet jeszcze wieżowce przy Cairo Road. Miasto ma w ogromnej mierze parterową lub dwu-, trzypiętrową zabudowę, a niewielkie centrum otoczone jest dzielnicami willowymi białych lub slumsami czarnych. Najwyższym budynkiem w centrum są silosy zbożowe przy torach kolejowych. „Moja Lusaka wieku kosmicznego" – głosi tytuł. Jego Lusaka. Obok rysunku on sam, wkracza w ten wiek, w to miasto, zamaszystym krokiem, w triumfalnej pozie z wyrzuconymi w górę rękoma (w jednej, rzecz jasna, włócznia). Jest listopad 1964 roku, od miesiąca na mapie świata istnieje nowe państwo – Zambia. Na kolejnych stronach listopadowego wydania „DRUM Magazine" z 1964 roku dyrektor Narodowej Akademii Nauki, Badań Kosmicznych i Filozofii wygłasza swój manifest: „LECIMY NA MARSA!

Widzę Zambię przyszłości jako Zambię wieku kosmicznego, bardziej rozwiniętą niż Rosja czy Ameryka. W rzeczy samej, w mojej Akademii nasze myślenie wyprzedza oba mocarstwa o jakieś sześć, siedem lat. To pech dla Lusaki, że nie miałem możliwości objąć stanowiska burmistrza miasta. Gdybym został wybrany, nasza stolica wkrótce stałaby się drugim Paryżem, jeśli nie Nowym Jorkiem. Gdybym został burmistrzem, przedmieścia

Matero, Kamwala, Chilenje szybko zapełniłyby się mieszkaniami i wieżowcami. Stare domy by zniknęły. Ale nieważne, jeszcze będziemy mieli nasz Paryż.

Gdybym dopiął swego, Zambia narodziłaby się w blasku rakiety Akademii lecącej w Kosmos. Ale Komitet Organizacyjny Obchodów Niepodległości był zdania, że rakieta może przestraszyć gości uroczystości, a nawet całą ludność. Zapewne martwił ich hałas i pył.

ZAŁOGA GOTOWA.

To wielka szkoda. Wszystko jest gotowe w naszej tajnej kwaterze głównej w dolinie, siedem mil od Lusaki. Rakieta mogła zostać odpalona ze Stadionu Niepodległości, a Zambia mogłaby podbić Marsa już w kilka dni po odzyskaniu niepodległości. Tak, to tam planujemy dotrzeć – na Marsa. Badaliśmy tę planetę za pomocą teleskopów, które mamy w bazie, i teraz jesteśmy już niemal pewni, że Mars jest zamieszkany przez prymitywne istoty. Załoga naszej rakiety jest w gotowości. Specjalnie wytrenowana astronautka Martha Mwamba, dwa koty (również specjalnie trenowane) i misjonarz polecą w naszej pierwszej rakiecie. Ostrzegłem jednak misjonarza, że nie wolno mu narzucać chrześcijaństwa siłą, jeśli istoty na Marsie nie będą chciały go przyjąć.

Jest jeszcze jedno wyzwanie, z którym musimy się zmierzyć. UNESCO nadal nie odpowiedziała na naszą prośbę o wsparcie finansowe w wysokości 7 000 000 funtów, a pieniądze te są nam potrzebne na nasz program kosmiczny. Wtedy będziemy mogli stanąć na czele światowej nauki.

Sądzę, że władze Zambii powinny się teraz włączyć, jeśli to my mamy stać się panami Siódmego Nieba Międzygwiezdnej Przestrzeni. Rząd powinien wprowadzić ustawy, by przeciwstawić się szatańskim spiskom naszych wrogów. Od dawna wiem, że w Zambii są rosyjscy szpiedzy. Amerykańskich też jest pełno w mieście. Oni wszyscy chcą złapać Marthę i moje koty. Chcą naszych tajnych informacji. Z tymi ludźmi musimy zrobić porządek jak najszybciej po odzyskaniu niepodległości, jeśli mam utrzymać pozycję lidera kosmicznego wyścigu. Więzienie bez procesu dla wszystkich szpiegów to jest to, czego potrzebujemy.

Poza tym jestem zadowolony z działań nowego rządu, ale musi on zachęcić młodych ludzi, by przystąpili do mojej Akademii.

Niedawno zburzono budynek naszej Akademii w Matero. To niedobrze. Mam nadzieję, że przynajmniej zbudują tam nowoczesne mieszkania i znajdzie się miejsce na nasze biura. Stolica nowej Zambii wieku nauki musi być piękna. Ludzie przyjeżdżający z daleka do światowej potęgi naukowej nie mogą przecież oglądać slumsów.

Zambijczycy nie są gorsi od innych narodów w dziedzinie nauki i technologii. Moje kosmiczne plany na pewno zostaną zrealizowane".

24

Nie wierzyłem synowi Mukuki Nkoloso, gdy opowiadał, że do Lusaki zaczęli zjeżdżać dziennikarze z całego świata, by zobaczyć, co dzieje się na tajemniczej farmie kilka mil od miasta. W ogóle wiele jego opowieści traktowałem z początku z przymrużeniem oka. Nie wierzyłem, dopóki w archiwach amerykańskich gazet na hasło „Nkoloso" nie otrzymałem ponad stu sześćdziesięciu wyników. Pod koniec 1964 roku i na początku 1965 o szalonym zambijskim naukowcu pisały gazety we wszystkich amerykańskich stanach, artykuły znalazłem również w periodykach kanadyjskich i australijskich. Śmiały projekt Edwarda Mukuki Nkoloso przyciągał znacznie więcej uwagi niż nowe państwo, w którym powstawał.

– Kiedy przyjechali ci Amerykanie – wspomina z dumą syn Mukuki Nkoloso – to mogliśmy im powiedzieć, że my już znamy gwiazdy i Marsa, ale nie ujawnimy im tego, bo to są nasze sekrety. Amerykanie już wiedzieli o tacie, że to, co mówił, to była prawda, bo on to badał, studiował. Wy, Amerykanie, myślicie, że jesteście najlepsi we wszystkim, ale to kłamstwo! My odkryliśmy już Marsa i gwiazdy! Krzyż Południa i Gwiazdę Polarną! OK, jesteśmy czarni, ale wszyscy zostaliśmy stworzeni na podobieństwo Boga, jesteśmy tacy sami. Oddychasz powietrzem? Tak. Pijesz wodę? Tak. Chodzisz do toalety? Tak. Więc w czym kłopot? Czemu uważacie, że czarni są gorsi?

*

W listopadzie 1964 roku do Lusaki przyleciał znany dziennikarz „San Francisco Chronicle" Arthur Hoppe. Przez dwa tygodnie Hoppe nadawał regularnie depesze prasowe, które przedrukowywały dziesiątki gazet w całych Stanach. Jeszcze w drodze do Zambii, gdzieś ponad Afryką, Hoppe napisał pierwszą notkę: „Wszystko, co świat wie o nowej Zambii, to pojedyncza depesza wysłana z Lusaki przez Associated Press. Według tejże depeszy tuż po tym, jak Zambia wywalczyła niepodległość, niejaki Edward Mukuka Nkoloso mianował się ministrem badań kosmicznych i niezwłocznie uruchomił śmiały program mający na celu wysłanie zambijskich astronautów na Księżyc przed końcem tego roku. Gdzie jest Zambia? [...] Depesza donosiła także, że pan Nkoloso zbudował już statek kosmiczny – miedzianą rakietę wysokości dziesięciu stóp – która w pierwszych testach wzniosła się na wysokość sześciu stóp. Napędem rakiety jest system Mukwa – napęd afrykańskiego projektu wywodzący się z katapulty. [...] Do tej pory pan Nkoloso zebrał dziesięcioro ochotników. Podobnie jak w radzieckim programie kosmicznym, wśród astronautów jest również kobieta, siedemnastoletnia Martha Mwamba. Jej celem jednakże nie jest lot na Księżyc, lecz na Marsa, który został zaplanowany w ramach ambitnego programu kosmicznego Zambii. Oprócz bardzo rygorystycznego treningu, jak donosi Associated Press, pani Mwamba zajmuje się też karmieniem kotów, które będą jej towarzyszyć w przyszłej podróży kosmicznej.

– Nie możemy ufać nikomu w projekcie takiej skali – podkreślił pan Mukuka Nkoloso na konferencji prasowej. – Niektóre z naszych pomysłów znacznie wyprzedzają plany Amerykanów i Rosjan i dlatego nie mogę pozwolić, by ktokolwiek zobaczył moją rakietę.

Jak w przypadku dwóch potężnych rywali, decyzja Zambii o przystąpieniu do wyścigu kosmicznego jest motywowana jednym, najważniejszym powodem: narodowym prestiżem. Jeśli, jak zakłada plan, w ciągu następnych sześciu tygodni zambijski astronauta zdoła wbić zambijską flagę na szczycie księżycowego wzgórza, konsekwencje dla całej zimnej wojny mogą być niewyobrażalne.

Dziś Zambia rozciąga się na powierzchni większej niż Francja, ma 3,5 miliona rdzennych Zambijczyków, 73 plemiona i dialekty, mnóstwo miedzi, fabrykę butów, 1 275 000 sztuk bydła, 175 700 sztuk kóz, ogromne ilości much tse-tse i demokratyczną konstytucję. [...] Prezydentem i ojcem założycielem Zambii jest dr Kenneth David Buchizya Kaunda, kwakier wierzący w niestosowanie przemocy. Gra hymny na gitarze, gra w ping-ponga i zdaje się bardzo miłym człowiekiem. [...] Czuję się trochę tak, jak musiał się czuć pan Stanley, gdy wiek temu wyruszał na poszukiwania dr. Livingstone'a. [...] Czy Zambia dogoni Rosjan? Czy może dogonić nas? Jakież to wspaniałe sekrety do odkrycia! Jakaż to przygoda przede mną! Aż ciarki chodzą po plecach, gdy pomyślę, że gdzieś tam daleko poniżej mnie, gdy piszę te słowa, cisza afrykańskiej nocy rozrywana jest rykiem lwa, lamparta i rakiety napędzanej systemem Mukwa".

Kilka dni później do amerykańskich gazet dotarła druga korespondencja, tym razem pisana już z Lusaki: „Z biciem serca szedłem za Okuno przez zakurzone ulice Lusaki, pośród kwitnących jakarand, splątanych krzewów bugenwilli, aż doszliśmy do zielonego, dwupiętrowego budynku, przystrojonego flagami i napisem »United National Independence Party«. Przeciskaliśmy się ciemnym korytarzem między kobietami w turbanach, z dziećmi na plecach, następnie wąskimi schodami w górę do małego zatłoczonego pokoju. Okuno wskazał na otwarte drzwi z napisem »Publicity Chairman«. Tubylcy wyszli, odsłaniając mały pokój z pokaźnym znakiem na ścianie głoszącym »SECRET« i tajemniczym kablem wijącym się po podłodze. Za biurkiem siedział niewysoki mężczyzna z bliznami wojowników Bemba na skroniach. Ubrany w bojowy hełm i mundur khaki przyozdobiony czerwono-złotym szamerunkiem i medalami z hasłem »Pokój i Wolność«.

– Pan Nkoloso, jak przypuszczam? – powiedziałem.

– Tak, oczywiście – odpowiedział z uroczym uśmiechem i przyjaznym uściskiem dłoni. – Przyjechał pan w najlepszym momencie! Właśnie podjęliśmy decyzję, który z naszych dwunastu astronautów zajmie honorowe miejsce w naszej kosmicznej kapsule zmierzającej na Księżyc. To będzie Godfrey Mwango, ten tutaj. Dlatego że wykazał się ponadprzeciętnymi umiejętnościami chodzenia na rękach.

Pan Mwango, umięśniony młody mężczyzna o szerokich barkach, również w pełnym mundurze khaki i hełmie, uśmiechnął się skromnie.

– Chodzenia na rękach? – zapytałem.

– Tak, oczywiście – odrzekł Nkoloso. – Właśnie przeszedł testy na przyszłego astronautę: symulowany powrót kosmicznej kapsuły na Ziemię i lądowanie w wodzie. Wsadziliśmy go do beczki i wrzuciliśmy do wody.

– Trochę się bałem – wtrącił Mwango. – Nie umiem pływać.

– Od jutra – powiedział Nkoloso – jako że został wybrany, zintensyfikujemy program jego treningu, tak by Zambia była pierwszym krajem, który zatknie flagę na Księżycu. Będzie nam bardzo miło, jeśli zechce nam pan towarzyszyć.

Nie mogę się doczekać".

Obok tekstu Arthura Hoppego jest zdjęcie. Godfrey Mwango demonstruje swoje zdolności, stojąc na głowie na małym stoliku. Z boku podtrzymują go Martha Mwamba i inny, młodszy kadet. Nad wszystkim panuje dyrektor Nkoloso w powiewającej pelerynie.

Wyobrażam sobie amerykańskie rodziny na rozłożystych przedmieściach, jak z serialu *Cudowne lata*. Z rzędami identycznych, równych, białych domków, z przystrzyżonymi trawnikami. Wyobrażam sobie otyłych panów siedzących na tarasach, z piwem w ręku i papierosem w ustach. To piwo właśnie im się wylewa na flanelową koszulę, gdy zanoszą się rubasznym śmiechem, czytając doniesienia Arthura Hoppego.

Trzecia korespondencja nadeszła dwa dni później: „Pierwszy zambijski astronauta został z powodzeniem umieszczony na orbicie dziś o godzinie 15:14:32 czasu środkowoafrykańskiego jako wstęp do planowanego lotu na Księżyc. Godfrey Mwango, lat 21, człowiek o stalowych nerwach i ponurej facjacie, okrążył orbitę 17 razy, turlając się w czterdziestogalonowej beczce w dół trawiastego wzgórza, zanim zatrzymał się na odpoczynek w cieniu drzewa. Test został oceniony jako »niezrównany sukces« przez dyrektora programu kosmicznego Edwarda Mukukę Nkoloso:

– Bardzo dużo się nauczyliśmy – powiedział dyrektor.

Wszystko odbyło się w centrum szkoleniowym przyszłych astronautów – na małej polanie pośród buszu, jakieś pięć mil od stolicy tego nowego kraju, Lusaki. Beczka po oleju to wierna kopia kapsuły kosmicznej, tej, w której dyrektor Nkoloso ma zamiar wysłać astronautę Mwango na Księżyc przed końcem przyszłego miesiąca.

Dzisiejszy test był pierwszym testem oglądanym przez dziennikarza i fotografa i w związku z tym dawało się wyczuć pewne napięcie, zwłaszcza podczas ostatecznego odliczania. Jak zazwyczaj dyrektor Nkoloso był ubrany w swój upstrzony medalami mundur i hełm. Lecz dziś, specjalnie na tę okazję, miał na sobie również parę czerwono-zielonych spodni oraz fioletową pelerynę.

Astronauta Mwango w mundurze khaki i hełmie bojowym leży nieruchomo na ziemi, podczas gdy inni podsunęli w jego stronę wielką beczkę po oleju. Jeśli czuł lęk, to dobrze go ukrywał. Potem na rozkaz dyrektora Nkoloso inni kadeci, w tym jeden z włócznią, włożyli pana Mwango do beczki, nogami do przodu.

– Wszystko OK? – spytał dyrektor Nkoloso nieco zaniepokojony, klepiąc bok kosmicznej kapsuły.

– OK! – usłyszał w odpowiedzi.

Dziesięć... dziewięć... osiem... – zaczął dyrektor Nkoloso, ale ostateczne odliczanie musiało zostać przerwane dwukrotnie w związku z problemami technicznymi. Astronauta Mwango okazał się nieco zbyt duży jak na tę beczkę i jego głowa wystawała na zewnątrz, niebezpiecznie blisko ziemi. W końcu jednak Mwango skurczył się w beczce na tyle, by spełnić wszelkie wymagania bezpieczeństwa dyrektora Nkoloso.

– Start! – wykrzyknął dyrektor Nkoloso, dając kosmicznej kapsule solidnego kopniaka. – Wszystkie systemy w gotowości!

Niestety zbocze okazało się nazbyt łagodne i po okrążeniu orbity kosmiczna kapsuła zatrzymała się na kępie trawy. Koledzy Godfreya Mwango ochoczo podbiegli, by pomóc mu się wydostać z beczki w światło chwały.

– Wow! – usłyszeli wszyscy.

Mwango sam bezpiecznie doprowadził kapsułę do miejsca lądowania pod dużym drzewem. Wszyscy świadkowie, w tym kilka miejscowych kobiet z dziećmi na plecach, podbiegli do miejsca lądowania, by zobaczyć, czy Mwango jest cały i zdrowy. Ten wyszedł z kapsuły sam, bez niczyjej pomocy, a na jego twarzy zawitał szeroki uśmiech.

– Człowieku, co za lot! – powiedział.

– Astronauci zawsze tak mówią – wyjaśnił Mukuka Nkoloso i skinął głową z aprobatą.

Spytany o to, jakie wnioski wyciągnął z przeprowadzonego testu, dyrektor Nkoloso skrzywił się i odrzekł:

– Z pewnością trzeba będzie skombinować większą beczkę".

W czwartej depeszy korespondenta „San Francisco Chronicle", którą wiele amerykańskich gazet wydrukowało w Wigilię Bożego Narodzenia, czytamy: „Dyrektor Nkoloso, kierownik projektu, dziś był życzliwy, aczkolwiek małomówny. Choć zgodził się, bym obserwował testy kapsuły turlającej się wraz z astronautą Mwango po zboczu wzgórza, odmówił mi wydania przepustki zapewniającej wstęp w pobliże platformy startowej rakiety. [...] Dyrektor Nkoloso zdradził jednak, iż tajemniczy »system napędowy Mukwa«, który miał ponieść rakietę, został odrzucony. [...]

– W zasadzie to był system oparty na katapulcie zbudowanej z drewna mukwy – wyjaśnia dyrektor. – Niestety okazał się daleko zbyt prymitywny jak na nasze potrzeby. Wykonaliśmy także kilka testów, używając łuku i strzał, oczywiście jedynie w celu opracowania trajektorii lotu i studiowania sił geofizycznych.

W ostatnim miesiącu, tuż przed dużymi uroczystościami związanymi z odzyskaniem niepodległości, dyrektor Nkoloso badał również możliwości wykorzystania dynamitu jako siły napędowej. Zaproponował nawet, by na środku Stadionu Niepodległości ułożyć kilka paczek dynamitu, postawić na nich krzesło z jednym z astronautów i wystrzelić go w Kosmos w szczytowym momencie uroczystości. Pomysł ten został jednakże odrzucony przez władze, choć dyrektor był przekonany, że takowa próba byłaby zgodna z mottem zambijskich astronautów: »Dokądkolwiek prowadzi przeznaczenie i chwała człowieka, tam zawsze będziemy«.

Gdy zawiodły obydwa systemy – system Mukwa oraz ten oparty na dynamicie – dyrektor zdradził, że obecnie pracuje nad systemem Mulolo.

– Mulolo to znaczy huśtać się – wyjaśnił. – Przywiązaliśmy liny do wysokich drzew i następnie rozbujaliśmy astronautę tak, by wyleciał w Kosmos. Do tej pory osiągnęliśmy dystans dziesięciu jardów, ale rzecz jasna wydłużając liny, jesteśmy w stanie polecieć znacznie dalej.

Czy Zambijski Program Kosmiczny wiązał obecnie swoje nadzieje z systemem Mulolo?

– O nie – odrzekł dyrektor – ten system ma niestety swoje ograniczenia, ale zamierzamy połączyć siły z Zambijskim Klubem Lotniczym. Oni pracują nad budową szybowca. Potem mamy nadzieję, że nawiążemy współpracę z Zambijskimi Siłami Powietrznymi.

– Zambijskie Siły Powietrzne?

– Są niewielkie – przyznał Nkoloso – ale zdeterminowane.

Lecz na jakim systemie napędowym będzie teraz polegał Zambijski Program Kosmiczny? Dyrektor spojrzał przez ramię, pochylił się w moją stronę i powiedział:

– Napęd turbulentny. Ale niech pan zrozumie, nic więcej nie mogę powiedzieć w chwili obecnej. Nie mogę narażać prestiżu kraju. Musimy pobić Rosję i Amerykę w wyścigu na Księżyc. Co oni mogą zrobić, my możemy także".

Obok tekstu zdjęcie Mukuki Nkoloso stojącego w beczce – kapsule kosmicznej. Ręce w górze w geście triumfu, w lewej oczywiście włócznia.

A może po prostu źle rozumiemy pomysł Edwarda Mukuki Nkoloso? Rozpatrujemy go w złych kategoriach, mierzymy złymi jednostkami racjonalnej miary? Któregoś dnia, patrząc na afrykańskie maski, które kupiłem, by powiesić na ścianie w moim mieszkaniu, przyszło mi do głowy, że być może jest jeszcze jedna, i to niezwykle ważna, warstwa tej historii. „Kansas City Times" pisze w październiku 1964 roku: „A co, jeśli czarownicy i tancerze odziani w lwie skóry wiedzą coś, czego my nie wiemy? A jeśli okaże się, że pierwszymi odgłosami, które dotrą na ziemię z Księżyca, będą dźwięki afrykańskich bębnów? Czy również będziemy się śmiać?".

– Nkoloso, jako Bemba, mógł być w jakiś sposób zarówno pod wpływem tradycyjnych wierzeń dotyczących pochodzenia jego plemienia, jak i wierzeń związanych z czarami – sugeruje doktor Walima Kalusa. – Bemba wierzą, że istnieje połączenie między nimi a sferą transcendentną, mityczną. Więcej, wierzą, że z tej sfery można czerpać moc i używać jej, by osiągać cele tu, na ziemi. Możesz korzystać z tych mocy, dajmy na to, by osiągnąć sukces w polityce albo w małżeństwie czy w pracy. Nkoloso zapewne był tego świadom. Tego, że jest pewna energia, która, choć mityczna, może być bardzo użyteczna, by osiągać cele w życiu. Niewykluczone, że czuł, że ponieważ należy do ludu, którego założyciele przyszli z niebios, to on może czerpać użyteczną moc z tej sfery, by wykorzystać ją w swoim kosmicznym projekcie. Mógł myśleć, że jeśli jego projekt zakończyłby się sukcesem, to on i jego współplemieńcy mogliby może powrócić tam, skąd pochodzili ich przodkowie. Lecz jest jeszcze coś bardziej istotnego. Bemba wierzą, że czary mogą dać ci możliwość przemieszczania się z jednego punktu do drugiego. Było dużo takich przypadków, gdy ludzie byli oskarżani o podróżowanie nocą z jednej wioski do drugiej, często odległej o wiele kilometrów, by wyrządzić jakąś krzywdę swoim wrogom. Podróżowali bez użycia samolotu rzecz jasna. To bardzo silne przekonanie wśród Bemba. Ci ludzie nierzadko byli potem atakowani przez tłum, oskarżani o czary, często ginęli. Oczywiście to przemieszczanie się w czasie i przestrzeni niekoniecznie musi służyć złym działaniom. Może być również wykorzystywane, by pomagać innym. Zatem Bemba mają pewne wyobrażenie o przestrzeni i Kosmosie, choć rzecz jasna funkcjonuje ono w bardzo mitycznej sferze. Nie ma ono żadnego związku z wiedzą naukową czy technologiczną. Sądzę, że Nkoloso czerpał stamtąd bardzo dużo dla swoich pomysłów, które funkcjonowały jednak w połączeniu z bardzo tradycyjnym rozumieniem rzeczy. Myślę, że w swoich działaniach inspirował się wieloma źródłami – chrześcijaństwem, mitami, własną wiedzą o Kosmosie, ale również współczesną nauką. Nie można wykluczyć, że wierzenia Bemba wpłynęły na to, co robił w taki czy inny sposób. Zwłaszcza jeśli chodzi o przekonanie, że człowiek może przemieszczać się bez użycia żadnej technologii, lecz korzystając z mocy czarów. To z pewnością było dla niego ważnym źródłem inspiracji.

W piątej korespondencji Arthur Hoppe donosi: „Umieszczenie zambijskiego astronauty na Księżycu, planowane początkowo na przyszły miesiąc, zostało dziś »nieuchronnie odroczone«. Przyczyna tego niepowodzenia, według dyrektora Nkoloso, jest jedna – brak środków finansowych na dalsze badania.

– Wraz z rozwojem naszego napędu turbulentnego jesteśmy technologicznie znacznie przed Amerykanami i Rosjanami – wyjaśnił Nkoloso. – Lecz w związku z promieniowaniem kosmicznym okazuje się, że będziemy potrzebować silnika o jeszcze większej mocy, a to będzie wymagało większych nakładów finansowych.

Pomimo faktu, iż w kwestiach finansowych Zambia pozostaje mocno w tyle w stosunku do Amerykanów i Rosjan, dyrektor Nkoloso nie traci wiary. Bezzwłocznie wystosował prośbę do rządu USA o »dodatkowe zapasy ciekłego tlenu i ciekłego wodoru oraz 7 500 000 funtów brytyjskich«. Przedstawiciele ambasady amerykańskiej odmówili zajęcia oficjalnego stanowiska w tej sprawie. Jednakże jeden z nich przyznał prywatnie, że nie widzi powodu, by USA pomogły Zambii w wyścigu na Księżyc.

Poinformowany o reakcji Stanów Zjednoczonych dyrektor Nkoloso bez słowa wyjął mały czerwony medalik ze swojej kieszeni i przypiął na piersi do munduru. Na medalu widniała podobizna Lenina. Czy to wskazuje, że będzie szukał pomocy w ZSRR?

– Proszę – odrzekł z rozbrajającym uśmiechem – to jedynie pamiątka, którą otrzymałem od rosyjskich delegatów podczas uroczystości niepodległościowych w zeszłym miesiącu. Zdecydowanie wolałbym robić interesy z Amerykanami, ale...

Dyrektor Nkoloso zdradził również, że zwrócił się o pomoc do ONZ. Pokazał mi kopię listu, który wystosował do UNESCO w Genewie, prosząc o wsparcie techniczne w budowie rakiety oraz 19 000 000 dolarów. Jak do tej pory nie otrzymał odpowiedzi.

– Nie mam wątpliwości, że mój projekt uzyska pełne wsparcie bloku afrykańsko-azjatyckiego.

Dyrektor Nkoloso wybrał się też do ambasadora Izraela, pana Avishaia. To niezwykle znaczące w kontekście trwającej na afrykańskim kontynencie rywalizacji między Izraelem a państwami arabskimi, prześcigającymi się w udzielaniu wsparcia finansowego i technologicznego nowym państwom.

Ambasador Avishai przyjął dyrektora Nkoloso uprzejmie, lecz również nie zajął stanowiska w tej sprawie. Choć ambasador nie udzielił żadnego oficjalnego komentarza na temat zambijskiego projektu kosmicznego, wyjaśnił motywy stojące za setkami izraelskich przedsięwzięć pomocowych w Zambii i innych krajach Afryki Środkowej.

– To nie jest z naszej strony altruizm – powiedział – to wynika z prostego faktu, że Izrael otoczony jest zewsząd milionami wrogo nastawionych Arabów i potrzebujemy jak najwięcej sojuszników.

Tydzień po wizycie dyrektora Nkoloso w ambasadzie Izraela premier Zjednoczonej Republiki Arabskiej Gamal Abdel Naser ogłosił, że on także zamierza otworzyć ambasadę w Lusace. Przyjazdu Rosjan i Chińczyków można się spodziewać każdego dnia.

– Mam przeczucie – powiedział z radosnym uśmiechem Nkoloso – że opóźnienie naszego programu nie będzie trwało zbyt długo. Sądzę, że z pomocą tak wielu przyjaciół Zambia wkrótce będzie na Księżycu".

Kilka dni później amerykańskie gazety od Florydy po San Francisco wydrukowały szósty tekst Arthura Hoppego: „Ale porażka jest porażką. By zbadać stopień rozczarowania wśród zwykłych Zambijczyków, niezwłocznie wybrałem się na wyprawę do serca rozległego afrykańskiego buszu. Jak wszystkie wyprawy w głąb afrykańskiego buszu, okazała się prawdziwym piekłem. [...]

To była niewielka, zbudowana z błotnej cegły chata, kryta strzechą, którą ona dzieliła wraz z ojcem, dwoma młodszymi braćmi i siostrą. Woda gotowała się w metalowym naczyniu postawionym na żarzącym się węglu. Po jednej stronie na ziemi leżały dwa koce, po drugiej składzik drewna, na nim niebieska walizka i tykający budzik. Zapytałem panią Ndongę, jakie miała odczucia w związku z Zambijskim Programem Kosmicznym.

– Tak, proszę – odrzekła, potrząsając głową – wyprawa na Księżyc to zadanie dla Amerykanów.

Ale czemu dla nas, a nie dla Zambijczyków? Pani Ndonga zakryła dłońmi twarz i zaczęła chichotać. Następnie, jakby przepraszając, uczyniła pewien gest. Zrozumiałem ten gest doskonale. A teraz mogę się jedynie modlić, by moja depesza dotarła do naszego świata. Ten gest bowiem, mówię to z absolutnym przekonaniem, podsumowywał to, co myśli zambijska opinia publiczna o tym, że Ameryka wydaje dwadzieścia miliardów dolarów, by wygrać wyścig na Księżyc jedynie po to, by umocnić swoją pozycję na arenie międzynarodowej.

Oni myślą, że jesteśmy niespełna rozumu".

Chciałem tego wszystkiego posłuchać z pierwszej ręki. Domyślam się, że do gazet trafiła jedynie część tego, czego świadkiem był amerykański dziennikarz. On sam mógłby zapewne powiedzieć o Mukuce Nkoloso znacznie więcej. Niestety Arthur Hoppe zmarł w 2000 roku. Pod koniec grudnia 1964 roku, w przedostatniej, siódmej korespondencji z Lusaki pisał tak: „Zambijski lot na Księżyc został dziś przełożony na początek przyszłego roku. Ponadto, kiedy tylko mierząca dziesięć stóp, napędzana systemem turbulentnym rakieta powróci z Księżyca, zostanie niezwłocznie wysłana na Marsa.

To dobra wiadomość dla siedemnastoletniej Marthy Mwamby, pierwszej zambijskiej astronautki. To ona została wyznaczona do tego historycznego lotu na Marsa. Martha umiejętnie skrywa podniecenie za maską dostojnego spokoju.

Zatem jeśli wszystko będzie przebiegać zgodnie z planem, Martha pójdzie w ślady Godfreya Mwango, numeru jeden wśród zambijskich astronautów, który został wybrany jako ten, który zatknie na Księżycu czerwono-czarno-pomarańczowo-zieloną flagę nowej republiki. Mwango został wybrany do tej misji, ponieważ prezentował nadzwyczajne umiejętności chodzenia na rękach.

Pani Mwamba została wyselekcjonowana do lotu na Marsa, ponieważ jest właścicielką dwunastu kotów.

– Jakie będzie zadanie tych kotów? – spytałem dyrektora.

– Proszę – odpowiedział, skinąwszy głową – po części koty zapewnią towarzystwo w długiej podróży. Ale przede wszystkim stanowią wyposażenie techniczne.

– Wyposażenie techniczne?

– Tak. Gdy Martha wyląduje na Marsie, otworzy drzwi rakiety i wypuści koty. Jeśli one przeżyją, wtedy będzie widać, czy Mars nadaje się do zamieszkania przez ludzi. – Odwrócił się w stronę pani Mwamby: – Czyż nie jest tak? – spytał.

– O tak, właśnie tak – odparła pani Mwamba. [...]

Jest poważną kobietą o krągłych kształtach, czarującym uśmiechu i uroczym chichocie, gdy wprawi się ją w zakłopotanie. Zazwyczaj ubiera się we wzorzystą sukienkę, sandały i, jak przystało na astronautę, wełniany wojskowy sweter w kolorze khaki. Ukończyła odpowiednik edukacji podstawowej – to bardzo dużo jak na dziewczynę z tych stron – a ostatnio studiuje astrofizykę, kosmografię, geometrię, chemię i astrobiologię, jak zapewnia jej nauczyciel, dyrektor Nkoloso. Do tego, w związku z przyśpieszonymi pracami nad programem kosmicznym, Martha bierze także udział w wymagających treningach fizycznych, takich jak staczanie się ze wzgórza w beczce po oleju. By doświadczyć uczucia podróży przez międzygwiezdną przestrzeń.

Spytana o to, czy owo przeżycie było dla niej doświadczeniem ekscytującym i cennym, czy jedynie rutynowym, Martha schyliła lekko głowę i zaśmiała się ujmująco. Sama zgłosiła się na ochotnika, mimo że, jak mówi, było to »trochę niepokojące«. W przeciwieństwie do astronauty Godfreya Mwango, Martha Mwamba nie przeszła jeszcze pełnego testu wodowania kosmicznej kapsuły, podczas którego beczka z astronautą jest wrzucana do wody. Mimo to specjalnie dla zdjęć zgodziła się stanąć w pływającej po rzece beczce. To również określiła jako »trochę niepokojące«.

Astronauta numer trzy spośród dwunastoosobowej grupy to Ruben Simwenga, lekko zbudowany młodzieniec w wieku dwudziestu dwóch lat. On poleci w Kosmos, gdy pani Mwamba wróci z Marsa. Cel jego misji pozostaje jednak nieznany.

– Całe niebiosa stoją przed nami otworem – wyznał ekspansywnie dyrektor Nkoloso.

Funkcja pozostałych astronautów w grupie nie jest do końca jasna. Jeden jest odpowiedzialny za noszenie włóczni, inny za trzymanie sztandaru Zambii, zadaniem jeszcze innego jest noszenie pękatej teczki dyrektora Nkoloso.

Spytałem dyrektora, na jaką planetę sam zamierza się udać w swojej zambijskiej rakiecie napędzanej systemem turbulentnym.

– Och – odrzekł, kiwając smutno głową – podjęliśmy decyzję, że nie mogę wznosić się na wysokości powyżej czterystu stóp. Muszę być tu, na dole, i nauczać".

A co, jeśli to wszystko było jedynie wielkim żartem? Afrykańską krotochwilą, na którą nabraliśmy się wszyscy, począwszy od poważnego prezentera ITN? Może Zambijski Program Kosmiczny to nic innego jak wieloletni artystyczny performance na najwyższym poziomie, którego nie powstydziliby się współcześni artyści? Teatr, przedstawienie, które trwa, mimo że główny aktor i reżyser już dawno nie żyje? Może nie doceniamy tego człowieka, lecz nie jego geniuszu, tylko poczucia humoru? Mimo upływu lat wciąż rozbudza wyobraźnię fotografów, malarzy i pisarzy.

Co, jeśli Edward Mukuka Nkoloso, siedząc w końcu na swoim Księżycu, omiatany słonecznym wiatrem, ze wszystkich nas się teraz śmieje?

Kilka lat później, w 1969 roku, w „Chicago Journalism Review" ktoś wrócił do tematu zambijskiego lotu na Księżyc i skomentował go w ten sposób: „Nie ma nic, co Afrykanie lubią robić bardziej niż naśmiewanie się z białych, którzy biorą wszystko tak poważnie. Oni mają mocno rozwinięte poczucie humoru, więc jak podłapią coś zachodniego, to lubią to naśladować". Z końcem 1964 roku jeden z zambijskich periodyków dla białych – „Abercornucopia" – poświęca dyrektorowi Nkoloso całą stronę tekstu: „Obecnie nawet najtwardsi zwolennicy afrykańskiego nacjonalizmu czują, że ten dowcip zaszedł już znacznie zbyt daleko. Dotarł do zagranicznych mediów, w szczególności do gazet amerykańskich, gdzie został wyeksploatowany na ogromną skalę. Jeśli opinia publiczna odczuje, że »dr« Nkoloso posiada jakiekolwiek oficjalne wsparcie, może to mieć bardzo niekorzystny wpływ na stosunek Amerykanów do Zambii, a w szczególności na wysiłki ich rządu związane z pomocą dla rozwijających się krajów. Ludzie nie lubią pożyczać pieniędzy i wysyłać pomocy w miejsca, gdzie hochsztaplerzy brani są na poważnie. Świat – który często potrafi być niezwykle głupi – nie może pomyśleć, że »dr« Nkoloso ma jakiekolwiek oficjalne wsparcie w swych »kosmicznych« działaniach ani jakiekolwiek związki z rządem lub otoczeniem prezydenta. [...] Nkoloso powinien bez rozgłosu odejść z życia publicznego i powinno się go trzymać jak najdalej od prezydenta, tak by w żadnym wypadku nie pokazywał się z nim na żadnych zdjęciach oficjalnych czy prasowych. Co więcej, w przyszłości nie powinien być dopuszczony do piastowania żadnych stanowisk rządowych lub partyjnych. Oprócz oczywistej szkodliwości jego działania dla Zambii nie ma przecież nic bardziej nudnego niż wielokrotnie powtarzany dowcip [...]".

W ostatniej korespondencji z Lusaki Arthur Hoppe pisze: „Więc poszedłem się pożegnać z moim przyjacielem Edwardem Nkoloso, dyrektorem projektu. Po ponad tygodniu spędzonym tutaj naprawdę zdaje się bliskim przyjacielem. Znalazłem go w jego kosmicznej kwaterze głównej na drugim piętrze starego budynku właśnie w chwili, gdy miał spotkanie z czwórką swoich astronautów. Powiedział ze smutkiem w głosie, że żałuje, że wyjeżdżam, i że on też właśnie przygotowuje się do podróży. Następnego dnia wyrusza do Ndoli, górniczego miasteczka sto pięćdziesiąt mil na północ, gdzie jego astronauta numer jeden, Godfrey Mwango, przejdzie »trening stoicki«.

Spytałem nieufnie, czym jest ów trening, bo prawdę mówiąc, pewne pomysły pana Mukuki Nkoloso, które poznałem podczas tego tygodnia, budziły moje podejrzenia.

– Tam jest stary szyb górniczy, zalany wodą, głębokości około czterystu stóp – wyjaśnił Mukuka Nkoloso, jak zawsze z radosnym uśmiechem. – Wrzucimy go tam. – Potem zwrócił się do swoich astronautów i jak to miał w zwyczaju, zapytał uprzejmie: – Nieprawdaż?

– Tak – odpowiedzieli zgodnie – tak zrobimy.

Astronauta Mwango kiwnął głową i uśmiechał się równie pogodnie jak pozostali.

Pan Nkoloso jest fascynującym człowiekiem. Ma czterdzieści lat, jest chudy, niewysoki i pełen szacunku. Ma również coś w rodzaju wrodzonej godności i gdy przechadza się ulicami Lusaki w swoim wystrojonym w medale mundurze i bojowym hełmie, w eskorcie swoich astronautów, miejscowi ludzie pozdrawiają go z szacunkiem, a europejscy dyplomaci traktują z przesadną uprzejmością. Jest bowiem także dyrektorem do spraw propagandy w United National Independence Party, partii znajdującej się u steru władzy.

Jego wiedza jest dość szeroka, począwszy od podstawowych robót technicznych, a na komiksach o Kosmosie i Bóg wie czym jeszcze skończywszy. W jednym zdaniu będzie mówił o teorii względności Einsteina (zgadza się z nią), potem o mitologii plemienia Bemba, którego jest członkiem, wspomni też o Dedalu i Ikarze i »napędzie turbulentnym«, który zaprojektował, by polecieć na Księżyc. Do tego będzie się ciągle serdecznie uśmiechał, a jego oczy będą bacznie obserwować twoje reakcje na jego słowa.

Tak więc gdy ściskaliśmy sobie dłonie na pożegnanie, zadałem mu pytanie, które nurtowało mnie od początku: po co w ogóle chce lecieć na ten Księżyc?

– Bo – odrzekł, przyjmując dziwną pozę – jest. Nieprawdaż?

– Tak – przytaknęli astronauci – właśnie tak.

– On nie jest jak chmury – kontynuował. – Leciałem samolotem podczas wojny i wiem, że przez chmury można przelecieć. A Księżyc jest ciałem stałym zawieszonym pośród nieba. I my także jesteśmy ciałami stałymi, więc z pewnością możemy do niego dotrzeć, nieprawdaż?

– Tak – znów przytaknęli astronauci – właśnie tak.

Spytałem, co zrobi Zambia z Księżycem, gdy już wygra kosmiczny wyścig. Po raz pierwszy Nkoloso wyglądał na zaskoczonego.

– Ale czemu? – odparł. – Księżyc należy do nas wszystkich. Jest tam, byśmy wszyscy mogli go podziwiać – znów się uśmiechnął. – Więc, gdy przylecą Amerykanie i Rosjanie, powitamy ich jak braci.

Uścisnąłem po raz ostatni jego rękę i powiedziałem, że ufam, że nowa zambijska republika wygra wyścig na Księżyc. I naprawdę mam taką nadzieję".

*

– Jak ta rakieta poleciała w Dzień Niepodległości, to potem Nkoloso zamierzał wystrzelić taką z człowiekiem – wspomina Devison Bambo Miti, dopijając coca-colę. – Ale nie było żadnych sponsorów. Partia i państwo też nie chciały się włączyć w projekt. Nkoloso był sfrustrowany tym brakiem pieniędzy, za wszystko płacił z własnej kieszeni. Niewielu ludzi pomagało, bo większość nie doceniała tego, co robił, nie rozumieli, że to bardzo ważne i że pomoże naszemu krajowi. Myśleli, że to strata czasu. A gdyby miał pieniądze, to na pewno wysłałby kogoś na Księżyc, przynajmniej małpę. Pieniądze są ważne. Bez pieniędzy trudno zbudować prawdziwą rakietę. A tak, jakoś rok po Dniu Niepodległości, Akademia przestała działać.

Osiem miesięcy po wizycie Arthura Hoppego, w drugiej połowie 1965 roku, do Lusaki przybył znany dziennikarz i fotograf Dennis Lee Royle. W jednym z jego artykułów, licznie przedrukowywanym przez gazety w całych Stanach Zjednoczonych, Edward Mukuka Nkoloso narzeka:

„– Po tym, jak zagraniczne telewizje i gazety pokazały naszych astronautów podczas treningu, otrzymałem tysiące listów z innych krajów. Ale moi astronauci poczuli się jak gwiazdy filmowe. Zaczęli się domagać wynagrodzenia i odmówili dalszego udziału w programie ćwiczeń.

A to nie wszystko. »Siostra Niebios«, Martha Mwamba, która ukończyła pełny kurs kosmiczny, czyli odbyła pięćdziesiąt »lotów orbitalnych« w beczce po oleju oraz przeszła pomyślnie wszystkie testy grawitacyjne huśtania się na drzewie, zaszła w ciążę. Zupełnie niespodziewanie. W związku z tym, zamiast lecieć na Marsa, wróciła do swojej wioski, gdzie rodzice odradzili jej dalszy udział w kosmicznych fanaberiach. – Mam kłopoty ze swoimi astronautami i astronautkami. Nie chcą się skoncentrować na locie w Kosmos. Zamiast studiować Księżyc, romanse im w głowie – przyznaje Nkoloso. – Dwóch spośród moich najlepszych kadetów – ubolewa dalej dyrektor – poszło na hulankę miesiąc temu i od tego czasu ślad po nich zaginął. Inny z moich astronautów przyłączył się do miejscowej trupy artystycznej. Mówi, że zarabia większe pieniądze jako cyrkowiec, bujając się na wysokim maszcie".

– KK starał się go zniechęcić do prac nad tą rakietą – komentuje Sikota Wina, siedząc w swoim pełnym pamiątek salonie. – A swoją drogą, ciekawe, co się z nią stało. Tak czy inaczej, była symbolem tego pragnienia wolności, które nas wtedy ogarniało. Ale oczywiście nikt nie brał go na poważnie, zwłaszcza w UNIP, gdy widzieliśmy te turlające się beczki. Chodziliśmy tam czasami to oglądać. Wszyscy mówili mu, że wycieczka na Księżyc to jednak trochę bardziej skomplikowana sprawa. Zresztą wielu myślało, że jest wariatem. Ale potem, gdy nadeszły zaproszenia z USA i Rosji, zaczęliśmy na to patrzeć inaczej. Przez pewien czas było o nim głośno w Lusace, to, co robił, cieszyło się sporym zainteresowaniem. Niektórzy się zastanawiali, czy może nasze uniwersytety nie powinny się zająć jakoś sprawą.

Ale nie zajęły się. Co więcej, Zambijski Program Kosmiczny nieuchronnie zbliżał się do bankructwa. Ani rząd, ani prezydent Kaunda, ani UNESCO nie odpowiedzieli na prośby Mukuki Nkoloso o wsparcie finansowe. Choć rząd Kennetha Kaundy kładł spory nacisk na rozwój nauki i edukacji, zapewniając ośrodkom uniwersyteckim znaczące, jak na rozwijający się kraj, środki finansowe, Edward Mukuka Nkoloso nigdy nie otrzymał żadnych pieniędzy. Kaunda, zirytowany i zawstydzony nadmierną medialną popularnością Akademii, tolerował jej działalność, lecz jednocześnie starał się zniechęcić Mukukę Nkoloso do dalszych prac nad rozwojem kosmicznych technologii. Choć lokalne media raczej wyśmiewały pomysły dyrektora Nkoloso, to dziennikarze zagraniczni podchodzili do tego, co robił, z pewnym szacunkiem. Do kosmicznej kwatery głównej płynęły listy ze słowami sympatii i uznania z całego świata. Ktoś podarował mały teleskop, ktoś inny komplet książek o Kosmosie, jeszcze ktoś inny przysyłał zapasy jedzenia. Lecz niestety w paczkach i listach rzadko były jakiekolwiek pieniądze. Z Indii jakiś młody miłośnik astronomii przysłał dziesięć rupii.

„Popatrz na te listy ze wszystkich stron świata – mówi w artykule Dennisa Lee Royle'a dyrektor Nkoloso – przynajmniej mam największą kolekcję znaczków pocztowych w całej Afryce! Jeśli program kosmiczny się nie powiedzie, będę mógł zostać kolekcjonerem znaczków. Może Amerykanie chcieliby wesprzeć mój program kosmiczny? – zwraca się do dziennikarza Mukuka Nkoloso. – Tylko jedno musimy sobie od razu wyjaśnić: jak już dolecimy na Księżyc, to zambijską flagę zatkniemy jako pierwszą".

25

Jadę na wschodnie przedmieścia Lusaki, w kierunku osiedli, których nazwy zawsze wybrzmiewają na dworcu autobusowym jako ostatnie, odległe przystanki. Chelston, Avondale – dopiero teraz uświadamiam sobie, że to się tak pisze. Wymawiane przez młodocianych autobusowych naganiaczy, często pijanych, brzmiały zgoła inaczej, jakby mówione w zupełnie innym języku. W Avondale mieszka Stary Mwaba, uznany zambijski artysta malarz, rocznik 1976. Miał już wystawy w kilku stolicach afrykańskich, potem także w Nowym Jorku. Jego ostatni cykl obrazów nosi tytuł *We Are Still Going to the Moon* i oprócz Lusaki prezentowany był w Berlinie w 2015 roku. Wchodzę do niewielkiej pracowni wypełnionej ogromnymi blejtramami, tysiącami szkiców, notatek i zaschniętych farb. Na ścianie, przypięte do sznurka wiszą szkice znajomej twarzy bez zęba, w bojowym hełmie i pelerynie.

– Sądzę, że gdy ludzie o nim piszą i mówią, to w większości bardzo upraszczają tę historię, posługują się krzywdzącymi stereotypami i kliszami, powielając fałszywe opinie – zaczyna Stary Mwaba. – Uważają, że ta historia powinna być taka i taka, należy ją przedstawić tak i tak. Nie próbują szukać głębszego znaczenia i kontekstu. A historię tego człowieka należy opowiadać prawdziwie, i nie chodzi mi tutaj o fakty, one nie są najważniejsze. Mówię o tym, by być tu, na miejscu, mówię o wrażliwości i szacunku, nawet jeśli on był niespełna rozumu, choć ja nie uważam, by tak było. Byłem w Nowym Jorku kilka lat temu i znajomy podesłał mi ten klip z YouTube'a. Potraktowałem to oczywiście jako żart. Dopóki nie przypomniałem sobie, że słyszałem już tę historię. Widziałem tego człowieka. W dzieciństwie. To było coś, co się opowiadało w domu jako anegdotę. Moja matka pochodzi z tych samych okolic co Nkoloso. Żartowało się u nas, że stamtąd pochodzą sami wariaci, no bo Nkoloso, Lenshina, Mulolani*. Zacząłem trochę badać sprawę i trafiłem na zdjęcia Cristiny de Middel.

Wybucham śmiechem, gdy okazuje się, że nasze zainteresowanie Edwardem Mukuką Nkoloso zaczęło się od tych samych zdjęć.

– Na początku byłem zachwycony tym, że ktoś już coś zrobił z tym tematem – opowiada Stary Mwaba. – Ale potem zobaczyłem wywiad, w którym de Middel mówi o tym, dlaczego zrobiła ten projekt, i poczułem głębokie rozczarowanie. Bo ona powielała te głupie stereotypy o Afryce. Na zasadzie: spójrzcie, ten kontynent to nie tylko smutne historie, głód i wojny, lecz także coś wesołego, na przykład grupa ludzi, którzy chcieli lecieć na Księżyc. Zatem ubierzmy parę osób w kolorowe stroje i zróbmy zdjęcia. Owszem powstały bardzo piękne fotografie, ale historia, którą nam opowiadają, jest niezwykle powierzchowna. To w jakimś stopniu świadczy o niezrozumieniu tematu, tego, czym tak naprawdę była w tamtych czasach idea Nkoloso. Kłopot w tym, że w zdjęciach Cristiny nie ma nie tylko kontekstu, ale przede wszystkim nie ma Mukuki Nkoloso. Nic nam nie mówią ani o Nkoloso, kim był i dlaczego wpadł na taki pomysł, ani o miejscu, w którym to się działo. De Middel te aspekty pomija, co w moim odczuciu czyni jej prace pustymi. To bardziej opowieść o niej samej niż o nim. Żeby zrobić te zdjęcia, podróżowała po

* Emilio Mulolani – zwany Piotrem Afryki, przywódca sekty chrześcijańskiej Children of the Sacred Heart (Umutima Walowa), w której głosił, że ludzie powinni być naturalni jak dzieci, chodzić bez ubrań, uprawiać wolny seks. Sektę zdelegalizowano, a on został ekskomunikowany.

kilku krajach Europy, szukała odpowiednich plenerów. Dlaczego nie przyjechała do Zambii? Znów ktoś przedstawia naszą historię, niewiele o niej wiedząc, nie próbując nawet jej zrozumieć.

Stary Mwaba pokazuje mi szkice do serii *We Are Still Going to the Moon*. Z zakamarków pracowni wyciąga też wielkie płótna. Na wielu z nich postacie zwykłych Zambijczyków i Zambijek uchwyconych w prozaicznych chwilach dniach – na ulicy, na targu, u fryzjera. Seria obrazów *Space Cadet Audition* to portrety przypadkowych ludzi – jest młoda kobieta z dzieckiem na rękach, jest nastolatek w rozchełstanej koszuli, jest dziewczyna z ogromnymi kolczykami. Na dużych płótnach uliczne sceny z Soweto Market (targowiska w centrum Lusaki).

. Na przepełnionych kolorem płótnach Starego każda postać jest potencjalnym kosmicznym kadetem lub może bardziej – mieszkańcem Kosmosu. Jest także obraz czarno-biały, duży, niemal kwadratowy. Na nim człowiek leżący na ziemi, obok dużych beczek po oleju. Nad nim cały wszechświat plam, kształtów, które za każdym razem, gdy mrużę oczy, układają się w inne znaczenia, skojarzenia, których nie nadążam nazywać. Obraz ma tytuł *Obsessed with Space.*

– Nasza współczesna sztuka, nasza historia, w ogóle wszystko, co robimy, jest zdeterminowane przez to, jak patrzy na nas Zachód – przyznaje z żalem Stary Mwaba. – Naszą historię zawsze piszą inni ludzie, a my się tego później uczymy. Wyobrażasz sobie, że nam się w szkołach mówi, że to Livingstone odkrył Wodospady Wiktorii? Lenshinę znamy głównie z opisów brytyjskiego Komisarza Okręgowego. A przecież to jest niezwykła postać! Kobieta, która zakwestionowała całą naszą tradycję, religię, państwo, całą afrykańską duchowość – dodaje Stary Mwamba po chwili. – Byłem wkurzony, że wszystko, czego możemy się dowiedzieć o Mukuce Nkoloso, zostało stworzone przez ludzi z zagranicy: najpierw ten prezenter ITN, a teraz de Middel. A dla mnie to jednak coś więcej niż grupa ludzi turlających się w beczkach – kontynuuje emocjonalnie artysta. – Wtedy stwierdziłem, że sam chcę opowiedzieć tę historię. Nie tak jak oni. Zastanawiałem się, jak historia Mukuki Nkoloso łączy się ze mną, jak odnosi się do mnie samego. Jest w niej tak wiele dziur, tak wiele pytań i brakujących elementów, że robi się z niej niemal legenda, nie wiesz już, co jest prawdziwe, a co nie. To, co mnie najbardziej poruszało, to to, że gdy przeczytałem kilka wywiadów z nim, obejrzałem materiał filmowy, to wiedziałem, że on naprawdę wierzył, że można polecieć na Księżyc. On nie żartował. Ludzie mieli go za szaleńca, ale on po prostu uważał, że można to zrobić. Sądzę, że to niezwykle znaczące, to kluczowe. Bo gdzie my teraz jesteśmy? Wszyscy patrzą na Zachód, na Amerykę. A tu mamy gościa, który rzuca wyzwanie Ameryce. I ta relacja między lotem w Kosmos a odzyskaniem niepodległości. Przecież ta niepodległość to był taki sam lot w Kosmos. Nie tylko dla Zambijczyków. W całej Afryce to był pewien symbol. W wielu nowych krajach wypuszczano znaczki pocztowe z kosmicznymi motywami.

Przyglądam się portretom Marthy Mwamby wykonanym z powyginanego miedzianego drutu. Na ścianie pracowni wisi ich kilka, są częścią serii *Life on Mars*. Na każdym z nich „Siostra Niebios" patrzy z tęsknotą gdzieś w dal. Stary Mwaba również próbował ją odnaleźć. Bezskutecznie. „Siostra Niebios" pewnie nawet nie wie, że stała się inspiracją dla artysty, a jej miedziane portrety zdobiły ściany berlińskiej galerii.

– Kłopot tylko, że wiele osób przestało postrzegać życie, jak widział je Mukuka Nkoloso – ciągnie Stary Mwaba, gdy wychodzimy z jego pracowni, wsiadamy do auta i kierujemy się w stronę Lusaki. – Mówię o marzeniach. Szukamy ich zawsze gdzie indziej, w ogóle ludzie już coraz mniej marzą. Utraciliśmy tę zdolność, zwłaszcza młodzi. W naszym kraju można dziś usłyszeć głosy, że niepodległość uzyskaliśmy zbyt wcześnie. Są ludzie, którzy twierdzą, że lepiej by było, gdybyśmy nadal byli kolonią. Sądzę, że mamy tendencję do zajmowania się rzeczami nieistotnymi, zadajemy niewłaściwe pytania. A Nkoloso zadawał właśnie odpowiednie pytania, poruszał wbrew pozorom ważne sprawy. Bardzo doceniam to, że mimo braku technologii i możliwości finansowych miał tę ideę, niezależnie od tego, czy u jej podstaw leżały wierzenia związane z czarami, czy wiedza naukowa. To, czy Nkoloso brał to wszystko na poważnie, czy nie, to drugorzędna sprawa. Czy miał świadomość tego, że jest na przegranej pozycji w tym wyścigu? Sądzę, że tak, inaczej byłby niespełna rozumu. Najważniejsze jest jednak to, że wierzył, że lot na Księżyc i na Marsa jest możliwy. Nie pomylił się przecież? Inspirująca jest dla mnie jego wytrwałość, upór i konsekwencja w podążaniu za swym celem. Ja go postrzegam zresztą bardziej jako filozofa niż naukowca. O tym są moje prace. Ja ciągle chcę żyć marzeniem Mukuki Nkoloso. Przecież my ciągle możemy marzyć o podróży na Księżyc. Nadal możemy lecieć w ten Kosmos.

*

Po powrocie do hotelu otwieram katalog berlińskiej wystawy, który sprezentował mi Stary Mwaba. Na jednej ze stron czytam opis przygotowany przez kuratora Davida Elliotta: „Koncentrując się na donkiszotowskim ideale, jakim była Zambijska Akademia Kosmiczna, która jednym krokiem podjęła próbę przeskoczenia absurdalnych paradoksów kolonializmu, niepodległości i globalizacji, Stary Mwaba jasno daje do zrozumienia, że nawet w czasach Nkoloso Kosmos miał znacznie większą moc jako metafora niż jako granica".

26

Ilekroć pytałem syna Mukuki Nkoloso o pozostałych członków rodziny jego ojca, zawsze odpowiadał wymijająco, zmieniał temat lub mówił, że wszyscy umarli. A przecież musiało być ich trochę. Bracia? Żona? Inne dzieci? Kuzyni? W Afryce ma się wszakże duże rodziny. Zacząłem nabierać podejrzeń, że syn Mukuki Nkoloso chce pozostać jedynym dysponentem historii swego ojca. Tak by wszyscy zainteresowani tematem trafiali wyłącznie do niego. Dochodziły mnie jednak słuchy, że gdzieś jest jakiś drugi Nkoloso, choć nikt nie potrafił powiedzieć, czy jest on bratem, kuzynem, a może wujem człowieka, którego odwiedzam w domu w Chilenje. Miałem nawet numer jego telefonu, kilka numerów. Ale w Zambii to nic nie znaczy. Ludzie kupują telefony na kartę, gubią jedne, kupują drugie, często mają po kilka numerów naraz i nigdy nie wiesz, który jest aktualny, jeśli którykolwiek. Nie sposób się dodzwonić. Jednak na kilka dni przed moim wyjazdem jeden z telefonów odbiera jakiś mężczyzna. Mówi, że wie, że ktoś go szuka, ale nie miał pieniędzy, by naładować kartę i oddzwonić. Po prostu. Teraz cieszy się, że w końcu udało nam się skontaktować. Poznaję go parę dni później. Znów miejscem spotkania jest galeria handlowa.

Fortunate Nkoloso przyjeżdża do Lusaki z oddalonego o blisko czterysta kilometrów Kitwe specjalnie po to, by się ze mną spotkać. Wysoki, chudy, naturalnie roześmiany człowiek po sześćdziesiątce. Przedstawia się najpierw jako syn Edwarda Mukuki Nkoloso. Potem jako brat. W końcu dochodzimy do tego, że jest kuzynem, synem brata Edwarda Mukuki Nkoloso. Ciągle jednak podkreśla, że Nkoloso traktował go jak swojego własnego syna. On nazywał Mukukę Nkoloso czasami swoim ojcem, czasami bratem. Koligacje rodzinne w Afryce są względne.

W połowie lat sześćdziesiątych Edward Mukuka Nkoloso został powołany na stanowisko osobistego reprezentanta Kennetha Kaundy w African Liberation Center. W tym czasie Zambia, oprócz Botswany, była jedynym krajem południowej Afryki cieszącym się wolnością. Instytucja stworzona przez KK miała w zamyśle wspierać narodowowyzwoleńcze organizacje w ościennych krajach – Rodezji Południowej, Mozambiku, Angoli, Namibii, RPA. W Lusace bezpieczny azyl znajdowali wszyscy ci, którym w ich własnych krajach nadal groziło więzienie lub śmierć. Mimo ryzyka rząd KK chętnie udzielał schronienia i wsparcia ludziom z ANC*, ZAPU, ZANU, MPLA, FRELIMO, ANC (SA), COREMO, PAC, UPA, SWAPO, UDENAMO. Naturalną konsekwencją takiej polityki była częsta obecność w African Liberation Center doradców ze Związku Radzieckiego i Chińskiej Republiki Ludowej. Przez Lusakę płynęła broń dla partyzantów. Niepodległa Zambia nieuchronnie stała się rewolucyjnym przyczółkiem środkowej i południowej Afryki. Były wojskowy i niedoszły astronauta Edward Mukuka Nkoloso został człowiekiem, który z ramienia zambijskiego rządu koordynował relacje z partyzantami i godził interesy często rywalizujących lub wręcz otwarcie wrogich wobec siebie ugrupowań. W jakimś sensie odegrał istotną rolę w wyzwalaniu ościennych krajów.

* ANC, zdelegalizowany w RPA, od 1963 r. do upadku apartheidu miał w Lusace nawet swoją kwaterę główną. Partyzanci byli rozlokowani w buszu dokoła Lusaki, a Liberation Center było jedynie miejscem pracy i spotkań. W 1968 r. lotnictwo RPA zbombardowało z tego powodu budynki Liberation Center. Pisze o tym między innymi Jacques R. Roy w książce *Don't Quit – Don't Cry*. Przebywający w Zambii przedstawiciele różnych organizacji narodowowyzwoleńczych często byli celami ataków terrorystycznych organizowanych przez władze krajów, z których pochodziły.

Młody Fortunate Nkoloso dzieciństwo spędził na wsi. Do Lusaki przeprowadził się w 1966 roku, zbyt późno, by zostać jednym z kosmicznych kadetów. Ale w African Liberation Center, przy boku przybranego ojca, spędzał całe dnie.

– Jak się wchodziło do Liberation Center – opowiada mi Fortunate Nkoloso – to od razu po lewej były drzwi z tabliczką „His Excellency Personal Representative of Kenneth Kaunda". Naprzeciwko biegł korytarz z biurami tych wszystkich bojowników. Każdego ranka oni przychodzili do pracy o ósmej rano i wykonywali swoje obowiązki. Od czasu do czasu, tak raz w tygodniu, Mukuka Nkoloso zwoływał ich na apel na podwórku. Ustawiali się przed nim w linii i paradowali. On robił im całą musztrę, wykrzykiwał rozkazy, a oni grzecznie wszystko wykonywali. Bo też się go bali. Nikogo nie faworyzował, nie utrzymywał przyjaźni. Dbał bardzo o dyscyplinę, jak w wojsku. Gdy ktoś się źle zachowywał, pił, sprowadzał kobiety, to Nkoloso dzwonił do KK i tamten od razu musiał wracać do swojego kraju. A ci ludzie to była banda pijaków. Jak ktoś się nie chciał podporządkować, to Nkoloso go wyrzucał bez słowa. KK ufał mu bezgranicznie. Choć czasami, gdy się go spytało o Mukukę Nkoloso, to potrafił się roześmiać.

Fortunate Nkoloso przynosi na spotkanie teczkę ze starannie powycinanymi zdjęciami i artykułami z gazet. Teraz rozkłada je przede mną na kawiarnianym stoliku, porządkuje, układa, dopasowuje te, które się rozdarły. Wśród rozłożonych na stole dokumentów jest też zaproszenie na państwową ceremonię pogrzebu Edwarda Mukuki Nkoloso i kilka nekrologów.

– W biurze miał bardzo dużo książek. Potrafił wziąć jedną, przeczytać trzy, cztery zdania i odłożyć na półkę. A potem następną i tak samo. A po chwili wychodził z biura i wybierał się do miasta. Czasami szedł na piechotę, choć przecież dostał od rządu auto, ale nie chciało mu się go odpalać. A potem w mieście przypominał sobie o tym aucie, zatrzymywał kogoś na ulicy i mówił: „Wiesz, gdzie jest Liberation Center? To leć tam i powiedz, żeby przysłali tu moje auto natychmiast! I powiedz, że

Mukuka Nkoloso cię przysłał!". I zaraz ktoś po niego przyjeżdżał. Czasami palił chambę, czyli marihuanę, w zaciszu gabinetu. Od czasu do czasu też papierosy, choć nigdy nie dopalał ich do końca, zaczynał i wyrzucał po chwili, potem odpalał następnego. To była raczej poza niż nałóg. Czasami mówił bardzo dużo, nikogo nie dopuszczał do głosu, a potem milknął i pogrążał się w myślach, widać było, że coś mu ciągle chodzi po głowie. Był zupełnie nieprzewidywalny. Wydaje mi się, że po tym więzieniu w pięćdziesiątym siódmym wyszedł zmieniony, nie całkiem normalny. Bardzo go tam bili, zwłaszcza w głowę, nie wiem, może nawet jego mózg został w jakiś sposób uszkodzony, bo to, co potem robił, nie było normalne. Czasami zachowywał się bardzo przyjacielsko, a zaraz potem brutalnie. Miał humory i nastroje. Potrafił wstać znienacka w środku nocy i pojechać do biura. I po chwili zawołać pomocnika, by mnie natychmiast przyprowadził. Bo ja zawsze nosiłem tę jego teczkę. A jak on wzywał, to trzeba było biec co sił w nogach. Biegłem całą drogę od domu do biura. Chodziłem za nim prawie cały czas, zwłaszcza w wakacje, bo tak to miałem szkołę. Nie miałem nic do robienia w domu. A on mnie często wołał: „Fortunate, chodź! Idziemy!". Więc byłem przy nim prawie cały czas. Tak naprawdę to było strasznie męczące, bo on potrafił latać po mieście cały dzień, to do sklepu, to na policję, to do Shoprite'u na drugi koniec miasta. Albo po frytki do centrum i z tymi frytkami na lotnisko. Tylko po to, żeby pooglądać samoloty. Wtedy jeszcze nie było nowego lotniska, tylko to stare tu niedaleko. Siedział godzinami i oglądał startujące i lądujące samoloty. Potem nagle wstawał i z powrotem do miasta. I tak cały dzień.

Czasami Fortunate bierze którąś z leżących na stole gazet do ręki, patrzy na zdjęcie wuja w oficerskiej czapce, wzdycha „Ech, Nkoloso, Nkoloso, co to był za wariat!". Każdy z wycinków budzi w nim jakieś nowe wspomnienie, prowokuje kolejną opowieść. Raz po raz widzę, jak szklą mu się oczy.

– On w ogóle rzadko chodził gdziekolwiek sam. Zazwyczaj szło za nim sześć, czasami siedem osób. On, potem ochroniarz z włócznią, dalej ja z teczką, ktoś z innymi rzeczami, a reszta po prostu, bo to była jego grupa. I nikt nie śmiał iść obok niego, szli gęsiego jeden za drugim, taki orszak. Jak on szedł ulicą, to auta się zatrzymywały z piskiem opon, nawet biali, bo przecież niewielu czarnych miało wtedy auta. Biali się go bali, niektórzy skręcali w boczne uliczki, gdy go widzieli. Jak ktoś widział tę jego pelerynę, to schodził z drogi. A gdy wchodziliśmy dajmy na to do hotelu albo restauracji, a w hotelach też przecież głównie biali, to ludzie po cichutku opuszczali salę, jeden w lewo, drugi w prawo, i nagle się okazywało, że jesteśmy sami. Był takim człowiekiem, że gdziekolwiek wchodziliśmy, kierował się od razu do drzwi dyrektora. Nawet do State House wchodziliśmy. Wojsko, policja, nikt nas nie zatrzymywał. A w State House bankiet, jedzenie, picie, zabawa. A jak zaczepił cię jakiś ochroniarz, to wystarczyło powiedzieć, że przyszedłeś z Mukuką Nkoloso. Ja wiem, że to brzmi nieprawdopodobnie. Jakby ci to ktoś opowiadał, to pewnie byś pomyślał, że zmyśla. Ale ja tam byłem, zawsze przy nim byłem. Widziałem to wszystko na własne oczy. Często to wszystko bywało bardzo śmieszne. Można było się śmiać do rozpuku. Miał gest i rozmach. Jak siadaliśmy w restauracji, to kelner przynosił napoje skrzynkami. Skrzynkami! Nkoloso nie zamawiał pojedynczych butelek. Stół był po chwili zastawiony po brzegi, nie uwierzyłbyś! Mogliśmy zjeść wszystko! I nigdy za nic nie płaciliśmy, ludzie bali się go poprosić o pieniądze.

African Liberation Center działało do początku lat dziewięćdziesiątych, do czasu, gdy ostatnie z sąsiadujących krajów uzyskały niepodległość. Mało kto pamięta, gdzie w Lusace był budynek Liberation Center. Zaprowadził mnie tam Zachariah Zumba, ówczesny sekretarz Edwarda Mukuki Nkoloso. Dziś po African Liberation Center, które miało siedzibę w dzielnicy Kamwala w południowej części miasta, nie został ślad. Budynki zburzono. Choć w tym miejscu decydowały się losy całej południowej Afryki, nie ostała się choćby tablica pamiątkowa czy napis na murze.

– On nawet w domu cały czas mówił o tym Kosmosie – ciągnie dalej Fortunate Nkoloso. – Obsesja. Chodził po domu i mówił: „Ci muzungu lecą w Kosmos, czemu ja nie mogę? A jeśli ci muzungu chcą tak bardzo na Księżyc, to ja polecę dalej, na Marsa!". Ciągle o tym gadał. Jemu często wydawało się, że nie ma rzeczy niemożliwych. W ogóle nie myślał w tych kategoriach. Mówił na przykład, że trzeba się udać do Kabwe. Ale jak? Co to oznacza? Że na piechotę? Autem? Samolotem? Nie, on po prostu chciał być w tym Kabwe jak najszybciej i tyle. Wychodził z domu i dopiero w drodze orientował się, że nie da rady dotrzeć do tego Kabwe! Bo to sto pięćdziesiąt kilometrów.

Zatem czy Edward Mukuka Nkoloso się poddał? Zrezygnował? A może pochłonął go inny, jeszcze bardziej szalony plan? Gdzieś na początku 1970 roku gazety rozpisywały się o tym, że Edward Mukuka Nkoloso prowadzi kampanię na rzecz zambijskich czarowników, domagając się, by otrzymywali stałą pomoc od rządu. Z gorliwego katolika Nkoloso stał się nagle zwolennikiem czarów i medycyny naturalnej. Czary, tak zawsze tępione przez polityków UNIP, uważał teraz za jedyne antidotum na chrześcijaństwo, które obwiniał za zniszczenie afrykańskiej, rdzennej wiedzy i mądrości, a czarowników widział jako równych naukowcom. Sam przecież czuł się znacznie bardziej człowiekiem nauki niż politykiem czy wojskowym. O nowej inicjatywie Nkoloso znów pisały nawet gazety w USA. Sam Nkoloso czarów ponoć nie uprawiał. Choć jeśli czarownik to naukowiec, to czymże innym jak nie czarami była jego próba lotu na Księżyc?

– Kiedyś Mukuka Nkoloso oświadczył, że tego i tego dnia odpalimy rakietę – przypomina sobie Fortunate. – Wzięliśmy auto, zapakowaliśmy tę beczkę, cały jego orszak ruszył z nami do Ngwerere, tam była taka mała rzeczka. Wieść się rozniosła i przyszli gapie, ludzie oglądali z odległości. Ustawiliśmy beczkę, jeden z kadetów wsiadł do środka, beczka miała nawet takie małe drzwiczki. Wszyscy wzięliśmy rakietę, unieśliśmy ją do góry, a Nkoloso zaczął odliczanie. Cztery... trzy... dwa... jeden...

start! I wtedy z całych sił wypchnęliśmy rakietę w powietrze, ale oczywiście nie poleciała zbyt daleko, spadła, stoczyła się po zboczu i wpadła do rzeczki razem z kadetem, który był zupełnie przerażony. Nkoloso machnął ręką i rzucił: „To gówno to porażka, przecież to nie doleci do Marsa! Dobra, wracamy do biura!".

Spytałem Fortunate, czy wie, co stało się z tymi wszystkimi rzeczami Nkoloso.

– Te graty z Akademii Nauki potem trafiły właśnie do Liberation Center. Mieliśmy auto rządowe, pojechaliśmy i wzięliśmy to wszystko, te jego rakiety. A potem wszystko gdzieś przepadło.

We wrześniu 1973 roku na biurku Edwarda Mukuki Nkoloso wylądowało pismo, które czterdzieści trzy lata później znalazłem w jednej z teczek Archiwów Narodowych. Wymówienie. Ministerstwo Obrony dziękowało za lata służby oraz poświęceń i zwalniało go z funkcji szefa African Liberation Center. Z następnych pism, wszystkich oznaczonych jako poufne, wymienianych między ministerstwem a gabinetem prezydenta, widać jasno, że państwo nie wiedziało, co dalej zrobić z Edwardem Mukuką Nkoloso, i starało się znaleźć mu pozycję, która nie wiązała się z żadną funkcją reprezentacyjną, a jednocześnie zapewniała jakiekolwiek środki utrzymania. Nkoloso został więc wysłany do Kafue Estates, niewielkiej osady pięćdziesiąt kilometrów na południe od Lusaki, gdzie przydzielono mu funkcję szefa ochrony znajdujących się tam zakładów. Na pocieszenie dostał niewielkie mieszkanie.

– On zawsze chciał być ministrem obrony – kończy Fortunate Nkoloso. – Ale taki człowiek nie mógł być przecież dowódcą armii. Czasami on był jak komediant, to wszystko, co robił, to była komedia.

W 1983 roku Nkoloso ponoć ukończył studia prawnicze na uniwersytecie w Lusace. W archiwach uczelni nie znalazłem jednak jego pracy magisterskiej. Bez względu na to w tym samym roku otrzymał od University of Zambia doktorat honoris causa. Dwa lata później, w uznaniu zasług na rewolucyjnym, afrykańskim froncie, został zaproszony do ZSRR. Od Gorbaczowa dostał Medal 40-lecia Zwycięstwa w Wielkiej Wojnie Ojczyźnianej 1941–1945. Taki sam jak generał Jaruzelski czy generał Rola-Żymierski i ponad jedenaście milionów innych obywateli ZSRR i krajów zaprzyjaźnionych. Jest nawet zdjęcie. Wielka pięcioramienna gwiazda, wieże Kremla, kolejka odznaczonych, a wśród nich jeden czarny.

27

Niektórzy mówią, że Narodowa Akademia Nauki, Badań Kosmicznych i Filozofii przestała działać w 1965 roku, gdy opadła narodowowyzwoleńcza euforia. I gdy nie powiodły się próby zdobycia jakichkolwiek funduszy. Inni wspominają, że Akademia działała do początku lat siedemdziesiątych, gdy księżycowy wyścig miał już swego zwycięzcę. Tak czy inaczej, zastanawiam się, jak czuł się Edward Mukuka Nkoloso 20 lipca 1969 roku. Gdzie zastała go wieść o tym, że Neil Armstrong i Buzz Aldrin wylądowali na Księżycu? Czy czuł się rozczarowany i zawiedziony? Czy wręcz przeciwnie – sukces Amerykanów zwiększył jego ambicje? Czy widział zdjęcia i filmy z powierzchni Srebrnego Globu? Czy Księżyc wyglądał tak, jak go sobie wyobrażał? Nkoloso nigdy nie miał wątpliwości, że człowiek prędzej czy później wyląduje na Księżycu. Fala światowej dumy dotarła błyskawicznie również do Afryki. Wiele osób urodzonych w drugiej połowie 1969 roku nosi imię Apollo.

„– I co, nie mówiłem? Wylądowali na Księżycu w 1969 roku! – odpowiadał pewnemu dziennikarzowi w wywiadzie wiele lat później, tuż przed śmiercią. – Ale sukces Amerykanów to sukces całego rodzaju ludzkiego. – Po chwili dodał: – Dziś, jak mówisz o lądowaniu i życiu na Marsie, ludzie nadal mają cię za nienormalnego. Człowiek nadal boi się zapuszczać w nieznane. A czas najwyższy, żebyśmy myśleli o osiedlaniu się w innych częściach

Wszechświata. Jeśli tylko ludzie zaczną myśleć w kategoriach naukowych, ten lęk uda się przezwyciężyć. – Dalej Nkoloso nagle zmienił temat i odniósł się do Starego Testamentu, Księgi Jozuego, gdzie Jozue rozkazuje Słońcu, by wstrzymało swój ruch. – To jest przecież jakaś histeryczna wypowiedź ze strony Jozuego. Nie ma w sobie ziarna prawdy. Badania naukowe wykazały przecież, że to Ziemia porusza się wokół Słońca. Jako chrześcijanin nie chcę być kojarzony z tak prymitywnymi wypowiedziami. Biblia powinna zostać poprawiona!"

„Jestem człowiekiem owładniętym przez naukową teleologię" – wyjaśniał dalej Nkoloso. Tłumaczył przy tym, że termin „teleologia"* wywodzi się od słowa „teleskop" i jego umysł, tak jak teleskop, jest w stanie widzieć znacznie dalej niż inny. „W prostszych słowach: jestem ogarnięty czymś, co ludzie mogliby nazwać naukowym szaleństwem".

Spytany o plany na przyszłość, powiedział: „Nie porzuciłem mojego projektu. Nadal mam wizję przyszłości człowieka. Wciąż wierzę, że ludzie będą się swobodnie przemieszczać z jednej planety na drugą. Człowiek był głupi, starając się odizolować od reszty Kosmosu. Człowiek i Wszechświat to jedność. Żyć w oddzieleniu od Wszechświata to głupota wyższego rzędu".

Tymczasem wzmianki o zambijskich planach podboju Kosmosu można było znaleźć w amerykańskich gazetach jeszcze pod koniec lat sześćdziesiątych. Nkoloso nadal zapewnia w nich, że pierwszy czarny człowiek już wkrótce stanie na Księżycu, a potem na Marsie. W grudniu 1968 roku pogratulował załodze Apollo 8, która jako pierwsza okrążyła Księżyc, i dodał: „Zbudujmy teraz zambijską rakietę! Nie możemy zostawać w tyle za innymi narodami. To kwestia naszego niebiańskiego przeznaczenia, naszej naturalnej ambicji i kulturalnej hegemonii". W połowie 1971 roku Edward Mukuka Nkoloso ogłosił, że zbuduje w Lusace potężny teleskop, by móc bliżej przyjrzeć się planetom. Lecz, jak

* Nkoloso myli znaczenie słowa „teleologia". Za Encyklopedią PWN: „Teleologia – nazwa poglądów filozoficznych uzupełniających lub zastępujących przyczynowe wyjaśnianie rzeczywistości wykrywaniem ich celowości".

w przypadku lotu na Księżyc, znów nie było zainteresowanych, by wyłożyć pieniądze. We wrześniu 1969 roku gazeta z Kalifornii „Redlands Daily Facts" poświęciła Edwardowi Mukuce Nkoloso dwie kolumny. Autorem tekstu był pilot, generał lotnictwa USAF Perry Bruce Griffith.

„Należy przypuszczać, że coś wysoce wyrafinowanego, dajmy na to radio, samochód albo nawet maszyna do pisania, w rękach przeciętnego Zambijczyka byłoby obrazem równie niedorzecznym jak brzytwa w rękach sześciomiesięcznego dziecka" – napisał generał. Ale jego ton zmienia się z każdym następnym akapitem. „Niemniej w tym ryzykownym wyścigu w Kosmos Rosjanie i my mamy towarzystwo – Zambię. Możecie ich nazwać astrozambianautami. [...] Szefem Narodowej Akademii Nauki, Badań Kosmicznych i Filozofii jest Edward Mukuka Nkoloso. Nie znajdziecie go w *Man of Science* ani w *Who's Who in American Science*. Ale to bez znaczenia. Nie sądzę, by Mukuka Nkoloso przejmował się tym, że nie jest zapraszany na konferencje Boba Gilrutha* czy von Brauna, ani tym, że nie może czytać raportów Gagarina czy Jakowlewa. On ma swój własny program i własne problemy. [...] Prace nad jego rakietą trwają otoczone największą tajemnicą. Można się jedynie dowiedzieć, że użytym paliwem będzie siarka. Mała buteleczka tej substancji stoi zawsze na jego biurku, a on spędza dużo czasu, wpatrując się w nią z uśmiechem. Pomocy w programie udzieliło kilku Amerykanów. Wysłano kaszę oraz inne składniki diety zambianautów, które będą im niezbędne, by trzymać ciało i przede wszystkim ducha w dobrej formie podczas orbitalnego lotu. Teleskop wysłany przez jakiegoś sympatycznego Jankesa jest jednym z najcenniejszych narzędzi, jakie ma [Nkoloso]. Niestety teleskop ten dotarł na miejsce uszkodzony, i to poważnie, ma bowiem pęknięty okular". Kilka akapitów dalej generał pisze: „Gdy ludzie się z niego śmieją, on jedynie wzrusza ramionami i mówi, że z Marconiego też się śmiali. I dodaje: »Nie ma sensu

* Pierwszy szef Centrum Lotów Kosmicznych NASA.

być niewolnikiem Ziemi. Podobnie jak Amerykanie my już nie chcemy być przywiązanymi do Ziemi«. Być może Zambia wyśle człowieka w Kosmos, nawet jeśli mieliby go wystrzelić z armaty, jak robią to w cyrkach. Jak mówi Nkoloso: »Nie ma sensu być niewolnikiem Ziemi«. Jedynie lotnik lub astronauta może w pełni docenić prawdę tych słów".

*

Mimo wielu wysiłków nie odnalazłem Godfreya Mwango, choć wiem, że jest gdzieś w Zambii. Apele w telewizji oraz w „Times of Zambia" nie odniosły żadnego skutku. Jak potoczyły się losy zambijskiego astronauty numer jeden? Czy Godfrey Mwango spogląda czasami na Księżyc, na którym nie dane mu było stanąć? Nie wiem. Syn Mukuki Nkoloso twierdzi, że spotkał go rok czy dwa lata temu, lecz nie potrafił wskazać, gdzie mieszka. Ponoć Godfrey Mwango pisze książkę o kosmicznym epizodzie swojego życia. Ani ja, ani kilku innych dziennikarzy zainteresowanych tematem nie odnaleźliśmy też Marthy Mwamby, „Siostry Niebios", która nigdy nie poleciała na Marsa. Wiem jednak, że Martha została pierwszą kobietą w Zambii, która kierowała autokarem rejsowym. Podróż autobusem z Lusaki do odległej Kasamy to niewiele mniej niż lot w Kosmos. Lecz w Afryce takie historie giną bardzo łatwo. I zanim ktokolwiek zdąży ich wysłuchać, przepadają w bezkresach buszu, blakną wypalone słońcem i rozmyte deszczem. Nikną pośród mozołu codziennego życia i już po paru latach trudno powiedzieć, czy naprawdę się wydarzyły. Nawet te najbardziej niezwykłe, jak lot w Kosmos, zasługują na niewiele więcej niż lekki uśmiech czy machnięcie ręką. Tak właśnie wyobrażam sobie reakcję Marthy Mwamby, gdyby dane nam było się spotkać. Ona pochylona nad paleniskiem gdzieś w wiosce na północy Zambii, ugniata nshimę ciężkimi, spracowanymi rękoma. Na podwórku niewielkiego domu, w cieniu szałasu krytego słomą, otoczona gromadką wnuków. A ja pytam o Kosmos. Do ostatniej chwili miałem nadzieję, że ktoś ją znajdzie w tej Zambii. Że ktoś przyniesie jej wydanie

„Timesa" z kwietnia 2016 roku i powie: patrz, mamo, babciu lub sąsiadko, tu jest napisane, że ktoś cię szuka. Wtedy wsiadłbym w samolot i poleciał się z nią zobaczyć. Ale na kilka tygodni przed oddaniem tekstu do wydawnictwa, w lipcu 2016 roku, doszła do mnie wiadomość, że „Siostra Niebios" zmarła kilka lat wcześniej w Luwingu, śmiercią zwykłą, ziemską, ani trochę nie kosmiczną. Nie miałem też okazji porozmawiać z astronautą numer trzy. Ruben Simwenga również zmarł wiele lat temu. Losy pozostałych niedoszłych astronautów są nieznane, prawdopodobnie większość z nich już nie żyje.

28

– A w siedemdziesiątym drugim pojechał do tych Stanów – mówi któregoś dnia syn Mukuki Nkoloso, gdy odprowadzam go do pobliskiego kościoła. – Zaprosili go na Florydę, na przylądek Canaveral. – Ścisza głos i gestem dłoni pokazuje lecący samolot, a może rakietę. – Dostał tam mały podarunek, który po przyjeździe dał Kaundzie. To ponoć był kamień z Księżyca. Ale ja go nigdy nie widziałem i nie wiem, co się z nim stało.

Znów myślę, że konfabuluje. Pytam więc każdego, z kim rozmawiam, czy wie cokolwiek o podróży dyrektora Nkoloso do Stanów. Dopytuję zwłaszcza ówczesnych polityków UNIP, oni przecież z pewnością wiedzieliby o tym. To byłby piękny finał tej historii. Wyobrażam sobie, jak Mukuka Nkoloso stoi na platformie widokowej, ze wzrokiem utkwionym w ogromną rakietę Saturn V. Może ktoś robi mu zdjęcie? Lub kręci film? Co mógł czuć człowiek, który tak bardzo chciał lecieć w Kosmos, w chwili gdy odliczanie dobiegło końca i potężne silniki rakiety Saturn V z rykiem unosiły członków misji Apollo 16 ku gwiazdom? Domyślam się, że to mogły być najpiękniejsze minuty jego życia.

– Owszem, z tego, co pamiętam, to chyba go zaprosili – mówi Sikota Wina – ale zdaje się, że KK nie pozwolił mu jechać.

– Nie pamiętam, by pojechał do USA – odpowiada Alexander Grey Zulu, który na początku lat siedemdziesiątych pełnił funkcję ministra obrony. – Za to Amerykanie przyjechali tutaj. Przysłali ekspertów, by zbadali jego pomysły. – Dziewięćdziesięciodwuletni Grey Zulu z trudem wymawia kolejne słowa. Po chwili uśmiecha się i mówi: – On byłby bardzo szczęśliwy, gdyby wiedział, że pan o nim pisze.

– Był zaproszony do Stanów – mówi Zachariah Zumba. – Naprawdę go zapraszali. Ale nie pozwolono mu jechać. Bo sposób, w jaki on się zachowywał... – Próbuje pokazać coś gestem ręki, tak jakby bał się powiedzieć wprost. – KK mu nie pozwolił. Bo on był bardzo trudnym człowiekiem, KK bał się, że narobi naszemu krajowi kłopotów. Zbyt często mówił, co mu przyszło do głowy, to było zbyt duże ryzyko dla rządu, przyniósłby wstyd. Pojechał ktoś inny. Poza tym ten cały projekt kosmiczny był jego prywatną sprawą. Zresztą nie tylko USA go zaprosiły, inne kraje też. Ale nawet jak pojechał do ZSRR, to ta podróż była trzymana w tajemnicy, nikt tego nie ogłaszał, nikt o tym nie mówił. Pojechał raptem na dwa, trzy dni.

Pytam również Vernona Mwaangę, ówczesnego ambasadora Zambii przy ONZ, a później ministra spraw zagranicznych, generała Kingsleya Chinkulego oraz kilku innych. Wszyscy zaprzeczają lub nie pamiętają. Informacji o wizycie w USA nie znajduję też w zambijskich gazetach. Lecz ostatniego dnia mojego pobytu w Lusace w Archiwach Narodowych natrafiam przypadkiem na pewien list, datowany na 9 października 1974 roku, adresowany do ówczesnego premiera rządu, którym był Mainza Chona. Pismo nadane przez instytucję o nazwie Zambian National Space and Astronautical Administration Programme podpisane jest przez Edwarda Mukukę Nkoloso. Dyrektor informuje premiera oraz cały rząd, że powyższa instytucja zamierza wkrótce rozpocząć prace nad budową niewielkiego silnika rakietowego i w związku z takim przedsięwzięciem prosi o wsparcie finansowe. Ale nie to jest istotne: „Przez ostatnie dziesięć lat Zambia zaangażowała się w prace badawcze, by zwrócić uwagę świata na możliwość zbudowania rakiety, dzięki której moglibyśmy dołączyć do innych narodów w eksploracji przestrzeni kosmicznej i wesprzeć ludzkość w odkrywaniu tajemnic Układu Słonecznego oraz dalszych światów pozazodiakalnych. [...] Dziękujemy Jego Ekscelencji Dr. K. D. Kaundzie, członkom Komitetu Centralnego oraz szanownemu premierowi za umożliwienie dyrektorowi E. F. Mukuce Nkoloso wizyty w NASA w USA i obserwację startu rakiety Apollo 16*. Ponadto zwracamy się z prośbą do rządu, by w ramach swych możliwości zapewnił nam wsparcie materialne oraz moralne, tak by Zambia również mogła osiągnąć cel, który inne narody już osiągnęły, to jest by pozwolić człowiekowi przed jego śmiercią, by mógł podziwiać to cudowne, najwspanialsze dzieło Wszechmogącego Boga w najodleglejszych zakątkach Wszechświata".

*

Przeszukując nieliczne dokumenty dotyczące Zambijskiego Programu Kosmicznego, natknąłem się też na taką korespondencję z wiosny 1988 roku:

„Szanowny Panie,

czy mógłby mnie Pan poinformować o rezultatach Zambijskiego Programu Kosmicznego z lat sześćdziesiątych?

Oficjalna nota prasowa z dnia 3 listopada 1964 roku mówi:

»Ameryka i Rosja mogą przegrać kosmiczny wyścig, twierdzi Mukuka Nkoloso, dyrektor generalny Zambijskiej Narodowej Akademii Badań Kosmicznych. Dziesięciu zambijskich astronautów oraz jedna siedemnastoletnia kobieta są gotowi do startu. Nkoloso:

– Do końca 1965 roku pierwsi Zambijczycy wylądują na Księżycu. Moi astronauci są w pełnej gotowości, jednakże napotkaliśmy pewne trudności... Używamy systemu startowego własnego projektu, który jest rozwinięciem katapulty.

Dalej pan Nkoloso oświadcza:

* Misja Apollo 16 wystartowała 16 kwietnia 1972 r.

– By dokończyć projekt, potrzebujemy około siedmiuset* milionów funtów. Wydaje się to dużą sumą pieniędzy, lecz wystarczy sobie wyobrazić prestiż, jaki zyska Zambia. Niestety mam też kłopoty ze swoimi astronautami. Nie są wystarczająco skoncentrowani na naszym kosmicznym locie; zamiast studiować Księżyc, w głowie im jedynie amory. Martha Mwamba, siedemnastoletnia dziewczyna, która ma zostać pierwszą kolorową kobietą na Marsie, musi również karmić dziesiątkę swoich kotów, które będą jej towarzyszyć w kosmicznej podróży. Przyzwyczajam je do warunków kosmicznego lotu, umieszczając je codziennie w specjalnej kapsule. To czterdziestogalonowa beczka, która później toczy się po zboczu wzgórza. Daje im poczucie przemieszczania się w przestrzeni kosmicznej. Zrobiłem także specjalną huśtawkę na długiej linie. Gdy są w najwyższym punkcie, odcinam tę linę – to daje im poczucie nieważkości«.

Domyślam się, że wniosek o siedemset milionów funtów ZNASR** złożyła do ONZ. Proszę zatem o informację, czy Zambia otrzymała te pieniądze i czy program lotów kosmicznych został rozwinięty.

Z poważaniem

Dr Kabunda Kayongo

Ministerstwo Technologii".

Odpowiedź nadeszła trzy tygodnie później:

„Szanowny Panie,

w odpowiedzi na Pana pismo z dnia 24 maja 1988 roku dotyczące rezultatów Zambijskiego Programu Kosmicznego.

Pragnę Pana poinformować, że kwestia, która jest przedmiotem naszej korespondencji, nigdy nie była traktowana poważnie przez rząd Zambii i z tego powodu wysiłki pana Mukuki Nkoloso

* Tu chyba błąd piszącego. Nkoloso zazwyczaj mówił o siedmiu milionach funtów.

** Zambian National Academy of Space Research.

nie uzyskały żadnego wsparcia. Zatem program umarł śmiercią naturalną.

Z wyrazami szacunku
E. N. Kamuyuw
Asystent Sekretarza
Ministerstwo Energii, Transportu i Komunikacji".

*

„*I was strolling on the Moon one day. In a merry, merry month of May* – śpiewali astronauci Apollo 17*, wylądowawszy w jednej z dolin księżycowego Morza Jasności. – *When much to my surprise a pair of bonny eyes... tup... turup... tup... tup...*"

Nie mogę przestać myśleć, co nuciłby Edward Mukuka Nkoloso, hasając w podskokach po powierzchni Księżyca.

Warszawa, marzec 2017

* 7 grudnia 1972 r. – ostatnia misja programu Apollo. Eugene Andrew Cernan, Ronald Evans i Harrison Schmitt byli jak dotąd ostatnimi ludźmi na Księżycu.

Bibliografia

Czasopisma i gazety

„Abercornucopia", grudzień 1964
„Ada Evening News", grudzień 1964–styczeń 1965
„Chula Vista Star-News", 6 grudnia 1964; 10 grudnia 1964
„DRUM Magazine", styczeń 1964; grudzień 1964
„Nshila Magazine", r. 1963, 1964, 1965
„Redlands Daily Facts", 24 września 1969
„San Bernardino County", 26 listopada 1964; 2 sierpnia 1965
„San Francisco Chronicle", grudzień 1964–styczeń 1965
„Santa Cruz Sentinel", 2 marca 1969
„The Cincinnati Enquirer", 2 marca 1969
„The Gettysburg Times", 18 sierpnia 1965
„The Kansas City Times", 30 października 1964
„The Ottawa Journal", 31 października 1964
„The Sydney Morning Herald", 22 listopada 1964
„Time", 30 października 1964
„Times of Zambia", r. 1963, 1964, 1989
„Tucson Daily Citizen", 28 października 1964; 1 sierpnia 1965
„Z Magazine", listopad 1988
„Zambia Daily Mail", r. 1963, 1964, 1965, 1989

Książki

Baldwin Robert E., *Economic Development and Export Growth. A Study of Northern Rhodesia, 1920–1960*, Berkeley 1966

Central Africa. Part I, Closer Association 1945–1958, ed. Philip Murphy, British Documents on the End of Empire, Series B, Volume 9, London 2005

Chazvemba Runesu, Other Worlds Untold. An Anthology of African Poetry, Johannesburg 2015
Chiwome Emmanuel, Zifikile Mguni, *Zimbabwean Literature in African Languages. Crossing Language Boundaries*, Gweru 2012
Drysdale Andrew, *My Neighbour Madiba... and Others*, Cape Town 2007
Encyclopedia of African Religion, eds. Molefi Kete Asante, Ama Mazama, Thousand Oaks 2008
Ferguson James, *Expectations of Modernity. Myths and Meanings of Urban Life on the Zambian Copperbelt*, Berkeley 1999
Flammarion Camille, *Astronomie populaire*, Paris 1880
—, *L'atmosphère. Météorologie populaire*, Paris 1888
From the Cam to the Zambezi. Colonial Service and the Path to the New Zambia, ed. Tony Schur, London 2014
Gewald Jan-Bart, Marja Hinfelaar, Giacomo Macola, *One Zambia, Many Stories. Towards a History of Post-colonial Zambia*, Leiden-Boston 2008
Gordon David M., *Invisible Agents. Spirits in a Central African History*, Athens 2012
Kalusa Walima T., Megan Vaughan, *Death, Belief and Politics in Central African History*, Lusaka 2013
Killingray David, Martin Plaut, *Fighting for Britain. African Soldiers in the Second World War*, Woodbridge-Rochester 2009
Macmillan Hugh, *The Lusaka Years. The ANC in Exile in Zambia, 1963 to 1994*, Auckland Park 2013
Magona Sindiwe, *Please, Take Photographs*, Athlone 2009
Marwick M. G., *Sorcery in Its Social Setting. A Study of the Northern Rhodesian Ceŵa*, Manchester 1965
Roy Jacques R., *Don't Quit – Don't Cry*, b.m. 2012
Stokes Eric, Richard Brown, *The Zambezian Past. Studies in Central African History*, Manchester 1966
The Road to Independence, b.m. 1972
Williams Gwyneth, Brian Hackland, *The Dictionary of Contemporary Politics of Southern Africa*, New York 2016

Internet

http://content.time.com/
http://news.bbc.co.uk/2/hi/8344170.stm
http://www.history.com/
http://www.itnsource.com/en/shotlist/ITN/1964/11/13/FS131164002/?s=zambia%20and%20astronaut

http://www.itnsource.com/en/shotlist/RTV/1964/11/14/BGY505190222/
http://www.times.co.zm/?p=57295
https://en.wikipedia.org/wiki/Space_Race
https://history.nasa.gov/

WYDAWNICTWO CZARNE sp. z o.o.
czarne.com.pl

Sekretariat: ul. Kołłątaja 14, III p., 38-300 Gorlice
tel. +48 18 353 58 93, fax +48 18 352 04 75
mateusz@czarne.com.pl, tomasz@czarne.com.pl
dominik@czarne.com.pl, ewa@czarne.com.pl, edyta@czarne.com.pl

Redakcja: Wołowiec 11, 38-307 Sękowa
redakcja@czarne.com.pl

Sekretarz redakcji: malgorzata@czarne.com.pl

Dział promocji: ul. Marszałkowska 43/1, 00-648 Warszawa
tel./fax +48 22 621 10 48
agnieszka@czarne.com.pl, dorota@czarne.com.pl
zofia@czarne.com.pl, marcjanna@czarne.com.pl
magda.jobko@czarne.com.pl

Dział marketingu: honorata@czarne.com.pl

Dział sprzedaży: piotr.baginski@czarne.com.pl
agnieszka.wilczak@czarne.com.pl, malgorzata.wietecha@czarne.com.pl

Audiobooki i e-booki: anna@czarne.com.pl

Skład: d2d.pl
ul. Sienkiewicza 9/14, 30-033 Kraków
tel. +48 12 432 08 52, info@d2d.pl

Druk i oprawa: Drukarnia POZKAL
ul. Cegielna 10/12, 88-100 Inowrocław, tel. +48 52 354 27 00

Wołowiec 2017
Wydanie I
Ark. wyd. 8,9; ark. druk. 13,5